SHORT TERM

By Jay Richard Kennedy

PRINCE BART

SHORT

JAY RICHARD KENNEDY

TERM

THE WORLD PUBLISHING COMPANY

CLEVELAND AND NEW YORK

PUBLISHED BY The World Publishing Company
2231 West 110th Street, Cleveland 2, Ohio

PUBLISHED SIMULTANEOUSLY IN CANADA BY
Nelson, Foster & Scott Ltd.

Library of Congress Catalog Card Number: 59-11536

FIRST EDITION

TO MY DAUGHTER, SUSAN

Chapter 1

THE Arc de Triomphe high above the Etoile was crowded with lovers who looked down at the chestnut blossoms and tulips, colorful spires, and traffic on the Champs Elysées. Some cars were already moving on the sidewalk. Kenneth Fenimore Preston had arrived late yesterday, April Fool's Day, his forty-second birthday. Now standing on the roof, alone and apart, looking down, he realized how much this need to view everything from above had been his prison. The last time he had been in France was nine years ago. In uniform. 1944. Grenoble. Also on business then. But business of a very different kind, serious and painful business, everyone's business and yet his very own personal and still unfinished business. What had brought him here now was nearly finished. That was something to see from above as he stood apart and alone. His life. It too was very nearly finished. Wasted. It brought the added, bitter discovery that a wasted life was lived twice, the second time with all the scattered parts neatly assorted into hard, compact, and inescapable decades confronting one. From now on, each day would be not only what he would become or do but also what he had done and once was.

The last time Ken saw Paris was before all this had begun, before his father's suicide, twenty years ago. That too had been tulip time, birthday time, Easter vacation time, but then hopes and plans ran high and wide for an instructorship in American history, an assistant professorship at Harvard—the chances for it were excellent according to the chairman of the department—and then, at long last, if he was good and he was sure he would be, a curatorship in some first-rate New England museum! Cousin Arthur had promised to help. Before that he had come to Paris so many carefree times with Mother. Oh, very young, very gay. Dismissing his regrets was a habit with pattern and purpose. First reduce remorse by ridicule. Then flatten realistic hopes into idle wishes. Soon wishes descended into whimsy: a constant whittling-down process until at length it all ended as nothing, with a wry smile. Only now the smile would not come. Like a remorseless quarterback on a timeless Monday morning, he saw his score. Zero. He was stuck with his current number, forty-two, on a fading unused sweatshirt. His role had been on the sidelines: the name Preston of Preston & Company had not been worth the game. Time! The signals had been all fouled up from the very first skirmish. Still you played in accordance with the rules so rah rah rah for absolutely nothing. Happy birthday. Happy Fool's Day.

The sun was beginning to set. A rim of gold lit the western outskirts, encircling the city in its fiery embrace, a cradled thing of rising shadows and misty purples with the faintest beginnings of night creeping through narrow, time-worn streets. A flurry of picture-taking absorbed the others on the roof. Two beautiful Chinese girls, Sorbonne students, wearing skirts and light pullovers, were resting, books in hand, their heads against the stone, smoking and laughing as they spoke about Ken in rapid French with Canadian accents, assuming he could not understand.

"Look at that American *ballot* wearing his vest on this warm day."

"He is protecting his heart of gold. Valuable property. Afraid it will melt!"

He hurried from their voices and laughter to the exit. This way down. This way out. *Ballot.* Stuffed shirt. Square. A verdict in slang, a vote in any language. Ballot. A vote cast and past recall. Standing beside him in the descending lift was a man close to fifty, holding hands with a woman in her mid-forties. She wore a cheap cotton dress and a plain wedding ring; he was tieless in an old windbreaker. When they reached street level, where the permanent memorial flame burned, surrounded by the freshly cut flowers, he kissed her lips and stepped aside gallantly. They smiled their love without embarrassment.

Ken knew he should not continue walking. He should return to his suite. There was little time left in which to change for cocktails and dinner with the lawyer for the French combine. He should not have come. Above all he should never have brought the reorganization of Western Hemisphere Industrial Power to the brink of completion at this point in his middle age. Its size, the length of time it had hung over his life and Father's before him, coloring and shaping all of it, was what had made him sum up.

He continued to walk among the crowds alongside of others. Everywhere he felt the nameless, persuasive pulse of love, surrounding, engulfing, beyond reach. The boys and girls body-close on park benches or walking the Champs Elysées hand in hand. The embraces unconcealed round the splashing fountains of the Tuileries. Time again! He retraced his steps, passing Fouquet's on the Champs Elysées instead of following the deserted Boulevard George V, though that would have been faster. At Rue Bassard he turned left. By the time M. Chanteuf, his wife and the young lady, Louise, had arrived, he had bathed, shaved, dressed, and was waiting at the entrance to the bar of the Hotel George V off the main lobby.

The lights were out in the last boulevard café. The oppressive evening was over. After saying good night to the Chanteufs and seeing Louise to her door, Ken walked down toward the Louvre to see the tulips once more by moonlight. But every few yards he was accosted by the bright, soliciting "Bonjour?" of the young, smartly dressed streetwalkers. He returned to the hotel, unable to sleep and lay awake open-eyed on the wide, soft, luxurious bed, alone with the twisted torment of remembrance.

The next morning he breakfasted early at a café across from Pont Neuf, paused at bookstalls on crooked, cobblestoned streets in Montparnasse, fed pigeons in the Luxembourg Gardens and watched the hundreds of eager children at play, free at last of restricting gloves, leggings, and mufflers. Near Notre Dame he lingered where the workmen at the stream below dug rocks out of the thawing earth. He paused frequently at outdoor cafés with gay signs painted on their windows and sat under multistriped awnings beside enthusiastic, arguing students in bright-colored corduroy pants and open shirts, sporting beards and other self-conscious emblems of freedom. At the bookstall where he finally found a French paperback copy of *César Birotteau,* he saw a man in his late thirties standing behind a woman, his strong hands clasped round her waist while she, smiling and rubbing the back of her head against his shoulder, leafed the pages of Racine. Her hair was unruly, short, and black. The man was of a height and build equal to his own, broad-shouldered and tall for a Frenchman. Ken did not want to see their faces.

He had made a reservation this morning for the night train out of the Gare de Lyon to Grenoble: probably one more mistake. What was unfinished this long should remain so. Then church bells chimed and he recalled his almost forgotten, final appointment with M. Chanteuf.

Even in the bright April afternoon sun, the Rue Boissière looked like a street of rundown apartment houses. The courtyard had no flowers, no garden, not even the charming old cobblestones of most of the St. Germain apartments. He rang the huge bell on the outside door and on the signal entered, crossed the yard, and ascended the dusty stairs. At the end of the ill-kept hallway, he knocked on M. Chanteuf's door.

The phone rang, interrupting M. Chanteuf in the midst of an eloquent if directionless outburst regarding the French combine's vast
holdings in Western Hemisphere Industrial Power—twenty thousand
shares. The call from a client who had innocently violated the cus-
toms, currency, and health laws of three countries was unwelcome,
but at least it afforded M. Chanteuf an opportunity to give vent to his
suppressed anger. Thus far he had tried and failed to bring M. Preston
around to the point of defending and persuading, the only time one
disclosed vital information without intending to. Each man had a
style. It was the fingerprint of his soul and until you saw it up close
you could not know who he was or how to deal with him. But this one
wore invisible gloves! Nor was this due to clumsiness on anyone's part.
Most well-to-do American bachelors Preston's age arrived in Paris as
boys to a brothel, eager, hot-blooded, avid, and indiscreet. Not this
one. Last night everything had been perfect. No doubt of it. With the
Lido so packed it had seemed impossible to find space anywhere for
another party; their table had been ringside and center where M.
Preston could see the superbly smooth nakedness of the high-heeled,
high-breasted show girls and sit in perfumed, sweet flesh-smelling
nearness to them as they promenaded and strutted, their marvelously
round and firm rouge-nippled playthings bouncing within touching
distance of his hand, as Louise, even closer in her tight white satin
and low *décolletage,* pressed beside him in the dark. Louise had been
impeccable as always, never overselling as most of them did, and as
always she had also been honest, his major evidence for the dignity of
vice. Before the floor show as they danced, Louise hit the target
squarely when she said, "I'll tell you something, little man. Your Kenneth Preston is the kind of American who will not touch a lady till he
has known her at least a month and if she is no lady he will not touch
her even if he knows her forever." He had thanked her for her frankness.
    "I expect to be paid either way."
    "Of course, my dear." He squeezed her bare shoulder. "But then you
will owe *me* the last twenty minutes of this evening."
    He collected after taking Mme. Chanteuf home and leaving her at
the door, when he went for his "evening walk." Louise had been both
furious and charming.
    "It was something *you* did, you pint-sized jack-in-the-box. And me
wasting a brand-new gown on the evening! I was ravishing." As she
paced, he had watched with relish her angry movements through the
parted front of her dressing gown. "Every male reeked of it, even the
waiters. If he knows my work, and others find out, I'm ruined. When
that happened to Claudine, she had to start all over again in Madrid."

He had soothed and reassured. She was magnificent. She was entrancing. She was the best in Paris. She was flawless. The American simply had no manhood.

"Nonsense! He is no *tante*. On this I never make a mistake. Never. Something went wrong. Something *you* did."

At last she subsided but there was still enough anger left in her and she discharged it in other ways.

It was all very puzzling.

Louise had used every artistry at her command. The fact that she had actually married an American millionaire and lived in Chicago for a year helped enormously. She had left her wealthy husband and returned to this work because she was bored! But that was a separate matter: she could not have been more perfect. A Parisian divorcée familiar with America, chatting gaily with Preston in both languages about everything from Broadway and Chicago's stockyards to Paris's spring weather and the multiparty system in France. Even Chanteuf had been amused by her notion of a new political party whose program it would be to abolish wine drinking as the cause of France's moral bankruptcy. Preston had actually smiled when she raised her parted fingers before her animated face, laughing her merriment, to say, "I can see us all on May Day, gathered at the Obelisk in the Place de la Concorde, our fists clenched high in the air, round glasses of lukewarm water as we sing, 'Arise, ye prisoners of the grape vine.'"

But when Louise's green eyes that dominated her foxlike face promised Preston more exciting, intimate things, to be exchanged only when they were alone together later, M. Preston had looked away.

The result of the evening had begun to come clear to Chanteuf at the high point of laughter when the featured comic, who salted and ate menus, collars, cuffs, burning matches, and matchboxes, finally shook salt over the tall naked show girl and, with wide-eyed delight and wonder, chased her off stage. It was then, as the Lido house lights dimmed for the last number, that he had ventured one unmasked, searching stare at his American guest's unamused gray eyes and disapproving mouth over the broad chin; the erect, black-haired, close-cropped head not even slightly gray and in no way relaxed, and had realized with sick certainty that neither Louise on her well-practiced back nor he standing on his toes would learn from this man what he did not wish to reveal. You could hear the audience breathing during the final production number which simulated a Pigalle street scene in lower Montmartre. Seven streetwalkers, six in tight black skirts, the most voluptuous one in red, were picked up by seven sailors. Their leader carried off the girl in red, to reappear with her upstage on a raised platform masked to represent a Pigalle house. At the open window the sailor ripped all the clothes off the girl except for her lace panties as for some perverse reason she fought for her honor, to the jeers of the watching sailors, the high, girlish laughter of the other streetwalkers, and the accompaniment of pulsating music and frenzied dancing downstage. Finally gripped by awakened passion, she tore off the panties and flung herself at the sailor who brought her naked body close to him, arms around her, his face and hands moving in time to the music and the dimming lights down to some unimaginable region of her body as the lights went out to a storm of applause. But when the lights went up, he had not been at all surprised to catch M. Preston in the act of stifling a yawn as he looked at his watch.

Chanteuf cut the phone call short and hung up. M. Preston seemed as bored now as he had been last night. Chanteuf picked up where they had been interrupted. "But the issue is whether something may happen you could not know about," he said.

"Such as?" Ken asked politely.

"Oh," Chanteuf waved a hand in the air. "Anything. Frankly, if you will forgive me, your firm has only one and a half million dollars—neither you nor your partners, Messrs. Coogan and McBride, have anything else to speak of outside your firm. This reorganization involves one and a half *billions,* monsieur! What is to stop your more powerful American associates from selling on favorable news out of Washington today or tomorrow because they expect unfavorable news later from the Federal District Court simply because of something they themselves will do to create it? You see the position?"

"Yes, I see it but it's altogether impossible. Such conduct would only result in less profit for all parties."

"No doubt. But it could still happen. There has been much passion in this matter for twenty-five years."

"In the first place, if it happened, we would certainly know. In the second, we should immediately tell you. You have my assurance."

"On which point?" Chanteuf smiled.

"Both." Ken was frowning.

M. Chanteuf nodded gravely. "That is sufficient," he said. "Have my assurance" were words to make him laugh. How often had he himself used them without the slightest notion of how to back them up and as many times again when his specific purpose was deception! Yet coming from this sober man, genuinely shocked at having his word questioned even half in jest, they were almost sufficient. A different breed. Not at all like other early American best family loafers he had met, gambling in Madrid, boating on the Riviera, acquiring mistresses, wives, summer and winter homes, and incessantly harassing their lawyers or property managers for more inherited money to squander. Too bad he was so humorless. But what a splendid throwback to Pilgrim landings and other legends of the New World's origins!

"Besides," Ken was saying, "even if one of the principal parties did anything so self-destructive, it could no longer prevent the reorganization."

"But timing, monsieur. The reorganization will take place without a doubt. The issue in any such speculative investment is *when!*"

"Now," Ken said. "No matter who does what. The Securities Exchange Commission will approve today or tomorrow. The Federal Court must approve when it convenes a few weeks hence."

"You speak with certainty, but it is exactly *that*, monsieur, we seek more assurance on."

"M. Chanteuf, have you ever been in South America?"

"I have not yet had that pleasure."

"There are millions of people in those countries who can neither read nor write." He spoke patiently and without emphasis. "And all because they do not have inexpensive light in sufficient abundance." Ken cited the example of Mexico, where out of twenty-five million people, only seven hundred and fifty-nine thousand remained who still spoke nothing but Aztec, all the rest now speaking Spanish—evidence of their readiness for literacy. "Only one thing is missing, cheap power and light. Now they are demanding it and that is the underlying reason the reorganization will go through without delay."

The top of Chanteuf's bald head was shining. "To be sure. It is exactly *that* we are attempting to decide based on the facts."

Ken frowned. "I assumed all the facts were known to you. I'm sure M. Coogan has fully acquainted you with them. You know that our State Department cannot afford to have this political sore festering so close to home. Besides, the native South American utility systems simply do not have the funds or technical skill to meet their new expansion needs and have been forced to admit it. As for the principals in my own country: Tamiami Utilities has been sold to the state of Florida. All they hold now is cash and stock in the parent company, North American Power, which in turn has only one remaining functioning subsidiary—Western Hemisphere Industrial Power." Ken sighed. "WHIP must turn its frozen pesos into dollars before anyone can start taking profits and for that there must be reorganization. The New England insurance companies have no alternative to our plan which gives them vast tax benefits in back interest on their senior bonds and also provides for their participation in profits. As for the Texans who dominate the parent company: for them this constitutes complete victory on the issue that interests them most—control. The time will never be more favorable for any of the principals. Even dollar balances exist for the first time in all major South American countries." Ken stopped, then added, "But you know all that. If these facts are not sufficient reassurance, monsieur, you really should get out at once and take the profits you already have."

Chanteuf's wide brown eyes blinked. His round face turned bright red. "Wouldn't that embarrass you?" he asked.

"Not in the long run. The stock must remain in strong hands until the Michigan court convenes. If not yours, then someone else's."

Suddenly Chanteuf felt that all his anxieties were provincial and ridiculous. "The idea of a little court in Michigan deciding a world-wide issue such as this is quite amusing," he said.

"The original founders of North American Power built their first utility systems on the outskirts of Detroit." Ken rose. "It was not until 1928 that they set up WHIP as a subsidiary to develop the native resources of South America."

How well he announces that the interview is at a close, Chanteuf admired. And without yet knowing our decision! What was it? The only American strength was money. Neither culture, character, reason, nor planning—only money. Lucky recipients of two centuries of accident. But Preston had no money, at least none to speak of. Not since his father had lost his entire inherited fortune of fifteen million or more in the WHIP collapse back in '33. Twenty years ago. "Of course I must bow to your superior knowledge of the facts as you have lived with them all your life. After all," he said, "it was your father who originally proposed setting up WHIP for the development of South American power."

Ken nodded. It was the only time Chanteuf saw something distinct and personal in his eyes. He was quite familiar with the whole tragic story of Preston senior's suicide following the crash and subsequent unrest in South America, the seizure of control by the Texas millionaires, and the inevitable bloodshed that had begun in Cuba and spread its red stain over the whole of Central and South America. That was just about the same time the Stavisky scandal had caused violence in the Place de la Concorde.

"Well! If all goes badly in Washington and we have not sold, or for that matter, should all go well and we do not acquire more stock today, we shall have missed the coach. Coach? That is not the word. Boat?"

"Yes. Boat."

He was walking Ken to the door. "On my last visit to the States I went to Detroit. What money there is to be made in America if only one knows how!" He said it with a sudden rise of warm enthusiasm on the wave of which his mind was abruptly and completely made up. He couldn't have said exactly what finally gave him full faith and conviction in both the man and his plan. His bluntness, the review of the plain facts, or perhaps his genuine indifference. "I'll speak to my people and recommend a stop purchase order of another ten thousand shares today on a favorable decision in Washington. If they agree, we shall remain in your Protective Committee, and at your complete mercy." He was beaming. "You truly believe it can rise another thirty points?"

"At least."

"I might be able to get some of our group together this evening. Could you dine with us?"

"I'm sorry, no, thank you. I leave early."

"A pity."

"Yes. I regret leaving Paris."

Chanteuf believed him. Another bond. Chanteuf loved Paris, whether occupied by Germans, preoccupied with general strikes, or overoccupied as at present by the infiltration from outlying districts.

"M. Coogan would have liked very much to be here," Ken said, "but as you know he had to attend the Securities Exchange Commission hearings in Washington. Unfortunately, I am only a statistician."

"Not at all. Not in the slightest. Believe me! As you said, at a time like this, what one needs is *facts*."

A cable message from Patrick Coogan in Washington arrived as Ken was checking out of the George V. It stated: STILL IN WASHINGTON STOP PRESTON PLAN APPROVED HURRAY ONLY ONE OBJECTOR UNIMPORTANT STOP TRIUMPH COMPLETE STOP ARRIVING DALLAS TWO DAYS SUGGEST YOU GO DIRECTLY OUR SHACK FLORIDA STOP WILL FILL YOU IN BY PHONE BUSINESS FLORIDA AND DALLAS.

He had no time to phone Coogan in Washington and congratulate him; not if he was to change his return flight, reroute to Tampa and still catch the train. It did not much matter to him whether he returned to New York or went to Florida. But he did not intend to miss his journey to Grenoble.

The last thing Ken remembered thinking of before falling asleep in his train compartment was finding his father's body twenty years ago in the gun room, his right eyebrow singed by gunpowder, a pistol in his hand, and a hole clean through both temples. His hair had been cut close by the barber that morning, the way he always had it done before he left for one of his big-game hunting trips.

Awakening in his compartment at dawn, Ken watched the sun come up and dispel the swirls of heavy mist as ewe lambs, calves, and colts awoke to gaze with slow blinking eyes into the ruddy east. Dotting the rich, rolling green fields were the thirteenth-century stone houses, darkened by time in their own unmistakable way, and the compact farmhouses with slanting roofs, slated, red terra-cotta shingled, or thatched, all with cheerful shutters and low doors. An occasional gray castle flanked by fat turrets stood high on some promontory. Smoke was beginning to curl from chimneys. In the distance, dominating and getting closer, yet always above and beyond reach, spread the vast, majestic sheets of white snow of the Alps with black patches of rock emerging from the elusive, curving symmetry. He opened his compartment window wide and stood stripped to the waist, breathing slowly and deeply of the crisp, cold air as one does after swimming too long under water.

Ken stepped out of the station into the warmth of the sun as it appeared from behind the low early-morning mountain clouds. Grenoble was the bottom of a wide, graceful cup completed by the rising foothill shoulders of the Alps. The rain had fallen into it like wine mellowed by apricot, plum, and apple blossoms, mixed with pine needles and snow, then chilled in the icy clouds. Now the soft rain had stopped, leaving a clean sweetness in the air.

Students were already on bicycles, alert and calling out to one another, some on their way to the University from the many run-down hotels or off to an early start for the mountain passes in pairs, lunch baskets and books fastened behind their seats. Tomorrow was Easter Sunday. There were still two days left of their holiday.

Old peasant women in from their farms to say a final confession at the big church before the Resurrection, and to make note of future purchases, walked by sedately in their black shoes and stockings, dresses, and head shawls. The window washers were well along with their jobs in front of the main stores. His back to the station, the low buildings of the town in between, Ken faced the glistening white-capped peaks high above, their wide ribbons of snow receding further from the green foothills each day as spring advanced. Ken asked the porter, "Which way to the Hotel Citoyen?" and was shown the narrow street close by. The porter indicated a building on the right-hand side one block away, and mumbled, "With the bright blue and yellow door and shutters."

Ken remembered the door and shutters as being a dull, ugly green;

the one night he had entered it after curfew so swiftly, that was the only thing he had noticed. At the hotel he paused. Yellow and blue. It was newly painted and even smaller than he had remembered. Inside were the same old low, narrow registration desk, the room keys hanging on their rusty hooks at the wall close by the worn, splintery stairs, and the open telephone fastened to the peeling wall opposite. The wall was still green. Only the chambermaid was new, a young girl fresh from the land in her dirty sweater, colorless dress, and shapeless canvas shoes. He asked for room 218, and it was available. It too was unchanged except for the linoleum, now more cracked, faded, and dirty. There were still no closets, no hangers for clothes. One tiny electric bulb hung over the bed, and another dangled over the washstand next to the old *bidet*. The room would be cold at night again and the mattress lumpy.

"A hotel owned by Milicien." Both of them had envisioned a regal, luxurious affair. They had laughed hysterically, realizing just how seriously dangerous it was to do so, yet incapable of stopping, hands over their mouths, as the shutters flapped, her long hair loose and flowing, catching between her palm and parted lips, making her sneeze and laugh anew whether because of the sheer ridiculousness of the place, their inability to lock the swinging shutters and door, the fact that they had made it safely, or the church bells chiming the quarter-hours all through the night and for them, commencing it seemed at that exactly inappropriate fraction of a second each of the three times until dawn.

The desk squeaked and its thin legs swayed with the moving weight of his arm as he filled out the police card. It might have been the same desk into which they had then placed the incriminating evidence of the shilling before they left, hoping it would cause trouble for the woman who owned the place. *Natalie had heard the shilling jingle and when she lifted his jacket she found his silver snuffbox. The shilling had struck against it in the pocket lining. Natalie wanted him to leave it behind along with the shilling and he had refused.*

"They will know it's American," she warned.

"Not unless they can recognize Paul Revere silver." Or the fact that the face sealed into the inside of the box was a daguerreotype of his great-grandfather done by Morse himself in 1839. For that they would also have had to recognize the wall behind Timothy Preston's face as the southeast one of the office of the President of the United States and the hardly visible décor as that chosen by Martin Van Buren.

"I always keep it with me," he said, *and Natalie had been obliged to accept it.*

Now his left hand fingered the silver box in his vest pocket as he studied the questions. "Reason for visit: Tourist, business, other reason—please check." Tourist. That's all he was here, now. He knew full well that the shilling could not be there. Nevertheless he opened the drawer.

Over *café noir* and *brioche* he watched the others reading newspapers, puffing their morning cigarettes, sipping coffee, or cracking hard-boiled eggs. They lived here, worked here, you could see that. The Italian waiter knew them and they were known to each other. This entire journey was senseless—a sentimental, foolish impulse; the result of running. But the earliest train back to Paris was not until late tonight and he knew no one else in Grenoble. He rose abruptly, paid his bill, sent off a cable of congratulations to Coogan, adding that he would fly straight through to Tampa and await his phone call at the cottage on Heron Key, rented by the firm two years ago as a stopover for the many trips taken by Coogan and their lawyers for conferences in Tampa and nearby Havana with the board members of Tamiami Utilities and the South American interests in WHIP. Then he went seeking the address.

The sign said "Novelties and Souvenirs." In the window were many overly decorated objects, cheap factory-made lamps, magazine racks, pipe stands, book ends, all excessively varnished and fashioned out of various woods hewn down in the nearby forests. There were also beads of cheap, painted glass, ornate beer mugs and busy gingerbread clocks from across the Alps in Switzerland. The store itself was not much larger than his hotel room. A lady customer was at the point of deciding to purchase a wooden shoe in which a clothes brush was kept. Removing the brush released a catch and caused a small music box inside the shoe to play—of all things—"Oklahoma!" until the spring wound down.

The man behind the counter rewinding the spring looked up at Ken and did not recognize him. When the lady customer nodded, he stuffed the brush back in the shoe, stopping the music. It was remarkable to see Angi, his brown eyes still bright, his face and body still lean, his cheeks still high-colored, and his straight black hair still falling across his forehead over one eye, as he stood behind the confining counter wrapping a ridiculous wooden shoe for a Parisian lady too old to go skiing.

The last time he had seen Angi, he was sitting on the stone basement floor, leaning with one elbow against the short-wave set, poised, his legs crossed under him as though ready to spring. He remembered Angi saying as he smiled, "When I want a good night's sleep, Major,

I go into the woods." At their first meeting Angi had explained how it had at last become too difficult for him to spend the days in Grenoble working at the factory. *"Considering the character of my night work, it became necessary for me to disappear into nature,"* he had said, his brown eyes twinkling.

"Yes, monsieur?" The lady had left.

Ken cleared his throat.

"Angi?"

The shopkeeper ran a restless hand through his hair, pushing it out of his eyes. He frowned. Then his face flushed.

"The Major!"

He seized both Ken's hands across the counter. "What sky did you drop out of this time? But you haven't changed a bit! The vest and jacket, you see. I remembered you as a French tutor in corduroy. Eight years." He laughed. "You—the Major—of course—my God!" He had come round the counter and was pounding Ken's back. "So here you are after all."

He led Ken through the store to an even smaller room with just enough space for two chairs, a table, stove, icebox, and one closet. He plugged in the coffeepot, still warm, removed an old shirt from one chair and a newspaper and a loaf of home-baked bread from the other.

When Ken told him he was staying at the Citoyen, Angi laughed, winked, and nodded. "There are students and students, eh?"

His face grew abruptly serious. "The fat pig who owned it? She was attended to after the Liberation." He lit a cigarette and added, quite bluntly, "My wife is ill. Nerves. Talk of our kind makes her worse. Otherwise I would ask you to stay with us." Ken said he really preferred to be at the hotel and Angi nodded.

"So! What brings you back?"

Ken smiled faintly and shrugged. His business had taken him to Paris. Having come over three thousand miles it seemed wrong not to go the short distance to Grenoble to see it once by daylight, to look up Angi and find out what happened to the others.

"The others," Angi repeated softly. Then in his normal voice he said, "Let me see. The ones in on your visit—"

"Maurice, Roger, *le patron*, the old man, the Mayor of St. Simon. The Polish Jew in Franco uniform."

"Yes, Montero who didn't speak Spanish." Angi laughed and stopped. "You knew he died."

"I was still here."

Angi nodded. "And *le patron*. I remember now."

"How is the old man?"

Angi's face softened with affection. "Died last year working a farm in Ste. Marie."

He unplugged the coffeepot and poured. "Yes, in the end he returned to the land. His sister's."

He peeled part of a lemon, placing the skin on a plate between them. "What an impulsive *tête brulée* he became! Simply refused to surrender his arms. Long after the Liberation, when it was a crime to still keep them. I got word of it and visited him." He waved his pen knife. "A small-arms gun—not so small, a Piat—" He laughed and shook his head. "Draped in blankets and a fancy coverlet, taking up half of all the room space he had. 'This isn't a bride,' I told him. 'You can't live here in sin with it or it's jail for you, old man.' But he would not give up the gun. 'What if we need it again?' 'Then we will take it once more from the enemy,' I told him. 'Didn't we start with two hunting rifles, my brother, you, and I?' Finally I reminded him, 'The young ones who refuse do not yet understand. What life have they experienced but the woods and the killing? But you—is there nothing else to it then? It was you who recruited me, old man. Will you now shame the adjutant of your sector commander who is like your own son besides?'" He winked, remembering its effect, and bit on a piece of sugar and drank the coffee. "We had to dismantle the whore of a gun and drop it piece by piece, night by night, into the Isère. As to the others, Roger is dead and so is Maurice."

"Maurice," Ken repeated softly.

"Yes. He had gathered medical equipment from the retreating Boche. He was going to practice in Paris. Specializing in female disorders, he kept saying, as it had been his natural gift from the day he was born." Angi smiled. "Roger quit the Communists. Natalie finally convinced him."

"I'm very glad."

"Later he saved her life." He hurried on. "They are both on our monument for Oisan in the Romanche Valley at the circle. You must see it."

The name of Natalie hung between them. "I want to."

"We built it ourselves. No one but the boys. It's less than fifteen kilos from here. I have no car—" He indicated the cash register in the empty shop. "But my daughter has a license. She's nineteen and drives well. A car can be rented here."

"If it would not inconvenience your daughter—?"

"Eugenia? No. No. Her vacation is still on. She's a Université student and works at the Jubilee Splendide in her spare time to pay her tuition. Speaks English as you do French, I am told. A terrible flirt."

He laughed. "A fine girl." He chain-lit another cigarette though the first was barely smoked. "Who else? No one except the Mayor."

"And Natalie," Ken said.

"Yes. Natalie. She and Maurice planned to marry." He paused, took Ken's cup and poured more coffee into it deliberately. "She became a nurse." He went to the icebox and returned with a piece of goat cheese and two apples.

"I'm glad," Ken said.

Angi handed a knife to Ken and peeled his apple as he spoke, his eyes focused on his knife. "Following Normandy, when the FFI and the FTP were joined, she went up"—his head indicated the Oisan foothills—"where Roger and seventy of his men had mopped up a small nest of Boche in a village and taken a few prisoners. There were plenty of wounded. Five hundred Boche coming down from farther north found them, killed half, captured the rest. They put the boys in trucks, the officers on burros, and made Natalie and the other nurse walk. A herd of cows coming up for the summer to graze the mountain pastures blocked the road and Roger called out to her to cross under the cows. There was a bridge below on the other side. He was up on the burro and could see past the cows to the bridge and the opportunity. 'Jump!' he said. The other girl was the wife of a Vichy naval officer bastard. She had been forced to go with Natalie and she was in no danger with the Boche once they saw her papers and checked, you can be sure. Roger swung his animal to block the way so Natalie could jump." He chain-lit another cigarette, chewing his apple as he smoked. "She escaped, reported in, and that night our boys were rescued. But Roger was already dead. They shot him a few minutes after Natalie escaped."

Ken nodded. "And Maurice?"

"Also in June, holding the Briançon Road in Romanche. Many fell there. Thirty thousand Boche trying to get out of Grenoble. You understand." He drew a deep puff, brought the knife with cheese on it to his mouth. "You will like to see the power plants in Romanche. Remember our God damn power plants?"

Ken nodded again.

"It will not be out of your way." Angi finished his coffee in one impatient gulp. "They are on the same road as our monument."

"And the Café des Oiseaux?"

"That's another road. Near Bulac up past d'Uriage. You forget we climbed over the slopes and ridges then. It is different by car. How long do you stay?"

"Tomorrow night."

"Time enough, if you start before lunch. You must get the car before then in any case. We still have two-hour lunches in France." He rose. "You can even visit the Mayor of St. Simon on your way to Bulac if you like. He has grown old and silly but he is still their mayor. His version of events is enough to make you laugh yourself sick. Not sentimentalizing or boasting," he added quickly. "But the civilian view. How he stopped the boys from doing impulsive things. How foolish we were to seize the towns and the plants so long before D-Day, as they had to be abandoned anyway and were not important to begin with."

Ken flushed. He was certain that Angi had heard all the tiresome explanations, defenses, and apologies for actions such as the one he had convinced them of. Operation Anvil versus Operation Overlord, Eisenhower versus Churchill versus Montgomery versus Stalin and the prematurity of the one or wise postponement of the other depending on how you chose or were forced to look at it.

Angi headed into the shop. Ken followed.

"The Mayor still bemoans the looseness of the women in the Resistance. But then it was always his business to perform wedding ceremonies."

He took out a sign reading, "Back in ten minutes."

"We'll find Eugenia swishing around the manager of the Jubilee Splendide. I told you she works there? Otherwise she will be at home doing her studies."

"I'm sorry your wife is sick."

"It was the aftermath. Raising a daughter all that time with me away. You have not married." It was a statement.

"No."

"So."

The Jubilee Splendide was only a few doors away.

"Where is Natalie living?" Ken asked.

"Paris." Angi opened the hotel door. "I don't know exactly where. We lost touch."

Each time the mountain road turned into places where the timeless trees and knife-straight towers of rock kept out the sun, they were totally engulfed in a deep fragrance of pines and silence, stranded on a hushed green island. The streams grew louder in the hollows as they splashed down from the heights of smooth moss-covered slabs to race across the road's slippery surface, dark and gleaming, leaving enough water behind to form a growing bank of ice at the decline before flowing on to gain force, dash against stones and trees, carrying pebbles and pine cones, and finally join the Isère River far down in the valley below. Even out in the sun the air was colder and thinner now. There were actual patches of snow clinging to trees and rocks a few feet overhead. The hairpin curves were more numerous, sharp, and steep. Suddenly the road rose straight before them, curving only slightly. Then all at once the world lay at their feet. The pointed fir tops, the hundreds of streams pouring down every side of the mountains, the flat green meadows with their neatly hedged-in plots, the specks of houses and villages, their own small ribbon of road twisting and turning like a thin, long string of gray silk, all appeared in perfect sparkling miniature.

The snow was everywhere, dry, white, and friendly in the hot sun— no longer mysterious. To the left of the lookout point where Eugenia had parked the small car, skiers were gliding over the wind-shaped Alpine patterns in ice and snow. The café was a hundred yards ahead.

"How I love it all," Eugenia cried. "I have lived here all my life and still—" She removed the gay scarf from her hair. "I would die to go skiing right this minute." She was dressed for it, in ski pants, heavy shoes, a woolen sweater. "Aren't you hungry?" she asked. "And you do want to see your café."

They walked from the car, pausing for Eugenia to lift handfuls of snow, taste it, then hold it to her cheek tenderly and throw the rest of it at Ken. As they neared the café she ran, challenging him by a wave of her hand to race her. He smiled indulgently, ran after her up the road and the stone steps and sank into a chair at one of the outside tables while she entered to let the owner know they were there. A fat dog waddled up to put its jowly chin on his foot, and its tail beat the patio stones as its soft, large brown eyes fixed attentively on Ken's face.

"You drove very well," Ken said.

"Father told me you saved his life and I was to satisfy your every whim and desire."

Ken smiled. "That does not sound like your father."

"That is surely what he meant. It must be! Besides, I have two personalities, one when I speak English as now and another in French. Which pleases you more?"

"Both are charming."

"You sound like a Frenchman speaking English while I—" She lifted her face out of her hands as the fat lady set down the tray of sandwiches, coffee, and apricot pie made of the preserves from the fruit that grew in the valley. The pie was still hot.

"The Mayor gave us a lovely lunch," Eugenia said. "But how he went on and on about being the one who saved everything here at the café! Is it really true? His statements about being questioned by the Boche over a single cow were without proportion. As for his views on women in the Maquis—altogether ridiculous! He almost ruined my lunch. Besides, I am always hungry, especially when I am happy. Do you know when I am made love to my appetite is enormous?"

"I think perhaps you should begin speaking French."

She laughed, and pouted. "I mean to shock you and I only bore you. What happened here? Have you really come almost four thousand miles just for this? I feel so privileged if that is true." She drank her coffee and her face, pink and clear, turned red. "I am usually very collected with boys. Truly. But you are different. A man. And my father hardly ever praises anyone. You seem terribly rich. Are you?"

He laughed. "If I were your father, I would spank you."

"But you're not and I am much too big for that." She was a tall girl with bright blue eyes, small ears, and a long, graceful throat. "All Americans are rich. I was eleven at the Liberation. So now you know I am only nineteen. But the last year I helped, putting up stickers, delivering letters. I wish I had been a woman then, with something to believe in." She lit a cigarette, suddenly serious. "We believe in nothing. We study and plan and have no faith. After all, what is there worth living or dying for?" She flicked a nonexistent ash. "You let me babble on and on," she laughed. "But I give you no chance to stop me. What was here? Why do you come back to it? Americans are not supposed to be sentimental and I hope you are not. I hate sentimentality."

"So do I."

"Did you love a woman here?" She lowered her eyes and put out her cigarette. "Excuse me. Now I have gone too far. I think you are right. I had better speak French. And very little," she added in her native language.

Ken answered her in French. "I never could come out when I was here except at night. Save once for a moment, behind this very café. I was in France anyway and I have always wanted to know what it would be like to be here free and able to see it."

"Are you disappointed?"

"Not at all."

"No, tell me, please! Have I spoiled it?"

"No. No. Definitely not. If you were older or I younger, your father would have something to worry about."

"Perhaps I should speak French and you English. We are both more sensible in our native tongue."

He laughed. It seemed as if years had gone by without laughter. He took her hand and laughed again. "This is a wonderful country and it makes wonderful people."

"Don't you love your own country and people?"

"I don't know."

"Why not?"

"And I don't know why I don't know." He rose. The dog followed. "In that basement were the munitions for the entire region, and the sector chiefs lived here when they weren't in the woods below. This road is new. There was only a footpath then. They thought the Germans would not dare go this deep into Resistance country and they were right except for that one time the Mayor mentioned. He spoke the truth. Didn't your father tell you?"

"Let us not refer to my father. Seriously. I am a woman. You are a man. Your visit here is very romantic and I am a cynic. So this is like a dream to me. All right?"

"All right."

They went inside, secured permission to go below to the basement, now laden with jellied preserves and firewood.

"An old man who recruited your fath—excuse me—one of the first Maquisards of d'Uriage from Isère guarded the munitions here night and day for two years. The last four months he had an assistant. Before that he was alone. The Mayor captured the Germans the only time they came. He had nothing but fourteen boys and two rifles so he pretended he was a lieutenant of the FFI with sixty armed men. Yes, they ran round the café and shouted. They wasted some shots." He omitted his part in it. "The old man reached the Mayor on a private phone hidden right over there." He pointed to the furnace. "We were here for two nights. Just the old man and us." He looked out the small window. "She was somewhat older than you. Not much," he hurried on. "She handled the short wave."

"And you?"

"I compiled inventory, listed required materiel."

"Then you are an engineer."

"A statistician."

"What is that exactly?"

"One who correlates facts, figures. Dust!" He stopped, his face suddenly pale.

She put her hand on his arm gently. "I don't think so," she said. "No. No. You have done more than that." She moved her body in front of him, offering her lips.

He kissed her. She clung to him, would not let him go. He pulled himself away.

"Please," he said. "I do not approve of myself in this role. Please. Forgive me." He walked ahead to the basement door and she followed him, feeling his pain, knowing he would permit few people if any to ever see it, not understanding but wanting to, needing something to which to give her unused love. The sun was dipping into the west. Weird, long-bodied, sharp shadows etched their blackness on the white snow.

On the descent, Ken sat in silence. She glanced at him occasionally, started to sing "Kiss Me, Kate," showing off her English, stopped abruptly, and hummed quietly. The sun was setting very fast. She saw Ken watching it and said, "You need not worry. I am a very good driver."

"I was thinking I will soon see it as I remember it."

They both spoke French.

"How did you learn our language so fluently?"

"My mother took me to France many times and when I was a very small boy we spent the summers on an island between Campobello near Maine and the French-Canadian border."

"Campobello? Where President Roosevelt lived?"

"Yes."

"You knew him?"

Ken nodded. "Sometimes our families met, picnicking on Treat Island nearby." He blocked out a rush of remembered sounds and smells. The cold bay, the herring weir, their campfires and songs: the hunt. "And how did you learn to speak such perfect English?" he asked.

"An Englishwoman lived with Mother and me during the Occupation. An expatriate. She taught me nursery rhymes. It is my holiday language. My childhood-memory language. In school they gave it rules," she shrugged. "If I do not marry, I would like to live in America. I am to be an engineer, and America is the best country for engineers, isn't it? If I marry a man I will never deceive him."

Ken smiled.

"Don't you believe me?"

"Yes. Of course. You are not capable of deceit."

"No. I mean it. I have slept with many boys but only if they appealed to my sympathy, because I am maternal and kind-hearted. Not good. Good women take, that is all. They are like glass, cold, breakable, without regard for life. They are moral and virtuous and beastly. But if I should love and marry, all I have to give would belong to one man only and forever. You believe me?"

"Yes."

"I tell you this because we will never meet again and I know you will not tell Father. Americans are strong," she paused, lost in something, then began again. "Father has lived so much and yet he is

"She is high-spirited. That's all."

As the train pulled in, Angi shook Ken's hand, and holding it asked, "What was it all for, Major? Seriously. Does anybody know?"

When the train pulled out, Angi was still standing there, waving his hand, the cigarette drooping from his lips.

Chapter 2

THE air smelled wet, salt-clogged, and storm-laden. For days now dense, gun-metal clouds hung motionless in a low sky turned black, contrasting with unexpected tiny patches of bright Florida blue high above. In the early morning, fast, white, puffy clouds had already moved southward escaping a cold jet stream of wintry air that rushed relentlessly in from the northwest.

Ken lay bundled up in the damp chaise longue on the lawn between cottage and sea wall. Crashing gray waves from the Gulf of Mexico broke high against the sharp point of the wall and became small ripples that tapped their way downward to be soaked up in an oblivion of sand. He had arrived at their rented cottage on this isolated tip of Heron Key on Florida's West Coast four days ago. The first night Coogan phoned from Dallas to explain Ken's mission. With the Securities Exchange Commission's approval, the last step—Michigan—was now at hand. The entire Texas crowd planned to appear before the Federal District Court and have themselves a big time afterward. It had scared the Tamiamians chicken-witless. Everyone knew of the bitterness Judge Keane still felt toward the Texans, and everyone knew why. When the Judge had rejected their unworkable partisan plan eight years ago, the Texans had swooped down on His Honor after the fashion of a cattle roundup. Their tactics included a newspaper campaign of near slander against Keane's son, exposing junior's high jinks, of which going AWOL and boisterously resisting military arrest in the red-light district of Detroit had been only the mildest beginning. The scandal almost cost the Judge his bench. Now someone *had* to persuade the Texans to leave their representation in the impersonal hands of North American Power Company's junior counsel in Detroit and stage their festivities in Texas later or there would be nothing to celebrate!

Ken might inform the Tamiamians that Coogan had already broached the touchy subject and the Texans were listening thoughtfully. Coogan was quite sure he could finish up the job in Dallas with a few more quarts of bourbon and two or three tactful days. Ken should so inform the Tamiamians. Then *they* had something to tell Preston & Company. It couldn't be done by phone or mail; Ken would understand why once he met them. Ken had met them and he understood well enough now. It certainly could not have been done by phone or mail.

The lease on the cottage did not expire until May 1, and he had no reason to return to New York. There were no special situations in work now and none in the offing; nothing further to do on WHIP—nothing at all left to do, in fact, except for confronting Coogan. But his fury at Coogan, who was already successfully back from Dallas, was still too strong, and his contempt for himself as yet too much to handle.

Yesterday for a few hours warm air blew promisingly over the Gulf from the south. Then the north wind reappeared, shifting eastward to become a land breeze heavy with swarms of small, hard insects from the nearby swamp grass, as well as masses of icy air from far-off Grand Banks. The result was a thick, choking fog that fully enveloped the Key. All morning Ken had shivered and watched straggling remnants of off-season tourists, loath to return North and unable to afford the move to more civilized parts of west Florida. They would emerge briefly from the fog at the far distance, mostly middle-aged women, alone or in braces of twos and threes, doggedly approaching like ghosts, wrapped in coats and scarves which flapped as they stooped to pick up a shell and shake loose the clammy, wet sand before they threw it away or placed a find acceptable for northern sale into a plastic bag. Sometimes they appeared with old men aided by walking sticks, as they exercised a stiff leg at a slow, halting pace. When an occasional woman approached in a bathing suit, her head erect, she was either scrawny with protruding neckbones or bumpy with fat rolling over the sides—hair dyed too red or too blond. Even when the sun came out for fleeting moments all their chilled faces remained turned from it as they shuffled forward, hunch-shouldered and pinch-faced, seeking small profit from empty shells no longer inhabited by the salty flesh of life.

Since noon the fog had closed in completely. Nothing reached Ken from behind it now except the muffled, mournful sound of the gulls and the even sadder sound of the sea. There was something between the gulls and the sea that gave them no joy in sound, only in motion, unless that was his own distorted impression born of a desperate need for sweeping and decisive action and an end to this inner paralysis. He had seen the ocean dance and play at Caleb Island near Campobello where so much of his earliest New England childhood had been spent. Through most of the seasons he had seen the sea blush with sunset, drip wet gold at high noon, or glisten on calm, clear nights like

a young, naked bride when moonlight paid tribute of infinitely frag-
mented silver ornament. But never once had he heard the sea sing a
happy song: either that or he could no longer recall it.

The keening of the gulls came to him from behind the fog, companions of bone-cold remembered places where, if it had rarely
snowed, it never thawed.

Last night when the fog was still gathering, Ken lay awake and
tried to trace just how he had painted himself into this corner.

Before leaving for London he had still been able to tell himself this
growing sense of futility was sheer biochemistry—the normal letdown
after three years of a most exacting effort. But his trip to London and
Paris, made mandatory by the need for Coogan's presence in Washington at the same time and for the same reasons, pointed the shape of
things to come: the years of cloistered isolation as head of his firm's
research and statistical department were over. Then a half-hour conference in Florida stripped away what remained of the years' lingering illusions.

The Tamiamians had been quite forthright and businesslike and Mr.
Otter, chairman of their board, was very glad to meet the son of
Jonathan Preston at last, peering over his glasses like an ancient owl
to say that at first they had resented the instigation of voluntary divestment of their utilities in Florida though they knew all along it
was the Texans who had used political influence so crudely and un-
fairly. Still the sale under the Public Utility Act of 1935 was inevitable.
Bygones were bygones. They had received a fair price, very fair.
Extremely fair. And his lower lip had combed the gray mustache down
as he assured Ken they recognized how the Preston Plan had made a
continuing, profitable existence possible for them through the stock
participation in the parent company, North American Power. So. They
were grateful for the diligent efforts of Preston & Company, and wished
to prove it. They were prepared to buy seventy thousand shares of
WHIP from Preston & Company though it was known they only held
fifty thousand shares at present. The purchase would take place away
from the market at the highest quote on the Floor during any one of
the five trading days following favorable Michigan court action. They
would also buy the shares held by the French and British groups but
at somewhat less advantageous terms, naturally. Such a block purchase
would remove one hundred and twenty-five thousand shares from the
market. It would raise the price at once and Preston's duty to the Floor
Protective Committee would be more than met! The added profit to
his firm in short gains on twenty thousand more shares would no
doubt defray the legal and administrative costs Preston & Company
had assumed in behalf of all parties.

While the air conditioner purred and black flies buzzed on the outside screen, the phone call came through from Havana. It was full of joviality, bad Spanish, and sly inferences. So the same offer was being made to the South Americans, who had spent twenty-five years and no small amount of human blood opposing outside domination of their national resources and would now surrender all of it overnight for a quick profit! Even before the reorganization was complete, the seemingly defeated minority in Tamiami was hard at work, seeking to wrest control out of it. It was legal enough. It was proper enough. It had nothing to do with the reorganization save to follow it. As they said, it was of no concern to the Michigan court. But if Judge Keane got wind of it, he would find some pretext for rejecting the reorganization: were Ken in his place he would do the same. He wasn't shocked by their conduct; only by his failure to expect it.

Though it doomed the fruits of reorganization to failure, his duty of office was quite clear—his was the duty of silence, acquiescence, and compliance. His duty to himself was irrelevant. His personal reasons for working on the reorganization—his private need to finish what had finished Father was irrelevant. So was his impossible naïveté in ever thinking he could reconcile such altogether personal reasons for the Preston Plan with the only sensible, practical reason anyone ever should or could have for being in finance. Profit.

He was irrelevant. This shabbiness was a fitting close to a pointless career.

When the Texans found out, they would retaliate. Doubtless the New England insurance companies planned some senseless intrigue of their own. The final victors might well be the off-stage private interests close to the New England group. Not really final. Nothing would be final, because there was to be no end to the madness, which would go on and everlastingly on.

In one unguarded moment his head was turned by catchwords like honor and duty, and behind his back half his life had slipped away. He had endured this distortion of his nature for nothing—an errand boy for double-dealers—quaint and ridiculous! He had entered the firm in the beginning and WHIP at the end to complete what Father had started; at the *actual* end, he would be known as the author of chicanery and double-dealing deceit. What was more, he would be admired for it as he had been held in contempt these past twenty uneventful years! and for all time to come this would be known by his name, their name, Father's, Grandfather's, and Great-grandfather's name! The Preston Plan. The lunacy was complete.

No doubt Coogan expected to get what he had originally bargained for. But he wouldn't—Ken would see to that. It was the only cold

comfort he could derive from this now. Coogan would not gain entrance into the Big League with a mere million. Not without Ken. Not
without the prestige Preston label, not yet.

At least that much honor was still left in the name.

Ken jumped up and began to walk, almost running into the fog,
stumbling in his haste and tripping over rotten logs. He was forty-two.
Wifeless, childless, planless, less and less, and still dwindling. He had
carried the title of senior partner and done the work of a glorified
clerk. He had been a tool, first for Father's chosen partners, junior in
name only, and then for those of his own choice, Coogan and McBride.
Preston & Company, once a creed, now a tarnished trademark, a
mockery, a pickpocket's key, an open sesame for others to enter each
open season year after year! He had made none of the history, past
and purposeful, nor present and when accounted for of no account at
all. Forty-two. Twice twenty-one. More than half his life gone so in-
conclusively he could scarcely detail the years, weeks, or days except
for isolated events burned painfully into memory.

Finding Father dead in his gun room, surrounded by his trophies,
stuffed lions' heads, kudu horns, snow leopards, and hippos. Hearing
Mother, already headed for hysterics, saying, "He ran out of targets!"

The summer of '29. His first at Preston & Company, in the statistical
department where Father had shrewdly placed him, away from the
ticker tape, ringing bells, cigar smoke, and smut of the customers'
room. There he had discovered an unexpected application of his
natural interest in social phenomena, historic and economic trends,
facts and figures, and their possible synthesis into some useful working
hypothesis. This discovery did not have the result Father had hoped
for. When the summer ended and he returned to Harvard, he knew he
would never prefer the firm to a faculty, a Seat on the Exchange to a
seat of learning, or the sale of securities to a studious life of scholarship,
with the ultimate aim of a career in curatorship.

Yet a few years later when Father failed and shot himself, Ken remembered the Rules. They had dictated the Only Right and manly
thing to do as the only son of the oldest son of Timothy Preston's
first-born son at the tender age of twenty-one, preordained to enter
finance rather than science, history, or education as other Prestons had
done and as he had wanted so passionately to do and almost had done
until predestination caught up with him.

He had manfully made the best of it. He had chosen to head up the
statistical department, reduced his share of profit and achieved, so he
had thought at the time, a compromise between what he actually
wanted to do and the only function in Preston & Company that was

almost but not quite like it—as like and no more like than a resemblance between the girl you passionately loved and lost, and someone who hauntingly had the same color hair, same cut of eye, same form of body and face, but none of the singing heart or vibrant spirit that had made you love a first and only time.

No one can say he hadn't taken those wasted years like a man. Done it like a man. Damn sight more manly by God than the dilettante works of other Prestons. Practical work, son, tangible work, boy, with its countable rewards like a squirrel's nuts, a cannibal's shrunken heads, or the barnacles on sea rocks. Damn right. For a man's work was from son to son and though a woman's or a pansy's might never be done, so doing while gathering garlands to entwine in maidens' hair was not for him. Hell no and Christ no and gotcha and roger and good show and other manly mannerisms like slap 'em on the back and attaboy, boy oh boy, man the deck and deal and cut and double deal and undercut the deck and cut the crap of cutting paper dolls or dreaming dreams of ghostly ships, curatorships and scholarships that would never go to sea like whaling ships or sailing ships, now crewless, screwball, ball-less ships and only real if time stood still which time does not. The Great Time had passed and with it great, truly great-grandfather Timothy Preston. The end of the line, the last male seed—and in this seedy way a journey ended.

Most of all he remembered France and *what was it all for, Major, seriously, does anybody know?*

WHIP would succeed, if that's what they called it, and everlastingly no one would ever know anything. The Prestons who knew nothing at all would no doubt approve the squandering of his life; their polite weekend guests on Caleb Island, knowing even less, would certainly agree. Ken Preston had done it—what do you know! He had carried it off. With a handful of pennies he had accomplished what his father who never ever *really* knew anything don't you know had failed to do with fifteen or was it twenty million dollars, no one ever really knew. Colorless Ken had cleared up the mess, wiped out a blot, and cheers for the family's good name. He was a good man of good stock with good breeding and good blood will tell and to tell the truth no one *really* knew how he'd done it.

One day he might even come to believe it himself. But only by day. That much he *did* know. That much he would never forget and *that* was what he had better remember now. Only by day could he ever believe it and no matter how many times you dismissed the nights, they never dismissed you.

It was in France in '44 that he had once decided to quit, but never did—another thing hard to forget.

He wanted to howl, to cry out, to be violent; yet all he could feel was depression, apathy, a decent, decorous despondency, all neat and of a proper, present-day, puny, prissy Preston size. Even Father, who had never raised his voice, as Great-grandfather must have for his crew to hear him above the gale, had been sufficiently moved if only once to decisive action when he raised his delicate gun hand against himself, the revolver discreetly muffled by a silencer.

The fog was thinner here, pierced and scattered against a high mass of tarred wooden pilings extending far out into the Gulf. He could see three pelicans flying in formation. They folded their wings in unison and divebombed for fish. One rose vertically from the choppy water with his prey. The second, less fortunate, followed, its wings unfolding swiftly like banners drawn by invisible strings. When the third sought to rise, it flew lopsidedly and fell back to bob on the waves like a wound-down toy. It attempted flight again—this time succeeding. With one wing only half spread it flew clumsily in the opposite direction, away from the other pelicans, toward the shore and the north—deeper into the fog.

No, he *hadn't* quit and that was almost ten years ago, when he was only thirty-two. Forty-two now. Fifty-two soon. Then sixty-two—seventy-two—

He could hear the Gulf at his left and the trees in the convulsing wind at his right. He could not tell whether it was the blackness of night or the storm about to break. Around the bend was only the tall swamp grass and beyond it the bay. He had reached the end of the sand spit. The tide was high, leaving at most a foot of beach to walk on; in some places there was no beach at all. He removed his wet shoes, rolled up his damp trousers, and walked back toward the cottage knee-deep in the cold water.

A sudden clatter made him turn. It came from a cluster of thick, curling stumps high up on a dune. It might have been the sheddings of a huge snake. It was only the water-shriveled, bleached roots of wild sea grass. Behind it, dimly visible, was a wind shelter of shaking southern pines. The wounded pelican moved again, huddling closer into the trees, and stared unblinkingly. Ken climbed up to the top of the dune. The bird lifted one usable wing against him, not permitting itself to be touched. Overhead were the silhouettes of other pelicans circling low. Ken watched them rise to a higher altitude, still circling.

"Stand up and hook up."

When the ground signals seemed correct, the plane had descended, and a sudden gust of wind had made the navigator worry in view of the smallness of the clearing and the fact that it was so thickly sur-

rounded by pine trees, rocky crags, and streams turbulent with the melting ice of the Alps and poorly visible due to the mists of early spring.

It was almost impossible to see anything now except down below in the far distance on the beach where the small yellow light of a storm lamp turned on the westward sea side of his cottage. The pine trees thrashing in the wind concealed and revealed the small light below.

"Sorry, Major, something wrong with those signals."

The wind blew, moving the branches again, and the light of the storm lamp was in the clear once more.

"All fine now, Major, and there's your pinpoint. Good luck!"

The fourth time around, he had jumped directly over the pool of light made by headlights of the four trucks and landed smoothly with only a badly twisted ankle but no serious damage.

The truck lights went out and many Frenchmen were embracing him, slapping his back, excitedly shaking both his hands. The trucks were gone by the time he had buried his parachute. Then he headed into the woods with three of the Maquisards. The youngest one supported his weight so that they could move as quickly as Ken's limp permitted.

Two hours later they were picked up by a truck. It drove recklessly around the trees, passing other trucks like their own, weird, charcoal and wood-burning vehicles. The parked gazogenes looked as though they were on fire as shadowy, slim figures, wearing berets, with rifles slung over their shoulders, piled wood into the flames at the open fronts of the trucks.

They reached the field hospital deep in the woods near midnight. Wounded men lay on cots made of the pines. Ken said that if time and the protection of night were being squandered because of his ankle it was quite unnecessary. He was told the stop had to be made in any event in order to pick up his short-wave operator.

Insects living this side of timber line sent constant staccato messages across great distances; sentries guarding the night.

"No worry. The Boche doesn't penetrate this deep."

In a steadier light Ken now saw that the boy who had borne most of his weight was barely seventeen.

His ankle was strapped by a well-built, dark-haired girl. There was a streak of gray that ran a half-inch thick through her unruly black hair and she kept pushing it out of her large brown eyes with the back of her hand.

"I could give you a sedative to ease the pain," she said in almost excellent English.

"*Thank you, no,*" *he answered in French.* "*I prefer to be completely awake.*"

She nodded, helping him into his shoe. "*How was your landing?*"

"*Ordinary.*"

The ankle had swollen considerably.

"*You were lucky,*" *she said.* "*We acquired this ambulance and the medical supplies only yesterday.*"

She told him how they had seized the Vichy ambulance after an important Milicien officer in a nearby town took critically ill and his aide called for emergency medical assistance from the Nazi-run hospital in Grenoble. They had captured the ambulance after a gun duel on the Oisan road. Another ambulance was promptly sent from Grenoble and picked up the sick Milicien. Meanwhile an Italian patrol from St. Simon, seeking the first ambulance, saw the second one, mistook it for the captured one and fired, killing all of the Milice, including the sick officer. She laughed and disappeared. When she reappeared she was dressed in ski pants, a plaid jacket, and a kerchief around her hair. She carried a small suitcase.

"*I am Natalie, your communications staff, also the medical supplies expert.*" *She smiled and pointed.* "*That is our transportation.*"

He limped quickly after her to the horse-drawn cart where men were tying the horse's hoofs and cart wheels with rags. She lifted herself to the back of the cart.

"*We passed curfew at midnight,*" *she said.* "*It is doubtful that the Boche will be up this far but if your plane was seen it is not altogether impossible.*"

They were watering the horse.

"*If we are stopped our story is we fell asleep and hitched this ride somewhere along the road. We were making love in the woods. I was visiting friends in Grenoble where we met. We have spent two heavenly days together.*"

There were two bicycles in the cart to substantiate this. "*You will be sleepy. I will do most of the talking. You have your cover papers?*"

He nodded.

"*Is your French as good as it sounds?*"

Ken said he thought it convincing enough if his sentences remained short. She told him that no story they used would really be believed if they were stopped by Germans, but it would be fine if they were stopped by Italians who believed anything for money. It was for this reason they had chosen St. Simon, policed only by Italians, for their safe house and the conference. In view of Ken's presence, French Milice would be the worst of all. She handed him a wooden box with cracks in it. When they had crawled far back into the cart, she drew

*one like it over her face. He did the same. A few meager slabs of cheese
were dropped in on them along with large quantities of rutabaga, the
inedible potato substitute on which most of South France now existed.
A smelly canvas covering was drawn over them and secured to the
cart by frayed ropes. His ankle pain was quite severe now. There was
no way of moving his legs. For many hours the horse jogged slowly
along. Ken slept a little. Mostly he lay awake listening. Once the cart
stopped when the horse urinated. It was a loud, unsafe sound on the
frost-hard road. Then once more for a long stretch he heard nothing
save for the creaking of the cart. Its monotonous rhythm put him to
sleep. Once the cart swerved sharply and he awoke to feel something
soft lunge against him. It was the girl's warm body.*

*When next he woke the cart had stopped. He heard a French-
accented man's voice call out with false genialty, "*Buon giorno.*"*

*It was answered by two sleepy male voices, both gloomy, "*Buon
giorno, patron.*"*

*The ropes were being untied and he felt the cool dawn air as the
canvas was partly lifted. Then the cart was tipped abruptly and he slid
forward, his feet hitting a wooden stay. The sharp pain rose from
ankle to knee. He was in an almost upright position when the wooden
stay dropped from under his feet and he hurtled downward, the
cheese and vegetables flying from behind, hitting his head and shoulders. When he rose from the stone floor, the box smashed, his nose
bleeding, three men dressed as peasants approached in the wine cellar
to greet him: Angi, Maurice, and Roger. Soon after* le patron *himself appeared with a banquet breakfast of* café au lait, *jelly, and
hot rolls. He bent his thickset neck and heavy shoulders forward formally, smiled and said, "My honor, Major. Likewise the village's.
Everyone is delighted you arrived safely. They know, of course. Even
some Milice, I am afraid. All but the Boche."*

*Then followed five days and nights as he argued for London's
proposal that the Maquis first seize the power plants in the Romanche
Valley and afterward the adjacent towns including St. Simon. Roger, as
Communist representative from Franc-Tireurs et Partisans, used every
reluctance of the others to abandon the safety of the woods for the
exposed dangers of the power plants and towns. He reminded the De
Gaullists that the African invasion of last November resulted in German occupation of South France, blaming it on "Wall Street's con-
nivance with British Imperialism." He objected to Stens because their
range was less than two hundred yards and they jammed. He challenged the authority of Americans like Ken who were junior in status
to British Intelligence, lectured on war as class struggle conducted
by other means, and once succeeded in sufficiently sidetracking Mau-*

rice to create a lively discussion of alternate plans for blowing up bridges and trains that gained power from the plants. Maurice favored using detonating cord, connecting all the charges with enough aluminum nitrate, while Roger advocated a different technique as they explored the comparative merits of explosives that pushed concrete against those that cut steel, until Ken interrupted to warn all of them that rejecting London's proposal would result in Allied bombers blowing up the plants and the consequence in ruin for the peasants of the area would be on their conscience. Twice Ken changed his recommendations to London, using the code virtually no one understood, including Natalie. Once he recommended seizing the towns first and the plants afterward, as well as replacement of Stens with Browning automatics, M-1's, and American carbines of the folding-stock type. The second time he proposed all materiel be dropped before any steps were taken by the French and that the Communists be given their full share in advance of any action. In between, Germans arrived in St. Simon with potatoes and tried to use them as a decoy for Maquisards as well as to gain information from the hungry townspeople regarding the conference which they now knew was taking place somewhere in the area. The next day, students from the University in Grenoble, who had hung a skeleton on the front door of the Milice chief in protest against the withholding of the potatoes, were captured on their way to the Tunnel du Mont Cenis and one had his eyes gouged out. Roger dismissed the action as infantile leftist nonsense, but twenty-four hours later a hundred German Gestapo were swarming in the town of a thousand people. In the wine cellar, they had reached a stalemate. All the De Gaullists agreed to Ken's plan as modified. However, Comrade Roger still held out for greater authority in the action, actual delivery of materiel in advance, and equal political authority in the towns once they were captured. The others had made Communist co-operation a condition for the plan's execution. So there was nothing to do but wait. In the tense atmosphere, Maurice spoke of his dream of the night before.

"Did I tell you?" he said. "What clams! Gigantic ones in seaweed, green, fresh, smelling of the sea. It all sizzled happily in a coal fire, but high, close to God with green grass in spite of all the ice and snow. Then instead of flames it is music. Warm, sweet, caressing to the ear. And for a plate, white, smooth, and cool, a woman's thighs, which I likewise bite ever so gently and lick clean."

Angi said, "Freud could explain everything."

"I know without explanation. I wish for the taste of a woman, a virgin woman fresh from her bath like a jewel in the sunshine. And music, endless music for the woman without coarse, hard pants."

Later, while the others slept, Ken paced. Snoring came from under the northeast window where Maurice lay on his stomach, face flushed, his right knee jerking fitfully, his left hand between his legs.

Comrade Roger had used the worst in them for his purpose, sharpening differences in the name of unity and seeking partisan advantage while proclaiming the Communists' right to equality. That's only as expected. But he uses what is here and real and is my problem. They all fear to leave the hills. They cling to the shelter of trees; they fled the towns simply to stay alive. Only later did they face the need to fight. They have yet to believe in their ability to do so where the fight finally has to be fought and won—not where they have been driven to and hide and barely exist but in the towns. They must take the towns and plants. I come and go. I will not face the aftermath of retaliation. Yet I must convince them of the rightness and possibility of seizing the towns and plants. Natalie understands this. Not willingly, but she cannot avoid understanding because she wants to live, to reclaim everything that belongs to her, and so she must understand. Angi can understand but by now he has confused fear with caution so that he needs guarantees I cannot give. After Roger, Maurice is the problem. Maurice is actually glad that he was driven out of society. He prefers the trees, rocks, half-raw food, danger, and violence. These very deficiencies of his are his strengths in this situation. Maurice is decisive: so is preventing Roger from using it all. Roger had tried to challenge Ken's authority by raising such extraneous matters as Marxism-Leninism, Imperialism, Clausewitz, infantile leftism, assuming they were foreign to Ken. There had been hours enough of waiting and if Roger knew nothing of what in fact the Soviet Union was, he had read everything of what it was supposed to be. Once Roger had been able to carry the subject sufficiently far from the plants and towns to get back to harping on the African campaign.

Ken said, "There are two sides to the African decision," which drew Roger's sneering statement that this was "the great American liberal disease of seeing two sides to every question when one is wrong and one right."

Ken replied, "Sometimes it is only a clash of equally legitimate interests," to which Roger said, "I think your so-called bourgeois democracy would look better to the world with my charge of naïveté than with your admission of immorality."

"I'm afraid democracy cannot be dismissed that simply."

"Bourgeois democracy. History is dismissing it."

"That is a good example of my point. I am not at all sure that is what history is doing and you are and those are the two sides of that *particular* question."

Etcetera.

It had all been plain nonsense and a mistake due to the waiting. The real issue still remained the towns and the plants.

Ken reviewed the map as drawn by Angi, fixing it in his mind to erase the grid-accurate map of the region shown him in London. Angi's map marked distances by meadows and hedges; cemeteries, trees, and streams. The water fountain in the square was life's center and the points of the compass were measured in yards, feet, and inches, not kilos and miles. Briançon had seemed much closer to St. Simon in London. The Isère River coming down from due north of their safe house to flow west to Grenoble and then wind around and come out southeast of him at Romanche had also seemed a simple matter in London where its winding had not been clearly stated. Another hazard. Roger's guerrillas would have to do some dangerous walking, crossing many exposed roads to join the FFI in the north for the seizure of the plants. Clearly St. Simon would have to be the FFI problem alone. The landing field, the same one London would use for the drops further east by northeast out of St. Simon, was a distance from Romanche measurable only in terms of danger. After it there remained the practical question of allocating a fair portion of the supplies for the Communists. Until the towns and plants were seized they could not take their full share back: the exposure made that impossible. This was an argument in favor of London's original proposal and he had failed to take advantage of it. But throughout the real problem was getting all of them to leave the woods and face exposure and their fear of it. He would have to reduce this to its proper size in all their minds. Once again he fixed the distance from the landing field to the Café des Oiseaux where materiel would be cached, measuring the hazard of tangled dead branches, twigs and roots underfoot, and streams to be crossed.

"You can't sleep."

Natalie had seen Ken's feet through the bottom of her screen and opened it. It was like a door to a tiny, separate, private room. He stood at a distance.

"Come in and close the screen," she said. She sat up as he entered. A blanket was wrapped around her. "Sit down."

As he sat she leaned forward for her cigarettes and briefly in the shadows he saw her flesh, white, from the billowing, rose-tipped breasts to the small toes, feet turned toward one another like a bashful child's. His hand lay tense but limp on the stones, his finger tips touching the edge of her horse blanket, coarse and hard. A motor shook the sky. Neither looked up. Maurice's snore stopped abruptly, brakes screeching in his mind behind some forest tree or mountain slope.

"You did well," she said.

"We are still deadlocked."

"No. Roger knows the January decision. He is weakening."

Then silence.

"I do not have hard pants on now," she said.

"Natalie."

"No words, Major. Whatever. But no words."

Fast breathing made her body rise and fall, revealing, concealing.

"So particular a dream?"

He nodded remembrance. "I think I must say good night," he said.

"Good night, Major." She said it softly. There was something glad in her regret, something she had set aside long ago that his declining reawakened.

The next morning, led by Natalie, they brought all their pressure to bear on Comrade Roger, and Roger struck back with countercharges. The ranks of the FFI were filled with peasant cowards, men who had fled to the hills not for love of France but out of fear of Hitler's Todt labor conscription; that and ex-stool pigeons or strike-breakers whose wives were still being paid their absent husbands' salaries by grateful factory bosses. Angi reminded him that the F.A.M.A. and its Communist leaders were the last to enter the fight against Hitler as well as the first to have collaborated with him, and Roger's answer that Communists fought Hitler in Spain when men like Maurice were stealing their neighbors' pigs and chickens finally caused Maurice to draw his gun out of its holster.

Fortunately le patron appeared at that moment to say, "You leave for the new safe house. Right now. Quickly!"

"All of us together?" Roger asked.

Le patron did not answer. He motioned them impatiently to the open door leading up to his restaurant. They climbed the stairs single file and walked through the darkened room round the tables with the chairs piled on them.

"Out front is a Boche truck," le patron said. "Walk straight to the open back and hop in."

"What is this?" Roger demanded.

Le patron did not answer. Maurice left first, Angi followed, then Ken and behind him Natalie. The rear of the truck was open. An Italian soldier stood by looking the other way as they entered. At the last moment when le patron and the Italian were closing the truck, Roger ran out, leaped in, and the truck raced away.

They could hear the driver and the man next to him conversing in the local patois. They spoke of the God damn Maquis, the Communist Jew-bastard students from Grenoble, the Jew-bastard American who

*had landed, and what they would do when they found him. They dis-
cussed the Spanish ex-Loyalist workers scattered throughout South
France and how generous General Franco was in offering them am-
nesty if they returned to Spain to work. They agreed that the Fuehrer
and Il Duce would surely win the war. The truck stopped, there was
a brief exchange, and the driver left. The man beside him took over the
wheel. They drove more rapidly now, with many turns and spins.
The truck stopped. Its back door was opened.*

"Whore of a ghost!" Roger said.

*Maurice knocked the submachine gun from Roger's hands. Before
them stood a slight, Spanish-looking man. He wore the uniform of a
Fascist Franco officer, medals on his chest.*

*"Montero!" Maurice embraced him. So did Natalie. They did not
explain and the little man with Franco medals drove off. He had
brought them as far as the truck could go up the narrow road. They
followed the footpath higher to Café des Oiseaux—their new safe
house and sometime headquarters for the sector commanders, ad-
jutants, and unit leaders.*

*Nearing it, Maurice motioned them toward the bushes and from
behind one he whistled in imitation of a mountain bird that never
sang at night. The sound was answered. They walked faster, now
using the center of the road. Soon they were inside. The old man embraced Angi, acknowledged the others, and answered Maurice's questions: nothing had happened except for the munitions brought to the
café after the ambulance was taken the other day. No materiel had
been depleted. They took Ken through the house and showed him
their total reserve of munitions for the entire sector. Angi told the old
man that Ken had joined them to see how much materiel they had and
needed. After that the old man opened bins, well covers, and furnace
doors willingly and on the upper floors the chests, drawers, highboys,
vents, closets, and other hiding places. Meanwhile Natalie set up her
wireless in the basement. The scarcity of munitions, from examination
of which Comrade Roger was not excluded, made him thoughtful:
clearly he had not believed it was that low. Nor had Ken. The old man
brought them cheese, wine, cold biscuits, and jellied preserves. Restrained from making fires and alone at the café, he could neither cook
nor hunt. For fresh meat, fowl, or vegetables such as there were, he
had to wait for the boys in the woods. Maurice proposed that they go
back and look in on their camps. Angi agreed.*

*"And you," Maurice said to Roger. "You wish to see how it is with
us?"*

"You don't mind?"

"You already know where we keep our munitions. Yes or no?"

"Why not?"

"I must remain for messages from London," Ken said.

Maurice grinned. "So must Natalie."

"I am sure they both have things to discuss with the old man," Angi said, winking to his sponsor. "For myself, when I want a good night's sleep, Major, I always go to the woods." He rose.

Natalie smiled and they left.

"You don't think there will be trouble for Roger?" Ken asked.

"No, no. Maurice knows we need the Communists right now. Such stunts are their stock in trade, not ours."

"Maurice was fingering his gun before we entered the truck."

"That is simply Maurice's sense of humor. We have shot one another in the past but that was over food or munitions when the drops were too few."

With the old man's permission, Ken re-examined the munitions inventory carefully, noting exact amounts and types. The shortage was quite serious. They did not even have enough to take one village, let alone five or the Romanche power plants. The old man asked whether they wished to sleep upstairs and Natalie explained she had to be near the short wave.

"If there is a message," she told Ken, "I could come up and wake you."

"No," he said. "I prefer to be on the spot."

Later the old man brought a goatskin bladder of wine, more cheese, some old blankets, and for Natalie a feather quilt left over at the café from peacetime when it was used by Alpine climbers and skiers. He tapped the pot-bellied stove.

"Up in the gooseneck is a wire," he explained. "When you pull it, the phone comes out. It connects to the Mayor's home. Once used it is to be cut. It is only in the eventuality of the Boche. I sleep in the room above, over there." He pointed.

Ken nodded understanding.

"No Boche has come yet." The old man waved his hand across the basement wall directly facing the woods, and affection restored life to his face. "They will not dare it."

He left them. Now there was silence broken by nothing, not even a wind in the twigs. After long listening Ken could hear a distant rushing stream. But the strange humming sound was his own excitement. She came from behind the cold boiler wrapped in the feather quilt. Then she lay down and spoke in a whisper.

"All right," she said.

The sound startled him. He turned.

"It was sweet of him about the quilt," she said. "He's a nice old man."

Ken agreed. She was smoking a cigarette, looking up at the bril-

*liant, starry sky through the uncovered window. A new moon was ris-
ing.*

"Should we cover it?" he asked.

She looked at him inquiringly.

"For security," he added.

She laughed. "Superfluous either way."

"That is very little munitions reserve for two thousand men."

They were twenty feet apart, facing each other from opposite walls.

"How does a man like you come to this work?"

"O.S.S. began as a research statistical project. That and my knowing
French."

"But you could have left when it changed."

"I suppose."

"Still you stayed."

"Yes."

"To prove to yourself you could?"

"Possibly."

"Now you know you can. That is no longer your problem."

"What is my problem?"

She raised her pack of cigarettes, then laughed and dropped it.
"And you don't smoke either."

"No."

"It reminds me of a joke," she said.

"I always remind people of a joke," he answered.

"God. Please." She said it with a comic roll of her eyes. "It is bad
enough to be alone with a man whom you desire who desires you
not, with such a sky outside and with who-knows-what facing us tomorrow. Don't seek my sympathy."

"Natalie."

"When your voice is so low, I cannot hear."

He rose and crossed to her and stood. She looked up.

"Natalie."

"You are going to talk again?"

"Well, mustn't we?"

"No. We must not. When each night can be your whole lifetime,
there are rules if you are to find a completeness. No talk. That is the
duty if there is still to be hope and humanness. Talk is for enough
time guaranteed to live the years, not the hours. Even then life is an
emergency. Here if we have many days, we have many lifetimes,
not to be all mixed up with one another by confessions, questioning,
and talk. They are the only faithlessness in this condition. Do you understand?"

"No."

"Then you are still only watching. For or against but not part of."

"That is not so."

"That is so. Also that is your problem now. Please don't touch me."

"Natalie."

"No. I despise fumblers in the dark, like ants who collide by accident. You wish to watch and wait and talk and chart through centuries, while you blaspheme against the life that is now."

"I'm sorry you're angry."

"I am always angered by waste and obscenity. Good night, Major."

He turned and started to go. *"I haven't touched a woman for years."*

"More waste and obscenity."

"No. Promiscuity is your ants fumbling in the dark."

"You think like a woman." She extended her hand. *"All right. Stay. I have no eternities and happily-ever-afters in which to teach you how to claim your manhood and you have an abundance of foolish virgin signs."*

"I am sorry."

"No. You are unused but not obscene. So in our lifetime together I will love you and show you." Her hand had barely been able to reach the light, but no part of her pulled away from him.

Choking, Ken woke against the hard palm tight over his mouth that held his jaws firmly. With the other hand the old man pointed upstairs and then touched his ear. Ken listened and heard boots approaching in unison on the road. Reading Ken's eyes, the old man shook his head, pointed to the woods, and shook his head again. Of course. Maquis would never make the approach this way. Boche? He released Ken. Ken turned to Natalie. She was sleeping. The old man nodded. Ken placed his hand over her mouth. She choked, struggled against it, and understood at once.

They dressed swiftly as the old man pulled the phone out of the pot-bellied stove. Natalie dismantled her short wave. Ken removed the loose stones from the wall space behind the boiler. Then Natalie went to the window. From the side she looked out and counted. The old man could tell by what he saw on her face—it was not a look for Italians or Milice. She held up all ten fingers, then lowered them and raised eight. The old man held the phone and nodded. First Ken pushed the short wave through the small hole in the stone wall, then the rifles; there were only ten in the basement. Natalie crossed both forefingers and made the zero sign. Gravely the old man understood. Then she showed him both her palms and the backs of her hands and made another zero. The old man lifted the phone from its cradle. Natalie reached Ken and pointed to the hole and then to him. As he started crawling through, feeling cloth and skin go at certain places, he heard the old man telling the Mayor in low tones that eighteen Gestapo, fully armed, were coming up the road. So far they could know nothing and could see no signs of life. There was no smoke from the immediate woods and no sounds carried on the wind. Nor had there been any since sunrise, less than an hour ago. Therefore the Maquisards were too far away to help. By the time they heard shots it would be too late.

Once outside, Ken drew his forty-five and took a step forward. Natalie grabbed his arm, stopping him, and pointed to the twigs underfoot, then to her ear and to the road. He nodded. She touched her chest with her finger, pointed to the ground on which they stood, and began to take off her shoes. Ken seized her and held her firm. Her silent anger made veins thicken in her throat as she struggled, but he would not let her go alone. The old man had put the loose stones back into place so all they could do was stand there silently with the ten rifles and listen and wait. At last they heard the old man at the café door facing the road overhead.

"Nein. No one, herren. I hunt and live here. Ja, ja."

They heard the sound when he was hit, and the door made a loud slam when it was shut. During the brief noise Ken and Natalie managed to advance over the crackling twigs to reach the edge of the rear wall of the café. Trees, bushes, and dead leaves still stood thick between them and the road. From the silence it seemed that all the Gestapo were inside now. Ken thought of London trying to reach them and pointed to the ground, to the road, and to both of them. Natalie shook her head firmly. They waited. At last she touched him and pointed to the path below.

In the distance they saw silhouettes of the Mayor approaching with the boys, fourteen in number and all under sixteen in age. They carried only two rifles. Natalie raised her revolver over her head and moved it back and forth but it was too low to catch the early sun. Ken lifted her to his shoulders. The sun was still not high enough for the blue steel to pick up its rays. The approach would take twenty minutes at the least. They had to avoid the twigs off the road or the sound fast feet made on it. If any of the Gestapo came out before the Mayor reached the café, it was over. If London tried to come through before the Mayor reached the café, and got no answer, it could be over. Finally the Mayor made the boys remove their shoes and they ran the remaining distance up the road. They were going to attempt the capture of eighteen Gestapo men with two outmoded rifles. They were breaking up into two groups of seven. Ken stepped out into view in the half light. Before the boy with the other rifle could shoot him, the Mayor seized his hand and nodded to Natalie as she appeared beside Ken, straining under the weight of the ten rifles. On signal the two groups of boys began running, shouting, and singing. The Mayor led one group, and the biggest boy with the second rifle led the other. They wasted shots as the groups crossed, picking up the rifles beside Natalie. The impression of many men relied on the speed with which they ran, the fact that the dawn light would reveal only shadows to the Gestapo inside the café, and the spacing of the shots from the dozen rifles and two guns—that and the loudness of their voices. After the two groups circled the café for the second time, the Mayor called out, "Boches! The invasion has begun. Your only chance to live is to surrender. The American major of an advance corps is here."

To Ken it seemed a ridiculous, foolhardy thing to do. They were all motioning him impatiently to speak. In German, Ken said, "Surrender as you are ordered or you will die inside in flames."

The Mayor said, "I count to three. One—two—"

The door opened. The first one threw out his arms and appeared, hands overhead. One by one the other seventeen Gestapo followed. The old man appeared, bleeding only from one eye and his cut lip. He carried a carbine.

"That is the last," he said. He waved to the woods. "They heard our shots. Soon they are here."

"Do you think the Boche knew or were they simply on reconnaissance?" Ken asked.

"They will tell us why they came up this far," the Mayor said slowly in his poor German, to make sure the captured men all understood. "Or they will suffer long and hard."

"We will have to change the safe house again," Natalie said. Her voice was trembling. She did not look at the captured men.

Changing the safe house proved unnecessary. Even before Angi, Maurice, and Roger had appeared with a hundred FFI men, Natalie had set up the short wave and they heard from London. Ken's proposals had been accepted. The drops would take place tonight at Boulac. The Maquisard were to be at the clearance station at 2100 hours with as many trucks as they had for transporting arms, medical supplies, food, and clothing. The FTP would get its full share. The hundred men emptied the café of everything.

"Roger is impressed with our camp," Maurice said good-naturedly.

"And with London too?" Natalie asked Roger.

Roger said he was now ready to wireless FTP headquarters, urging co-operation for the seizure of the plants and towns under unified De Gaullist command.

At 2200 hours there was still no sign of the planes. Then suddenly they heard distant explosions, saw the pink puff of ack-ack in the sky, and four gazogene trucks appeared out of the forest ready to form a semicircle and begin signaling with their headlights.

"The red, white, and blues!" Natalie shouted and pointed. The first plane was circling. It made a perfect pinpoint with ten parachute drops. The second plane dropped bazookas. The Maquis appeared out of the woods carting materiel and medical supplies. The charcoal-burning trucks were racing around the clearing. There were four planes in all and at the end a message for Ken advising that Jeds would be arriving tomorrow to aid in training the Maquis in the use of bazookas as well as to supervise the engineering of the power plants.

In the woods they ate bread and cheese while Natalie checked off her medical supplies. Men came by and met Ken. He was embraced, shaken by the hand, slapped on the shoulder, and kissed. L'Américain had delivered the goods! It embarrassed him. He did not see how his role had been of any real consequence. Natalie bathed his scraped skin and from somewhere a new shirt and trousers were provided. It was then she saw the silver box as he transferred it from a pocket of the old clothes. Angi whispered to Ken, "I think we go for St. Simon tonight."

"Who was the man in the Franco uniform?" Roger asked.

"A whore of a ghost," Maurice answered, smiling.

Gunfire cracked. They listened. It cracked again. Maurice jumped to his feet, grinning.

"God damn Boche. Forced him to come to us." He leaped lightly across a ditch. "This way."

He ran. Ken, Roger, and Angi followed. Natalie ran the other way. Ken worried about her.

"Now we try out tonight's drops," Maurice told him.

They were on their bellies, concealed by low, straggling bushes facing a stream. Ken was handed a new submachine gun. Suddenly soldiers appeared, frightened Italians. They began to cross the stream cautiously and unhappily.

"Macaronis," someone whispered. "Poor bastards."

The Italians wasted a few shots. A Maquis came running from behind and whispered to Maurice.

"Decoys," Maurice explained to Ken. "Boche salopard!" He smiled and crouched. "Idiots." At last the Germans were forced to appear. Behind Ken someone laughed.

"Now!"

Maurice signaled them to follow and started running. As they ran, shots rang from the woods overhead. It was the Maquis. They ran until Ken's ankle was ready to give out. Now they were high above the stream, protected by boulders, their three-quarter circle fully manned by well-armed Maquisards. The Germans down below were trapped, a steep cliff at their backs. They continued heading across the stream to their deaths. Still following Maurice, Ken descended as they stepped over some dead Germans.

"No undershirts," Maurice said, turning one over with his foot. "And their jackets get skimpier." It came to the dead man's waist. Maurice lifted it and the rib cage showed. He kneeled and removed the soldbuch from the man's breast pocket and read quickly. "Seventeen," he said. "His first battle. A squab."

They dragged the dead Germans and placed them in sitting positions. From below one could not tell whether they were German, Italian, or French, dead or alive. Using the corpses as shields they shot more Germans. Then they ran up to complete the circle from above. On the way they stepped over more dead Germans who had attempted to cross the stream higher up.

"Pot bellies. In '43 they came wearing black shirts, with round arms in yellow tanks. Blond, tall, and proud. Now they leave small boys and old farts."

There was a low whistle. Maurice rose and ran off, telling them to wait. Angi was explaining to four men who had joined them about the approach to the power plant. "Straight down the hill," he was saying. "And then the road. Across it is a sign no bigger than your palm. It reads, 'Briançon 85.5 kilos.' Every fifteen minutes the two Boche patrols meet—"

Maurice returned with fifteen men, all grinning, some wounded. "Watch our American. He has not seen our lovely landscape by daylight."

He left with the fifteen men. Angi, Roger, Ken, and the four to whom Angi was explaining the approach to the power plant remained behind. They were shielded by the tall pines and boulders high above the stream now. At their backs in the distance silhouetted by the moon were the Alps, their tips and slopes dark and looming. One of the four men passed a flask around. Their breaths exploded against the night in sheets of silent steam. The cognac burned and evaporated, leaving nothing but a small warm spot in the belly. Ken kept worrying about Natalie. A voice from behind called out in an audible whisper, "Foutez le camp!"

They scattered. The four men left together. For the next ten minutes, shots rang out on every side. A young Maquisard who had attached himself to Ken beckoned him to follow. It was the boy who *helped Ken the night he had landed. The shots re-echoed, bouncing off the mountains on all sides. A piercing scream, high and female, came from below on the other side of the stream. It started almost above hearing and wound down to a whimpering, dying sound like liquid fire, turned to sick jelly and quivering itself into stillness. There were distant shots from below, in or near the town itself. Ken still followed the young Maquisard, his submachine gun getting heavier with each step. As they ran, the boy skipped ahead happily, like a child, leaped over a rock and clicked his heels in the air. They now seemed to be on the other side of the stream, facing the Alps directly and higher than before.*

"Romanche," the boy said, pointing down. "The power plant." He looked even younger than seventeen.

He kicked Ken's leg above the bad ankle and motioned him to silence. Some yards away Ken heard the faintest rustle of twigs. The boy had a knife in his right hand, the rifle hanging over his shoulder. The thrumm! of his knife cutting air was followed by a gasp and then a bubbly sound. They pulled the dead German to them and faced in the direction from which he had come, using him as a shield. Ten Germans appeared. Ken's gun responded automatically. Then silence. The French boy who had clicked his heels in the air was dead, surprise on his face. So were the Germans—their faces were blank. Ken wondered whether to sit and wait, or to move, and if so in what direction. He had been balancing himself on his good foot when running and jumping, keeping the raw ankle out of it as much as possible. The air washed by a mountain wind blew up his sleeves, creating goose bumps. A figure was approaching, coming up from the side nearest Romanche.

"Don't shoot, Major."

It was Natalie. He rose, extending his hand to help her.

"Stay down!" she hissed.

"I was so worried."

She crawled over bodies to sit beside him. "I hear you have done well."

"What is happening?"

"Almost over. We have the main plant. Also Ste. Marie d'Uriage. And St. Simon, I think. Comrade Roger did well too. When he forgets the Kremlin he can hate Germans and aim well." She looked up at the sky. "Some night."

"What are we waiting for?"

"It will take a little while. No more Boche will come that way." She pointed toward Romanche.

The moon lit up a long shaft of rock. Over the valley below a mist was gathering. She let her head rest on his shoulder and looked toward the Alps.

"All around us dead men and boys," she said. "While life sleeps below. How everything opposes itself."

She felt him shivering. "You are cold." She took his gun hand and placed the fingers between her lips, inside her mouth where it was warm. "Too bad it is April instead of June. Soon our fraise de bois will be ripe and the lavender in full bloom."

"If the invasion isn't soon, Roger will be right and for all the wrong reasons." His voice quavered.

"Don't speak of it. You are still shivering. Your foot must be badly infected."

"No," he said. "It is the killing."

His teeth chattered. She opened her waist jacket and put his other hand between her breasts. "Are you better?"

He was not. But it felt less like a nightmare, less a violation of his nature. He could smell the pines again, see the snow peaks once more and hear the streams. The hideous smells, sounds, and sights receded a small distance into the vanishing night.

"London was kind to us," she said.

"Yes. The drops came at the right time."

"They dropped you first."

"What if someone comes?"

"Not for twenty minutes and we will hear them when they reach the stream. It is the way the mountains are formed here."

"You give yourself so freely to me."

"Love is not war. To win, you must surrender."

Later they heard a distant rumbling sound and then a whistle. She buttoned her shirt quickly. From down below signal lights appeared similar to those of the reception committee at the dropping field where Ken landed. Was that only six days ago? The forest came alive with voices, first low, then a shouting and singing to the bold crash of dead twigs and branches underfoot. Ken hurried with Natalie, following her down the slope to the level ground leading back to St. Simon. There were four German trucks. Maurice stood on top of the first one, his arm around the shoulder of the man with the Franco medals. Maurice whistled for quiet.

"So. Any Spanish workers or peasants who wish to return over the Pyrenees to work for Franco?"

There was laughter, whistling, and catcalls.

"You have heard of our Spanish Fascist friend. Here he is."

They cheered the little man in Franco uniform. Maurice held up his hand. "But what you do not know is that he is a Jew come to us from the north of France and has helped hundreds of patriots to hide in the Alps. Actually he is Polish and cannot speak one single word of Spanish."

Laughter.

"He can hardly speak French besides."

The laughter became hysterical.

Natalie had brought Ken to the trucks. Maurice whistled again. "This is our American." They cheered loudly. Ken had to climb to the top of the truck. Maurice embraced Ken. So did the Polish Jew who spoke no Spanish, little French, and wore a Franco uniform. Ken felt foolish and unworthy. He wondered at the cost of this break in security if any of them were captured. But he enjoyed it as he nodded and waved back.

"Here is our comrade from the FTP. He also fought well tonight." They cheered. "With and for us as a Frenchman against the common enemy."

Roger gave the salute of the Front Populaire. He could not resist making a speech. "I bring warm fraternal proletarian greetings and return to my comrades of the FTP and the glorious French Party to urge the seizure of the remaining towns under co-ordinated French command. Long live France!"

They cheered again.

"So," Maurice said. "Now these trucks have another fraternal greeting. For the people of St. Simon—potatoes! With the aid of our comrades from FTP we will take the other towns and with the aid of London and the Allies we will hold all of it for D-Day."

They cheered Ken once more as symbol of the Allies and D-Day. Both seemed almost at hand. The truck lights went out. The Maquis disappeared into the woods almost as quickly as they had assembled to bury the dead and perhaps find more wounded. Natalie, Ken, Angi, and Maurice entered the first truck. Roger, the man in Franco uniform, the old man from Oiseaux and the Mayor took the second. All the trucks formed a victorious procession into town. Maurice told them how le patron had died. The Boche butchered him with a cleaver a half-hour after they left the restaurant basement for their new safe house at the café. Le patron had told them nothing, but they learned which way the truck had gone and the eighteen Gestapo followed the tire tracks to the footpath and their footprints and the broken bushes to the café. All this they had smoked out of the captured Gestapo before killing them. So German headquarters knew nothing and the munitions could be returned to the café. Then Angi related the story of their seizure of the mairie. It was guarded by Miliciens who asked for the password. The German uniforms taken from the captured Gestapo before killing them were bad fits and there had been no time for a Parisian tailor! Besides, the Maquis did not know tonight's password. When they failed to show themselves or answer, the Milice fired. Then one of the boys whose uniform almost fit stepped into the light and said in German, "Same thing with these idiot Milice. Constantly! Twice this week they have shot at us." In the Milicien's moment of hesitation, they had been killed and the mairie *taken. Gestapo headquarters had been preposterously easy. They approached in the German trucks, drove to the wired enclosure and simply killed the patrol as it approached to open the gate. A few grenades inside the building finished the job.*

The trucks drove into the center of town and stopped beside the ancient Roman water fountain. Maurice had them honk horns. Then he whistled with his fingers and shouted, "Pommes de terre! Vive la France!"

In a matter of minutes the entire population was swarming the square in their night clothes, carrying baskets for the potatoes and little flags for the Maquis. There was weeping and laughter. The two remaining students from Grenoble were cheered as were Roger, Ken, and Montero. The story of the Mayor's heroism was told. He received the greatest ovation. A naked little boy, laughing with sleepy excitement, ran through the crowd from its mother. Other women, hysterical with laughter, aided her in the chase. A few dead Milice lay faces down at the far end of the court square. Most of them had escaped. Potatoes rolled down the street and people bumped into one another.

"Why so silent?" Natalie asked Ken. "Are you ill again?"

"I am thinking of le patron."

"That was in another lifetime," she said.

Before dawn Roger was off to make his report and recommendations. He promised to be back shortly after nightfall. Maurice told him they would use le patron's *basement again as their safe house. Montero, who had drugged the Franco consul in Grenoble and pushed the clock back four hours in the event he woke, had to leave and "set things right."*

In the basement Angi found food and wine. Natalie sent off messages to London for Ken and to Algiers for Maurice. They ate cold chicken washed down with wine, smoked cigarettes, and went to sleep.

They were all waiting in the wine cellar, Angi for word about engineers from London for the power station, Maurice for reconnaissance reports on Boche movement out of Grenoble, the old man for instructions concerning his return to Café des Oiseaux. Mostly Ken waited for Roger's return with evidence that he would keep his word. He knew that right now the FTP decision was the most crucial fact so far as London was concerned.

"Since we have taken the plants and three towns already, little Moscow has no choice," Maurice pointed out.

"Not necessarily," Ken said.

"Still Roger fought well," Angi said. "What is wrong with many Communists like Roger is the Kremlin. When Roger thinks for himself he is almost reasonable. When he speaks with a gun he is superb."

"They claim to be scientists," Maurice said. "And the business of science is to predict, they tell you. Each time they predict. Of course little happens as they predict, but it does not stop them from predicting again and again."

"I wish I could predict," Natalie said. "Instead all I can do is wish."

"Wish then," the old man said.

She turned on her stomach. "Oh. I would wish for a farm like the Mayor's. It stands high on the slope," she told Ken. "Against it you see the mountain snow. It is very neat with brown hedges, very green and very fertile."

"I wish for it to be quite different from before," Angi said.

"Not I," Maurice said. "Let me go back to medical school and pick up where I left off."

"No. In return for what we have endured and must yet endure, it should be better. Less accidental and insolent. Less indifferent." Angi flicked his cigarette against the stone wall. By habit the old man walked to it and stamped it out.

"Also I would like the lunch time to be reduced," Angi continued. "Tell me, Major, is it true that in America lunch time is only an hour?"

Ken nodded. "Sometimes half an hour."

"There," Angi said as though it explained a deep mystery. "In France we take two hours. An hour would be just right. Both dignified and healthful. There would have been no Maginot line if we had taken only one hour for lunch."

"Tell me, Major, before we left here for the café why were you so concerned about the crop shortage north of Oisan?" Maurice was smiling.

"Because we might have needed additional food with supplies from Grenoble cut off." Ken was also smiling.

"Still what could facts and figures do? We could not eat them."

"True," Ken said. "But they could, when compared to previous years, explain that the crop was being removed from the area out to *the north with neither you nor the Boche in a position to collect it."*

Maurice laughed. "That could be possible."

Ken nodded. "Yes, that could be possible. The result of a shattered bridge perhaps. You like to shatter bridges, I have noticed. The Boche do not destroy a bridge that cuts off food. Therefore you might have done it."

Natalie burst into laughter. "I told him nothing, Maurice. I swear."

Maurice nodded. "Your statistics look harmless but they have sharp teeth. It is true. My men destroyed the bridge. The peasants sell the food for gold. Also the Boche take some to send home to their families. I am myself a Jura peasant. They are peasants. It is a family matter. I could not tell you. You understand?"

"I understood four days ago," Ken answered gravely. "But I did not tell London."

They all laughed.

"And are you satisfied to return to things as they were, Major?" Angi asked.

"I suppose I would prefer it more active," Ken said.

"This is not active enough for you?" Maurice laughed.

"Stupid. He means more active than his life was before." Natalie smiled to Ken. "Now that he sees how well he can do it."

Ken smiled back. "Yes. For a good reason I can do it."

"And enjoy it."

"Yes. And enjoy it. I may quit what I did before the war when this is over. There are better ways to spend my life. I never wanted to do the work I'm in in the first place."

"Good for you, Major!" Angi said.

"All you philosophers can kiss my ass," the old man said. "What I wish for right now is more wine."

"And I predict you will get it." Maurice jumped up. He returned and handed a bottle to the old man.

"Your idea of the telephone saved the day," Maurice said. "Without it, we might never have heard from London, and the Boche perhaps might have been waiting at the clearing to pick up our munitions, the sector heads captured—it is almost too much to think of it."

"It was fear," the old man explained. "Not of the Boche but of the silence. In the first eight weeks I lost seventeen kilos. All from being alone. I have never lived that way before. Then, knowing the phone was there, I could talk to it. Not using it, you understand, or taking it out of the stove. Simply talking to it, knowing it was there."

The report came that Ken and Natalie would be able to try for entrance into Grenoble after dark. It was the only way he could get to examine the Vichy police records. A meeting had been arranged for the purpose at the Hotel Citoyen, run by Milice. That was as far as their man on the Vichy force dared take it. Copying was impossible. Now that they all understood the connection between knowing these records thoroughly in which Vichy reflected principles of work beyond local matters, and the need to keep the thirty thousand Boche trapped in Grenoble, the Armée Secrète in Grenoble agreed that the risk was necessary. Maurice's men arrived. He spoke with them outside and then came in, buttoning his shirt. "Twenty trucks, three hundred Boche troops all from Grenoble toward Vercors." He grinned to Ken. "The Boche leave. You enter. See you get out. I guarantee they won't get back in."

"Maurice," Ken walked up to him. "Have you a chemist?"

"In the woods, yes."

"Does he have equipment?"

"Yes. Sometimes Algiers asks him to examine this or that." He grinned. "When there is time, he does so."

"Can he go with you?"

"We could not support the delay."

"It is important. I want the trucks examined. The axle grease and oil. Also the used toilet tissue and stools of the Boche. They may all be recent replacements from Germany."

Maurice began to laugh.

"Listen to him, blockhead," Natalie said. "The Major is a statistician. Such facts tell him where and when we must fight."

Ken saw Maurice thoroughly angry for the first time. Also for the first time Ken realized that Natalie and Maurice, so casual toward one another for six days and nights, had been intimate before he came.

"Our job is dead Germans," Maurice said. "The dead smell alike."

"Maurice," Ken said. "Though you are a peasant you are also a medical student. You know that specific facts reveal specific things." He looked Maurice full in the face. "Once out of a garbage can in a German prison camp we took a scrap of paper. It was the sketch of a new bombing sight."

"Getting the chemist and his equipment will cost an hour and will delay us afterward," Maurice insisted.

Ken simply looked at him and waited.

"All right," Maurice said at last. "The chemist. Toilet paper. Merde." He laughed. "And let us hope so." He nodded and shook Ken's hand. "Only because you shoot so well, Major."

When he left, Natalie said, "He will do it because you did not tell London of the blown bridge and the Oisan crop shortage."

When Ken and Natalie returned from Grenoble in the morning, Roger was already there. So were Angi and Maurice. The old man

*was gone, ordered back to the café. With four times the previous
amount of munitions, he had been assigned an assistant. Maurice had
a bandage on his left arm and seemed cheerful. He took a sheet from
the breast pocket of his torn shirt.*

"Chemist's report. He worked until an hour ago. If you want him,
there he is." *The chemist lay sleeping, his head on his rucksack, both
legs higher than his head, dangling limply over a wine barrel. His
report on the men showed an even further reduction in protein diet.
The axles of the trucks suggested the possibility of a shortage of
molybdenum. They had broken down when the first few shots were
fired. Ken noted the serial numbers and types of trucks for London's reappraisal.*

"Important?" *Maurice asked. Natalie was rewinding his bandage.*

"Very. If true, they are half beaten already."

"If Chico says it, it's true. And the leaflet—" *Maurice took it out
of his boot.* "I had the boys search very carefully, as you can see."

*The leaflet was in German, issued by FFI to judge from the paper
and content.* "You understand it?"

Ken nodded. " 'Der Fuehrer denkt für uns; der Fuehrer führt uns;
der Fuehrer führt uns im Stalingrad zum Todt!' *Fuehrer means leader.
It also means driver. It says,* 'Our leader thinks for us; he also drives
us; he drives us to our death in Stalingrad.' "

"Not bad," *Maurice said.*

"You bastard, how long do I have to wait?" *Natalie exploded.*

Maurice smiled. "Oh. The Major didn't ask. Three hundred Boche
in twenty trucks as reported. All finished. We caught up with them
southwest of Grenoble in the Vercors. We and Roger's boys together. They cost us fifty men."

"Out of one thousand?"

"Yes. One out of twenty to get a hundred out of a hundred." *His
mouth was smiling. His eyes were not.* "Three hundred Boche. That's
one out of a hundred of what they have in Grenoble. And one in two
thousand of all they have in France. I too understand statistics,
Major."

"Are you saying the delay for the chemist raised your losses?"

"He is speaking of the need for immediate invasion," *Natalie said.*

"I agree on the need for immediate invasion," *Ken said.*

"And what else?" *Natalie asked Maurice.*

"The usual." *He rose and walked to the other side of the basement.* "Montero is dead."

*He worked silently on arrangements for bicycle squads of girls
who would bring word to wives, mothers, sweethearts, families, and
friends of the fifty boys killed in last night's battle.*

Ken wrote out and put into code the range of power services of the plants, the problems and conditions of the towns taken, all eight of them now between the joint efforts of FFI and FTP. He detailed the results of the first unified action in Vercors and Oisan, and briefly stated the principles of the Vichy hostage formula used in Grenoble with its system of authority and so forth, as well as the heavy losses of the night before. He stressed the uniform expectation of immediate invasion. When he handed the message to Natalie, she said, "The chemist is waking. Do not congratulate him. Do not congratulate Maurice, either. It was a fine victory but they do not wish to be congratulated."

Later Angi left for the power plant to meet with the Jedburgh engineers and Maurice returned to the woods. They were to meet again the following morning at the safe house. Ken and Natalie were alone in the basement and the window was uncovered. The sun shone in, washing everything with its brilliance. The food drops had included a surprise—bananas. She held one, peeling it mischievously.

"So handsome. Adorable. A pity to reduce the symmetry." She bit a piece and placed another in his mouth. Her head was in his lap. "How did you get your silver box past the security search in London?" He didn't answer. "Why is it so important to you? Is it family pride?"

"Knowing the beginning," he said.

"Here, that is bad." She turned her shoulder so that the top two buttons of her shirt opened. "This is a trick. Close the buttons. I will show you again."

His hand lingered.

"No. Close them. I must show off."

He did. She twisted. They popped again.

"I can't do it with a brassiere on. Only this way."

"You and Maurice were close," he said.

"In another lifetime. Can't you forget your silver box?"

"Not easily."

"We can. But then we are a very ridiculous people."

"No. You are not ridiculous."

"Oh, yes," she insisted. "Very ridiculous. But also wise. Both ridiculous and wise. Is that possible for a statistician to whom two and two make forever four? Yet sometimes one and one make three."

He sat up. "You don't really think—"

She laughed and pushed him down and fed him the rest of the banana. "No. The calendar is our friend. But just think. If I had a little major in your land of silver boxes I should be turned out of my house in disgrace. Here a girl has a baby out of love, no one despises her. Even in peacetime it is not the greatest tragedy. Except for the very young. Now it is war and I am not very young."

"Yes, you are. Very young."

"No. Twenty-five. Very old."

"Nonsense. I'm thirty-three."

"A silver-boxed baby. I am very much older than you." She opened her screen. The short wave was flashing its recurrent signal. *"My little monster is chattering again."*

She walked to it with her long, coltish yet military stride. It was FFI. *"We are proceeding throughout the area,"* she called to him. *"More British and American Jedburghs have landed at specified fields. The Boche is trying to recapture the power plants and the towns. Security measures are back on our agenda."*

They covered the window with burlap again. They heard a plane, a shot, ack-ack, an explosion. It all sounded very far away. *"If the Boche recapture these villages it will be a massacre,"* she said.

"The Boche will capture nothing," he said.

"Five hundred thousand of them in France," she said. *"Still so far I think it goes well. If only D-Day comes very, very soon. What were we talking about?"*

"My silver box."

"No. That the French were ridiculous. Or was it the symmetry of the banana? But all of it is gone now."

Her short wave was signaling again. This time it was London with a long message in Ken's special code. She took it, held it, then handed it to him. He had seen her hesitate a moment.

"I would explain the code to you if it were permitted," he said.

She shrugged and sat watching him read. He was to leave at 0400 Saturday. More Jeds would be dropped tomorrow to facilitate bazooka training and resist Boche efforts to recapture the plants. He was to be congratulated on the unified action. He was to destroy all factual material taken from Grenoble if he hadn't already done so and trust to memory. Speaking of memory, Major, do you recall the unofficial rule that our men are encouraged to team up with women who handle short wave? The French girl could come with him to London. The chances of his staying in London with the girl for the next many weeks were very good. Major, you are a lucky man and good-by.

"Bad news?"

"I leave at 0400 Saturday."

"Oh? Nothing else?"

He didn't answer. She walked the basement in silence. It lasted over ten minutes.

"We were speaking of the silver box and the photograph," she said, breaking the silence.

"*It is a daguerreotype.*"

"*Ah, yes. Not a photograph. A daguerreotype. By Daguerre. Another Frenchman. Another pioneer in the ridiculous. He invents a photograph that is not a photograph. Do I have it right?*"

"*What's the matter? Is it because I'm leaving?*"

"*Nothing is the matter. The French are all for a gesture. All for the moment. That is why the French are ridiculous. Is it right? Am I learning your silver-box views?*"

"*Natalie, what is it?*"

"*Statistically all our gestures will be taken for granted. If we win, the price we pay will be taken for granted. If we live, in time we ourselves will be taken for granted. If Hitler wins, his crimes will soon be taken for granted. Any outcome will be taken for granted. But in that case, you see, even the permanence of your silver box is ridiculous.*"

"*Natalie, there was something else in my message.*"

"*The moment to tell me what was in your message has passed.*"

She went to sleep in her shirt and pants, wrapped tight in her blanket, closing the screen behind her.

Roger was the first to return after dawn. Maurice and Angi came together. They shouted at one another in French so quickly that at first Ken could not follow. When finally Maurice turned to him and asked, "What is your opinion?" Ken answered, "I don't know what you're arguing about."

"Not arguing, discussing. The issue now is road blocks. Whether to keep roads open from here to the Alps or to block off the roads and the tunnel so no Boche or Macaroni can come through from Italy. Your Jeds have no opinion on it."

"Blocking roads and the tunnel will prevent our own use of them when necessary," said Roger.

"If necessary," corrected Maurice.

"We must expect serious Boche retaliation and the need for retreat," Roger insisted.

"We are already getting serious Boche retaliation," Maurice said.

It went on for quite a while and then stopped when Angi said, "Roger, you can't advance by thinking always of retreat."

"I absolutely agree," Roger said, and the innovation of it left them all speechless for a moment.

"The Boche can't make up their minds either," Maurice said. He was happy. "Now that we are in the villages we can use them like forests. Surprise—mitraillage—évanouissement—is also possible in the towns. As you said, Major, and you were right, a house for a tree, a street for a ditch. It's good. If D-Day were tomorrow, it would be absolutely fine."

"They are at a disadvantage," Roger agreed. "If the invasion is soon."

"It is soon," Maurice said. "I can feel it. I can taste the fresh-water friture *fried in butter, with goat cheese, dry wine.*"

"—and women without hard pants," Natalie added.

He turned to her and smiled. She walked to him and put her arm through his. He patted her, accepting her proffered friendship again.

There was a message from London. Natalie did not seem to look at it when she handed it to Ken.

"It is confirmation. I leave at 0400," Ken said.

They reviewed requirements to be put to London by Ken upon his return. When he said, "I will fight for these requests," they nodded, believing him. Then FFI instructed the others to clear the safe house by tomorrow and return permanently to their field stations. The Mayor appeared with dinner. He said that arrangements would be made for each of them to leave separately. Shortly past midnight the Mayor returned to take the first of them. It was Angi. When he embraced Natalie he said, "And if I do not see you again—merde."

She shook her head and turned away.

An hour later it was Roger. His mouth produced its reluctant smile. "Till D-Day." He gave the De Gaullist salute, followed by the clenched fist of the People's Front. Roger's boots scraped to the door. The door clicked open and then shut. Ken relocked it. Maurice sat, holding Natalie's hand. Twenty minutes later they heard the Mayor's heavy step approaching. Maurice shook hands with Ken. He took Natalie by both shoulders, looked into her eyes, and said, "If I do not see you again—merde."

"You will see me," she said angrily.

Maurice continued smiling and he was gone.

"You broke my code," Ken said.

"After three or four messages it was simple."

"Let me tell you why I hesitated."

"You hesitated. That is enough."

"No, it isn't. If you came this way in their eyes you would be compromised."

She looked at him with scorn and turned away.

"You don't believe me."

"Oh, I believe you." She puffed her cigarette.

"It is not only that. Once I am reassigned it will be to a strange place. Here you are known, you are with people who love you. You are safe."

"Safe?" She laughed harshly.

"Natalie, after the war—"

"I told you before—no talk. No talk of safe and after, probably and maybe. Never now, never yes, never no! You are brave. You are smart and kind and inside you are nothing! Because you are not man enough to accept the life at hand. Therefore you are nothing. You think and try always to understand the whole by looking ahead. By breaking it down into all the little pieces. So you are stupid and you are a coward. Yes. You are brave and you are a coward! You are smart and by trying always to see and foresee everything you are stupid. Because you do not respect the one small part that is here and now— that is you and me—us. And that is all there is to life. But that is what you do not see. And so I am compromised here, in this room, by you, now. Not later. Not in London. Nor in Paris. Nor by danger elsewhere. Not even in America or after the war."

"I see."

"I see. I see. You see. You do not see! Why do you always say I see when you do not ever see anything?"

"You think I hesitated because I don't care?"

"I think nothing. I feel. Imperfect and in my small part, I feel. You think." She nodded. "You think of the one little century from the beginning of your worthless silver box. Even when you took me with your eyes closed, you were thinking. And that is why it was simply temporary necessity, disgusting and ridiculous. And so are you."

"Now it is you who are full of words."

"I am full of words because I am filling the time, Major, waiting for the Mayor to come and for you to leave."

"I told you how they would look at you and what I feared if I took you elsewhere. If you still want to come, I want you to. Will you come?"

"Certainly not."

"Then when it is over?"

"No, for heaven's sake."

"Natalie, I am trying to tell you that with all my heart I care."

She looked at him. "The worst of this is," she said, "that it is the truth. You are as free as you will ever be and for me it is not enough. No, not even now."

She heard the Mayor approaching the door and turned her back. He knocked. Ken walked to the door. She called after him. "Major."

He turned. "You will come?"

"No. But it is not only you. It is me and everything. All too far apart."

He walked back and kissed her. Then she turned away and he left.

Chapter 3

AT THE cottage, by the narrow strip of light from the storm lamp on the floor of the wet porch, the caretaker was fastening the canvas coverings west, north, and south against the wind whipping in over the Gulf of Mexico.

"Worried where you was," he told Ken. He smelled of salt and seaweed. Coogan had hired him three years ago. He sold bait, rented out deep-sea fishing boats, and captained more serious trips on the side. "Phone's out of order," he went on as he pulled hard at the canvas facing north to secure it over the last metal button screwed into the porch. "Damnedest season. If it ain't fog or frost, it's storm." He turned the button horizontally in the rough eyelet on the stiffening canvas so it would not slip out. The canvas slapped loudly against the wood.

"I was walking."

"Bad idea in this weather without a flash." The man sniffed at the air. "Gulf will pitch its last boogie for the winter tonight. Maybe drive the snowbirds home early." He laughed. "That's them northern folk come in October with a ten-dollar bill and one shirt and don't change neither till they go back where they come from soon as summer moves in."

Ken asked him if he wanted to come in for coffee and he said no, he'd better get crackin' before the storm broke. If it got too bad, he'd return and fetch Ken. It wouldn't hurricane, that was certain, and the best thing to do unless he wanted to head for the mainland right now was keep candles handy, the storm lamp by his bedside, and stay indoors. Extra water was already drawn in the bathtub just in case the electric pump went dead.

Ken thanked him and said he preferred to stay, and the man left.

The Boche *had* recaptured the towns and plants. The Allies *had* bombed and burst the dams after all. He *had* wanted to say I love you to Natalie but he hadn't and it was not until a week later in London that he realized the depth of his loss. He had lost Natalie. And he had *not* quit.

With peace came the letdown so well known at the end of all wars that it had a name like other minor disorders: *la grippe* for aches and pains; the common cold for running nose; and postwar disillusionment for the played-out feeling that proved the joy of peace to be an intoxicant known only to those who had never been at the fighting front. Stirred and revealed to himself in new places, he had returned to the States expecting a world that would also be new: instead he had found only novelty. Its trash had predictably tarnished, swiftly turned old, and died. As others returned to factory and farm, he had returned to Preston & Company. Then, when Mother died, the hydra-head unexpectedly returned again, nourished on five years of sleep. Quit! Except that there was WHIP—the last holdout of debris from the crash of '29 and the subsequent failures of the early thirties: the hemisphere's chained colossus of power and light—unfinished family business—*his* business. Quit or take on WHIP. He had taken on WHIP.

It was finished now—the end of a comedy or tragedy composed of all latter-day Preston errors.

To want to be but not to be. To wish to do but not to do. What was the answer? The more you remembered the less you knew. Always the same.

Years before he had planned his life from Commencement to curatorship but had gone into the firm instead. Always long on plans—plans galore—as recently as the Preston Plan. But short on deeds; on the here and now that added up. As recently as this very twilight moment and as far back as the early summer of '28, in the shipping basement of L. Burton & Company near the Bowery in Manhattan. That was Father's bright idea for "making a man out of him" when the conviction that Mother had made him dangerously soft had alarmed Father into action.

He had met Mario in that shipping basement—his good Cuban friend Mario who, alone when the others laughed, had helped him. That was the day they killed the rats creeping overhead on the old pipes to slide down on skittering claws into the packing barrels and steal someone's lunch and sometimes take someone's fingers as well. He had stood dazed, club in hand, the rat bleeding, poised on the barrel beside him, dying, moving forward, desperately ready to spring, when Mario had pulled him back. As the rat brushed his leg and scurried off, trailing blood, the others laughed and Mario finished the job for him.

He had *wanted* to do something for Mario. Wanted to but had never done it.

As he had also *wanted* Muriel—the same summer in the same place and he had lost her too as Father steam-rollered him into that summer and then steam-rollered him out of it. The story of his life.

Twenty-five years ago. A quarter of a century. A fat chunk of time falling away to fly forever through space, and how time can fly, old man and boy. Multiplied by four it was a century—the longest possible distance between any two points known to any man, including freaks who never drank or drank too much, chewed tobacco and lived in Turkey with twenty-one wives, or only drank goat's milk in Tibet with no wives at all. A man who lived to be a hundred would probably feel the full oppression of inescapably knowing how short it all was. You are born and you die: what little lies between is yours to do the best you can with, or the worst, and indeed you *had!* A cripple's marching song. Grin and bear it. Make it count. Leave something behind. A short life and a merry one. Chin up in this vale of tears and don't make waves. It's all unsound fury signifying whatever each man's own whistling-in-the-dark song meant to him and you made it up as you went along, while all along it remained unalterably a distance shorter than any fool's journey right next door to your unattained heart's desire. A quarter of a century. If you let yourself you could remember only too well the smell of summer air, the hot, empty streets, the narrow, musty hallway into the kitchen where she stood fresh from her bath and her sixteen years, frankly teasing and scared and trembling with wanting you as she waited, tiny and barefooted behind the ironing board in her altogether transparent cotton nightgown and whispering, "Mama and poppa are gone visiting and my sister's at the beach. Go inside and take a bath." They had left the lemonade to grow warm on the kitchen table, *and honest, Ken, please, Ken, the bedroom isn't the coolest room in the house and don't or do, I just don't know, Ken, so you tell me* while you wondered how does a girl know this is the boy I want to take me, to see, feel, and know me, and the way it happened with all the torturous doubts and then the certainty as for three months you knew it and then were ripped out of orbit. *Now, son. Son! I am your father and you're only seventeen. Listen to me, son.* Then you had nothing but the naked, gnawing, guilty hunger, and the pain of having lost her.

In all these wasted years one thing stood out and one thing only. Then, now, and always he remembered the Rules and obeyed them. *That* was the answer. From the very beginning in the summer of his first love when Muriel, like a miracle or a catastrophe, had altered his personality into something unlike what he had ever been before or since, but had clearly not altered him enough, down to WHIP, here and now. Everything in between was more of the same. Birth and death were done to you, one being the price for the privilege of the other, and which was price and which privilege depended on what you did to the portion in between. That tenuous, tentative part, flanked by the rasping birth cry at the beginning and the waxen lump of flesh at the end, the part *you* did to life. If which was which depended on *that*, in his case with nothing in between, with waste and failure in between, more and more of the same in between—

The summer of '29. All through the Friday morning sessions in Father's office as he listened respectfully to the senior statistician's deferentially submitted charts that meant no more to Father than a white worm's view of the world, his mind had bubbled with plans of his own. But *only* his mind. Friday after Friday, he had built his dreams; the exact museum, the exact exhibits, the papers he would write. Friday after Friday holding fast to the belief in a place for himself in a world where such work was respected, where it mattered, while the statistician pointed out a declining business index; unsound, rising credit; the "cats-and-dogs" stage of the market, through July, August, and early September of 1929, Friday following Friday, and Father's jovial responses to statistics of shrinking profits, rising unemployment, problems growing in England; from Friday to Friday all through that summer growing slowly as his own plan grew in his mind, but *only in his mind* growing steadily until Father had to concede, "Well, yes, it *is* growing," and the statistician's timidly eager answer, "Yes, sir, that's just it, Mr. Preston, it *is* growing, sir." Then Father pushed the papers to a far corner of his desk, locked his hands behind his sun-tanned neck, leaned back in his swivel chair as the ticker tape rolled merrily along, and confidently predicted, "But it won't ever grow up, you see. That's the point. Never grow fast enough to catch up with all the favorable factors. Why, brokers' loans increased seven hundred million dollars this month alone. The total is now seven billion. Do you suppose everybody's gone mad? No, sir! Never grow up fast enough. You can count on it."

"Yes, sir."

"Good summer, son?"

"Well—"

"Growing to like it, boy?"

"Well, sir—" Not really, not growing half fast enough to like it, no sir.

The day he prepared the first paper of the semester at Harvard was the first day of the news. October 24, a Thursday, and then again on Tuesday, October 29, with no Friday meeting in between on facts or figures. What had not been growing up, boy, not half fast enough, sir, had suddenly reached full stature on the heels of the Hatry panic in England. In its manhood it stretched and sent the market tumbling and with it industries and homes and lives, and people like Mario, his good friend, Mario, and Muriel, his first love, all tumbling down, with

Ken walked along the deserted beach, inspecting the results of the storm and the new splendor it had washed ashore: tree trunks, mounds of seaweed, the wood of boats and docks, fruit from distant tropical places, and boxes from ships' holds. There was a man's hat, its lining and label ripped out, the stained sweatband still attached. They shared the beach with the remains of previous storms. Ripped-up water-front pines, their mahogany roots a tangled pulp with countless small shells embedded in them and their upper branches whittled to fine points by the wind, stabbed in disarray at the air. Moss grew on their undersides, submerged each time the tide rose. Near the cove a six-foot shark lay on the sand, intact but dead. The sand cactus was still red-tipped from frost but spring was already at work. Young terns were in training under the watchful eyes of parents. Black-eyed Susans were unfolding in the sea grass. A large turtle strolled by like a miniature elephant in armor, enjoying the morning sun, its heavy front legs bowed under, the rear ones stolid, rough-skinned, thick, and straight. As it lumbered over a freshly dug hole and flattened the curls of sand left behind by a retreating crab, it saw Ken, tucked in its head, and stood still. Ken began to run. A long-forgotten feeling, something like freedom, burst within him. Still running he turned to the Gulf, plunged in, swam swiftly through the waves, then ran back to his lawn, stretched naked on the cot, and lay there for hours facing the sky as a soft breeze played over him.

It was not too late. Late, yes. But there was still time. The sun rose steadily and the beach became a dazzling reflector with etched-out dark places of built-up sand shoulders, stored seaweed, and newly upended trees. The sun drew raw fragrance from the spears of stubbled grass and pungent savor from the caverns of countless shells. The Gulf had become a vast warm bathtub, giving off the briny smell of heat.

When Ken sought relief he crossed the sea wall, walking farther each time as the tide continued to move out. Then, putting on his trunks, he went inspecting the beach, this time in the opposite direction. A mile south of his cottage lay the dead pelican, its face turned shoreward, the beak opening and closing as the tide spread its hingeless jaws and pulled them shut. He continued down the beach, curious and interested, following it as it bent inland, seeing it for the first time. The storm had been kinder here. A sea urchin's shell caught his eye, a bracelet of pale blue tiny dots rising from the circular background of rich purple—fragile and perfect. He picked it up carefully and turned it over. The other side repeated the design in white, like rare old lace.

Up ahead were two girls, young, firm-breasted, lean-legged in shorts and halters, their pert, pretty faces reddening attractively in the sun. The south wind carried their voices to him. They were touching a small fish with their toes.

"Feels funny," one said. "Furry." She laughed and shivered. "What *is* it?"

"I never saw anything like it before. It *is* furry!"

Ken approached them.

"It's a sea mouse," the first one decided. They laughed. "Yes. A sweet brown little sea mouse." They saw Ken and smiled tentatively, embarrassed at their whimsy being overheard.

"It *is* a sea mouse," Ken said.

"Really?"

"Yes. That's its name."

"Imagine!"

"And it's a very long way from home. The north wind must have blown it."

"Chasing spring," one said. They both laughed.

"Poor little thing, even if it is a Yankee."

The other giggled. "Let's give him a decent burial."

When Ken looked back one of the girls was still watching him. She turned away and then looked straight at him, waved, and smiled. The other was burying the sea mouse. Both of them began collecting shells.

The sun approached the horizon, a brilliant paleness on the water.

Ken had his coffee and sandwich on the porch. Even the cottage seemed new to him, a functional sunward place, uncluttered, from its straw matting and simple woods to its vast wonderful window facing the endlessly active blue-green water and western sky. The herons had gathered on the wall, faces turned to the sun. It was setting white; he looked straight into it. It could have been a New England spring sunset, with its lacework of feathery clouds and the pale blueness in the darkening east. Only the air was tropical now. The smell of grass, sea, and sand had subsided.

He thought of the young, pretty girl who had waved and smiled. Chasing spring. Vaguely it brought to mind a poem by Tagore. *Gitanjali* 27. He felt as if its subject should have been love but he knew that wasn't so. He had the book at home. When he returned, he would look it up.

Next morning he heard the phone ring and ran in from the Gulf. No one answered. As he turned to leave, it rang again. It was Coogan. He said, "Michigan court convenes day after tomorrow, nine-thirty A.M."

"I see."

"We've got to talk about that conference you had down there before then, you know."

"Yes, we do."

"And not by phone. You can make a day or night plane tomorrow just so long as you're here before the bell."

Ken said nothing.

"You still there?" Coogan asked.

"Yes," Ken said.

"I'm sending Riley to Michigan. Might as well keep my face out of it. Judge Keane still thinks I'm Johnny-come-lately."

A pause.

"We made a big bet, Ken. Thanks for the vote."

No answer.

"One thing I knew all along. Judge Keane can't be reached. He'll make up his mind on the facts as he sees 'em and a higher court will cut no ice—which could cut our throats of course but there you are." Coogan forced a laugh. "We know what he thinks of our colleagues and isn't it the goddamned truth! So it's all up to how much he's impressed with the fact we got those bastards to agree on something."

"That's probably so."

"Anyway *we* think we're good. What makes us a team." Coogan laughed. This time it sounded genuine. "Day after tomorrow comes teacher's report card. I hope you got your winter coat. It's still snowing to beat hell up here."

Ken reserved space for the last flight on the following night.

As he was driven off in the caretaker's car the baby blue heron was promenading up and down the sea wall. It was the only moving creature. The terns, gulls, pelicans, and crabs all along the beach were motionless in the setting sun, facing it and listening. The sky was painted like an inflamed proclamation except for the southwest where milky clouds cast a solid shadow over the shore-bound waves, darkening them to a blackish green until the tide carried them across the sun's fiery orange path on their diagonal northeastern journey to shore. There the small gentle breakers turned a bubbly gold, their last spume flying like the manes of wild horses coppery red, leaving the shore line a thin transparency of shimmering golden wetness spread over the sand. Ken still had his head turned back to look at the strutting heron as the car rounded the sandy bend.

In the east the sky was clear and full of stars. The glow of last day-light persisted behind them in the west. When they rumbled across the wooden pre-Civil War bridge where Negroes leaned over the rotting rails with fishing poles, they entered the first of the fog bank.

By the time they reached the little airport it was thick. Ken said good-by to the caretaker and climbed in beside the pilot of the single-motored plane for the short hop to Sarasota.

"We'll be lucky if we make it before this soup closes in," the pilot told him. "We'll hedgehop all the way. Can you imagine! Still snow-ing up North. Sure looks like spring ain't never coming."

Ken's short flight from Sarasota to Tampa where he was to board a nonstop to Idlewild was canceled. So was every other flight. Sara-sota was fogbound. There was a shortage of buses and cabs. An old man with hanging jowls was demanding information; some throat affliction reduced his voice to a thick, tremulous whisper. Behind his glasses the right eye seemed smashed. The airline ticket agent was shouting his answer. Two elderly ladies were asking other misin-formed passengers how they were to get to St. Petersburg. As the time went by, a porter, sweating as he cleaned up wet rubbish, kept remembering aloud that his day had been over at eight and here it was close to nine. An old man with a calm, passive face, broad and childlike, stood near Ken at the passenger desk. He wore the black, deep-crowned hat of the Amish who lived in large numbers in Sarasota. He squeaked in his black, pigeon-toed, tight shoes as he fumbled in his buttonless jacket for his ticket and asked how he would get to Tampa.

"By cab, sir, with this gentleman." The agent indicated Ken and Ken smiled.

"Oh? Well, that's very fine."

The old Amish gentleman sat up front in the cab holding his cloth bag on his knees. Ken sat in the rear beside a young lady. She seemed no more than twenty and gave the impression of someone tensed and alerted as most people never are and only a few in rare moments of joy or pain. Ken turned away quickly, with no clear impression of her features or appearance, yet it jolted him into painful remem-brance. At the last moment a lean, roosterlike man appeared, calling out to his friends, "If my proposition sounds right, I'll be back in a week, *hear?*"

He was very drunk.

"Good boy."

"Just so long as it sounds right to you."

"Gotcha."

"This damn cab goin' to Tampa?"

The cab driver said yessir, the young lady nodded, and the drunken, roosterlike man headed for the front seat.

"Mind sitting in back, sir?" The cab driver weighed some two hundred and fifty pounds—it was a close squeeze with even the small Amish gentleman beside him.

"Don't give a damn where I sit." He got in on the other side of the young lady. As he rolled down the window he called out to the people who were seeing him off, "Just so long as it sounds right to you, *hear*? I can come right back down in a week."

He asked the driver, "How long does it take to get to Tampa out of this damn airport?"

"About an hour and a half, sir. With the fog it could be longer."

"Cab ride like this costs a damn fortune in New York." He said it to no one in particular.

The girl turned slightly away from his alcoholic breath and Ken saw her face again. This time he really looked at her. The green eyes were large and perfectly spaced under naturally shaped brows. Her nostrils started widely apart and came to a point, the nose small and upturned like that of some animal vividly on the scent. Her lips were red without lipstick and shaped in an impossibly perfect bow. The ears were small, almost lobeless. It was a face from which the mask had been ripped, or because of her youth was not yet habitually worn, and Ken felt guilty of indiscretion. It was like watching an unsuspecting naked woman. He turned to face the window. Why did she affect him so strongly? Feature for feature there was no resemblance. Perhaps it was the nakedness of what he saw, or the darkness, his uneasiness at going back, the abrupt change from his solitude. The cab was speeding through the fog, the road intermittently visible and lost. It was slippery wet.

"Does the plane fly north or south to Tampa?" the Amish gentleman asked.

The cab driver let it pass and the old man asked him again.

"Don't really know, sir." He didn't understand the question. Nor did anyone else. For a while there was silence.

"Lots of planes crash," the old Amish gentleman said.

The belligerent drunk in the rear caught Ken's eye with a wink and as Ken turned his head away, he saw her profile again. Such resemblance was impossible. So was the idea that he could not truly remember any more.

"Lots of other things crash too, sir," the cab driver reassured. "Trains, buses, boats, lots of things."

"Yes," the old Amish agreed. "The world is full of crashing things. Changed." He nodded. "Very changed."

He was speaking to himself in a clear unself-conscious voice. "I'm not at home in the world any more."

"Who of us is, pal?" said the drunk in the rear.

The headlights were feebly yellow. The gigantic driver shifted his massive weight, mopped his brow, and wiped fog from inside his window with the handkerchief. Ken looked at the girl again. She *did* remind him. It suddenly brought back Tagore's poem. "*He whom I enclose with my name.*" It seemed she was looking at him too, now, but perhaps it was only to keep her head turned away from the smell of alcohol.

Then the Amish began to sing.

> I want to go on that journey,
> I want to go on that journey—

He realized his hat was still on and removed it, continuing to sing the hymn as he might have at a prayer meeting.

> I want to go on that journey, Lord,
> And leave without saying good-by.

There were several stanzas, all sung in that same clear voice.

"Death," the belligerent drunk whispered to the girl, "the last promissory note." He grinned and shook his head. The others remained silent.

The Amish spoke again. "Yes," he said in a refreshed, almost cheerful voice. "It's certainly true. That's what I'm here for now. Ready." He nodded his bald head with its white fringes, his hat still resting on the cloth bag that covered his knees.

At the Tampa airport departure of Ken's flight had already been announced. His plane was crowded as all northbound night tourist flights were even in off-season. As he strapped himself in, the feeling of a moment long forgotten returned. More remembering? A warm night in the late twenties. Indian summer. After losing Muriel. Right after losing her. When he still hated Father. Mother and he at Carnegie Hall. The Indian poet, Rabindranath Tagore. He was their house guest and they sat on the platform. The proceeds of his recital were to be used for the university in India. Later at home the soothing voice with the warmth of many smiles and mysteries. The great black eyes and white flowing beard, the brown long graceful hands holding the cup and saucer, and Ken timidly requesting that he recite the stanza again. Then the soft voice read Ken's secret and spoke straight to its raw wound, chanting:

> I take pride in this great wall and I plaster
> It with dust and sand lest a least hole

Should be left in this name
And for all the care I take I lose sight of
My true being.

"Please fasten your seat belts and obey the No Smoking sign."

The plane was rising. The sky was suddenly clear, the fog gone.

"I beg your pardon."

He had been staring at the last passenger to board—the girl be-side him. "We came from Sarasota," she reminded. "In the car."

She looked entirely different now. Her face was pale but very beautiful. She couldn't possibly have been in the sun. Perhaps it hadn't been shining where she was, or she might have been ill.

"The old man was very touching," she said.

He nodded and looked down at his hands. He was fingering his silver box. The sea-urchin shell was in it.

"Rather bad weather most of the week," he said.

She nodded. He wanted to account for the mirage of resemblance. It seemed important to him to render it rational.

"Isn't that early American?" she asked.

"Yes." He put the box back into his vest pocket quickly. "Federalist, actually. 1791."

"I'm so pleased I almost guessed." She smiled. "I work at the City Museum in New York," she explained. "The authenticator's office. I'm only just beginning to learn."

He took out the silver box again and handed it to her. She looked at the sea-urchin shell inside, saw the faded daguerreotype and then the silversmith's mark. "Hey, Paul Revere."

He nodded and looked at her while she admired the box. She saw him looking.

"It's beautiful," she said and handed it back.

He was still looking at her.

"What?" she asked.

"It's all so remarkable," he said.

"What's remarkable?" she asked, smiling again.

"Why, everything. I mean you being here and working for the City Museum." He flushed. "It's the only one I haven't been to."

"Oh?" He amused her. "You visit museums?"

He nodded. "Constantly."

She opened her purse to find cigarettes. He reached for matches.

"My name is Laurie Dugan," she said.

"And I'm Kenneth Preston."

Chapter 4

FRANCIS XAVIER MCBRIDE ran the back of his huge, red-hair-covered hand over his dry mouth and blinked his bright blue eyes rapidly as he looked up at the Stock Exchange clock. Since the opening bell at ten o'clock he had been on the Floor, waiting. He had, in fact, been waiting three years, two weeks, four days, one and a half hours, and McBride was a man of uncontrollable impatience when faced with even the most minor frustrations. He was not at all built for waiting. Nor was he built for measured caution or careful listening. No doubt he should have stopped, looked, and listened for all he was worth when Pat and Ken had gone into all the fine and fancy points of this WHIP operation. Instead he had been satisfied to gauge their right to confidence in it by his right to confidence in them, and at the beginning, over thirty months ago, had almost dismissed it as a vague, grandiose notion for the far-off and unlikely future. Well, here was that distant future now and wasn't it simply grand!

As the sweeping second hand brought it closer he found himself incapable of stopping this chain of belated bitter thought.

Item: Judge Keane had pissed on the Securities Exchange Commission in 1946 when he forced the issue up to the Supreme Court for a stalemate, and back it had gone to the SEC where it stayed dormant for three more years.

He could do it again.

Item: Judge Keane hated the guts of all major contending parties, their lawyers and all their arguments too: he freely said so.

Now was his chance to prove it.

Item: When young Keane was caught getting laid in a Detroit cathouse, his old man had vowed to make them pay for it.

This could be payday, *and thank you, Texas!*

Item: Now even Coogan admits that Judge Keane's mother-clucking over WHIP after fifteen years as its trustee bordered on the insane—and trust His Honor to make everyone toe the line every time and brush your teeth or Mama spank.

Keane could paddle their asses without mercy in his little padded cell until doomsday.

No riddle why no one had ever figured out a workable plan for WHIP: it was a deathtrap for boobies and he was caught in it.

Once he had actually enjoyed the hard work of acquiring WHIP a hundred or two hundred shares at a time—even harder work now to believe it or recall the pleasure that had ended a few months ago. It began last spring with the rising chances of Dwight D. Eisenhower's running for president, still rising on his victory at the polls, steadily rising right up to the merry week between Christmas and New Year's when the Dow Jones averages had hit a buoyant and promising high of 295, and investors, traders, brokers, and speculators all in on the buying bandwagon anticipated the fabulous new dramatic rulings. Relaxed margin requirements. Lowered interest rates. A balanced budget. An end to the useless war in Korea. Reduction of taxes on corporate, dividend, and personal income. Even a shortening of the holding period for long-term capital gains! He had picked up block after block of WHIP in that rising market as the active Floor absorbed the gay moods of the world of finance, and greedy customers listened to brokers while brokers drew new courage and faith from increased buying until at last America itself had joined the festivities as six million, five hundred thousand investors acquired holdings listed on the Big Board and the Curb, or traded Over-the-Counter. The Floor men had appeared every morning like gladiators, high-spirited and alert, ready for swift and decisive contest, eyes open to every trade, awaiting the moment when gossip, feuds, and horseplay disappeared and the big third phase of the Booming Bull Market would begin. Short selling had reached an all-time low, confidence an all-time high, and in that atmosphere with commission business plentiful McBride had been a happy man—a standout figure in any crowd, whether executing customers' orders or buying WHIP for the firm's account. He'd been on top of each situation, tall, rawboned, lean-jawed, explosive, and high-tempered, a gambler and a fighter. A practical joker when trading was dull, a piston-rod pile driver when the tape was active. Buy! There was no problem with WHIP no matter what happened so long as what was happening went right on happening and led as it must to the Big Bull Market while America continued Christmas shopping early with visions of sugarplums dancing in each head-on collision which kept sending the market up higher on every hotly contested trade.

But incredibly it had not taken place. The false start reached its peak right before Christmas then stopped while all through the House, both Houses, in fact, nothing was stirring at all as the stocks hung in mid-air with such care in hopes that gifts of generous legislation soon would be forthcoming but they weren't and now sixteen weeks later the Street had passed through successive stages of disbelief, impatience, indecision, and outrage, finally to reach this dull, chronic disappointment as all hopes went up the chimney.

Taxes had not been reduced. The war in Korea had not ended. The holding period for a long-term capital gain remained unchanged. The market fell on no volume from 295 to 264 as evil whispers rustled softly out of Washington like the flutterings of a shroud foreshadowing the threat of a hard money policy to take away what little candy was left. Some of the boys were even saying that the proposed new, high-interest bond would not get the time-honored buying support of the Federal Reserve Board. If such a government bond ever came through, it would cause the banks to raise interest rates overnight. Discourage business expansion. Curtail installment buying. Cripple building prospects. Reduce cash surpluses. The market would crash!

His two geniuses had put their heads very close together and here he was, caught in the middle, with all his capital trapped in WHIP, and WHIP itself trapped in a motionless market since New Year's. If ever this dead market moved it could go only one way—down! and with it every last penny he had earned, begged, and borrowed.

Unless the Michigan court came through today.

He turned his back on the sickening sight of the harassed young man who was spending his first day on the Floor. He had picked the worst week of the year to become a regular member of the Stock Exchange and was getting the usual hazing. The punk was trying to buy the usual nonexistent stock, British Roofing and Tile Limited, for the usual nonexistent customer, and the usual fake crowd of Floor men were pretending to buy, thus "preventing" the Harvard Business School graduate from doing so. The boys had nothing but time and fury and they were using both to do the hazing up brown. Sucker!

Normally McBride would have been in the thick of it, shouting in the newcomer's ear, ripping the buttons off his brand-new broker's jacket, shoving, and mauling. Kid stuff. Story-book crap. Time wasting for holidays when nothing real happened. That's what *they* thought! He'd show the bastards a genuine crowd today. A rally! Just as soon as word from Michigan came through. Then the Floor would take on its authority, led by him, no snot-nosed errand boy for the nation's wealth.

His thoughts had started his body moving involuntarily in the direction of the specialist's post where WHIP was traded. He stopped, remembering that others, members of their Protective Committee, all of whom had helped defray the legal and publicity costs, were watching him. Every move he made today was a signal—Santa Claus or *Malchamovis*—and he didn't dare approach the post until he had word. Word, God damn it! Word word word!

The pain of waiting made him vindictive. The perverse desire to start a false rally was almost uncontrollable.

There, there, little rookie, don't cry. The young man's jaw was quivering, and the boys in the fake crowd could hardly contain their laughter. Mac was out of step, sympathizing with the victim while despising him, but most of all hating himself. Well, come on, eager beaver, get wise. Get dry behind the ears. When your family bought the Seat, surely there must have been lectures, warnings, and a fast run-through. But no doubt in all that preparation they had neglected to tell this Harvard Hero to *look at the tape*—the first and last rule of the Floor. If you ever get out of this alive yourself, lummox, remember it. Look at the tape, screw the hot tips and cold charts. In the future when Mr. Preston gazed into his crystal ball or Coogan peered down the corridors of bankers' clubs, just make sure it wasn't for you. If it isn't happening on the tape then, mister, it isn't happening.

Still the rookie didn't look. They never did. No one did. He hadn't. That's how they all learned the first lesson. When in doubt or hung over, when confused or in the dumps, when you don't know up from down, or are in panic, just step on the brakes, man. Stop, listen, and look—*at the tape!*

After the hazing was over, if Joe College didn't smile pretty and say it was fun, and thanks a lot, fellas, he might as well quit. On the Curb, the name of the stock they used for this initiation was Kennicott Mining Association—KMA, and at the end of the harmless gag, the victim was usually told what it stood for—*Kiss My Ass* if you don't like it!

The sudden absence of familiar sound made McBride look up in alarm. The tape was standing still. It was days like this one made brokers stay home just to keep out of trouble. Many of them hadn't even bothered to come down today. Those not in on the hazing were either asleep in the heavy leather chairs, their feet hanging limply on the marble floor, or playing backgammon and gin in the smoking room.

But he had to stay on the Floor. He just had to stand there and watch both doors and wait because through one of them at any moment could come that cold-blooded, blue-blooded, masterminded son of a bitch Ken Preston to give him the Word.

He flexed his husky shoulders inside the checkered sports jacket that no longer fit. It made him feel better. This was his good-luck jacket. He had worn it every Thursday since the one in early spring ten years ago when he was only a customers' man, barely eking out a living. He'd come a long way since that Thursday and lady luck was his girl. Count on it. She knew when to lift her pretty little skirts, pull down her silken panties, and jiggle on his red-hot knee. She'd done it then when he first wore the good-luck jacket and gone short on a tip, to leave for a long weekend fifteen thousand bucks ahead. That seed money had grown. With it he had put up the front that bagged him his wife and from that bag had borrowed the money with which to buy his Seat. Later he had borrowed two hundred thousand more from her father—unsecured, of course—and here he was, a Floor partner of Preston & Company. So take it easy, chum, and cool off. When the killing came through he'd stuff the Seat money down his wife's throat, the working capital up her old man's ass, and just for laughs an extra something between her legs and he'd *still* be a millionaire. Sweet Jesus, after the killing he'd throw that jacket away and wear the green tie he'd put on for the first time this morning just as long as he lived! Killing. His mind ran from the word and he fixed his thoughts firmly on victory.

Fifty thousand shares at an average price of 55 thanks to his hard work and sweat. Today's quoted market was 107 offered, none bid except for the specialist's nominal 103. They'd bid! Soon as he had word.

The hazing was over and the rookie was smiling a sick, pale, miserable smile. That's it, sonny, you grin and bear it. The tape was moving again. The world lay ahead. But not if the court turned the Plan down. A fifty-point sell-off. Not at all impossible. Not with WHIP. Not in this market. In this market more like seventy points, eighty even, if the government came through with that long-term bond and the added blow of no Federal Reserve buying support. In a crazy tumbling market, WHIP could sell off ninety or a hundred points. Why not? It had done that and worse before. Fifty thousand shares, the largest Floor holding in WHIP common, thanks to his goddamn partners, and may God damn you both to hell!

Still all the market had to do was bull the stock up one point and there was an additional fifty thousand bucks. But what if it went down one point, chum, just one lousy point? Or two or—

Get out of that squirrel cage, chum. Out of the trenches by Christmas or New Year's or Easter or May Day or noontime or never, but just let's have it, one way or the other. For a million or for broke, let's have the word! Word, damn you bastards! Sure, they could have sold out on the rise when the Washington decision came through but it's too late for that now, chum. No more trading in the stock, chum.

Not till the court rules in Michigan. Maybe right this very minute, chum.

He looked up at the clock. 11:46. Christ Almighty. He looked toward the main entrance of the Floor, then at his phone-order clerk who merely shook his head. Lunch time soon. The thought of even trying to drink water made him ill. The Federal District Court in Michigan would recess. More waiting. Another hour of it at least—with Riley, senior partner of the law firm of Riley and Caldwell, sitting in on the rear bench of the Federal District Court in Michigan, waiting for Judge Keane's decision. As soon as it was announced Riley would instruct his spotter, a lawyer too, who'd speed off in the waiting limousine driven by a lad with police-card courtesies to the nearest public phone booth away from the courthouse. The phone had been kept open to their office upstairs, paying overtime on the New York end, since ten o'clock this morning. Waiting. When the spotter reached their man at the phone, he would take it and say yes or no, or repeat very quickly but also very clearly the substance of a muddy legal decision to Coogan who had Caldwell of Riley and Caldwell at his elbow. Waiting too. Then Ken would appear on the Floor. Meanwhile Coogan's unmarried secretary was on that phone eating up the quarters and cracking horny, corny jokes with the Michigan man—waiting— just so the long-distance operator wouldn't plug in on the line and think no one was using it. If the decision went against them, that phone call wouldn't make the difference; nor would it if the word was favorable. As for a muddy decision in this market: that was a death sentence!

I can't wait much longer.

I'm not going to be able to sweat this out. I *have* to sweat it out. Where were the cruddy customers' orders that always came through when he was too busy to handle them? There aren't any, chum. No one is buying. Not today. A loud wolf whistle rose from the Floor. McBride looked up at the Eastern Gallery. Over four hundred thousand visitors had appeared there this year. They would no longer buy but they still appeared daily, fascinated by the myth of Wall Street and the lure of money. A female visitor, young and attractive, had leaned far over the rail in her low-cut white silk blouse. Even McBride's loins were dead today. The wolf call continued for a good two minutes, a chorus of four hundred male whistles from pursed mouths in faces momentarily upturned to the east. He could not stand it any more. If Ken came right now it was too bad. He signaled to the clerk and hurried away from the nine hundred silent phones, the gapers in the Gallery, and the crotch-itchy idle Floor men. Small groups loitered around the door to the smoking room. A few days ago a fist fight had broken out there over a two-bit card game. The Floor men had long since passed out of the aggressive, high-stakes gambling stage in which they whiled away idle days with bets ranging up to five thousand dollars on whether Tom, Dick, or Harry walked away from the specialist's post by turning left or right and whether the next guy out of the washroom would still be zipping his fly. McBride had always been in tune with the collective will, the split personality of the Floor. When specialists were bullish and the rest of the boys bearish, or customers as a group bearish and the Floor therefore predictably bullish, he was tuned in. Today they were as one and he was an outsider, joined to them only in fear. A lot they knew of fear. Even less did those dimwits in the Visitors' Gallery know anything about any of them. You had to be part of it, one of the thirteen hundred-odd men caged in that one square block, trading the same securities, watching the same tape, responding to that same glib and greedy world outside with its maddening, unpredictable moods and outrageous demands to know how they felt today. He knew. He was out of step but still he knew. The rest of the Floor was also waiting. But it was waiting for nothing and some bad news from Washington. The smart boys. Out of positions, or only sensibly in. Worried but safe. On the side lines. *He* was suffering the excruciating anxiety of an immediately impending future—no bloody customer's—his own! Committed fully, inescapably, and may God help him.

McBride entered the smoking room as an old-timer was once again telling the tale of the Floor man who had received an order to sell Urban Service during the crash of '29. "Sell how many, you fool?" And he had been told to sell, you fool, until ordered to stop. He had sold one million shares from an opening price of 100 down to 55 and still going down at the bell. That night the janitor found him in his office, crouched on all fours on top of his desk with a pair of scissors, cutting designs in the desk blotter. After that three months in a sanitarium. Then retirement. The listening group laughed. Crash and bust stories. Depression stories. This was a new note. It seemed only yesterday they still recalled glory like a temporarily routed army, readying for new triumphs by reliving great battles or recounting the antics of the High Command. Sentimentalizing in musty reminiscence like goddamn chambermaids at the bed of a temporarily indisposed or rejected king's mistress as they waited for new events to stir new passions and give new delights befitting the great, the vigorous, and the mighty. Eunuchs and pimps! He moved on quickly into the washroom. So now it was the crash of '29. He lit a cigarette and sucked the smoke in hungrily. Coogan should hear these tales. He was probably sitting upstairs in their office calmly listening to Caldwell's half-assed lawyer's jokes. No smoking rules there. He would like to see Coogan or Jesus H. Christ stay calm if he had to face the firing line and live through the empty hours of kibitzing, shooting of water pistols, and all the other goddamn high-school pranks day after waiting day. And Preston. Their absent-minded mastermind. His mind could afford to be absent; with over a quarter of a million outside the firm's investment, why not? Even the fifteen or twenty million his father lost back in the thirties and the inheritance taxes paid when his mother died three years ago couldn't change that. If the court ruled against them and they were wiped out—he felt the urge to vomit as the words slipped through—even *then* Preston would go on as before, just because his name was Preston. Just because he was the fourth generation of Prestons to head Wall Street or State Street firms. No matter what boners he pulled, he could always set up another Preston & Company as its senior partner. A statistician. A high-class accountant worth no more than fifteen or twenty grand a year. Someone opened the door and shouted, "Mac, your number!"

McBride ran and then stopped: running was not permitted on the Floor, and this was no time to be violating rules. He walked as fast as his legs could carry him. His red hair, usually unruly, was now electrically charged, standing on top of his square, massive head. As he reached the Floor and saw his number on the Board, all fear left him. Word at last. Michigan! He rushed up to his order clerk.

"Sorry, Mac. Just a customer's order for five hundred shares of Zed at the market."

He walked away, his legs trembling. 12:05. By now the court in Michigan was recessed. Or was it an hour earlier there? The Floor was emptying, the members off to lunch. He filled the order, left the post, and handed the slip to a squad boy. A Floor trader, part of their group, moved up alongside him.

"Think it's safe to go to lunch, Mac?"

"You're in the wrong business for safety, chum!"

"And you're getting nervous in the service, ain't you, Mac?"

"Kiss my neck. I'm saving my ass for Coogan."

There was a time that would have ended in a fight, a beaut. Many were the fines he'd paid and was then forced by the Board of Governors to make formal apology as well. He couldn't afford to lose control today. So take comfort. From what? Well, Ken, for instance. Ken was the best statistician on the Street. And Coogan knew his business too. WHIP had not risen from 25½ to 107 for nothing. They knew where the body lay. Naturally it stood still. Who would sell an hour before victory? And only a madman would buy at these prices without knowing reorganization was now an absolute, recorded fact. For all his la-de-da, old American silver, and sweet little whatnots, Ken had something; he could penetrate a hopeless maze. He had done it before. He had something and he had it like no one else Mac knew in this business, where time was money and a research job that took eighteen hours a day for two years with no guarantee of success was an unheard-of, fantastic speculation. Maybe their iceberg wonderboy had seen the answer once again, this time where the giants had not. If so, it would make them all rich today. Unless of course the insurance companies or banks or Texans or Florida group had pulled a last-minute fast one. They had the power and power did not have to yield to logic. It didn't have to be right. It didn't have to be smart. It didn't even have to be sane. Take the government with all this talk about hard money. So it was nuts. But would that stop it? McBride went to his phone and called upstairs. Coogan's voice came through exactly as Mac had expected. Smirking, manipulating bastard.

"Yes, Mac?"

"Any word?"

"No, Mac."

"This market won't rally for the Second Coming of Christ."

"They'll rally, Mac. The minute they see you heading for the specialist's post."

Coogan made it a practice not to mention WHIP on the Floor phone.

"Everyone's out to lunch."

"They'll scurry back fast enough."

"What's Ken doing?"

"Staring out the window at the boats in the Battery. Dreaming about our next big project, I hope." He gave it just the right amount of contempt. "Save your strength for the news, Mac. You'll need it then."

When Coogan hung up, he shook his head and smiled. With Caldwell sitting opposite him, he had to smile. Of course the market was dead. If nothing else, it was still hung over from March 15 with those morning-after-the-year-before tax-return shakes. And of course they were worried about hard money and the like. Children! The government would most certainly launch its thirty-year bond at 3¼ per cent without Federal Reserve support and no doubt, either, that both bond and stock markets would tumble badly when it did. As long as it didn't happen today. Once they got out of WHIP in a nonpanicked market, they would no longer be dependent on customer commissions. Then what difference could a bear market make to them except for a stiff sell-off in volume which would simply create some added commission business on the way to their next big project? He tapped the subpoenas and legal complaints on his desk.

"Now what about this drivel, Joe? How fast can we expedite it?"

"Three or four months."

"I want it done in days."

"You can't, Pat."

Famous last words. Coogan restrained a smile. McBride had pulled a purchase out from under the nose of the Floor man for Naughton & Company a month ago. Now Naughton's customer had brought suit for the profit and Naughton in turn had named Preston & Company in a third-party action.

"If Naughton were the only one contesting Mac's purchase it would go to the Stock Exchange for arbitration. The whole thing would be over in a week. But their customer has a right to bring a court action. What with suits and countersuits, motions for dismissal on the law, pre-trial depositions, and motions for dismissal on the facts—"

The phone rang. Caldwell stopped short, his mouth still open. Coogan listened and hung up.

"No news yet. Tell you what, Joe. Naughton's customer is suing for twenty-five thousand. Offer them five and settle for seventy-five hundred. I want this over with in the next two days."

"Fine. It'll still take a few weeks, Pat. I'll get right on it tomorrow."

Coogan smiled. "Get on it now. Use the phone in the conference room. Michigan won't call any sooner because you're sitting here. When they call, I'll tell you."

He wanted Caldwell out of the way. He marveled at the naïveté and stupidity of people. Caldwell was a reputable lawyer. McBride was a first-class Floor man. The so-called experts and economists with their dismal charts and bearish market letters, who really believed Eisenhower and his advisors would abandon business to help the banks to higher interest rates at the expense of the whole economy, were supposedly well informed. They were all such simple-minded idiots. He picked up the phone again.

"Get me Naughton. If Michigan calls, cut in."

Two weeks for this flyspeck with all the things he had to do after WHIP came home today!

"Naughton? Coogan. Yes. Now what's all this I hear about Mac and your Floor man?" "Oh?" innocently. "You're joking—No, Caldwell hasn't told me yet—After all, the specialist *did* give Mac the trade." He laughed. "Oh, sure. I guess Caldwell had a right to accept service. Well, that's what comes of principals not dealing directly. What are you doing for lunch tomorrow?"

Naughton was turning him down. Coogan waited patiently. "Pity.

And to think we could have avoided all this if I'd followed my instinct Wednesday night at the Blue Goose Club in Montauk. Sure I was there." He hadn't been, but the report from the detective who had would do. "I was halfway to your table when I saw the lovely lady and thought it was Mrs. Naughton till I got closer. I never remember that gal's last name. Quite a colorful female." His smile broadened as Mr. Naughton twisted and squirmed to accept the lunch date after all. "Righto. Tomorrow at one. Bankers Club."

He hung up. Seventy-five hundred dollars saved. If Mac had been more careful there wouldn't have been the problem in the first place.

Overgrown ape!

Still, Coogan sincerely believed he liked people. They were fascinating; full of unexpected fears, weaknesses, and superstitions, distorted turns of mind, high hopes, and despair. And such astonishing abilities and preposterous failings where least expected. He liked being in the thick of them, taking his chances on how he compared in conflict and foresight. He enjoyed meeting the unexpected without preconceived notions and bending it to his will, or swallowing his pride and losses while learning his lesson when he failed. The government's move would shake out the free-ride artists now in on a button, bank money, and a gambler's prayer. It would wallop the market and probably create four or five million unemployed; in his opinion, Washington's target. He'd heard that government receipts from taxation would probably fall three and a half billion short of the estimate set forth in January for this coming June. Yes, business was off for the moment. Finally all of it would stabilize the economy. And away we go for the third phase of the bull market. What of it if the new bond pledged the American public to pay an additional annual nine hundred and seventy-five million in taxes? It would all be made up in the prosperity that resulted from it. The New Era! He was altogether prepared for it if WHIP came through. If it didn't, an adverse decision couldn't stop it or him, merely cause delay—a crushing blow, no doubt, but somehow he would sweat it out. If the sell-off were only moderate and Michigan ruled against them, then the firm could solve the cash problem by using customers' deposits for their own credit. He had carefully thought this through. By cutting it fine they could get by with the Board of Governors and if it was too severe he had already found personal sources from which to borrow. It violated Section 9A of the SEC but that couldn't be helped. It was all part of the calculated risk. Ken could meet his end of it by simply dipping into private funds, and of course McBride would be tossed out. His replacement would be more carefully chosen. Naturally any Floor man remained just that—a Floor man, subject to the Floor's moods and whims, living from moment to moment, keen to the fast trade and the two-point profit, following the action of the tape like a sparrow the droppings of a horse. Still they could do better than McBride—find someone more able to have grasped the essence of this WHIP reorganization in the first place. WHIP had been paralyzed for exactly the same reasons that the economy itself had been held down for almost a quarter of a century. Appeasing leadership. Skeptical masses. Red tape. A field day for backbiting underminers and theorizers of liberal labor and leftist libel.

America was back on the track. The size of the project had widened his own horizons. He was not yet fifty years old and he had grown with it. The youngest nation in the world, leaving out the so-called new state of Israel and other similar provinces with their withered hands out. The same old cow-pasture countries with a new set of rulers and fanatical notions of their right and place. They were two centuries too late with or without Russia's help. This was America's century. Just young enough but not too young. With all the know-how and the necessary guts to reach out for it with a ruthless hand of steel on an arm of lightning, the strong fingers tipped with gold. This was the beginning. He could feel the endless twisting, turning, spitting, glowing vitality of it in his blood. Contest, conflict, conquest. For months it had challenged his imagination and now thanks to WHIP he was on hand not only to see but also to be a part of this miracle. Thanks also to his stubborn courage and foresight. Nor could he omit Ken's passionless brilliance. Ken's way of sighting treasure was something special and it was too bad that the fact of finding it rather than possessing it was all that mattered to Ken. With his name and knowledge and a mind to match, Ken should have had at least twenty or thirty million by now. He needed Ken. One without the other could not have carried off this feat. Between them they had used a mysterious physical law—the same one that allowed a ten-pound pitchfork to lift a thousand pounds of hay. With their puny capital, they had done the trick and, no doubt of it, Ken's farsighted realization of the possibilities in the Public Utility Act of 1935 leading to the voluntary divestment of Tamiami's holdings had proven to be the flip of the farmer's wrist that tossed this fortune into their wagon. But it was he, Coogan, who had driven off at full speed to the market place, his fists firmly closed on the reins, certain of every precarious inch of that narrow, winding road. He smiled. That made McBride their jackass. He regretted the tension between Ken and himself, but it was unavoidable. He was not unaware that Ken had wanted to have it out with him this morning. Of course he had expected Ken to be offended by the purpose behind the offer made by the Tamiamians.

But he had not anticipated Ken's outrage at being its beneficiary. Old school ties and similar abstract ethics—the pretentious luxuries of those who never had to scratch for it. Well, Ken would get over it. Meanwhile the bonus would pay for the legal and promotion expenses and it would teach the arrogant, swindling Texans a lesson for their years of rough riding. It would also show the Tamiamians he was no sucker. All this work for a million dollars? A peanut out of the total loot the others would share, thanks to his effort! A sum ridiculously small, less than a finder's fee. Sitting still for that was no way to earn their respect.

Finding the method for getting paid that served the Tamiamians' own interests helped further to build character. If Ken didn't understand it now, he would later. Just how did he think his great-grandfather had amassed the millions in the first place? Surely not the way two following generations of Prestons had damn near lost all of it. You would think the fact that the Texans had driven his father to his death would make Ken enjoy paying them off and delight in knowing they'd wake tomorrow not half so high and mighty as they were today; it should have made the extra profit especially sweet.

No matter. He could afford to avoid Ken for a few weeks while he cooled off. With a market sell-off due any day it would be months before the buying public was ready for his next Big Step, and Ken was not one to sustain strong passion for very long. The very idea made Coogan smile. He had the patience to wait, the persuasiveness to win Ken over—and the realization that he was getting the best of the bargain helped. So was McBride, only Mac would forget it as he forgot everything that didn't suit him. But he would remember. Each of them shared one third of the profit: clearly Ken was entitled to three quarters all by himself on WHIP, the last of the big special situations. Ken had known something about all of them, grown up in the midst of them, could have made a fortune in any one of them. His father and uncles had either been involved in some way in their underwriting or had arbitraged, traded, or invested in their securities when these companies had been launched in the twenties, only to collapse with the crash and languish during the thirties and forties until plant and capital expansion in 1949 gave them a new lease on life and gave Preston & Company these rare opportunities, of which WHIP was the rarest of all.

This was an interesting moment, an amusing one, for after a fashion he was praying. Please, God, let Judge Keane have had a good night's sleep, an easy bowel movement, a pleasant hop in his own fresh hay last night, and an excellent breakfast this morning. Let the Texans stay home as they promised and keep Riley from getting carried away by the melodious sound of his own voice, just this once. Let no one irritate His Honor on the way to the bench.

Then the reputation won would be worth ten times the dollar profit. His name had spread far and wide in financial circles. The friends he had made were the biggest asset of all; these and the things he had learned. The hidden possibilities—like the use of publicity, unknown in the world of securities and finance. Industry had learned that lesson decades ago while finance shied away from it in the doghouse of public opinion. This was the time to come out! Advertise off the business page. Use radio and television. Plant squibs in gossip columns. Merchandise. Use public relations, sex appeal, human interest! From this lesson had come confidence and the germ of his new idea; a public funds plan on the installment basis to sell securities to the masses for the first time in financial history. A check-off against wages, like pension funds or union dues for investment in America's future. No less than six million workers who could qualify and forty million members of the middle class. He had already looked into the technical aspects. It was doable. A public funds plan that would build a new kind of empire in tune with the times, tied in with the New Era. A public funds plan to capture a market of forty-six million customers!

And for all this he needed Ken. He needed Ken's know-how applied to new credit opportunities and the tricky migration of capital that lay ahead. Then he would be ready to deal with the ins and outs of front and back doors to interlocking and dissolving directorates. With Ken at the drawing board he could play the SEC, the PUD's, the ICC, and the Federal Reserve Board like a symphony as at long last the red tape was cut while the vast public appetite for profit would lead America to the tape! *Coogan* Public Funds. Ken despised publicity and that was how he wanted it. Ken was shy to the point of a sickness; he hated people, and that was fine with Coogan. He had sent Ken off to London, Paris, and Florida no less to remind him just how much he despised being in the midst of them than to pin down the Tamiami offer with Ken as both witness and participant. He also needed Ken to deal with the old cliques. They were not ready to accept him, they probably never would be—perhaps it was too late for that. But it was *they* who were too late when it came to the touch that counted. The people's touch. That and nothing else would tap the new market of the New Era in a new and prosperous America. Such thoughts made him calm. They were not impractical or far-fetched. This was no dream. He had gone all out for WHIP but he had never lost his head. He had simply taken the full chance on his total conviction. It was exactly for this he had joined Ken in the first place. The Preston tradition, the Preston name, an asset worth a fortune that Ken did not know how to claim.

A big man's future was in Judge Keane's hands today.

His secretary entered, her face flushed. "Michigan!"

"Put Preston on the other wire. Turn on your recording tape and—"

Caldwell entered at a run. "Michigan!" He picked up the second phone.

Coogan nodded. "—and type it in triplicate the moment the conversation is over," he finished telling his secretary.

He reached for the phone. "Coogan speaking. You there, Ken? Operator, put Michigan on, please." He was totally confident of what the court decision would be.

McBride was eating peanuts and watching the listless tape when someone hissed in his ear: "Preston!"

He dropped the bag, turned, and headed for the water cooler near the entrance to the bond room. He tried not to run. McBride was already at the water cooler as Ken passed the smoking room. Move, man! Move, you crawling son of a—

Ken reached him, filled a cup, lifted it, and said, "The court has approved our plan."

McBride had a swift intake of breath. His eyes widened, then he grinned. "Here we go!"

McBride bolted across the Floor to the specialist's post. The others had seen Ken enter and watched the whispered conference from a distance. Now they hurried after McBride.

Ken ran the bond tape through his fingers, noting the dullness and softness in trading.

Suddenly a roar went up. Ken raised his head in time to see McBride, high above the growing crowd, shoulders looming, his arms spread over all the others.

When he reached the specialist's post, evidence that the Preston Plan had gone through, the thirty Floor men who had rushed up behind him expected McBride to sell. None of the Floor men except for a picked few in the Protective Committee expected that his first trade would be to buy!

"Buy 500 WHIP at a quarter!" McBride shouted.

"Buy 500 WHIP at a half," he called out again when his first bid was met by the startled specialist.

"100 WHIP to buy at seven-eighths," he boomed. For a moment it created confusion. Preston & Company were not only holding their position: they were *enlarging* it. Were they becoming long-term investors in the reorganized WHIP? What hadn't the Floor considered? Then several who had joined the crowd to sell on the rally abruptly changed their minds and followed McBride's lead. They competed with him and it sent the price up on each trade. Others were signaling their order clerks for instructions from upstairs. In a matter of seconds bids outstripped offers. The buyers, including McBride, lifted their ceilings half a point at a time with no chance for the specialist to maintain an orderly market.

In the Eastern Gallery the visitors pushed to the rail and leaned forward, thrilled by the sudden burst of excitement below. There were boos and cheers, shouting and shoving as the Floor men bid, offered, matched coins, and the latecomers pushed frantically to get into the crowd. Paper was piling up swiftly underfoot. The squad boys scurried back and forth. The tape was moving steadily.

Two governors had reached the post. A third one was hurrying across the Floor. Ken looked up at the tape. It was a ribbon of motion, not all of it on WHIP of course but it alone was rising. 100 WHIP 110½; 100 WHIP 111.

Brokers who had left for lunch were suddenly back, gulping the last of sandwiches or wiping milk from their chins as they ran. Preston & Company wasn't selling WHIP. They were *buying!* Buying? With over fifty thousand shares already? 500 WHIP 113; 500 WHIP 113½.

The trend of Floor men following McBride's lead was gaining size. Many who traded for their own accounts and had waited for this moment as a signal to get out of WHIP on the rally were buying instead. Brokers who had not been in on the speculation were being carried by it, abandoning a traditional position and entering an investment situation even before outside investors had begun to buy. Others who lacked the will or stamina to hold out were selling. Still others, until this moment unsure, afraid to buy anything in the stagnant market, were suddenly buying, indifferent to price and chasing the stock until they got it. They were all buying the future of the reorganized company. A speculator's dream come true. The unlimited possibilities in Latin America for abundant light and power had at long last burst upon the Floor. The slow-growing far-off chorus from beggars in slums joined by children on sugar and tobacco plantations, pious hill-country peons, descendants of heathen conquerors, and transplanted slaves now factory workers thundered in the pent-up force of the Floor, its months of paralyzed waiting finding at last this avenue of release.

"300 WHIP 114½; 300 WHIP 115; 500 WHIP 115½."

Many who reluctantly sold now at these rising prices did so to free capital in order to cope with other long-range positions that might sell off later because of Washington. When for an instant selling paused, McBride led the shouting bids of buyers and others sought to match him at ever higher figures. "200 WHIP 117½; 500 WHIP 118."

Unprepared for McBride's action, the specialists had sold too much in the first minutes, and now the tide of buying multiplied by McBride's unexpected switch had whipsawed them. The governors were on hand to make sure the specialists would not be understocked for later today and tomorrow. It left them no alternative but to compete with McBride and those who were following his example as buyers.

The oldest member on the Floor reached the edge of the WHIP crowd, puffing. He was dressed as always in striped trousers and tails, a three-inch-high celluloid collar, his carefully parted white hair pasted to his head by sweat and his pince-nez trembling on the bridge of his nose, as he shook in palsied disapproval. Ken saw the new broker, obviously initiated into the Street by a fake crowd earlier in the day to judge from his buttonless, ripped coat, as he pushed past the old gentleman, spinning him around and plunging into the thick of the crowd, his white-knuckled fist clenching bona-fide orders at last. He would never mistake the fake for the real thing again as long as he lived. The news ticker was now confirming what the Floor already knew. Soon it would bring more buyers from Eastern and Midwestern states. The old gentleman was still trying to enter the crowd. As he bent and rubbed his shin a voice sang out, "Wait till the sun shines, Nellie, and the clouds go drifting by." The remaining two hundred Floor men not at the WHIP post picked up the refrain in a harsh chorus that surrounded the old man as he limped around the edges of the crowd vainly seeking a soft spot.

"Then we'll be happy, *sweetheart!* You and I—I—I."

The old gentleman's firm—originally on State Street—represented none but the most conservative investors. It surprised Ken that any one of them should be placing WHIP buy orders so soon. They were not buying a long-term growth picture at all. They were buying a new batch of lawsuits and Ken wished he could tell him so. He turned from the sight and looked at the Big Board tape overhead.

"WHIP 121; WHIP 121½."

Most of the nine hundred phones were ringing now. The singing Floor men beat time with their metal cigarette lighters on the rails of idle specialists' posts.

"Buy and buy—y—y—y!"

McBride was pushing his way out of the crowd away from the deafening din. He rushed up to Ken, his good-luck jacket torn down the back. One sleeve was gone. He pulled off the other sleeve, ripped the two separate halves of the jacket, and threw them all to the floor.

"Little old jacket, screw you to high heaven," he shouted. He threw his arms around Ken. "We've bought, boy! Eighteen thousand shares and we could sell them all right now for another fifteen-point profit! Seventy thousand shares even. A millionaire! Kiss my prat!" he called out to the entire Floor of the New York Stock Exchange. "I love you like brothers." He was almost mad with joy. "Screw you all!"

A Floor man whose only interest in WHIP was arbitrage watched the crowd from a distance with a worried frown. McBride gulped water. Then he doused his head under the spigot. He took out his water pistol, filled it, and shot a fine spray fifteen feet across the room into the face of the arbitrageur. "Cheer up, you bastard," he called out. "There's lots more at the top."

The arbitrageur, who could not trade until the new when-issued WHIP common was offered tomorrow, shook his head and wiped the water from his face with his handkerchief.

"Not if they bull that old common much higher," he said.

McBride laughed. "We're buying it and if you want to know why, you schmucko, here's Preston. Ask him."

He had his arm around Ken's shoulder. "I almost forgot," he whispered. "We're selling."

Ken nodded.

"Maggots," McBride grinned. "We sweat it out and they complain about the size of the crumbs." He took a breath. His red face went pale. "Jesus!" He grinned again. "Twenty-four years," he marveled, "to get WHIP out of jail."

"Longer than that," Ken said quietly.

McBride looked at him with admiration and hostility. He was suddenly lightheaded and a little sick to his stomach. Ken's calm was a damp, unfathomable thing. If he didn't know him so well, he would have sworn it was an act. "I'm going to call Coogan, the jerk." He felt fine again and removed his arm from Ken's shoulder. "Then I'll go out and buy me a brand-new jacket," he said gaily. He stopped short and looked around for a moment to make sure no one could hear him. "Why stop? Look at them. With our seventy thousand shares and the fifty thousand from the frogs and limeys out of the market, all committed to Tamiami—and that's *still* not counting the spicks—we can sell everything we pick up now right back into the market later today and tomorrow."

Coogan had already covered that with Ken, using fear of the new government bond as his excuse. Otherwise, Coogan said, there was no doubt that buying more to sell directly into the market was perfectly sound.

Ken looked again at the old man. He was still outside the crowd. His left hand was shaking. Both his legs were twitching. McBride felt Ken's active disinterest and some undercurrent besides.

"Forget it!" McBride said quickly. "This is your baby, and I'm with you." Sweat was running down his face. He was unaware of it as he hurried off.

One thing Ken knew. No one would ever place him in this position again as long as he lived.

That late afternoon and early evening, reporters, customers, brokers, and customers' men jammed the office of Preston & Company. The financial reporter for the *Herald* asked McBride for a statement. McBride, his arm around a secretary from a firm three floors below, his hand under her blouse fumbling with the hooks of her brassiere, waved his glass of scotch toward Coogan and said, "Ask him, chum. I only work here."

Coogan's answer was, "Mac and I are the arms and legs. Ken Preston is the brain."

Everyone started looking for Ken. It became a game. Find the Brain. They called his name as they ran from room to room. No one could find him.

"The brain's gone, man," McBride shouted. "Real gone, man!"

It sent up a gale of hysterical laughter. Finally Coogan made a formal statement. "In behalf of Mr. Preston, who has worked tirelessly on the reorganization of Western Hemisphere Industrial Power, inspired by his father's original vision of hemispheric unity that would bring the God-given privilege of low-cost light and power to the masses south of our border, and build an even richer continent based on mutual trust and free enterprise, let me say that the abiding faith of both Kenneth Preston and his father has at last been fully and finally vindicated. A new era is opening for America and that, my friends, includes *all* the Americas. We're happy to have played a small part in its inception. On behalf of Preston and Company I wish to thank everyone whose confidence, courage, and effort have made this triumphant moment possible."

The next day, April 15, 1953, the United States Government launched its long-term three-and-a-quarter bond without Federal Reserve support and the bond market collapsed. Many holders on margin were wiped out. The stock market soon followed. One Floor man, who held a twenty million dollar top-grade bond position on only one million dollars in cash, died of a heart attack. He had lain dead in the bond crowd for fifteen minutes before a doctor reached him. An important money broker died that night. WHIP rose another five points despite the general sell-off. The sale by Preston & Company to Tamiami took place as agreed before the end of the trading day.

All that weekend Coogan held open house. McBride had meant to attend. When he got home he told his wife he stood within ten thousand of being a millionaire after he deducted taxes, paid off her father for his Seat on the Floor, and the fifty thousand he owed her. He insisted on working out all the figures to prove it.

"Oh, Mac, I believe you. . . ." "It's wonderful, Mac. . . ." "Mac, oh, Mac, how marvelous."

He cut her ecstasy short. "Jerk. You miss the mathematical issue. The mathematical issue is *this*." He reviewed the figures for her again this time on paper while she was torn between delight and the wish to call her father at once. There was also the fact that if she did not get her husband into bed soon he would be off on one of his really wildly dangerous nights. She listened for the fifth time. Then she tried to soothe him. "It doesn't really matter, Mac. What's the difference, darling, everything we own has always belonged to both of us."

McBride shouted, "Makes a hell of a difference to me. *Me!* What we do is this. We cut for the high card." He pulled open the desk drawer and took out a poker deck. "If you win I pay you fifty thousand plus a bonus of ten. But if *I* win you only get forty and I'm a millionaire. Me." He paused and brought his head forward to make sure she understood it. "Millionaire *net*." He ordered her to draw. She turned up a nine of hearts and smiled with happiness. He drew a jack of spades, lifted her off the floor, and kissed her wildly.

"I'm a millionaire, your ever-lovin' husband is a millionaire!"

He had dinner and went to bed with her. When Mac started snoring she phoned her father and told him the great news: he had of course already heard and had discreetly decided to wait for his daughter's call lest his son-in-law think he was in any hurry to get back his two hundred thousand dollars, which he most certainly was, before McBride's gambling temperament destroyed the winnings and left the unsecured debt unpaid. Besides, the bond market collapse had hit part of his portfolio and he could use the ready cash.

Unfortunately McBride woke two hours later. Despite his wife's protests he left the house and drove with drunken deliberateness out of Scarsdale back into Manhattan. Coogan's open house was completely forgotten. McBride started with seven or eight scotches at the Oak Room. Then he wandered east to a bar where he was known and called a girl friend who wasn't home. Later he went to another bar and worked out in detail how he would tell Coogan to drop dead if he thought he'd sit still for this profit being invested by the firm in any- thing at all. When this market sell-off and hard money caused deflation, and these and other factors created a depression, his million would be real money, worth two or three times as much as it was today. *Then* he would decide how and where to invest it. Maybe sell his Seat and retire. Break up the firm right now, if necessary. Whore his head off. He had waited long enough. By two o'clock he was lean- ing on another bar shouting over the muted three-piece orchestra, "Anybody here thinks I'm stupid, just say so, that's all. I'll beat the shit out of every Jew bastard in the place."

A man as big as McBride, considerably younger and nowhere near as drunk, left his girl friend on the tiny dance floor and tapped McBride on the shoulder. "I'm a Jew, big mouth."

The other man sprained his right hand. McBride's jaw was badly lacerated and his wife and father-in-law picked him up at City Hospi- tal. All through the stitches, the burning alcohol, and the dressing, he remained insensible to pain, still drunk and babbling that Coogan wouldn't sell him, never ever again never never never in at the bottom or out at the top. Baruch had the system all right. Trust those sheenies and no use trying, son-of-a-bitch egomaniac, no highfalutin plans from him or their Fancy Dan stick-in-the-mud stuck-up statistical stinking senior partner either. "A millionaire net," he mumbled half asleep. Then he sat upright, eyes clear, voice hoarse and strange and full of hate as he taunted his wife. "You want to *know* why I married you?"

He fell back, sound asleep, slept all through Saturday, had a light dinner in bed, and said to his watching wife, as he moved his jaw with effort, "I'm sorry, ever lovin', what say we celebrate?" A half-hour later he was asleep again. He slept until late Sunday afternoon. When he woke she was still watching him. "I gotta thank Pat and Ken right away," he said. "And the right way. Great guys!"

Coogan humored him and said he understood. Ken was out.

Chapter 5

THE CITY MUSEUM closed at five on Sundays. Ken reached the authenticator's desk a few minutes before. A young man was leaving, carrying a large package wrapped in newspapers under his arm. Then Laurie Dugan was smiling up into Ken's eyes and saying, "Well, hi, how are you?"

He busied himself unwrapping the silver urn and placed it on the counter.

"This is supposedly eighteenth-century New England but I doubt it. Can the silversmith, year, and place be traced?"

"I think so. We can't give you its worth unless the museum wishes to buy it, but any dealer can tell you that."

"It doesn't interest me."

She looked up, amused.

"Do I pay the charge now?"

"It's a free service of the city."

"Ugly, isn't it?" he said.

She nodded, controlling a mischievous twinkle.

"Well," he said.

"Well," she repeated.

He hesitated, said thank you, and started to leave.

"You've forgotten your receipt." She smiled. "It's Kenneth Preston, isn't it? What's the address?"

He told her and asked how soon they'd have the information.

"Either in a day or two or it will take weeks."

"Well," he said once again.

She smiled and waited. He looked miserable, frowned, turned, and left. Downstairs he realized he hadn't taken the receipt after all. He returned and opened the door. The receipt was not on the blond wood counter. There was no sign of her. The top light was off now. Where she had stood he saw a short ladder hooked into a horizontal slot that ran the long stretch of wall space along the green files of index cards.

"I thought you'd come back."

He turned. Half concealed by the open door at the coat rack was a mirror at which she was fixing her lipstick. She held the receipt.

He took it and they left together. On the stairway she stopped. "My umbrella."

"It's not raining now."

When they reached the street it was pouring.

"It is too raining."

"I can drop you off in my cab."

"It's out of your way. I live on West Twenty-third Street."

"Then you can drop me."

She was amused again. "I take the subway."

"Oh, I'd be glad to pay for it."

When the cab was a block from Fifty-third Street, he asked, "Have you had dinner?"

"Up in the office?" She was laughing again.

He flushed. "Would you like to join me for dinner?"

She seemed to weigh it for a moment without amusement. "All right, but just for dinner. I have an appointment later."

He took her to the French restaurant with the small awnings over the inside windows that duplicated in miniature the pink and red tablecloth design. There were tiny flowerpots on little glass ledges and a rough paper on the wall that looked almost like red brick. Wooden pillars at spaced intervals from ceiling to floor had ivy growing on them. All the lights were masked by straw bread baskets.

The waiter, a boy in his teens, approached and in French said, "You have been away quite long."

"I was here last night, René."

"It was my night off."

"I have been traveling."

"Are you hungry tonight or so-so?"

"Very hungry."

"You seem at home here," she said as the boy left.

"I live round the corner."

She nibbled at a breadstick, watching him.

"Why do I amuse you?" he asked.

"I don't know," she said. "You just do. Besides, there were two of you in a row. The one who left when you came in."

"Oh? Is he a friend of yours?"

"No."

As they ate, she told him how the ex-GI had appeared exactly two weeks ago carrying the same newspaper-wrapped package Ken might have noticed. It contained a clock liberated in Germany some years ago. He and his fiancée wanted to know whether it would go with the imitation English furniture they had selected for their apartment in the Bronx. The curator had established without difficulty that it was an original twelfth-century Nuremberg clock—the rare kind with melodious chimes that still kept perfect time and had a little soldier in uniform who marched out and blew his trumpet on the hour. The museum had one almost like it but not nearly as good and it would definitely match the imitation English furniture. Also it could be traded for a houseful of original English furniture with enough cash to spare for a good-sized down payment on an English-style home in Massachusetts! The museum would be glad to purchase it for seventy thousand dollars. This had been going on for two weeks.

"Know what he finally did, hey? Said thanks a lot, ma'am," she imitated his tone, "but I think I'll just let it sit on our mantel for a while!" She laughed and shook her head. "Now you come along and you don't want to know what your urn is worth."

"He sounds very sensible."

"I suppose that's what you would have done."

"I hope so."

She nodded and sipped the wine. "Not me."

"Why not?"

"Seventy thousand dollars! Do I need a better reason?"

He didn't answer.

"What are you anyway?" she asked. "A schoolteacher, an antique dealer, or what?"

"I'm a statistician."

"What's that?"

"It's easy enough to do but rather difficult to explain." He stared at her. "You know you remind me of something."

"So you said on the plane."

"Well, you do."

"Maybe a human being, hey?"

"No. It's associated in my mind with a basement and rats."

She burst into laughter. It made people at other tables turn their heads. "You are without a doubt the goofiest guy I ever met."

The waiter, René, smiling broadly, left the check.

"Would you like to do anything this evening?" he asked stiffly. His cheeks burned with embarrassment.

"I have a date."

"I see."

When they reached the cashier's window she said, "You dropped your receipt."

He put the receipt inside the silver box.

"That's twice now," she said. "I don't think you really want that urn."

"Perhaps I don't."

They walked toward the corner.

"I'm free tomorrow night," she said.

"I see."

"Do you? What do you see?"

"Why do you keep laughing at me?"

"Because it's warm enough not to wear a vest or a black coat and a Homburg hat is really very corny."

He smiled. "May I drop you?"

"No. My date is near here."

He removed his hat and extended his hand.

"Well, you do want to see me again, don't you?"

"Yes, I believe so."

"Don't break an arm trying, Mr. Preston."

"May I pick you up at the museum tomorrow?"

"If you'd like to. You *do* remember my name?"

"Oh yes. Laurie Dugan."

He heard her laughter as he tripped getting into the cab.

The next night she had the information on the urn. It was in most of the catalogues and he was right. The year was 1728, it was made in New York and was once owned by the widow of Captain Kidd. The silversmith was in doubt, for which reason, whether he cared or not, the museum would offer only four hundred dollars for it.

"Imagine Captain Kidd having a wife and such a gal owning that ornate pot."

Ken smiled. They were back at the French restaurant again. It seemed to please the waiter very much.

"You remembered what I remind you of," Laurie said.

He nodded.

"Yesterday when you said my name."

"Yes."

"I guess what you did wasn't good enough for her."

"You might put it that way."

"Long ago?"

"Twenty-five years."

"You're kidding. You're not that old."

"I'm forty-two."

"Then you were—" she worked it out backward "—only seventeen. Why, you were just a baby."

"I suppose so."

"Without ambition?"

"Quite."

She ate, watching him. "And you still are."

"I'm afraid so."

"You don't seem very put out about it."

"Why? Are you ambitious?"

"You bet I am!"

"With what goal?"

"I don't know. Just ambitious. It's only a feeling so far. But a strong one. No fooling around."

"And how does that go with working in a museum?"

She didn't answer. After a while she said, "Not that I owe you any explanation, but I'm in love with a married man." She looked up. "And for God's sake, don't say I see!"

He remained silent.

"He's in love with me, too."

He said, "I see."

She laughed.

"Do you have an engagement tonight?" he asked.

"I thought I did with you."

"Would you like to do anything in particular?"

"No."

"I live close by. You might like to see my silver collection."

"Brother. How corny can you get!"

"Pardon me?"

"The etchings."

He frowned. "I don't understand."

She studied his face. "You really don't," she said finally.

"You mean you would rather we went elsewhere?"

"No. But no funny stuff." She smiled at his blankness. "You kill me. Funny stuff. Making passes," she explained.

He said, "I see," and she said it in unison with him.

As they left the French restaurant she said, "Now you've forgotten the urn."

He went back in to get it.

At first glance his living room seemed larger than it was. Then Laurie realized it was due to the absence of clutter and the way the floor space had been preserved. Bookshelves were built into one wall, a gray fabric couch and dark butler's tray stood against another, and a dining table was close to the third, with chairs placed around it facing the windows in a way that made her feel no one ever ate there. At the fourth wall on shelves and a low captain's chest were pieces of silver and the hi fi. She knew about hi fi's. This was a fine one, custom made with the files for records inside it. She was certain it was carefully indexed and constantly used but always closed afterward with the records back in their proper plastic jackets and hard paper sleeves. Nothing would ever be out of place here; nothing left exposed. She felt a house unvisited and unlived in. It made her voice louder than usual, the way places long uninhabited can unless they compel you to whisper instead. He sensed her appraisal.

For a moment he had the impulse to show her the rest of the apartment, his study where the desk was littered with hundreds of sheets of paper, the exact content of each known to him, but that would have meant leading her through the bedroom.

Ken took the more interesting pieces in his silver collection and placed them on the butler's tray—where she could examine and admire them. There was a tankard by Sanderson, some of the smaller pieces by John Hull, and a salver by Edward Winslow.

"What's the charge you get from these things?"

"They're a part of our past."

"Is that good?"

"I continue to hope so."

"I still don't get it. But I love your Paul Revere box. It's perfect."

"Not actually. John Hurd was the master snuffbox maker. Paul Revere only made a few for close friends. He did this one in 1791."

He had taken the box out of his vest pocket and handed it to her. "You see that fluting?"

His fingers grazed her hand as he pointed out the design.

"It wasn't in any of his earlier work."

"How did you get it?"

"It was a gift to an ancestor on my father's side."

She opened it. The box was empty now. She studied the faded daguerreotype sealed inside. "This the ancestor?"

"No. That's his grandson, Timothy Preston. Timothy was my great-grandfather."

"I can see why the past means something to you."

"But not to you?"

"It doesn't send me. So you're some sort of blue blood?"

"Hardly. Timothy started as a cabin boy. His grandfather was a snuff grinder."

"All right. An aristocrat, then."

"I think of slave owners as aristocrats. Prestons fought slavery."

"You know what I mean."

"No, not really."

She looked at Timothy Preston's face and closed the box. "Aren't all the Founding Fathers' present-day brood supposed to be rich or something?"

"I'm not."

"This box alone should be worth a fortune."

"It's not for sale."

She indicated the silver display. "Aren't all those things valuable?"

"Only to me. Most of them belonged to Mother."

She handed him the silver box. "So his grandpa was a pal of Paul Revere's. He must have been something."

Ken smiled. "I believe he was."

"How did you rate it?"

"It's always been given to the eldest son in each Preston family since Timothy's grandfather."

"Eldest son? I think I visualize that. No, not really. I mean brothers have sons and they have sons. Isn't there an army of cousins?"

"I'm the only male Preston descendant of Timothy's eldest son."

She curled up on the couch. "I have a brother. Just an ordinary kid. I did have a sister. She killed herself."

"I'm terribly sorry." He paused. "So did my father."

That made her look up.

"He lost all his money," Ken explained.

Laurie nodded. "My sister thought she was a Lesbian. I'm sure that wasn't it at all. My father never grew up." She said it as though she had not changed the subject. "He liked garlic in his food but was ashamed to let Mother buy it if he was with her. He coached neighborhood kids in football on his days off, and though he wasn't any good at it, he'd spend more time with them than with his own family. Then when the boys were old enough to ask us for dates, he wouldn't let us go out with them." She opened her purse for a cigarette. "Do you suppose that happens in lots of families?" she asked. "Suicides, I mean."

"I don't know the statistics but I shouldn't think so."

She brooded a moment and then seemed to shake it off. "Just what do statisticians do?"

"Nothing much. Just check facts and figures."

"You told me that. But I don't seem to be able to picture it." She smiled. "It's like your family tree. I have to see things."

"It's really nothing. You examine financial situations. Mostly adding and subtracting, that's all. I specialized in those that went into bankruptcy in the thirties."

"Past tense?"

"Pardon me? Oh. Why, yes. I'm thinking of changing my work."

"I hate figures." She rose from the couch. "It must be very dull."

"Not if you enjoy it, I suppose."

"And do you?"

He didn't answer.

"Then it's profitable?"

"No. Not very."

Laurie had walked to the bookshelves. She picked up a book. It was a first edition. She smiled quizzically. "You have expensive tastes."

"That was my mother's. Most of what's here was."

"Also not for sale?" She squashed her cigarette in the ash tray. "When I found out that urn was Captain Kidd's widow's I thought maybe you had pirate blood." She found her bearings and headed for the kitchen. "Weren't any of your ancestors horse thieves or pimps?"

"No one ever told me."

"That's supposed to be standard equipment," she said over her shoulder.

In the pantry she found the coffee and the percolator and saw the tray for his morning breakfast. It was all carefully laid out. Cup, saucer, plate, glass, napkin, sugar. "I'll bet you're full of all kinds of little rituals," she said as he entered the kitchen. "Like brushing your hair back on each side twenty times and then forward twenty times."

"Fifteen. How did you know?"

"Aren't all bachelors?"

"I suppose so."

She fumbled at the stove. "Did she matter *that* much?"

"She? Oh, no, I don't think it was just that."

"Mama's boy?"

He flushed. "No, I don't think it's that either."

"Well, what then? Do you like your freedom that much?"

"I'm not even sure I know what freedom is."

"Then lust for lots of women. Is that it?"

"I'm probably undersexed, if anything."

"You're probably slightly bats if anything."

"You remind me of her very, very much."

"And you remind me of nobody."

At eleven o'clock he took her home. "May I see you again?"

"Not tomorrow. I have a date. Wednesday."

"At the museum?"

"Why not let me go home first and bathe this once?"

"Of course."

"You don't have a car, I suppose?"

"No."

"I do. Borrowed. I thought maybe we could have dinner in the country."

"Fine."

"It belongs to my married friend."

"I see."

"You don't mind?"

"No. Why should I?"

She started to explain and said, "You're way beyond me," and she was gone.

They went up to Teaneck for dinner. Then they danced. He held his left shoulder high, his hand low, barely touching her back, and took the long, slow steps popular in the late twenties.

"I love to dance," she said.

"I'm sorry I don't dance well."

"You dance very well. Old-fashioned but very well."

"No, I'm stiff."

She laughed. "To me that means drunk."

"We said that too."

"Well, you may be stiff but you're graceful."

"No, I'm not. I know what I am. I'm stiff."

"You think you know what you are and you're stiff because you think you're stiff. Someone could teach you to relax. You're graceful.

The time after that he had tickets for the theater. They went to a Broadway drugstore for a quick snack and planned to eat supper afterward. A pasty-faced, long ropy-armed man waited on them. He wore thick glasses. Behind them his eyes glittered with harassed hatred for the small pen he was confined to and the rush of people on their way to the theater. Ken waited ten minutes before the waiter took their order and called out the beverage part of it to the counter clerk at the other end.

Another ten minutes went by. They were getting uncomfortably close to curtain time.

As the long-armed waiter loped by with someone else's order, Ken said to him, "I'm not sure whether your partner heard you."

"He heard," the waiter answered.

"Because we're in something of a hurry," Ken explained.

"You're not the only customer in the place."

"There's no need to get impertinent."

The man paused before Ken.

"No? And no need for you to get snotty, either."

At that moment the other counterman placed the malteds before them.

"Thank you," said Ken.

"And if you don't like it," the man with the thick glasses said, only he said it very softly as he leaned forward, so the manager couldn't hear him, "just say so and I'll knock your ass right off that chair."

Ken considered him for a moment and then turned to Laurie. "I think we'll make that curtain all right," he said.

When they left the drugstore she demanded, "What kind of a man are you, anyway? To let a soda jerk or any other kind of jerk say that to you in front of a woman and do nothing about it?"

"I suppose your married friend would have pulled him right over the counter."

"You bet he would."

"I see."

During the first act curtain she said, "Wallie was free tonight and wanted to see me. I said I was working late."

Wallie.

Later she said, "I don't know whether I like you at all, and if I do, why I do."

"If you do, I don't know why either," he answered.

"O.K. I give up," she said.

During supper she said, "All the way from Tampa we talked. Now we meet, we talk, we talk, we meet. I still don't know anything about you. You could be a middle-aged Jack the Ripper who's kind to young girls and drinks their blood."

"Yes. That's exactly how I spend my time."

"Go to hell," she said.

"Does that mean you don't want to see me again?"

"It should for a fact but it doesn't. Would it matter to you, hey?"

"I think it might."

They finished supper and walked.

Next time she suggested, "Let's live dangerously and eat someplace else tonight. All right?"

"Fine."

She took him to an Italian restaurant. They knew her there and examined Ken curiously. He had tickets for the theater again.

"If you're not rich, you shouldn't be buying so many tickets and picking up expensive restaurant tabs all over the place."

"I'm not poor either. It's only three theaters and six restaurants so far."

"You keep track of everything?"

"It's a habit."

"You're loaded with habit."

"Would you rather we did something else?"

"No. But there's just no point to you spending your money on me."

Two men entered the restaurant and left the door open. Ken went to the door and shut it. "I suppose," he said when he sat down again, "your friend Wallie would have ordered them to shut that door or told the waiter to do so."

"Is that still eating you?"

"Oddly enough, yes."

"Then next time don't shut the door."

"And pick a fight and gouge somebody's eyes out?"

"Just so long as they're not mine. You like the food?"

"Very much."

"I love the garlic," she said.

He nodded. "What does your father do?"

"Sells insurance in Chicago. He and Ma are separated."

"That's too bad."

"Only for my kid brother. He has to live with him. I guess some men should never marry."

"I suppose you're right."

"Those that don't grow up."

He didn't answer.

"Once Ma went to the country after her appendicitis operation. That's when we lived in the city. I must have been ten. My kid sister was going on eight. My little brother stayed at Grandma's. Helen and I waited for Pa on the stoop stairs till two in the morning. She slept with her head on the marble. I had a big time. You know, visions of Pop dead or leaving us or out in the country because Ma was sick again or he was hurt and needed help or was in jail. All he was was drunk. But he *was* genuinely surprised to see us there. He said he'd told the janitor to let us into the house. He was lying, of course. Still he was actually surprised to find us. He had a few drinks and just forgot he had kids, that's all. Maybe that's why he never earned more than forty-five a week, and had daydreams of being a country gentleman."

She finished her wine and Ken refilled her glass.

"I love wine and I hate whisky. It does bad things to me." She sipped. "You know that silver of yours? It's worth twenty-three thousand dollars."

"Really?"

"Yes. I asked the curator and he had a dealer look it up." She fished in her purse and came up with a slip itemizing the tankard by Sanderson, teapot by John Hurd, salver by Winslow, and the John Hull spoon. A price had even been placed on the Revere box.

He toyed with his spaghetti. "The colonials used to keep their wealth that way in the sixteen hundreds," he said. "The silversmiths were like bankers then. There weren't any banks at the time."

"It seems I'm always bringing up money," she said.

He didn't comment.

"And you hate talking about money," she persisted.

"Well."

"You think it's vulgar."

"Probably."

"You seem to have such a head start on other people."

"Meaning your friend Wallie?"

"Among others."

"I suppose if you never had it at all, you invest it with power it doesn't possess. And if you made it by yourself you can use it as some measure of your capacity. Neither of these things ever happened to me, nor wealth either. Perhaps that's it."

"Well, I like your not caring about it."

"Do you?"

"At least it's different."

"My great-grandfather made a great deal of money. My grandfather lost most of it in arbitrage after a most conservative career. My father lost the rest by speculating."

"You getting angry with me?"

"No, not at all. I'm just explaining."

"O.K. Explain. What's arb–arbitrage?"

"It's much too complicated and very unimportant. Some other time."

"O.K. Skip it."

"If you're really interested I'd be glad to explain it now."

"It's none of my business. Skip it."

"Now *you* sound angry."

"I'm not angry," she said. She sounded angry. "Why should I be angry? It's none of my business. Just skip it."

She finished the wine. "I told you I'm in love with Wallie."

"Yes. You did tell me."

After the theater they went back to his place for coffee. While it heated she looked through his books and found Ivan Turgenev's "A Lear of the Steppes." The author had inscribed it to Ken's grandmother.

"What does Wallie do?" he asked.

"He's a distributor. Radios, TV, and hi fi. He started as an errand boy." She tapped the book. "I tried reading this once. Just couldn't make it."

"That's understandable. The innocence of his individuality makes him inaccessible to the twentieth-century mind. Like Emerson in a way."

"And what are you, hey? A nineteenth-century ghost?"

"In some respects."

"That's true, you know."

She continued exploring the bookshelves. "No mysteries?"

"All of them."

"I mean who-done-its."

"Sorry, no."

"I love them. I like soft-backs because they're only twenty-five cents. You can afford to leave a book at Penn Station or a restaurant when you finish it. A sort of unofficial circulating library." She walked from the bookshelves. "Someday I'd like to read a mystery story where the hero doesn't shack up with a sleazy dame on page one, get beaten up fit to die on page two, and is in there slugging again on page three. One that doesn't have it all figured out at least a hundred pages before the police and three months before the reader understands the author's mile-long last-minute explanation."

"Is that how they all go?"

She fished out a cigarette. "And you don't smoke either," she said.

"No, but if you have a twenty-five-cent copy of a who-done-it you think I ought to read, I'd be very glad to try."

"Just tell me this. What have you and I in common? I mean it."

"I don't know."

"You think I'm born and bred on bubble-gum wrappers and I think you're an ossified mummy. It's silly."

"I suppose it is."

"You suppose. I know. Besides—"

"Yes?"

"Never mind." She stood up. "Look, I only see you on the nights he can't and have dinner with you when he has to eat home with her."

"You've already told me that."

"If he could see me every night I wouldn't see you at all."

"I know that too."

"And money *does* matter to me. It's on my mind. Maybe that's why I talk about it. Because I never had enough and there's a lot of it around and I want some. And your silver and your rare books bore me stiff. Because childhood on Long Island was very dull and my job is very dull and most jobs are very dull. I don't want to steal it or inherit it or get it as a gift either. I want to earn it. And I like plain talk, even four-letter words sometimes if you don't mind, which you do, I know. And a man who loses his temper and raises his voice and has the guts to insist he hailed the cab first when he actually did, like you wouldn't do tonight." Her voice had risen to a shout.

"I'd better take you home now."

"Oh, drop dead!"

He went to the closet for her coat.

"I'm sorry," she said, following him out to the foyer.

"I understand," he said.

"Like hell you do!"

"Please. Laurie, let's not get—"

"Just say vulgar and I'll clout you with one of those God damned colonial pots."

"I am what I am," he said. "I too would like to be different."

"Who asked you to?" She pulled her coat from him. "And who said I wanted to be different?"

"I despise myself when I sound—"

"Stuffy!"

"Yes. Or snobbish and tiresome."

"It wouldn't make any difference. I told you I'm in love. If you tried to kiss me I wouldn't let you."

"I haven't made a—pass."

"No. But you could. So could I. Anyone can cheat on anyone. Biology makes us that way."

"You're too young to be that cynical."

"I'm not cynical!"

"Very well."

"Then for God's sake what—" She dropped the coat and headed for the kitchen. "The coffee!"

They drank the coffee in the living room. She asked him to explain the book's inscription, "To Juanita Trumbull Day." It was his mother's mother and she'd been a good friend of Turgenev's.

"In what way was he like Emerson?"

"He believed in freedom but thought that respecting privacy and adhering to strict principles was the only way to get it. I mean unlike Thomas Jefferson or Maxim Gorki. Jefferson made deals with free-soilers and slave-holding Democrats to further freedom. It ended with Huey Long and Mayor Hague, the Southern Democrats of the Civil War and the Ku Klux Klan. Gorki made similar deals with Lenin and Stalin. When his genuine belief in freedom inconvenienced them, the Kremlin had him killed by poison. Being practical doesn't have anything to do with it. When you compromise the principles of freedom and honor, every effort you make thereafter only intensifies corruption and leads to further slavery."

"That's what Turgenev wrote about?"

"Oh, no. Though Emerson did say the end pre-exists in the means. Turgenev simply pointed out the meanness and barrenness of human existence."

"And you believe that?"

"I'd rather not."

"I think love makes everything worth while."

He smiled.

"Now *I* strike *you* funny," she said.

"No, not a bit. That was Turgenev's main point. Love. Also Gorki's."

"Christ said it earlier."

"Lao-tse said it before Christ."

"Now what are you driving at?"

"Nothing. I suppose it all proves that the past and beginnings *are* important."

"O.K. I'll buy your silverware."

He smiled. "Everything didn't begin in 1900."

She laughed. "Make it 1931. That's when I began."

"Your parents would argue otherwise."

"I said I'll buy your silverware."

She asked him how it was made and he explained the uses of draw-ing irons, stakes and anvils, boiling pans and the sand cushion.

"Was your father interested in these things?"

"No, only my mother in a way. Father's passion was hunting."

"So you *are* a mama's boy."

"I suppose if I'd been a girl I would have been better off."

"Ye gods! How can a man say that about himself!"

"Why not? It's true."

"It's unnatural. No wonder you never got married. Don't you like being a man?"

"Liking it doesn't make it the best thing that could have happened to me."

"That must be an occupational tic. You add, you subtract. You never get a score."

"I've committed myself on occasion."

"Well, at least I have that to look forward to."

When they parted, she said, "I'm going to be busy. I'll call you when I'm free."

She did not call.

At the end of the week he phoned her at the museum. She agreed with silences in between to meet him that evening at the French restaurant because she would be leaving the museum early.

When they met she kept her eyes averted and toyed with her food.

"What's the matter?"

"As facts and figures go it doesn't add up. Nothing you'd understand."

They ate in silence. The proprietor came over to greet them warmly in French. After a few exchanges the proprietor left.

"What was all that about?"

"You."

"Great subject."

"He says it is bound to turn out for the best."

She looked up. Huge tears welled and fell. "I didn't want to do that."

She left the table, stayed in the rest room for quite a while and when she returned said, "I'm really not hungry. I think maybe I'd better go home."

Ken paid the check and they walked out.

"Don't you even care to know what it's about?"

"If you wanted me to know, you'd tell me."

She walked ahead. He caught up with her.

"It's not a pretty story and no mystery who done what."

He waited.

"Why I work at the museum? You asked me, remember?"

He nodded.

"Because I had to clear out of where I worked before. Chorus line of the Esquire Club where a certain gentleman saw and charmed me."

He nodded again.

"When I became his mistress he wanted me out of there. As far away as possible. I got a room by myself, to make it easier for him. That's why I've been seeing you. I was alone too much. He has political connections in the city. That's how come the museum because I wanted to work. He didn't want me to work at all but I have to. If I had all the money in the world I'd still want to work. Doing nothing drives me crazy. Then I got pregnant. I couldn't find a safe abortionist in New York but he knew one in Cuba. Then I rested up in Florida. We were supposed to go away this past week to Vegas where he'd get a divorce. I was going to write and tell you. That's why I stopped seeing you."

Her chin was trembling. She held the tears back by staring hard at the sidewalk.

"But now he can't go," she finished.

"That's too bad."

"Yes, it sure is. He can't go because his wife is pregnant. Naturally he has to stay with her. She isn't going to Cuba—" She was sobbing uncontrollably. Ken took her into the side street away from Lexington Avenue.

"I'm quite the kid, don't you think?" Her sobbing had subsided. "Now I better go home."

He pursed his lips and studied her face. "And where was your mother?"

"In Calterston, Long Island, with troubles of her own."

She wiped her cheeks and put on her lipstick. "So," she said.

His face was expressionless.

"You agree I should go home?"

"I think so."

She gave him a half-smile. "This is one time it's safe to commit yourself, professor."

She turned and walked off.

The next day he phoned her and asked to see her that night.

"I have a date."

"You can't mean that."

"Yes. He called and I actually made a date with him. I'll break it."

They drove out to the country. Neither spoke except once when she said, "I called my mother. Late last night. She said, 'Are you in trouble?' You know what a mother means when she asks her daughter who isn't married, 'Are you in trouble?' *Now* she asks."

Finally Ken spoke. "Why did you tell me about it?"

"I don't know. Because you're kind, I guess."

"What did you expect me to do?"

"Realize I was a dirty, disorganized tramp as well as an ignorant kid and he's not the first man either. Just stop wasting your time on me."

"I see."

"And for God's sake, stop saying I see!"

"You want to work. Do you like your job?"

"Oh, really—!"

"No. Answer me. And look at me, please."

She did. He stopped the car.

"Because I wondered whether they would give you time off again if they knew you were going on your honeymoon."

She was staring hard again.

"Do you suppose they would?"

"Why marry me? You can hire a far more literate companion for conversation."

"You grew up too soon and I too late. That might be as good a basis for marriage as any. Only don't sell yourself short. In fact, don't sell yourself at all. Of course, if you can't see yourself marrying someone my age, with my dis—"

"Wallie is thirty-six. You're not older than God."

"With my disposition," he continued. "So different from what he must be. I'll understand."

"You don't know what you're doing," she warned.

"Does that mean yes?"

"I don't know."

When he reached for her hand, she pulled it away gently.

"I don't know, Ken. Honestly, I just don't know."

Chapter 6

EVEN THOUGH it was the third of May, the temperature stood at forty-three degrees and the sky looked as if it would snow. Gulls flew angrily over the motionless train, stranded on the track halfway to Laurie's destination, Riverneck, Long Island.

Engineers and brakemen had probed and examined the engine for one wasted hour. The trip should have taken less than two hours to start with. She could have been at Mary's already if she hadn't returned the car to the rental agency. Laurie settled back in her seat and watched the gulls swoop over the pond. On a single tree stump, half submerged in the shallow water, a bird perched motionless on one slender leg. Its immobility irritated her. She wanted to tell Mary the news, return to Manhattan, and get it over with. All this going through the motions was too much.

She knew what she had to do. No more recklessly treating each day like her last or idiotically believing the future is forever.

The train started with a sudden screech of releasing brakes and grinding wheels. Aided by the insistent wind blowing strong east by northeast, the thick smoke pushed forward only to dissipate itself against the sky heavy with its stubborn low blanket of gray clouds. This weather was going to be like Fanny Brice's comedy farewell she'd read about. Good-by already!

She turned her face back to the window just as the ruffled surface of the stream disappeared round the bend.

It was going to snow, and a good thing she was wearing the fur coat and woolen dress and carrying her lighter clothes in the traveling bag. The coat was paid for by Wallie. So were the dress and her silken underthings: if she was to carry it that far she would have to throw out practically everything and close down Ma's store.

There would be no more acting on impulse—that was the point of it all.

She'd arrive a good hour late and Mary would not think of calling the stationmaster: not Mary. She'd either worry helplessly or more likely avoid worrying at all by pretending no one had told her when to expect her daughter. That was the one thing Ma was good at.

Her mind hopped unbidden to the image of the small boy she had passed in the air-line limousine on her way to Cuba and her own last fruitless effort to make time stop. Again she saw the child throwing his big red rubber ball earnestly against the side of a warehouse building. Close by, its leash strapped to a fire hydrant, the boy's puppy, tiny and fuzzy with its coat of baby fur, peered up at each passer-by. Laurie had felt its smallness and astonishing newness, its brown eyes innocent of all experience and with that wonderment deep inside them that suggested how much the puppy still belonged close to its mother. It had torn at her for the thing inside herself she was keeping this appointment to destroy.

That night when she appeared at the doctor's Havana office, her features were composed and expressionless. All else about her person was aloof, relaxed, almost motionless except for the wedding ring she wore, borrowed for the occasion, on which each of the fingers of her right hand in turn played repetitiously. When the moment of sharp pain came, it was the ring she had bitten into to keep herself silent. Love oh love oh careless love was strictly for the ballad-singing birds and saying so slipped the expressionless mask back over her young face.

When the train reached Riverneck, a chilling rain was falling. Dick's Cab Service was at the station and old Paul, the driver, brought his wind-burned hand to his cap so that his thumb seemed to touch his beaky nose, pink-tipped from the unexpected cold. He smiled, a yellow, snaggle-toothed smile. Then his leathery, jowled face fell back into vacantness as he drove south of town in the direction of Calterston.

"Looks like this winter ain't never goin' to end," he said.

She mumbled agreement.

Talkative bitch. He knew where the Dugans lived, no need to ask that. Since way back when Laurie's pa was still under one roof with Mary; far back to the early time before Laura—they called her Laurie now—or her younger sister Helen who had killed herself three years ago were even born. They were customers when he had first started his own oil-burner service company and was still a welcome, indispensable man on winter nights. Who'd a' thought then he'd end driving a cab, much less working for someone else!

Strange family, the Dugans. Dead Helen and her ma, Mary. Small and timid like field mice. Dan and this one were alike. Polite, big-boned, and violent. He recalled the fights between father and daughter he could hear from the basement when delivering fuel. Many were the times Paul had tiptoed up the basement stairs and pressed his ear against the door to their living room. The trouble he had been put through when the Dugans had changed from coal to oil! Mary had agreed right enough to the need for a new motor and larger ten-inch pipes leading to their living room. But Dan canceled the order. He insisted that asbestos on the six-inch pipe running twenty-eight feet under the house would do as well. Of course it hadn't. Also putting the thermostat in the hallway was Dan Dugan's idea. Naturally the damn heat shut off before it got to the main part of the house. Dan had refused to pay for the extra work caused by his own fool stubbornness and that wasn't all his stubbornness had cost him. Lost his family. When Laurie started work as a model it near drove Dan half crazy. Weird how Dan's business affairs had improved only after his personal life was shot to hell. Ain't that the way. He'd never forget the day he called Dan in Atlantic City. Dan was there for the insurance company convention. Mary was out—he'd come to refill the tank, entered the house to check the thermostat, smelled gas, and found Helen. Afterward, at the funeral, Dan thanked him, saying, "I thought when you said you were Paul it was Paul McCarthy from my company. We were working together on a prospect. He was supposed to bring this fella to Atlantic City for a good time. When you said 'I got bad news for you,' I thought the contact had gone cold, but what the hell." It was queer to see him smile the salesman's sad smile with his daughter's self-stopped body in the casket a few feet away as he added, lying in his teeth, "You get hardened to such things. That's why I said 'Let's have the bad news.'" Paul slowed the car down; the road was getting slippery now. He knew damned well what both of them actually said. "This is Paul Sutherland. Mary's not home and I found your younger daughter, Helen. She took gas." Dan had asked, "How is she?" and Paul had replied, "She isn't," and that was that. This one had behaved well at her sister's funeral. Dignified, held-in-like, face pale, eyes wide and Lord that girl had a pair of eyes and that wasn't all she had a pair of! Even then when she was only a kid, not yet eighteen. Something! And strong. Too strong for a girl.

Three years ago. That was the year before he went and sold his business. Helen was sixteen and this one had come up for the funeral. A well-paid model already. Only two years older than Helen but much more grown up by a damn sight. Helen hadn't ever left the nest except through death.

So she was almost twenty-one now. A secretary. Beautiful, like no one else in the Dugan family, not even her ma, who was pretty enough, but a standing-still, waiting kind of pretty, like a vase of flowers you had to reach in and pluck, not a get-up-and-go and get it for yourself pretty like this one. Though it was the damnedest thing how their faces and voices were so much alike. Twins, almost. She was a mistress to married men, he'd heard. For money. Hard to believe. Still, so was Helen's suicide at the time, or this one's leaving before it happened or Dan's deserting Mary one year afterward for that matter. Damned if what most things folks did and were made any sense, himself included. Selling out like a fool instead of explaining how lonely that woman said she was at first and only later— What meat she must have on her bones. He'd like to get just one long, unhurried, uncovered view! "Lucky you're dressed for the weather," he said to her profile in his rear-view mirror.

"It's cold in the city too," she replied, not turning her head.

Real conversational. To hell with her then. She *is* too hard for a girl, comes from bein' a whore—too independent and proud. Like a man. Only she sure as sweet little apples and big round grapefruits didn't look like one!

Laurie had been watching the familiar countryside. Gnarled branches, their young green killed by frost; houses, barns, wires, and fences were all shaking now under the gathering wind. The northeast side of the landscape facing its force glistened wet and shiny. The side away from the wind looked dirty and black.

Paul had no family she could ask him about. Strange things had been said about how Paul lived, even when she was a grade-school kid, and what he used to do on cold nights when he came to fix a faulty furnace and the man of the house wasn't home. Something about selling his business to settle one of those scandals with money. There was that about living alone: it made people goofy. She ought to know.

Except for Ken.

"How's my ma?" she asked.

"Never gets any older."

That was silly too. She'd spoken to Mary only three nights ago.

It was the distance between their lives that was vast.

She wished again to get there, tell Ma, have it over with, and leave.

When they reached the front door, the rain was slowing down.

"You're still the most beautiful girl around, Laurie."

There was always something faintly lascivious in the way Paul said anything; a senile lechery that could only perform its unwelcome caresses now with finger-feeling words. Still she felt sorry for him. Appetites out of hand or past one's means were a heavy cross as she should know. He repeated the hand-to-cap motion that looked like thumbing his nose, thanked her for the tip, and left.

Laurie found a note fastened to the front screen door.

"Waited," it read. "Had to go to Riverneck. Back by four. Put up pot roast if you want. Something came up."

Yes. Me. I came up. She thinks I'm pregnant, but so long as I can't face her and say so it won't really be true. That phone call at three in the morning a few days ago had been misleading.

Inside the auxiliary warmth of the electric heater gave off an unused, slippery smell. Furnace trouble. She should have paid for a new one while still with Wallie. Too late now. She disconnected the heater and went up to her old room. An hour. She would put up the pot roast and have it almost ready by the time Ma got back. The first thing Ma had to know was that there was nothing wrong. Not any more.

As the pot roast cooked, she cleaned up the kitchen. As usual, it looked clean but was dirty in all the hidden places, inside the stove, at the base woodwork under the sink, on the upper shelves in the closets. Pop always had a zeal for a clean, spotless kitchen. Mary would go to the library on Saturdays and it was a time of happiness for Laurie, cleaning up the kitchen and making it shine. There had been just enough of that to make it hurt.

She wandered about, inspecting the house. It had cost Pa twenty-eight hundred dollars above the mortgage when they first moved in. Mary said she could get sixty-five hundred or seven thousand now, but where would she live and what good would it do her? Each time in the past when Laurie had returned after that stormy time, the house seemed to grow smaller, dingier, and uglier. When they first moved in it had seemed huge. That was after their one year of apartment house living in Brooklyn at Ma's insistence, sick as she was of small-town life, endless repairs, cesspools, and faulty water heaters. She remembered how happy both Pa and she were when they returned to Calterston. She had run to him from the front lawn, shouting, "Daddy, Daddy, there are a hundred rabbits on it." Actually there had been quite a few, five or six, and he had lifted her to his shoulder and kissed her dirty, dimpled knee. Returning to Calterston was like living again. Dad could spend Sundays coaching the football team, laying out the laundry cardboards from his shirts on Saturday to map the line-up of Notre Dame so that long before television they spoke of "seeing" Notre Dame on radio. The pipe-tobacco smell in the parlor. A snowman in the back yard. Blossoms near the bedroom window in spring and summer. Today its size felt neither falsely large as it had at first nor oppressively constricted as later on—only rather pathetic. Splendor was no longer attractive. The unpretentious was no longer stifling— another result of having made her choice; perhaps also of having made peace indirectly with whatever it was here she had fled from.

She remembered the times she and Helen and their friends had left the house to go to someone else's place because "that room is too small to dance in."

One should have a house, big and roomy, or else live in an apartment: this was neither. It sent her mind to Ken's apartment. *Live* in an apartment. She would try. Really try.

Laurie had run through all the sanitary napkins she brought with her in the hasty leaving of New York. She hunted through the house. There were none. Typical of Mary. She would overlook what she found distasteful even though she would have to make terms with it regularly for some years to come. Laurie left a low flame under the pot roast and walked the three blocks to the drugstore.

It was twenty minutes after she had returned that she heard her mother at the door, thanking someone for the ride home, bustling in cheerfully, calling a laughing good-by from inside the door. She was early. Poor Mary. She knew that cheery side of her. Disaster had hit twice. First Helen's suicide. Then Pa's leaving. Now me.

She thinks I'm next.

Mary Dugan was thirty-eight. Married at sixteen, mother to Laurie at seventeen. She was small, pretty. As Laurie was twenty-one and looked twenty-five, so Mary at thirty-eight seemed thirty and somehow less mature than Laurie. They were like sisters, and at a quick glance it was Laurie who should have been the older one.

"Hi, Ma," Laurie called from the kitchen. "I've got the roast on." She addressed her as Ma but still thought of her as Mary. It was pointless to do otherwise, like a battleship saluting a ferryboat because the silly little thing had accidentally been built earlier.

"You come home for a rest. First thing I do is put you to work. Imagine, practically freezing in May!" Ma stalled over removing her galoshes. "Some new sets arrived at the store and I had to go back." Laurie had entered the hall to greet her.

"Paul told me he drove you up. Whatever is going to happen next to that Long Island Railroad?"

"Look, Ma. Hey." She turned her mother around, holding her by the shoulders, towering over her. They both had the same green eyes, the same lovely mouth. "Slow down. Everything's fine."

Mary made no reply.

"I'm on vacation."

"You told me. Three weeks. I couldn't understand. You just came back from a week in Florida."

"That was different."

"Oh?"

"I'm spending one week here with you and two on my honeymoon."

Mary looked up quickly. She tried not to show her joy. There were always so many bad strings attached to the smallest good news.

"Goodness! How sudden."

Laurie nodded. "His name is Ken Preston and I met him coming back from Florida. He has a little shack near Canada."

"Gracious! Then I don't know him?"

Which meant Ma now realized it was over with Wallie, who had never intended to leave his wife for her or any of the other girls who had come before and would surely come afterward. A few more steps and she would have it all except for the visit to the Cuban doctor. No need to tell her that now. Breaking any new facts of life to Mary was like preparing a child for a serious but unavoidable operation.

Laurie kept her arm on Mary's shoulder as they moved into the kitchen. "He's a statistician. He's gentle and kind."

"How old is he?"

Laurie looked into the pot on the stove. "Forty-two. Never been married before and says I can work or not as I see fit. What else?"

She could feel Ma stiffen. Pa's age.

"A bachelor. Well. That means he'll appreciate you." Ma was getting dishes out of the closet opposite the stove. Their backs were turned to each another. "What's a statistician? Something like a bookkeeper?"

"Sort of. Not quite. More tone and it takes knowledge. He checks up on stocks and things to tell people whether they're good for investment. Has his own firm, with two other men. Preston and Company."

"Oh? He's rich?"

"God, no, not at all. But he's not poor either."

"Mm-m."

Laurie turned from the stove. Mary still faced the closet.

"Look'a, Ma."

Mary turned. "Well, of course, if you're madly in love—"

"I'm not madly in love."

"I gathered."

"He isn't rich and never will be. He's early-American *Mayflower* or Boston, rather. There seems to be a difference, if that means anything and in hard cash it doesn't. What matters to me is that he's *kind* and thoughtful. He's honest and decent. He likes to stay at home and listen to music—"

"Well, good. I'll sell him some records."

"Hold up with the jokes, hey." Ma's unhappy eyes softened Laurie's tone. "Sure, we'll order all our albums from you by mail. That way we'll keep the fortune in the family."

Mary smiled. "Maybe it's the way you describe him," she said softly.

"I'm describing myself. Those are all the things about him that count. I'm sick of people who kick everybody around trying to dance the Great Expectations waltz. Ken's no world-beater. He's shy and a little quaint. I guess he earns ten or fifteen thousand a year and I know he inherited some early-American silver worth about twenty thousand dollars and some books worth another five. That's the extent of his fortune. He's sort of fuddy-duddy and I suppose he's too old for me and there'll be no yearning burning under the hide of me and stuff. But he's what I need. I'm marrying him because I want to."

"Have you met his parents?"

"They're dead."

"Oh."

Laurie turned quickly to the stove. "Golly, how fast!" The pot roast was beginning to burn. "It's done. Smell." She moved the pot over. "Snatched from a fate worse than death." She turned off the flame. "His father lost whatever money they had after the '29 crash, I gather."

"At least it's his own firm. Is it—you know—promising? Can it get big?"

" 'Big' doesn't go with Ken. Except his height, I guess. I can't understand his work too clearly, though God knows he tries to explain. What difference does it make? If it's Ken you can be sure it will always be—" she sought the word "—medium."

"You don't seem to know very much about him."

"I know *him*. That's enough for me."

"Okey dokey. Do I get invited to the wedding?"

"Sure, goony. You can give the bride away." Laurie turned her head. This is the day Ma gives baby away with half a pound of TNT. She walked to the door, keeping her head averted.

"Going to the john. Be right back."

She hurried up the stairs, into the room she had once shared with Helen, went to the window, and lit a cigarette angrily. Your wishing-well window. Stop wishing. Just you pull yourself together, Miss Once-upon-a-time and stay on your track. You knew how Mary would react. You should know by now how her own dream-world smoke half chokes you to death. Outside, the unseasonably cold rain gained new momentum. The wind whistled in a wilder key now through the tossing limbs of tall trees, rocky crags, and crevices in the weakened backs of stubborn old weatherproof houses. It howled across the flustered stream that ran near the house and past the fence she used to jump over on snowbound mornings for a short cut to the station and the 7:32. Then very ladylike and looking anything but her sixteen years with the feeling that she was a masquerader, she would appear sedately at the model agency, gloves and all, proper and correct, and ready for the day's calls. The landscape was being washed into an indefinite gray.

Not for me!

Black or white. Clear cut. You pays your money and you takes your choice. I've taken mine. Life must be taken in small doses as the one drug that's really habit-forming and very dangerous medicine, so shake well before using and take only when strictly needed. I give myself completely to nothing and no one. I will know in advance what I will or won't do. I will reckon the cost. That's where clear-cut decisions begin. The well-advertised Full Life includes all the pain as well as the pleasure, in which unfortunately pain outdistances pleasure two to one sold American but I'm not buying any more. I need kindness. Peace! A life I can call my own and the chance to plan it—things in their fixed places, even disappointment where I left it and can find it again. I'm bruised and aching with the need for it, having learned that the only birthday really worth celebrating is the first one. After that you sink lower each year through disillusionment, breakdown of youth and strength, to death, and I didn't invent this hoax, I only discovered it. I am marrying the mild and mundane. Amen. I am doing it deliberately, and I hope to be good enough to deserve it, please God. *Please!* And I will please Ken in every way I can, I swear! And I also swear to avoid climax and the quest for it which only leads from one letdown to another, avoids middles and ends, trying to experience only beginnings; the road to promiscuity, self-contempt, and self-destruction.

Ma—Exhibit One. A passionate, unsanctioned weekend with Pa, planting me, and then two people made it good so as to hate themselves every morning after till neither sickness nor health nor poorer nor richer could hold together what should have been rent asunder in the first place and which too late, by Helen's death, did them part.

She opened the window. The wind was tossing sprays of the little stream into the air. Rain dashed blindly against the side of the house, rattling the screens, streaking the windowpanes, gurgling impatiently down the drainpipes, and pounding insistently against the roof top, seeking a force equal to itself to tame it.

Ma had never reckoned the cost of things, only their attractiveness, and here she was. So there was a price for reckoning the cost of things too. Banked fires and the mind's eye forever policing the headstrong heart. But she knew now the price for not doing so. There was Mary who had given her heart its head and who had cringed ever after from any feeling whatsoever out of remembered pain, freeing herself only once in a wild grief when she had stood over Helen's casket and had found incoherent poetry in her uncontrollable agony, swaying, hands clenched as she said, oblivious to all others present, "We're so lucky,

Dan. Our beautiful, brilliant child is wax! Helen. You were tired. You wanted to sleep. I know. Listen, I understand. I'll join you. I'm tired too. The next time I'm sick I won't fight and we'll be together. Come, Dan, look at her. Come with me. See your lovely daughter."

The marriage between Mary and Pa had been breaking up and Helen could not stand it. She was better off dead. Now Laurie felt only a softened sadness for all their confusion and its results. Mary never did get sick enough to die—another promise she lacked the power to make good on.

Laurie had run upstairs, afraid that she would break down and cry. Old habits cling. She wouldn't cry. She might have once. This numbness felt good to her. Safe.

She shut the window against the wind's short, loud cries and turned her back on the rain, now not touching earth at all, then abruptly changing its course and forcing its wetness into the soggy ground to blast frost permanently out of each last tenacious hideaway.

She hurried downstairs. I'm upsetting Mary again. I came to put her at rest and so far I'm drawing one large blank. When she entered the kitchen, the table was set.

"Well, what's doing with your love life, hey?"

Mary shrugged her shoulders. "I still get invited of a Saturday night to the Harvey Smith Hotel. One time it's a big potato buyer, another it's a cabbage man. My newest flame looks like Pinocchio and sounds like he's eating celery when he's only chewing bread. Roscoe is in the fertilizer business. He says if he didn't have taxes to pay, he'd have money to burn. Only I keep seeing a big pile of you-know-what smoking instead." She brought her palm to her face so it touched her nose and she giggled, a small-girl gesture. "Which reminds me, I saw Norma Holmes the other day. Imagine her crust coming back here! Remember Norma? She had the riding academy out toward Hampton Bays."

Laurie did. She had learned to ride, paying for it out of her first modeling fees, and had stopped going when Norma's husband made vigorous passes at her. Norma was the first woman in Calterston to start whispers about Laurie being "fast" and "loose."

Mary went on to tell Laurie how Norma had sold the farm and stables to strike out for Buffalo—now there's a place to strike out for —leaving her two children, one six, the other four, in the hands of a twelve-year-old girl in their house in Hampton, and stayed away for three months. Then she returned to take the children back to Buffalo.

"There were two calves, three cats, and a dog she'd left with her kids at Hampton. I think it was having them made it possible for the youngsters to hold out. Well, she took those animals out in the back yard and cut their throats and the poor kids saw her do it from the kitchen window."

"No wonder her husband left her. There's always a reason." Laurie stopped short. "Her husband, as I remember, was a decent sort of egg, except for roving hands."

Mary nodded. "Wrecking your marriage is a terrible thing," she said defenselessly.

"Or your love affair. I've done it often enough to know," Laurie said. "Shouldn't you write to Dad and tell him?"

"Dad can go to hell," Laurie said calmly. She reached her hand across the table. "Honest, Ma. I know what I'm doing."

Mary nodded at a mystery. "I believe you always did."

"No. I always didn't. But I do now. It still leaves me with appetites, big ones, for all kinds of things. But I'm trying to satisfy the most important one, and if it's at the expense of all the others, why then I guess that's part of growing up. I want peace and quiet. I want to know where everything is all the time. Even if that means there's less of it. That's the biggest damn hunger of my life right now."

The next morning spring was a three-dimensional uprising, the sky cloudless, the smallest twig in the distance as vividly visible as a nearby barely budding tree. The air throbbed with the smell of young greenness and the stirring muck of earth. Laurie and Ma rose early. Mary told them at the music shop that her daughter was home for a week— was getting married—and she'd be in late in the afternoon. Yes, she agreed, it was wonderful and twenty-one *was* just the right age for getting married. They went out before breakfast to examine the house for storm damage.

Later they ate breakfast on the tiny front porch, basking in the long-awaited sun. The persisting dampness of the wood gave off a sharp but cozy fragrance.

"I want to see Doris." Doris was Laurie's closest childhood friend.

"She's visiting her in-laws in Jersey."

"Damn! Make sure you tell her I asked for her."

Mary nodded. "I suppose you won't be able to go to Chicago next month."

"What for?"

"Your brother's high school graduation exercise."

"No, I won't."

"I guess I have to."

"You know how much seeing Pa upsets you. Why not phone Tommy and arrange for him to come in for a week?"

Mary sighed. "Yes, I suppose you're right."

"I'll wire him too and send him a present."

"Should I turn off the oil heat yet, do you think?"

"Better wait and make sure."

"I hope winter is over," Mary said with a little sigh.

"So do I. But wait and make sure anyway, hey."

"What's he really like?"

"Colorless until you get to know him." *Which no one could say about Wallie.* "Ken's set but he's set in just the way I want him to be. Underneath he's strong. I can't quite explain. I just know that if I ever go off half-cocked, he'll bring me back."

Mary had been buttering a piece of toast slowly, her eyes fixed on it. "When you phoned the other night—was it about this?"

"Yes."

"You sounded so upset." She was removing the butter from the toast now, scraping it off the knife onto the edge of her plate.

"Not upset. Unsure."

"And now you're sure?"

"Definitely."

Mary looked up. "I mean, if there is something else . . ."

Laurie put down her cup. "Like what?"

Mary shrugged. "I don't know, really. But if there is . . ."

"I'm not pregnant, if that's what you mean."

Mary flushed. "I'm so glad! I thought maybe . . ."

Anger was rising in Laurie now and she was trying to control it. *She musn't let go.* "You mean Ken made me pregnant so I was making him marry me?"

"Heavens, no!"

"Then what? Wallie made me pregnant and I was palming the child off on Ken so Wallie and I could keep up the good work?" *Don't let go, I said.*

"No. Really! What's the diff—as long as you aren't?"

"Were you all set to tell me if it was Ken, don't make the same mistake you made in marrying Pa, and if it was Wallie, don't enter marriage with another man based on such a disgraceful lie? You really know that little of me?" *Don't let go, honey. Oh, don't let go.*

"I've been many things, but a cheat or a coward isn't one of them!" *That's your department. That's why your husband is gone, your home wrecked, and me out of it, with your other daughter dead. Because you tried to reduce life to the size where your little hand could clench it, never looking at it, and what runs over the sides you just pretend isn't there. Well, life isn't that way! It never was! It never will be! And you've shriveled to the size of your own palm pretending it can*

be, and we've all run over the sides, falling and breaking our bones
and our hearts because of you.

She rose to her feet. *"Don't let go, honey," Wallie had said when she
was close in his arms. Oh honey, don't let go.* She beat one clenched
fist into the open palm of the other hand.

"God damn it," she said. "I swore I wouldn't do this. I'm sorry, Mary."
"And why shouldn't I let go, hey? I've got a bear by the tail." "Don't
pay any attention to what I say. I'm sorry, Ma. But I'm still bleeding
from it. I'm raw all over. Whatever I've been, I've tried to be straight
with myself. If nothing else, I've been that."

"What do you mean, bleeding?"

"Yes, I was pregnant. *Was.* That's why I went to Florida. Wallie
knew a doctor in Cuba. Your grandchild was killed before it was born.
And Wallie was its father, which is why it's dead now. That's why
I'm staying here for a week before the honeymoon. The doctor said
six weeks. It's only five now."

"Laurie."

"And I told Ken all this so he would know what kind of a screwball
I am and stop wasting his time, and *then* he asked me to marry him."

She was pacing. *"Just pull and you'll see what you got by the tail.
But don't let go, baby."* "Honestly, Wallie!" But she had to let go.
She had to let go.

"I didn't mean to hurt you, Ma. You're so unable to take it. I swore
I wouldn't all the way out. I'm really sorry." She ran her hand through
her hair. "Ken knows I don't love him with a capital L. He knows
how I've lived. He knows I'd prefer him to a trainload of Wallies and
all their lechery and loot. I'm not conning him or myself or anyone
else. I know what I'm doing."

She'd let go. She had to. Suddenly she was sobbing, "It wasn't for
you, Ma. Honestly. It wasn't for you."

Chapter 7

THEY COULD have been married at the First Presbyterian Church in Manhattan with a reception at the Water Club. His father's name was still on the plaque. Ken dreaded the prospect and was going to leave it up to Laurie but it never got beyond the question of type of ceremony. Laurie said Pop was in Chicago where she hoped he'd stay. Her aunt was in California. She preferred that they just go to City Hall or some such thing. Ken arranged a simple, unattended ceremony at a minister's home in Connecticut. Afterward they were going to drive straight from there to his camp on Lake St. Terese. Cousin Alicia teased him about picking a Unitarian minister and reminded him of his mother's quip after they had moved to New York and she abandoned that church for Father's Presbyterianism with the pronouncement, "Unitarianism requires its own trilogy: the brotherhood of man, the fatherhood of God, and the neighborhood of Boston."

Before leaving, Ken had met briefly with Coogan. Since his return from Florida, at first Coogan had avoided him, and then Ken had either avoided Coogan, or the new and only important fact in his life, Laurie, had pushed all matters of the firm out of his mind. He didn't really care which it was. Coogan had shaken his hand with warmth on hearing of Ken's good fortune. Then he raised the matter of the Tamiamians himself so candidly that it was only after their meeting Ken realized he hadn't stated in unequivocal terms his intention to quit.

"I know you've been upset by the lack of ethics of those Florida crooks," Coogan had said. "But they'd have done all of it anyway. What did it take? A visit to Rockefeller Plaza to commit the French and British? They had the South Americans in their pocket all the time. They'd have simply picked up our fifty thousand shares on the market through dummy buyers at lower prices. Now let's face it, Ken. We *did* foot the whole bill for the reorganization and they profited a damn sight more than we did."

The closest Ken came to stating his decision was to say, "I don't care to be in a business any longer where such things can happen," to which Coogan had replied, "Nor I, and thank God we don't have to any more. The big men of finance are fundamentally honest. The robber-baron days are over, and now we can stay on the gentlemen's side of this business all the way. But why figure it out? We have plenty of time. It'll be months before this dead market starts moving. You just go away with your bride. We can discuss it all when you return."

Ken had not disputed it. It seemed a distant, trivial thing now: all that was urgently close and real was Laurie.

She was traveling up to the minister's near Westport with her mother and Cousin Alicia. It would be easy for her with Alicia. She too had married late and not quite in the expected Preston manner, although her vows had been attended with the full complement of ceremony. She would sympathize with Laurie. He was driving up with Alicia's husband and that was not so easy. Ken had wondered before how the son of a one-time night watchman from Allentown, Pennsylvania, who never really had the opportunity to know his father-in-law, could be so much like him. From the first, George Tucker had taken naturally to his wife's private house with the elevator and wine cellar, and the fourth largest cottage on Caleb Island: he was in fact now telling Ken their current plans to find a place of their own in Canada with enough acreage for a private hunting preserve. He was a promising engineer, all the more promising, but still not delivering since he had engineered his marriage to the oldest of Stuart Preston's five daughters three years ago, and the latest edition of the *Social Register* had at last included his name as husband of the Married Maiden, Alicia Preston.

He had commented favorably on Ken's car, acquired yesterday, and spoke with vague condescension as though to a poor if legitimate member of the family. He knew of course all about Ken's father and how the family had resisted his glowing proposals for speculating in South American utilities as well as Ken's recent, belated first step forward toward recoupment of his father's losses.

"The girls all hope you're coming out to the Rock," he was saying.

"I doubt it. I guess Laurie and I will just stay at the camp for a while."

"Opening the camp is a good idea. It's an awfully nice little spot. Awfully."

Exactly like his father-in-law. As a boy, Ken had resented his father's younger brother and felt somehow that he mocked his father or knew things he would not share with him. Uncle Stuart's discreet image came and went, smiling imperceptibly into a gray mustache as he said nothing, while Father clowned and was evasive in his presence. A mystery born of a mystery that had outlived its origin. Whatever it was in Uncle Stuart that led him to marry Aunt Betty, of a good but flashy New York family that retained a cook at three thousand a month and a kitchen staff of twelve, had also led him to go along with his wife's determination that all of the girls' "comings out" would be in the Little Season. When Cousin Margaret changed her mind at the last moment and wanted a certain singer for her debut, Uncle Stuart had located him at a two-week engagement in Rio, paid for its cancellation, met the price of the celebrity, and flown him back. Perhaps the secret was that Uncle Stuart saw nothing special in being a Preston and took the privileges it provided for granted, as Father had not.

". . . might drop in on you on the way back," Tucker was saying.

Tucker had been to the camp only once—during the summer he courted Alicia. Even Aunt Betty had disapproved and so Mother had invited them, four months before her death.

". . . awfully. Beautiful girl. Bright and vivacious." Tucker nodded approval. "Though I must say the female faction of the family resents your depriving them all of a crack at her in true Preston style." He laughed, a high, dry squeak. "You may be sure the boys all understand."

He meant the four husbands of Alicia's younger sisters who had taken their full crack at Tucker on that unbearably hot summer day in Old Boston when Ken was the usher assigned to the center entrance doors of the church and had tried in vain to persuade the house servants of the Prestons, Aunt Betty's people, as well as distant relatives, minor associates, and casual acquaintances to help fill up the right-hand pews traditionally reserved for the groom's relatives and friends. Finally two hundred guests sat in the bride's section and only twenty in the groom's, among them Tucker's father and uncle, both perspiring. They had sat five rows back, sunk in their seats like terrified janitors mistaken under grave circumstances for royalty.

Later at the Fundy Club, Alicia's mother had excused herself from an elder statesman, and chatted with the two petrified gentlemen, while the four other husbands and Ken had gone upstairs to the bedroom and watched George Tucker shed his white linen dinner jacket and dark trousers as his best man darted in and out the door. Tucker had walked aimlessly about, sweating in his undershorts while other husbands of Prestons lounged and itched on the damp beds and rough fabric chairs, nursing their melting drinks, their wilted collars open as they waited and watched; because of that night they had all gone skinny dipping out at the Rock. There were various versions. The accepted one was Archie's—a weekend guest of Margaret and Tuffie's. Alicia suggested skinny dipping. When George, shocked, had asked, "Naked?" and she smiled and said, "Of course," by which as any fool should know, she meant wearing their bathing suits down to the beach where the girls would strip and go in first and the boys would follow. Tucker, the last to appear, was seen approaching in the hallway stark naked. Alicia succeeded in reaching him before he entered the room. She tossed him a robe and said, "Oh, we wear things on the way to the beach, dear, because it's more comfortable in the carriage." There had been some question as to the adequacy of George's anatomical endowment ever since.

After showering, Ken saw Tucker watching them in the bedroom through the bathroom mirror, a towel draped round him, finally making up his mind and dropping the towel. He walked into the bedroom, naked once more, picked a fresh shirt, socks, and tie while the other four examined him slowly, appraisingly, up and down, down and up. The eldest broke the silence.

"Now, George, it's too late to pull out of this." Laughter. "So you might as well be set straight on a few points. Most important, once you let one of those Preston females make you get up in the morning to fetch coffee that's just how it will be forever." He spoke slowly as befitted a man now not only senior among Preston husbands but also in his sixth year of work on a thesis for his Ph.D. on the philosophy of Mach. The next in seniority said, "They're spoiled, George. Centuries of spoiling. They take handling. Now here's a secret. They're very biological." More laughter. "That's the only safe way to keep them happy and make them toe the line."

Each took his turn at the ritual, including the youngest, who at twenty-four mourned the contemplated demolition of the Ritz Carlton and often wore a cutaway on Sundays. George had smiled and listened, his eyes wary, resentful, and attentive behind the glasses, and Ken had been sick to his stomach.

"Seventeen Whittier Row," Ken said and stopped the car.

"Right. There's Alicia's heap up ahead. They've gone in."

"Rituals are barbaric," Ken said in a flat tone, without moving.

"They certainly are," Tucker agreed cheerfully. "Awfully."

Ken suddenly began to tremble. "That's odd," he whispered to himself and then with no seeming connection, "there was another woman, you see—two, in fact—" Ken was seized with a fit of dry, racking sobs. Tucker managed to put an arm around him gingerly. "—when you wait this long," Ken said. His sobs sounded like the hoarse barking of a wounded animal. Strange behavior for a man on his wedding day. Awfully. And for a Preston. But then so was not being married till the age of forty-two. Under the unexpected breakdown, Ken had shriveled and grown older, then inexplicably he looked younger.

"Thank you," he said and smiled with puzzled embarrassment. "Strange, wasn't it?" His face was still white when they entered the minister's home.

Ken said, "This is Saranac," and stopped the car. "About an hour away now. Would you like some coffee?"

"No. I'll just run into that shop. Only be a minute."

She went in to buy two pairs of flannel pajamas. The last time she had worn flannel pajamas was when she was fifteen, but the silk nightgowns in her bag were all gifts from Wallie and as they drove up through the farm country, despite her determination to be matter-of-fact about it all, she found she simply couldn't wear the nightgowns. She came out with the package under her arm and Ken took it.

"Pajamas," she said. "I didn't realize it would be so cold up here."

"There's a fireplace in the bedroom." He stopped abruptly and stepped back into the car and started it.

Their conversation since Westport had been steadily growing more strained, less personal, and they seemed more like strangers now than on that fog-bound night in Sarasota when they had first met. Once Laurie said, "Your cousin Alicia kept talking about the 'Rock.' What's that?"

"Caleb Island off the coast of Maine. My great-grandfather bought it in 1859 for a few thousand."

"You make it sound like prison."

"It is. We left when I was seven."

"Not to hear dear cousin Alicia tell it. She went on and on about the time Mummy lived at Mansion House and it was *such* fun and Cooze Arthur is *such* fun too and so is Cooze Sarah. And of course, Cooze Theodore who is the master of Mansion House now. She called you 'cooze' too. Seems everybody on the Rock is a cooze."

"Means cousin. A figure of speech." He remembered Cousin Theodore, past his eighty-sixth birthday then, disapproving strongly when Aunt Betty removed her own treasures from Mansion House after Stuart's death, but Theodore had considered the matter beneath both Preston comment and contempt.

"Mmm. When we were kids 'cooze' was a figure of speech too. Short for 'coozy' which was a very dirty word. I take it this is the rich end of the family."

"That's right."

"She also told me how whenever you or she were naughty at dancing school you were left off the lists. Is that why both of you didn't marry sooner?"

He didn't answer. Later they talked about the weather, the countryside, and finally about nothing at all. Ken pointed across the street. "That's our summer theater. Opens in two weeks. They do good work."

"We'll be gone in two weeks."

"We don't have to," Ken said.

"Well, we'll see."

When they reached the mainland dock at Lake St. Terese, a man with gray hair and a very young face came out from behind the counter, smiling as he took Ken's hand.

"This is Mrs. Preston."

He nodded, still smiling. "Mr. Sands says he can come pick you up in the work boat."

"No. I'll use *Silver Box*. She gassed up?"

"Sure thing. Put on a new propeller when we heard you were coming. We're hammering out a small dent in the old one. We checked the rudder." He ducked back behind the counter. "I'll get your food box."

"You might throw in some flashlights." Ken turned to greet a small, delicately formed old lady who approached them, her bright blue eyes on Laurie.

"Well, now, how are you, Mother Brooks?"

"Just fine, Mr. Preston." Her bright eyes sparkled behind the glasses. Her white hair was piled high on her head in the fashion of the late nineteenth century. "It's been such a long winter." She extended both her finely veined hands to Laurie. "And this is Mrs. Preston?"

Laurie nodded. The old lady smiled. "You're very welcome to St. Terese, child."

Her son carried the food box down below to the slips. *Silver Box II* was a twenty-foot-long motor launch. It responded quickly to the starter, backed out straight despite the strong drift, and picked up speed as Ken turned her forward, headed toward the point. "You all right?" he called over the motor.

"I'm——"

The wind swallowed up her voice as she laughed and nodded. The lake was sparklingly clear, the hills and mountains visible in detail, vivid and overstated as in a colored post card. Ken pointed straight ahead and shouted something. She pointed to her ear, still laughing. The spray drenched her face and the wind was tossing her hair. As the boat slid smoothly into the slip, they were greeted by an excited cheeping and fluttering about of barn swallows in the dock.

"They have eggs in their nests," Ken explained, pointing overhead to the eaves. "They'll carry on each time we appear till the little ones are hatched next month."

A man came down the road pushing a wheelbarrow. He wore an old-fashioned hard straw hat and garters on his shirt sleeves.

"Mr. Sands, our caretaker." Ken waved and called out, "How's the weather been, Mr. Sands?"

The old man nodded and smiled as he approached. "Lake just cracked back two or three weeks ago. There's an icehouse full, all packed down good with straw."

"This is Mrs. Preston."

Mr. Sands removed his hard straw hat an inch from his head as he kept nodding and beaming. He and Laurie shook hands. Then she ran out of the boathouse a distance up the road. Mr. Sands, still nodding his head and beaming at Ken, said, "Well, well, Mr. Ken, I must say. Well, well, well."

"Ken," Laurie called out. "Come here."

He went to her as Mr. Sands leaned over for the food box and placed it in the wheelbarrow.

"You crazy, idiotic, goony— It's like autumn! Only there are no insects. A shack near Canada? Now look. You said you weren't rich. I'm not talking about money. I could be awfully God damn mad at you."

"Do you like it?"

"Like it? It's too much. But what do you mean a shack and not rich?"

"I'm not."

"O.K. I'm your wife, right? I mean, I should know, shouldn't I? So what's not rich?"

"Of course you should. We have a little more than a million."

She thought he hadn't wanted her to know until they were married so at least that reason for accepting him would be ruled out. She had no way of realizing that by his lights he had told her the truth.

Mr. Sands reached and passed them with the wheelbarrow.

"I wanted to thank you, Mr. Ken, for selling my WHIP."

"Thank you for holding on to it."

"Well, when it comes to that, I bought mine back in '28. That and Telephone. Never had a minute's doubt about either." Then, to Laurie, "Only time you'll have insect life here, Mrs. Preston, is after the rains. A few little gnats and the like. Bees of course, but they don't bother."

"And deerflies next month," Ken reminded, smiling.

"We won't be here next month."

"Why sure you'll be here," Mr. Sands said. He kept pace a little ahead of them. "But the deerflies, they won't, Mr. Ken. Not since last year. Something those fellas down to Paul Smith Ag College doped out."

Laurie was running up ahead again. Ken followed her.

"You won't find nicer country anywhere," Mr. Sands told Laurie, and turned off the road toward the kitchen door. There was a stone patio some fifty feet long on the lake side of the main house with a ladder down into the lake and a diving board. Some hundred yards back, Laurie could now see that there were two floors above the dock at the boathouse.

"What's over the boathouse?" she called.

"Game rooms," Ken said, joining her. "Darts, ping-pong, card tables."

"Golly, I love this." She walked to the edge. "Is it ever warm enough to swim?"

"You get used to a nip in the air."

She raced around off the patio and back up to the lawn. "What's that?"

"Sunhouse," he answered, following. "Mother used to have tea there under an awning."

"It looks Chinese."

"It is." He smiled, remembering. "From her Tao period."

Laurie ran to the far end of the lawn. "And that?"

"My father used to work there. You see how far back it is from the lake? It's quiet and the trees keep out the sun."

She whirled around. "Is this an island?"

"No. A peninsula. But it's awfully narrow and grown over from the mainland. The only way to and from is by boat."

"My God," she said. "There's another house."

"That's Mr. Sands's. Mother left him the acre it's on in her will and paid for having it built. If we ever sell, it's subject to that."

"You must never sell!" she cried. "Not if you get as poor as J. P. Morgan's umpteenth cooze. I love Mr. Sands. I love the smell of the air. I love everything. I'm afraid I'm going to have to stand on my head," she announced. She somersaulted and lay on her back in the young grass, smiling up at the sky. Ken sat down beside her.

"You do like it."

"Promise you'll never sell it. Never! Never!"

He nodded.

"Upside down I thought I saw another house."

"You did." He pointed back to where the pines were thickest. "That was the first house after we left Caleb Island in 1918. It still has no electricity. That's how Mother wanted it. All her things are locked in there." Sadness had crept into his voice. Laurie rose.

"I'll make coffee. Then let's drive around the lake."

"Coffee's ready," Ken said. He nodded toward a window from which Mr. Sands was beckoning.

They went out in the sailboat. When the wind died down they returned and he took her on a tour of the lake in *Silver Box II.*

"You handle boats real well, hey."

"Been doing it since I was eight."

He pointed out the few camps, less than a dozen spread round the long lake shore. As the motorboat faced their dock, the setting sun behind them, she said, "And that's ours." She put her arm through his. The backwash sprayed over them on the front seat. Her face was damp and shiny.

"I didn't know you were rich when I married you and it's the last time I'll ever mention the subject again. But I *didn't* know. Admit it."

He smiled. "I admit it." The fact that they weren't rich wasn't worth arguing about.

"All right then. Will you teach me how to handle this boat?"

"Right now if you wish. Nothing to it except for docking and pulling out."

"No, not now. I'm a little afraid of it. Besides, I'm still on tour."

He had slowed down the motor. It purred softly. He left it that way.

"Stop it altogether," she whispered.

He did. They listened to the silence. The lake was turning red as the sun sank below the horizon.

"How old were you?"

"When I first came here?"

She nodded.

"Almost eight."

"Has it changed?"

"No."

"I knew it." She turned to face him. "I think—I mean I—I'm beginning to—" She turned her head away. "We mustn't let it change, Ken."

The soft wind was turning the boat slowly.

On the way back from the boathouse he stopped at a big tree, lifted some horseshoes off a long, rusty nail. "Ever pitch these?"

"Nope."

He threw one at the far peg into the dirt.

"You're good, hey."

"Not very." He threw the other. It scored a ringer. "Mother was. It was her only exercise. She used to play Mr. Sands by the hour. That's why it's next to his house."

"Your mother moved from that damned Rock. I like her. I wish I'd met her."

"She's all over this place one way or another."

A bell chimed softly. "That's dinner," Ken said, taking her hand. Then he dropped it and she took his arm and held it.

The dining room was directly under their bedroom. Its walls were made of yellow pine with silver birch pillars from floor to ceiling. The furniture was cedar except for some Chinese pieces that didn't jar. A high window ran the full length of the room facing the lake, the mountains, and the sunset. Two sailboats were caught in its last rays. The room was flooded with it. In the adjoining living room, Mr. Sands was piling logs in the fireplace. The smell of burning pine mingled with the aroma of freshly ground coffee.

"I don't know if I can stand it. It's too much," she said. She lowered her voice. "Isn't he putting an awful lot of wood in there?"

"It gets cold very fast once the sun is down."

"We won't be staying up that late."

"I'll have the fires set downstairs bright and early," Mr. Sands said, entering. "If there's anything else you want, just buzz me down to the house." He shook Ken's hand, then extended his to Laurie. "This has been a happy place for many seasons, Mrs. Preston. Now I know it's going to be that way again and stay that way." He started to leave, then turned. "Shall I leave the steak bones out?"

Ken nodded. "I meant to ask you, has any mail come from my Aunt Sarah or Cousin Arthur?"

"No, sir, Mr. Ken."

He left.

They sat in the living room. The chairs and couch were covered in a bright red material with gold piping. It kept the illusion of sunshine on the many days of summer when it rained steadily. The sun had set and it was night.

"What are the steak bones for?"

"Raccoons, then the squirrels, and finally chipmunks. They take turns."

She laughed. "Can we watch?"

"If we're still awake."

"He's awfully nice."

In a little while, the moon was out.

"I'm ready to go up," she said.

They paused before the fireplace. By its light she saw a metal emblem set in the rock. There was a motto inscribed in French on its dark red and blue background.

"What does it say?" she asked.

" 'Here reigns love,' " he translated.

She nodded seriously. They went upstairs.

She was lying in bed, facing the window flooded in moonlight. She turned her head as he entered.

"I hope you don't mind," he said. "I only wear bottoms."

"I don't mind. You have a nice chest."

He went to the fire and poked at it.

"How do you put out this light?" she asked.

"Right behind you."

With the light out, the fire gave the room a warm, private glow. "Which side do you sleep on?"

"It doesn't matter."

"Yes, it does. Which side, hey?"

"Left."

"Everything you do matters to me now. What you eat, read, wear, everything."

He had come to the left side of the bed and sat down on the edge. The moon's silvery brightness was intense. A small cloud passed over it momentarily and was lit up with a pinkish hue that shone through its center like a luminous heart. Then the moon slid out from behind it like a ballet dancer.

"You can see inside the boathouse," she whispered.

The detail of shore line, even to the single, separate needles of the pines, was clear. She could see the rocks and submerged tree branches in the shallows of the still, clear water. Far off the mountain appeared to be coated in silver-blue ice. A day bird called out very fast, "*Weep! Toodla—toodla—toodla—Weep! Weep!*" It was misled by the moon's brightness into behaving as though an early dawn had come. Ken rose. "I'll be right back," he said.

"It's as bright as sunlight," she said.

"When that window is open wide you can smell the pines from across the lake."

She bent forward and opened the window wider.

Another bird called out, "*Ba-ba wheet! Ba-ba wheet! Ba wheet! Ba wheet!*"

"Was this your room?"

"Yes," he answered from the bedroom alcove.

"How could you sleep on nights like this?"

"Sometimes I didn't."

His voice sounded strange.

"What are you doing?" She hopped out of bed.

He was sitting in a chair, his face buried in his hands. She went to him and knelt on the floor beside him. "What is it?"

He shook his head.

"Are you sorry you married me?"

He lifted his head quickly. "God, no."

"I could understand it if you were. Honest."

He shook his head again and buried his face in his hands once more.

"Then what?"

He simply shook his head.

"Is it being back here?"

"No."

"What?"

"Me," he said.

She took his hand. "Come on, hey," she said. "Let's go look at the moon."

They lay there. She stirred beside him. He was looking straight ahead. When he turned, he saw her pajama top lying on the foot of the bed.

"Laurie."

"Hush. Let's look at the lake. I'm not at all sleepy. Look. The pine trees and stars and everything are all reflected upside down in the lake."

"*Ba wheet! Ba-ba wheet! Wheet! Wheet!*"

It was a male bird and his cry had grown more urgent.

When he took her she was surprised—almost fought him off as though he were someone else. That couldn't be Ken. But it was and surprise became joy, was no longer surprise, would never be again— for under all the reserve, inside that dear self-doubt and gentle hesitation, stripped of the cold, imposed things outside, this boy hunger and fury was Ken. In infinite grace, with unexpected force, yet ease and an astonishing understanding and willingness to wait, that which she had given up any hope of in her choice of him was part of him, now part of her, of them, as they were of each other.

She threw off the soft velvet-covered down quilt Ken had put over her during the night. Holding it up against herself she leaned forward out the open window. "Good morning!"

Ken waved a fishing pole from a rowboat the other side of the lake. It was a day for windbreakers, mufflers and gloves, hot coffee and rosy cheeks. There were ripples on the water racing the wind, never quite reaching the point of whitecaps. The sun was warm and the hills were washed bright green. "Coffee," he called out, pointing.

She saw the thermos at her bedside and nodded, opened it and poured a cup, raised it to him and drank quickly. She showered, dressed, and hurried down to meet him.

He was already at the dock, waiting with an extra rod baited for her in the boat.

"Oh, it *is* a good morning."

"They're all like this."

They rowed back to where the rocks were and Ken caught two trout and one sweetwater bass. When the ringing of the bell reached them, she rose and exulted, "Breakfast!" and almost fell out of the boat.

They rowed back quickly. After breakfast he took her walking through the meadow where the carpets of white and purple clover grew along with tiny forget-me-nots and giant buttercups. By noon the bees were drunk with nectar. The young leaves of the silver birch trembled like banners up above in the sun and murmured like secret conspirators in the shadows below. It was the kind of day to let a man innocently believe the world was made for him.

Mr. Sands managed somehow to clean the upstairs when they ate and the downstairs when they fished, and did his chores, using the work boat, going to and from the mainland, when they swam. The rest of the time when they wanted privacy, he was out of sight and they were altogether alone.

When it rained they sat close to each other before the bright living-room fire, playing music, reading. He taught her caliente gin. She kept winning.

Ken said, "My father thought it was a real test of mental stamina if you could win at caliente gin."

"Clever fellow."

"Of course, it's different when you play with many people."

"Hmm."

"Especially when you see any card and want it. You must be the first to shout 'I want it.' Mother always shouted whether the card was good for her game or not."

"Greedy."

"Yes. She was very greedy."

She saw his troubled frown come and go.

Once while reading she looked up and said, "You'll never guess who-done-it."

"Who?"

"Aristotle." She held the book up. "But the real mystery is, what does it mean?" She found the place and read aloud: " 'Virtue is concerned with action, art with production.' Does he mean art is like childbirth but action is the only real test of character or what?"

Ken thought. "I don't really know."

"You have it underlined."

"No, my mother did that. She was always underlining things she liked, even in first editions."

"Then she understood it?"

"Or at least she imagined so." He smiled. "All the evidence since Aristotle suggests that action is concerned with evil for which reason the business of art should be virtue. Maybe that's what he meant."

She studied him. "You think action is evil?"

"Judging by results it seems to be."

"You find your work evil?"

"Statistical research is not action."

"Is it art?"

"It's neither. No one knows what it is. Besides, I don't intend it to be my work much longer." He extended the book he was reading. "Read aloud to me. Do you mind?"

She looked at it. Tagore. "You really want me to?"

"Yes. You read very well."

"Did your mother read aloud?"

"To my father."

Also to him but he didn't want to linger on it or his work. Or action. Or the meaning of Aristotle's statement.

"All I ever recited aloud was in high school English II." She made a face and mimicked herself. "Ah, distinctly I remember it was in the bleak December—only I don't distinctly remember anything else at all about it."

" 'The Raven,' by Poe," Ken said.

"Oh, yes. Poe. He was a spook."

She began to read timidly at first, laughing at herself. But soon because of the way he listened and what it was Tagore said, she forgot and it wasn't poetry on parade and she wasn't being foolish. She enjoyed the sound of the cadence with him and for him and began to hear in it what he did.

The haze before the sun softened everything. The ripples on the water followed one another to shore, more shadow than substance. The sun's gold was pale, sparkling at the shore edge in a pool of quiet water over which rolled the sighing last of each gentle swell. Sun, shore, water, and sky were indistinguishable, horizonless. Laurie was sleeping on the couch on the patio, covers half off, her breast pressed against her arm, the nipple taut. Her cheeks were flushed, the tiny, almost lobeless tips of her ears pink, her lips half parted. A breeze made her bangs rise and fall against her forehead as she breathed deeply. Ken went to her and covered her. He ran his finger tips over her tousled head and whispered her name soundlessly. Clouds had materialized out of the thin haze, swallowing up the waning sun. The lake turned gray-blue, with deepening shadows. Jumping fish left small bubbles on the surface. He moved carefully to get another blanket. The moon would be rising soon. When he turned, she was watching him.

"I woke you." He whispered as though doing so would make her fall asleep again.

"I'm tired out."

"I've sent Mr. Sands away. Dinner is ready." He came to her.

"Loving you so much is what makes me tired," she smiled. Her arm hung at her side. He kissed it in the soft place.

"How long have we been here?"

"Ten days."

"No, I mean here."

"I don't know. Hours."

The sun had won out in the end, appearing beneath the clouds nearer to the water's edge. All was horizon once more—separate parts of earth, water, and sun-red sky. Her face seemed suddenly aflame in it.

"You are so beautiful."

"You make me beautiful." She turned to him. "When I was a kid, I grew too fast and I was clumsy. I thought I was ugly. It comes back sometimes."

"Here?"

"No. Never here." Her gaze stopped at the window of the dining room behind his head where, standing on the table, was the hand-wrought candelabra with its many thick, tall, firm, pink candles coming to graceful points. She smiled, eyes half closed.

"What?" he asked.

"I had a dream."

"Tell me."

"No. It would shock you." She turned her drowsy face toward the setting sun.

"Nothing you do will shock me."

"All right." She told him in sleepy tones, her eyes shutting and opening. As he reached for her she was asleep again. The sun, round and ripe, had slid below the horizon. A flock of birds silhouetted against the sky headed for the pale northern star. The moon had risen full. Where there had been haze and gold there was now cool, clear silver.

"You know what tomorrow is?" she asked.

"Sunday or Monday."

"Monday. The end of our two weeks. The museum said if I was a few days late they'd understand."

"I see."

"I don't want to go back," she said. "Do you have to?"

"No."

"What about your partners?"

"They don't need me." Then he added quickly, "There's nothing happening. The market is standing still. So if you really want to stay—"

"I really do. I'll call the museum tomorrow morning," she said. She dived into the lake off the patio dock. The fish swam away.

She came up out of the water and asked, "Did you ever play house?"

He smiled. "No."

"What a marvelous place to do it this is. I was always playing house. It's the female instinct. Sometimes I feel as though you and I are playing house."

"We're not playing anything," he said.

"No. The world's playing house. That's the truth. We're all that's real."

The trout returned. She dived back into the water. He dived in after her and the trout darted swiftly away again.

The letter from Aunt Sarah arrived at last. Enclosed with it were the minutes of the Board of Trustees for Caleb Island. The section pertaining to the Preston clan's conflict with the mainland county over the price charged per kilowatt hour for electricity was underscored in red. The town, with the approval of the Maine Department of Public Works, had originally charged the Island $0.06 per kilowatt hour, then raised it to $0.2775 and now, after stormy controversy, proposed a compromise of $0.10. Since Ken was an expert on power, did he consider it equitable and please advise. Her letter carried the good news that the contemplated museum in north Maine for early New England arts, crafts, and lore, now in the final formative stage, had luckily not yet chosen a curator. She intended to submit his name to the provisional organizing committee meeting in a few days.

"You look real happy, hey."

"I am. I enlisted Aunt Sarah in my quest for a curatorship and her letter is most encouraging."

"Where's the museum?"

"It will be near Trubeck when it's finished, a year from now."

"A whole year? Jeepers!"

"Yes. She suggests I write one paper for the *Philosophical Journal* and another for *Curatorship*."

She nodded thoughtfully. "Well, I can work in your authenticator's office."

"I don't have the job yet."

She nodded again. "I suppose you'll stay with your firm till then," she said. He didn't reply. They had played to a standoff at a game of checkers and it had begun to rain. She told him how as a child when the weather was bad she would worry about old people and animals outdoors and pray for them.

"Now I really can't make my suggestion," he said.

"Why? What is it? Go on and make it."

"I thought we'd go fishing. The rain brings them up."

"You go."

"No, let's play another game. This one's a draw."

"No, really, go ahead. Please. We've been together twenty-four hours a day for three weeks now."

"Are you bored?"

"No, Master Kenneth Preston of the S.S. *Silver Box*, etc., I am *not* bored. But I won't charge desertion if you go off by yourself for an hour now and then."

"All right. Only for an hour."

When he was gone she read Aunt Sarah's letter. She watched the rain. Then she went outside.

"You'll catch cold, Miss Laurie."

She looked up. It was Mr. Sands at his open window, reprimanding with a wagging finger. He beckoned her to come in. His small living room was a jumble of old colonial furniture, books, and small models of schooners and brigantines. Against the wall, shaped by hand, wind, and time, stood the ten top feet of the summer topmast of what must have been a large schooner.

"What a wonderful place you've built here," she said.

"It wasn't built. It was accumulated." He was pleased. "A tin can here, a shingle there."

He poured tea.

"What's that?" she asked.

"Peak of the topmast of the *Silver Box*. Are you Irish?"

"Don't I look it?"

"Dublin?"

"On my father's side."

"Well, then. This will interest you, as they say. I suppose you know there were a lot of Irish in Boston." He always spoke of Boston in the past tense. Then he told her the story of the Irish famine and how Mr. Ken's great-grandfather Timothy had helped save the lives of Dubliners in 1847 by sending the *Silver Box* with gifts of food and medical supplies, a mercy ship, a friend ship. The Sons of St. Patrick had held a special banquet in his honor.

"Mr. Ken's Uncle Stuart tried to take the topmast. But Mrs. Preston, Mr. Ken's mother I mean, she wouldn't hear of it."

"You've worked for the Prestons a long time."

"Since 1890, and my father before me."

She admired his window plants and then suddenly remembering said, "I saw a flower the other side of the little house. Purple with white centers like wings. And four tips that point to the ground from the top. Over it there's a sort of white, heart-shaped crest. What is it called?"

He laughed. "That don't sound like a proper description of anything. Of course, we've lots of wild flowers growing here. Why don't you pluck one and bring it along?"

"I hate to pluck flowers and let them die."

"Mr. Ken's mother was like that. In Quincy she'd stay up all of a winter's night just to prevent their freezing. You might take Mr. Ken to it and ask him. He knows all their names."

"Really?"

"Yes indeed. Flowers, rocks, and birds."

He moved off to a desk and returned carrying a hummingbird's nest perched on a small, slender branch.

"Mr. Ken found this." He invited her to place her finger inside the nest. It was no larger than a chicken's egg. Carefully she felt its softness, delicacy, and warmth. Pleased with her response, he fetched another nest.

"This here's a northern parula warbler, off of Caleb Island. That moss camouflage is so near perfect, only an expert could have found it."

"Mr. Ken?"

"On his last visit when he come home from the war." He poured more tea. "All the Prestons loved flowers. His mother kept a plantin' book in her room and many's the time she sent me hightailin' for spruce that was budworm proof all in a hubby-bubby about it. Of course there's no such thing but it was her love for growing things made her never stop seeking." He rambled on as old men do. "Worried me nervous about the stumps being too high at tree-cutting time and bawled me out for not finding woodsmen willing to bend their backs down far enough to cut low stumps. The trouble was Mr. Preston wouldn't pay well. Tight as Dick's hatband, he was, with working folk. Not at all like Mr. Ken or his mother. But a fine gentleman. I suppose it was also his wishing to get back to Caleb Island. The minute he went off to war, Mrs. Trumbull Day, that's Mrs. Preston's mother, went right ahead and found this place and bought it. Heard about it from Robert Louis Stevenson, who lived not too far from here in Saranac. She never did like Caleb. Said she missed the lilacs and the

flag root and even new-mown hay had a tinge of herring on the Rock."
He smiled to himself. "Of course the real thing of it was that the Rock
was all Preston, as they say. I'm glad you favor flowers. Mr. Ken's
mother would have liked you surely. It's too bad you didn't meet him
when he was back from O.S.S. and she was still alive." He laughed.
"Though I suppose you'd have been little more than a schoolgirl
then."

Laurie nodded. "You say Mr. Ken was in O.S.S.?"

"Yes, indeed. A major. Did dangerous, important work in France and
Belgium."

"He never told me."

"Well, now, that's his way. Not much for talk as they say. It's not
he lacks pride. He just don't care a cent for showing off and don't
know how to tell a body. Still his father told enough for both of them."
He looked out the window. "Well, the wind's blowing those black
clouds off and dying down. Mr. Ken should be coming in soon. You
ask him to show you the letters from President Roosevelt and General
Montgomery one day."

She left him and waited for Ken at the shore. There was no sign of
him. She stood there realizing she was worried. There was so much
about him she did not know. Why hadn't he answered her about the
year of waiting for the museum? The sky grew blacker. Then she
smiled. She felt suddenly quite sure of his strength, his knowledge and
self-reliance.

She went back to the patio, behind the icehouse where no one
could see, and removed her clothes. She was dancing in the rain and
then became aware of the fact that Ken was watching her. She covered
herself with her hands. Ken waved a string of fish at her from the
porch.

"Six trout."

"That's marvelous. Now stop looking at me."

He dropped the fish. "You should have seen them leaping." He
smiled. "You were leaping a bit in the air yourself."

"You stay away and hand me a towel."

"I can't do both."

"Then give me the towel and my slacks and sweater and be quick
about it. Jeepers, you do smell fishy."

"You smell of lemon, pine needles, and rain."

"Mr. Sands gave me the lemon with my tea. I think you're terrible.
I thought I was alone."

"Liar."

"Yes, I'm a liar. Now you just wait."

He didn't.

The outdoor couch was wet. "Hello," he said afterward.

"Hi." It was like returning from a far place. "Or getting there," she said.

"What?"

"Nothing. Everything." She turned so her leg was free of the wetness. "It's like knowing you for the first time, every time. But never as a stranger. You know?"

"Yes."

She rubbed her nose up and down against his shoulder. "I wasn't prepared," she said.

"You're lying again."

"Not that way, goosehead. Don't smile. I might get pregnant."

"I hope so."

"I don't. It shouldn't be an accident. I was born by accident."

"Whatever way you were born is right for me."

"If you hadn't swept me off my feet I was going to ask you about a flower." She was putting on her clothes. "Why didn't you tell me about O.S.S.?"

"What else did Mr. Sands tell you?"

"Things. It's nice to know your husband is a hero."

"Mr. Sands used to call my father a distinguished international financier."

"Well, wasn't he?"

"Certainly not. He died a failure. When I joined O.S.S., it was simply a research organization. I was a statistician."

She took him by the back path to where the flower grew.

"Was there a girl there too?"

"Where?"

"Come on, hey. Was there?"

"Yes."

"Twenty-five years ago and then again in 1944. What's in between?"

"Why do you want to talk about it?"

"Because I have to fit into place so there are only two of us and no shadows."

"There are no shadows."

"I'm entering your world, not you mine, so I see the shadows. Were any of them big like me?"

He smiled. "No one was like you."

"Was your mother big?"

"Now what has she to do with it?"

They were passing the small house now. "What was the first one like?"

"I don't remember."

"Yes, you do. I reminded you of her. Was she big?"

"She was tiny. Her face was something like yours. Not much. But she was tiny."

"You're not going to tell me anything, are you?"

"I'll tell you this. You're the only girl I ever loved."

"I don't believe you, but why?"

"Because you know how to laugh and love and live and you wipe out all the grayness and you're very beautiful."

"Blarney. It must have been awful doing it all alone that way."

"What's that?"

"Killing."

"I was with the Free French."

"And she was French?"

"Yes, she was French."

"Still it's not the same as our own army, is it? I mean when everyone does it and there's no choice, they all share the responsibility."

"Killing is killing. Each of us does it with his own hand."

"I can't see you killing ever."

"Nor can I."

"I can't even see you hurting anyone."

He didn't answer.

"You always did want to be a curator, didn't you?"

"Yes. I suppose I did."

"Because there are no living things around in museums to hurt?" She went on quickly, changing the subject. "If it weren't for your great-grandfather I wouldn't be here." She told him the story of the Irish famine. "I can't picture your great-grandfather Timothy waiting one whole year for anything."

Before he could answer, she ran up ahead.

"Here's my flower."

Chapter 8

Ken BEGAN working on his paper for the *Philosophical Society Journal* immediately after Aunt Sarah had phoned to tell him his name had been submitted to the Provisional Committee for the museum and had been very well received. She suggested that his paper for *Curatorship* be on something specific with which he was completely at home, like the change in style of silver from the Colonial to the Federalist period. She thought the other paper for the *Journal*—naturally more general in nature—might deal with fundamental changes in cultural trends and their consequences in the seventeenth, eighteenth, or nineteenth centuries in New England life. He had tentatively chosen the collapse of Transcendentalism and the subsequent emergence of fads and cults with their impact on art, architecture, literature, and religion shortly after the Civil War. For the technical piece, he considered tracing the decline of wood carving as an art with particular reference to shipbuilding, from its original integral place as part of the ship to its subsequent projection beyond the ship's bow as a mere accessory, and its ultimate elimination. He planned to treat it in terms of the dominant role of functionalism in folk art as differentiated from the academic and classical without voicing any preference. For the past several days it had been raining and he had been working on the piece for the *Journal*.

Laurie had gone into town early to shop and on the way Mr. Sands had at last taught her how to handle the boat. She burst into the study to announce, "I docked the boat both times myself. Going and coming. All Mr. Sands did was watch."

"Now if you do it at night, you're all set."

"Not yet. That still scares me. How on earth did your mother and grandmother ever manage it?"

"Grandma never did. When she bought the place, she was promised the right to use the road from the mainland. It turned out the agent for the elderly sisters who owned it spoke without authority. I suspect the discomfort those boats caused Grandma was the main reason Father was willing to stay. But you're a young, healthy girl."

"I'm still afraid to do it at night."

"Shame on you."

"That's just what that little old lady on the dock says all the time. 'Shame on you. A girl like you, big and strong as a man.' I don't like that."

Ken rose from the desk and went to her. "Well, you certainly have long, lovely legs."

"My feet are off the ground right now just the same. Let me down. No. I can't. Don't you know we've been here a month, you greedy thing?"

"Already?"

"It's the twentieth. We're getting like Tarzan and his mate up here. I was surprised and disappointed. I hoped I was pregnant."

"At the time you said you hoped you weren't pregnant."

"I changed my mind. Do you still want me to be?"

"Of course."

"When?"

"At once."

"Be serious."

"I am."

"Mr. Sands and I examined that other house."

"Father's?"

"It's yours now. It looks like a perfectly marvelous place to work but it has termites."

"It always did."

"That's no attitude. I've hired an exterminator."

"Fine."

"And the stuffing is coming out of the pillows on the couch. We're picking fabrics and getting it reupholstered."

"All right."

"Don't sound so vague. It's practically vandalism. And that reminds me. I've thrown out all your vests. Do you mind?"

He looked up. "No."

"Am I interfering with your work?"

He put down the pencil and smiled. "No."

She had come around to the desk and was looking down over his shoulder. She read:

> The matriarchal character of Boston after the Civil War is commonly accounted for by the exodus of Boston's best sons to the undeveloped West or the self-exile to England and Europe of those who did not care for the new industrial class. It is generally conceded that the

ethnology of Boston fell more and more under feminine domination and that the culture proved the worse for this emasculation. However . . .

Her eyes ran to the bottom of the page:

A woman without maternal instinct is a sport, a mistake in nature. She may be compared to a planet possessed of all things for human habitation save oxygen and gravity. If she be as beautiful as the cool crater of the moon, or as dazzling as a meteor, without the maternal instinct she can at best inspire only mental interest in a civilized man, whereas for the primitive male if she be as ripe to the eye, as fragrant to the smell and touch as a childhood hope, she will create only the fleeting appetite of lust. For a woman to inspire love in any man, he must feel in her above all that mystery of the cosmos which she embodies in the human species . . .

She looked up.

"It's much too subjective and horribly overwritten," he said.

"I like it. Are you a primitive man? And where did you learn all that?"

He smiled. "I'm not sure I did."

"What was she like?"

"Who?"

"Your mother. Was she beautiful?"

"At the end only in her face. She had theories about everything." He smiled. "At the age of fifty-five she became interested in water colors. She was very good but she stopped because she refused to become a 'menopause painter.'"

"She would have found me very ignorant."

"You? I learn from you every day."

"From me?"

"Yes. That all this is to be enjoyed, not simply investigated."

"When I actually was—pregnant, I mean—do you mind my talking about it?"

"No."

"Yes, you do."

"Yes, I do, but go on."

"I hated myself and I hated him and all mothers and fathers and children but I still wanted my child. Isn't that strange?"

"Not at all."

"I mean for all our big talk are we that helpless? When nature issues orders, must we just roll over and go zoom?"

"There are approximately two hundred million sperm released in the split second of an orgasm. Only one sperm enters the single ova. There's your zoom. They live together precariously for ten days in the

Fallopian tube and if they survive that trial they are permitted entrance as one into the uterus. I suppose the woman inside whom that happens must be persuaded by nature to welcome it regardless of whether society does or not."

"I can't stand it when you talk that way!"

He picked up his pencil again. "Sorry."

"I *am* interfering with your work. Now for instance, where did you learn that sperm, ova, and *zoom* business?"

"A reference book, I think. I don't recall. Besides I had an excellent biology tutor."

"Tutor? Didn't you go to school?"

"Not until college. I was educated at home."

"You remind me of a magician I once saw at Radio City. He came on stage without tables or magic wands or props. Just a handkerchief hidden in his hand. Then for twenty minutes he kept pulling things out of it."

"There's really nothing mysterious. Father wanted me to go to private school. Mother didn't. It was one of the two serious arguments they ever had."

"Only two? They were lucky."

"Perhaps they never got to know one another well enough to seriously disagree."

"What was the other time?"

"When Father insisted I work in a shipping basement in New York. That time he won. He felt I was too soft. Perhaps if Mother had lost when I was seven, he wouldn't have won when I was seventeen."

"And that's where you met Muriel."

"Yes. How did you know?"

"When we first met, you said I reminded you of a basement and rats."

"Yes. That's where I met Muriel."

"I'm not at all sure I would have liked your father."

"I'm not at all sure, either."

"If we still have a maternal instinct, why don't we have a mating season?"

He put the pencil down again. "Well, in a certain sense we still do. I suppose that's why most marriages take place in June."

"Ours took place in May."

"Our courtship was faster than most. I believe we still retain some of the relics of the lower mammals."

"I'm glad I'm a mammal with all my relics."

"I can get back to this later."

"No, you go on with your work."

He shook his head and smiled.

"I'd hate to think you found me ignorant," she said.

"I don't."

"Because I learn new things from you all the time," she said. "You know the day we got married in Connecticut? I thought I was being terribly unfair to you. My mother thought I was being unfair to myself. I almost didn't go through with it. Did you know that? I felt awful because you deserved someone—I mean all of someone—someone who would die if they lost you. And I didn't feel that way then. I told you so beforehand."

"Yes, you told me."

"But now I do. You see? I do. I love you so I'd die, I really would, if you were—if—"

He had come from around the desk and was at her side. He stopped her mouth with his fingers. "So would I," he said solemnly.

She walked back to the desk with him and sat on the floor at his feet. "Don't," he said. He put down the pencil. "Now stop it."

"Why should I?"

"You're a hussy."

"You're my fella." She was smiling happily.

As the end of June approached, early house guests for the long Fourth of July weekend began to appear at the various camps, and with them daily practice sessions out on the lake, with sails red, white, and blue for the Fourth of July Regatta. The Club had phoned Ken, inviting him to join in, and he had been gracious in declining. As they sat on the patio and watched, he told her how seriously his father had taken the Fourth of July and Labor Day regattas. The one time they had added an official regatta in August, Father actually cut short his hunting trip in Canada. For him, that was taking it very seriously indeed. Sailboats practiced every day now regardless of weather. Today had been clear. Only after dinner was the lake empty. The moon shone bright. The air was still but cool. They could hear the voices from the widely separated porches and patios, low and laughing, accompanied by the sound of music. She made him dance to it and said, "You see, you aren't stiff any more." Then she said something else that made him flush, laugh, and shake his head.

They heard the tinkling of ice in glasses from half a mile away. "Let's buy dance records."

"All right."

"Let's go out on the lake."

"Fine."

"Right now. Without clothes."

"Wear shoes," he said. "The pine needles are sharp, and you'll want a robe. It's quite cool."

She wore the terry robe over her shoulders. In the boathouse they could read the gas, oil, and speed dials by moonlight. Day birds were singing again. Ken started the motor.

"Wait," she said. He turned off the motor and they listened. It was silent. "No mother birds," she said.

Ken stepped back on the dock and flashed his light at the nests. "The eggs are still here."

Laurie laughed. "The moonlight went to mama's head. They're off on some impossible adventure."

"Yes." He re-entered the boat. "It was clever of you to notice the silence."

"I have my ear to the ground. I even hear ants growl."

They drove slowly out to behind the uninhabited island. She removed her terry robe. He stopped the motor.

"We may drift into the rocks," he said.

But he left the motor off.

The way they had lain, she saw nothing but the stars. He saw the sky and the island shore.

"Could they hear us?" She laughed and blushed.

"I hope not," he said.

"Now I'm cold."

A shelf of clouds shimmered from behind the moon. Their prow cut the stillness of the water and left the reflected stars, trees, and houses a trembling velvety confusion in the lake like a jigsaw puzzle finished in silk and falling through space.

"Now how about you docking us tonight?"

"No," she said. "I just can't judge distance at night on water."

"It's as clear as glass."

"Not yet."

Back at the house they heard noises and tiptoed through the living room to the kitchen to watch a big fat mother raccoon who had lifted the cover off the garbage bin outside. She removed the steak bone, took it to the asphalt landing where her two children feasted on it. When they finished, she herded them off with one last careful look over her shoulder as they disappeared into the woods. Then the squirrel appeared and perched its back feet on the base of the bone. It was twice as high as he. His front paws held the upjutting point as he nibbled away as close to the tip as his mouth could reach. Then he tried to climb it and fell and raced away.

"They're comics," she said.

"They do it every night."

"You only like steak twice a week. You told me in the restaurant in New York."

He smiled. "Mr. Sands cooks some things better than others. He doesn't know."

"He knows now because I told him. Three times a week I'm cooking dinner. Do you mind?"

"Mind?"

"I mean interfering with shopping and checking bills and measuring your clothes and throwing out all your vests. That reminds me. Your slacks are a half-inch tight in the seat. I measured them while you were fishing. I've told the tailor. I hope Mr. Sands doesn't mind."

"I just didn't want to bother you."

"I want to be bothered. I want you to tell me everything. The things you like and don't like."

"All right."

"I'm Mrs. Preston now."

"You certainly are."

The rain was falling in fat drops. It made the mud slippery and thick. The air was cool, almost cold. Ken had shut the window of the small house to keep out wasps.

"Ken!"

He opened the window.

"Your sandwiches." She pointed to a plate, its contents wrapped in a napkin, on the back porch floor. Beside it was a thermos of coffee. "Come get them. I don't have boots on." She wore her dressing gown.

He pulled the poncho over him and ran across.

"You treat me like a bear who must come out of the woods for his sugar."

"I'm sorry, angry bear. Here's a kiss. Now take away your honey."

"So fast?"

"The wind is blowing up my legs and on my tummy."

He kissed her again, and putting his lunch under his poncho ran back to the little house. The mud sucked at his boots and made a satisfying sound. The fir tree smell was heavy in the cool air. He kicked up the fire, returned to his desk, attacked his sandwiches of cold steak, and savored the aroma of freshly ground and brewed coffee before drinking it. Get back to your paper. Considering its beginning —you are always considering something's beginning. Yours. Your family's. Wood carving. Great-grandfather Timothy's secret, a life lived in the open, publicly, where everyone could see, and yet no one understood his score of lives lived with just as many tries and trades and tirades against the only mortal sin he knew: neither the waste of station nor of fortune but only of precious life. You know something? This honeymoon is a beginning too—perhaps the only one starting at the top that rises instead of declining into anticlimax. Why hasn't man enough sense to know when he's happy? Why must it always be clear only long afterward so that it is a bitter pleasure, a lost perfection remembered? Were the joys of being and knowing too much to take simultaneously? I know. Do you? Yes. I know I am happy. Good. Then put down your paper. You are happy. I say I am happy! Deliriously happy and these happy sandwiches are delicious. So is this coffee and the wasp outside my window is begging so earnestly to come in and taste it while I am so happy, I might even let it in to drink my coffee, noisy wasp. You *are* crazy. Yes—happy crazy. I am a crazy bear full to the brim with the honey sweets of love and gratitude of being and knowing. I know I love her with all this hunger and I am happy, happy, happy.

Alicia and George Tucker arrived, phoning from the dock, and Mr. Sands picked them up. They could stay only for an hour or so, Alicia explained, if they were to reach the city today. They sat on the patio watching the practice races for the regatta and George enjoyed the martinis as they recounted their five weeks on the Rock. Ken asked how Aunt Sarah was and George said, "Same old Aunt Sarah. Just try to stop her when her mind is set on something."

Alicia gave him a warning look and tried to change the subject but George was enjoying the martinis too much to notice. "You certainly have an awfully fine advocate in her. When they said a Wall Street fellow your age could never adjust to the 'reflective life' and curatorship was not a rich man's hobby, she told them where to get off."

He laughed and reached forward for a refill. " 'For my one hundred thousand dollars, my nephew can adjust to anything he wants to.' She was awfully good, awfully." He drained his glass. "Money still talks, but you can't take it away from Aunt Sarah. She knows how to pick the right words."

Alicia made one lame effort to change the subject. In the stillness that followed, they watched the sailboats. After they left, Ken put through a call to Caleb Island and told Aunt Sarah, "I don't like your buying me this job."

Afterward when Laurie asked him what Aunt Sarah had said, Ken told her, "She says George exaggerates and that when they read my papers they'll understand."

"You have a job. You're your own boss and damned good at it. You're nobody's idiot cousin."

Ken didn't answer.

"I think your exalted family stinks."

The last practice for the regatta took place against a clouded sky and a bucking wind. They sat on the patio and bet peanuts and crackers on who the winners would be. The starter shot the gun once, not for a race but as a greeting to Ken, and Ken waved back.

"Do you sail very well?" she asked.

"Father made me take it most seriously."

"Do you enjoy it?"

"If he hadn't made me take it so seriously, I might have."

"Your father took Preston and Company very seriously, too."

"Very."

"Why won't you ever talk about it?"

"There is nothing to say."

"But it's your work. I want to know about your work."

"It's not my work any more."

"It will be for another year. At least another year."

"What do you want to know about it?"

"The whole thing's a mystery to me. You haven't quit yet. How can you stay away this long?"

"It's a declining market. It will continue to go down with brief breathers for quite a while."

"There's nothing one does when it's that way?"

"Yes, you can go short each time a security rises a fraction before going further down again."

"And after it goes way down, then what?"

"That depends. If and when the government changes its hard-money policy, it will turn around and go up for quite a while."

"I thought money was money. What's hard money?"

"Not really. Hard money means interest rates are high and money is 'hard' to borrow. The government creates this condition by paying high interest to the public when it borrows by issuing government bonds. That makes all bond interest go up and interest charged by banks and installment stores and by everyone else."

"That's what the government is doing now?"

He nodded. "To prevent inflation. Last week employment was at an all-time high."

"Is that bad?"

"Some people think it causes inflation."

"Do you?"

"Not *per se*. Even if it did, the solution is not in creating unemployment."

"I should say not!"

He smiled.

"And what they're doing makes the market go down?"

He nodded.

"I'll never understand this. But go on."

"Well, the government removes money from banks by borrowing more from them through the Federal Reserve Board. That leaves the banks less money to lend to the public and at higher interest because money is scarce and harder to get. That restricts business expansion and future earnings which also forces the market down."

"That's silly. Shouldn't they stop?"

"They will, I think. When they ease credit, we'll have a bull market. That's a rising market."

"A big one?"

He was thinking far past her question, looking past the sailboats fighting the strong wind in front of the deserted island.

"It might be the biggest in history," he said.

The way he said it made her turn her face from the lake and look at him. He rose suddenly. A sailboat turned over, its mast snapped. Two people were thrown into the water. Laurie ran to the edge of the dock. Ken followed her.

That night she asked, "Are there women in your work?"

They were lying in bed. A stiff wind kept billowing the curtains.

"There are girls in my department."

"We'll fix *that*. But do they work at it the way you do, I mean?"

"I believe there are two or three women chief statisticians on the Street."

"Do they work in the Stock Exchange?"

"On the Floor, you mean? No. It gets pretty rough down there sometimes."

"Could I learn your end of it?"

"Yes, you could. It's quite simple. But why?"

"So we could be together all the time."

"We are together all the time."

She frowned. "When you go back."

"If I take the museum, we can be."

"But if you don't?"

He said nothing.

"Even if you do, we have to go back sooner or later," she said. "We can't sit up here for a whole year."

He didn't answer.

"What are your partners like? Why didn't they come to our wedding?"

"I didn't ask them. They're all right, I suppose."

She rolled over closer to him and kissed his arm. "Tell me more about going short."

She offered him a puff on her cigarette. He took it. "I'll get to like that yet," he said.

"Going short." He took one of the two pillows from under his head and threw it to the foot of the bed. "Here are three pillows. Identical. Yours, mine, and that one. They all serve the same function."

"No, they don't either."

He continued, smiling. "There's a man over there—"

She pulled up the covers quickly.

"He wants to buy a pillow at today's price of one dollar. It was ninety-nine cents at the last sale so I have the right under the laws of the Securities Exchange Commission to sell him a pillow I don't have."

"But you do have a pillow."

"Yes, but I'm not selling him mine."

"Nor mine either, hey."

"Yes, yours." He bit her finger gently. "Only I don't know it's yours yet. Nor do you or he. And he doesn't care."

"I hate him and he's a Peeping Tom."

He kissed the tip of her nose. "I just sell him any old pillow I don't own at today's price of a dollar. Now why?"

"That's right, hey. Some nerve! Selling a strange man my pillow right from under me."

"Not yet. I sell him a pillow for a dollar because I believe the price of pillows will go down. Meanwhile I borrow a pillow and deliver it to him."

"Is someone else here too?"

He kicked the pillow at the foot of the bed to the floor. "There's his pillow borrowed by me and delivered to him and I'm through with him."

She put her head on his chest and her pillow on his stomach. "That's very smart," she purred. "Just for that you may share my pillow for free."

"No. One week later—"

A bell was ringing. He picked up the telephone. There was no one on. "Wrong number, I guess."

"One week later," she reminded him.

"Yes. One week later, pillows sell down as low as fifty cents."

The bell was ringing again. He sat up once more.

"That's funny," she said.

He hung up. "The operators aren't used to all the guests up for the Fourth. The telephone service on this lake is privately owned."

"Fifty cents," she persisted.

"All right. You want to sell."

"No. I gave you my pillow."

"You can't. That's not business. I buy your pillow for fifty cents." He took it off his stomach. "Deliver it to the person I borrowed from." He threw it to the foot of the bed. "And I've made fifty cents by going short."

He turned closer to her.

"You're brilliant. But I think I lost fifty cents, didn't I?"

The bell was ringing again. He sat up and jiggled for the operator. She told him his number had not been rung at all.

"I couldn't help you in your work," Laurie said. "I wouldn't know when the price of pillows was going up or down."

"You study charts of general trends and specific industries." He dismissed it.

"No," she said. "Go on. What if I study charts of general trends?"

"There are graphs for particular industries, earnings of specific firms. It's all very dull."

"No, it's not. Go on."

"Well, you watch the moods of buyers and sellers by the growth of short positions in the market, for pessimism. Increased purchases of certain stocks in strong volume are barometers of optimism."

"Then why did Peeping Tom pay you a dollar?"

"He followed a tip, or didn't get enough facts or true ones, and he and his broker might have misinterpreted them."

"Is that what your father did?"

"No. He was misled by a dream. He wanted something to happen so badly he stopped facing or studying the facts."

"I'll have to help you some other way, until you get your museum." She snuggled.

"By loving me."

"No, that way I'll be helping myself."

"Same thing."

"No. Go on and finish. You made fifty cents."

"Let's stop. You're not really interested."

"I am too. Somehow you got my mind off it."

"There's nothing else to it. I made fifty cents by going short."

"What's the opposite of going short?"

"Going long."

"That's much more becoming to you."

"You're very fresh."

The bell rang again. Their heads turned and they looked at the wall behind them and began to laugh. It was the buzzer to the kitchen pressed by the weight of their heads and shoulders when they came close together. Mr. Sands had pushed the headboard too close to the wall that morning.

"Lucky we found out now," she said.

Ken got off the bed and pulled it farther out while she lay in it.

"Did you get that strong in O.S.S.?"

He was picking up the pillows.

"Did you parachute?" she persisted.

"Yes."

"Why won't you talk about it?"

He lay down and the bell rang again.

"Oh, no." She looked behind their headboard. "It's not us this time."

It rang once more. "Imagine. It must really be the telephone and at this hour."

"It's only ten-thirty," he said, picking it up.

"My God," she laughed. "Is that all?"

Ken said, "Long distance," and handed her the phone. "Your mother."

"Hello, Mom?"

She sat up abruptly.

"It's me."

It was Wallie.

"I'm in town. Yes, *your* town. At the country club. Got the hat-check girl here to give that pitch about long distance and your mother. Don't hang up or I'll come out by taxi boat and it'll be one hell of a night for the three of us. I must see you. You better say Mom again or Fancy Pants will start wondering about the look you must have right now on that lovely face."

"All right, Mom. I'll mail it tonight at the post office. They still pick up air mail till eleven o'clock."

"You come to the club. I'm in room 1014."

He hung up.

"Mom needs a loan of a hundred dollars right away. She was afraid with the Fourth weekend coming up, she'd be stuck. I'll make out a check and go in with it. Take me half an hour."

"I'll do it."

"No." She was in her slacks and buttoning her blouse quickly. "I'd rather."

"All right," Ken said, and started to rise. "We'll do it together."

She came to him. "No," she said firmly. "You said finally I had to handle that boat alone at night and you're undressed and this is it. Please, Ken, I want to."

He nodded slowly.

"I'll phone you when I get to the dock." She kept her voice bright. "And I'll phone before I start back so you can come fish me out with the work boat if I take too long."

Mist clung to the lake and fog rolled in over it. The dock walls and floor were wet, the eaves dripping. The mother birds were back and complaining as she started the motor. She knew Ken would be listening for the motor and she was careful not to flood it. Backing out, she bit her lip and tried to keep evenly between the rough, V-shaped buoys because of the rocks on either side. At last she had the prow facing the point. The lake was dense under banks of white, thick mist. She drove slowly, shivering. The cold spray stung her face. As she rounded the point, she suddenly saw the red warning light almost alongside her. She swung quickly away from the grass concealing the big rocks. She thought she had heard the ping of metal on stone but she was light-headed with fear and couldn't be sure. This could be a night full of misgiving, rashness, and ruin. From out in the deep center of the lake the mainland dock seemed far away, a small forlorn light. The water rolled menacingly close to the top side of the boat, splashing black and cold. She shivered again. In her haste she had not put on a bra or taken a sweater. She feared to go fast but she also dreaded the creeping time out there alone. She kept looking at the bottom of the boat fore and aft for signs of water coming in. Then she realized she had forgotten to put on the tail light. She flicked the button left of the panel. It made a pale spot that left no imprint on the blackness. When she finally docked she came in too fast and at an angle, hitting the slip hard. It killed the motor. She worked her way forward with her hands along the dock, pulling the boat into the slip. She had to remember all over again how to tie the knots securing the wet rope to the steel ring in the dock floor. Her fingers were stiff and trembling.

"Black night, Mrs. Preston," the relief man said from above.

Mrs. Preston. She fortified herself with it. In the garage she remembered saying she would call Ken and jumped out of the car to do so. Keeping her voice gay, she told him about forgetting to put on the tail light and being mixed up about tying the knot. She didn't mention coming that close to the red warning light at the rocky point or hitting the slip so hard and killing the motor when she docked at an angle.

"You forgot your checkbook, too," Ken said.

"There's another in my purse," she lied.

At her knock the door to room 1014 opened at once. Wallie stood there a moment, and looked down quickly at her slacks. He always hated her in slacks. A chastity belt of sorts. His eyes were hot and moist. The cleft in his chin still gave his red, too heavy face an incongruous boyishness. Then he stepped aside to let her in. She had almost forgotten how huge, strong-boned, and muscled he was. He was wearing a silk robe over his naked body. There was a poured drink on the table. He held another one in his hand. He was sweating. She remembered always feeling clean in his sweat and knew she had better leave soon or she would be sick.

He pointed to the drink on the table. She refused it with a shake of her head and he sipped his watchfully. Watchfully. It brought back competing with her roommate Katherine, who had described him as a free spender, virile as a bull, and good for kicks, competing by dancing an improvisation to the wild African jungle-rhythm records as Wallie sat in the room she and Katherine shared, sipping his scotch watchfully like a judge at a beauty contest, a buyer at a cheap costume-jewelry bazaar, or a sultan picking his favorite concubine. She had won. He had picked her and she had felt foolish and guilty and then proud. The next time around he had called for her, not Katherine, and she hadn't seen Katherine ever since. A short week later she moved out and quit the Esquire Club, at his request. Then he moved in and took her over.

"I'm on my vacation," he was saying. "I planned on taking it earlier and spending it with my sweetheart."

She didn't trust herself to speak yet.

"You're getting plenty of loving, I see. Always gave you a certain look."

"Stop that. The only reason I came was that I didn't want Ken to know."

Her hands were trembling and her face was white.

"Yeah. Mr. Fancy Pants. I hear he's the shy, retiring type. Hates scenes. I expected you'd come for that reason if nothing else."

"All right." She had her voice almost under control. "Say your piece. I'm expected home in half an hour."

"What's the hurry? I drove eight hours in this holiday traffic to get here." He smiled, then he frowned. Suddenly his eyes filled with tears. She had never seen him this way before. "Laurie, don't walk out on me. You're the only reason I've been slugging. What have I got to try for if you leave me?"

Ah distinctly I remember it was in the bleak December and the first Christmas he promised to go with you and didn't, sending you to

Miami to mourn the old year out instead where the sun he said would
replace his warm kisses while the laughter, lights, and song broke
your heart as merrymakers in funny paper hats broke colored balloons
with toothpicks and swung the wooden noisemakers round and round
to the hot whirling midnight. The telephone, a call reserved twelve
hours earlier whirling round and round as he made it sound like a
business call for the benefit of the affectionate voice behind him coming
clear over the wire when he didn't want it to. His wife. The hated,
despised woman according to him with whom he saw the new year
in and her out. At the end of the ridiculous conversation still assuming
rights as he said, "Don't do anything I wouldn't do," a piece of advice
she could have, should have followed and didn't though enough
drunken slobs were available with auld lang syne at the hotel, advice
better taken by not doing anything he wanted her to do including
coming here tonight. Oh God, you shouldn't have come here, you
shouldn't have come here tonight.

"I'm married now," she heard herself saying. "And you'll get on
without me as I had to without you."

He was at her side, kneeling, his arm across her, his fingers high
on her leg.

"You wanted security. You couldn't wait. Now you're married and
so am I. We can see one another just like we used to. Come back to
town. You won't be lonely when I'm not there and he won't know
about me any more than Diana knows about you."

His other hand had moved down her shoulder. His fingers were
opening the buttons of her blouse round and round as she pulled back,
the scraping noise of the chair good for her. The movement ripped the
buttons of her blouse open. She was standing.

"You pig. You nasty, evil son of a bitch. Keep your hands off me.
Don't ever call again or I'll put Ken on the phone. That Fancy Pants
is just influential enough to cost you your distributorship."

He rose from the floor slowly.

"I despise you and detest everything I ever thought I liked about
you. Your big noise, show-off strength, and false promises. I hate you!
I love Ken!"

"And his well-heeled Wall Street firm." His voice was low and un-
steady.

She had been surprised at herself for using Ken's power in the financial world. What would she have used if Ken were the curator of a
small museum in Maine?

"*Him!* You understand, you big sweating slob? Not his company or
his money."

"Sure. That's why you acted so innocent and asked me, 'Who is

Preston of Preston and Company, a sweet, quaint old man who came in today with a funny silver cup?' Thought I forgot, huh? You were being laid by me while you were selling wedding bells to him. Think I don't know, huh?"

The doctor had said six weeks. She had told him that and tried to make the time easier for him. So much for his stated concern for her inside wounded self.

"Well, what if I was?" she asked calmly. He would never believe what Ken was like and talking about him to Wallie made her skin crawl. "Sending me off to abortionists while your wife was under the tender care of a gynecologist. Who are you to tell me what's right or wrong?"

"How about Fancy Pants? How about telling him you spread your legs for me the day you and he got married? How about that? If you try, you can get witnesses for anything, you know. How would you like that?"

"Try it and I'll kill you."

He took one step toward her and slapped her hard across the face with the back stiff side of his open hand. "Don't threaten me," he said. "You know I don't let anyone threaten me."

The welts rose red and long across her cheek. Having lost his control, he could only regain it by losing it further, chasing it to a dead end. That had to come now.

"You could have had a real marriage with love. You didn't want that. You got what you wanted. What you still want. Miss America from the skin out. You give yourself to nobody. You hate men, all men. You think I don't know, you horny bitch? Only you got a hole that has to be filled and you can't help it. What do you daydream each time you need it so you can let it slide in?" He laughed, a quivering laugh that shook with rage. "I've made it with women to whom it comes natural and I can tell the difference. Only a Fancy Pants jerk like you hooked would be dumb enough to break up a family to spend his old age with you. Except he had no family to break up for your boobies and other standard equipment that'll all wear out one day."

He nodded as she stood there trembling.

"They ought to invent a new rubber and name it after you. The merry spider. Love 'em and eat 'em."

She looked wildly around the room. She saw her drink on the table, seized it, and hurled the glass in his face and ran for the door. He ran after her, the whisky burning in his eyes and streaming down his cheeks.

"Laurie, please. Please, honey, please. You know I can't divorce Diana till the baby is born."

"I couldn't be a real woman till I met a real man!"

She forced her shaking fingers to the buttons of her open blouse and touched something warm. It was her breast, exposed, the thin network of veins and its fine full modeling rising and falling rapidly. She saw Wallie staring.

"Want Mama's titty, do you, you overgrown, vicious crybaby?" She was buttoning the blouse deliberately. "I hope you took a good look. It's the last one you'll ever have."

She pushed past him and opened the door. This time he didn't try to stop her. She stood a moment outside his door, still buttoning the blouse, smiling in a whitefaced rage. She heard a buzzer, the slamming of an elevator door, and she ran to the end of the hall.

She drove fast. The country club was just on the outskirts of town nearer the dock. The relief man answered her good night as she entered the boat. There in the sheltered darkness of the slip she put her face in her hands over the wheel and sobbed, one palm over her mouth so the relief man wouldn't hear. After a while she stopped, examined her cheek in the mirror, using her flashlight. She rubbed the smeared lipstick from her chin. The welts were still there but fading. If she drove fast enough the cold air and wind would remove the last traces of them. She lifted the glass windshield the way Ken showed her to, so the strong breeze would blow straight at her. She stepped out of the boat, used the open phone at the lower dock, and told Ken she was on her way.

She sped across the lake unmindful of the hazards so frightening on the way over. All she feared was being by herself with the need to repeat that it's not true I hate men though it is true I must still tell myself loveless things of violence and rape but less each time less and less while more and more it was hating not men but Wallie and all the others like him who clutched and clawed and the image of herself they gave her and the contempt in self-defense but not what I want to be or am becoming and can and will be for Ken because of Ken and because he makes me feel the way I must and want to with him not against him. Ken is a man. He is *my* man. And being his is breaking up all those hateful habits if as he said I grew up too soon and he too late which means he understands and that will save me. Without a word he understands and I must not lie to him for that too is a kind of hate and fear. Not reach into the rotten dregs of dirty daydreams to coax love and desire into clean things like willingness and surrender so it's not me or it won't be and each time it is me less and less and Ken will make it go, will make me forget the face, the voice, the vicious charges and their

vanishing untrue truth this Ken will do for me and I will be for him.
"Ken!"

He was there waiting in the shadows of their dock. He helped her
out of the boat, not looking at her. "I have a surprise," he said. He
turned his searchlight on the eaves at the barn swallows' nest. It sub-
dued the small dock light and shadowed her face. Three newborn
birds woke with their tiny mouths opened wide, heads held back, expecting worms. The mother bird sat calmly, only spreading her protective wings.

Ken held her hand, his flashlight pointed ahead as they walked up
the unlit road to the house.

"Everything all right?"

"Of course. Why?"

"Just so long as everything is all right," he said.

The next morning Ken woke to find her sorting out dresses, under-
clothes, shorts, and shoes all piled up neatly on the chaise longue.

"I saw Mr. Sands this morning," she said.

That meant 5:30 A.M.

"He's bringing all these to his granddaughter, the one he's always
worrying about who works in town."

"Yes. Clementine. She runs an elevator at the country club."

"I don't want any of them."

"Let's go to town and do some buying," he said.

"And you pick everything?"

He nodded, kissing her neck. She held on to his face.

After breakfast the phone rang. Ken answered it. "It's long distance
again," he said.

She felt her face pale as she watched Ken leave the room. When he
reached the outside patio, she was telling him through the open window in a weak, relieved voice, "It's for you, from New York. Mr.
Coogan."

Chapter 9

FOR THE LAST twenty minutes on the plane up to Saranac, Coogan had tried to achieve a positive frame of mind by fixing his thoughts on the great opportunities provided by his plan. The fact that McBride had insisted on coming with him didn't help. Each specific argument he marshaled only reminded him that the major opportunity was slipping away. Their capital had been tripled by WHIP. Money brokers offered the facilities of fifty eastern banks at better rates than they had ever enjoyed. The curiosity of newspapers and magazines as to future plans had not diminished. But none of it had value if it remained unused. Something had to be announced and Preston, not he, had to be there to announce it.

The question of when Preston was getting back into harness had become embarrassing. Last week the secretary of Howard J. Cavendish, president of Central Life Insurance, phoned to invite Mr. and Mrs. Preston to dinner, "and Mr. and Mrs. Coogan, too, of course." *Too.* Of course. His advance was completely bound to Preston's. A few nods at a piece of wood, if they came from heads high and mighty enough, transformed mere lumber into idols, and the nod was still to Ken, not to him. Ken's indifference and inaccessibility and the time slipping by had kept him up nights smoking, reading, and making notes in the pad Melanie had given him for Christmas. During the day he continued to accumulate arguments: he had more arguments now than he knew what to do with. He hated this kind of fact-finding. That was Ken's work. But this time roles were reversed. Ken was the customer, the man to be sold and convinced, and Mac's tactlessness was an added burden in the circumstances. What circumstances? He wasn't quite sure except that Ken was married and they hadn't even been invited to the wedding. Ken had remained closeted with his bride for months now and time was vanishing. Interest in them was still high. But news was expected—demanded. The nation was becoming more curious daily about the market, the Street, the possibilities it offered. Who could say where their role would stop once properly set into motion, with their victory in WHIP properly consolidated? Except that it hadn't been consolidated. They had impermissibly lost precious, irreplaceable time! To make his frustration complete, after the first unpleasantness with Leatrice, who kept asking why Ken hadn't invited *her* for the two days at St. Terese—surely the bride wasn't that young or ignorant and here we are canceling our Fourth of July weekend plans and what was she to do—he then came upon his son, Hal, moping in his room. Only the week before, Hal had been all excitement over his acceptance at M.I.T. to study sound, light, physics, electronics, and short-wave frequency. When Coogan had asked, "All set for the weekend, son?" Hal kicked his tool kit with his canvas sneaker and answered, "Sure. All set. I'll tie a flag to a firecracker and shove it."

Coogan couldn't understand it. He had pressed severely as to its cause, thinking perhaps Hal's dating plans had backfired; he tended to keep too many girls on a string at once and he had told him so before. Finally Hal blurted it out. "How do you expect me to feel, this fine Independence Day weekend? I'm eligible for the draft. All the other kids are way ahead. That calls for influence. I told you this six months ago!"

"Would you rather be in a Mongol slave state? Or a foreigner getting charity from Uncle Sam?" Coogan had demanded. "We've got the ball and we're running with it. If that costs a price, by God, we pay it. I'll use influence when the time comes to get you *in* right, but not to keep you *out*." His wide blue eyes had narrowed. His round, cherubic face hardened and he saw how startled Hal was by the tone of his voice. "You get nothing for nothing in this world. You're an American, with all the privileges that go with being one. Defending your country is part of that price."

Then Hal said, "Oh, Christ, the main Fourth of July speaker is loose in my bedroom!" and stormed out to set the time and place for picking up his date. To complete the picture, his daughter Melanie had no date at all.

Ken's two-week honeymoon had stretched to two months, so here he was now in the untenable position of having to sell Ken his public funds plan, instead of revealing it.

Then he got his first sight of Laurie. Sun-tanned, golden-colored, beautiful, young, full of appetites, her eyes alive with lights and responses as she advanced through the airport gate holding Ken's arm. Just one look at her and Ken together told the story. This was what he had needed! Coogan saw the whole thing at a glance and his brooding vanished at once.

After introductions, Mac said, "You look like you got monkey glands," and Coogan agreeing said, "By Jupiter, you do look fifteen years younger! Doesn't he, Mac? Look at him."

Mac had looked at him and then at her and then constantly at her and had been looking at her ever since. "I just said he did."

On the way to the dock, Coogan chatted cheerfully about the city heat, how incredibly cool it was up here, the fact that he regretted deeply bursting in on their honeymoon, and through it all McBride kept staring at Laurie.

In the boat, Ken drove. Laurie sat in front with him, her knees up on the seat, face turned back, answering Coogan and uncomfortably aware of McBride's steady stare. Before dinner they drove round the lake, swam, and had cocktails. During dinner Coogan told a funny story, a true one, he hastened to add, about a Floor man who had been institutionalized for the past five years at a fancy sanitarium for the mentally ill. He was let out a month ago for a trial period after pleading and submitting to endless tests for several weeks. All unknown to his family he had returned to the Floor long enough to go short some thirty securities. While the family and lawyers were frantically turning heaven and earth to invalidate his transactions, his short position made a profit of two hundred thousand dollars in two weeks. Then of course the family abandoned their fight against it and the Floor man closed out the positions, took the profit, and asked to be sent back to the institution. He had simply wanted out long enough to go short, make the money, and satisfy himself he could still call a bear market, crazy or not.

"Of course," Coogan added, laughing, "we weren't that smart. Couldn't do much of anything while you were gone."

Laurie caught Ken's eye and the corners of her mouth twitched with amusement.

After dinner they sat in the living room. Laurie placed the new dance records bought earlier in the day on the long-playing hi fi and served and freshened their brandies and highballs.

"Marvelous dinner," Coogan said.

"Laurie's work."

Coogan nodded. "Well, Ken, you're the world's best proof about the old adage on still waters."

McBride laughed and Coogan smiled at him but his eyes stayed cold.

"Ken knows how to pick winners," McBride said. "I'll take a refill on the bourbon, please." His foot was tapping to the music. He stood up as Laurie went to the bar. "Pat has some hot news," he said to Ken.

"So I assume." Ken looked to Coogan.

"Well, I thought you and I might just sit out on the porch together and chat about it."

"May I listen?" Laurie asked, approaching with McBride's drink. Coogan looked swiftly from Ken to her and back again.

"Of course," Ken said. "You don't mind, Pat?"

"No. No. Wish my wife tried to understand. Don't mind at all."

He did, but there was no way out of it.

"I don't understand a thing," Laurie told him, sitting on a pillow at Ken's feet. "But I just feel I ought to try."

Coogan nodded. You try all right. You try real fancy. All right, use her then. Jujitsu. I will use you fine, my avaricious, oversexed female friend. He looked across the room at the hi fi. Laurie jumped up and went to it.

"Just turn it down a little bit, please," Coogan said. "It's nice as background."

She turned it down. Coogan lit a cigar.

"I seem to always have things that can't be gone into by phone or mail. Of course you know the market's at its bottom." He blew at the end of his cigar. "Some of the boys have been to Washington seeing Secretary Humphrey about this hard-money fiasco and I've talked to them. Bingham is among them and you know he's no windbag. They're all pretty certain Treasury is sour on it now. They've said as much on the Hill. Of course the President claims the Federal Reserve Board has autonomy and all that but the inside word is even Sherman Adams feels the sell-off has gone altogether too far and they're none of them happy now with Winthrop Aldrich's sudden trip to Europe. The boys are convinced we're going to have easy credit and a large supply of money by Labor Day." He smiled. "Now what do you make of that?"

Ken looked down at Laurie, then out of the window. "Hard to say." He studied his drink.

Hard to say! I've done all the work. All he has to do is say he agrees. But *that's* hard to say. Does he know at all what I went through while he sat and read and computed harmless figures? If he really wants to know what's hard I could tell him. Working like a nigger. Breaking my back. Bribery, flouting Exchange rules, drinking myself sick with the Texans and living in that Florida shack with scorpions and cockroaches for playmates. Benzedrine. Sometimes so dirty I stank, while he never missed a meal. High-yaller whores and clapped-up spicks. Hard to *say!* Even talk is hard for my aristocrat and I'll be completely and absolutely God damned if I'll sit still for it. But you will. Yes, you will.

Coogan was still smiling. "You don't think it's safe to say that easy credit would start a rally?"

Ken's face was expressionless. "I don't know, really."

Laurie looked up at him sharply. *"If they reverse the hard-money policy—the biggest bull market in history."* Those were his exact words in answer to that very question less than a week ago. What was all this?

"That's exactly how the Floor feels," McBride said. "Not at all sure. They're not a bit sold it's hard money that's sitting on this market."

Coogan relit his cigar and blew at it again. If McBride didn't shut up, his hard-won control wouldn't last out the discussion. He looked straight at Laurie for a moment. She turned her eyes away. "Best sign in the world, Mac. The Floor is always bearish just when the market is about to rise." Then he turned back to Ken. "Still, if you *had* to say, Ken, how would you call it?"

"I suppose the market might rally on such news," Ken answered.

"Now, Ken, I'm really surprised you're unsure, because that's what I've always admired about you most. Your accuracy. I seem to remember just before you went to Europe, you said capital goods expansion was only beginning and existing savings were way ahead of product supply or new industry."

Ken fidgeted. "Let's assume Washington eases money and it will release a genuine bull market. What do you have in mind?"

Coogan relaxed. He reached for the black brief case on the floor. "You'll find this very boring, I'm afraid," he told Laurie.

She looked at Ken and said, "I'll get coffee."

She rose from the pillow and went to the kitchen. Mr. Sands was very glum.

"Anything wrong?" she asked.

"No ma'am, Miss Laurie."

She helped him with the dishes.

"Now you take Mr. Ken's father and his partners. They never would have busted in on a young married couple this way. Real gentlemen, as they say."

"I think it's something very important."

"Nothing's that important. I don't care a cent for folks with bad manners."

She smiled. "They'll be gone tomorrow and it's sweet of you to care. I came in for more coffee."

"Just about ready, Miss Laurie. I'll bring it along. Guess I should have had Clementine down serving."

"Nonsense," Laurie said.

When she returned, McBride was standing at the hi fi. He turned it up a little as she approached. Ken and Coogan were at the coffee table where Coogan had spread several charts.

"Dance?" McBride asked her.

She hesitated and he had his arm around her. McBride's dancing was smooth, graceful, up to the minute, and close. When the side ended, she disengaged herself, her face flushed, and walked to the coffee table. McBride followed, smiling.

"Then why should the average stockholder be fifty-two years old, most of them over forty when the majority of savings accounts are started by folks in their early thirties? Why are we so far behind?" Coogan looked up. She saw his resentment but was determined to stay. It wasn't that dancing with McBride didn't please her. She hadn't danced that way since—

Coogan was using her to make his point. "—and you're married to a man whose business this is. Now if you wanted to buy stock," he said to her, "and you couldn't ask Ken to do it for you, how would you go about it?"

"I don't know, really."

"Of course you don't. And suppose I said to you, buy PK or ISN or RT, what would that mean to you?"

"Why, nothing."

"Exactly. Nothing." He turned to Ken. "But that's all you'll ever find on the financial page. It's a miracle six and a half million people hold securities as it is. According to Brookings Institute there are twenty-one million family spending units made up of forty million adults with liquid resources and income sufficient to invest in corporate shares, and I'll tell you that they all have faith in free enterprise. Every single one of them would buy securities if they knew where and how to go about it and someone had the sense to invite them to. Besides, there are another five million with high enough salaries who are accustomed to buying everything on the installment plan. And they're good for it. Government bonds, insurance, homes, cars, clothing, jewelry, everything on the installment plan. Except securities. We're as outdated as the one-horse shay." He turned back to Laurie. He smiled. "Now you've been with Ken morning, noon, and night for seven weeks. Did you ever once look at the financial page?"

"No," she said, flushing. "Why should I?"

"No reason at all. Whose slogan is 'It's Smart To Be Thrifty'?"

"Everybody knows that." The flush had left her face.

" 'All the News That's Fit To Print'? 'Fifty-seven Varieties'?"

She smiled.

He turned back to Ken. "I could throw fifty of them at Mrs. Preston and she'd recognize them all. Because every product in America advertises where people can see it. And they do so in human terms. Except for securities, brokerage firms, and the New York Stock Exchange.

Why, everybody knows what Frank E. Campbell's is, and they're an undertaking outfit! Hard selling isn't swindling. It's just recognizing human nature. You want to get a message across, you have to clown, rant, rave, bleed, and wiggle your ears, invent fables and legends, give a hundred examples. Just handing out a bushel of statistics in a one-inch ad in dead type was all well and good when a handful of Americans could afford to invest in America's future, but this is a new era. Anybody who goes courting against competition will tell you, you gotta primp up when you go to the market place. There's nothing vulgar about it. Hell, courtship looks like claptrap to an old married man, but it's the body of the letter." He smiled. "Romance and exaggeration aren't lies. You know the old story. You like Bach—Martin Luther took the best product in the world, the Bible, and made the world believe in God by translating it from dead Latin. Now we have a success story like few other Street firms and we did get off the financial page with some of it. If we go straight into television, onto feature pages, into magazines, proclaim the biggest damn bull market of all time, blow our horn a little, and pick our securities in the proper order, we can become the number one firm in America, the number one firm in the world!"

Mr. Sands came in with the coffee, served it, and asked, "Will there be anything else?" He addressed it to Laurie. She looked to Ken and back at Mr. Sands.

"Are the fires set in the guest rooms?"

"Yes, ma'am."

"Then I guess that's all, Mr. Sands. Thanks so much."

"Pleasure, Mrs. Preston."

"Now before you react, Ken, I know how you feel about publicity. This thing can be sold as American Public Funds or Public Funds Associated or even Coogan Public Funds if you like. I don't mind publicity." He smiled as though making a frank and innocent admission. "My idea is you pick the stocks, I work on financing and personnel. Mac executes the orders. We make a special approach to unions on their strike and pension funds. Get the whole country involved in buying America on the Big Board. From a dollar to a dinosaur-sized diamond." He stretched. "At least study it. I'll leave you all the facts and figures. Riley is working on the legalities, margin restrictions and such. I've sounded out the Board of Governors and the SEC. They have no fundamental objection. Now why don't you dance with your wife while I have a drink? That's enough business for one night."

"Yes," Laurie said. "Let's dance."

Ken was stiff and self-conscious. Laurie's face was red. Each time they turned she could see McBride, his bourbon in hand, leaning against the patio window, smiling as he watched. They played gin rummy, sat on the patio, had a few more drinks. At eleven o'clock, Coogan asked if he could be excused.

"It's still early," McBride said.

"We're leaving on the seven A.M. plane," Coogan reminded him.

"Oh?" Ken said. "I thought you were staying through tomorrow."

"No." Coogan smiled and patted his arm. "I told my wife I'd be home by ten o'clock. We have a date with friends for the last two days of this holiday. I didn't want to barge in but you can see how important it was. If the market starts to rally within a month or so, there's an awful lot to do."

"There's still vacations to go into," McBride said.

"We can cover that over breakfast."

"How about one dance before the last record's over?" McBride asked Laurie.

"In that case, I'll just finish my nightcap," Coogan said.

Laurie danced with McBride and felt Ken watching. When Ken walked to the coffee table and began collecting the charts, McBride said to Laurie, "Don't let our absent-minded professor fool you. He takes in everything."

"Who is that?" she asked.

"Ken. That's what we call him."

"That's not what I call him."

McBride smiled.

"And what is it Ken took in?" she asked.

"Everything," McBride said easily. "The facts, the figures, and all the opportunities. Just about everything."

The music ended and they went to bed. Ken came downstairs to separate the burning logs in the living-room fireplace so that they wouldn't fall still blazing against the screen during the night. When he returned to the bedroom, Laurie's light was out and her back was turned.

"Laurie?"

"Yes?" She didn't face him.

"Are they bothering you?"

"No."

"Will you join us for breakfast?"

"If you want me to."

"It's up to you."

"I'll be at breakfast."

"Well?"

"Well, what?"

"How do you find them?"

She turned to him, an angry snap in her eyes, and said nothing.

"Mac dances well," Ken said.

"Oh, shut up." She put her head on his shoulder. "I don't like them," she said. "I just don't, that's all. McBride is a slob and Coogan thinks he's the smartest and I don't."

"You really don't like them."

"I said I didn't. Who do they think they are, treating you like a junior?"

"I don't mind," he said mildly.

"I thought you were quitting. If you're really quitting, why didn't you say so?"

"As you've pointed out many times, there's still a whole year."

She didn't answer. She lit a cigarette. "Could Coogan have pulled all this material together since you left?"

"Possibly. I don't think so."

"Nor do I and I don't know anything about it. So he's had this on his mind from way back."

"Yes. I'd say so."

"Why didn't he tell you before?"

Ken shrugged. "Waiting for the result on WHIP, I would imagine. And making up his own mind. Then I've been gone for over two months."

"I don't believe it. I think he always planned to spring it on you and shove it down your throat."

"Does it matter?"

"Yes. It means he's using you."

"I'm afraid I encouraged that sort of thing."

"You're no rubber stamp," she said. "And nobody's going to use you as one any more or call you one either." She squashed the cigarette. "And all that public fund business. Where does he come off proposing it be named after him?"

"It is his idea. He knows I dislike publicity."

"Do you like the idea?"

"I can't say. It might have possibilities."

"It's your brain they've been riding on, the stinking pitchmen."

"I didn't know you had such a temper."

"There's a lot about me you don't know. Putting it to you as though it were a foregone conclusion, two against one."

"Laurie," Ken said. "There's a fundamental difference between them and me. I'm leaving the Street and they like this business. Naturally they want to consolidate on our small success."

"You made that success and it wasn't small. So it's up to you to decide what comes next. If you stay and for as long as you stay. You despise this public funds thing, don't you?"

"Do you?" he asked.

"I don't understand it. Coogan sounds like a crook but that could just be a lifelong prejudice against Wall Street. You're from Wall Street too. You're no crook and you've told me about the high ethics of so many people you know down there. It's what you think about it I'm interested in."

"Coogan isn't crooked. He's aggressive and very competent. I don't care for the flamboyance and unwieldiness of the idea but that may just be my bias from a lifelong prejudice against selling securities like soap on a Woolworth counter."

"Why is it your bias, damn it? Why isn't it your conviction? They think your being quiet means you're slow-witted and your mildness is weakness and I resent it, damn them to hell."

He smiled.

"Don't smile. I mean this. It's very important to me. You're my man, that's why."

He drummed his fingers on his chest.

"Remember I told you at the beginning, I'm not ambitious."

"And I told you I am." She seized his arm. "For you. I want people to know what you are. I hate it when they patronize you and smirk at you and work rings around you behind your back; like your Aunt Sarah trying to buy you a job with Coozy Tucker rubbing it in, or Coogan trying to sell you one. I could brain all of them for doing it and I could brain you for letting them."

"Right now I have only one ambition," he said, putting out his light.

"What?"

"To dance like McBride."

"Oh, shut up!"

She kissed him with anger and hunger.

At breakfast Coogan outlined the vacation problems of customers' men, order clerks, research staff, and the need for staggering authority through Labor Day.

"Of course I could delegate responsibility," Coogan said. "And you're still on your honeymoon." He smiled self-deprecatingly. "But it has been a long year for all of us."

"I want to go on a trip is what Pat means," McBride said.

"Of course," Ken said. "I see no reason why you can't leave now."

"I mean for the rest of July and August. You're the only other firm member who could be on the Floor."

"There's little to be on the Floor for."

"All July and August?" Coogan asked him.

Ken nodded.

"For customers as well?"

"That's my opinion."

"How about September?"

"September may be active."

Coogan smiled. The girl hated him. Hated him on sight. But she would be his ally in the end. He suddenly knew it.

"Well, Mac," he said, "there you are. If Ken thinks we're losing nothing of consequence till September, it's good enough for me. You haven't been too anxious to take positions anyway."

He turned to Ken and managed to include Laurie. "That makes the rest of July and August planning months. Strategy time. Your time." He turned to Laurie. "That's the remarkable thing about Ken. He could plan the whole public funds project from right up here. Needs none of us. That's how he did all of them. We just provide some facts and a little leg work. He'd have the securities picked in their right order from here to Christmas."

He rose. "I hope you'll go for it, Ken, after thinking it through. It's the challenge of a lifetime."

At the airport he thanked Laurie, apologized again for intruding, and said, "Maybe you can convince him to be less shy. I'd prefer to call the project Preston Public Funds."

McBride said, "When you get to town, come see the Floor."

After the plane left, she took a deep breath. At the dock she wanted to drive the boat. On the patio, Mr. Sands served them coffee. He wore his straw hat and was cheerful again. He smiled to Laurie behind Ken's back.

"I suppose I should have insisted they stay," Laurie said.

"No. Pat was expected home." Ken was looking over his final version of the paper for the *Philosophical Journal*.

"We surely don't need any more money," she said.

"No, we don't."

She tapped his manuscript. "And that's the kind of challenge *really* interests you."

"Yes."

"Is it finished?"

"Yes."

"How is it?"

"More appropriate in tone."

"May I read it?"

"Of course."

"And then let's go mail it."

"All right."

"And then let's go fishing."

"Fine."

Chapter 10

HE HAD TAKEN her for a drive around the countryside as far south as Lake Placid, where they visited the grave of John Brown. On the way back along the Ausable River, they descended the rocks at one of the gorges and swam in the wild current, letting it push them around bends and carry them down small falls and cascades. Then they stood in a quiet pool of sun-speckled water and two fish approached to swim between their legs, dart at Laurie's feet, and nibble at her toes. She kicked, the fish swam away and returned. She stood motionless and the fish explored her toes again until she couldn't stand it any more and burst into laughter.

"How can you ever catch a poor little fish after that?" she asked.

When they returned to camp, Mr. Sands gave Ken an envelope picked up in the morning mail. It was his manuscript to the *Philosophical Society Journal,* rejected with polite suggestions for changes but no promise of publication if their objections were met. They had lunch and went out walking.

"I'm sorry they didn't approve."

Ken nodded.

"When are we going back?" she asked.

"I don't know."

"You've been thinking about Coogan's plan?"

"I don't want to go back to the Street at all."

"All right."

"We don't need the money, as we agreed. Why I've done it this long is a separate matter. But since I don't want to do it any more, why go back?"

"Just do what makes you happy."

"Being with you right here makes me happy."

"I mean makes you happy for the next forty-five years," she said.

They walked past Mr. Sands's place. Ken turned off the path abruptly and held the branches back so she could get ahead of him.

"You'll rewrite the article?"

He nodded.

"And then what will you do for the next twelve months?"

Twigs cracked underfoot. The big closed house stood between them and the sun. It imposed a wide, dark shadow.

"You were surprised that 'Battle Hymn of the Republic' originally came from 'John Brown's Body,' weren't you?"

"Yes. Ken, let's get back on the path. It's cold here."

"I hadn't noticed."

He led her through to the other side and approached the lawn.

"What about 'Battle Hymn'?"

"There's confusion about how it actually came to be written. Our history is full of such things. Snow says that Julia Ward Howe was approached by Abraham Lincoln to take the John Brown song and give it pious lyrics. Van Wyck Brooks credits this to James Freeman Clarke, the time he was with her in Washington when she was helping the soldiers and heard them singing the John Brown song as they tramped by. I once tracked both their source materials and both seemed to be accurate."

She sat down on the bench, a small frown on her face, listening attentively.

"I think it's important to know," he went on, "whether impersonal authority or intimate friendship was the force that gave her the impetus and inspiration that still makes our hearts beat faster."

He paused. "It's only an example of the kind of thing I mean," he said.

She waited.

"I'd like to track down such inconsistencies and get at the truth." He hesitated. "That's what I'd like to do with my time," he finished. "Maybe even after twelve months."

She looked at him another moment and then burst into laughter.

"You find that funny?"

"You must be kidding."

"No, I'm not."

She stopped laughing. "All right. No, damn it, it's not all right. I mean sure, it's fun reading Emerson and Thoreau and discovering Sarah Orne Jewett and Mrs. Fields and all those others. Really learning it the way they're never taught in school is wonderful. It's a brand-new world and I love it. But—" She took his hand and pulled him down to the bench. "Darling, I didn't mean to laugh and I can see it's sort of what you must have always wanted to do so that makes it fine." She was squeezing his hand hard. "It's just I don't see you that way. The library dry-as-dust way. I can't help it."

"How do you see me?"

"I hurt you. Ken, I didn't mean to. I don't care what you do, it's you I love. And that's not just three little words, like I love you. If that's what makes you happy, do it. And if you don't mind your Aunt Sarah buying the museum job for you, do that too and go on rewriting articles till these people are satisfied with them."

"I won't return to the Street."

"You're young. You have to work."

"But I don't have to work for money, so it should be something I want to do."

"That's right. But is all this what you want to do?"

"Of course it is."

"Then why does it sound so vague? I don't know any more about Wall Street than I do about museums or journals or early American history. If anything, less. When you talk about the Street, it's real and all this other stuff sounds like a dream or something. Long ago and far away and worn out. If you must know, it sounds farfetched and unreal. I'm sorry, but that's how you make it sound."

"I see."

"No, you don't, darling, and I guess I don't either. So let's just get started on it and go ahead. But let's not talk any more, Ken. Let's just *do* it. I—" She stopped.

"Yes?"

"No. I think you're perfectly right. You do what's right for you."

"What were you starting to say?"

"Nothing. Except, well, can anyone be good at what they don't like?"

"I doubt it."

"Then why were you good at what you did on Wall Street for twenty-one years?"

"That's not easy to explain."

"Ye gods, I'm not asking for an explanation! You don't owe me any. I'm just trying to help if I can."

"All right. Go on."

"Well, maybe it's the *way* you did it you don't like."

"No. The way I did it made it bearable."

"What I mean is, aren't you head man in name only?"

"That's also part of what I mean."

"I'd better butt out. I don't know enough about it and it's really none of my business. I just care about you a lot and I know you a little. That's all."

"You know me more than a little."

"O.K., then. You're so, oh, I don't know—modest, I guess. Retiring. You're not competitive at all because you don't have to be. I know that. Just like you don't need to show off on water skis or have bulging muscles and you can still lift the boat and you don't have to be domineering for me to—" She put her face against his. "You know. These are the things I love in you. But others take advantage of it. They don't understand it and you never ever got the pleasure, the recognition, the *respect* is what I mean, I guess, for what you did. Now maybe that's why you hate it."

He said nothing.

She rose to her feet. "I'll shut up."

"No," he said. He was staring at the ground. "That may be. It may well be." He didn't believe it, not for a minute. But he *did* believe because he knew that right now *her* respect mattered more than anything else.

The next morning rain beat hard against the window. It woke him out of a nightmare. He was still shivering from it and the nightmare was very clear. She had somehow led him to walking. It was winter. They were walking on ice. It wasn't the lake, nor was it the gorge. And he did it with misgiving. She had been ill. Then she took a step ahead of him, downward, and the ice broke beneath her and she was in the water. He rushed forward and the ice broke under him, too. The water was cold and wild. It was carrying her away. Yet swimming fast in the same direction to save her, he was held back. Struggling, he thought, she's sick. Now she'll never get well. This will kill her. Then all at once there was a large ferryboat approaching. He called out. The boat would save them. Then he saw its paddle wheel churning the water. Its suction pulled in cakes of ice and drifting wood as it came nearer. She had moved toward it and its suction was pulling her. With all his force he exerted his freezing limbs to reach her and save her. Just as his hand was about to touch her foot, the paddle wheel dragged her in. He thought of it mangling her and reached out to her. The suction caught his arm and was pulling him in when he woke. Beside him, Laurie was sound asleep.

After that it rained for a week, during which he tried to work on the rejected paper. He didn't get very far. The rain had stopped yesterday. He came in to find her vacuuming the hand-woven Indian rugs.

"What are you doing?"

"I need the exercise."

"Let's play tennis. The court is dry now."

She turned off the vacuum. "Ken, I'm losing track of days, weeks. I feel like a parasite. I typed your paper and it took all of three hours. That was three weeks ago. I've done nothing but sun and swim and sleep and sloth or huddle in front of that fireplace. I'm like a vegetable. I've been vacationing for almost three months now."

"You shop and cook and—"

"Oh, jolly. Worn to a frazzle I am," she said. "I'm not needed."

"I need you."

"I mean for the wheels to go round. There are no wheels. I'm playing house again."

"You're wanted. Isn't that important?"

"I have to be *necessary*. How can I know what I'm necessary for till I know what you're going to do?" She forced a smile. "I'm a restless girl. Always was. I'm finished in here anyway. I'll shower and let's play tennis."

She took the little box with the absorbent cotton and the field mouse outside. She shook the mouse out onto the bottom porch step. It had been born during the rain and she had taken it in and fed it with an eye dropper and tried to remove the fleas, saying they were larger than it was. The mouse stood for a moment, confused. Then he heard the sounds under the house and disappeared in their direction.

"Poor thing forgot where he belonged."

She took Ken's arm and they went off to the tennis court.

On the twenty-seventh, when the cease-fire at Panmunjom ended the Korean war, Coogan phoned to ask Ken whether the peace in any way altered his market forecast. It did not. Had Ken made up his mind? He had not. Did he have any idea when he would? Ken didn't. Another three weeks were gone. Ken knew it. When he hung up, Laurie was sitting on the couch, watching him with a levelness and sadness in her eyes. Then she rose, sighed, and left the room.

The air was very still. Small gnats were circling in groups over the low pine hedge between the patio and the lake. She rocked back and forth in the swing. It creaked. Ken was reading his manuscript. He heard the creaking and looked up.

"What's the matter?"

"Nothing," she said. She threw her cigarette to the ground and began pacing. She stopped and sighed. "I wish there were a breeze."

He looked out over the lake. It was motionless. There were no clouds.

"Would you like to go indoors?"

"No. I need the air."

"Are you all right?"

"Yes, I'm all right." Her voice had an edge. "I'd like a martini."

He nodded and rose. "I'll have Mr. Sands make them."

"I'll make them." She walked swiftly inside.

He sat down again and put the manuscript on the outdoor metal table and looked at the gnats. The nights between them were still good. The days were not. They could have been for him if they still were for her, but for her it had all gone wrong since Coogan and McBride had visited weeks ago, since the phone call for her the night before that. Since George Tucker had blurted out the truth about Aunt Sarah and the museum, and the *Journal* had rejected his manuscript. They all seemed to have happened at the same instant. The two separate parts of his life had to be joined. Perhaps it was impossible to find new work at his age, but the youth of his love for her belied it. So did his need to work. Somehow he had to make clear to her why all of the old life was over. Still she was right. They could not stay here suspended. He *had* to work. But it was not work, it was love that had been the absent force in his life. No longer missing now.

Laurie appeared with the drinks and said, "Let's go to the summer theater tonight."

"Fine. I'll find out what's playing."

"I don't care what's playing. Let's just go. And have dinner in town."

"Of course."

"I'll go tell Mr. Sands," she said, and was gone again. When she returned she said, "Mr. Sands was disappointed."

"He'll get over it."

"It's so damn still," she said. "I just wish there were a wind."

"Would you like to go back to New York?"

"Mom says the city is hotter than hell now. Hard to believe."

"How would you like to spend a weekend at the Rock?"

"No, thanks. Not unless that would settle this museum business."

"We could drive up to Canada."

"I'm quite happy here. Another drink?"

"Not for me."

"I'll have another drink."

"Laurie, you have to understand why I don't want to go back to the Street."

"Don't just keep at me about it, Ken. It's very still here and I'm restless. That's all. The air is very still and you're still and I'm happy here."

"I merely thought—"

"I'm happy here!" She shouted it. "I'm sorry. Look, I'll just go in and get myself another drink."

The phone was ringing. She ran to answer it. Ken saw her face light up and he went inside.

"Yes, Mom. He is? Hey, hey. I'll bet. Him and Einstein. Has he grown?" She laughed. "Just tell him not to use it on me. Hey! Tommy? Oh dear, you've gone and lost your voice and found it in the basement." She laughed again. "You'll have to tell me all about it in simple English for nonmathematical nitwits. Wonderful. Put Mom on. Yeah, Mom. Why can't you both come up here? Oh. Now wait." She cupped the mouthpiece. Her eyes sparkled. "My kid brother is in from Chicago for a week. Mom wants to know if I could fly in for two or three days to see him. They can't come up because of the store."

"I'm sure we could get you a reservation today."

"Mom? O.K. Now wait. Say hello to Ken." Their eyes met. He had heard the voice himself. He could tell it was female and recognized it as her mother's.

"Yes, she looks very well," Ken was saying as Laurie checked the air-line schedule card that hung from a nail over the desk. "I'm sure she can leave today. I'll put her back on. Thank you, that's sweet. Well, I'm not quite sure just when at the moment."

She told Mary to expect her in time for dinner tonight unless she called back. Then she phoned the airport and secured a reservation on the 3:30.

"Sure you don't mind?"

"Not at all."

She was quite excited. "You don't want to come in?"

"No. I think your family reunion should be unencumbered."

"Oh, really."

"Well, you've been away almost four months and there's lots to talk about. Come on, we'll get a swim before lunch and then pack."

She kissed him. "I'll be glad to see the little stinkpot. It's just for two or three days."

She forgot about the other drink.

He drove her to the mainland dock and then to the airport.

"You're sure you don't mind?"

"Of course not. Mr. Sands has been wanting to clear the undergrowth near the mainland. It will give me some exercise."

He waved as she boarded, turned and walked fast until he realized he had passed his car. Perhaps it was as well to be alone. After so many months and years of being alone, spending every morning, noon, and night with someone else made self-location difficult and yet he didn't want to be alone. That was exactly what he did not want. For some reason he found himself working out the mathematics of her age. At the time of Pearl Harbor, she was nine, born after silent pictures and the crash of '29. Laurie had once laughingly told him how early in 1944 at the age of twelve, when her mother worked in a war plant on the second shift, she had hurried home from school to find that Mother had hidden the alarm clock in the refrigerator and grumbled when Laurie shook her and said, "It's time to get up and win the war." He could still remember riding a horse-drawn streetcar in Boston and gaslight on Charles Street. In 1944 he had been in France with Natalie.

He rose early the next morning and rowed out to the deserted island. The water was an undisturbed pool near shore, mirroring its own submerged mysteries of moss, watercress, and stones, a complete and self-contained liquid jewel. He felt a hot thirst, a yearning to reach the outposts of his own incompleteness and weld the disjointed parts of experience and need together. Laurie and he had been with each other twenty-four hours of each day for weeks and months; never for a single minute of it had he needed diversion or change. She had. She could not help it.

But this fulfillment lived a life apart: it was almost impossible to pin down. Their union and his love for her were separate from his whole life rather than a new phase of it.

After breakfast he went to the thick woods with Mr. Sands. Clearing the underbrush did not interest him. An hour later he found himself at the dock where all the birds seemed to have departed. Then a mother bird appeared, a worm in her beak, and the three fledglings materialized, emitting happy, hoarse, peeping sounds as they opened their three little beaks wide. They had already taken on the protective color of the dark dock wood. The mother flew over them, tempting them with the worm. Then she flew out under the dock to place the worm on the piling. She repeated this performance many times, her mate appearing from somewhere to fly, dive, and pirouette while he sang, trying to make the experience of flight to fight and fight to live as attractive as possible. By the time Mr. Sands had rung the bell for lunch the most courageous of the young birds had ventured as far as the eaves where it huddled, peeping in agitation.

After lunch, Ken returned. The last of the three fledglings had left the nest, sorry ever to have started on the precarious adventure. A flock of flying cousins, uncles, and aunts were happily engaged in the aerial pyrotechnics, now soaring round and round the dock, buoys, and lawn grass, swooping and darting, to encourage the fledglings. Finally hunger drove them out as far as the pilings. By sunset all three, rewarded with worms for having met the full test, were flying with their parents and other relatives, returning frequently to perch on the dock, warming in the sun, hardly distinguishable from the shingles on which they rested.

Ken was sorry Laurie had missed it. He'd have to tell her all about it when she called. If she called.

After dinner he walked aimlessly around the peninsula, avoiding the marshland. Laurie had loved the insistent, intractable, pungent smell of it before her restlessness had become acute. He had always found it offensive and unbearable. Mother had liked the smell too. Father hadn't. For some reason it was pleasing to women but not to men. He stayed in the woods where a north wind now carried the tangible scent of pine needles and air sweetened by rains that left syrup in the fallen leaves and mellowed needles underfoot.

Too bad the wind had not come sooner, before Laurie had left. By an hour after dinner, Ken had passed an interminable, torturous day. He missed her. He was sick with missing her. Was it only four months ago that the long familiar self-sufficiency and passion distilled to civilized and chilling safety had first been replaced by hunger that demanded sanction and release? Since then love had created new boundaries of personality, a new limitlessness but also new limitations. He needed her. He needed her presence. He needed her respect. When he had spoken of John Brown she laughed at him. He had chosen the poorest example of his point. There were weightier cases of historical inconsistency. The liberal civil laws and religious tyranny as brutal as the Inquisition, side by side in the same people, the same Pilgrim Founding Fathers. She would still have laughed. His quest for new work was not a last ditch, don't-take-no-for-an-answer effort. He didn't seem capable of one and he didn't know why. But he knew she had fled from him. Don't avoid that. She fled. And if these injured bruises define your new length, width, and base, they also reveal your peril. You found freedom but you lost something. Now you need something more important to you. You need Laurie. And she needs evidence that you are her man. She needs it in neon lights with claws and fangs, club and cave. She can't help it. On all of America's Madison Avenues and Market Streets, Wall, Broad, and State, city, town, and country streets, there were well-dressed men whose clubs if now exclusive were still built for pressure, in the handshake of course not the closed fist, and who called victims prospects, while cave-ins were all a matter of health, wealth, or marriage with full regard for law and orders like catch the 9:15, take probanthine or antacids at ten, and no martinis before noontime. But it was still the warrior bringing home the bacon crisps with olives and pretzel sticks not stones to break the little woman's bones on the 5:37. Why did everyone sneer at it only after going through it? Why was its rejection only the dream, not the fact of middle age? Why couldn't she see it *now*? Why couldn't he explain it to her? What better way to spend their time than together? He did

not know why he couldn't make her see any more than he could make
up his mind and act on it. Not only Coogan was waiting for action.
Laurie was.

When Laurie phoned, he was nervous, dry-mouthed, and ridiculously
reassured. Had he really thought she might not call at all, might never
come back, might have realized it as an insane error on the rebound
from Wallie?

She was telling him how much she missed him, and asking had
he been fed properly, did Mr. Sands remember to call the laundry?
She had forgotten to tell him. And what about the underbrush? She
was sorry to call this late but she had been chewing her family's ears
off about him and the place and its beauty, and God, it was stinking
hot in New York and she was delighted about the barn swallows and
all their uncles and their cousins and their aunts and wasn't it wonderful that the wind was stirring at last and was he as lonesome for her
as she was for him? Then she laughed at something at the other end
and lowered her voice and whispered certain things to him and he
knew that she did love him and that making up his mind was not a
dark, banishing, solitary thing but one more bond that could draw
them closer together.

"Mother and Tom would love to see the Floor of the Exchange."
She laughed. "You should hear me making noises like I know all
about it. Bonds and stocks, hard and soft, short and long." She laughed
softly. "Anyway, can they, do you think?"

"Of course. Phone Coogan in the morning. He'll arrange it."

She reminded him she would be coming back the day after tomorrow
and said Mom wanted to say hello. When they hung up Mary laughed
and said, "Goodness, he sounds like a lovesick cat."

"No jokes about my husband, hey. If he's lovesick, that's two of us."

Tom rose. "Well, there's my exit cue loud and clear if I ever heard
one. There's a radio forum on I want to hear anyway." He pecked
Laurie's cheek. "At least marriage hasn't changed you for the worse.
Thanks for the Wall Street bit."

He went up the stairs three at a time.

"Isn't he getting awfully big man for seventeen?" Laurie asked.

Mary giggled and put the flame under the coffee. "All talk," she
said. "What I don't understand is how he became a physics quiz kid.
Your father was just as terrible at math as I am, witness his bank
account, so it can't be *his* influence." Mary fanned herself and smiled.
"I'm awfully happy things are turning out this way for you."

"You've no idea, Mom. I didn't know such a man existed. It's corny
but true. He's wonderful."

"I suppose you'll be coming back once the heat spell breaks."

"I don't know. He loves it so up there. I do too," she added quietly.

"But he can't be that well off."

"He can't, but he is." She opened a closet for coffee cups. "He's worth over a million dollars."

Mary's jaw dropped. Laurie laughed.

"I have to sit down," Mary said.

"You should have seen my face when he told me, and he doesn't think that's rich. He doesn't care. Nor do I, would you believe it? I couldn't care less." She took the pot off the stove. "At the airport Ken asked me to tell you if there's anything you need—he said make out a check to your mother in whatever amount you both think."

Mary laughed and blushed and laughed again. "Now that's another thing I'll never get accustomed to."

"How much do you think, hey? Three, four thousand?"

"I don't need anything, really."

"Now look, Ma."

"No. You're always bullying me but this time, no." She put sugar in the coffee and went on quickly. "It's funny. I always knew you'd have money. Some people are just meant for certain things. You never reached for it. I remember what you said about him. When you first began to model I knew it. That reminds me." She told her of Lucy, a high-school friend of Laurie's already twice divorced, finally finding what seemed to be the right man. He had given her a present, a parakeet. A week before the wedding, Lucy caught some infection from it—psittacosis, she thought it was called, and the day that was set for the wedding she was dead.

"How awful. I have to phone her mother right now."

"You can't. They've moved. This happened three months ago. I wasn't going to tell you that on your honeymoon. Lucy always gave me the feeling that she was marked for tragedy. Your father would explain it by Ecclesiastes and your brother by extrasensory perception and wave lengths and what not. Now how on earth did I ever get on to that? Oh, yes, marriages. The feeling you get about certain people. By the way, Tom says your father was simply furious about your wedding. Not because he wasn't invited. Because it was to a non-Catholic."

"Don't you believe it. He knew that much about me a long time ago. It's because he wasn't invited. Now let's settle the finances, hey. If you'd rather, I'll send you whatever Pa does so you can tell him to use it for Hail Marys."

"No, Laurie. It's funny. I didn't mind sending you off to work modeling your last year in high school, or taking your last dollar from you when your father left. But—well, I'd rather he knew none of us Dugans married him for his money. You know? Now let's not talk about it any more or my strength of character will break down."

A horn was honking. Laurie jumped up, parted the curtain, and waved out the kitchen window.

"There's Doris. We're going to have an old-fashioned high-school-type banana split and gab fest."

She picked up her cigarettes. "Be an hour or two. If you change your mind about the small stipend—"

Mary shook her head. "Run along."

Doris said, "Let's go to Stouffer's instead of Howard Johnson's so all our green-eyed alumnae can ogle how you look and sing auld lang syne into their hemlock."

Stouffer's was the expensive ice-cream emporium in Riverneck. They charged a dollar-fifty for a banana split.

"Golly, your tummy sure is way out front."

"Something about the way I'm built, the doctor says. It's only seven months. Maybe I'm carrying the London Tower lying down."

They laughed.

"It's good to be together again, hey. How is Toby?"

They had been friends since grade school, two ugly ducklings before adolescence did its astonishing work on Laurie, when she was still too big, with clumsy legs shooting down from skirts, and the braces had not yet straightened her receding jaw line. Then all of it suddenly took on shape and form, her eyes vividly brownish green, hair silky, nose turned up with a flare of nostrils, and her proud, strong, feminine figure became lithe and full in perfect proportion at five feet eight inches. By high school, Laurie had completed the infrequent transformation from worm to butterfly and the summer in between had permitted girls to say enviously, "Gosh, but you've changed this summer," and boys to watch her progress up and down the stairs from the best vantage point and dream delinquently about how she filled sweaters and how her skirts gave way at each marvelous move. Doris felt she had been a beneficiary of this miracle. She remained plain, not actively ugly, just nondescript, and grateful to Laurie for having drawn her into the select circles. Doris knew that Laurie had prevented her from becoming a bitter old maid, teaching her how to dress and make the most of her passable legs, slim waist, and winning smile. She married a former member of the football team at Riverneck High in her senior year. He was playing semiprofessional baseball and football at the time. Now Toby Foote was a fireman and except for occasional weekend drinking, straying, and the brooding that came to him after close calls on duty, he made a good husband and father. Doris worshiped Laurie, whose transformation had been her own good fortune. Laurie seemed a sort of magic to her now as she had then—the dark-horse walkaway winner in life's perpetually perplexing popularity contest.

"I always knew if you wanted money or society or anything," she was saying as they drove up to Stouffer's, "all you had to do was just go get it."

So Laurie explained again how that wasn't the way it was at all, and how much she loved Ken.

"The way you look, any man would go down on all fours and do parlor tricks just to have you go live in his kennel."

They laughed and Laurie said, "Sometimes I wake up and feel I'm like I was before. Then I look in the mirror and I just can't put it together."

"You were a mess before high school," Doris conceded.

"I don't mean that. I mean before falling in love with Ken."

"Oh."

Inside Stouffer's, Doris admired her strapless dress and they ordered. Laurie asked about Toby Junior, who was now three years old. He had a rash from the heat, Doris said. She didn't know how to ask the doctor but she was sure it came from playing with himself too much. "He's something awful. Isn't this ice cream the greatest? He's even worse than his father. It's got raisins in it! Well, I never! I can't imagine how he'll be by the time he's ten. When I take a bath or go to the john he reaches up and grabs and his mouth opens and—"

They both giggled and bent over their banana splits as the college boy waiting table for the summer brought their water. Then a woman walked by sucking a raspberry popsicle. Doris kicked her under the table. Laurie saw it and said, "Lemon," and they both burst into wild laughter.

This was one of their more wicked intimacies. It came from a terrible post card Doris found in her older brother's desk when she and Laurie were in the eighth grade. They kept the post card for four days while her brother searched in frenzied silence in his gym locker, in the attic, and through his sports paraphernalia. Each day after school over their homework, the picture concealed in a history book, they faced it and giggled and blushed and were outraged and whispered and wondered and wished. Then they went outside with it so they could really talk about it and just look at it. They had bought lemon popsicles from a street vendor. Just as Laurie was about to suck hers, Doris knocked it from her hand and said, "I can't, I just can't."

Finally they put the picture back because they were getting obsessed with it and falling behind in their homework and it was close to graduation. Every time afterward when they saw popsicles, one of them said, "Lemon!" and they broke up.

Now they laughed as uncontrollably as they had that early summer day in the eighth grade. Their relationship was built of such things. Its roots were in those years, and afterward when they had gone their different ways, they were still part of one another's growing up and loved each other for it. But it had never got past the silly sex talk, signs, signals, and partisanship—something vaguely and conspiratorially "anti-boys."

"It's good to see you again, hey. We shouldn't have drifted apart." Doris nodded.

"So what?" Laurie said. "We'll drift back together."

Doris shook her head a bit sadly. "Toby and Mr. Preston?"

"Look, goony, this isn't feudal England in the Middle Ages, you know."

"I'd be more discombobulated than Toby. He was even embarrassed to see you, now you're Mrs. Preston."

Laurie remembered dating Toby in junior year before easing him off on Doris, who, with some sound advice from Laurie, took care of the rest. If ever there wasn't an embarrassed type!

"Toby embarrassed. That's a picture," Laurie said and they were off again. The picture this time was of Toby, the one taken by the chain-store people and placed in the grocery window when Toby, aged fourteen, was towheaded and smiling. They wheedled a copy of the picture out of the grocer and spent afternoons kissing it. The other girls, five or six of them, took turns kissing the picture of Toby's face. It was after one of those sessions that Doris agreed to renew a game of their earlier childhood with her older brother. Sitting on his lap, her thin little summer dress up to her knees, on the rocker in the backyard where the bees buzzed and the birds sang sleepy in the sun, a game of rocking back and forth and chanting, "Rock the little baby, rock the baby rock her rock her rock rock rock a baby babee—rock rock rock rock!" while the chair squeaked, gaining momentum, and her toes twisted backward around his calves and she pressed her arms close and outside the circle of his arms, his hands clasped hard in front of her, her own tight little fists clenched, held down straight on either side. She had told it to no one but Laurie and asked was it a sin and would she go to hell for it? They had never concealed anything from each other. When Laurie went on her first serious date she reported it to Doris in full detail and Doris worried that Laurie would be pregnant and Laurie became more explicit until Doris had to admit at the age of fourteen she didn't really know what had to happen exactly. Laurie explained and cleared up all the confusion Doris's mother had caused and then loaned her a book on it. By the time they reached high school it was only necessary for one of them to point a finger, raise a shoulder or an eyebrow, for the other to know exactly what was meant. When Doris went into labor, Laurie was at the hospital making the long night shorter for Toby, just as Doris had been the first to see Laurie after her tonsils had been removed when she was ten, and had given her all those books for keeps not for lend, even though they were part of Doris's very own library with her own handmade index cards and the jackets carefully pasted in.

Laurie had even gone to Doris with her first serious love affair, the one with the pianist, but these problems were shared by them somehow as children involved in the torments of an adult world.

"—and if I tried to talk to a man like Mr. Preston I'd die," Doris was saying. "You know I never had your nerve."

They sat in silence and ate their banana splits.

"You're not insulted?" Doris asked.

It hadn't occurred to Laurie to be insulted. "I was just thinking you and Toby are still a couple of half-grown cluckheads," she laughed.

Doris really thought she'd married Ken for his money.

"You're both down with the heat, or all three of you, I should say."

This started them giggling again. But it wasn't the same. Laurie didn't feel like laughing any more. None of the old gang showed up at Stouffer's and in less than an hour or so they left. That's what Doris thought, all right. Married Ken for his money.

At Mary's door, Doris said, "Toby asked me to tell you we've saved up two thousand dollars. A little more, actually. It's in his savings account now. I just didn't know what to get you as a present," she added with embarrassment. "But that's not what Toby asked me to mention." She squirmed uncomfortably in the darkness. "You know he never gambles and we're looking to buy a larger house. We'll need more room now. Firemen hardly ever get bonuses except for losing an arm or a leg practically. So if you hear of something, a stock, you know, if you thought it was all right, we'd like to take a chance. I told him to ask you himself but—" She trailed off.

"Sure. Any bargains on Fort Knox, I'll send you a night letter."

She still liked Doris. They could still giggle together and Doris was glad for her, but why couldn't she of all people understand? Or maybe it was just hashing up how she'd been ugly before high school, and the small, hidden scar it left way inside where she continued grateful for any attention, vulnerable to the type of male who naturally had his pick of natural beauties and her naked defenselessness when one of them assumed she had always been in that category. Even the years that followed and the specific pursuing males hadn't cured it, hadn't quite taken the overeager fear of being left in spite of her readiness to take life and demand it. Until Ken. Yes, Ken had made her believe in herself. There had been one time before in her life when she couldn't make contact with Doris. That was when her childhood had seemed a fairy story cut off and beyond recapture, the brief nightmare time of disorder and confusion when out of wanton rebellion the slightest accident could have made her a whore or hophead, anything at all, or could simply have driven her to follow sister Helen's example. When Laurie's breasts had first ripened to full splendor she and Doris had admired them and then, feeling silly, had painted faces of pigs on her breasts with their lipstick and Laurie recited, "This little piggy went to market, this little piggy stayed home." Only four years later, in the dressing room at the Esquire Club, the line girls had played the same game and one of her recent, haphazardly chosen boy friends had watched at the door and made her do it for him afterward when they were alone. It marked the point of factual removal from Doris, for this little pig or that big swine in a home or a house were all at the market on display in such self-disgust and shame and confusion that she could find no way to laugh at it or share it or escape it.

Now it was as though the terrible interval she had never discussed with Doris had been known to Doris all along and she judged Laurie and her marriage in the light of it. They could never drift together again.

Laurie saw the light on in the kitchen and went in.

Tom was at the table, eating pretzels and reading.

"You still up?"

"Don't I look it?"

"What're you reading?"

"*Mysticism and Logic.*"

"God, what's that?" She leaned over his shoulder to take a pretzel and read: "There is first the belief in insight as against a discursive analytic knowledge: The belief in a way of wisdom, sudden, penetrating, coercive which is contrasted with—"

"It's Bertrand Russell," Tom said. "And you should never start reading in the middle."

"Way beyond me."

"He wrote that by 1917. It's just coming into its own."

"Now that you're here to claim it?"

"What's impossible about that?"

"Nothing but you. Where's Mom?"

"Sleeping, I hope. Was that Doris?"

"Yes. She sends her regards."

"Mm—m."

"And thank *you* too."

"When did you last have anything in common with Doris?"

"We'll always have things in common." Her eyes were angry.

He shrugged and returned to reading Bertrand Russell.

She saw the light go out in Mary's room as she was halfway up the stairs. She frowned. Doris thinking that! It made her forget whatever it was about Mary that puzzled her. That's all it was. Afraid to meet Ken, my eye. She thought I married him for his money. An ancient bag of gold. That's what she thought, all right. And what does that make me?

The next day the temperature reached 100 and Mary decided at the last moment not to go into Manhattan with them. It would have meant closing the store because the two regulars were on vacation and one relief girl was sick from the heat while the other's bewilderment over the cash register was even worse than her own. They would return on the 5:49 and she would pick them up at the station.

In the Visitors' Gallery at Eleven Wall Street all that Laurie and Tom could see below were frequent sailings of paper planes made out of order slips flying from one end of the Floor to the other. A group trailed one man. He had a sign on his back. It read, "Hit me. I love it," and the other Floor men were doing so till he removed his jacket and crumpled up the paper sign into a small ball. Once there was a loud shouting. They couldn't make out why. Soon after, several hundred of them began beating a rumba rhythm on the booths and posts. The guide explained this was their way of showing displeasure at the event that caused them to shout earlier. The quarterly statement of a certain distillery company had been announced on the broad tape along with the news that they had invested their profits in a new rum factory, instead of raising the dividend as expected.

McBride welcomed them at the exit and Tom said, "It's all pretty childish."

"Tom!"

McBride smiled. "Just intermission time, chum. Come back in about two, three weeks and tell me how it strikes you."

"I think we'll go up and thank Mr. Coogan now," Laurie said. "I know you have to get back to the Floor."

"What for? How about a cool drink?"

"No, really. Thanks a lot."

He nodded, grinning.

Tom said, "It's one-forty-five. We have four hours and I'm going up to see the Sound and Light Exhibit." He had explained it to her on the way in from Long Island. It was at Grand Central. She said she couldn't care less but if he wanted to, they could meet on the lower level at Penn Station at five-thirty. She had said it to shut him up but now he reminded her that she'd said so. McBride listened, still grinning.

Tom went to the IRT, McBride returned to the Floor, and Laurie went up to see Coogan. He wore a black silk jacket and white paper cuffs as he led her around their offices. Somehow the customers' room gave a stronger impression of action than the actual thing it reflected downstairs. Maybe it was because she could hear them giving orders and the fact that the tape dominated everything in the small room. He showed her Ken's office. "It sure is waiting for him." Then he offered her a Coke.

"Now tell me. How is Ken?"

"Fine."

"I'm more than a little mad at him. I've written him four times. He hasn't even answered."

He caught her surprise.

"I suppose he's thinking it over," she said.

"If he has some other idea, why doesn't he put it on the table? We can't sit with the doors open and no merchandise. Not after WHIP. You know about that?"

She nodded.

"It was a big one. Our share was nothing like what most people imagine but it was big and it was ours. Now we have to move on. How long can he just do nothing?"

He patted her hand.

"I know. I understand. A man like Ken marries only once. Believe me, I don't want to intrude but even in young love, after six months a normal, healthy person just plain has to do *something*. Now you look like someone who needs to mingle with people and enjoys keeping busy."

He saw it register and she saw him see it.

"Yes." She met his eyes. "I do like people and I certainly like to have work to do."

"Of course you do. You're a young, healthy girl. It's natural. Now it's almost four months. It's not that you don't love him and don't enjoy being with him but you're bound to get a little restless, now isn't that right? The time to get to work is before that happens. For you of course that's something different than what it is for Ken. He's a man. He has a profession and obligations."

"If he doesn't want to do anything, I don't see that he's obligated to anyone."

"My dear Laurie—may I call you Laurie?"

She nodded.

"Fine, and you call me Pat. He's obligated to *himself*. I'm a simple soul but Ken is complicated. A contradictory man with very high standards. That's why it took him so long to marry. You've been with him and love him. So you know. He's no loafer. He never was. A man who has to find the roots of things. With his bold, active mind—" He laughed. "McBride is something else. All he needs is activity. I'm talking about *action*. First place, Mac has more money than he ever dreamed of. Second place, he wants to keep on the move and drink and think he's enjoying it. One of these days I suppose he'll quit, put it all into tax-free municipals and drink himself to death, or just get so restless he'll gamble and lose it all. But Ken. I'll be perfectly frank. At first I thought it was you. But I know now that's not so." He smiled. "I have some impression Ken isn't even sure he wants to come back to the Street. It's not like him to ignore my letters and let almost four months go by without a plan." He looked out the window. "He had other plans for himself as a boy. Who of us didn't? Something about early American history." He turned back. "When you try to recapture a dream you usually break your heart. His real world is waiting for him right here. With every reward any man could dare hope for. A chance to make his own history. Besides, you get a good inflation and his million won't be worth more than half, maybe less. The German mark was worth twenty-five cents once and the Germans wound up papering their walls with them." He smiled again. "You one of those people who hates money on principle?"

"No, I don't hate money. It just doesn't mean that much to me."

He nodded. "Still there are many things. You'll see. Fine paintings. A nice home, works of art, donating to civic activities you believe in. Entertaining the kind of people you like, leaving something behind. There'll be children, God willing. But the real point is the challenge. This is a new era. Most people don't even suspect it exists. But Ken sees it plain as your face, plainer than I ever will though I hate to admit it." He smiled again. "You disapprove of Wall Street?"

"I don't know anything about it. I suppose I always thought of it as a place for people with plenty of money who gambled and made lots more."

He smiled. "Some start with nothing. I did. Others with fortunes go

broke, like Ken's father. Those of us who work at it aren't gamblers
and Ken is the least gambling man I know. Oh, I don't mean he's a
coward. But he has to reduce everything to graphs and charts, you
know." He was smiling again. "I sometimes wonder whether he doesn't
look at the sunrise and break its mystery down to facts and figures.
He's smart. I admire him and I know he's got to get moving. It's a
great relief to know he's married to a level-headed girl like you. Well."
He rose. "I certainly didn't intend to go into all this but I've been
sitting here watching the months go by and naturally with time running
very, very short, it's begun to bother me. Credit will be easy right
after Labor Day. That's a fact now. You might tell Ken that. I hope
you don't think I've been unfair?"

"No," she said. "I can't say I really do."

They chatted a few minutes longer. When he opened the door,
McBride was waiting outside. He told Coogan he was calling it a day.

Coogan nodded.

"When's Ken coming back?" McBride asked bluntly.

Coogan merely shrugged and smiled.

McBride addressed Laurie. "I've got an air-conditioned car downstairs and I'm headed uptown. Like a lift?"

"No, thanks. I'm not sure what I'll do."

He waited till she left and went down in the elevator with her.
Outside the sun slapped her face like an angry hand. She tried to
imagine the soft rain on the lake at St. Terese, the need for a sweater,
the invigorating wind, and the welcome crackling of logs in the fireplace.

"My car's right here."

"All right, thank you," she said. "I think I'll go to Bonwit's."

The car was a blessed relief, cool and fast. He had tuned in on a
radio station with commercials only on the half-hour. Soft and easy
dance music came through. He gave her a cigarette and said, "If you'd
like a Tom Collins just press that gadget next to the glove compartment."

She did, mostly to see what happened. There was a small bar, drinks
ready. All she had to do was pour.

"Some deal, eh? I bought it right after we hit our home run last
April."

It was the first time she had felt comfortable since waking that
morning. "Weren't you supposed to take two months' vacation?"

"Yeah. I bought a piece of property on the Sound and we're building.
We were going to spend time kibitzing the contractor and then go to
the Coast and maybe Canada. But I had it after three weeks. Anyway
I didn't want all of us out in space if the market started to go."

It made her feel apologetic.

"I don't mind," he said. "If you know how, you can buy all the things you want right here in this city."

There was just enough left for one drink each. When they reached Bonwit's he stopped, looked at his watch, and said, "I have two-ten. You'll be finished in there in half an hour. That leaves three hours in which you can roast to death."

"It's all right."

"I have a date at the gym at five. We can have one more tall drink where it's cool."

She could see the heat waves rising from the sidewalk and the pasty, tired faces, the droopy, wilted clothes. It *did* seem senseless. What she really should have done was make Tom take an earlier train. Then they could have gone to Mary's store where it was cool, or to the beach. Well—

"All right. I suppose so. I'll come back to Bonwit's later."

Chapter 11

THE Carlton Cocktail Lounge was cool, the music was silky soft, the cucumbers were crisp, and the gin dry. Everyone looked unhurried, unsticky, and refreshed. The city was a reasonable, exciting place again. Two more Tom Collinses had pleasantly surrounded her in a carefree, swimmy haze. It felt good in all that half-lit, almost chilling cool to have the warmth of another body close up on the dance floor. Too close. Too hazy. Just a minute, hazy Mazie. A rumba. She pulled back and wiggled her right hand in his to break the palm-close pressure.

"Let's stop," she said. "I just feel like waltzes."

On the way back to the table, Mac looked off suddenly with a frown, and then relaxed again. "How about that? Thought I saw my wife with another man!" He laughed. "I wouldn't want to wreck this joint on such a hot day."

"Why make assumptions? You're here with me and it's not sinister."

"That's different. I'm a man," he answered. "Besides, anything that's mine has got to be the best. And once it's mine, it is, believe me."

"That's too farfetched for me."

"Go on. I'm the easiest fella to figure you'll ever know. Get all the fun you can, when and where you can. The story of my life. They're playing waltzes again."

She had finished the Tom Collins and it was all hazy again. Not dizzy. Just easy breezy and flowing to the rhythm of the—now wait a minute. Sleazy. She pulled back. He was grinning down.

"You're like me. Dole it out. When I don't want to frighten I just say Mac, dole it out. A hundredth part at a time. Never all at once. When I've made my point I turn it off like tapping a wine barrel."

What was he going on and on about?

"You're talking in circles again," she said.

The gin and the orchestra and her head were talking in circles too. Round and round. Buzz buzz and fuzz fuzz. Round and round and I remember it was in the bleak—he was close again. She pulled back and looked at him.

"Too close?" he asked.

"Much."

The music stopped. When they were back at their table, he ordered two more drinks.

"None for me, thanks. I'm not used to it."

"Much."

"Much too much. But not as a rule."

"Celebrating?"

"Just trying to stay cool."

"How are you doing?"

"Fine, thanks. Cold, in fact."

"Why, sure." He eyed her, still grinning but with some added dimension of amusement. "Doling it out. Just like me. But at my age it comes in longer strides, you know. I'm thirty-five. Almost old enough to be your father if you were say ten or eleven." He laughed and raised his glass to her. "Here's to rolling adjustment."

"What's that?"

"Rolling adjustment. Sounds like a lot of things, don't it? What the Washington boys call business when it goes bad in easy stages. Step by step. Like distributorships. TV and hi fi that are overpriced and sell mostly on installment." He laughed. "That rolling adjustment is busting our mutual friend's business wide open."

"Who's that?"

"Our mutual friend. Victim of the rolling adjustment. He's a customer of one of my buddies on the Floor. Wallie is who-is-that. You know Wallie?"

She took a slow sip. "I wasn't aware you knew him."

"But I was aware you knew him. Mutual friends. Dole it out. That's my method."

"I don't know him any more."

He grinned. "I know you don't know him any more. Dance?"

"No, thanks."

"I told a pal of mine why Dale Carnegie is all wet, washed up. The real answer on how to make friends and influence people is just don't ever lose your money."

"I think it's time for me to go now."

"Still over an hour and it's hotter than hell out there and you're cool in here. Remember you told me? Practically cold, you said. Like me. Now don't get sore. I was only kidding. You know I know someone who knew Wallie's wife, while Wallie knew you. I still know the friend and he still knows Wallie's wife and poor Wallie doesn't even know it yet. Thought you'd be interested."

"We've been under some serious misunderstanding since we first met. I'm leaving."

"Little old Mac is never under anything. First, last, and always on top. Have another drink?"

"You must be deaf as well as dumb. I said I'm leaving. And I want to tell you about this undertone—"

"Undercurrent, undercurrent."

"Undertone. If my husband is to work with you and I'm to see you, we might as well get it all straight."

"All straight, Mrs. Preston and Company, is how I like it."

"You're a good dancer. I thought you were a gentleman. I had time to kill. It's a hot day. It's cool here. And that's that. Period. Do you understand?"

"Perfect."

"No, I see you don't. Perhaps if I tell Ken, he might help you to. While he's making up his mind what to do about the business."

"Rough player, huh? All right. What am I doing that's wrong?"

"Just about everything."

"I told you I was only kidding. So teach me."

"What? Manners? That's impossible. You're too old. Or recognizing the signs when you're drawing a blank? You're too conceited."

"Look, I just mentioned a mutual friend so you could place me."

"That's what I'm trying to do. Place you. Way far away where you belong. I love my husband."

He was grinning again.

"Mr. McBride, I'll say it once more before I leave. I love my husband."

He raised his hands, palms up. "So do I. So does Coogan. So do all the old fogies at the banks and insurance companies and all our old-line customers. I know a fella sells male-female perfumes. He loves broken-down Hungarian princesses and syphilitic Italian counts who give testimonials he uses in high-priced ads."

She rose. He did too.

"O.K. That's how you want it. You love your husband. So what happens next?"

"I leave." She picked up her purse.

"Come on. Don't overplay the climax. I approve climax. I go for it. But why overdo it?"

"I think perhaps I'd better tell my husband."

As she walked off, he was still standing. And he was still grinning.

The fan had broken down on the Long Island train and breathing was a precarious undertaking. Laurie had the window open and her head out. The cinders and heat didn't help. She turned away from it and looked down at Tom's book: "In introspection we seem to be immediately aware of varying complexes consisting of objects in various cognitive and conative relations to ourselves."

"What are you reading now?"

"Same book. I told you not to start in the middle."

He looked up. "Holy cow, do you smell of gin! Better buy some chlorophyll gum at the station. You're getting like Mom."

"Thanks for telling me. I had four hours to kill in that dirty furnace waiting for you so I cooled off. Is that Pop's latest flash from the front? Mom doesn't even drink beer."

"Take a look in her bedroom closet if you believe that. That big redhead cooled off too, didn't he?"

She wanted to box his ears.

"I know each time the silent generation opens its big mouth it's supposed to put both feet in it, space shoes and all. But not today, hey. Don't exaggerate your so-called role in history."

He smiled. "You sound like something sired by Mickey Spillane and raised by Sartre. It must be the alcohol or your new social standing. It releases and inhibits you at the same time. That's an interesting kind of reaction."

"Ye gods." She turned back to the window. Then she forced herself to speak to him again. "You just made that up about Mom to sound smart, didn't you?"

"No. She's a lush. Solitary drinker."

"What proof have you got? And don't be so God damned detached. She's your mother."

"I can count the empty bottles in her bedroom closet, can't I?" He returned to his book. Then he looked up. "I'm supposed to tell you to write to Pop."

"You can tell your father to write to me first." She preferred the open window after all.

"Why does your kind of person get that upset about family?"

"What kind of person is that?"

He ignored it.

"You know you're growing up to be some kind of a monster," she said.

"You think so? I don't know."

"You have contempt for love and hate, even for simple affection and respect. You're becoming a monster all right."

"Each of us has a right to support till we can support ourselves and this society makes it the burden of parents. What has that to do with hate or love or even respect?"

"And what do you do about Mass and Confession?"

"I go. Why argue? The Holy Trinity—Daddy-O, J.C., and the Spook.

It's all part of the arrangement. Just write to him. What difference can it make?"

"I told you. If he wants to hear from me, let him write first."

"It's not his idea, it's Mom's. He's much too angry."

"Oh, is he!"

"Look, he's just a simple soul who still keeps Notre Dame scores. I observe phenomena. He judges. He's a moral dinosaur." He shrugged and returned to his book.

"Now that we've entered this high-level conversation, please don't stop."

"Ugh. That gin smell. I've half a spearmint. You want?"

"No, thanks. What is your father so incensed about? What is this moral outrage bit?"

"You knew he'd be wild when he heard you married an aging, coupon-clipping gloop. I suppose fundamentally that's why you did it."

"You'd better stick to your algebra or very soon I'll stop playing big sister."

"You returned to the subject, I didn't. All I said was I don't judge you, and Pop feels it's his duty to. You don't have to work up adrenalin in this heat because of your childhood reflexes. And don't embroil me in it." He rose and moved over to sit down alone across the aisle.

The train arrived on time and Mary was not at the station. Paul was and they took his cab home.

"I hear you're in for congratulations," Paul said.

"Thank you."

"Big Wall Street man. Sure glad for you."

When they reached home, Laurie told Tom to go upstairs. He refused.

"Go work out an equation. I want to talk to your mother."

"Please don't give me orders."

"Now what happened between you two?"

"Go upstairs, you snot nose, or I'll put your head through this wall!"

"Go on, Tom," Mary pleaded hastily. "Please."

He mumbled, "Hysterical female," and ambled out.

Laurie washed her face at the kitchen sink and dried it with a dish towel.

"For goodness' sake, what happened? I was sure the train would be late." She stopped helplessly and began again. "I know Tom's very hard to take. It's his age and trying to be smart in all this heat."

"Tom says you're becoming a lush. Are you?"

"I don't think you have the right to talk that way to me."

"Is that supposed to be an answer?"

Mary turned to the stove and lowered the flame under the coffeepot. "So now you're a drunk. Well, that's peachy."

"I'm not a drunkard. None of us is perfect."

"What does that mean?"

"It means none of us is perfect, that's all."

"I know none of us is perfect but don't you have any more sense than to drink with that kid in the house?"

"When Helen got stuck on that woman teacher and did what she did—well, it comes back to me sometimes and maybe I take a drink now and then."

"Why should it make you drink? That was Pa's fault."

"Even if it was, it makes me take a drink now and then."

"There's no use looking back, Ma, you know that."

"Yes, I know that. But we all do, don't we?"

"What does that mean?"

"It means none of us is perfect and we all look back whether it's our fault or not and Helen wasn't your father's fault. She was mine." She walked across to the closet for cups and saucers. "God knows he isn't much and maybe that's why I picked him. But Helen was my fault."

"Now look, Ma, I mean that's plain silly. It's stupid. For God's sake, take off your hair shirt. It's Pa's fault, we both know that and Tom's being snotty is Pa's fault too. Now just how do you figure that Helen is your fault? Tell me, how do you figure that?"

"A lot of things are my fault," Mary answered. She put down the cups and saucers and turned her head away.

"Why did you give Wallie my number?" Laurie asked.

"Laurie, you know I can't follow you when your mind jumps that way."

"Nothing's jumping. I asked you a question. Why did you do it? Giving that bastard my number. Why?"

"He knew you were at Lake St. Terese anyway and he also knew your husband's name. What difference could it make?"

"You did it for the same reason you won't take my money, isn't that so?"

Mary sighed. "I'm sorry, Laurie, I can't follow you."

"Don't follow me. Just answer my question. Why don't you want my money? You took it in the past."

"I told you why." She turned off the flame under the coffee.

"No. I thought you told me but you didn't tell me. So tell me now. Why?"

"Really, Laurie. Must we? In all this heat?" She poured the coffee. "I'm just a simple soul—"

"Look, I'm up to my chin in simple souls. What I need now is an honest one. Somebody who can answer a simple question with a simple answer. It's not that hot and neither of us is that drunk so I'll ask it again. My husband and I offered you money. You can use the money. Why won't you take it?"

"I don't need any money."

"That never stopped you from taking it before or sending me out to earn it. What's new?"

"Drink your coffee."

"I don't want any God damned coffee. I want an answer to my question."

"I'm trying to make do without taking money from my own husband now."

"Because you detest and despise him, because it humiliates you, because you don't love him."

"I guess that's right."

"I don't detest and despise my husband. It doesn't humiliate me." She nodded. "You don't believe me. You don't believe I didn't know he had money when I married him. You don't believe I meant what I said about him before I married him or that it's changed the way I said it's changed. Isn't that right?"

"It's no use arguing with you when you're this way, Laurie."

"I'm not arguing. I'm asking questions. Wallie's money was all right because at least that was love and he's our kind of lug, only lucky. That's what you believe, isn't it?"

"Laurie, I don't know what happened today or what you want me to say—"

"Nothing happened today and I don't give a damn what you say. All I'm trying to do is get an answer. You think my husband's a middle-aged sucker in his second childhood and I've organized a well-run, one-woman whorehouse. Answer me!"

"You seem to be asking questions and answering them without me. Why make it so hard on yourself?"

"Yes. That's what you think and Tommy and Doris and her husband as well as Ken's partners and Pop. Any comments?"

Mary looked away.

"Just don't tell yourself you're drowning my shame in your alcohol, that's all."

Laurie went to the phone, called the air line and asked for a reservation on that night's departure for Saranac. There wasn't any. She booked the earliest available flight the next morning and sent a collect wire to Ken to expect her.

"I'm checking into the Riverneck Hotel tonight," she said. She walked out of the kitchen.

"Laurie," Mary said softly. "I want to tell you something."

Laurie didn't stop.

Mary struck the kitchen table with her small closed fist. She struck it so hard the dishes jumped and the coffee spilled. Laurie turned.

"I said I want to tell you something."

Laurie walked back as far as the kitchen door and waited.

"You can tell yourself all kinds of things when you're young. Then all at once you're old and telling yourself doesn't help unless it's the truth." She turned her head so that she could see Laurie. "I don't know whether you love your husband or not. But I know there are worse fathers than yours."

"Really? Under what rocks are they hiding?"

"All he wanted was for you to go to college. He knew you were bright and he wanted you to be prepared. I was against college. I guess I was in a hurry for you. Or for me. I don't know. Your modeling hurt him. And your earning more than he did hurt him too. Not having enough to send you to college hurt him also: and making you and Helen always laugh at him hurt. Like the time he was ashamed to carry all our worn shoes to the shoemaker and I threw them one by one out into the snow and he had to kneel and pick them up. When I told you and Helen about it to make you laugh, you were only fifteen and Helen was thirteen. Such things can hurt a man a lot."

"Well, now, I'll tell you a few things that can hurt a daughter!" Laurie said. "When your sister kills herself and you cry your eyes out for four days while she's unburied so the kids in her class can be at the funeral and you've cried yourself dry. Remember what he said at the funeral? 'You unfeeling bitch!' Unfeeling bitch is what he called me. 'In front of all those people not shedding a single tear,' he said. Do you know that can hurt a daughter? And the conference with the priest afterwards. 'God punished us.' That's what he said. 'Father, God punished us because my older daughter was about to marry a Jew.' Which was a lot of crap in the first place because Sidney didn't mean to marry me. So if that's what you called me back for, I'll leave now."

"No. I said I don't know whether you love your husband. That isn't really true. Let's say I find it hard to believe you love your husband because I don't see how you can."

"I love Ken!" She shouted it.

"How can you? You never learned what love is. I should know. Lord, I should know."

All at once she began to cry. She held both sides of her jaw with her hands to stop the trembling and it made her look almost funny. Laurie walked into the room and stood a small distance from her.

"You ask where are fathers worse than yours? Take mine. The night he died. I was Tommy's age and working. Because Pa was sick and I had to leave school to help out. The only thing I bought for myself was one pair of silk stockings. One pair. My only pair. My older sister, Bertha, had put them on. I could have killed her—I—she—Bertha—she wouldn't take them off, wouldn't give them back. My only pair of silk stockings. I pulled at them and they tore and I shouted something. I don't remember what. 'My God, you ruined my only pair of silk stockings.' Something like that. Then my father was screaming for me to come into his bedroom. He wasn't supposed to get excited. I was worried sick. And there he was sitting up in bed. His face was so red, I can still remember. 'I'm dying while you blaspheme about parading your body in silk stockings,' he said. 'May your soul rot in hell.' Then he died right there. He cursed me and he fell back and died." Her chin stopped trembling. "I know there isn't any hell and he was sick and old-fashioned and I was just a silly kid and it was all long, long ago. But you see, I never forgot. I was glad to be alive. And I hated him. I did want to love him but he just never let me. I think your sister couldn't be glad to be a girl because I never forgot it. I know your father was driven out of his own house by it. Do you see?" She put her small hands quietly on the table. She was biting her lower lip hard. "Do you see?" she repeated.

"I think I do. And I don't know how Ken got through all that but he did. Ken got through to me, Mom. I don't want to tear him down or take him. I don't fear him or resent him or hate him." She held Mary. "I love him."

Mary nodded against her, not believing it. Laurie stayed the night.

It was a bumpy flight back in the two-motored plane, full of head winds and air pockets. The clouds that sat below like pink and white mountain peaks looked solid enough to walk on. The plane descended through them into the rain and was tossed up, down, and sideways. For a while it seemed they wouldn't land at Saranac at all but at some private field in the farmland area seventy miles away. Ken was waiting with her woolen sweater, rubber boots, and heavy raincoat. She leaned her head on his shoulder as they drove to the dock where the Brooks family greeted her warmly. Do they believe that of me too, she wondered. She had been so sick with it she hadn't noticed the unpleasantness of the trip. Now she felt her ears pop and the queasiness in her stomach. Ken's cousin Alicia believed it. She realized the subtle ways it had come out on their trip to Westport. At the time she'd thought of it as a rich cousin condescending to the future wife of a poor one. Coogan was certain of it. It was there in all of them. Did Mr. Sands believe it?

"How's your mother?"

"Fine."

"And your brother?"

"He's too much. The return of Frankenstein. Kept reading something by Bertrand Russell in all that heat. *Mysticism and Logic.* I looked at a paragraph and got dizzy."

He smiled and caressed her head as they got into the boat. The canvas cover was up. It was still raining hard.

"Lord Russell can make anyone dizzy at times. He ridicules the *a priori* assumptions of metaphysics and rejects the claims of dialectical materialism that all things are knowable and yet his own brand of mathematics-bound magic—"

"No," she pleaded. "Not now. To hell with Russell and my brother. I've hated being away. Kiss me again."

He did and the boat raced toward the rocky point and passed it. As they approached their dock, she could see Mr. Sands beaming as he waved his hard straw hat. When he helped her out he said, "Too bad you missed the barn swallows leaving the nest. Major event, as they say."

"Mr. Ken told me." No, not Mr. Sands. He didn't believe it.

"It's nice you're back now," he said.

She felt like crying.

They sat all bundled up and close together on the patio under the awning and had coffee. Then they went for a fast, freezing swim in the rain. Later they sat rubbed dry after stinging hot baths, close to the bright fire. Ken offered her a drink and she refused it.

"Can we get to New York in time for me to enroll in college, do you think?" she asked at dinner.

He looked up with surprise. "Enrollments ended in July, I believe. Perhaps earlier. Aunt Sarah knows people on the Board of Trustees at Columbia. I'll phone her tonight. When did you decide to go to college?"

"It just came to me. You don't think it's silly?"

"No, it's fine. I'm very pleased, in fact. What will you study?"

"You'll have to tell me. I just want to stop being so ignorant. If you go back to the firm, maybe I should enroll in secretarial school and learn shorthand, bookkeeping, and business English so I could help you."

"No, you must study what you want."

"You don't really think it's too late?"

"We'll see. I'll phone Aunt Sarah right after dinner."

"I mean too late for me at my age."

"At twenty-one?" He laughed. "That's a perfect age to start anything."

"Only if your plans allow for it. And if you're really ready to go back to New York."

After dinner they returned to the living room. She picked up the newspaper. It was open to the financial pages. "The Dow Jones averages closed today at 255," she said. "Did I read that right?"

"Yes, they fell to 255."

"Does that mean the bull market isn't coming?"

"No. There was no volume. I think the sell-off is drying up."

"And then comes the bull market?"

"In all likelihood."

"If the Federal Reserve Board eases credit," she said.

Mr. Sands entered with the coffee tray.

"Mr. Coogan asked me to tell you he's certain of easy credit by Labor Day," she went on.

"Mrs. Preston's going to know it all pretty soon," Mr. Sands said, smiling.

When he left, Ken said, "You're really trying to understand about the Street, aren't you?"

"How am I doing?"

"Very well."

"I guess if a pig like McBride can understand it so can I. Which will rise first—the—" she hesitated over the words "—industrials, utilities, or the railroads?"

"Not utilities. They move slowest. And the rails are too depressed by chronic internal difficulties. The industrials will rise first. What happened with McBride?"

"He makes passes. Nothing I can't handle but I resent him thinking I can even know there's another man alive except you."

"That's just Mac's manner."

"I don't like his manner!"

"Are you angry with me again?"

She was seated on the couch, swinging one leg crossed over the other in swift, restless kicks. "No, but Mr. Coogan is. He's very upset about not hearing from you. Polite but very angry."

"I'm planning to write to him tomorrow."

"He says he wrote to you four times and you didn't answer."

"That's true."

She took his hand, pulled him down to the couch, and stretched out with her head in his lap. She was looking backward at the flames. They stayed that way for a while. Mr. Sands appeared to take the coffee tray.

"While I'm remembering, Mr. Ken, when do you figure on dismantling the dock?"

"Must you?" Laurie asked.

"Yes," Ken told her. "It freezes. We have at least four weeks," he told Mr. Sands.

Mr. Sands frowned. "Mebbe. Frost's coming early. A light touch of it on the bushes this morning."

He jerked his head in the direction of the mountain where small patches of yellow dotted the green in the cold curtain of rain. "Four weeks is all right I reckon. We'll have our ice bath then."

Ken nodded. Mr. Sands smiled and left them.

Ken was looking through the great window at the mountain. Laurie raised her head and took his hand.

"It's beautiful," she said.

"Wait till it turns red. Like a fiery bush in Giantland, tinged with orange, gold, and purple. Later on when it snows, pure ice cones hang eight feet long from the evergreens."

"It must be something."

"I'll phone Aunt Sarah now."

She put her head back in his lap. "It can wait. It was just a crazy idea. Wait, hey." She looked up. "Is that when we go back? When you take down the dock?"

"We don't have to."

"I'm sorry I missed the barn swallows."

"Tell me," he asked. "What if I do nothing for a year?"

"It's up to you." She looked back at the fire.

"No, tell me. Suppose I do nothing but stay here or travel or, if you go to school, I go back to school with you for a year. Get my Master's and then teach history in some small-town college where you can continue as a student while I earn my curatorship."

"It's entirely up to you." She sat up. "Ken, don't you honestly feel the need to find something to do now?"

"I believe I have found it in loving you."

"But Ken, darling, we can't just sit around doing nothing but making love. It's not natural. Let's give half our time to it, hey. You know I'd rather help you in your work than do anything else, if it's at all possible. I'd much rather do that than go to school. But we can't become two sticks of dead wood from doing nothing."

"I'm concerned about what we could become from doing the wrong things."

"I fell in love with the man who did whatever it was you were doing before."

No. You fell in love with a man who had just *quit* doing what he did before.

"Your father ran the firm."

"Yes."

"Like Coogan does now."

"If you wish."

"But your father failed. Is that what you're afraid of?"

"I'm not afraid of anything."

"Well, I'm certainly not afraid of how you'll show up in comparison with others."

"You'd like me to be like Coogan?"

"Now, Ken, you're silly. You can't be like Coogan. You'll never be like Coogan. Nothing you do can make you be like Coogan."

"You don't know much about the Street."

"I'm willing to learn." She rose and crossed the room to the bar and poured herself a brandy.

"Wall Street is supposed to be a mirror of the economy, by classic definition discounting events three months in advance. Actually it's a highly respectable gamblers' den with a lot of greedy, spoiled, aggressive, and overprivileged boys dressed up as men. Their handshake is good and they are very proud of that. But the dishonesty is in the very premise of what they do, not how they do it. Some are there for power, others to get rich, and many of them think they are still back at Princeton or Harvard, bucking the line at a football game. Wall Street shapes nothing. It means nothing. For a man who has enough money and no need to prove himself at the expense of others, it's both dull and tiresome. To a man who half understands this economy it is disgusting and parasitic. It's a debasing waste of time. Now, that's Wall Street. If you treat it like anything else, you end up as my father did. I learned that finally."

She lingered over her brandy glass. "Everybody thinks I despise you and I married you for your money. Did you know that?"

"No."

"Do you think I married you for your money?"

He smiled.

"Well, do you think I despise you?"

He continued smiling.

She sipped her drink. "Do you know why they think it?"

"Does it matter?"

"I think so. They can't imagine a twenty-one-year-old kid like me who isn't on your high intellectual plane wanting anything else from a dusty, old-fashioned, 1953 model of the Late George Apley like you except his money. So it matters!"

"What our love is made of is our own business. No one can make it theirs unless we permit it."

"What we do in *bed* is our own business. What we do in the *world* is the world's business. They *make* it their business and we can't stop them, because we live in this world. I don't give a damn what they think about me. Well, yes, I do, but not that much. Only I can't stand what they think about you! If McBride thought you were a man he wouldn't make a pass at me. If Coogan thought you were one he wouldn't try to use me against you. If I were a man and my wife told me about McBride—look—my mother won't take money from me any more because that's what she believes too. Everyone thinks I'm for sale because they think you're no bargain. Aunt Sarah buying you a job. If you don't care at all what anybody thinks, let's just get away from the whole human race. This camp isn't half far enough away. Let's just get where there's nobody at all. Only let's do it. *It.* I don't know what *it* is any more and I don't care just so long as we go ahead and get it done and over with."

She gulped down her brandy.

Ken nodded slowly. "You want me to go back to the firm. That's true, isn't it?"

"Ken, stop torturing it and me and yourself with it. All that's important to me is that you reach a decision. If we're still sitting up here when the snow flies, I'll go out of my mind. Make up your mind like a man and act on it like one. That's all I ask."

"No, that isn't all. You've been asking me from the beginning to go back to the firm."

"Well, if it's that awful, why does everybody else want to wind up there?"

"Because they don't know what it is."

"I don't think *you* know what it is either. How could you? You've been playing second fiddle and rubber stamp and hiding behind research. Well, you told me so yourself. You've never really tried."

"Then it *is* what you want."

"Ken, I never know what you're driving at when you get off on one of those indirect things of yours. O.K. Yes! I think you should go back to the firm and this time take it over—my God, the look on your face. I don't care. That's *just* what I think and I don't give a damn if you lose every cent doing it so long as you take over once and for all and get counted. Now just remember—you asked me."

"And you told me," he said quietly.

"Yes, I told you," she shouted. "How else can I get through to you? You won't rant or bang the table or spit in my face. Oh, I know what you think but does anybody know what you *feel?* Do you?"

She stormed out of the room. At her feet on the patio lay a red leaf. The wind and rain had stopped. She looked up at the trees. As far as she could see, they were all glistening green with only faint touches of yellow. She picked up the leaf. It lay in her palm, perfectly shaped and still. It was red, a small dead maple leaf. The very first one of autumn.

She lay in bed, waiting. She wanted him, wanted him to want her. When he appeared, he was fully dressed, wearing his windbreaker and carrying a storm lamp. She lay, knees up, her covers to her chin, watching.

"I'm not sleepy," he said. It sounded like an inscription on stone. She nodded, scared.

"You want a sedative?"

"No, thank you. I prefer to be awake. I'm taking a walk. Perhaps I'll read. If it gets terribly late, I might sleep downstairs. You don't mind?"

"No, of course not."

He left.

But I do mind. If I lose, him, I'll die. I want to help him by loving him, but loving isn't enough. It is far from enough. When a man like Ken has lived this long that way, trying to help by making it up out of love alone is not enough. You have to *know*. I don't know and there's no one can help me to. There's something else to all this. I know that. But *what?* What is the hidden part? The part he can't talk about. The part that maybe he doesn't even know himself. Just sensing it's there isn't enough. I know the part I see. And I love the part he'll let me see. I love him. But the rest of it, like a world glowing in the dark, is the part that matters now. All I ever see is the tip, the tip of an iceberg. No! That's what he thinks of himself. And that hidden part is the part that's pulling him under. God help me find some way of not wrecking the only thing I've ever wanted. Ken's not a parasite. He's a man who knows how to make up his mind. But he wants something and he's tracking its roots and origins. He can't explain or find it and I don't know what it is. Don't let him get lost and don't let me lose him.

She could see him, shadowed by the swinging, fitful yellow of the lamp as he walked down the road behind Mr. Sands's place. Lucky Mr. Sands. Life made up his mind for him long ago. He had his work and he had to work. He knew his work and he did it every day because he *had* to.

Ken was headed for the thick pines, the cold place behind which was the old, boarded-up house. He was carrying something in his other hand. It was a hammer. He disappeared in the shadows. God help me. God help me to know.

Chapter 12

THE HARD OAK planks crossed one another diagonally over the locked log door. By the rays of the storm lamp he removed the nails. Spiders had used the years to work out intricate designs in corners and from the overhead beams. Mold had formed on the pine woodwork near the warped windows. The inroads of termites had created piles of damp sawdust under the beams. In the fireplace, paper, kindling wood, and logs were still set from that night three years ago, just before Mother had suddenly felt better and said she wished to return to the city. In a sense both Father and Mother had retired to this dark place before returning to the city, seemingly recovered, only to die. He stood for a moment in the center of the room, the storm lamp on the floor. To his left was the long, narrow hallway and sharp drop leading to his childhood bedroom. Past it was the smaller one used by Grandma until she died. To his right the master bedroom Mother and Father used during the early twenties before the new camp had been built. No electricity. Yet Father, who had sat in this very darkness, in that chair facing the lake, had been possessed by light, consumed, scorched, and killed by it. That was after he had "grown strange," as Mr. Sands put it, saying so without embarrassment as though describing an act in nature. How little he or Mother really knew about Father—as little as the people living closest together ever knew about one another. He had vaguely begun to understand that—after the funeral, before he and Mother went to Cuba, when Father's will had been probated and Mother handed him the silver box. "It's yours now," she said, and he had felt something move inside when he shook it.

"There's something inside."

"Yes. He always carried something in it."

Ken had held the box in his palm, reluctant to open it. "Carried what?"

"I don't know. It was his."

Naturally she wouldn't open it. Ken had hesitated, afraid to find out what his father might have treasured all those years. Then he opened it. Inside were locks of hair, soft and golden, tied together with a blue ribbon.

"Why, it's your baby hair," Mother had said. "I never did know where it went to."

They had both stood there, naked with a feeling of never having known Father at all. Then Mother asked if she could have the baby hair.

Each night Father sat with a kerosene lamp and his case of scotch, allowing Mr. Sands to treat it as a normal event, bringing soda and ice; "pulling himself together," Mother called it at first. Later Father ignored the ice and soda, ordered Mr. Sands to leave him alone, and rarely used the lamp. Thereafter he kept the warm glass filled to the brim and sat in that chair, solitary in the darkness, looking out over the lake. It had made him physically ill, liver ill, all in a hurry and from the Nembutals he washed down with it, never more than half awake yet hardly ever asleep. The asbestos they had tacked to the rug near the chair where Father's lighted cigarettes fell constantly was still there. The night Mother pleaded that he return to the new camp, Father had looked at her with the raised eyebrows of a well-prepared, mildly reproving conversationalist and said, "You must surely know it was *you* who destroyed my self-confidence, my dear." Even then—his eyes bloodshot, his hands shaking—he hadn't raised his voice. "By permitting your mother to purchase this house during the Great War and leaving Caleb Island," he pointed out. "And keeping my son from Round Green School," he explained. "Every male Preston went there, you know. That's why he's an outlander. It was a form of infidelity, my dear. The kind the chaps spoke of at the front."

"It's the alcohol talking," Mother said. Finally she permitted the psychiatrist to come and she was told to stay away from him. Ken spent the days and nights with Father, rarely sleeping. Very soon they would decide what was to be done with him. They could of course remove him from the cold room, by force if necessary. The matter would be settled within the next few days. Ken had spent those days and nights in this room. At first Father ignored him, looked through and past him. Then all at once he began to speak. Not to Ken, never once looking at Ken. He spoke of things long past and, one would have thought, forgotten. Trivial things meticulously remembered, beginning usually in the middle of some silently formed idea. "—that walking stick. My father's. Not a strong man. Grandfather outlived him by several years, you know. Father had it made in—yes—on March 17, 1895. The seventeenth. Twelve days past my fourteenth birthday. It was a beautiful stick. Ivory and ebony. At eleven-fifteen in the Charles Street place, in Boston. He held it and pointed it at me." His eyes lit up. "'You'd best know your Latin lessons well from now on, young man,' he said. 'The head of this stick weighs five pounds.' But he never had the natural force of Grandfather. Never. Nor of my son. He was more like me, Father was. Except that Father wouldn't take a chance. Two per cent municipals and streetcar preferred. He lost it all in arbitrage, just the same. That stick was good for me. Best thing that ever happened. The real trouble is my boy. He spent too much time with his mother. It's not his fault. She kept him away from his own kind, except for Cousin Arthur, and he was a bad influence. Yes. She made him that way. He'll never overcome it. Well, what with the firm," he said it almost apologetically, "at the moment, you see, that's my big problem. Perhaps if he'd had a brother. But my wife wanted no more children. She valued her figure too much. Although I had a brother. My business was making money and he had no business. Yet he made more money than I did. 'Because I just leave it alone,' he said. He went over my head to the rest of the family, warned them to stay out of it—" He trailed off.

Then he put on his glasses and looked at Ken for the first time as though he were a person, not his son but someone he vaguely knew— an invited guest perhaps, or at least a stranger who meant him no harm. The fact that Father had acknowledged his presence at last led Ken to say, "Sir, can't we continue this discussion back at the house? It's terribly cold here."

"No, no. Not back at that house." And Father laughed as though a joke had been exchanged between them. He winked and shook his head and took another drink. "Not the other house," he said. Then, still smiling, his manner grown confidential, he tapped the side of his nose. "I have things to unravel. Can't be done around women. Women are unstable, moody. But don't ever let that deceive you. They have other strengths. Yes, women have their own ways. One should never underestimate them. Not at night. That's the time a woman eats your heart away and your manhood too. At night." His tone remained affable and confidential but his eyes had darkened. "Women are night creatures. You don't want to ever forget that. If you have things of moment to see through, stay away from women—especially at night. Oh, they're safe enough and dull enough during the day. Night is the time they come alive." Then he filled his glass again, and just as Ken thought he had lost all contact, Father said, as an important after-thought, "Not my wife, of course. She's never dull. A remarkably stim-ulating lady. She can banish you into the coldest exile in the brightest sun of day with a quip, a smile, or a hug." He nodded, ratifying it as though it were a compliment. Ken could not make his father return to the camp that night.

Remembering it brought back Mother's deathbed reference to the incident with the cat Pinto when he was thirteen. Their only battle-field. That summer Father had taken time off to be with him, probing, evaluating, frowning as he smiled, listening as he spoke, checking up as he made lighthearted proposals befitting the carefree summer hours together. They had returned from the trails and Ken ran ahead to chase Pinto away. When Father said, "What is it, boy? Don't you like Pinto?" Ken, his face pale and his voice trembling, had replied, "I don't like him killing squirrels and chipmunks." "That's his nature." Ken shook his head, rejecting it, and Father's frown deepened. All that summer Ken had watched the squirrels and chipmunks at play, blending into the landscape except for the tips of their tails and the tops of their backs, rushing straight up and down tree trunks, defying gravity and scampering out on a slender branch to the very twig that should have cracked under their weight but miraculously didn't or, suddenly tiring, sitting on the ground munching something, their little eyes darting in all directions and then, at some mysterious signal, dashing off again carefree and curious, seeking what only they knew in their endless freedom. But the moment Pinto descended the back stairs they would vanish and from high in a tree or hidden under the eaves above the cornice of the house their insistent cry would mock Pinto whose bushy tail and reddish eyes gave evidence of his murderous rage. Sometimes Pinto outsmarted them; concealed under the house or lying flat over the space between concrete platform and earth. On bright days he lurked at the boathouse or behind some shrub for hours, crouched and silent. Then one of the rodent families would mourn a member and all would be more cautious. This was the same Pinto who crawled up his trouser leg, slept like a feline angel with paws over its nose, or purred as it settled in his lap. The same tongue that lapped up the warm entrails of his blameless, butchered prey without the excuse of hunger caressed his hand. During the winter months Pinto was docile and mild; it was the joke of the kitchen staff that a mouse could have lived safely in his fur. Everywhere in nature all that summer the same lesson, down to the still cloistered buds of a not yet unfolded daisy growing at the top of a long stem. He had marveled how well covered these stems were with prickly leaves, not sharp enough to hurt the human hand but sufficiently knifelike to ward off insects and bees till the daisy was in full flower. Then the prickly leaves disappeared and its beauty became unprotected prey to the hunger of the insect world for pollen and honey. Why, he had wondered then, were the young and weak protected and misled into false security only to face maturity in a hostile world that defeated them with wanton force or by blind acci-

dent, and if this was not a plan why was it so uniform? How unfortunate it was to grow up, he had thought many, many times. How
wonderful to be forever young and dependent, safe and free to observe
the mystery of it all! At first it had made him appreciate his mother's
decision to keep him at home and he had worked hard with his tutors
to prove he could learn in this familiar place as well as away from it.
Afterward he had questioned the rightness of his mother's scornful,
vivid statements to Father about Round Green School with its "lights
out" rule at eight P.M. even in springtime with shades drawn unnaturally against the still setting sun, evoking the picture of her home-
sick, lonely boy not permitted to phone her, crying his eyes out, a
prisoner actually, and made to feel guilty and weak because of a natural,
loving instinct. All arbitrary rubbish from headmasters, who delighted
in assuring parents that they knew what was best, having done it for
years and years, but not knowing the child himself for more than a
matter of days while the mother who gave it birth and knew its every
nuance was obliged to sit still for it, and pay good money besides, all
on the theory that this brutal deprivation of love "prepared" the boy for
the world and taught it "self-reliance," "community living," and other
rot which failed to meet the simplest test of whether it hurt or helped
his inner security here and now. It might have been true as she said
that such schools were run by money grabbers as joyous over the robbing of one young soul of its freedom or coercing one young boy into
writing letters that dutifully said, "It's grand here, Mummy, and I
wouldn't want to come home for the world," as a missionary was in
winning a native away from paganism by force of arms. And yet one
had to be prepared for what *was*, not for what should be. When he had
spoken to Mother about Pinto and his other disquieting thoughts, she
had said quite cheerfully that the meaning of it was in the process:
each was an offering to all, and all a sacrifice to each. The struggle and
surrender were meaningful only when taken as a whole. The beginning
when you were not yet fit timber to be tested, to triumph or be destroyed, was but a part. *That* was the true preparation.

"If your father does not leave willingly within twenty-four hours,"
the doctor told Ken the next morning, "he will have to be taken by
force."

All that day and far into the night, Father ignored Ken. Then he
looked up and said, as though no time had intervened, "That is what
women are, son. Spiders binding a man with long slender threads.
They can't do otherwise, that's how God made them. Take your mother.
When she ridiculed Round Green School, she was only being true
to her nature. Very eloquent. That's women. She just wanted to hold

on to you. That's all a woman ever wants. Except for one." He repeated it. "Except for one."

He pushed the bottle toward Ken and motioned him to come closer. "Have a nightcap, son." It was going on toward four in the morning. Their breaths could be seen by the light of the lamp. Father rose from the chair, stepped over the fallen blanket, and walked, almost not shuffling, to the cabinet where he fetched another glass. "Ice?"

There wasn't any and Ken said, "No, thanks, Dad. I'll have mine neat."

"Well, drink up, boy."

Father had found a cigar and searched for a taper. There hadn't been a taper in the room for years. "Can't stand sulfur ruining a good cigar." He lit a cigarette instead.

"She was my secretary. In the spring of '13. Just a girl. No family. A very ordinary girl. Nothing at all." His eyes lit up behind the film of Nembutal and alcohol. "Nothing at all. Completely ordinary." He smiled and the outlawed tenderness flooded through from behind the dark curtain, uncreasing his face and firming his mind for a passing moment. "Of course it was out of the question. Things have a beginning and an end as well as a middle. You understand." Then his eyes were clear and his voice was his own as he looked straight at Ken and repeated it. "*You* understand." A current ran through him, leaving a shudder. Then he was void, chilled, like a man electrocuted but still alive and twitching. At last he fell asleep. Ken carried him back to the camp where he was put to bed in the guest room.

The next day when he woke, Ken was sitting beside him. "We came back last night, Dad. Mr. Sands says there's too much frost to heat the old house by fireplace now."

Father whispered, "I need a drink." His hands shook and he bit his lip. Tears welled in his eyes. "God help me, I need a drink." His voice was a hoarse, tortured whisper. Ken gave him a handkerchief and Father kept rubbing his glasses that he held in his hands as the tears ran down his face. "I don't want to die. That's the main difficulty."

He slept again. When he woke he asked for the Bible. He put his left hand on it and swore to Almighty God that if ever he got past this illness and shame he would never drink again. He did get past it— the doctors agreed it was something of a miracle.

They had managed very nicely bringing Father back to New York City in the overnight train, compartments A and B, where the porter showed Ken how you pulled the handle and made two rooms of it.

A month later, Father started on light vermouth with the doctor's reluctant approval. Then followed champagne, sparingly, and Mother said, "See, your father is really well again; he's bargaining and trading over light wines and beer with God Almighty. Or is it the devil? Either way he deals only with principals."

Two weeks later the doctors had to forbid him permanently all forms of alcohol. He began chewing gum, packs and packs of it, incessantly.

Except for the night of the event Father had been preparing himself for all along—his suicide—and Ken's first morning down at 25 Broad Street, the worst of it had been right here in the cold darkness opposite that chair as the best of it had been in New York, afterward, during the false recovery. In his seeming convalescence, Father rambled on in some ways as disconnected as before and yet it was somehow different. Only once had he spoken of the catastrophe and then again as though to a stranger. "I was trying to bring light to South America, you see. The idea of it fascinated me. But this other crowd used it for manipulation and so we lost the faith of the natives." His eyes took on a milky, faraway look. It was the same look he had in the photograph taken when he was still quite young, in Africa, at the end of a kudu hunt. And then, as though still discussing the catastrophe and making you feel that he was, he went on to say, "My father never quite understood things in the same way his father did. Of course, that was a different time. Your great-grandfather Timothy was captain of his own ship, *Silver Box*, at twenty-one. At twenty-seven he was a builder of ships, a shaper of trade and, at thirty-seven, of railroads. When he was forty he recruited and financed one of the first all-Negro regiments out of Massachusetts. He was advising Lincoln when he was forty-two. He wasn't a man, he was a force, a furnace. The sparks flew from him and never cooled off. What was his secret? His journals up at Caleb Island tell you everything and yet, what was it? Have you seen what Dr. Channing wrote in one of the journals? That your great-grandfather was one of the fifteen most remarkable men he'd ever known, along with Emerson, Longfellow, Parkman, and Thoreau; it was written after one of the hunts in November. It was the time and place, the circumstances. In his day you bet on men and he talked to me man to man when he was seventy-seven and I was ten."

He smiled. "Hell, he was a cabin boy at eleven. Went over my composition with me. I had to cut out a couple of pages. He said, 'It's all right to snip and trim, boy, but never cut the balls off a stallion.'"

He laughed. "This bringing of light to South America was his kind of project." His thoughts wandered. "At first there were fiestas, prayers, and incantations in the hills. Witch doctors. Rituals. Cuba was the key. So long as Machado y Morales felt sure of himself, before he went too far with his damned *colecturias*, lotteries. And our crash, of course." Then his thoughts returned to Timothy. "It was very flattering, his talking that way to a boy of ten."

Somehow Father had bridged the years of Great-grandfather's childhood and his own and the catastrophe, treating them all as one. " 'Now, boy, you're pledged,' he said to me. He meant Preston and Company, since I was the oldest and that was the tradition he'd established with my father. So I took over the company." Father lay back pleading with something in the far reaches of his mind, his eyes seeking to find it, and then as at the old house he saw Ken as his son, his only son.

"I wanted to be an explorer," he said. "In the thick wild country where your mother never let me take you. Where mornings banish night. A place where words would get you nothing." His eyes had that same faraway, milky look.

The thick, wild country had lured him in, ravished him, and shaken his reason. As the chart of his delirium rose, the ticker tape on WHIP fell, beginning with the Cuban uprising in 1933, as WHIP dropped from 280 to 240, followed by Machado's answer of *ley de fuga*, taking fathers from children and husbands from wives, to be shot in the back while "trying to escape," down to 220. As others died of hunger, torture, and drowning in the rat-infested Cabana Fortress, down to 200. Indignant American newspapermen wrote headline stories: one filed by the correspondent of the *New York Times* landed him in jail —down to 180. Then came the Cuban general strike. 160. The massacre at the Palacio followed by retaliation—150. The sacking, burning, and looting of houses of Porristanos and Machadistos—140—130. Then the fever spread through South America. Violence, conspiracy, attempted *Putsches*. Country after country. 120—115—110. And Father still shuffling about in house slippers, drinking constantly despite the doctor's orders, chewing gum, the wads of it stuck to chairs, paintings, and furniture, sometimes hanging from his chin as he sat half asleep, drooling, his cigarettes burning holes in the rugs, setting fire to wastepaper baskets. Then swiftly the rage ran amuck. The storming of the palace in Havana—90—80—70—60. The panicky exodus of leading executives of WHIP and other American corporations from all points in South America to the safety of New York, Chicago, and Los Angeles. 50—40—30. The slitting of hogs' throats dragged from the palace cellars and chunks of the red, dripping meat eaten by shouting, starving mobs before the statue of ex-President Zayas—29—27—26. At last the night of the desecration of Machado's pornographic theaters, when WHIP stood offered at the bell—25½—no bid.

The subsequent slow restoration of sanity over the years did not matter to the Street until Ken made it matter with the Preston Plan, the end of the Depression debris and, as Coogan was so fond of saying, the beginning of a New Era; the last of the workouts, a relic like bath-tub gin and the dinosaur, worked out twenty years too late to matter to Father, that long ago wiped out, and shortly thereafter dead and buried. The doctors could find nothing. Nothing specific. Not even some definable statement about illness of the mind. When Ken had said to his mother that there surely must be something that someone could do or find, she had answered, "No. Nothing. Your father is dying from that rare, well-named, and incurable Bostonian disease called grandfather-on-the-brain." Thus each in his own way had stood by powerless as they watched him die, so that insurance money could bridge the gap of debt.

The bridge table was still in front of the chair where Mother had last sat, playing solitaire in the summer of 1950. She too had managed nicely in the overnight train back to New York in a double compart-ment A and B where once again a porter explained how you pulled the handle and made two rooms out of it. She too had rallied. Then she too died. Originally when the house was lived in, the bridge table stood near the other window where the shade of trees kept out the noonday sun. Later they would return to it and play caliente gin. The last time they had done so was after some weekend guests had left early. Mother, still hot from defending the work of an obscure Ameri-can artist against the criticism of a popular Spanish one, a house guest, was playing furiously as she mimicked this guest and imitated the way he rolled his black eyes.

"Eet ees not arrt when eet ees so grrim, too grrim. All weeth thee rrocks, thee clouds, and dirtee watair. Thees grray, stoneee beesiness ees not arrt beecause eet ees not beeooty." Father had laughed and won the hand. Ken said, "I never expected you to use prejudice as a substitute for argument," and Father had reproved good-naturedly, saying, "Now, son, the Trumbulls and Days were as staunchly Aboli-tionist as the Prestons." Mother had shuffled the cards and answered, "Of course you're right, son. It was despicable of me. But on bended knee, please don't get sanctimonious. At least not before your Master's degree." He had not felt sanctimonious, only loyal to a memory and a wound he had learned to live around but only barely. Loyal to Mario, who had helped him in the shipping basement with the rat cleaning, all tied up with Muriel, who missed her lunch hour that day waiting outside till it was over. He had told Mother of it. She knew of it. Yet she did not understand at all, as she went on to say, "I have always sympathized with minorities as you may remember," obviously re-ferring to her chairmanship of the local Committee to Free Sacco and Vanzetti and her public denunciation of Governor Fuller, Judge Thayer, and District Attorney Katzmann to the infuriated horror of all Trumbulls, Days, Prestons, and assorted friends with the exception of Ken, Aunt Sarah, and Cousin Arthur. "Hence my concern for talented, civilized Americans," she went on to say, "who are today the smallest, saddest, and most persecuted minority on earth. No doubt that is the reason their art is no longer funny or lyric but stony and grim."

It should not have surprised you. Not after what she said when you were ill with pneumonia following the mad and fruitless search in New York, hatless and coatless in the snow and rain. That was before Mother encouraged your invalidism, when she still tried to make the love itself invalid.

"Sometimes restlessness makes one as sensitive as you only *think* he's in love. Isn't it better to face biologic facts like rational people? Then let me say it. Satisfying oneself in the customary way for a young man is less hurtful to everyone all the way around. I should have thought your father had already told you where and how one finds the—outlets available for that sort of thing."

What did he want here? He did not wish to return to the past, or reopen its pain. He did not want to dust off the labels or the name on that door: Preston & Company. He did not want to return to the Street through the back door or the front! This chamber of darkness, of times and people long past, this place of failure should be torn down. It should never have been opened again.

But it is you who opened it. You are the ghostly moving man, haunting rather than being haunted. With Laurie had come light and sunshine, laughter and hope, energy, hunger, and pride. She restored your right to your body as a place to live in and call your own. If she goads, it is for you, not against you. Then why do you leave her alone to come here? You're a reasonable man. You're sane. Sometimes the things that happen in your head can almost pass for thought. Then think! She loves you. In so many devious ways your unsolved problem makes her position untenable. So she seeks an answer. She turns to you for it. Why not? You're her man, like Helen Morgan's man who'll never know she loves him so what's the difference if I say I'll go away? Now look. Stop it. I know all about you: when you start this figure-eight skating on thin ice I know you best of all. That's part of Mother's little legacy. Only she verbalized with lucid wit and you rip yourself down in silence. Just what do you want? Life. Then take it as you find it. Not so fast. To take it as you find it means finding it acceptable. Otherwise the future is a senseless repetition of the past. But if you don't accept it, what is your choice—your *free* choice? Surely there's no choice without freedom and no freedom without choice. Otherwise what is the sense of understanding the past? Who said there was any? Who but you finds that dusty road back a sensible one? Has anyone ever proven that it makes any sense at all? Once you took it as you found it and as a result it took you. Took you for almost all the life you had. Did *that* make sense? No. But nor does this. You have earned the right to take your time and decide how to spend the rest of your time. In exchange for twenty-one years on the Exchange doing what you despised you have earned that right of free choice. Listen to me. Listen! Free choice is an illusion. No, wait. Believe me. That is a fact no matter how you figure it. Aah, so it's facts again. Well then, facts. Number one: I have the money. Number two: I'm not that old. Number three: I never wanted the Street. Number four: it's clear to me at last why I drifted into it. Really? With your eyes wide open you're still dreaming. Start with simpler facts. You drifted? Yes. That's clear at last. Why? Father pro and con; this way and that. Father breaking your heart while breaking your back. Ho ho and ha ha. Likewise ho hum. You did not *drift*—though flotsam and jetsam you are and oceans away from the starting point. *You* are afflicted with the incurable disease. Great-grandfather on the brain. Yes, you. Amen and so be it. You did not drift into it. You flew! Remember Mother hanging on your coattails trying to bring you to earth as you flew? As late as her death and as early as Father's, in Cuba. That first morning at the cemetery outside Havana when you and Mother had the place to yourselves except for the two beggar children, the old flower woman, skin-and-bone thin, and lastly the man almost toothless, his eyes intensely black and burning, his hair silky, long, and pure white. He wore a straw hat, ripped at the crown, his feet bare, his torn dungarees and red shirt faded as he held one leg out before the other, his long arm outstretched as though commencing some medieval dance with a courtly bow. "Look," Mother had whispered, "the mad prophet." The intensity of his eyes, his grace, and the way the beggar boys teased him had moved Mother to give him a five-dollar bill. He had looked at it in his hand without clutching it, as though it were a sacred bird resting for an instant in a strange place. Then his body sagged and he began to cry. Mother had stared, frightened—her first Cuban. Then she turned and hurried off and you followed her. The beggar boys trailed behind, first in silence and then—the spell broken when Mother blew her nose—they rushed up to her demanding centavos and cigarettes. "Not to worry, señora. He is loco." Both tapped their heads solemnly.

"Don't speak pidgin English to me," she commanded. "*Porqué está enfermo de la mente?*"

The boys had exchanged questioning glances out of dirty faces and shrugged thin shoulders.

"He worked in the sugar, señora," one explained. "Now he has twenty-five years. The sugar cane has taken the tooth and from the sun he is no longer in the head."

The other nodded.

"Only twenty-five years!"

"I have eight years," the first one said. "This one has seven and we would please you to have cigarettes and centavos for each."

She gave them her pack of cigarettes, a dollar apiece, and hurried off. Once again you followed her. Later she said, "No wonder it killed your father. He couldn't profit out of the blood of such people. He was a man of conscience." And at the look on your face, "Oh, don't just sit there like that! What do you know about it?"

Later that evening. The Prado. After a day marked by silence as you visited churches still following her, where old women tapped their heads against cold stone floors, and then you shopped surrounded by beggar children, and bathed luxuriously in well-attended splendor at the Nacional. That night on the Prado, as their boy friends hovered protectively at a distance, young Cuban girls had stopped at the boulevard table, and flashed black eyes, shook long hair tied with red and orange ribbons, sashaying as they sold raffle tickets for their night school. Mother gave them twenty dollars. Then she said, "That small girl, the pretty one? She reminds me of Gertrude something-or-other when she was a girl. My school chum, Gertrude. You remember her?" She had become a serious music student and later a devotee of Mary Baker Eddy or some similar high religious disorder sweeping Boston at the time, Mother chattered on, but no matter. When she was young and terribly talented so that love and the free development of her talent were the obvious goals of her genetic fate, she fell madly in love with her music teacher. "That was before you were born. Or she fell in love with the fact that he believed in her talent and knew how to bring it out at that point. Same thing, really. He was twenty-five years older than she and quite ugly, but she turned Episcopalian heaven and Unitarian earth to get him. Of course he was already married and she paid for it as only what was left of Back Bay could make one pay. Well. After three years of punishment and exile in New York and California, she left him. Why?"

She waited so that you would realize you had not the slightest idea why. "'Because he makes noise when he swallows.' Her exact words! Said it was leave him, go mad, or kill him. Now she knew perfectly well that love was more than a matter of sounds even for a musician and her explanation was idiotic. But deep down where language can't reach, it was still the truth, do you see? She couldn't explain it, not even to herself, and it made no sense at all but she had to accept it because senseless or not, it was true! Talent and love were her fate and now he stood in the way of both." Then she frowned and with her gift for abrupt transition, demanded, "Why are you doing this? Why don't you close the firm?"

"You know the reason."

"Yes, the reason, but what's the *purpose?* Your father paid his debts with his life. Legally his creditors can't take your inheritance in which he was only a life tenant anyway, or my few pennies and the house Mother left me. We can go to Europe. You can study archeology. Become a tutor. Do anything at all that suits you! I'll brush up on my French and Italian. Visit museums or repay Tagore's visit. I could even take up hand-loom weaving. No one with a shred of decency can expect you to do this! You're just not made for it. You're neither a gambler nor a mixer, and you couldn't kill a trapped fly in cold blood! What else is there to it?"

"I can try to make something else out of it."

"*Noblesse oblige* and fiddlesticks. It can't even make something else out of you."

"Mother. Please. Stop it. I'm no longer a boy, I'm a man."

"Is that always the accepted explanation for ruining one's life?"

"I'm a Preston."

"Oh, for God's sake!"

Yes, for God's sake. Father this way and that indeed. Father abdicated and it became *your* opportunity. Call that point one. As for point two: you aren't "that old," we'll let it pass and come to point three. After twenty-one years, you've earned free choice. Which leads to point four. That you know what *it* is. *It,* you idiot, the *it* that Laurie can't define and through all these weeks and months of nights and embraces you have not been able to explain to her. Can you explain *it* to yourself? Name this *it.* You know what you *don't* want but do you know what you *do* want? Unmasked by the rigmarole of words, this is your kudu hunt. So name it. Take your time. Don't rush. Here is your free choice. So please choose. Oh, do. All well and good about the twenty-one years. But nothing has intervened for the past four months. Optimum conditions currently exist, as we statisticians so fondly say, so freely choose and take your time. But put *it* into words now. Perhaps afterward will come deeds. You haven't, you know. That's why she's impatient. Take a month, take three or five or fifty. Do take your time while she sits up there breaking her heart. Just the two of you on an island. Sorry, I have no stop watch; no one does because there is no such thing. But take your time which is of the essence for you're not that young which covers point two. All right? A thousand minutes, shall we say? Well, choose, damn you, you stuffed shirt! You careful, mincing, accurate, impossible, wool-gathering excuse for a man, speak up! We're all waiting. Stand up straight and tall, there's Mommy's good little boy now. Breathe deep the rarefied atmosphere and tell the little girl you like to play with so much what you want to do, there's a dear little soldier. Figure-eighting again on even thinner ice. Watch yourself. She isn't playing house. She is your wife and she loves you. She has a right to ask. Summer is ending. You cannot hide here forever. The city waits. The city without lakes, fish, rising suns or sunsets, borning birds and visibly changing seasons. Even here in a few weeks there will be only ice and if we are still here when the snow flies I'll go out of my mind, she said. Here is your historical inconsistency and no scholarly magazine editor to turn you down.

Recall the plane ride to London? As the other passengers ate or drank, chatted or dozed, and you stared out the window, away from them, apart from them, dimly aware of the plane rising higher, ever higher, more distant from the green growing earth until what only a moment ago was a mile long seemed but a yard long, a foot high, an inch wide, scale-perfect though ever smaller, soon only a foot long, inches high, inevitably growing smaller, then only an inch long, ever higher and knowing that if it continued—this flight Away From—in order to see, to locate design and order, so you had constantly told yourself—to observe in sterile and detached safety, you then admitted —with enough of gravely seeing, enough of quiet, passionless, and isolated skillful seeing, one could at last without warning pass the point of gravity, finally seeing life itself as a dead geometric figure, a ball, and other earths and figures and facts and meteors, brilliant gases, galaxies ever rising, ever seeing, ever more clearly, ever so coldly, so knowing, until all at once with the heat of panic you saw that out there instead of love or longing or living there was left only the Olympian timelessness of brilliantly poisonous radiation and the deadly rising, speeding, chilling distance moving ever farther away and apart from and outside of as the brain grew colder and clearer, ever more remote until the things seen and studied and probed and calculated and analyzed and charted out of all their human, earth-bound nearness vanished into a statistical speck and all that remained on the whirling path to logical madness as a rapidly vanishing speck was *you!*

Laurie is the green earth, the life with purpose. She is your wife. She has a right to ask, the right to know, what you did, what you do, and what you are going to do. Of course *you* never ask. Naturally. Privacy is something to be respected, with respect to which here and now and just between us, did we not ever respect her right to privacy when privately she took the boat and went to town and how far she went to town we'll never know with her checkbook in hand or was it in her wallet which she said was in her pocketbook while all along it sat on her dressing table, staring you in the face along with the sound of the male voice the operator said was her mother while she told you also by phone, not face to face or cheek to cheek but from the privacy of the mainland dock and you listened from the left side of the bed as she told you she had it with her in her pocketbook, as in further respect for her privacy you kept the revealing dock and path lights off so she might be spared the possibility of your clear view of her guilty, anguished face. There's a privacy for two. For better or worse, in sickness, in health.

Listen again. She loves you. She goads you out of love. Not *out* of love, *into* love, *because* of love. With love she goads you. Shall we make it two thousand minutes or three thousand or four? Can this be: *it* is nothing but a childhood wish, a lingering vagueness, a fable of fog and false landings, a youth-time dream outlived and when made concrete by the timely test you don't really *know* what you want to do at all, except relive the wasted years. One can't. So you don't know what you want. Or even whether what you want exists. Know this then: pursuing *it* you will lose what you have to be alone again with all the minutes from here to eternity. So you see. A starting point or a stopping point. Or both. You won't be beguiled into wasting your life doing things you despise, seeking power and money you don't need, or pretending that doing so will make others understand why she loves you.

I do not understand why she loves me. How can anyone else? But I *do* know that doing things I hate will not make it any clearer. It can only destroy whatever there is in me she does love. Whether I can name it or not, I want freedom of choice and I need the freedom to remain uncommitted till I have chosen. But you *have* chosen and if born to be free is neither mystic nor euphemistic, it is equally true that free choice implies cost. You *did* choose. Out of necessity you freely chose. You chose Laurie and let us not suggest that you were rushed —you did not move with headlong haste. You are forty-two. You may feel like twenty-five *but you're forty-two,* and there is another historical inconsistency if such things still interest you. Here is a third: you chose a child; all right then, a girl—a young woman, if you persist. She is twenty-one, half of forty-two, as old as the length of time you wasted, and in her your appetites found freedom, because she alone makes possible this new-found contact with yourself and you alone can testify to the changes that choosing her have wrought. Good God and sweet dreams, at long last you love and are loved and if this very love makes the prospect of tarrying among the polite highwaymen of Eleven Wall Street who use pencils instead of stilettos unthinkable, that is only another historical inconsistency! Now listen and stop being ridiculous.

Your life is a cavalcade of the ridiculous. Listen carefully. You need Laurie as much as you need air. She is more freedom than you ever dreamed of having. Without her you will wither and die. Keep this up and you will *lose* her. Call her innocence ignorance or her ignorance innocence: you love her *and she loves you.* The thing you must do is go back, call Coogan, take hold of your firm as you took her, and for her now firmly take the bull by the horns and that is a lot of bull for any man to take and horns aplenty for any newly wedded husband to seize by the dilemma of the checkbook not in her pocketbook but on the bedroom dresser.

Take over your firm, I said. You know this business in your sleep. In that at least you are typical of your time. When it comes to Know-How you know all the answers. How to buckle down, how to make a buck, how to buck the line, how to line up projects and project a future program of plentiful profits you surely know. You have Know-How all right: so do trained seals, monkeys, and even fleas. But the question is *why.* And know-*why* is a very different matter of which you know damn little but at least this much: Life is here to be lived, waded through, not wasted, and in its fullness is your only freedom. You have chosen. She has already entered your life and you have already entered hers. She would laugh at the word entered. She would repeat the word entered and whisper it and you would feel a wildness that has nothing to do with watching, waiting, or wishing and you would feel an abandon you never knew or hoped to know before, so abandon all hope ye who have entered here for hope is faith while faith is blind belief, which all human history of wars between believers proves is nothing but illusion and the fact that every single human being, cynics included, cannot live without it is simply the rock-bottom inconsistency of all. Some riddles are best left unanswered. The only one that *you* must answer and have answered and can no longer question is that you are happy and whole and human only when you are with her. Laurie is your answer. You are hers and you have found each other. That is your hope, faith, and belief. Must her image of you square with reason? Can *you* state why only her smile, the particular tilt of her nose, and only the feel of her fingers tug at your heart? Explain the wonder of firmness in the miracle of her arms, thighs, and other delights denying category like laughter, tears, and whispered nonsense —inconsistencies all. Yet without them you will perish. You can say there is this and that and I do or do not understand but for all these senseless reasons I love her. Then what can she say except what she has already said as honestly as she can time and time again? Respect became rapture and affection love when tenderness burst into desire, and her need is to see you doing, being, acting. That is the part of you

she sees, the essence of musk smell for her, for Laurie the magical
materials of matehood. The cave man brought home more skins and
carcasses than were needed for dinner and warmth, and tales of heroism
beyond the time span of a dying fire. That's all there is to it. Your time
is up and adolescence is unbecoming indeed to a man past forty.
That is how she needs you. That is how you need her. Now you know
what you must do.

Laurie woke with a start. He was not there and his pillow had not
been slept on. She leaned forward to the window. It was night everywhere but in the east. The lake mist hung unmoving and low. A full-
bodied, clear, melodious bird song came to her across the water from
the uninhabited island. She heard the fish jump and land in soft
splashes. Ripples widened on the surface of the transparent rock-
bottomed stillness. No light shone from the old house. The clock said
five-twenty-two. Smoke curled from the chimney of Mr. Sands's place
and hung on the air, pleasing to the smell as it floated slowly by. She
put on her robe and slippers and went downstairs. A raccoon scurried
off the back porch at the sound of her approach. Mr. Sands had set up
the living-room fireplace but it was still unlit. She put a match to it
and walked through to the kitchen, seeking signs of Ken. Then she
went outside and through the thick dew-wet tree cluster down to the
old house. The oak planks still lay about on the ground. The door was
locked. He wasn't there either. A wild thought sent her running across
the lawn onto the graveled path to the boathouse. Both *Silver Box II*
and the work boat were securely tied in their slips. Overhead the
deserted nests rustled faintly and gave off the beginnings of a crackling,
dried-up sound. She shivered against the cold and walked back to the
path, rubbing her arm where it had been bruised rushing into the
boathouse. Then she saw the light in "Father's workhouse." She started
running and stopped. The surge of anger was followed by relief and
she walked the rest of the way feeling tight in her chest and watery
in her legs. The windows were shielded by tacked-down curtains. She
knelt low at one and looked in. Ken was seated at the desk, reading.
Books were spread out before him, some open, others closed, strips of
paper marking certain pages. The fire had died in the fireplace. For a
moment she hesitated. Then she went back to the main house, brewed
coffee, fried eggs and bacon, buttered toast, squeezed orange juice, and
carried the tray down the path, up the porch, and kicked at the door.
When Ken opened it, he looked at her distantly.
"Hi. Come see the sunrise. It's too much."
She walked in and placed the tray on a small birchwood table built
into the floor. Irrelevantly she noted that the fabrics she'd chosen to

reupholster the chairs suited the room. Then she went to the fireplace and started to shovel the cold ashes to one side.

"I'll do that." His voice had the hoarseness of no sleep and many hours of silence.

"No. You eat. Just pour me coffee."

As the fire began to crackle, he ate; then he walked to the door, opened it, and stood there.

"It's a marvelous morning," he said.

She was beside him. They drank coffee and watched.

"You're up early." He put his hand on her shoulder. He was hers again. There was something blocked off and held away in it but he was hers. When she went back for the tray she saw the titles of the books on the desk. They had to do with corporations and tax law. There was something called Prentice-Hall. A very thick book with the word Moody's on its cover had the most slips of paper sticking out of its sides like pics in the carcass of a mighty bull.

He looked at his watch. It had stopped.

"It's about six-thirty," she said.

"I'll have a quick swim and phone my secretary at home before he leaves for the office. Things I want him to get for me on the outside."

She waited.

"We'll leave here in a week. That will get us in the day after Labor Day." He put his arm around her shoulder. "I'm going back to the Street."

He had been on the phone for the past half-hour, first with his secretary, then with Coogan to whom he gave reassurance he had not rejected the public funds plan—it was simply that for the present he believed it premature and would explain his views in detail next week. She didn't understand his clarification of why the twenty securities he named to Coogan would be first to lead the market in the hedge-hopping buying pattern they both agreed would take place at the beginning. Then Ken told her, "Pat wants to say hello."

She picked up the phone to hear Coogan's pleasant voice say, "Congratulations. I've got to hand it to you. You did the trick and my hat's off to you." She understood that. She understood Coogan believed she, not Ken, was responsible for this decision. She understood Ken believed it too. Whatever happened, she would be responsible.

It gave her no feeling of relief, achievement, or pride. The only thing she felt was fear.

Everything was moving south led by the birds, their batlike silhouettes against the western sky, wings outstretched, swiftly rising and falling. Leaves somersaulted across their lawn and over the pine-needled earth to lie flat up against the side of the house or reach the lake, landing and sailing, pushed by the breeze, their stems upright. The air smell was of burning leaves, hardening earth, and fresh paint on weatherproofed camps and docks. The mountain opposite their big window was ablaze with red and bedecked with bright yellowing maple leaves that put the continuing green of the pines to shame. The sun appeared in splashes of warm gold on the brown tree trunks where it broke through the bushes. Against the silver birches it became a soft, rosy pink. The somber, bullet gray of the lake was spotted at the horizon in broken purplish rectangles, oblongs, and other changing shapes each time the clouds moved over and past the setting sun. At the dock, Mr. Sands had placed their bags in his work boat.

Ken said, "Meet you at Brooks's. We'll follow in *Silver Box*."

Mr. Sands pulled out, half standing at the wheel, steering, raising, and lowering the gas as he allowed for the strong leftward drift of the rising wind. Once past the buoys, he pointed her north against the blow and sped away.

"Let's drive slow so we can see everything," Laurie said.

Ken was looking up at the eaves. The nests were all dust now.

When Ken passed the rocky point, the wind was close at their backs, their own wake dashing over starboard and port sides, striking hard against the windshield, their faces and shoulders. At the far shore, a lone rowboat was struggling, unable to make headway. Lightning streaked once and struck trees somewhere on the top of the mountain in the west. The black clouds were now directly overhead.

"We'd better hurry," Ken said.

The rain came down all at once in a thick sheet. By the time they reached the mainland, it had turned to sleet. The wind howled and the lake convulsed.

"Golly," Laurie said.

He took her arm and they ran up the wooden stairs to the office. He had to pull hard to open the door. Laurie stood inside, her face pressed against the glass while Ken settled up their account for the summer. The hail struck the dock with loud bulletlike sounds and rolled over the lake in a constant barrage like wet stones in an avalanche.

"I wonder what happened to the poor soul in the rowboat," Laurie said when Ken rejoined her.

"I told Mr. Brooks about him. As soon as it subsides, they'll have a look."

A man appeared, running up the stairs; they couldn't see him until he was a few feet away. Ken pushed, the man pulled, and between them they forced the door open.

"Were you in that rowboat?" Ken asked.

"Not me."

It was a caretaker. He was drenched to the skin. "Don't tell me some fool is out there in a rowboat."

"You'd better be going along to dinner, Mr. Ken," Mr. Sands reminded.

"I wish we could find out about the man in the rowboat," Laurie said.

"Not too much time," Mr. Sands told her. He walked off to load the car.

They waited another ten minutes and the storm cleared. The sun spread red just above the lake shore, a long thin line of vanishing color. They could see the rowboat in the cove far off. It pulled out slowly.

"We'd better go now," Ken said.

Mr. Brooks hoped they'd come up for winter skiing. His mother nodded. When Laurie said, "We'll see you next year," the old lady's finely veined, thin hand squeezed hers hard, the bright blue eyes misted swiftly, her wrinkled face broke into an unexpected merry smile, and she said tentatively, "The Lord willing."

Yes, she could be dead by next year. So could Mr. Sands. Laurie walked away quickly to the dock garage. The sight of Mr. Sands vigorously putting their bags into the car trunk reassured her.

"We'll see you after dinner then."

They drove to the country club. The sky had clouded over again, but not with storm. Now it was simply rain, cold, fine, and steady, promising many more dead leaves by tomorrow. Their table faced the big bright blaze in the lobby fireplace. They danced and drank martinis and had an excellent charcoaled steak with Caesar salad.

"You're not very talkative," she said over coffee.

"I'm sorry."

"I hope Mrs. Brooks is alive next year."

"She's said that every year since I was ten. I hope so too."

After dinner they drove to the railway depot where Mr. Sands was waiting. With him was Ralph, the chauffeur for the Stoddards across the lake. The Stoddards had left by car yesterday. Ralph saluted Ken and removed his chauffeur's cap for Laurie.

"Everything all right?" Ken asked him.

"Yes, sir. Mr. Stoddard says it's O.K.—I'll have it at your door tomorrow afternoon, and thanks a lot, Mr. Preston."

Ralph was staying behind to help the Stoddard caretaker close camp. Originally he was to fly back, until Ken had asked Mr. Sands to scout the possibilities of someone willing to drive his car back to New York tomorrow for a fee.

Mr. Sands had already removed their bags from the car trunk and was handing them up to the train porter. Ken planned to complete his work for the conference with Coogan, McBride, Riley, and Caldwell scheduled in their offices tomorrow morning. He hadn't wanted to do it on their last day. He would work tonight while Laurie slept—those were his best work hours anyway, he assured her.

"Well, Mr. Sands," Ken said, "you take good care of yourself. I'd just as soon you hire some town people if the camp needs heavy repairs this winter."

Mr. Sands stood beaming and nodding. Ken knew he'd do no such thing. When Mr. Sands shook Laurie's hand, she leaned forward and kissed his cheek. It was pink and shiny bright.

"You must try to get up for skiing," he told her.

"I don't know how to ski."

"Now you'll learn fast enough with Mr. Ken here to teach you," he said.

She laughed. "We'll see."

The cold rain was black on the gravel. It stirred up agitated puddles and they moved around them carefully on their way to the train.

"Come for Thanksgiving and Christmas," Mr. Sands called after her.

She waved to him and the train started to move. Mr. Sands, his face still blushing and shining with the beads of rain running down it, stood holding his hard straw hat a few inches over his head.

They found their compartment and Ken put his brief case down next to the window. He straightened up suddenly. "My silver box."

"You left it on the dresser. I took it." She removed it from her purse and handed it to him. He dropped it into his jacket pocket. The porter appeared with their bags.

"Compartments A and B to New York? Yes, sir."

"You might open that wall table," Ken said. He explained he would be up during most of the night working. "Do you suppose you could get me a pot of coffee around midnight?"

"Yes, sir, we'll manage that nicely. And let me just show you how you turn that handle. You can make two rooms out of it."

"Thank you," said Ken, cutting him off. "I know how."

TWO

Chapter 1

MAC went to the guest bathroom. If he barged in on her, the outraged outburst would be good for some laughs. But he had other things in mind tonight: like the fact that it was the day after Labor Day and Preston would be back tomorrow. In the beginning, each time he brought home a new pair of those novelty panties, with red hands painted or sewed on, and laid them out on the bed, she was offended, hurt, and humiliated. Later when she wore them it made her resentful and sullen. Her disinterested eyes would stare blankly at the far bedroom wall, and she would always throw them out the very next day. Recently she'd tried to act as though it flattered her. Like hell. He showered, shaved, used a lotion, and whistled a tune: words went silently with the melody. *Rags to riches, hags to bitches, bags to witches, nags and gags and sags and twitches!* She'd do. She had better do. You are staying home, chum, and so she damn well *will* do. The Floor was really rocking today—only one day after Labor Day, and since the big bull market began right after Labor Day two years ago in '53, there hadn't been a day like this one. Man! A crowd, rushing the specialist's post fourteen seconds after a broad tape announcement of a three-for-one split in a blue chip stock this morning, and this joker-broker out front was pushed forward by the others until his head crashed against the post. Really rocking. Concussion. If it was action you wanted, the Floor had it. He stopped whistling. Why all the fuss and feathers? Down to cases, what did any man want? Make enough dough to quit if you felt like it, have a few laughs, kick some guys around, and never get kicked yourself. The furry, fiery feeling that came from a few stiff drinks and get me laid and down to sleep. You got 'em all. So what's with the riches, bitches, witches kick? Why the complaints? Man, you got it all made! Like hell you do, so long as Preston comes back from Shangri-La tomorrow and that's no *mañana.* Two years now since Fancy Dan took front and center so it's forward march as the boss-man, top sergeant quiet Harvard-style gives the orders. At first he'd stayed away so long you practically had to go bring him back. Four months the year of his honeymoon, or was it five? Last year only a couple. This time less than three weeks. It wasn't so much the fact of Ken's being around but the feeling of it, even when he wasn't there. Who the hell needed him and for what? But you couldn't keep him away now. The market was swingin', really swingin', every day, hand over fist. The Indian rope trick and Tarzan's act, with Jack and the Beanstalk thrown in. Thermometer without a top and gaining more altitude every day. From 255 in '53 to 481 and still rising. Who needed him in this market? And who could stand much more of him? How Coogan does it I'll never know but I'm not Coogan and that I do know.

Picture of a wife panting to get laid. Her black hair hanging to her shoulders. Her large brown eyes with that cowlike, expressionless look: that "I'm above it so it isn't happening to me" look, "and I don't really care, so *there!*" Joyland. You know how your ever-lovin' hates it when you walk in this way, without a stitch. Especially when you're that ready: it fascinates her, makes her want to grovel. Then she remembers childhood rules and gets angry and ashamed. Don't tell me again, I know. "*I'm sorry!* I was brought up to believe that a lady is always modest." Who was that lady I saw you with last night? Preston's piece was no graduate from *that* finishing school.

The black lace panties were not on the cover and she was under it. He watched her turn away and light her cigarette. How rude. How crude. How lewd. Nuts to you, my ever-lovin'. Get angry. He smiled. Go on, get sizzling mad: fry. Give me the icy treatment. Tonight I love it. Tonight no favors, just action, any kind or unkind, every kind and plenty of it! Go on, papa's girl—lie stiff. He got in beside her, spreading himself wide, crowding her, and pushed the covers off.

"For heaven's sake, Mac!" She drew the covers back. He bunched the satin at its center, pulled it to his side, and let it slide to the floor.

"Heaven's sake, *what*, ever-lovin'? Strip tease panties look good on you. You lost a little weight around the belly playing tennis this summer. More like you used to be."

He was certain Barbara spoke about him to her girl friends, spoke with disgust, scorn, or indifference. He had gotten closer to barfly pickups with whom he'd spent no more than a disordered hour of his life between wrinkled bed sheets, never to be seen again.

"Mac. Please!"

"Always aim to."

He forced himself on her and held her down with his weight. "Stop wigglin', ever-lovin'. This is your husband calling."

But the sight of the Floor man bumping his head into the post and the sound of cracking bone came back to him. Three for one. *Split!* Wide open split. *Wider.* Split three for one, all for one. The Three

Musketeers. All for the one and only Kenneth Fenimore Preston to
whom the three for one split and news of it leaking to the Floor only
meant a means by which companies diversified ownership into smaller,
less powerful hands and all that bullshit about let's see the balance
sheet and it doesn't necessarily mean an increased dividend and all that
ice water he poured from way upstairs, just as far from the Floor and
the uproar as any man could be. He opened his eyes. Action! God
damn, there's a world full of action, chum. The little old world is spinning with it: just hop on. He tried again, failed again, and blamed it on
Barbara. He was sick of the sight of her. Doing me a real favor. I need
you like I need him. There's real action jumping everywhere. If that's
what you want, go find it. Well, after the first big winning back in '53,
and following the WHIP workout, was the dull, safe period all that
bad? He shut his eyes again, this time so as not to see her. There was
something soothing nice about night-in-night-out easy peanut eating
scotch highball watching boxing, wrestling, football, baseball on TV
and going to sleep early, spending the slow-moving daytime hours
uptown, picking imported fabrics downtown for midtown fittings at
custom-made tailors, massage and flattering sun lamp, fresh air and
the appetites of getting the Long Island house built, opened, and lived
in weekends. Was that bad? Once in a while you went on a bat, tore
off a piece, but staying home, lapping up the gravy was *it*. So she was
content; you were too and you enjoyed looking back at the perilous
times. WHIP and your crazy faith in the judgment of Coogan and
Preston—faith in *yourself*, chum. Still it made you weak just to think
of it, and what might have happened. You violated every rule in the
book, half the Stock Exchange regulations, common sense, sanity, for
Christ's sake, to come out rich! The luck of the Irish. Like winning a
losing war. In that long, long time from May to September of '53, only
two years ago, how often did you tell yourself you would *never* go
through that agony again? So *if*, just *if*, you want action, bear in mind
that you've *had* action and that's a real word of caution, chum, of
which you have had all too few of late. You know what you're like—
how easy it is for you to throw everything on one shake of the dice.
You know, too, don't you, that you almost gambled life itself with
WHIP? So better be good and sure you can go it alone and avoid
temptation. It was easy to stay away from those swinging doors the
summer of '53. There was nothing doing on the Floor and the tape
stood still. It's the bull market now. The big bull market. So it's
different now and what goes up, comes down. But when? Can you
buck those head winds without a policeman? When the bull market
came, right along with it came Ken, your timid, soft-shoe Fancy Dan
himself, right out of nowhere, equipped with wife and all, bucking

head winds on the wing like you never dreamed of! Man, drunk to the gills you wouldn't have dared! And Coogan went right along with the game: figure that out if anyone can. It worked. It still works. Only now it works on you. Not it. He. Preston. Without him all that magic still has you in its spell. The zing and steam, jolt and bolt, bell to bell, toe to toe, tingling your spine, and it's man alive, because that's what life boiled down to. Safety or satisfaction: but just how long can any man get enough of both without spoiling either? Nuts to the safety belt! Screw safety. I can take just so much of safety. Safety stinks. Preston stinks. He stinks to high heaven. To hell with Preston and the Preston prestige, the Preston tradition, the Preston and Company. I have my own tradition. My uncle Jim was on the Street before his father was and my father is bigger than your uncle's mustache.

He opened his eyes. Son of a bitch if she wasn't lying there, reading a magazine, with her bare can high in the air! He slapped it and grinned. "Too sweet to resist, ever-lovin'."

"You hurt me." She was close to tears.

Before she could turn he had pinned her down, bottom side up. "I'll fix it."

"Get away. You're disgusting."

He failed again and he swung to the floor, picked up the blanket, and threw it at her. "Play with yourself," he said. "I'm going to New York."

She huddled under the covers, tearful and frigid. In spite of despising him, she could not stop the process that always took place just when she resented him most. She saw him as a lifeguard diving to save her, a lumberjack felling tall trees, the athlete who won the meet, the steel puddler, and all of them at once. Then she remembered how he sat on his haunches before an open wood fire high up on a hill, stirring bacon with a green branch and testing the coffee by pouring it into the green grass, and long before that, all through childhood, adolescence, and college days, the sound of a horse's hoofs, her cheek close to the stallion's proud throat, her soul singing in happy harmony, and who cared if some homework remained undone? Yet always at the peak of this recaptured, carefree bliss she recalled his contagious laughter when Mac, calling it the story of his life, explained that God had invented the wheelbarrow to teach the Irish how to walk on two feet and it would bring her back to where, who, and what she was, to what *he* was, and the resentment as she stared at him and wondered why this mechanical mating, those stupid, insulting pants, and this soft, collapsing mattress with all the sickening frills had fouled them up. She was convinced if their life weren't this way, he wouldn't be either. Each time she wanted to tell him so. But seeing his sneer and knowing his plans, she would not, could not, give him the satisfaction.

"Suit yourself," she said.

"That I will and God damn well you know it."

His thick neck itched under his collar and his flesh felt prickly. He wriggled his toes inside the big shoes to scratch the dry skin. He was driving the car at a reckless speed. What was the missing gimmick? Well, her for one thing. Her, from top to bottom, or the other way around. Every damn thing about her. Once she was too tight, now she was slack—like driving a car over slippery roads with tires that had lost all traction. He saw the gas station from the corner of one eye, jammed on the brakes, burning rubber, went into fast reverse, and told the attendant to gas it up. He phoned a girl he knew would be home because he'd told her to expect him. Then he'd changed his mind and now had changed it again. What if he hadn't shown up? There was almost as much pleasure in contemplating that as there was in what he had finally decided. Nice girl. Bachelor girl. Batches of snatches in the sleepy city. All you had to do was go and get 'em. Girls, girls, girls. He had another obsession. Oh, he knew it all right, but there was nothing he could do about it. O.K. Say he had three million bucks. If the inflation was what they said it was, the three million was only worth one and a half. Now one day the market collapses. You know it has to and you're in, right up to the ears. So you're clobbered. You lose, say you lose half. Then the value of what's left is only three quarters of a million. But the living scale you're on now demands more than fifty grand a year, and that's what? Seven per cent, the top any dividend could hope to yield. So you have to take chances. You take them. Then there's another stiff sell-off and you're caught. It was full of holes—he knew that but he couldn't stop it nor the sweat it started and the steam it created and the thirst for scotch and dames that went with it.

When he got there, she had almost given up and was ready for an argument. But under her housecoat he saw she still wore the black panties. Trademark.

"Flat tire. Stuck on the road. Had to walk a couple of miles." He tore the housecoat from her without preliminaries.

She smiled skeptically and felt him. "You're damp."

"Just daydreaming."

In the Murphy bed it started again, only this time he didn't even whistle. Two silent tracks with the drumbeat of a head crashing against the post. Three for one! Split! Crash! Smash! One, *rags to riches*, two, *bags to bitches*, three, wham bam and the head beaten into the post again. Knock it off which is what they almost did to that poor bastard's head. You need action, chum. I mean you *need* it. Your own. Altogether your own and no one else's. Now you don't call this waltz time action.

Swing that baton. Change the beat from *oomp*-pa-pa, *oomp*-pa-pa to a high up, far out da-da-da-da- *zoom* ba! da-da-da-da- *zoom* ba! Far out. Far in. And out and in and out and in and Yeah! Yeah, nothing. Something else is eating you, not this. No? What then? Ha! What! Change the beat. Change oh the beat oh, presto change-oh the beat oh—it's time for a change-oh. A damn quick double quick very quick change-oh! *That's* what's eating you. His Majesty Mastermind is returning from the Summer Palace. He and that long-legged piece of ass who has his name and won't stop till she's taken him for all he has and I have had it. Two years ago no one could get her out from under him long enough to put him to work. He's been working everything and everybody ever since, especially me. Calling all the shots. On my back. Not buy and sell orders, just orders like they give a busboy. How and what and when to buy and sell. When it was Coogan and you it was good enough just to have the phone local, and then a correspondent firm, till along came Preston and three years later his bride, and after her the new look and now five branches with wire services, our own clearing, and three other men on the Floor. That was the most direct affront, the least tolerable fact of all. Coogan could send Caldwell or Riley—lawyers, not even members of the firm! —to serve as his proxies. Preston assigned hired hands to cover securities analysts' meetings, bank conferences, underwriters' caucuses. But only partners could work on the Floor. So Hawley, Curtis, and Rourke were partners. They shared the domain of the Floor with you. The fact that they got only five per cent each and their partnerships were nominal and this was a rule not of the firm, but of the New York Stock Exchange, didn't matter. Nor did it help to know that all they did was execute customers' orders, hands without a brain, while he alone handled the firm's trades and the personal ones of Preston, Coogan, and himself. O.K. screwy, but he couldn't help it. There was a man on the Floor who had thirty-five brokers covering every post. They ran thousands of shares each day while he played gin in the smoking room and never handled a trade. From the card table he exercised absolute control over each and every broker, each breath drawn by every last partner! Well, why can't you look at it that way, stupid? You got three mules pulling your wagon for you. What's wrong with that? What's wrong with that is whatever made me try to handle every trade myself, running from post to post until even I, built like a bull, couldn't take it. I'll tell you: here's what's wrong with it. Listen carefully, get the wax out of your donkey ears. That cold-blooded, ice-watered adding machine sitting upstairs pulls the strings and you dance like a puppet is what's wrong with it. *You* are a nominal partner, understand? You're a jerk: in exchange for money, he's taken your balls. That's what's wrong with it.

Preston is eating you. Hating Preston is eating your guts. It's almost a full-time job now, hating Preston. You've got nothing but knots in your belly to show for it, and there'll be rocks in your head pretty soon if you don't watch out. A simple, normal guy like you can go batty from this. That's how it is. You can't laugh at him any more. That happened somewhere along the line. So long as you could sneer, it was O.K. Velvet pants. Blue-blooded blah. Fancy Dan Mastermind big Brain big yock. From the distant days before WHIP, through all those long range positions. Northwest Utilities. Rocky Mountain Light and Power. Technical Engineering. Preston dreamed them up, Coogan finagled financing, you bought them. Then when we sat in those positions for a year, two or three, and from day to day in bread and butter trading down on the Floor, *you* were Boss. *Boss*. Nobody told you. You called them on the Floor. There are no long range positions now. Everything is day to day, and Preston calls them all. In! Out! In! Out! Right face and forward march like a monkey on a string, and bachelor girl had music there to *in out* and music to read by, think, play, sway, and lay by and dancing Preston's piece on the Carlton Cocktail Lounge floor had promised so much two years ago that had come to so little since. You waited too long. You thought you had time. So long as you could laugh at him, you did. Now he's no one you or anyone else can laugh at. Not any more. You're still dancing like a monkey on a string and bachelor girl and all these girls don't have what Preston's chick has. How the hell can you forget about him with his name on the order pad every hour every day Preston & Company *bought*, Preston & Company *sold*, *by* Preston & Company, *for* Preston & Company. Where does the feeling come from that he's paying you back and paying you back for nothing? You're hopping, boy. In out out in *bounce* like a rubber ball! *Dance* like a monkey on a string. In and out. Back and forth. Faster. Out! In! Back. Forth. *Harder* back and forth and tougher and harder and back and forth and in and out and that's it, chum! Out.

He lay on his back, breathing hard, not from pleasure but frustration. "You lost me, honey. Some other time."

He looked her over as he dressed. Pale. Furious. Her face had a startled look. Good thing he closed his eyes sometimes. A pretty broad. But all of a sudden she looked like a rag doll from the chin up. It was the way the eyebrows ran like V's upside down. Turn 'em upside down and they're all kind, any kind, unkind. "Listen," he said. "I don't owe you anything. Why is it always you dames who have to be in the mood? I'm not in the mood."

"You picked a fine time to find out."
"Better late than never. I'll see you."
"Like hell you will!"

Red light again. Red light *still*. Driving in this city is damn near like being on the Floor these days. You stop three times, you start once, and someone else calls all the signals. It would be worth it to run one of these bastards down. A hell of a city. All right, red light, let's go, let's move here! Let's get green and go, man, go. You got it, Buster. That's *my* horn blowing. If I don't blow my horn, who will? So I'm blowing. Me. Francis Xavier McBride. My horn. There's plenty more like Bachelor Girl around. Women. Complaints, demands, airs, and pretensions—strip them down and you'll find conniving cats and dogs with a permanent mating season, what else? Give any one of them an edge and that's all, brother: the sweet talk time is over. That was another thing about Mastermind. Sweet talk. He had it real soft and easy like a woman. Till he got that edge—then murder! Hell with him. It's not I don't like women, I like women. I *want* to like women. But for just how long can you go on liking them when under all the flimflam there never was a woman who didn't hate men and want to keep as many of them as possible under her thumb, hating all of them all the time she needed them. Whores, every last one—no exceptions. That's right, including your own mother. Damn whore, nothing else. Why did she stay with the old man if it wasn't to get her share of Uncle Jim's estate? That's all it was. How many times had you heard the old man bellowing it at her? Staying, clinging, and denying him his rights in the bedroom. Hell with the bedroom, too. First comes clearing your mind. There's plenty more beds you can lay in, but you can lay even money and odds besides there are not plenty more three million buck bundles lying around to lay your hands on! So stay with the subject, chum, and you can reach in your jacket pocket just in case you've lost track of it: you'll find an order pad there. *Preston* & Company. We make more trades in one day than some firms our size do in a week and I'm the boy who makes 'em. So he's made no mistakes so far. At these prices, how many do we need? I'm nobody's rubber ball. When the Preston kind go nuts, they really go. You're taking no more chances, chum, and no more orders, either. End of story.

He stood at the bar and drank bourbon straight. If that slob behind the counter wasn't kidding, this was his seventh double. Double trouble.

The girl beside him was admiring his jacket. Cashmere. May I feel? So soft. So sexy.

"So go blow," he told her. No more chances.

Later he was downtown where Seventh Avenue and Sixth got all screwed up from Fourth Street to Eleventh. The Up and Up Club, haunt of the beat boys and the girls with Italian bobs and one hundred per cent American bubbies. Far out. Really far out. The young, hung, and stung generation. Bearded boys on H, and girls breaking a stick, no filters, while the horns wailed and the walls came tumbling down, way down. Like cars without brakes. No breaks at all, so they kept complaining. Junkies and seniors, freshmen and flips, democracy in action and plenty of it while all these hipsters and hops acted out a ball, blew up a storm higher than kites, feeling no pain. If lightning struck this joint and killed them all, some saint would have a hell of a time selling these spooks that afterlife was a better deal. Christ, the things you found out about in this town if you had a taste for tail! At least he could thank Hawley for that. He owed finding the Up and Up to Hawley in a roundabout way, backwards, actually. Hawley spoke of going there on someone else's recommendation, taking his fiancée with him and then realizing what an awful sort of place it was. "All that beat stuff. Girls who want to pick up with strangers. Thrill at any price. I just grabbed Fay by the hand and out we went."

He was right about that much. What these girls wanted was a thrill at any price. Hawley was just a kid, a college boy. All of these new ones were like that. If it weren't Hawley on the Floor, it would be someone else just like him. Kids learning about the Street in college. Tie that. Who taught them and what did he teach? If a teacher really knew the Street, why wasn't he there himself for the biggest bull market in history? Yet these kids knew the stocks and symbols, all the old forbidden hand signals to order clerks. They could read a balance sheet, chart, or the tape and knew Floor history he had never heard of. Football and track team boys. *Three-for-one split! Hags and rags and—* slow down. I smell a sweet one in the dark. Right near that wall. Hear her rustling. Lone wolf, get ready to howl. Lone wolf was a horse-laugh from the days of the buggy. Lone wolves are getting old-fashioned on the Floor. Can a man of thirty-seven be old-fashioned? Team team team. And all of them absolutely queer for joint accounts. Queer is right. That sweet smell is a boy. Boy! Well, your eyes are getting with it. What with gay boys and bull dikes, and long hairs all equally in the dark, it's a good thing I'm not night blind. Would anyone believe there were that many balled up dames and unballed boys in the world, and all of them right here in one joint? This was better than Saturday night in the good old college days. Take your pick. The tony ones under

twenty-five who could make it only with men pushing forty, falling
now and then for the line of the other pushers, or the wide-eyed ones
under twenty-one. Dark. But he knew the way.

"Hi."

Hi dee hi.

She made room for him at the tiny table.

"Doesn't that horn make you shiver, honey?"

"Phallic."

If you wanted it any darker than this, you'd have to lie down with
a sewer cover over your face. He had drinks and she took whatever it was that made her stay that way. Six, seven, eight. Who do we
appreciate? Who cares? The more drinks the merrier. *There's* a tradition. Holding your drinks. Uncle Jim sure could hold his drinks. Good
old Uncle Jim. Whereas you learned how at college midst the girls
with the soft knockers, he learned how in the office on Pine Street in the
school of hard knocks. Four-thirty A.M. every A.M. in that office so as
not to miss the London and Paris stock market openings. Five o'clock
New York time. From then to the time the bell rang on the Floor, he
sat in his office alone, pouring three fingers of bourbon every fifteen
minutes to race the engine and keep the brain sharp as he arbitraged,
trading dollars for pounds, pounds for francs, francs for marks—and
no easy mark Uncle Jim, who never had a partner in his life. *That's*
tradition. There's always a bull market somewhere in the world, Uncle
Jim said. Smart secret.

"How is it, honey?"

She nuzzled. "The most."

"My car's outside." Dark world's a nice world. Let's see. Yeah.
Pounds, dollars, francs. Very francs. Very laissez faire. Very fair. And
soft, and pretty as she leaned against him quietly. Man, you're half
asleep yourself. You're losing track of trouble. Good old Jim never lost
track. Day and night on the ball. Name, please. Three million bucks.
Profession? Do as you're told. Place? I know my place, God damn it!
His identity leaped forward with a start, jerking his muscles, tingling
his skin, and charged through his limbs. He was suddenly alert with
fear. Francis Xavier McBride, the Floor, my Seat and nobody tells
me! A student in his mid-twenties with a silky beard was trying to
horn in. Everybody trying to horn in. Wail, horn. Phallic as hell, horn.
But don't horn in on me, you snake-hipped creep.

"Beat it, punk, or I'll lean on you."

The indifferent young man moved off.

Mac turned to the girl. "Let's go, honey."

"You lost me," she said. "You goofed. You snored! The right moment's come and gone. I think I want to talk life with a cafeteria bus-

boy. I mean it's just all flesh to you and I can see that now. The bitter."

Whatever she did to stay that way was wearing off. "Let's try again." He did things to her in the dark.

"You have hands," she murmured. "Real hands. Like frying pans. I'm fixed on food. My mouth leads the way. You dig?"

"Yeah, honey, I dig plenty. Little fried eggs, sunny side up."

She giggled and moaned. "Oh God. I'm shivery again. Let's go before you lose me."

They moved through the grunting, circling, sweet, sweat-sick blackness and in the street he saw that she had long blond hair worn in a pony tail and was very young with trusting tired eyes. Her stockings were black and she wore a green wrap-around skirt, flat shoes, and no make-up. The sweater was black, too.

They sped up the East River Drive, across the bridge. Now somehow they were on the Hutchinson Parkway. Baby, it's cold outside and the sky is full of stars. Nice and warm inside. Way inside. He parked the car on a side road but before anything serious could happen a police car went by and he started driving again. The way Preston had spoiled his good luck. If Preston could interfere that much from the Canadian border, what would happen when he got in? Waltz time to radio rumba, hotcha, cha-cha, and last year had been worse than the year before. Now this year—a million or three million—what difference if he felt no different! If it wasn't freedom, what the hell good was it? Only the slack spring and summer of '53 had been a happy time. Not that you liked it slack, you didn't: ask the missus. But there was no good in getting rich if you just kept feeling poorer.

"Where are we going?"

He had forgotten she was there and turned, surprised.

"You a pro?" he asked.

"I like *that*."

"All right. So you're a lousy amateur."

She laughed. There was a gas station up ahead. It was closed. Just past the pumps was a public telephone booth. He stopped the car. They got out. He locked the doors and put the keys in his pocket.

"What gives?"

They were somewhere on the Hutchinson Parkway again. He took her hand. Man, the stars in that sky tonight! Living dangerously.

They walked to the phone booth.

"I don't dig."

"Calling a friend."

She nodded, thinking she understood. He opened the booth, stepped in, sat down, and reached one hand out toward her. "I just want to kiss you in here, honey."

"*Doctor* honey," she corrected. "I'm going to be a Ph.D."

She laughed, came in, and pushed the door closed behind her. When she started to protest, he slapped her face. If a state cop came by with her skirts up and him exposed, *that* would be something. And you don't want to take chances? You don't want to take chances, my foot, chum! My *own* chances. I want to take my own God damn chances! Consummation at last. He kicked the door open with his foot. "Now walk home. It's that way." He pointed. "I still have to call a friend."

She smiled. Joke. She stood outside the booth, waiting. It was cool. She shivered. He shut the door and phoned Coogan. So it was past midnight or one o'clock or two or three o'clock. If it woke Coogan, just too God damn bad.

"Pat? Mac. I want to talk to you and Preston first thing tomorrow morning. No . . . it couldn't. And it can't wait till lunch time tomorrow, either."

He hung up before Coogan could answer. She was standing near the car. "I thought I told you to go home."

She smiled. "I'm hungry," she complained. "And I have kids to tutor at ten o'clock."

He pulled a ten-dollar bill from his pocket and handed it to her. She looked at it, puzzled.

"By the time you get back to town, you'll be hungrier. Sleep's bad for you."

He unlocked the car and got in. She waited on the other side. When he stepped on the gas and left her standing there, the last thing he saw of her in his mirror, she was putting on glasses and looking bewildered. Good pickup. The car, not the broad. Each time he thought of her surprised face starting to smile as though he were kidding and then open-mouthed when she realized too late that he wasn't, he grinned. She might have taken your license number. So? So you can be expelled from the Stock Exchange. You're a member of the fussiest social club there is. Legal, moral, ethical, for Christ's sake, even *fashion* restrictions! They can refuse to admit, they *have* refused to admit anyone who displeases the Exchange or any Member who cares to say so effectively enough to the Board of Governors. Remember the men they kept out for the way they dressed? Even after you were accepted, before air conditioning, when you sweated like a pig on that Floor, you still couldn't take off your jacket. What could they do to a guy for the way he *undressed!* Any broad could write down a license number. She was over eighteen. Probably. You hope. He saw the state cop approach and slowed down to the speed limit and then slower for the toll gate. My *own* chances.

The clock over the booth said four-thirty. Exactly the time Uncle Jim used to get to work. Without partners. It was good enough for Big Jim to support my old lady, Dad's two sisters, their husbands, and Dad till he died. Then Jim's trained nurse took over his home, became his tootsie, and split his estate with Mom and the sisters. Not his fault there was nothing left when my turn came. What the hell has Uncle Jim got to do with it? Proves all women are whores, that's what he's got to do with it. And how to move fast and hold your liquor, that's tradition.

"Hold it."

"Yes?"

"Your change."

"Thanks."

Big Jim could hold his bourbon. So can you. Good training. A three-finger shot every fifteen minutes from four-thirty to ten, all alone most of the time and when the bell rang, there was Uncle Jim on the Floor every trading day from 1907 to 1938 and he never traded a single share, which is overdoing it the other way. Crazy. Everyone is crazy. That's a world-wide tradition. But Big Jim ran his roost—that's the *main* tradition, the only tradition. Jim sat at the head of his own trading table like a king on a throne, lording it over twenty men at the other tables. First time you ever saw Big Jim was in the twenties, when you were a grade school kid: a few days after Al Smith had appeared in the Visitors' Gallery and some nasty bastard hired a runt to come dressed in a diaper, looking enough like Mahatma Gandhi to cause a riot and take the sting out of Al's visit. Uncle Jim carried on about bigotry, raving and ranting from five after nine until nine-fifteen sharp. Then, in his black alpaca coat, frayed and dirty, he descended from his throne, walked the length of the room to his wall safe, shoulders bent by arthritis, his ugly face parallel to the floor like a big crab as he opened the safe with the key that hung from a long gold chain across his vest. He took out the bourbon, poured himself a shot in full view of the trading department, Mom, and a ten-year-old, wide-eyed boy, and swore. You got one hell of a long way to go to be like Jim, you do. Another thing. Jim spent it damn near as fast as he earned it. So remember that one and watch out, chum. That's tradition, too. The last time you saw Big Jim, you had a girl friend on each arm. Remember how Jim eyed them carefully, smacked his lips, said, "Not bad," and called out loud and clear to his head runner, "Joe, get out of that cage and come down here. I want you to take these two bitches on a tour of Wall Street." Those broads had thought he was something! He'd had his day, his lay, and his say, all of them to the full, all of them his way and with no strings attached! When all his juices were drained he was ready and willing to die and that's for me. That's mine. That's how I'll take it. Jim lived to be seventy-five. Who could ask for *more*? Don't know why I got on good old horny Uncle Jim. The state cop had turned south. The toll gate was far behind. I'll take my own chances. The gas pedal was light under his foot. Obliging. If I wanted to, I could press through the God damn floor of the car! But dole it out, chum. Just *dole* it out. Your trademark. If it's action you want, it's action you'll get. But dole it out. Yours. Not his. Not Preston's. I'm nobody's God damn & Company! Not any more.

"Preston residence."

"May I speak with Mrs. Preston, please?"

"Oh, yes, Mr. Preston."

"Hello, Ken?"

"Laurie."

"Ken, why didn't you wake me?"

"You looked too peaceful."

"You should have. If I don't, you must. Every morning."

"All right."

"Know what I'm doing?"

"No, what?"

"I haven't a stitch on and I'm looking out the bedroom window at the boats on the river. It's gorgeous."

"I'm sure."

"There's a bird in our big tree looking back. I think he's impressed."

"Hypnotized."

"Mmm—yes. Hypnotized. Please come home early."

"I'll try."

"God, I miss our lake! Don't you?"

"Yes."

"How soon will you be home?"

"The first possible moment."

"At least two hours before we go to your Aunt Betty's."

"I'll try."

"At *least*. Are you wearing one of your new ties?"

"Yes."

"Which one?"

He looked down and described it. "A bit gaudy but very nice."

"You'll wear it and like it."

"I do like it."

"Then what time will you be home?"

"My conference with the television people starts at three. Rockefeller Plaza. Depends on how soon it ends. What will you do today?"

He heard the quick sigh.

"I'll be busy. There's all the unpacking. My soul is still up at Terese. Next time let's come slower." She laughed. "By car or train, I mean. Did we have to return so soon, Ken?"

"Day after Labor Day and tonight's our date with Aunt Betty."

"Who else will be there?"

"Some of her daughters."

"Say twenty or thirty and their motley mates."

"There seems to be a new crisis about Mansion House at the Rock. Cousin Theodore is leaving."

"So what?"

"Nothing. I'll suggest they tear it down."

She laughed. "They'll love you for that."

"I'm sure."

"*I* love you for it."

"Good."

"I love you for many things."

"Even better."

"Say you love me too, you stinker."

"I love you too, you stinker. And I do love you but I must go now."

"Like fun you do love me. You don't even know what day this is."

"September the seventh, 1955."

"Oh, bother 1955. You're supposed to be the one with a memory. You just don't care any more."

"Wednesday? Our first day back?"

"You should *know*."

"Then tell me. I'm late for a meeting."

"The second anniversary of the first time we ever slept together in New York City."

He laughed and apologized for forgetting. "Happy anniversary," he said.

"*Now* will you come home early?"

"I'll try."

"You won't be late?"

"I hope not."

"Aren't you sure?"

"Yes. I have got to go."

"Ken, next summer let's leave in June and really stay away."

"All right."

"Did you like it at St. Terese this year?"

"Yes. I must go."

"But you will be home early?"

"Yes."

"Promise?"

"I promise."

He hung up and buzzed for his secretary. His new office space still faced out on the Battery with its ships and tugs. It would be nice if she could go about her business: school, planning meals, getting his new ties, whatever else she did, and still stay up there in the bedroom on the second floor looking out at the river whenever he phoned. Hypnotized.

Mr. Sloates entered. He was a Harvard man in his mid-thirties, lean, impersonal, alert, and attentive.

"The information on Lewis Limited, please."

Mr. Sloates left quickly and Ken picked up the Floor phone. He told the order clerk, "Mr. McBride."

Sloates returned and spread the Lewis Limited data on the desk before Ken. Ken read the summary as he held the phone and waited. Then he frowned. "Have Mr. McBride call me the moment he shows up." He nodded to Mr. Sloates and pushed the data toward him. "Tell Mr. Coogan I'm ready when he is."

"I did," Sloates said. "He's waiting."

Ken came from behind the desk. "I'm expecting Mr. Slezak of Midway Bank to call back, and I want Mr. McBride the moment he gets in. We'll be in the main conference room."

"Mr. Coogan said the meeting would be in his office."

Ken paused a moment, nodded, and left.

He walked the long corridor parallel to the new glass-enclosed well for clerks and secretaries. A battery of automatic computers flanked the south wall. He could still smell fresh paint and varnish. This was their latest addition in the past two years since the beginning of the bull market; the last for a while, pending the decision for or against launching Preston Public Funds. Floors thirty to thirty-four were all Preston & Company's now. He paused at the enlarged customers' room. The bell had rung only twenty minutes ago and already the green leather chairs and couches were fully occupied. Customers' men were littering the floor with crumpled up balls of paper from their order pads. Most of the men had suntanned faces. Ken nodded briefly to those who greeted him. For a few minutes he followed the tape racing by. When he saw 400 Lewis Limited trade at 17⅝, he frowned with irritation and turned to leave.

"Mr. Preston?"

It was Laemle, one of their customers' men. "Can I talk to you?" He lowered his voice. "It's about Kirkland."

"Yes, what about him?"

"It's hard to discuss here, Mr. Preston. And it's important."

"Can it wait till noon?"

Laemle looked unhappy. "If it has to."

"It does. Catch me after the meeting."

Ken left and followed the el-shape of the hall past the margin clerks' offices into Coogan's room. Pat's secretary swallowed the hot coffee in her mouth with a gulp and said, "Morning. Good vacation?"

"Fine, thank you, Martha."

"And Mrs. Preston?"

"Excellent. Mr. Coogan busy?"

"No, sir. He's waiting for you. Mr. Caldwell's still with him."

Ken had left Pat with Caldwell half an hour ago. Coogan raised one hand in greeting as he listened to Caldwell, who nodded to Ken, and continued, "So this British judge, his first day on the bench, realizes the case of the Crown against the little Limey is for buggery. This gives him the jitters. He recesses Court for ten minutes to think it over, paces the corridor, and he's lucky enough to find the most experienced judge sitting in chambers, wig on the table while he smokes a cigar. 'My lord,' he says, 'I should appreciate your generosity.' 'Certainly. Anything I can do, my boy.' 'What does your lordship give for sodomy?' The elder looks the young judge over carefully and says, 'In your case, two pounds ten!'"

Coogan leaned back and laughed. Ken had run the tape through his fingers.

"If you like that, I got another British one for you. There was this whore on the East End—"

"Save it for some other time," Ken said. "This is a crowded morning."

Caldwell flushed and reached down for his brief case. The light went on over Coogan's squawk box. He pressed the lever. "Yes?"

"The outside call Mr. Preston is expecting."

"I'll take it in there. You might find out what's holding up the bond men and whether McBride's on the Floor."

Ken retired to Coogan's back office. Coogan instructed Martha to round up Neil and his assistants and check the Floor for McBride. Then Caldwell said, "I always believed that fable about leopards and their spots, but I'll be damned."

"He's just serious business, that's all."

"Used to be a nice guy."

"A shnook, you mean. Now he's boss."

"And you don't mind?"

"No." Coogan smiled. "Though everyone else seems to. That's what I teamed up with him for."

The door opened and Martha told Pat that McBride was not on the Floor. Ken re-entered and looked at Caldwell for a silent moment. Caldwell fumbled with his papers. "Would you mind leaving us, please?" Ken asked.

"Sure thing." Caldwell lifted his tall, stoop-shouldered, bony frame out of the chair.

"For a moment," Coogan said. In recent years, the lines around Caldwell's mouth had accomplished the impossible of making his pinched face pouchy from the nose down, like a starved red squirrel with too many nuts in its cheeks. Red squirrel was right. His face and nervous eyelids, lips and scant eyebrows were identical; red, boiled, and peeled looking. The trouble with Caldwell, Pat decided, was that he held himself in contempt and he should know. But then he had no right to expect anything else from others.

When Caldwell was gone, Ken said, "According to Slezak, they will raise the discount rate to two and a quarter per cent tomorrow. Off the record, the Federal Home Loan Board will put a new squeeze on early next week to slow down mortgage money. He expects the overall dollar flow to be cut by no less than thirty per cent this month."

"That should make the tightest money in twenty-five years. I guess that tells our main story for this month's market letter."

"No," Ken said. "There'll be bargains later on in convertible bonds with a strong chance the stock market will go right on rising."

He walked to the tape again.

"Ken, do you think it's good for our lawyer to think you don't trust him completely?"

"No, and it's worse that I don't. Wasn't our lunch meeting with Mac pushed up to before the bell?"

"It's damn peculiar," Coogan said. "Calling me at three o'clock and then not showing up." He buzzed and Martha appeared. "You might try Mr. McBride at home."

"Is there some reason for not meeting in the conference room?" Ken asked.

"Kirkland's in there, waiting for you. Didn't Laemle tell you?"

"He tried. Why me?"

"Dunno. The bank sold out Kirkland's bond position. Had all his chips in bonds since mid-July and just managed to meet margin calls after that August 2 shellacking. Last week's bond sell-off knocked him out of the box. He's flat."

"If the banks sold Kirkland out, what can we do for him?"

"Nothing. But he insisted on waiting. Slightly hysterical, Laemle says."

Coogan's secretary reappeared. "Mrs. McBride says he's asleep and she can't wake him."

"I'll speak to her," Ken said. He took the phone. He exchanged a few pleasantries. Then he said, "Unless Mac is ill, I'm afraid you had better wake him and tell him I asked you to." When he hung up, Coogan shrugged and tried to behave as though he felt defensive in Mac's behalf. The result of this could be Ken's proposing they get rid of Mac. What a break that would be!

"Remember Cliff Keaton?" he said. "Last week he turned up on the Floor at eight-thirty drunk as a hoot owl. Fell into one of those comfortable leather chairs in the smoking room and began snoring. When the bell rang an hour and a half later to start the day, he jumped up and went home." He laughed.

Ken buzzed. "Would you get me Hawley on the Floor, please?" he asked Martha.

Coogan was delighted. Hawley was Coogan's choice for handling personal and firm accounts, once Mac was gotten rid of. Ken could hear the Floor crowd in the background.

"Yes, sir?"

"Good weekend?" Ken asked Hawley.

"Not bad, sir, thank you."

"How's the volume?"

"Four hundred thousand already. Wild. Looks like everybody wants to make a million dollars before lunch time."

"I'd like the market on Lewis Limited."

"In a sec. Seventeen to a half."

"Volume?"

"Not quite up to snuff."

"Sell ten thousand shares short at the market for my personal account. Don't rush, but try to complete it before midafternoon." He hung up.

"What about the firm?" Coogan asked.

"I'm not that sure of my facts."

"All right if Caldwell comes back now?"

Ken nodded. Coogan buzzed. "What's the story?" he asked.

"Lewis Limited may have been bluffing up a balance sheet the past six months. If so, it's coming to a head this afternoon. I'm counting on certain discrepancies in their inventory and the fact that at least one of the buyers called for a showdown. If I'm wrong, the stock should run away tomorrow morning, after they exercise their option to buy. If not, it will tumble today, before the bell. Pure gamble."

"Just so long as it's pure."

Caldwell entered. Coogan picked up the Floor phone and waited. "A pure gamble," he said. "Over a hundred and fifty G's for a short-term gain?"

"Our commodity straddle will make it long," Ken reminded.

"Only if there's enough of a move in soy bean futures in the right direction."

"There will be," Ken said.

"Get me Hawley."

"I still don't understand that commodity straddle operation," Caldwell said. "Oh, I get the tax law all right; separate months of the same crop are not substantially identical property and all that. But the damn thing's like a shell game. I don't seem to be able to keep it fixed in my mind. I mean, how do you still make out if the price goes down instead of up?"

Coogan was about to explain, but Ken's fingers tapping on the desk stopped him. "Just so long as you understand the law," Pat said.

"Why didn't Laemle warn Kirkland of a new hard money attack?" Ken asked.

"He did." Coogan moved the phone piece away from his mouth and put his hand over it. "But he also went along with Kirkland's fear the stock market would sit down to catch its breath. It's been scaling straight rock for two years now, Ken; in fact two years to the day, from 255 up to 481. That's more headway than the averages made from '27 to '29."

"There's no comparison," Ken said. "This market has a right to be where it is on an earnings basis. Are you telling me Laemle went counter to our forecasts?"

"No, no. It's just that he was worried enough not to crowd Kirkland."

"And why did he let Kirkland go in so thinly margined?"

"I'm not making it clear. Kirkland wouldn't listen." The green light went on over Coogan's Floor phone. "Hawley? Coogan. When you clean up Mr. Preston's sell order on Lewis, go five thousand short for me."

He hung up. "Kirkland's like all those other eggheads. Thinks because he's a mathematical genius in electronics, he can blueprint the stock market. All that gentlemen-prefer-bonds crap."

Neil arrived and with him his four assistants from the bond department.

"Laemle covered us with Kirkland, dangers, the need for a hedge position, and even wait-and-look-see advice. It's all in the record. Now." Coogan greeted the newcomers. "We should be able to settle this bond letter in half an hour, wouldn't you say, Ken?"

"All right if I leave?" Caldwell asked. He wanted to go short some Lewis himself. Ken nodded, Caldwell left, and Ken told Neil, "Take full notes so you can dictate the page and send it off to the printers before noon. I won't have the time." Then he said, "We must keep time open for the lunch conference with Mac."

"You still think we need it?" Coogan asked.

It was about public funds and expenditures for TV on which Mac had as yet stated no views.

"Yes, I do."

"Fine. All right, boys. The meeting is called to order."

Matthew Kirkland had been sitting in the main conference room for two hours now, trying to think. His tapered fingers clenched and unclenched. They were woman's hands, but suited to complex and special manual skills. In his spare time, he carved chess pieces: no less than ten unfinished ones always lay about in his study. His huge nose was emphasized by the sunken sallow-ness of his face. His scrawny body bent over the high, long table. Usually Kirkland's face was arresting despite his ugliness, and his eyes glowed behind the thick glasses with subtle intelligence. But now his chin was covered with a stubble of unshaven gray and all that was evident was his ugliness and age. Each avenue of his mind had led nowhere. Its desperate energy ran like blind electric current into a lead wall only to retrace itself and scorch his brain. He had lost track of time sitting there in a miasma of regrets, with occasional spurts of anger like this one at some aspect or other of his mistake. A life of discipline had made him mechanically list the possible paths to solu-tion. Now he looked at his notes on the Preston & Company order blank that lay before him on the conference table. He stared, un-willing or unable to read his own words. Irresistibly his mind hovered over the core of his mistake: the failure to enter convertible bonds as Laemle had urged. He invented ways in which it might all never have happened. Buying convertible bonds later, after the sell-off, and then as the stock market rose—he could have made a fortune! It was all so clear now. And then he would—he caught himself smiling at the cleverness of what he might then have done. He drew his thick lips back to reveal large, yellow teeth, widely separated like those of a horse. He shook off the fantasy and stared at the sheet again, paralyzed by full realization. There was no path to solution. Only escape. Run away? Appeal for mercy? *Die.* But what of his wife and child? The thought brought back his wife's remarks of last night and with it even darker rage that might have mobilized him out of this despair were there some path, any path at all, to action. No doubt it was all con-nected: things were. Disrupting his life of research for marriage to this fat, impossibly vulgar, pretentious toad! But she had been thirty and he'd needed her simply because he had denied himself for so long. She was his aberration and he knew it; a poorly trained, undisciplined research worker. She had married him to advance in his world. He knew that too, and had retaliated by excluding her from his projects, counting every penny she spent, exposing her ignorance in the presence of colleagues. She had reciprocated with flirtation and infidelity. Thanks to her repulsive nature and appearance, the weapon lacked the power it might have once had when she was twenty, not yet so fat, and her childish pouting was still relatively charming to some. Advance in his world? She had not bargained for this. Wandering again. But bonds were safe and this was a bull market. He didn't understand. Never before in his life had he been reduced to this dull stupor. Trapped. This was the very meaning of the word. No way out. Waiting for Preston was more madness. What could he tell Preston? What could he ask of him? Why should Preston help him? In what plausible way could he? Yet it had seemed logical this morning; even inevitable. Preston was a cultivated man. It was Preston's integrity and wide range of interests that had made him choose their firm after avoiding the market since the '29 crash. Now the market was rising. Simply couldn't understand. A year ago, he began following it, making imaginary commitments; keeping track of imaginary gains and losses. You were far ahead on April 18, the day Albert Einstein died. That's when you read the appreciation by Ken Preston in the business section. It was deeply felt. It had understanding. That and the *Wall Street Journal's* editorial condemning those who fostered peace scares for profit, had between them given you a feeling of something decent, civilized, and trustworthy in the financial community. So you'd made your appointment and even spent twenty stimulating minutes with Preston himself discussing chess and new trends in electronics. Besides, Preston had also married late in life and to a younger woman. He respected the academic world. He could realize the worth of your work as chairman of the American Electronics Research Institute. But what had that to do with the issue? The training of his logical mind made his position clear to him. The door opened.

"I've been in conference and have another in a moment. You wished to see me?"

"Yes." He whispered it as Ken came around to face him across the table. Kirkland could not look up. He was suddenly crushed by shame rather than disaster.

"Once your equity was gone," Ken said, "the banks had to sell you out."

Kirkland huddled over the table and his shirt front billowed away from his sunken, rickety chest. "All my life I've shunned public events, banquets, theaters. As a boy, sports. I have never written a potboiler or sought gain in my life. Not even glory or pleasures." His voice broke. "Only my work," he whispered.

"Was it all the money you had?"

Kirkland nodded.

"You receive a fair-sized sum from industry consultations and the Institute."

Kirkland sat motionless.

"You are close to retirement age. Surely there won't be an issue of need. Later, I assume you have ample insurance."

Kirkland still sat silent.

"Dr. Kirkland, I'm pressed for time."

"All I can borrow on my insurance is twenty thousand dollars." He looked up at Ken. "I used fifty thousand of the Institute's funds to cover margin in August. I'm an embezzler." He sounded incredulous at his own words. "The Board meets in three days. And my daughter is only five years old. You see I married a woman of thirty when I was fifty-five. A mistake of course but—even if I died it couldn't help them. Not this way. Not in disgrace." He began to sob.

"What is it you expect of me?" Ken asked quietly.

Kirkland shook his head. "Nothing. I have no place to turn. I never made friends. No gift for it. Only my work." He rose. "I'm sorry. It's just—" he stopped, his large head bent forward, more weight than his body could bear. He stared out the window at the skyline where the skyscrapers were clearly etched black, long, and narrow against the sky, looming over the leveled-out rubble of the city's crisscrossing clotheslines, yards, warehouses, tenements, and rubbish. "I planned to use the profits for personal research. A theory I have—"

"What do you earn, Dr. Kirkland?"

"Nothing. I have nothing."

"Yes," Ken said impatiently. "But what is your annual income?"

The phone rang. Ken walked to it and picked it up. It was Mr. Sloates to tell him that half his short sale order on Lewis Limited was completed. Now the stock was rising more substantially against him in strong volume, trading at 18⅜. Did he still want his original instructions to stand? "Yes," Ken said and hung up.

He walked back. "What did you say your annual income was?"

"Mostly the Research Institute. Fifty thousand."

"Then you could repay me in two years. Fifteen thousand a year. Borrow the remaining twenty thousand on your insurance."

He walked down to the far end of the table in the direction of the door. "My secretary will give you the check for thirty thousand,"

Ken said. "Also a note which he will witness, admitting the circumstances of this loan, establishing that it is not for securities, and pledging that you will stay out of the market. Should you violate that or fail to pay me promptly, your signed note will go to the District Attorney's office, with copies to the Research Institute and the press." He walked to the door.

Kirkland ran to him, but Ken reached the door first and left quickly, pulling it shut behind him.

He instructed his secretary and told him to get proper language from Riley with respect to SEC regulations on the matter of personal loans. He cautioned Sloates not to reveal the reason for the inquiry and warned him the entire matter was to be kept confidential.

At noon, Mac had appeared on the Floor, red-eyed and stuporous, to complete Ken's short sale of Lewis. By lunch time he was halfway through Coogan's order. Their discussion of the launching of Preston Public Funds was confined to Ken's doubts about the value of his personal appearance on television. Despite the fact that the various open letters of Preston & Company, signed by him and appearing from time to time on the financial page in major newspapers, had yielded remarkable results in the accelerated bull market, Ken saw no connection between that and personally appearing on a television show. Mac had no views, or, if he did, he took care not to express them. Pat argued that they should be guided by the advertising agency for whom, after all, failure in the first trial period of six broadcasts meant the loss of a client and they knew it. To the network the strong rating mattered even more because of the air time that followed, and the network agreed with the agency. "Their reasons are sound. Our industry has never approached the general public. Our product still seems too abstract to most people. They got to see you and know who you are, connect your name with the name of the firm and our five out-of-town branches. They identify you, they identify us. Unless of course the whole idea of being put on display is too distasteful to you. Up to you entirely."

"I can't help feeling that hiring someone would be in better taste and more effective." Ken mentioned a well-known television personality.

Pat smiled. "Well, of course, there's the problem that we'll only broadcast locally where we have branches. You can't afford such talent for local time. But whether we use TV at all is entirely up to you."

"What are your views?" Ken asked Mac.

Mac shrugged.

"Today's meeting isn't decisive and the Atwater executives won't be there. Still, each meeting is a step closer to commitment."

Mac stared at him.

"Well, you must have some feeling about it," Ken said.

"I'm not sold," Mac said.

"On what feature?" Coogan asked.

"On whatever that chart meeting proved. Or the customers' men. I watch tape. The market is due for a kick in the head."

"We're talking about the public funds and television right now, Mac," Coogan said.

"Sure. Right now you're talking about television. You're talking about public funds right now. You're talking about buying more stock. You can't tell people to buy stock if we're going to sell and I'm telling both of you that this God damn market is due for a kick in the head."

"You mean a technical sell-off, profit taking?" Coogan asked.

"I mean we should shorten our positions," Mac said.

"I'm late," Ken said. "Do you suppose you could manage to be coherent?"

"I'm coherent. I'm saying we should shorten positions. When the cops raid the whorehouse they pick up the customers along with the girls. Now is that coherent?"

Ken looked at him thoughtfully. "And that is what you wanted to see us about before the bell?"

"Partly."

"What's the rest?"

Mac's eyes shifted. "You're late. It'll keep."

"There may be a technical sell-off," Ken said. "If so it will be quickly absorbed. This market is on a proper basis and any decline in industry productivity is due to a shift of labor to services and research development from direct production. That means it will all show up in accelerated increases later. Fifteen times earnings is a proper basis for this market." Ken looked up at the clock. "A technical sell-off can have no bearing on our launching of the public funds. It would be months before we made the necessary changeover. I doubt we would want to sell in any case."

Ken waited. Mac shifted his bloodshot eyes again. "I say we should shorten positions," he repeated sullenly.

"And I say we probably should not. It's ridiculous to take short gains and assume all the problems of getting back in."

"You think I don't know how to pick up a stock after a sell-off without chasing it?"

"I'm sure you could if you happened to be on the Floor at the time and in a condition to do so. It's senseless to lose our long-term standing."

"I still say we shorten positions."

Ken addressed Coogan. "I'll be at Rockefeller Plaza in Mr. Fremont's office or their conference room on the forty-fifth floor with that agency woman, Miss Hinkson." He turned to Mac. "Keep me posted on moves of half a point or more in Lewis."

"What if George Devlin gets in from Chicago?" Coogan asked. "Shall I bring him uptown?"

"I promised Laurie I'd be home early. We have a dinner date tonight. What can Devlin raise that's new?"

"The rumor that the Soviets won't be able to meet Czechoslovakia's soy bean order. George says if it's true we'll see a rise of twenty cents a bushel on our March-May spread."

Ken computed. "That's true. And quite possible." He turned to Mac. "If that happens, we have the tax basis for transforming an additional one million of short gains into long-term gains. In that case I would agree to shortened positions."

"Thanks a lot." Mac grinned. He raised his martini to Ken. "King Midas. You touch it. Presto change-oh! Presto change-oh is pretty good, eh? From Preston to presto. Presto to change-oh and no small change-oh either. King size change-oh. Midas size. Gold size."

Ken rose. "You drink too much," he said. "And bluff too much. That's dangerous." He nodded to Coogan and left.

Mac said, "I'm gonna cold cock that bastard one day."

Coogan sipped his coffee slowly. "You really *do* drink too much, Mac, for your own good."

"Balls to him." Mac twirled his iced martini glass. "You know what he's talking about with all that services replacing production shit?"

Pat smiled.

"Or all that crap at the chart meeting," Mac went on, "about double tops, bottoms, triangles, and concentration points?"

"No, sir."

"All right! I'm on the Floor. I know the Floor. And I know the tape. There's going to be one hell of a sell-off, fifteen times earnings or not."

"You heard me on Devlin and Ken said if that happens, he agrees with you."

"I don't care whether it happens or not."

"Ken's the boss," Coogan said.

"Who *says* he's the boss?" Mac shouted.

"Mac, essentially it's his firm." Yes, full of bluff but almost ready to quit. No doubt about it. And when Mac quit, it would be with a knockdown brawl: Pat was sure of that. Interesting to see how Ken would deal with it when the time came. Brawn was a fact like breeding or money or brains and Mac had brawn: another reason for making sure that all his rage was turned on Ken. That was an issue, not a joke. To make him leave, it had been necessary to goad him like trainers poked caged lions with hot irons. This damn fool brute was a maniac—he could inflict real damage. Better on Ken than me. Deceiving Mac was so simple. It was Ken he was concerned about. He had hoped to use the time pressure and Mac's failure to show up before the bell to get Ken to cancel this meeting: a little more grist to the mill of Mac's resentment. However. Mac was only a matter of time. As for Ken, it was necessary to make him believe he was all for the public funds, all for the tour, all for the television appearances, and he felt he had succeeded. That was vital if he was to find the way of preventing it. What couldn't a man achieve with patience! Mac here, whose time had come, whose time for enjoying a third of the profit was over, with three Floor men replacing him at only five per cent each, was in the bag. The Floor was for feet and the best feet were those that knew they were no part of the head. Mac was on schedule, or almost. He might have quit today if Ken hadn't taken the wind out of his sails. That was *your* mistake: mentioning Devlin.

"And those customers' meetings," Mac was saying. "Talking out the possibilities of profit that way. You know it brings bad luck."

Coogan nodded. "Ken's not like us. He doesn't think our way. But that's not what's got you. What is it, Mac? What's the matter?"

"Matter? Nothing's the matter. We're making a fortune—out-Fennering Beane, out-beaning the Russians, and out-rushing the tape." He gulped down his martini and snapped his fingers for the waiter. "I just wouldn't want super-duper man to be wrong about anything is the matter, that's all." He ran his hand through the air. "B-z-z-z-z. With the greatest of ease." He nodded.

"He won't do anything wrong," Coogan said. "You or I might, but not Ken. Timing and knowing are in his blood."

When Mac did quit, he would have to believe absolutely that it was his own idea. The waiter appeared.

"Another martini. Double," Mac said.

"You mustn't let it get you," Coogan soothed.

Mac licked his lips. "Nothing's going to get me. But I'm getting just one more drinkie and back into the stable to clean up your short sell order. Then damned if I won't go a few thousand short on Lewis myself."

Chapter 2

FRANKLIN FREMONT looked up at the wall clock and frowned at the second hand as it moved in its endless circle. Each day he entered mortal combat with it. Now this. The chances for Preston & Company taking on coast-to-coast time after the six-week trial period were slim and the chances of Kenneth Preston agreeing to appear personally even slimmer. The prospects of audience identification on any other basis consistent with a budget for local time in each one of six cities, slimmest of all. Now here was his golden opportunity to have a drink with Ben Noble, who faced their time spot eight A.M. to nine, the housewife's favorite—and the chance to talk a little dirty business. His instinct told him that for fifteen hundred a week more than he was getting, Ben could be snaked away. But he couldn't see Ben and sit on this meeting—it was one or the other and there was no important talent present from Atwater Agency. Damned if he saw why *he* had to waste the time!

He asked Milt Bright whether he had read through Mr. Preston's rough notes on the topics suggested. When Milt glumly said that he had, Fremont asked Kathy Hinkson, from Atwater Agency, the same question. She told him that at Mr. Atwater's request, she had spent her time working up the biographical data on Kenneth Preston himself.

"Then may I suggest you kids exchange files till he gets here?" Fremont looked at the clock again. "We all want to see eye to eye. Since this is just a getting-to-know-you meeting and I have already had the pleasure, I'll stay out of your way. Of course, nothing will be decided. Still, every meeting counts, so may I leave one thought? This will be a soft sell. Now we all see eye to eye on that. Real live types at the studio. Americana. Questions and answers. With the subjects very general. Otherwise before long he's pitching a head-on sale of securities, which is all wrong. Now here's how you help. We're seeking a focus, a pinpoint. We want to merchandise through the man himself. Our theme is obvious: Wall Street mirrors the world around us. Put it this way."

He turned to Milt. "When I say *security*, what comes to your mind?"

"A sexy old widow with lots of money," Milt answered promptly.

Fremont smiled and turned to Kathy. She raised one finger delicately in the air. "Same thought. Different sex."

"That's what Preston Funds will sell. Lots of money. Security. Make it plural. *Securities*. Get it? Take bonds. It may be the peasant in me but to me the word bonds means ties, affiliations, neighborhood, family, nation. As for preferred, it's a natural. So is common. And I hope I don't sound too much like a peasant when I say that these labels touch on the warmest, closest, personal things to everyone from coast to coast, from cradle to grave."

"Especially common," Milt agreed.

"Common doesn't only mean cheap," Fremont pointed out. "Though even that's appealing when identified with price. But there's the common touch, common man, common sense."

"Also common-get-it," Milt said and shrugged when neither laughed.

"The trick is to shape Mr. Preston's comments on bread-and-butter subjects with that in mind. But for this we need his help. Nothing superimposed. Broken field running and a soft sell all the way. Do we see eye to eye?"

Up to the fifty-yard line, Milt thought, and said, "Frankly, Mr. Fremont, I don't think he's got the makings of a TV personality. Does that matter?"

"Now, Milty, he's not running for president."

Milt shrugged. "He still needs Bob Montgomery."

"We're counting on you for the common touch."

"Well, thanks, but I've read his informal notes. I had to wear my arctic gloves to turn the pages."

Fremont smiled. "Warm him up. Actually he's pretty brilliant. There's going to have to be direct identification of name and product. It's the only substitute for a year of missionary work that Preston and Company can't and won't invest in. So we've *got* to make good in six weeks. That is, if we make a deal." He looked from one to the other. "Remember that, kitty cats. So far all we have is conversation. No deal. God bless." Fremont left.

"God bless my foot to foot and eye to eye and F and double F you." Milt shoved the file of Ken's notes over to Kathy. She was sitting ankles crossed, her feet on the chair in front of her, her right arm resting on the table. She leaned sideways to pick up the file.

"Do *you* think Mr. Preston's pretty brilliant?" Milt asked.

"His nervous system is rather pretty on cold paper in an austere sort of way. O.S.S. Reconstructing the family fortune. Marrying an Irish-American working-class plebe. That last cost him his place in this year's *Social Register,* which is even worse than wearing yesterday's mink. Now *that's* pretty common. Or do I mean uncommon? I'll tell you one thing that's pretty and brilliant—his market letters. I've read over twenty and checked them against what happened. Fabulous."

"Plenty of free advice?"

"Just getting to know our product."

"If you ask me we should find out first whether it *is* our product."

"I'm having fun." She tapped the open folder. "Whose questions are these?"

"F's," Milt said. "And your agency's. Nothing superimposed, you understand. Fremont sells time, I buy trouble. Wall Street may reflect the world around us, but not through this frosty mirror." He lingered over some sheets. "Now what in Kee-rist is the Saturday Club?"

"Meeting of the great minds of New England. Holmes, Emerson, Howells, Longfellow. And Great-grandfather Timothy Preston."

"I dig this Groton and Bible Society bit but who cares about egghead gatherings? Hell, no one even reads Longfellow any more."

She saw the genuine distress on Milt's face and laughed. "We might give Mr. Preston questions with instructions to confine himself to a simple yes or no answer. Yes for investments, religion, and profit. No for confiscation, communism, and constipation. By some miracle, that's exactly six broadcasts."

"Funnee. But I have to show writers how to get scripts out of this New England clam chowder."

"We have had it too easy, Milt, and Mr. Preston would quote you Thoreau." She was still scanning Ken's notes.

"I wouldn't doubt it."

"I'm giving you a clue, Milt. Thoreau said, 'Not that which lulls us as luxury and suffers the nobler faculties to sleep the while, but what we stand on tiptoe to read is worth reading.'"

"My nobler faculties are hanging by their thumbs and I'm very sound asleep already. If Preston's ego needs publicity, let him buy a newspaper."

"It doesn't."

"Digging into his childhood tells you that?"

"He *doesn't,* Milt. You may find him more against this than you are."

"It should only happen. I can afford to be frank if it's safe."

"It's safe."

"All right. This kind of selling went out with Grandma Rochella's matzo ball soup."

"You miss the whole point," she said. "Modern man's story is a story of defeat."

"A real drag," Milt agreed. "So?"

"There was a time you got old and gray surrounded by loved ones and could look back on a life of service. If you timed it right between wars, the last lap could look a little like the glory of a journey's end. Today it's ulcers at thirty and a prairie dog's carcass served up to the vultures midst sand and tumbleweed. Now that's Mr. Preston's appeal. He's smart, decent, rich, lucky, and in love. He has a background that's good enough to keep any man self-satisfied cutting paper dolls to the end of time. But no. He wants to go out and do! And he's got all the weapons to give him a fighting chance."

"What's left to fight about? In his case, there's no room for argument!"

There was a knock at the door.

"Come."

The uniformed reception boy looked in, admired Kathy's legs, and said, "Mr. Preston, by appointment."

"Prompt," Milt said. "By appointment yet. He's got the hired hands behaving like the royal guard. Send him in."

Kathy brought her feet to the floor, folded her skirt under her knees, and turned to the table.

"Neither my modes of thought nor my means of expressing them are folksy," Ken was saying, "and you will find my views are even less popular. What practical purpose is served by attempting to build interest in public funds around me?"

Kathy continued to watch Milt with growing amusement.

"You have a very winning personality," Milt protested. "And Mr. Fremont feels the results of your open letters give us quite a following to build on. So do the top brass at the agency. Isn't that right, Kathy?"

She nodded slightly.

"Those open letters we published were rephrased by the agency and their subject matter was securities," Ken said. "All that people saw of me was my signature."

"Both the agency and network have writers for rephrasing," Kathy explained, "and I believe your photograph was effectively used several times."

"It's not quite the same, is it?"

"Many strong men have camera fright," Kathy said.

Ken smiled coldly. "All I fear is defeating our purpose."

"It's hard to see ourselves sometimes. You *are* very photogenic."

Ken felt color rise in his cheeks.

"You have poise and your voice is good," she went on. "A little like F. D. R.'s; I hope that comparison isn't odious to you."

"There is very much I admired in Mr. Roosevelt."

"I knew a fella once," Milt said. "Fraternity brother. He told me his father hated Roosevelt because before the New Deal he was able to live on the income *from* his income. After F. D. R. he was forced to live directly on his income." He laughed.

Ken looked inquiringly at Kathy and she shrugged.

"I've been over your views on the subjects suggested by Mr. Fremont," Kathy said. "Take these: education, courage, individualism," she continued. "I find your comments original and provocative."

"Oh?"

"I'm not that different," she pointed out.

"Perhaps you are. As you say, it's difficult for us to see ourselves."

"Who can miss seeing Kathy in that tight green job she's wearing?" Milt asked.

Now Kathy felt her color rising. She busied herself finding a cigarette. "Human exchange through speech isn't quite the same as silent, reflective writing. Why don't we try talking out these subjects, Mr. Preston? Let's take individualism."

"My views won't change."

"But let's try," she persisted.

"Very well."

She pulled her notebook toward her and reached for a pencil.

"I prefer to call it individuality," Ken said.

"Rugged individuality?" She smiled. So did he.

"Well, there's not really much to it. I think individuality is being destroyed by a ridiculous paradox. Orthodoxy is on the order of the day. But actual orthodoxy is branded heresy. In Asia, orthodoxy should mean Marxism, but Marxists are banished there. In the Catholic world, orthodoxy should mean the Sermon on the Mount, but love thy neighbor rigidly excludes the so-called godless. Our Anglo-Saxon Calvinist ethic should mean absolute individuality, but individuality has been relatively outlawed in the name of protecting national security from the enemies of individuality. What little of it is left is being regimented to the lowest possible level by standard slogans, standard brands, and the willing assistance toward mechanized mediocrity of such media as television. Experts stalk about the world like medieval apothecaries, sniffing obscenely at men's souls as though they were dirty bottles in which they hope to find, or failing that, willingly invent the presence of alien vapors. I believe in individuality and I sincerely mourn its passing."

"Gevalt!" Milt said.

Kathy looked up at Milt's face and laughed aloud. "And I suppose Wall Street is the last stand?" she challenged.

"Not at all. It completes the spectacle by appealing to the egocentricity of the savage, his greedy impatience, his faith in magic."

"Then why should anyone stay there?"

Ken paused. "We all have to stay somewhere, don't we, Miss Hinkson?"

She stopped smiling.

Milt said, "I agree with you one hundred per cent, Mr. Preston. You won't get customers that way."

"Then I have made my point."

"Unless you're pushing to make your point," Kathy said.

"Distorting? Not at all, Miss Hinkson. Those are my views. I certainly won't alter them to get customers. We want customers. It seems fairly clear that exposing me or my views is not the proper method for securing them."

Milt said fervently, "That's between you and the powers that be. But I buy it."

"You *are* a complication, Mr. Preston," Kathy said.

The phone rang. Milt answered it. "For you, Mr. Preston. Mr. McBride."

Ken left the table. "Yes, Mac?"

"I've been trying to get you for ten minutes. That God damned extension of yours was busy."

"Really? The line was free."

"That's great. All this efficiency is gonna put our message across to the public?"

"What is it?"

"Lewis got murdered all right. Off five and a half points. Traded at twelve, ten minutes ago. The story of doctored books is on the broad tape and Pat covered his short position five points to the good. So did I. There's only eight more trading minutes left."

"Keep my position open," Ken said. "Lewis's true book value is nine on a corrected inventory. The loss of public faith should discount at least an additional three points."

"You made yourself over fifty grand today," Mac couldn't help saying. "Why not cover half?"

"No. I'll stay open on all ten thousand."

"O.K. It's your dough."

"What are the averages?"

Mac told him.

"And the volume?"

He told him that too. Another strong day. Ken hung up and returned to the table.

"Good news?" Kathy asked.

"In a way. Yes, I suppose you'd call it good news."

"Was that Lewis Limited?" Kathy asked. "Because I hold a hundred shares at fifteen. It opened at seventeen this morning, didn't it?"

"Seventeen to a half. It's down to twelve now. I should sell if I were you. It will go well below ten tomorrow."

"And here I started the day thinking I was two hundred bucks ahead!"

She hurried to the phone. Remind me to remember this. One system at a time and the Preston letters never recommended Lewis. From now on your cigarette, car, toothpaste, and what-have-you is Preston & Company. The customer is always right. Damned if this one actually isn't! He *must* become a customer.

While Kathy reached her broker and instructed him to sell, Milt asked, "What's the matter? Is the market crashing?"

"Not at all."

"Thank God. I have Southwestern Steel and Amalgamated Alloys. A hundred of each. You think that's all right?"

"They will do nothing spectacular but they'll keep rising in a rising market. Their dividends are assured."

"Funny. That's just what my broker said. I like playing safe."

"Well, we're sure proving the point, Mr. Preston," Kathy said, returning to the table. "A year ago, playing safe, Milt wouldn't have dreamed of owning any stock. For other reasons, neither would I. Now we're pumping you on company time. See how much we like your personality?"

"That sort of affection should make IBM come up with a stainless steel Mr. America of 1955," Ken said.

She laughed. "That's funny."

"Only ridiculous," he said. "At this time of day, all serious things suddenly seem ridiculous."

"After the gong?"

"We call it the bell."

She bowed. "As yours are the Goldenest Gloves there are, I accept the correction. *Bell.* Now guess the price of the dress I was going to buy and you get a free box of candy."

"One hundred and sixty-five dollars."

"You're very close."

"You two just lost me," Milt said.

"Poor boy," said Kathy. "Lost in the land of lucre. Or is it licentiousness?"

"I thought it was Nod," Ken said.

"No, that's off-with-your-head land. No heads on our mainland, skipper. Secret of our success."

"Wynken and Blynken still have their heads," Ken said.

"Now you have just found the name of our show. 'Don't lose your head, man', also 'where is our headman?' or which side are you on?"

"It's all the same to Robespierre."

"And there you have our timeless theme. '*Make* them eat cake.' "

"With their heads tucked underneath their arms," Ken agreed.

"And *that* is our mid-show announcement," she said. "For a break in the tedium instead of the market, as headless man nods awinkin' and ablinkin', as our one and only headman says, 'Let others eat bread. We want cake.' "

"Now wait a minute," Milt pleaded.

"Milty, stay with it," Kathy said. "Our broken field client is pinpointing the product, finding theme, format, and soft sell all at once. Can't you see eye to eye?"

"Then are we well ahead of the game?" Ken asked.

"Way out in front," she said.

"Pooling our brains," Ken suggested.

"And bringing it home double F as in March Militaire. So on to our next topic. Education!"

"Sometimes a reflection of your teacher's prejudice. Never a gauge of true knowledge. Consider astronomy in the middle ages. Today's answer would have cost you your life then. What shall tomorrow's answer bring?"

"Mars, Jupiter, and jumping Venus. Which leads us straight to our next to last subject, courage."

"A polite name for desperation. Only the coward dares to hold back and consider both pros and cons."

"And pros and cons are *so* often alike, don't you think, Mr. Preston?"

"All too frequently, now that their fields of endeavor have merged."

"No mergers, Mr. Preston. Our program *never* touches the subject of finance. It's the soft sell all the way. But to get on."

"Yes. That's our real theme. We *must* get on and most of us don't have the strength to get off, to hold back and consider because doing so leaves you alone. Therefore solitude is the only courage and the only true hero is the coward."

"Dying a thousand deaths instead of one. Score for the prosecution. We are getting on swimmingly."

"Drowningly," he corrected.

"We *must* get your views on sailing and whaling in good old New England, but time flies, so perhaps after the bell—or is it a buoy now? However. Our last subject—man's soul."

"May I substitute immortality?"

"If you can."

"Thank you. Everyone knows that cleanliness is next to godliness. Therefore sanitation walks arm in arm with sanctity. But when the road narrows, which should go first? I am all for the street cleaner."

"And there's the bell to tell us we have just spent another relaxing half-hour with that jolly tar and his delicate feather, Mr. Kenneth Fenimore Preston of your street and mine, cleaning up on his Floor and yours. Now remember, what's good for the bell is even better for America and so at the count of ten, good night!"

"Clowns," Milt said.

The door opened. Mr. Fremont appeared. "Ah, Mr. Preston, how's it going?"

"Gone," Kathy said.

"They're seeing eye to eye," Milt told him.

Fremont and Ken shook hands.

"So close we've exchanged lashes." She turned to Ken. "Speaking of which brings to mind WHIP. Isn't there a safe, sweet story of simple faith buried somewhere in that?"

"No. Judas and the silver all over again. They're back in the courts, calling names."

"Pity."

"Part of the *Zeitgeist*."

"Seems our *zeit* has given up its *geist* and if I'm not very careful, the mood I'm in, Mr. Preston," she started laughing, "I'm going to be fired forthwith. There's a double F if I ever saw one."

"If so, this network will lose my account."

"Where did you hide the shaker?" Fremont asked. "I'll have a snort myself."

"See?" Kathy said. "No one believes in high spirits any more. If you're young at heart, the cause is aged in the wood and the spirits are the lowest there is."

"Are," Ken corrected.

"I can tell something real good came out of this meeting," Fremont said.

"A horrifying friendship," Kathy answered. "But I believe we are positively agreed that a program sponsored by Preston Public Funds should go on the air."

"Wonderful," Fremont said. "Let me get a real bottle and we'll drink on that." He walked to the other end of the room.

"But not with me," Ken added.

"Not so fast, Macduff," Kathy said. "I'm more convinced than ever. You *should* go on. Can you imagine hell without laughter?"

"Dante did."

"And look at his rating!"

"I wish you'd catch me up," Fremont said, looking at Milt.

"Another one who wants to get caught. You see? The criminal's delight. You're in."

They were laughing again.

"They're gassed. On fresh air," Milt said, "but she means it."

"There's a serious disagreement in policy," Ken explained. "The lady in green—"

"For a hundred and sixty-five dollars—"

"—answers the question in the affirmative. Quite seriously, Mr. Fremont, despite my protests, Miss Hinkson seems to think I'm a—"

"Natural," she helped.

"That's it. A natural born—"

"Personality. Providing the show goes on after the gong."

"Ask not for whom the bell rings, dear Kate," Milt warned. "It may count ten for you."

"Welcome aboard."

"But I have serious doubts," Ken went on.

"*Humorous* doubts," Kathy insisted. "The source of our sober disagreement."

"Do you follow them?" Fremont asked Milt.

Milt nodded. "It takes time. Like cultivating a taste for oriental dishes."

"Such as cockroaches and grasshoppers," Kathy said.

"Who toil not, neither do they spin," Ken said. "Or is that spiders?"

"Tops," she said. "And he is, Fremont. Batty and unbowed but tops. A hard-boiled egghead. And now you *must* turn it off, Mr. Preston, *please*, or I'll get double F'd to a fare-thee-well forthwith, whether you withdraw your account or not."

"Actually I'm quite serious, Mr. Fremont," Ken said, smiling.

"Go on," Fremont said. "Have fun. So long as you're making headway, don't let me spoil it."

They both burst into laughter again. Milt was laughing too. Fremont still wanted to get to the subject of pinpointing sale in the five localities where Preston & Company had branches: where the local broadcasts would take place before the finale in New York. Above all he wanted to confirm that this was not just talk, that there actually *was* a deal.

"Mr. Bright tells me you're impressed with the response to our newspaper ads and now Miss Hinkson has the mistaken impression that my after-hours hysteria is a substitute for humor. I believe it would be wiser—" Ken smiled again "—or let's say, *safer* for all parties concerned, to hire someone and not try to make something out of me that I am not."

"As who is in our troubled times?"

They were laughing again. Fremont decided it was the wrong time for the short strokes. He laughed with them. A deal. Imagine!

Kathy and Ken had left Milt. They were walking toward Park Avenue.

"You're a simply terrible television personality and I enjoyed every minute of it. Even if it's only after the bell."

"Why do you suppose Mr. Fremont was so delighted with our conference?"

"He sees a sale. Besides, he thinks we warmed you up. My agency's account executive wasn't there. Skulduggery. I don't count and we met at network headquarters. So if there's a sale it's a feather in his cap."

"I thought court jesters wore bells."

"Your wife must have a high time when you get going."

"It never lasts more than half an hour."

"Length of show."

"The wrong half-hour."

"Hysteria gone?"

"Quite."

"Leaves you a bit hung over."

"I'll be fine by the time I get home."

"Might I make a small two-word suggestion?"

"Please."

"And not get double F'd?"

He nodded.

"Slow down."

He didn't smile.

"Sorry. Is my credit good for one small question?"

He waited.

"That ten thousand Lewis. Was it dollars or shares?"

"Shares."

"From seventeen to twelve. Sold short. Meaning fifty-five thousand dollars profit."

"You listen carefully."

"Is that an everyday occurrence?"

"No."

They reached Park Avenue.

"I'm relieved. Because fifty-five thousand a day is almost two hundred and seventy-five thousand a month or fourteen million a year."

"You multiply fast."

"That's a woman's function," she said.

They laughed.

"Over fifty-five thousand in one day and you still don't consider that good news!"

"It's all right."

"You absolutely won't get me fired?"

He smiled.

"I have a theory." She paused. "You shouldn't be doing this."

"TV?"

"Wall Street either. Any of it."

"That's interesting. All my life women have felt I should not be doing exactly what I am doing at any particular moment."

"Want the rest of my theory?"

"There's more?"

"Yes. I think you're dangerous."

He smiled again. She smiled back.

"I do. In the arena one day, instead of laughing, you'll run amuck."

"Now that *is* a theory."

"Brand new?"

"Indeed."

"I'm flattered." She gave him her hand. "That was a hell of a conference. We must do it more often. If you stay on the Street and launch Preston Public Funds, I think you should go on the air. Humor is always in demand."

"Humor is disguised self-pity," he said. "And I don't think I could self-pity myself." He paused. "Self-pity my self-pity." He laughed. "Myself. Pity myself. Pity my self-pity. One could get caught in that twister forever."

"Some do," she said.

They shook hands.

"Thanks for the tip on Lewis. I'll name my next dress after you."

Ken had arrived too late to change. Laurie was dressed and ready, waiting in the living room. The melted ice in the martini pitcher made the gin wet and tasteless.

"How was the market?" Laurie asked.

Ken told her.

"What else happened?"

"Nothing special." The usual. Plus embezzlement and prophecy. What prophecy? Not remembering nagged at his mind. "How was your day?" Ken asked.

"Nothing much. I sent our summer clothes to the tailor and laid out menus for the week. Then I went to school to find out when classes begin. I could have phoned but I wanted to get out. They begin September 27." She handed him his martini. "Then I waited for you."

"I know. I'm sorry. The meeting was interminable. I couldn't find a cab, so I walked."

"Ken, I don't like sitting and waiting. And I don't want to spend all our evenings out again." She sipped her drink. "Are you going to leave town to sell that public funds?"

"I don't know. I don't think so."

She nodded and poured herself another drink. "That's what you said about the quarterly checkup on your branch offices. 'I don't know. I don't think so.' You've been doing it every four months ever since. One week out of sixteen."

"Because the problems shifted from selling and organization to investment, chart reading, and tax saving."

"Before the summer started I asked you if you were going to work June and July. Remember? You said you didn't know, you didn't think so."

"The bull market demanded it."

"Something is always demanding it. When will you be leaving?"

"Now, Laurie, I haven't said I will. In fact I'm pretty sure I won't."

"I know. But when?"

"It would start next month. But I keep telling you—"

"Yes, you certainly do."

"Laurie, you make it sound like I'm trying to stay away from you or avoid our being alone."

"Is that how I make it sound?"

He put his glass down and went to her. "Now, Laurie," he placed his hands on her shoulders, "you know what's the matter with us? Our first day. We've been home one day. We're not used to it."

"Only one day!" She bit her lip. "Nature beat you home by an hour."

"Oh! I *am* sorry."

"So am I." Her lip was trembling. "I keep trying to get pregnant and I can't. Still," she was crying, "I was pregnant once. Maybe that *thing* they did spoiled me so I won't ever be again."

The floor of Aunt Betty's dining room tilted and in place of windows there were portholes. A brass ship's bell hung from the ceiling beam and spliced ropes adorned the fireplace. The captain's wheel, compass, and binoculars stood between the portholes. A mariner's map of the currents and harbor entrances to Caleb Island occupied one whole wall. At first, Aunt Betty had done the room up this way as a lark, all but the tilting of the floor, of course. When she saw Uncle Stuart's delight, the tilted floor had been put in. Since his death, marine curiosa had been added from time to time. All this had happened after the last of the once frequent meetings of Republican party leaders at the house. In that discussion, Herbert Hoover's despondency had led someone to suggest supporting the Democratic candidate, F. D. R., in view of the emergency. That had marked the end of Uncle Stuart's interest in politics. The dining room was the result of Uncle Stuart's last years, a reversion perhaps to his earlier days, in which the passion for sailing amounted to a mania. Laurie remembered Mr. Sands telling her during their honeymoon how Uncle Stuart had tried to take the ten top feet of the summer mast of the *Silver Box* and Ken's mother had not permitted it.

Ken and Laurie were the only guests invited for dinner. Aunt Betty's daughters and their husbands would be coming over later. She chatted about her month on Caleb Island and told Ken how old and failing Cousin Teddy had become. She was careful to include Laurie as she related that Cousin Arthur attended the last meeting of the Board of Trustees of Caleb Island to formally decline his privilege under the terms of Ken's great-grandfather Timothy's will which entitled Arthur to occupancy of Mansion House once Theodore left it.

"Of course, Theodore is still there but he leaves after the hunt. He'll be going to the hospital in Boston for observation. Before next spring the issue will surely have to be settled."

"I imagine Aunt Sarah will take over Mansion House," Ken said.

"As the last male Preston, you would have to decline first."

"I shall."

"Then I suppose you may as well know your Aunt Sarah has already told the board she won't accept. She's eighty-three now, Ken. She's resigning as chairman of the board at the next meeting."

"I wasn't aware you kept such close track."

"On the whole, I don't, but after all, Mansion House—"

"It's only a house. It can always be torn down."

Aunt Betty's mouth opened and shut.

"We tore down the old house at St. Terese this summer," Ken went on. "When a thing outlives itself, why preserve it?"

"Your grandmother entertained Dickens in Mansion House. Dr. Freud was a guest there in 1909. Lincoln and Grant visited in your great-grandfather's time."

Ken said, "I know all that. It's past history."

Laurie kept her eyes fixed on her coffee cup.

After dinner, Alicia and Margaret arrived with their husbands, George and Tuffie. They went to the living room where George mixed drinks. Reggy, the youngest, came soon after with Randy, Corinne, and her husband, Clarence. Marcy, second in seniority to Alicia, and her husband James had not yet arrived. They were having dinner with Marcy's old Bryn Mawr roommate, Dierdre, and Dierdre's new husband, Bruce Davenport.

"Not too new," Reggy said. "Bruce is her third and he's well over forty."

"Marcy's not so new herself."

"Cat."

"Dog-female."

They laughed.

"Al," George said. "Would you tell the kitchen we do need some limes out here?"

"Of course, George," Alicia said.

"I hear some great reports about you," George told Ken.

"That so?"

"Yes. Awfully. Cornering markets and things and stuff."

"It's not permitted to corner markets any more," Ken explained.

"Well, then, however you do it these days." George laughed. "And going on television too, I hear."

"I'm not sure. The firm may, just locally in a few cities, to introduce us to larger groups. Then we'll decide whether to launch our own public funds."

Reggy, Margaret, and Corinne had gathered around Ken. Laurie stood at a distance.

"I suppose you would do a market analysis that recommends stocks?"

"No, nothing like that. Just express views on topics of general interest so the public knows we're not outside society."

Aunt Betty was supervising as the boys set up card tables and laid out the scrabble sets.

"But Ken, you must! I think it's splendid. How can you help but? Imagine! Airing your views on *simply* everything. When do you start?"

"Ken said he won't," George told Reggy.

"But he *should*. You will, Ken, won't you? I mean you look at least as attractive as—who is that fellow?"

"Ed Murrow," Corinne said.

"Lord, not *him*. He's too darling. The other, dreadful one."

"I think it's simply marvelous. And you must keep your suntan," Margaret said.

"Yes, do," Reggy insisted. "I can't *stand* those white-faced ones. Especially on color TV when their make-up doesn't cover their ears like—what *is* that awful creature's name?"

"Not Ed Murrow?"

"No, dear, the *other* one."

Ken caught Laurie's attention. She looked at him, then up at the ceiling. Alicia returned from the kitchen. Randy had joined them to announce that card tables were ready. Ken asked him how his paper on Mach for his doctorate was going and learned that Randy had set it aside last year. Having rested up, he was now ready to begin again with a new theme—his own. "That the only security there is comes from making peace with the fact that there is none," Randy said. He paused and looked at Ken as though he were an open pepper shaker that might make him sneeze at any moment. "You see my meaning?" he asked anxiously.

Ken assured him that he did and George called out, "Al, your mother says there's Rose Marie candy in the music room."

"Of course, George."

"I wonder why Marcy isn't here yet," Reggy said.

"Because of Bruce Davenport. He's crazy."

"We're all crazy. We're bound to be. How can we help but?"

"There's crazy and crazy," Randy pointed out. "You've got to separate the sheep from the goats."

"What?" Aunt Betty asked from the other end of the room.

"Randy told Reg you must separate the chic from the gauche."

"Now, Randy dear, you know there are no goats on Caleb Island, only sheep."

"Whatever are you saying?" Aunt Betty demanded.

"That we must separate the sheets from the ghosts," Reggy said. The girls all doubled up with laughter while Aunt Betty shook her head.

"Speaking of goats, do you remember my nanny?" Alicia asked Ken. "And how furious she was at the way we played cowboys and Indians?"

Ken remembered, smiling. "Yes. The way we played it the cowboys were always bad and the Indians good."

"Yes, that was your father's idea," Aunt Betty told Alicia.

"It infuriated Nanny and it certainly confused you. You were really very good about it."

"Was that on the Rock?" Laurie asked. It was the first time she'd spoken.

"Yes," Alicia said. "When Ken still came for part of the summers. But I would play 'soldiers' and drop-down-dead by Ken's rules. That made us even."

"What were Ken's rules?"

Alicia blushed. "I don't remember."

"Nor I," Ken said, uncomfortably.

"Speaking of rules and nannies," Corinne said to Reggy, "remember our game of hide-and-seek?"

Amidst gales of laughter, the younger sisters recalled playing their memorable game of hide-and-seek one day before they were to sail for Europe. They were getting acquainted with the new nanny and they had locked her in the closet. Then every ten minutes for five hours they heard her well-bred knocking from behind the locked door and the muffled but unperturbed, "Hello there?"

"Yes," Aunt Betty said, laughing hardest of all. "Luckily I happened to be passing through and heard it."

"Otherwise we might have gone off to Europe and left her in there, still politely tapping."

At eleven o'clock, Ken told Aunt Betty he thought they had better be going.

"I'm sure Marcy will be here any minute."

"I'm not," Reggy said. "Bruce Davenport drinks a simply tremendous amount. They may just not be able to get him to move any more."

"Did Marcy *have* to see them tonight?"

"They're going to Europe tomorrow. Bruce Davenport had passport trouble, Marcy says. It's a matter of principle for him to leave now."

"He's the one used to be a Commie fellow traveler," George told Ken. "He was 4-F in your war. Flat feet, bad vision, and hypertension, I believe. He volunteered for Coast Guard Reserve and put in a few safe hours of harbor assignments. Got himself photographed in uniform, and now he keeps the picture on his piano."

"Still he's a fun person," Reggy said.

"He's crazy," her husband said.

"Awfully," George agreed.

"Everyone's a little crazy. I mean how can you help but?"

"Didn't he used to write under an assumed name for one of those *new* magazines?" Aunt Betty asked. "*Trends* or *Streams* or *Trees* or something on that order?"

"*Mainstream*," Randy told her.

"He also wrote books," Margaret said.

"Some were quite good," Ken said.

"Al, dear, my pipe is in my topcoat in the foyer."

"Of course, George."

"Don't you agree, Ken?"

"On what, Reg?"

"That we're all a little crazy. I mean can we help but?"

"Probably not."

"It's from all those little things," Reggy went on. "Like what Alicia and Marcy did to me."

Alicia returned from the foyer with George's pipe and pouch. "What did I ever do to you, squirt?"

"There. You see? Squirt. When I was five, Marcy was twenty and you were twenty-two," she told Alicia.

"Cat."

The daughters laughed.

"She and Marcy would shut me out. But *completely*. Marcy was the intellectual. Books books books. And Alicia liked to gloat over her maturity. So once when they were out, I went into their bedroom and wrecked everything I could find. Then I told them and it made me feel ever so much better."

"I remember that," Aunt Betty said, smiling.

"An hour later we invited her to show us the destruction," Alicia reminded.

"Yes," Reggy broke in. "And when I went to their bedroom, everything had been repaired, but simply everything."

"I asked her 'where is the destruction, dear?'" Alicia told Ken.

"And there wasn't any," Reggy said, earnestly. "Just as though I hadn't done anything at all. As though it had never happened and I simply didn't exist."

The sisters laughed.

"Well, all right, but it wasn't funny to me then," Reggy said. "That's why we're all crazy. We just can't help but."

"I do believe we must go," Ken said, rising. "I have a very early conference tomorrow."

They left the card tables and clustered around. Randy asked Ken whether he'd visited any museums lately and Ken said he had been too busy. Randy thought it must be fun to be that busy. Meanwhile, Margaret was telling Laurie, "We must have lunch."

"I'd love to, but make it before the twenty-seventh. School starts then."

"Oh, of course," Margaret said. "You're going to school now, Mother mentioned. Bryn Mawr, isn't it?"

"No. Columbia, so I can stay in the city and spend the nights with Ken."

"How is it going?"

"The nights?"

Margaret flushed and Ken coughed behind her.

"Oh, school, you mean," Laurie said innocently. "The term hasn't started yet. It starts on the twenty-seventh. That's why I said let's have lunch before the twenty-seventh," she added patiently.

The doorbell rang. It was Marcy, her husband James, and the Davenports. When Dierdre Davenport was introduced to Ken, she said, "At last I have a Wall Street tycoon all to myself and I can ask my question. Dear—" she called to her husband, who was heading straight for the bar, "I'm going to ask Mr. Preston my question."

"You do that," Davenport said, opening the gin bottle. "Then maybe he'll tell the rest of us when the next depression is coming."

She asked Ken if a stock was good, why would anyone sell it, and if it wasn't good enough to keep, why should anyone want to buy it. Ken tried to explain.

"How about the next depression?" Davenport demanded.

Ken looked across the room at him. He was tall and massive, rangy and blue-eyed with a bald head, shining red, and a fringe of graying, bristly, blond hair. It occurred to Ken that the story of his being 4-F or ex-Communist might just be another one of George's many malicious inventions. "Are you expecting one?"

"Sure. Aren't you?" Bruce was drinking straight gin over ice.

"Not with your apparent relish," Ken answered.

Bruce laughed. "That's good." He drank the tall glassful in two gulps. "So when is it coming?"

"I'm not at all sure it is."

"Course it is. Always has."

"I hope not."

"Why? Sell before the collapse and buy cheap afterwards. Isn't that the system?"

Reggy said, "Oh, good! Bruce is about to attack the system again."

"It attacks itself," Bruce said. "To each his own."

"He isn't writing these days," Dierdre said. "That makes him combative."

"Yes, it makes me combative and this gin is God awful." He refilled his glass. "Well, George, what are you engineering these days?" he called out.

Alicia and Margaret left for the powder room.

"Because he hasn't any ideas," Dierdre explained, though no one seemed to listen. "No ideas any more."

She approached Laurie and said, "You're going to school."

"Yes."

"I've been going for some time." Her lusterless eyes remained expressionless. One eyebrow lifted. "Last year I studied short stories, medieval universities, and computors."

"Computors?"

"Yes. Monroe calculators and percentage adding machines. Very fascinating. Year before that I finished Elizabethan culture and the year before that, advertising layout, the German poets, and fencing, I think. All postgraduate."

"I'm trying to graduate."

"I seem to be running out of courses, so we're going to Europe." She looked up at Laurie as though she were an oddity. "The main thing is to fill up time," she said.

Ken signaled Laurie. She excused herself and left for the powder room. Ken went up to Aunt Betty and told her, "We'll just leave without any fuss."

"What's the matter?" Bruce demanded. He was standing beside Ken. "Am I driving you out?" His voice was loud, dominating the room.

"No. We were leaving when you came. I have work that starts early tomorrow."

"Wall Street. You call Wall Street work?"

"Mr. Davenport, you do seem to be itching for an argument."

"Why not? Spice of free speech. You afraid of free speech?"

The room had fallen into a moment of silence. The silence continued.

"Means it's twenty to or twenty after," Reggy said.

"What does?" Aunt Betty asked.

"When there's silence like that."

"It's only nine minutes after," her husband said, and there was silence again.

Corinne giggled.

"What is it you'd like to argue about?" Ken said.

"Anything. I'll take the opposite side. Should be a natural. I'm an ex-parlor pink. You're a current fink."

"Whatever is a fink?" Peggy asked.

Corinne giggled. "Sounds like a Jewish midget."

"A strikebreaker," Ken explained. "A stool pigeon. In labor parlance, an enemy of the people. Isn't that right?" He turned back to Bruce.

"Right."

"Come now, Bruce, behave yourself," Aunt Betty said. "I'm sure you're planning to write something terribly amusing so do sit down and play scrabble and tell us all about it."

"No, he isn't," Dierdre said. "He hasn't any ideas."

"I'm not writing and I won't play scrabble. I'm not planning to write and not because I haven't any ideas." He smiled at Dierdre. "You know why publishing has fallen off, Preston? My agent told me. As a retail industry, it's now in forty-ninth place out of fifty, because apartments are smaller than they used to be! People don't have room for books any more. Come to think of it, that may also explain the new fiction. Everything's getting too small, even the planet. Destiny's just a thing called real estate. No more room. So in fiction, it's I, not you, not he, her, or they. No plot, no names, if possible no events. A noun and vowel fiction. No room for verbs and consonants. Just I, oo, and oi. No room and no time. I met a chump who was in the Navy with me. He didn't ask what my new book was about, only how long it would be. I told him it's a comedy, pal. It takes place in jail. Six Communists, old, loyal standbys, veterans of the Spanish war, unemployment demonstrations of the thirties, and the fight for the forty-eight hour week and social security, share a cell together; sort of collective solitary confinement. It's in the fifties and they're all past fifty, too old to quit, too young to die, too persecuted to forgive or forget, and too burned out to start anew. So they talk. What else is left? But they talk as though it's still 1936. Then one of them, the youngest, he's fifty-two, gets his hands on a newspaper by bribing the guard and sees what's fit to print. He sees the facts, the year, the day, what time it is. So he makes a soapbox speech. 'Comrades,' he says, 'we're living in a dream. We've been misled. The Kremlin is corrupt. Socialism is a mirage and Stalin is dead. In fact, he never lived. We've wasted our youth on a criminal fraud. Ten or twenty years ago we could have gone to our graves believing our lives spent in the best and noblest of causes. But now we know better and it's far nobler to die knowing the truth than to go to our graves believing a lie.' Quite naturally the others turn on him in the cell. They beat him to death. Then they burn the newspaper. And when it's almost ash, one seizes the flame with his hand, puts it out, and preserves a small patch of paper with a comic strip on one side and a piece of a bargain basement ad on the other. 'Why did we do it?' he asks. 'He was our only hope.'" Bruce drained his glass. "A very funny idea. Right? But my friend hadn't heard a word. He just asked me again, 'How *long* is it?' I said six hundred pages. He said, 'You just lost a reader. Who the hell has the time to read that much?' When apartments get larger, maybe I'll write again. Meanwhile it's no loss. I never was a real writer anyway. Always needed a timetable. Real writers know you can't find or beat time—that's what makes them write. I'm just not desperate enough. But all this gas has made me thirsty." He refilled the glass. "Leave it to the H-bomb. It'll make room enough for all of us."

Laurie reappeared, wearing her evening jacket.

"Do you have room for books in your apartment, Preston?"

"Yes, and respect for those who write them."

"Don't be silly. Why respect? Writing's a racket like everything else. You tell a bedtime story. You get paid for it. You tell another. Everything's a racket. If *you* don't know that, *I'll* tell another."

"I don't think I really do, Mr. Davenport." The room was silent again. "I believe people who write books honestly perform a great service, even when their powers are limited."

"Ha!"

"And I imagine the writer risks considerable ridicule, scorn, and pain by pausing slowly to distill things the rest of us pass over too quickly and lightly."

"Ah, life. Yes, life. No, life," Bruce said.

"No. Just fragments. A paragraph, a sentence, even a phrase. Sometimes only a word." He turned to Aunt Betty. "Good night, dear."

"Ken, you *must* go on TV," Reggy said. "I mean how can you help but?" She ran up to him. "You will, won't you?"

Ken smiled and pecked her cheek.

"Sorry you don't want a fight, Preston. I'm in a rare mood for one. Your mother was always ready. Great believer in free speech. I liked your mother."

"Oh?"

"Sure. She wrote me a letter once condemning my first book. Called it a dreary inventory of temporary sordidness. Said it lacked red cheeks and honest sweat. Nice thought. True, too. I never forgot it. We met years later and argued about it. During the war. Had a real ball."

Ken remembered Davenport's book, *Crust,* and Mother's disapproval of it. It was part of their wartime correspondence and he had defended it.

"She believed there was more truth in poetry than in history," Bruce said. "That's true too, though why I never could convince her I was a Marxist and not a Darwinian, I don't know." He was pouring himself another drink. "She attacked Darwin and I kept agreeing, but she went right on attacking. Said it was true enough that living creatures change in a changing world, but all that survival of the fittest trash based on an ingrained lust to kill was refuted by the very fact we were talking about it. 'Asking creates change all by itself,' she kept saying and I kept agreeing. Didn't know better at the time." He drained his glass and poured a refill. "All part of the great adventure," he said. He drank again. "Tell me, Preston. You finding the great adventure on Wall Street?"

Ken looked at Bruce's gin glass. "Why? Have you found it somewhere else?"

"I know worse places to look. And I've tried them all. What do you say, Preston? How about it? Anybody you know *really* find it, the great third path?"

"What path is that?"

Bruce looked him over for a moment. He laughed. "The one that separates us. Never mind, Preston. You've given up asking. I can see that. Well, I suppose there's no harm in still asking. Or is there?" He raised his glass. "Here's to the day after Labor Day, Preston. And how do you suppose the first Christian martyrs, early Protestants, and Pilgrims spent that first day after harvest? We'll never know. Your mother believed everyone should have money and leisure and when they did, life would be beautiful. Well, everyone damn near does. Is it? Just questioning, Preston. You were born on April Fool's Day, weren't you? My last question. Up with scrabble, gabble, and dabble. Down with the rabble." He drank. "You should try this. After a gallon or so, you're right in there pitching headlong up that golden middle stairway to the solid eighteen-carat Pearly Gate."

Ken and Laurie said their good nights. George told Ken in a lowered voice that he had hoped for an opportunity to pick Ken's brains on some good market buys and Ken said he would be glad to have his office deliver their new market letter by hand tomorrow. Aunt Betty took Ken's arm. Laurie held his other arm and they walked out into the foyer.

"What a perfectly dreadful man," Aunt Betty whispered. "I must forbid Marcy to ever bring him or Dierdre around again."

"He's sick," Ken said.

"You weren't serious about Mansion House?" Aunt Betty asked.

"Yes, Aunt Betty, I was."

"You really tore down the old house at Terese?"

"Yes, Aunt Betty, I did."

"I thought you once wanted to be a curator." Aunt Betty's voice was very angry.

"Once. I don't any more."

"No. Well. I'm sorry. I'll tell Aunt Sarah your views."

"I'll write and tell her myself."

"Don't forget we're all going up to the Rock second week of November for the hunt. It's Cousin Theodore's last. I've given you two months' advance notice."

Ken stared at nothing, then turned back to her and patted her arm. "All right, Aunt Betty. I will try to make it."

"You call him a writer?" Bruce was bellowing in the living room. "He has a tic instead of a talent."

Someone must have answered Bruce, for he was shouting even louder. "Not a point of view! A *pose*. I knew him in the old A.P. days. He was a phony even then when it was actually *easier* not to be."

George was at the door. "Ken, before you leave you must help us settle one thing. It's important. Awfully."

The others were at the door too, except for Bruce and his wife. Bruce stood amused, turning the captain's wheel with one hand and holding his drink in the other. His wife sat on the couch, sipping brandy.

"Wasn't the Fifth Column substantial in France?" George asked.

"It was a force," Ken said.

"So is an enema," Bruce said.

"When it became the Milice," Ken added, "it had to be dealt with seriously."

"And that was part of your job," George prodded.

"Yes, in a way."

"The only force that matters comes from what people *want*," Bruce said, twisting the captain's wheel. "*Natural* force. Hitler took France because the Germans wanted France. The French people were split over socialism and communism. Didn't know what they wanted. So they lost. Had to. Fifth columns means absolutely nothing. If your job was fighting the Fifth Column, you were on vacation."

Ken licked his lips. His face was suddenly white as he took a few steps back into the room. Laurie was still holding his arm. She felt his muscles tighten.

"I can understand anyone who served a Fifth Column with alien propaganda wanting to believe it meant nothing," Ken said quietly. "Then he couldn't have helped the enemy. It absolves guilt. Especially if one drinks enough to blur reason, memory, and conscience."

"So you do want an argument."

"No. Argument is a waste of time. But I won't mind knocking you down."

"He argues because he has no ideas," Dierdre said.

"Sure. Knock down a drunken man. Said so yourself. Proves my point. What you want, that's all. Everybody gets what they want. Today they want prosperity which breeds fatuousness. There's a word to try when you're drunk. But you never are. Fat you, fat us, fatheaded everyone. Synonym—there's another tongue twister, for immorality, mediocrity. Same old babble, gabble, and scrabble. World's dying because that's what all two-legged termites want. Everyone." He leaned forward. His tone seemed suddenly to belie any drunkenness at all. "You hear me, Preston? *Everyone.* You, me, Dierdre. And the reasons we give ourselves for what we do and get and are are bunk. We can't face the real reasons. They're too small and disgusting —too embarrassingly ridiculous. That's what makes them true. A man like you calmly burning up on Wall Street and one like me red hot with nothing to heat, telling you—we're both God damn liars." He raised his glass to Dierdre. "Damned and liars. And if you would ever drink to me only with your eyes, I should gladly drink with mine." He turned back to Ken. "Our real reasons are too grotesque."

Color had returned to Ken's face. "I don't believe you're in any condition to fight or argue but when you're sober, you might remember my telling you that people do not always get what they want. Propaganda misleads them. Innocence, ignorance, need, unalterable circumstance. Sometimes out of pain they confuse their dreams with reality."

Bruce had turned his back. He whirled on Ken. "We get what we *want!* You're not worth arguing with. I've changed my mind." He turned his back again.

"You've changed your mind in more ways than one. I seem to recall a book you wrote. *Freedom Bell,* wasn't it? That ended on the idea that the human unit built on love was life's answer to death?"

" 'Wherever men and women love and the fruit of their union is brought forth, death receives the invincible, permanent answer.' Unquote." Bruce said. "You might as well state it accurately. But I wrote that before Byron swam the Hellespont."

Dierdre rose from the couch and walked unsteadily. Ken saw her face in the mirror as she passed it on her way to the bathroom. It was a lopsided thing, as though she had suffered a stroke or a fractured jaw. She had not looked that way earlier.

"Ken, now that you're back anyway," Aunt Betty said brightly, "you'll stay for coffee."

Bruce let out an explosive laugh. His face went purple with it. "There's your answer, Preston. Everything is just too too. So why bother? Have your bloody coffee and go back to the counting house."

"You mean Wall Street?"

"Yes," he shouted. "I mean Wall Street!" The pressure behind each word was like the exhaust from a huge, overheated, overburdened truck going uphill.

"What's wrong with Wall Street?" Ken asked. His face was getting white again.

"Don't ask me. You're the expert."

"You're the expert on Lenin and Stalin but that doesn't stop me from having views on their criminality."

"Ah," Bruce gave him an owlish smile and returned to the bar. "I *used* to be an expert on Marx and Lenin before it got all mixed up with Stalin. But you're still on Wall Street."

"And I think you're still an expert on Leninism, which gave birth to Stalin."

"Because I don't swallow this muck?"

"No. Because you don't seem to be able to vomit up the muck you swallowed in the first place."

"I must have said something. You want to argue now. What did I say?"

"It's just the way you say it."

"No. I said go back to your cage on Wall Street, back where you came from. That got you. That's it, isn't it?"

"I don't have to stay on Wall Street. That's more than you can say for anyone in the Soviet Union before, during, and after Stalin."

"You want to argue, I'll argue. But argue about something you know. You don't know a damn about Stalin and you don't even know how to pronounce Lenin."

"Everything that's happened since the turn of our century pronounces Lenin. The thief of a democratic revolution, murderer of the best freedom-loving intellectuals in Russia and mass assassin of the most numerous, most oppressed of the Czar's subjects, the peasants. He forged the name of Marx to a nightmare parody of proletarian power. He was a gangster who ruled only by the armed force of a desperate minority. That's what the word bolshevik means. He relied neither on justice nor reason and never on popular support. That's how you pronounce Lenin, isn't it? All Stalin had to do was follow without deviation."

"Oratorical gas. You blame Stalin on Lenin, you might just as well blame McCarthy on Lincoln."

"If you'll credit Lincoln with preserving a form of government that made it possible to get rid of McCarthy by due process and without bloodshed, I will. Gladly."

"Poppycock. Hindsight."

"For us. Not for Lincoln or the democrat Jefferson before him."

"O.K. You're free as a bird. Fly home. There's no cage on Wall Street. I'm free to write a book. Dierdre is free. George is free. We're all free to spend our evenings just exactly the way we spend them. You're free, George, aren't you? Don't you feel free, George?"

"Never mind about George," Ken said. "I'm free to stay on Wall Street or leave or do anything else I wish and you're free to defend the Kremlin by demagogic word games."

"Get off it, Preston. I'm not defending communism. I'm just asking questions. That's the only freedom I have. I'll ask you again. Are you free?"

"Yes!"

"Take a look at your face in the mirror, Preston, and go peddle your freedom. I'm not buying any."

"Ken," Laurie said quietly.

He waited a moment. "You should get a look at your *own* face. I don't need one big answer. No mortal god of flesh, no one single road or any one *anything*, and that's what freedom involves. Choice. With a sufficient abundance of paths and alternatives open and available as well as all the pain that goes with it. Yes. And that's what you've lost: the ability to face freedom and re-enter a world of choices. That's why you're still an expert on Lenin *and* Stalin."

"Ken, you simply *must* go on TV," Reggy said. "Don't you think so, Bruce?"

Bruce laughed harshly. "I can't wait. Only loosen it up, Preston. We're all stuck in the same elevator and it isn't going up or down. So what's the difference how we don't get anywhere?"

When they were outside waiting for a taxi Laurie asked, "Did you enjoy yourself?"

"I tried to stop. I was like a dog with a bone. I just couldn't let go of it." Or it of you. Free! "I behaved like an ill-mannered fool bullying a helpless drunkard, exposing a beaten man to himself in the one and only area in which he thought he wasn't beaten."

"Don't be too hard on yourself, dear. After all, he exposed you first."

A cab stopped and they got in.

They were undressing. Laurie said, "I overheard Alicia telling Margaret in the powder room, 'Why do you suppose I always say, "Of course, George" when I want to say, "George, you're a mangy bahstard!"'"

They could hear the low, casual voices of tugboat captains on the river, clear and distinct as they gave informal orders.

"God," Laurie whispered. "I didn't realize the sound carried that well. Do you suppose they heard me?"

He managed a smile. "They have microphones."

"I think George got you into that argument with Comrade Bruce on purpose."

"Quite likely." Ken had removed his jacket. "Our George."

"Just call me Al," Laurie said.

"Thanks."

"You mean thanks *awfully*."

They laughed.

"Hearing their voices makes me think they can see me. Do you mind if I put out the light?"

"No. Senior Preston by marriage pretty soon," Ken went on in the darkness. "After Arthur and me came Aunt Sarah and as Aunt Betty is widowed and out of it, it's Alicia's turn next. So George gets Mansion House." Ken wanted to fling his jacket across the room but he hung it carefully on the silent valet, feeling his way.

"Did Aunt Betty upset you by talking about your once wanting to be a curator? Is that why you flew off that way with Bruce?"

"I was tense when I got home."

"It was nasty of her just the same. And I was nasty to you myself, Ken. I'm sorry."

"We're both wound up. First day back."

"And me with my period."

"Yes."

"Your cousins certainly make childhood sound like a carefree time."

"It was, for them," Ken said.

"They still sound carefree."

"I suppose they still are."

"Like the Dinsmores, the Little Women, and the Rover Boys."

Ken didn't answer. They were in bed now, their heads close on the pillows.

"Do you like them?" she asked.

"Who?"

"Your cousins."

"Sometimes."

"They become paler copies of Betsy-wetsy the later they get born."

Ken turned his face away. Betty's dining room brought back the summer when he was eight, and used to go with Cousin Arthur from Caleb to the mainland, visiting the old houses on wharves where retired sea captains lived among lobster pots. Arthur had taught him not to be fooled by the beds but to keep a lookout for the hammocks. When the rest of their families were sound asleep, the captains returned to the men they once were for their outdoor sleep and the smell of salt which a life at sea had accustomed them to. In these houses, there were companion and hatchways, ladders and places not too unlike a captain's walk from which they still could survey the ocean. After each visit, Arthur came away having made a Yankee trade on some item which he added to the Thorpe Museum. The sea captains were the first adults Ken had ever seen unashamedly unreconciled to the present with one loveless eye for their asparagus, potatoes, and pastures and their heart's desire rolling away before them in the endless azure acres of the sea, where the careless flood tide of their youth still lived. Aunt Betty's dining room bore the same resemblance to these homes that his place on the Street did to those who could conceive of no other way of life. While all of them no longer explored wider possibilities, at least for a dyed-in-the-wool Street man or a genuine seagoing captain, it was real. *They* were not play acting as Uncle Stuart did and I do.

"Ken?"

He turned with a start. "Yes, dear?"

"I have nothing to say to them."

"They're hard to talk to."

"Am I hard to talk to?"

"No, dear."

"Are you getting bored with me, Ken?"

"Certainly not."

"I'm not carefree. I never was. My childhood was more hell than anything. I can't break up with girlish laughter."

"I don't want you to."

"Are you just getting used to me?"

"No."

"Ken?"

"Yes?"

"I didn't mean the things I said when you came home. You know that. I just get a strong nesting instinct this time of month and what's a nest without chickens, hey?"

He patted her shoulder. "We'll have them," he said.

Suddenly she was furious with him. The very thing she once cherished in him, she now resented: his total lack of excess, the fastidious fairness amounting to uncertainty and passivity. Just when she wanted him to be unreasonably asserting and demanding he yielded and robbed her of something, impinged on her separate identity, *her* free choice. The preciousness of being a unit of one, herself. His entire way of life had become a yielding to her, for which in the end she paid. The times he was gone, the restlessness when he wasn't, his silence, his screaming, roaring, accusing silence were all part of the price. It made her cry out with a need to fill the void. Not fill the void of time, not like that postgraduate running out of courses, damn her to hell, no, but a living void to be filled by a living thing. A child. Yes. That's what I need. All right. Separate yourself. You can still enjoy the dubious freedom of separateness, of fantasy, and a vagrant spirit, the bachelor-girl joy of being alone during the long, aimless days. Unburdened and unfettered. You are just uneasy. You are not at home with these people; you never will be. It has nothing to do with Ken. Except to be part of his carefree cowboys and Indians childhood, manhood, family. Tomorrow I'll go shopping. I'll call Doris tomorrow. It's not a filling of time, not for me, believe me. Good for you, I

believe you. I try to believe you. I know you'll know and when you
know, I'll know what all this school is preparing me for. Go slow, go
easy. Please, please, go easy. Things can get mucked up right now
without too much trouble at all. I don't know why! I wish I did. I also
wish I knew why I am aware of my identity, my sense of self only when
someone seizes hold of it, demands that I surrender and relinquish it,
which is the one thing Ken will not do. His generosity suffocates. No,
it's something else. You are going through something, a desperate
sickness from which only good can come. Does that make sense? I'm
wasting time and yet it's necessary. There's no way to circumvent the
waste, no shortcut.

"What are you thinking about, Laurie?"

He felt her body jump.

"Nothing," she said.

During the early part of the evening, Reggy had spoken of her
third child, a girl, as "so gratifying." All the Prestons are girls and all
they have is girls. I'd take an ungratifying child! "You won't be the
last male Preston," she said.

Ken took her hand.

She said, "What else happened today, hey?"

He told her about Kirkland and the new attack on the bond market.

"How terrible. Did it ruin many people?"

"Enough."

"It's indecent and cruel and stupid."

"The government thinks it's a corrective measure."

"How can it be if it destroys the weak and benefits the strong?"

"The government should impose high margin requirements on bonds
if that's what they want," he said.

"What does that mean?"

"No, really, let's drop it." He told her of making fifty-five thousand
and lending Kirkland thirty thousand. "Do you mind?" he asked.

"No, I don't think so. Still what does that really help?"

"Nothing but my conscience, I imagine."

"What have you to feel guilty about?"

"Nothing, I suppose."

"You've had a terible first day back, that's all."

"Yes, perhaps that's it."

Perhaps. I imagine. I suppose. Why didn't he strike out, disagree?
She fumed: He *should* have knocked Davenport down! Better *we* than
I, she warned herself, remember that. I certainly *will* call Doris to-
morrow, first thing. Then I'll go window shopping. And flirt on the
Fifth Avenue bus. And get my hair done a new way.

"I've more or less decided not to appear on television," he said.

"I'm glad."

"And we *should* try not to get involved in all those dinner date merry-go-rounds the way we did last year," he said.

"We'll just stay home alone together."

"Yes."

Going on vacation for even three weeks was a bad idea, Ken thought. It was like swimming far out in a wild sea with the waves so high you couldn't see beyond your moving arm, simply believing that shore lay somewhere ahead. But once you were lifted out to rest on a boat a few minutes you could see just where you were, namely nowhere. You could gauge the size, range, and number of breakers and where you stood. Nowhere. Then you were thrown in again, burdened with the price of respite: the horror of knowing. But you've been back in the swim now for one whole day. A day? Only one day!

"Ken, what are you thinking about?"

"Nothing."

She knew it was not nothing. There was no such thing as nothing. Knowing that, in his answer she knew their separateness. It wasn't so much that Ken wasn't with her as the *feeling* that he wasn't with her, even when he was.

"I sometimes wonder," she said, "why you don't have a special friend, a man, I mean, like, say Doris and me?"

"I don't know. Being alone so much as a child, I imagine."

"What *were* you thinking about before, Ken?"

He suddenly recalled the prophecy forgotten earlier. "*You will run amuck.*" Kathy had said it. "Nothing, Laurie. Nothing at all."

Moonlight and disappointment flooded their bedroom. The voices of tugboat captains had ceased. There was only the small sound of a guitar drifting from across the river. Laurie sat up.

"What is it?" he asked.

"The moonlight," she whispered.

Its silver crossed their bed and he could see her face, throat, and fine young body in it as she sat upright, looking directly into the moon's bright beam. She sat that way, motionless, and he lay back, watching.

"When I was a child, I would look at the moon. I would stare into its face for hours," she said, "losing myself in its whiteness that surrounded me like a circle of silver—distant yet near—and I was lost in the middle of it, counting the dark ridges, just to hold on. My eyes wouldn't blink and I couldn't stop. But time stopped, because I wanted it to." Suddenly she was crying.

He drew her face to him. "What is it?"

"Nothing." Two can give that answer. Careful. Even a tortured *we* was better than the separate *I*!

"Please," he said. "Is it something I've done?"

"It's nothing," she repeated. She knew that he knew it was not nothing. She had expected something; she could no longer even state what it was. There were many things one could not name. But that did not make them nothing. "My mother once found a lovely dressing table in a secondhand store. She scraped and sanded it pure white and gave it to me. Maybe I just remembered how beautiful it looked in the moonlight."

He moved her head gently to his chest. Then abruptly, before he could tell her that living minute by minute he sometimes lost track of the days and how he understood her wanting a child and feeling both the days and herself empty and how twisted and turned everything got and how much he did need her and knew he needed her, she was asleep. She was breathing heavily. It brought to mind the time he'd boarded a train at St. Terese with Mother and Father when he was still a child. Two people, Father's friends, their names long lost, had come to the station on horseback and sat there waving them off. He had looked away from the window for a brief moment, then bent down to pick up a toy dropped to the compartment floor, he now recalled. In that split instant, when his head was turned, the steam hissed and the train twisted out of the station. When he looked back through the window he saw only a high wall of solid rock. The people on horseback were gone without benefit of transition, their smiles never given a chance to fade or their figures to grow small in the distance. One instant smiling and waving. Close, here, *now*. Another gone, past, *then*. For that reason they had remained a haunting, tantalizing fragment of the incomplete and always would. He suddenly felt as though his manhood were running out of him into dry, hot, and insatiable sand. But why and through what hidden path? Through time, he thought: your youth, your unused moments or half-used and abused ones. For nothing, to nothing, a nothing that covers all the somethings that can make everything go wrong. Her nothing or mine. Ours. The indescribable, immeasurable *nothing* when major parts of your self go untapped. And that brought back for a fleeting instant his wedding day, the sobbing in George's car, the anguish in their bedroom when the moon had shone so bright and she had waited on the bed. Had Mother told Davenport he was born on April Fool's Day? You usually did not discuss it. Laurie puzzled over the births she yearned to account for that couldn't seem to take place while you puzzled over your own that sometimes felt as though it hadn't fully happened. April Fool's Day. You were in your teens, you had refused to have a birthday party on April 1, and Mother had treated you like an adult. She had said, "Unless you are prepared to believe signs of the zodiac, phrenological

charts, and all the other assorted lunacies that raged over a once spiritu-
ally flourishing Boston, how can you attach significance to a day?"

Then she had laughed. "You know, actually you were born in March,
not April at all. At one minute to midnight, the last day of the month
which supposedly comes in like a lion. The doctor arrived after you
were born—three minutes after, according to the nurse—and he
couldn't abide a permanent record that proved all went quite well without his interference. So like all men faced by their superfluousness he
rewrote history. In your case, by only a minute. That's why your
certificate says April 1. You see? Not only doesn't it matter, but it isn't
even true. Besides, births should really be measured from the moment
of love and conception, in which case you were born on July Fourth.
I know *that* for a fact! Now what more illustrious birthday can a
Preston have?"

A Preston. The last male Preston. Moonlight had not made her cry
in St. Terese. But now that he'd done what she wanted, she wished
it otherwise. Not it, him. Wished *he* were otherwise; the kind of man
to whom all this came easily, naturally, so he could do it and stop at
five o'clock and not need a twenty-four hour vigil over himself in
order to do it for the customary eight. She had shed no tears in the
only moonlight that lit the lake the night the phone call came and she
told him she left her checkbook on the dresser. A Preston. A man was
what he was and if the most enduring part of one's heritage was kept
in that safety vault called the genes, what was his true net worth? Not
too long ago you believed that things done *to* you and *for* you, not the
things *in* you were the decisive ones. This shift in view was the result
of the past two years, just how, he didn't know.

He was facing the river. At his back, Laurie was breathing evenly
in her sleep. On the mantel the clock showed the phosphorescent
second hand moving. The moon had once hypnotized her and made
her think that time had stopped. But time rushed by the righteously
innocent and the world-weary foolish at exactly the same pace. Even
if it was relative, in this it was constant and absolute. Each had his own
time that left no alternative but to keep pace with it, consuming time
as time consumed you or else rot. There was the tragedy of time. For
one the adolescent moon, for another gin, for a third love, and for all
of us, action. "Scrabble, gabble, dabble, and rabble." It was outrageous.
It made all talk of continuity madness. What continuity could there
be in living the immediate moment of sensation in each lickety-split
fractional segment of a second like a firefly lost in an ocean of darkness?
Yet to do otherwise was even more outrageous. You knew.

Green and red lights moved north and south on the river. They were
thinning out now. A last ferry was approaching from Welfare Island.

The tugboat captain was speaking again, his voice intimately low and confidential. Over a game of cards he was confiding to his first mate about a woman, loved, mistreated, and lost somewhere long ago, and how he missed her now when it was too late. He was unaware that his microphone was still alive, broadcasting his secrets to both sides of the river. There was no sense to living now for later. Later never came, for the very simple reason that we don't learn from our errors in a way that redeems or undoes. We only say we do because we know we should. We should but we don't. We haven't yet found out just how that's to be done. So if we change, we only change the nature of our errors. To really learn and correct, one would actually have to stop his portion of time and who can do that?

Consume time while time consumes you, or mark time and rot. Those were the only choices. He was doing the one, Laurie the other.

She turned and her hand fell across to rest on his chest. We mourn the same thing, Laurie; the hopeless, one-sided contest. At least I am more free than she. Her choices are bound by biology. Mine lie outside myself. I'm glad you see that. Now feel it. Believe it. Try. I am traveling at the fullest speed I possess. In what direction is a separate matter. She isn't. Still time is beating both of us and for this we blame each other. What can either of us do save what we are doing? Shall I stop till she goes faster? Shall we compromise my ripeness or her unavoidable maturation? It would not help either of us. There is no way to live in the moment with a sense of eternity. Men speak of it but no one has found the way. I know her loneliness. I visualize her days. I see her waiting now for school to begin and then waiting to complete it. And then still waiting. And waiting for the life within herself. And learning. I do see it. Mine the freedom to err and hers the freedom to prepare. As Mother said in the twenties, there's freedom and freedom. Pointing to the Ouija boards, the bathtub gin, Dadaism, gang wars, and hello, suckers, is everybody happy? *It was the same story in the eighties when Mrs. Jack Gardner appeared at balls with a lion on a leash and a page to carry her train. The New England of the New World had ended. So Boston was free to rename Back Bay streets with bully old English tags and for St. Paul and Groton to revert to British educational methods. The young men were free to go West. The young women were free to perish on the vine. Everyone was free to believe in swamis and seances, to secede from democratic forms and facts to the old fetal state before the great Declaration and its full assumption of the responsibility of freedom.* I would like to sleep. I don't know what the responsibility of freedom is and apart from empty phrases, I don't think anyone does. She doesn't want your child, she wants *a* child. This is the time of month that reminds her she was born to do so and hasn't. Just as you wanted to be a curator, not of any one museum, simply a curator, one who preserves, and you are both free to do so. Well, what could she do? She did it. What can you do? Use her downtown as a file clerk? Invent work? Fire servants? Retire? Your anger has deeper roots than that but let them sleep. Let everything sleep. Let her sleep. Let me sleep. My way we could be spending whole days and nights together, always together. Yes, and shoring up even more untapped force to leave behind, to lose forever the time that is past, unused. So we do as others do. Excellence is only man's failure to achieve perfection and this unsatisfactory estrangement is called life. Sleep! That is a foretaste of death but in it at least you can rest.

He brought his face closer to hers, thinking, dear Laurie, you mourn your childhood time when the moon could hypnotize you into believing that time really stopped. It cannot be done. You cannot relive, or correct the uncorrectable. We are here. Your perfect little white table and our honeymoon are not. We exist. Even though we are messing it up, we exist and we love each other. He brought her hand to his lips. Everyone is messing it up, don't you understand? What else can anyone do? Some do it slowly, others fast, some noisily, others in silence. One may almost know it and another never know it at all. At least, dearest Laurie, we are messing it up *together*!

A muscle twitched in his left hand. He clenched and unclenched it but the twitching would not stop. He hung the hand down over the side of the bed but it still throbbed. Laurie's face was turned toward him again. In the moonlight he saw her long lashes and parted lips. Her hair lay tangled across her forehead. She hypnotized him as the moon did her. Time might have stopped in her for him. She seemed now more than ever a child, not a woman at all as she lay on her stomach, her face still turned toward him on the pillow. Then, still sound asleep, she sang in a warm, gay, confidential whisper, "Patsy oree oree ay, early in the morning."

He smiled and kissed her.

"Love you," she whispered. "Let's leave. Europe. Asia. School's out. Work's nothing. Together. No al—" She snored once gently and stopped.

Al—Did she mean alternative? Alteration? Alicia? She was sound asleep. All of us will come to our senses. I know we will because we have again and again in the past or the human race would not still be here, trapped and seeking escape as it does.

What had that to do with any of the intangibles that were keeping him awake, that rose only to dive and get lost in the nameless depths? He fell asleep.

Chapter 3

KATHY took a long last look at herself in the vestibule mirror as she heard the elevator stopping on her floor. Lovely. Check. Ladylike. Double check. The elevator door opened.

"Ah, good morning, Miss Hinkson."

"Morning, Mickey." She loved his thick brogue.

"Pretty cool out today, Miss Hinkson?"

The impossible things he did with the o's in a word like cool. "Certainly is, Mickey." Mickey always asked her views on the weather when she left in the morning, before she could possibly know. Months ago she had given up telling him she hadn't been out yet and took her cue from his loaded questions. She hummed. This was one of the few apartment houses in Manhattan that called the thirteenth floor exactly what it was. She lived on it and felt very lucky most of the time. It was a small vanity but whenever she thought of how being on the thirteenth floor didn't bother her at all, it started a chain of clean, cobweb-free reasoning that made her feel alert, present, and fully accounted for. Incredible that her rent was the cheapest in the building simply because it was the thirteenth floor and they admitted it!

"So you know 'Kevin Barry,' do you?"

"Why, I guess I do, Mickey. Yes, I was humming it, wasn't I?"

"I knew Kevin himself," Mickey said and saying it changed something about his waxy, double-chinned, overweight, pixielike face with the wisps of sandy gray hair over large bald spaces.

"Did you really?"

He stopped the elevator between floors six and seven. "That I did." He turned to her. "I was to be by his side that very morning, you know, but an incident detained me."

Now that his eyes were no longer glazed, she saw how china-blue they were, and there was color in his cheeks, usually veal gray except when he drank too much.

"There were these British soldiers chasing us and up I went over this fence! Well, what should greet me but a strange and beautiful lass with green eyes and a tiny waist. She throws her soft arms about me and puts her rosebud mouth on mine. When they flashed their lanterns this way and that, she cursed them out and said into their lights, 'For shame a girl can't make her own love in peace.' They left and she smelled of a sweet perfume and I stayed awhile. It was afterwards she showed me the way over other fences." He sighed, all fake joviality gone from his voice.

She knew somehow, that wreck of a man though he might be, on that night he was a slender, graceful, handsome boy.

"Now you're not Irish," he said with mock accusation to cover his embarrassment.

"No, please forgive me, Mickey. I'm not."

"And you've never been to Ireland?"

"Guilty again."

"A pity. If ever I had a few pennies put away, I'd go back before my time was up. Now I hope you don't mind my taking up *your* time." He stood straight, his hand on the lever, and started the elevator. "But you have a bit of a rosebud mouth yourself. That and your singing 'Kevin Barry.'"

She whistled it all the way to the corner, where she picked up a newspaper from the wizened, sour-faced misanthrope who never greeted his customers or even replied when they greeted him. Kathy was one of very few exceptions.

"I seen in Earl Wilson your firm is taking on some Wall Street house for TV."

"Yes," she said. "I'm on the account."

"Nice to have an inside track. If there's a good tip on a stock, don't forget me. I still have a grandchild to get through college."

"You serious?"

"Who jokes about money?"

"I mean you're not old enough to be a grandfather. In that case, I'd be glad to tell you right now." She gave him the Preston & Company recommendation which wouldn't reach their customers for at least three days and told him that too.

"Thanks! Thanks a lot!"

She walked on, aware of men eyeing her. She had to remember to tell that to Ken—Mr. Preston. Even the newsies were buying stock now. It was in the air. Still the firm name hadn't registered at all, even though Earl had mentioned Preston & Company in bold type. The "& Company" part was Irish. Coogan and McBride. Had to be. So was Ken's—Mr. Preston's—wife. I should have told Mickey about that stock. The only way to get those few pennies for a trip to the old country I can think of! Up to here in shamrocks, begorra. The

British are coming. Up the rebels! Mr. Preston came from Boston which was full of the Irish. It was also full of the general notion among good and dead—really good and really dead—Back Bay backbiters, that the Irish, like a hospital transfusion, were new blood, red, raucous, and fresh. There was more than one fresh Irishman who had tried to give her a transfusion. You can't tell Mickey about the stock tonight. He won't be on that late. Monday: Dad's night. Tomorrow morning then. That's still two days ahead. Almost like playing God. God is a man, dear. O.K., then, goddess. You walk like one. You are crrrazy! So was Frank Boyle last night. Another fresh Irishman. Nice boy, really—twenty-five, up and coming in the agency business. And, like many a lad before him, he had tried to deflower her. Of course he hadn't realized that having his way with her would have involved deflowering. Both his campaign and his surprise had been similar to most. Cocktails, dinner, theater, dancing, a late snack, then hugs and kisses at the door and some adroit feeling of vital spots along with giving her goose bumps by skillfully running his hands up and down inside her sleeves. It was perhaps unfair of her to have permitted the inference inherent in the invitation into her apartment for the well-established alibi of a nightcap, but perfectly safe. She had been successfully stimulated by all the methods known to well-bred, presentable unmarried young men who recognized the crucial difference between a masculine offensive and masculine offensiveness and knew just how and when to stop them. Frankie found it hard to believe, as hard as every young man gone soft before him. Then followed the conversation which she had come to look forward to. Different young men responded in such unimaginable ways! It seemed that most young men without marriage on their minds found virginity a depressing obstacle. If one were to believe the literature of eighteenth- and nineteenth-century romantics, such was not the case then! However—she had told Frankie, "I like to pet. I like being made love to, up to a point. I'm flattered to hear you say that not sleeping with me makes you feel robbed of your manhood." Though if that's really true, it can't be very much, she'd thought, going on to say, "But honest to God, Frankie, I'm still saving myself for that one and only guy."

The effect of this on some was to make them come back again. She imagined Frankie fell into that category. Yes. He would be back, and getting back to Mr. Preston and good old Boston, who still feared and hated the Irish: if *he* did, why these partners? And did he hate his wife too, she wondered. The air was clean and smelled mountain stream sweet, a rare thing in Manhattan. She was humming "Kevin Barry" again. Breathing deep with shoulders squared brought her chest up high. Does his wife have a rosebud mouth and a perfect thirty-six like mine? Now, Kathy girl, keep it clean. It *was* clean, part of why her mind was clear, not murky—she always knew how she felt. Well, how *do* you feel? Fine, thanks! And you? Oh, I really do feel very very fine, thanks, and the way I feel is made of so many many things! Like? Oh—putting out the light at night to fall asleep in no time at all and then waking in the morning with a bone-deep feeling of having enjoyed something delightful that used me well and left me ravenously hungry for the day ahead. I'm bright, that's another thing. Smart. Well, it's true. Look at how most people frown and fret just trying to understand the simplest things. And from the way all the boys keep eyeing me, how can I help noticing I'm pretty? Oh, stop being coy. I'm healthy and pretty and I love my job. Anyway I love the fact that it's an interesting job and the knowledge that I don't need it. I *don't.* Dad has told me often enough that I don't need it and he could support me without it being any burden at all until I got married. How very nice for our side that the profession he is so successfully engaged in is itself so successful among successful people who always need it and usually can afford it. If, for some reason, I never marry, Dad can support me and give me psychoanalytic treatment at the same time. Don't want that either, thanks. Still, knowing Dad's there is good. Gives a girl an added edge in competition and I *do* feel competitive this morning! I feel like taking on the world this morning. I want to gamble, go way out on a limb. That's the only way to enjoy competition, when you feel good and look good and isn't it marvelous to be grown up enough to be overjoyed that you're young? To be blessed with the imagination to appreciate it! Young, free, and without entanglements and not the slightest desire to be older or crawl back to the half-baked stage so recently and gladly left behind. Everything I am meets harmoniously in the immediate present. Pleased to meet you. Harmoniously delighted to meet you too, I'm sure. Very sure and also confident. That's about as much good fortune as any girl can hope for. Let's see, almost two weeks—no, not quite, twelve days but it feels like more than that since I first met Ken—Mr. Preston. The newsie was right. An inside track on Wall Street is real nice. More than nice. It's terrific. Something like having a personal copy of every map with the strikes in the gold rush of '48. '55 model, frontiers of finance. Wells Fargo, Diamond Jack, and here comes high-steppin' Kate, so put your money on the reds and keep your eye on the spinning ball. He saved me four hundred dollars the day we met and reading those market letters and listening for those few offhand remarks in two meetings, I am now nine hundred dollars ahead. Reminds me—remember to inquire about that info I found about the Preston family heirloom, talisman, really, that Paul Revere silver box. *Box* is a bad word for television: sounds sort of obscene. Silver isn't much of a word, either. Hi yo, Silver; silver threads among the gold. Judas and the thirty pieces. No. It simply wouldn't do. Nor would the House of Preston, a poor man's House of Morgan. More like the name of a pompous Chinese-American chop suey joint. A problem. Many problems. But I don't mind problems this morning. I don't even mind possessing my maidenhood this morning. Oh, I know it's not the result of deliberate design or virtue or anything like that, but I'm feeling right virtuous today. Well, you dear, designing, sweet virgin. I'm as virginal as any adolescent if you please and equally entitled to criminal disregard for established rules on adult daydreaming. So. So if Mr. Preston—Kenneth—Ken—would look me up and down just once it would please me very much. Hussy. Would you like that proposal placed geographically? I know all my geography, thanks. Reading from north to south, my silky hair, smooth brows, hazel eyes, lovely lips—I mean real geography, dear. Seriously. Like out of bounds, out of order, out of this world, nowhere. O.K., O.K. It's out. As you see and I'll say, the boys are really looking you over this morning. There are such nice boys everywhere. But don't ever send a boy to do a man's job of work or play. What is it about girls today anyway that makes them go for men old enough to be—for heaven's sake, don't horn in on Dad's business. And it isn't they—it's you. Sweet Dad. I'll swear he doesn't have the faintest idea I'm still a virgin. Monday. Monday night. Our night. Ever since I got out of Wellesley. It's fun seeing Dad. I wish it were to see some of these young Lochinvars. Why are they so nerveless, flat, and dependent? Natural-born vice-presidents. All Madison Avenue babes in the woodwork. In the king's English, natural-born meant bastards and am I ever in the middle of them! So are we all in the agency business, honorably in the middle of the boys and men destined to be vice-presidents. Tens and hundreds of vice-presidents. All agency life is *we* life. *We* this and *we* that, and *we* who are about to salute you with a die dee die die have wee wee in our veins. You may call it madness but we call it Team Work. Sweetie pie and honey lamb and baby doll and when something comes off, *we* did it co-operation-wise. Like *so*. But when something fails, it so swiftly becomes second person singular in a hurry, like *so! You* goofed it, sweetie pie, judgment-wise. But when *we* get high enough up the ladder, *you* never get fired. You just resign, diplomatic-wise. And if *you* don't, baby doll, we make it most unpleasant for you contact-wise. Behave and *we* even help you get a job somewhere else: we keep your secret. Still whenever *we* make it, somebody always gets a raise: in this instance, *you*. If *we* sell Preston on personally appearing in local TV like *so* and then afterwards *we* sell Preston & Company on a thirteen-week cycle nationally, like *so*, then *we* at Atwater Agency made it but *you*, sweetie pie, honey lamb, baby doll, will get the raise! Putting "s" for sex, before "he," by simply being she and staying wise, *we* can make him like it. Then *you* get the raise, which, like praise coming from Atwater, has to be measurable like fever or the mileage on a hired car. Ken's going on the air *is* good for you, I mean him. Well, both. Truly! All right, all right, it's right for him, and his firm. And all that business about boys and men to one side, men like Preston are shaped in a different furnace. Wall Street is still lone wolf country. The vanishing American, and speaking of wolves, the boys are really howling this morning. What was it he said that first time about individuality? It will come back. Whatever he said, it was very true. I remember it feeling true at the time he said it. You felt many things when he said whatever he said. There are men and there are boys and you are not alone in that. Just look at the names that still sell tickets and get ratings: Jimmy Stewart, Gary Cooper, Cary Grant—give me that old-time religion! It was good enough for mother and it's good enough for me, I, us, and aren't we-you-I in a real merry mood this morning, miss. Just full of forbidden thoughts. Just so long as they're only thoughts, pleasantly wicked little ideas. But as Mr. Atwater has so often pointed out in behalf of Think Sessions, "If it's sound, what starts as the germ of an idea ends as action." It wasn't sound. It was most unsound. She nodded, telling herself firmly how unsound it was. Still she continued to smile, happily aware of walking faster than the others headed for the subway. Brazen, that's what I am. The result of four years at Wellesley, where girls were at long last permitted to marry—but not until they took an oath to conceal from the other students the secrets of the marriage bed—and the girls called the boys for dates. Girls without boys. There were some girls who didn't mind being locked up with other girls all the time: they just *loved* it. But for those like herself, after they had enough lonely weekends and the Cambridge boys didn't phone them, why, they just learned to phone the boys. In the beginning the aggressiveness of it was too much for her. But the first time she had forgotten duty on tea-serving at the dorm and again deliberately avoided the duty the following Sunday, her peers had voted the punishment of social probation, two whole weeks of it, restricted to campus grounds with nothing but girls, girls, girls, so that by the end of her second week she had overcome her reticence sufficiently to call a boy for a date, and imitating the others, ask, "What are you doing Friday night?" Then she learned to fence off the male assumptions that followed such feminine boldness. How many of the others preserved virginity to Commencement Day as the targets changed from Harvard seniors to young instructors to profs and Boston bachelors, she did not know.

By now the procedure of making the first advance and preventing the last was part of her higher education, along with Arista in high school, the dean's list later on, and graduating with honors. First it was a point of honor, then a contest, soon a pattern, now a habit in which by one technique and another, release of tension no longer demanded the sacrifice of virginity. Keep it up, dear, and one day you'll be the most brazen, unsacrificed, middle-aged virgin in town. But right now do wipe that smile from your face or the cop on the corner will think you're flirting. Some construction men whistling. See? The cop may even take you in for soliciting. Everyone thinks you're on the make. Not at all. Just admiring. Who would believe that you're still a virgin? No one. Sometimes even I don't. But virginity is not a state of mind: it's a biological condition. It's almost embarrassing to be twenty-three and that free or unfree or whatever I am. *Ah so!* as the Japanese generals say—you *do* concede that virginity is likewise a state of mind. Well, what with contraceptives and penicillin, what is there to fear biologically or logically? Nothing. I'm glad to hear that because I feel quite fearless this morning. Before she had gone to Wellesley, adolescent Kate, with no mother to guide her, had watched Dad squirm as he put on his best psychiatric manner and uncomfortably say, "As to boys, if and when you want to, do. And if you don't want to, don't." I guess I just never ever wanted to. At least not enough. Not yet. She was humming "Kevin Barry" again. His wife was Irish too. Can you imagine little roly-poly Mickey with the courage to jump fences, kiss green-eyed colleens, and stalk the bloody Irish night to try and keep a date with doom around that little bakery where they fought them hand to hand. To think that Mickey lost his great, historic moment for love! You just don't seem to be able to get your mind off romance this morning, do you? This is a working day, girl, and you are a working girl, and one hour from now there will be serious business to do with Mr. Preston, for Mr. Preston, on Mr. Preston and please do call him Ken. Thanks loads, I will. Ken. Conference with Ken. Ken, what pains you so much and why do I feel that all your strength and youth and wonder at life haven't even barely been touched yet? What can anyone do about it, Ken? Isn't there something I can do about it? There must be something, to bring you back from wherever it is so many miles away you seem to be, even when you're right across the table. I'm going to walk to the next stop. It's early and a good and mercifully abundant God has given me a simply scrumptiously beautiful day. I'll window-shop, that's what I'll do. It's early. I'll go down Madison. Feeling this way, I know how good that will be. Blouses and scarves and gloves and leather bags and shoes will all sing out their beauty. Yes, color and form do make music. Red will be the bloody brass of sunsets seen, field-fresh tomatoes and orange is yellow raised to its outer limits of ripeness fortissimo, like pumpkins bursting in autumn. While green is young spring, the whisper of new grass, made for bare feet to run in, dewy wet, or mysterious perfection in the shape and feel of an emerald, streams drifting swiftly over watercress in bright, spanking sunlight. The old, deep browns of leather and the pungent new smell of it will send shivers through you when you feel like this! Rough, thick, leathery things evoking village smithies of centuries back and their coarse aprons resistant to the sparks that flew as strong-fingered, male hands shaped hot metal for horseshoes and wheel spokes and the distant, well-used, smoothed out leather of coach seats on a racing carriage, careening down some crooked, cobbled road in sixteenth-century England. Old England, New England, masculine fingers, the traditional countryside. Mr. Preston, Ken, you and yours are really on my mind this morning. I'm full of a greedy zest for life. Past, present, and future. I glow with it. Ken, watch out, for I mean to explore any and all discoverable infinite possibilities.

Dr. Hinkson maintained his relaxed, casual expression as he sat listening to the dying man in the hospital bed. This was their first meeting. Very likely it was also their last. The patient had cancer, and metastases had spread far beyond surgical control. At most he could live only another month. When he died, his friends would repeat and repeat that he had had everything to live for: there were such corpses. He was the successful sales manager for a London fabric house in the United States, a prosperous Englishman, married, father of two adolescent girls and not yet forty-five. Everything lay ahead. Especially death. The patient had put his affairs and estate in order. Now he refused to eat or drink and fought sedation. The moment he regained consciousness, he ripped the intravenous from his veins. The internist had requested this consultation in hopes that perhaps Dr. Hinkson could get the man to eat and accept medication without the need to resort to restraints. "Anything that psychiatry can do in the face of a somatically hopeless situation," the internist had said. As the man knew he was dying, it was possible for Dr. Hinkson to be forthright without being tactless. He had pointed out that the man owed it to his wife and children to make the last months easier for everyone by agreeing to sedation and eating; trying generally not to upset his wife and children—in short, making the best of a very bad deal.

"Think of the happy years you had together. More than most. None of us knows everything about our future."

Now the Englishman was slowly answering and each word was

painful. "But I *do* know my future. And as medicine won't help me, I must hasten it myself."

"Come now. The same decent instincts that led you to put your estate in order should likewise—"

The nurse appeared and whispered, "Doctor, your daughter is calling."

"Calling?" In his total concentration on this crucial conversation the words meant nothing but intrusion. *Calling* meant something. Then suddenly that phase of his life fell into place and jolted the rest to make room. "Take the number," he snapped, "and don't interrupt again."

When she left, he locked the door, faced the patient, and their eyes met.

"*Your* daughter," the dying man said.

Somehow it lifted a curtain between them and made something clear to Hinkson. We are torturing this man. He has already been tortured beyond endurance. This organized effort to make him stand on the side of life, regardless of what absurd or grotesquely impossible depths his part of it has sunk to, is barbaric. He is not even dying on his native soil.

"Very well," Hinkson said. "I will admit it should be entirely up to you and I'll urge that fact upon the others. Now won't you admit that this proves you are still in command of your fate? Some of us wait for death in total helplessness, believe me, that's true. Since all of us must die, to control how we do so is the most any of us can expect when the time comes. Now don't punish the living any more than you have to."

He accepted the emaciated hand the patient offered him, pressed it, and left.

Outside he told the internist categorically not to attempt any further forced feedings or imposed sedation, and to firmly abandon any notion of the use of restraints. Yes, it was aiding death. He knew all that. His professional advice had been asked for and he was giving it. The wife was waiting, her daily preparation for widowhood begun.

"How is he?" she asked penitently when Dr. Hinkson approached.

"How should he be? Dying and knows it. How would any of us be? Help him to get through it as quickly as possible. I know how hard it is for you and your children, the guilt you feel, and your fear of a future you are trying not to face as yet. And he reminds you. Let's try to remember that for him there is no future, only the past. Help him take pride in it, instead of mourning where he can still see. Tell him how he has provided for his family and that because of it you won't have to worry and that your deep love for him frees you to think only of the joy of your life together. He won't find that heartless, believe me. Speak of the times you will always remember and try to believe you actually will. Convince him you cherish it and it will always bind you." He felt suddenly sick of himself and of all words. "Make him believe in the life he has had. It may hold him to life an extra moment longer for your children's sake and remove some of the resentment of death from his face."

The woman was weeping wildly. She stopped, her face drawn and pale, opened her pocketbook, and powdered her long, thin nose.

"You're quite right, of course, doctor," she said, matter-of-factly, "but it has been a bit of a knock."

Would he never grow accustomed to Monday, the disturbing day of his week? The rest of it he practiced in his penthouse suite and the weekends pleasantly passed at his country place in Danbury. They were easy days on the whole, quite unlike the clinic or the occasional private consultations such as this one in the medical wing across the green from the new psychiatric building. His old English desk, his spacious office, and the manageable neuroses of his patients in his private practice made him feel quite often that he knew things worth being paid for. Sometimes he actually brought about permanent cures. But here, where except for an occasional nominally paying consultation like this one, he wasn't paid at all and worked a longer day than any in his office, he always finished with the feeling that he owed something to someone and had no way of making good on it. Monday was his day of inadequacy, his day for heroes and heroines—people to marvel and wonder at—how and why they could and wanted to survive.

This week's hero was Danny, a nine-year-old boy. In a day of incredible things, the simplicity of Danny had stood out. Brought in as a truant, he had stopped eating. His school grades were good, his attendance record excellent, his I.Q. high, but one Tuesday morning almost two months ago, he had simply stopped going to school. More than a month later, the day he was picked up, he was sitting on the bedroom floor with his three-year-old brother, watching carefully as the little one tried to build an imposing edifice of wooden blocks. Without shouts, tears, or protest, Danny had clutched the bedpost in a death-grip and silently held on despite the frantic, unsuccessful efforts of the huge, powerful female truant officer. The boy's mother, the officer noted in her report, had stood at the bedroom door, sad-eyed and mute, observing, understanding, it seemed, but not interfering. Brought in eleven days ago, Danny had refused to eat until those four days later when Dr. Hinkson had first met him. Then under Hinkson's skillful questioning, the truth came out. Danny's mother had tried to poison his father and Danny had heard all of it. When his father said, "What next?" his mother had shrieked, "I told you after Danny I didn't want another baby and I don't."

From then on the question, of course, before interviewing either parent, was whether the boy was lying, hallucinating, or telling the truth. It had been Dr. Hinkson's conviction that Danny had spoken the truth. After that, Danny said, he had sat guard over his baby brother. Today Dr. Hinkson had managed to get him to recall that it was his mother who had told him, "You are the bigger, older brother and if you want Mommy to love you always, you must protect Andy from danger at all times." The mother had been interviewed during the week. He read the case report; obviously paranoid and fighting a losing battle against mental illness. Her effort to poison her husband was none too serious—ammonia in coffee—the smell alone was sufficient warning, had her manner not been. They had fortunately found room for her in the city hospital where a course of electro-shock treatments was scheduled. At the end of the interview with Danny today, he told him, "Your brother Andy is fine, your daddy is fine, and your mommy is now seeing a doctor and will get all well again."

Danny kept his face turned away. When Dr. Hinkson placed his hand gently on the boy's blond head, Danny looked up at him with a grown-up knowing in his eyes and in a sad voice said, "No. No, we're not fine. We can't be. I come from a bad family."

Dr. Hinkson sighed. Arson. Suicide. Addiction. Prostitution. Murder. Rape. Poverty. Ignorance. Did the classic psychodynamic patterns of a safely middle-class Victorian age still function in the face of this modern, streamlined inferno and bedlam?

The elevator door opened. He was stepping in as the nurse called from behind him, "Dr. Hinkson, you didn't take your daughter's number."

Freud had once said you could outlaw neurosis. Perhaps one could outlaw humanity as well. We're certainly trying. He stepped back and followed the nurse down the corridor.

Kathy had called Kenneth Preston and said she very much wanted to see the Street and the Floor and to kick some ticker tape with her own shoe so she would know what they were talking about.

Then, after the Visitors' Gallery, a peek into the customers' room followed by a walk down Wall Street and across Pine, she returned to his office and asked him questions, which he answered with reserve.

"But how do you find the projects?" she persisted.

He described the machinery of research, the tape, charts, industry earnings reports.

"I don't mean that," she interrupted. "You must have some personal sort of gift, something uniquely your own that you do."

"If so, it's hard to explain."

"Please try."

He thought. "Well, I suppose once you know the thirteen-hundred-odd stocks listed, and remember their symbols and price ranges, and have read annual reports on most of them over the years, any new piece of information brings to mind old memories. The product, specific individuals in the company, some bit of history connected with it. The security comes alive for you. Does that make any sense?"

She nodded. "Something like Sarah Orne Jewett's way of finding a story?"

Ken smiled. "That seems an odd comparison."

"I don't know. Didn't she say that whenever she saw an old house and thought of an old woman, something clicked and she knew she had a story?"

"Yes. I'd forgotten. To whom did she say that?"

"Willa Cather."

"That's so." He was still smiling.

"I've been rereading both of them lately," she said.

"I haven't read that kind of book in almost two years." Saying so felt like a betrayal of Laurie and he became abruptly formal again. She felt it and tried to re-establish balance.

"As part of preparing to understand your background better so that the public will," she explained.

"That presupposes I intend to appear on a program."

She sought some short cut to head him off. If you don't keep your mind on business, she warned herself, you will defeat all your aims, both your aims. All? Both? There was only one—

"And I must tell you," he was saying, "the more I consider it, the less I care for it. In fact—" He went on to tell her quite plainly that he was moving firmly toward the decision not to participate in any of the six television broadcasts. He admitted that his reasons ranged all the way from personal aversion to well-considered principles of sound policy. On all counts, perhaps it was best that the idea be dismissed, and that future proposals of the agency or network be based upon the premise that neither he nor his associates be expected to appear or have personal messages read in their names.

"Besides," he said, "five weeks away from the office is quite impossible at any time other than the summer which is now ten months away. And even then summer belongs to Mrs. Preston and me."

"Of course it's your decision to make, Mr. Preston. I did think you had tentatively decided to keep an open mind on it as we explored the relative advantages and disadvantages." A bad day for trying to clinch matters and a bad way to have started. It had seemed so promising this morning, but his phones kept ringing and that little man in the pin-striped suit who was sir-ing Preston all over the place bounced, flounced, hopped, skipped and all but jumped and flew in and out while the tape kept up a constant buzzing, clicking, and ringing, and Preston's aloof reserve kept increasing. Some specific pressure, an irritation or a disappointment—she couldn't place it. "Shall I slit my throat here or let the blood run downstairs over coffee?" she asked.

"I should celebrate if I were you. We can have coffee sent up."

She declined. One phone call in particular had intensified that look of irritation, impatience, whatever it was. She had tried to fathom what was being said at the other end.

"If he wants to terminate the relationship," Ken had said in reply to something, "I see no reason for prolonging it at all. We can sell enough positions, all of them, in fact, if need be, and pay him out this week. Our soy bean rise will take care of it and Hawley's quite capable of taking charge." Then he listened while his face grew more serious and he said, "I assume you did remind him it was considered that a sell-off could take place, and in the light of developments there's no objection to shortening positions." Something seemed to straighten up inside him and he put an end to the discussion. "No," he said. "Let's sell all positions at once and pay him out."

She found the earliest opportunity to suggest coming back later in the day in the hope that he might be able to spare twenty minutes away from the office at that time. She was back at three-thirty and Mr. Sloates said that Mr. Preston was on the telephone and would she please wait.

Ken was talking to Coogan. Pat was saying he thought Ken should speak to Mac before he left the Floor. "Just tell him you appreciate his offer to wait two months, even though we don't need it. I don't want him thinking there's bad blood here, Ken. It will only make him talk his head off on the Floor and that can't do us any good with the Board of Governors or our customers or the general public."

"If you think so."

"I really do, Ken. His big beef seems to be we didn't ask him his views on the public funds and the spending of money for TV in particular."

"But we did. We had lunch for that express reason. I quite specifically asked for his views."

"Hell, I know that. And you know Mac. Let's just not give him any fancied grievances to raise with the Board of Governors."

"Very well."

Ken told Sloates to listen in and take down a transcript of his conversation with McBride. When he got Mac on the Floor phone, he invited him to come up to his office.

"Haven't the time," Mac said. "What's on your mind?"

"I merely wanted to thank you for the offer to wait two months."

"Our contract calls for it."

"In any event, we won't need it. You'll be able to draw down your capital within three days."

"Suit yourself."

"Also I get the impression you feel the public funds, and, in particular, the television aspects of it weren't discussed with you. For the record, that's what our lunch conference was intended to cover the other day and I did ask your views. You said you had none. Pat said he left it entirely up to me. Now, also for the record, the entire issue is still open. The firm has made no commitments of any kind whatsoever."

"For the record I don't give a good God damn about the public funds and I am not a mama's boy who goes running to the Board of Governors. It's your snotty attitude I object to. I don't need you to tell me you don't dare leave town to go on TV."

"Really?"

"Yeah, really. Because you can't afford to take the chance of leaving your well-padded wife alone for five whole weeks and I do mean *hole*. H-o-l-e."

Ken hung up and was around his desk, flinging his door open, striding for the elevators nonstop to the Floor.

"Mr. Preston!"

Ken stopped. He turned. He caught a fleeting glimpse of Mr. Sloates, red-faced and bent over his typewriter. *You'll run amuck.* Prophecy. The prophet. Why was she here? Oh, yes, appointment. You are doing exactly what that gutter bum wants you to do. Public spectacle on the Floor. Scandal. News. I'll deal with McBride though. I'll destroy him.

"Yes, Miss Hinkson?"

"Are you all right?"

"Quite. Come in."

"I thought we were going out."

"Yes, of course. Out." Lucky she was here. And Coogan was about as wrong as anyone could be. Mr. Sloates was pointedly tearing up his notes. "Mr. Sloates," Ken said. "I am going out."

They sat over coffee in the drugstore, where she had taken the offensive. "I'm going to be blunt, because you are a gentleman and I know you won't strike a lady. To begin with, I'll admit I know absolutely nothing about Wall Street, and—forgive me—but you're in

the same predicament on public relations. If I entered your domain, I'd
have to forget my personal prejudices, wouldn't I? You are entering
mine. All I ask is that you do the same. If the evidence shows that it
serves the best interests of your firm to accept my proposal, bow gracefully. Now, the first time we spoke, you said you had no fear. I accept
that. So I'll ask you, what evidence have you to support your opinion
that your appearance on TV is unsound policy? I've brought along a
good deal of evidence to the contrary." She opened the brief case,
showed him the high ratings received by Monsignor Sheen when he
spoke on subjects like reverence and immortality, and certain programs
of Ed Murrow's dealing with politics, art, religion, philosophy, eco-
nomics, science, and democracy. She had charts on successful television campaigns relating to cancer and muscular dystrophy and data
on the broadcasts of President Eisenhower, as well as unofficial records
of professional public relations planning and the actual presentation
of the President of the United States to the rest of the world.

"None of these success stories deal with tangible products or flashy
personalities. They're all public-minded and nonprofit making, and
the personalities maintained their dignity and sold ideas to millions
of people. Now, other than prejudice or fear, how can you reject this?"
Again the word fear. Again the response.

He said, "All these people had standing. It made their views important." But his voice was not steady.

"How can one's views become important unless he expresses them?"
That's a lot of control and plenty of control, she thought. Like putting
your finger on a buzz saw. She went into the issue of pinpointing sales,
getting people to go to a store, pick up a phone, write a check, send
letters, and told him how one brought such things about through
proper television preparation and display. She had statistics on high-
priced quality products sold through the medium of television: dia-
monds, mink coats, luxury cars, first-class trips to and around Europe;
items costing no less than three thousand and frequently more than
ten thousand dollars and how television found their potential buyers
and made them buy. *He isn't listening* and you are missing the chance
of your lifetime. Then she showed him the records of new companies
and new industries, those that went on television to educate the public
as to their existence and those that didn't, and above all, those who,
going on television, went all the way, using a personal approach to
make the missionary work less abstract; showed the results of these
against those who were timid. In the midst of it she saw the clock
over the pharmacist's counter and jumped up.

"I have to call my dad."

"I beg your pardon?"

"I said I just remembered having a date with my father."

She phoned her father's answering service, then reached the hospital and returned to ask Ken if he minded changing tables to be nearer the phone so that she could prevent anyone from using it till her father returned her call. It would only take a few minutes.

"You ask questions most effectively," he said. "Where did you get the training?"

"I had to know how to ask questions in order to survive. Before I joined Atwater I was a nursery school teacher. But getting back to the subject while we wait, unless it's fear, how can you expect—" *That was it, all right. Fear, and you are going to stay on it.*

She had a way of turning her head from him after asking a particularly pertinent question so that he faced her profile as she listened to the answer or alertly waited out his silent reluctance to give one.

He couldn't be offended, really. You either had to listen to her or postpone this discussion. You either had to defer McBride or go back there now and destroy him. Her use of the word fear was accidental. But not with Mac, no, not with him. Well, do you? Is that what you can't face?

A man, red-faced with anger and speaking in a gravelly voice, was saying, "All right, operator, stop arguing and return my coins. Return my coins, damn it."

Kathy smiled. A lady sitting at the next table sighed. His wife, poor dear. They turned their heads away but Kathy had stopped speaking so they could not help but overhear.

Clang. Clung. Clunk. They heard the man scoop up the coins. "Well, all right," he said. "Now let's start all over again." They heard the sound of a quarter as it slid into a slot and down into the bowels of the phone's receiving box with its responsive gong; the gong had a faintly flat sound. "All right now. I *just* dropped in a quarter. Now is *that* a quarter?" His voice rose to a shout. "What the hell is the *matter* with that quarter?"

The phone Kathy was guarding rang. Laughing, she ran to the booth and pulled the door shut.

We are all of us ridiculous. The statement was ridiculous. Remove the provocation, there was nothing left. Remove your prejudice and what's left here? Her arguments were sound and so was she. There was a wholesome definiteness about her face, the space between nose and mouth, as well as in her firm chin and dimples. It brought to mind a strange combination of words and impressions: chastity and the English countryside, all glowing with boundless health. Have you really heard anything she said? A challenge. The question is to what? No more false challenges. Not any more.

She came out and said, "Dad couldn't talk before because of something about an Englishman."

"That's strange," Ken said. "I was just thinking of you and England."

"And I thought of you and England this morning," she said, and blushed.

They had a last cup of coffee. "I wonder how much of your reluctance is garden-variety modesty," she said. "Most of us hide our vanity—and greed too, I suppose—behind a mask of generosity, but somewhere deep down we know just what we are. Maybe you do the same thing in reverse. Hide generosity and a low opinion of yourself behind that get-tough, inscrutable mask. If that's what we're up against, my arguments are worthless. Because then you *do* see that you should do it and you know you can, but it offends you to admit you want to, so no matter what evidence I submit, you just won't."

"You make a bad weakness sound like an attribute. I will admit you've made me feel less certain. I'd like to reflect on all this. May I have those charts?"

"That's what I brought them for."

"I must go back to my office now," he said.

An elderly man's voice, hurt and indignant, came to them from another phone booth. "No, I won't see him. It makes me cold. I don't want nothing to do with strangers. You didn't ask me, you *told* me. So now I'm telling you, and it's enough now."

Kathy shook her head and rose.

"What made you leave teaching for the advertising business?" Ken asked, outside.

"What makes any of us leave the thing we always wanted to do for something quite different? More money. A greater challenge. The wish to show someone we love that we can. Some need, I guess, we never understand till years later, to prove something to ourselves, that's even more important than doing what comes naturally."

He flushed and she pretended not to see it.

"Of course, opportunity, too," she went on as he walked with her to the subway. "Mr. Atwater's granddaughter was in my class. She was having some trouble adjusting and her mother invited me to dinner to discuss it. He was there. I think Mr. Atwater was all set to threaten me with exile to Alaska if his granddaughter didn't take over as head of all the kids within forty-eight hours. I explained how I thought you got resistant pre-school tots to think and accept new and sometimes unwelcome ideas and values. He said that was exactly the principle of his business, but it paid ever so much more, so here I am. Of course I still can't use singing folk songs, playing the guitar, or drawing funny pussy cats: the major equipment of a private school kindergarten teacher. But I'm sure all that will come later."

They were at the subway station. "I appreciate your efforts," Ken said. "I shouldn't like you to think they've been wasted."

"I don't," she answered him confidently. "And I don't know why I'm telling you this, but I'm way out on a limb. I'm nobody at all and I had no business seeing you or showing this to you. The agency thinks your sales resistance to personal appearance is hopeless. I don't. They think it's conservatism. I don't. They think you can't adjust to streamlined techniques and that you are afraid. Mr. Preston, I don't. So if you are still undecided by tomorrow morning, this is as good a time as any to say good-by." She extended her hand.

"There's no need to," he said. "I've just decided I'm going on that tour."

Dr. Hinkson sat at the bar in Twenty-One, sipping his second martini. It was just as well that Kathy would be half an hour late. This Monday had been more Mondayish than most. He probably would never know what it was about the clinic that unnerved him so. Perhaps the knockdown, no-mercy nature of the emotional emergencies, the drastic destructiveness confronting unprotected existence, the lick-spit-and-a-promise character of clinic assistance. Still, it was better than nothing: but how much better? Monday brought him face to face with colleagues, and not in the same way that conventions did, where, drinking between times and being armed with the paper he invariably was presenting, it was possible to meet them on his own terms. He knew their unspoken criticism—unspoken to him, at least— that reached his ears every time. *Glib, arrogant charlatan.* No less than the orthodox zealots did he consider his position well founded in Freud. If diagnosis led to cure, there was one secondary gain to Mondays. Colleagues saw him in action on Mondays whether in case interviews, supervising psychiatric residents on the wards, or in conference. They had to face the fact of his ability and knowledge, and the further fact that while his views on many theoretical matters did not coincide with those of their various groups, he did help both patients and residents. Monday brought the feeling of being on trial. Gentlemen of the jury—sheep! It is of course true that without tender affect a human being is seriously disturbed: the one central characteristic of psychosis is absence of tender affect. But the other side of that matter, what was usually described as "head-over-heels in love" and was more like heels-over-head, needed some additional probing, and that suicidal state was not unfamiliar to him. He had experienced it with Kathy's mother before she ran out without warning fifteen years ago in San Francisco and left him there to raise an eight-year-old daughter. It had taught him how lunatic is the state called love. Its ecstasy created the pathological need to surrender one's self, be the sacrificial goat, abandon self-interest, intelligence, reason, and all the minimum needs of survival. Now, Dr. Freud, isn't that psychotic too? I, a respectful disciple, ask the question. He now had such love only for his daughter. Frankly faced, that was suicidal enough and because he had this suicidal love only for Kathy, he had taught her to live by this view, which, he supposed, made him a traitor to his sex. If in order to live without it, one needed evidence that love is unimportant and impermanent, Kathy certainly was prepared. It must not be she who sacrificed herself at the altar of someone else's pleasure. In short, you want her to be like your wife, the kind of woman you hated —because you loved her. Well, well. The picture of himself as a hopelessly infatuated father, victim of his pretty daughter's every tyrannical, feminine whim, made him smile. At least no carnal appetites were entailed; not consciously, anyway. As for other women, appetites and their gratification were sufficient. At forty-five he was still as trim as any boxer or professional dancer. Sun lamps and weekends prevented pallor and his face was handsome with the kind of gray at the temples and black, neat mustache that were almost summer-stock-theater perfect. He had no trouble in finding sensitive young women who ardently believed his profession endowed him with a sixth sense, secret knowledge of the human heart, and he was not above taking full advantage of this popular misconception. Ah, Monday, Monday. How good it was that he had managed to arrive in time for a couple of drinks before Kathy joined him. The Monday clinic was necessary as well as unavoidable. It reminded internists, residents, and the hospital administration of his existence and his skill. It remained the major path to referrals. Sometimes he felt that the change of pace from the relatively minor ailments and safety of his office to the vast, free-playing interdependence of the hospital assaulted him more than it was worth. Perhaps one Monday this change of pace would have the effect upon his return to his beautifully appointed, quiet office and his middle-aged, middle-class, middling-neurotic patients that abrupt deceleration of a fast-moving car has on an icy road. He would be spun over on his back, the four wheels of his equilibrium spinning in space, his ego jangled like bits of flying glass in a car wreck. He wiped the martini from his mustache tip deliberately, telling himself: I suspect you of wanting a vacation or resenting the fact that there are so many private patients available at present, with not enough time in which to see them. If so, be consoled. The dying Englishman was a private consultation. His widow will pay. He flushed under the statement as though a stranger had said it to him, insultingly, challenging his integrity. He ordered another martini, this time for Kathy. She should be here at any moment now. In fact, should have been here already. Each week she began with a drink and the idiot-of-the-week story at the agency. Last Monday it was the campaign slogan proposed for a match company introducing a foot-long match for starting fires in country fireplaces. "Nero never had it better." This week?

Seeing her every Monday was also disturbing, as well as stimulating. She meant too much to him. Perhaps the ritual should be abandoned or at least he should make the offer. She was so fully in possession of herself and so gaily forgetful of what he had put into making her so. The fact is she was no longer his. She was almost a casual stranger now with whom he had once intimately shared joy and sadness. They met in a key of comedy, high spirits, and frivolous superficiality. Perhaps his colleagues were right after all. Yet his paper on "Neurotic Latency Origins of Some Postpartum Depressions" continued as a classic in the field both for psychologically oriented gynecologists and, whether they admitted it or not, the members of his own profession. Kathy didn't mind his attitude toward love nor his candor in speaking of it. At all events, his view of the matter was stated frequently in his lectures and papers, in which he defended its consistency with Freud's theories on nonreciprocated overinvestment of libidinized narcissism, differing only of course as to conclusion. Small point. It was sheer self-defense and he knew full well that he did not draw this conclusion so much as this conclusion drew him: it was what he felt and lived by. As with others, thought merely followed as elaboration. So far as the foolish young ladies were concerned, at least no one could deny that he always made himself clear from the very beginning and never, ever, had any of them been past, present, or future patients. He had a standard disclosure, a standard disclaimer before seduction and he never failed to make it. "You fascinate me completely and I count the days until we meet. But holy love, marriage, and all that sort of thing are no longer for me." Meanwhile, his eyes gave the hot, smoldering impression that the words were dusty shibboleths not to be believed at all.

"Greetings, Daddy dear."

Dr. Hinkson made a swift transition, turned to her with a mocking smile, caught her wild elation, leaned over to kiss her cheek, and then handed her the martini.

"Yum and yippee." She took a sip and sat down. They saw the curious looks of others and smiled like conspirators.

"You look lovely today." He said it in a voice loud enough to complete the illicit impression and they laughed like wicked children.

"Why so late?"

"Very important business."

"Successful?" he asked seriously.

"Successful indeed!" She finished her drink. "God, that's good. I feel as if I've returned from no man's land. Remember I told you about Kenneth Preston?"

"How could I forget? The man to whose market letter I'm indebted for some sizable profits the last two months."

"Yes, well." She waved his remark aside impatiently. "Atwater's son wasn't getting anywhere with him. Nor was the network. I felt I was. So I took my life in my hands—" She told him the day's events. "Now if I only had your profession and knew just *what* it was I did that made him change his mind, I'd be on top of the world."

"You succeeded. That's enough. My sincerest congratulations."

He signaled the bartender for refills, raised his hand for the head-waiter, and they left the high bar stools for their table. She was explaining what was at stake, seeing Preston without the account executive. She couldn't control the sheer pleasure of violating the rules, of ignoring proper channels. It seemed almost as delectable as the success itself. "I think I probably would have been fired and of course they would have lost the Preston account."

They clinked glasses and sat down.

"I'm glad for you, rabbit. It must have been difficult. I see the differences between the securities business and medicine, but somehow one doesn't expect Wall Street to advertise itself, either."

"Very old fashioned, Daddy dear. Everybody's interested in Wall Street now. It belongs to the people. The public has a right to know their story."

They studied menus.

"Frogs' legs and *escargots*," she said. "I feel garlic hunger tonight. Maybe it's a craving for dry wine and lots of it. I never talked that hard or fast!"

He ordered. "Everyone's interested in psychiatry, too, these days. Do you think *I* should go on television?"

"You would be devastating."

He laughed. The waiter brought their refills. "And how devastating is Mr. Preston going to be?"

"Marvelous. He can go on doing it for years. The ideal type for the future."

Hinkson had located her exact mood and was trying to adjust to it. "And here all along I thought with his background he was more typical of the past."

"Only to savages," she assured him.

He interrupted her to urge that she taste the cheese spread on celery.

She did so and licked her fingers, then went on, "You take the kids of today, the ones growing up into the age when war will be outlawed if we are to survive. Are they going to admire all that rootin', tootin', shootin' stuff? Never! It's like admiring your own executioner. And please don't give me any of that masochism-sadism, death urges stuff. They'll change their tastes. Women have already and when these kids do too, the civilized man will be their new hero. So long as he's colorful and you can love him. Preston is and you can." She took another helping of cheese and celery.

"Are you planning this as a children's hour?" he asked, teasing. "I mean you *are* planning all this."

She smiled.

"What does this lovably intellectual giant look like?"

"He's about your age."

"Aha!"

"Aha! yourself. He has no thinker monstrosities, no high forehead, bushy hair, bulging eyes, or thick eyeglasses. He's a big man, but graceful. Black hair, gray eyes, nice chest that I'm certain isn't hairy like so many are. And let's see. A dimple on his left cheek, fairly flat bellied. And altogether a most presentable figure."

"Very observant."

She went over the entire story again. It was still too much to be taken for granted. "And now all these dodo birds will go ahead to make the money and take the bows. All they have to do now is lead him through six broadcasts in six cities and not make too many mistakes."

"Come now, enjoy your triumph."

"That's what I'm doing. I'm reflecting on it. Brooding. It's my triumph."

"Did it hurt anybody?"

"Not a soul. The account executive still gets his override."

"You sound envious."

"Aren't you clever. I am. Envious, enterprising, and still thinking. This caravan doesn't start for a month. A whole month." Her mind was racing. She had taken it this far. Why not? "I made up my mind and you may be the first to congratulate me."

"What happened now?"

"I'm going on that tour."

"Is that for you to decide?"

Her face was flushed. "Why not? I decided to sell Preston and did, didn't I?"

The insane thing was that he believed she could. "You've grown quite ambitious in one week."

"In one *day*," she corrected. "It will be a relief not to be around that agency. The second-class atmosphere gets me down. It's their attitude toward themselves. Each of the owners came from a top agency but they weren't in a top spot when they left. You know? And they have fine clients, second, third, or fourth in their fields. There's a glory attached to first."

"And is Preston and Company first?"

She laughed. "Not even fifteenth or twentieth. But he could be, if it mattered to him. If it was the place he really wanted to be and felt he naturally belonged, had to be. He *could* be first."

Yes, he believed it. He would be missing Mondays soon. Another free night to be filled, the freest night of them all. Modern father and daughter. Cheerio. *Arrivederci. Auf Wiedersehen.* It was humiliating that it should hurt him so. It made his manner more supercilious. "The part that will interest me," he said, "is how you convince them that it's quite all right for a pretty, unattached young maiden to travel in the company of a handsome, married gentleman, for five weeks, to Pittsburgh, Detroit, Chicago, and Los Angeles."

"You left out Boston. And I do thank you, kind sir, for the complimentary language."

The waiter appeared with the dry wine and the ice bucket. "Does your employer know that Mr. Preston has agreed?"

She looked up. Then she began to laugh. "I forgot to tell him."

They both laughed and when they stopped, he said, "Well then, naturally they haven't the faintest idea of the rest of your plans. Does the client have any intimation?"

"None," she assured him.

"I do congratulate you," he said.

She nodded.

"And all this. Won't it hurt somebody?"

She shrugged delicately. "*Quién sabe?*"

Chapter 4

THE trees were turning scarlet and yellow. The wind that blew from the Palisades defined Laurie's thighs and pressed the blue sweater against her breasts. This morning at Morningside Park and on the Drive, she had watched mothers fussing with babies, adding blankets, avoiding the wind. All through French, Lit, James Joyce, and whatever, the little faces had come back, defying her to concentrate. She propped her right foot on a bench and pulled the dry leaves out of her sandal. Boys whistled and she thought, I should be mad at them or something, but I'm not. Not even "or something": they're so young. Still, there was something mighty mixed up about giving them all that instinct, energy, and so forth, especially *so forth* and then sending them off to school like kiddies who had to ask Daddy-o for an allowance. Your maternal instinct is overboard. James Joyce could have used a mother. The air was colder but the sun was still warm. Too bad for those babies with nurses. You could tell the ones who had love, whether mommy's or nurse's or big sister's or grandma's by the way they held darling or shifted him or her. Get your mind on your textbooks. Next week means midterm exams. Get your mind on that. How do you expect me to? You're going to the doctor for the last tests that matter. In the morning a schoolgirl, in the afternoon a would-be mother, on weekends a bride. Morning, noon, and night. Jekyll-Hyde. For three weekends now, flying out to join Ken. Boston. Pittsburgh. Detroit. Now Chicago, and then Los Angeles. He was waiting to hear about Chicago and that was a longer ride what with tests next week if it happened to snow and the plane was delayed and you know damn well that's not the reason. Pop lives in Chicago and Ken's office has already heard from him—*that's* the reason. Mr. Dugan hoped to meet his son-in-law. You will go anyway. But right now it's the doctor's you're going to, to find out. You will find out. You have been finding out for over two years now every single month. You'll adopt a child. But that's not where the hunger lies! She phoned home and got her messages. Aunt Betty had called again. She always called when you were at school. Doesn't believe it, or refuses to accept it. Ken called from Chicago. An hour earlier there. During the weeks of his absence, resenting it, you really made something of those phone calls. Hello hello. How are you how are you? How is it going how is it going? Fine fine. I miss you I miss you. I love you I love you too. Good good. Good-by. Me too.

No doubt my fault. I gave him a hard time before he left. He gave me an even harder time by leaving and between weekends time yawned, bored by your existence and with excellent reason. No need to be petulant about reality. You are bored with it, too. First during the weekdays, Ken called every day, then every other day. Now twice a week. He's busy. So are you: a schoolgirl who wants to be a mother. You've seen how busy he is. The press, the staff, the public, the network, the agency, and publicity. Questions, answers, and receptions. Flights, trains, planes, and schedules. The events were a whirling dervish with skirts of many colors, meant to make you dizzy. How did he do it? Why did he do it? All she could make of it was a rising tide of greed for money, a zest and enthusiasm that made him a hero and the closed door sessions with his colleagues, which she sat in on to a welter of mumbo-jumbo the like of which could not be equaled! Charts and Wall Street. The Pit and pitfalls. New customers and taxes. Tax law and the ignorance of new members of the staff. It was all like the baking of a strange, mysterious cake. You watched the ingredients go in, saw the light go on in the oven, felt the heat, smelled the smells, and then for some reason had to leave before it all came out a cake, to be eaten. Friday night, Saturday, and Sunday, the long weekend. But the broadcasts were on Monday and in these weekend reunions your resentment vanished. Some part of the excitement rubbed off on both of you together. Then when you left on Sunday night you felt the big door shut with you outside, a door behind which you yourself had placed him. The week before Ken departed, you gave him the hardest time of all. Could be because of what Coogan did: either that or all those emergencies that began with McBride leaving the firm. Then came President Eisenhower's heart attack, and what that did to the world of finance, Ken's world. Afterward, there was that bright young man with the dimpled cheeks, curly brown hair, and cereal box-top smile, Stan Hawley, taking every last night that stood between you and Ken, "familiarizing himself." The more Holy Hawley familiarized himself, the more she was estranged from Ken. The more hours they were locked in Ken's study, the more locked up inside herself she became. Finally Ken said, "Really, Laurie, you might offer Mr. Hawley a cup of coffee or invite him to dinner, at least once." She might have, but she didn't. She had in fact said, "You don't even know whether he's going to stay. So why waste all this time on him? Or is it that you've nothing better to do with your nights?" By the time Ken left, she was ready to admit, but only to herself, of course, that the size, shape, and disorder of her conduct came from her own size and shape, the disorder of barrenness. The wish, the need, the obsession to be a mother. Going to school was a joke. Then the jealousy came like a sickness and vanished only when Ken suggested she join him on the weekends. Cute Coogan. Coogan had quite a style. No doubt because he does not want this tour and what follows it and he came real close to using me to prevent it. A man to watch. All he had done was call and ask was Ken home. No, he wasn't. Would he call back and tell Coogan whether he was leaving for the five weeks next Monday or Tuesday and was Miss Hinkson the person to keep in touch with while he was gone or was he right in assuming that Miss Hinkson would be touring with him? Cute. At that point Ken had not yet even told her that he was going on tour! Put in another dime and around we go. Sure, he hadn't told her because of all the pressure. McBride leaving. Eisenhower sick. Hawley needing assistance. When she mentioned Kathy Hinkson, the blankness on his face should have been answer enough. "Miss Hinkson? Certainly not. Why should she go on this tour?" But only visiting Ken on the weekends could assure her. Nothing could assure her or reassure her now but what the doctor had to say.

She was not sterile! Dr. Claud repeated it. Not sterile. Today's test ruled out the only remaining possibility: low thyroid. The ovulation test had been repeated and her careful daily taking of temperature made Dr. Claud firm and definite. She was fertile. She could conceive. Her womanhood was vindicated. Before leaving, she paid the nurse in cash; she was still in a daze.

The doctor frowned at the cash and all it implied. "We must get around, Mrs. Preston, to having your husband examined." He frowned again with active disapproval.

She apologized, "You know how men are. I don't want him to feel— well, you know. If it's his fault—"

"It's nobody's *fault*," Dr. Claud said. "That's a most primitive way of viewing it."

She left, her heart on fire with song. The back alley slinking to Havana, the strange doctor, the pain, the biting of the wedding ring that wasn't hers, all this had left a scar but it had not maimed her. She could be a mother; she could and she would. A *most* primitive way of

viewing it! Being man and wife was primitive. Being mates was
primitive. The fruit of your womb came from the beginning, the seed,
and the egg. What could be more primitive? I'm primitive. I never said
I wasn't. The feeling of joy and vindication stayed with her halfway
out to Long Island. Then it came to her as a shock. Past instinct lay
the dark side of this truth. She was fertile. Then Ken was sterile. She
drove in silence as that took on its own life and penetrated. You have
it in you to create, but you won't because he can't. Once you wept
because you were pregnant. Then because you weren't. Now because
you can be. Look at it this way. Motherhood did many things. Take
Mary. Losing Helen wrecked her. Over six years ago: how long could
you let a shadow chill your heart? Forever, in a mother's case. It
brought back last night's conversation: the reason for this visit. Mary
had phoned to talk baby talk in a small girl's voice. That meant she
was very drunk again. So you had decided, first school, then Dr. Claud's.
Afterward, if the news was good, a shopping spree and either way, a
visit to Mary, maybe Doris for dinner and home again. Was it good
news? Ken is sterile. How is that for news? Bad news travels fast. A
good thing this week coming up he was in Chicago and you had midterm exams. Better not to see him. Not till you're used to it, till you've
figured out how to tell him. Why tell him at all? For all of his quiet
authority, Ken needed so much babying himself and didn't know it
because his mother-bitch had held out on him. Held out in more ways
than one. I wish it were me. Bad news. That's why we're headed
straight for Long Island. Yes, very primitive. So primitive in fact that
you forgot. "It takes two to create the bargain of life and the argument
of it, but only one to prevent it." Unbidden it came to her that she had
blamed Wallie for something done in Havana and a doctor's knife.
He had not been guilty of it. The wind blew dead leaves against the
windshield. Where did all the roses go? A good thing Ken called early
and you were out. This morning you woke, crying for the child of your
own: little old unnecessary me. What's so great about motherhood?
Mary is your mother; apart from the sheer fact of life, what else did
she give you? If some other woman had raised you, someone who
really wanted a child, desperately wanted one, to whom you were not
an accident but an act of choice, how would it all be now? You can't
spend too much time with Mary. Not today. Better call Doris.

She stopped and phoned and Doris was delighted.

"Let's see, it's two. I'm due at the beauty parlor from three-thirty to
five. I can cancel that." She sounded unwilling to.

Laurie said don't. She didn't mind the beauty parlor. Doris would
pick her up a little after three. Before she hung up, Doris said, "I
need some advice," and they cracked the usual jokes about the halt

and the blind. Doris said, "Gosh, it must be heavenly to do what you want, when you want, and everything."

"Sure." Indeed. *Certainement.* Heavenly, absolutely. Then why does it feel like hell!

The new girl said, "Mrs. Dugan's out to lunch." She gave the word "lunch" a curve that told Laurie everything she didn't want to know. Pretty soon this new girl would be replaced by yet another new girl and still another. It happened more frequently now. Did she only imagine that there was a connection between the length of time they stayed and the frequency of her own visits to Mary? Were these get-togethers as tough on Mary as they were on her? It was two-forty-five. *Lunch.* Don't tell me, let me guess.

The store had certainly grown. So had its inventory. Mary had never taken a penny from her in spite of the fact that beginning as a source of fury between them it had become one of humor and now of silence. Sound management. Mary hasn't the character to resist the bottle but she can say no to my help and make the store pay. Probably due, as Ken's market letter said, to "an upsurge of prosperity unparalleled in history."

A corridor connected Cleary's Chop House to Cleary's Bar. Just one door away. Convenient. It was a nice place and the prices were high. Laurie looked through the restaurant, went to the ladies' room, and with that excuse paused at the entrance to the bar. Sure enough, there was Mary at the farthest point from the window, talking to a man and laughing shrilly. The bartender rubbed a tall glass with his towel. The tiny mouth in his fat face, parted like a thin slot in a juke box, was on the ready for the punch line to a joke. First Laurie felt anger, then squeamishness: it ended as anger at herself. She walked in and up to the bar.

"We have an appointment, Ma, remember?"

The look of panic in Mary's eyes softened her. She nodded coldly to the bartender, ignored the other man, and took Mary's arm. "Is there a check?" she asked.

"Mrs. Dugan's credit is good here." He made it sound like Laurie's wasn't. Mary pulled her arm loose, a child defying its— *forget that.* She led Mary back through the restaurant.

"How about some coffee?"

"I don't like coffee. It takes away the spell of the drink."

They came out on Main Street through the other door. Then Mary said as though ending an argument, "All right, all right. I'll tell Maureen and we'll go."

"Oh, is that the new one's name?"

Then Mary looked as if she were going to be sick.

"I'll tell Maureen. Just stand there and get some air."

On the way back to the house, Mary kept up her patter. Laurie had learned how to turn it off and not hear: almost like the deaf did with hearing aids. Maureen's girl friend has a boy friend. Maureen's girl friend's boy friend wants the girl friend to go to Florida, but the problem isn't whether a single girl does that with a married man. It's "do you tell the boss where you are really going, or pretend to be sick?" Maureen gives advice: Tell the boss. It's wrong to tell a lie!

They were back at the kitchen table. Reluctantly Mary was drinking the hot black coffee. Her patter had grown progressively faster, more scattered and pointless. Listening was like watching a chicken without its head, racing in a narrowing circle. Something about old Poop, that's Potter, widower, big man now in flower nurseries. Very big. Two hundred and forty pounds. Rich. And *all* in the rubber business.

O.K., I get the inference.

Before he got rich he weighed one hundred and thirty. Guess why? The food he eats, the amount of it, and a quarter of a million dollars worth of canned goods in some place he owns in the woods "in case of atomic war." Nuts? He married a girl, she weighed ninety pounds. Now she weighs two hundred. Weird?

"O.K.," Laurie said. "O.K."

"What's O.K.?"

"Just O.K.!"

"I called last night because I was scared," Mary said. "I'm not scared any more."

"What were you scared of?"

"I don't know. Yes, I do. I woke in a strange bed. I didn't know who I was. He begged me to stay and I wouldn't." Her defiance rose. "When I got home I was scared."

"You need a doctor."

"Is it sick to be popular?"

"Is that what they call it now?"

"I don't like sleeping with them." She rose from the kitchen table and went to the pantry where she kept her supply of scotch.

"O.K., Ma, let's drop it."

"You mean stick to coffee. You think I'm drunk. You know how many people have a drink after lunch? I'm certainly *not* drunk."

"I didn't say you were."

"Oh, ho ho." Mary's voice was coquettish with an undertone of malice. "I know you, my daughter."

Your daughter. My mother.

"If you don't watch yourself in strange beds with strange men and not knowing where you are, you're going to get hurt. Really hurt. And you'll come home with a souvenir."

"A souvenir? My doctor checks me regularly."

"I'm talking about getting pregnant."

Mary laughed. "I guess I've lived longer than you."

"I guess you have. And I guess I was an accident because you told me so and I guess you still don't know what time it is."

"Yes, you were an accident." She took down the scotch. "Your brother Tom was your father's way of showing he still had rights. Helen was planned. *She* was no accident. You were. Now if you're here to give me lectures, you can go right home again. I pay my own way. I don't need lectures."

She walked out and into the bathroom where she scrubbed her hands. The number of times per day had increased now. I must scrub my hands fifty times a day. So what? It keeps you clean. And the house is clean, too. No one could say she had let go. Clean as a pin. She vacuumed the rug in the living room after supper; when she didn't have dates, she vacuumed it for hours. Lots of baths. Sometimes during the day at the store, the need to take a bath was—well, not quite as bad as the need for a drink. Then there was this looking in the mirror business. Wanting to look in the mirror and not doing so. Passing mirrors in the store and keeping her head turned away until the last moment. In the end, she *had* to look. Something about a mirror. This one right in front of you now, look at it! First you see yourself without clothes on. Then to stop that you think of Tom and you see him but *you* are still there. The idea of rushing down Main Street without clothes on was the one she stopped in its tracks by bending her head forward till she felt the point of her chin on her breastbone. There was one sure way to get rid of it. She smiled. Just at the moment when they were relaxed with their arms around you and the lights were out, when their guard was down and they least expected it, could you ever reach a high, shrill shriek when you wanted to! Did you ever know four letter words! *She* doesn't want to be an accident. I didn't want to have one. Telling me I need a doctor.

Mary came out of the bathroom and returned to the kitchen. "I get lonely," she said. "Maybe if I had grandchildren it would give me something to do."

Is that an accident too or did drunkenness give her an evil accuracy? The strangest thing was Mary still looked young. Still lovely. Only that fine network of lines at the corners of her eyes. You can see the resemblance. You *do* look alike: except she was more like a woman should look—small and delicate. Quite accidentally you inherited the big-boned frame of your big-boned father and seeing Mary this way makes your hatred of him rise in your throat.

"Are you going to Chicago?" Mary asked.

The clairvoyance. "No."

"You still hate your father."

Evil accuracy. "Chicago's too far and I have exams."

"Why hate your father? I don't."

"Maybe that's what's wrong. If you stayed sober long enough to hate him, maybe hating him would *keep* you sober. He wrecked your life. Why don't you hate him?"

"Because I never loved him." So all that's left is indifference with a few small jokes on the way. But you can't put such things into words and explain to Laurie, that accident or no, she's lucky. She hates her father because she once loved him. The closest you ever came to it was Helen. None of that. But I did love Helen, poor baby. The only one in this house who was even less than me so I loved her. Little baby, you shouldn't have done that. Made me lose you and made me hate you. So that even when the dead leaves fall and the green grass grows in the whispering, lovely silence of the cemetery, where the old, smooth stones are soft to the eye and surround invitingly, I cannot pity. Because I loved too much. Even your shadow is muted. The only love I knew. And lost. So I split myself down the middle with a glass and its liquid content even sharper, seeking my own way to death. Without love you live in a narrow, closed room without sun or air and the choking advances from in front and behind and both sides, a tighter, deeper pit beneath the rug, the floor, beyond the bar, seeking escape from the gray indifference and the one small spot that's black for death, seeking the cheated colors, exploding rainbows, its mysteries debased and humiliated, the price you pay for blasting the walls so they don't close in. And all because the only love you ever had was so fragile, so insignificant and temporary. You cannot stand this one standing there staring at you with your own face and form set on the larger frame of his body, judging what she does not know.

"I'm going up to my room." Mary took the bottle and the glass and left.

The Wetland birds were active as they always were along the sandy barrier beaches this time of year. From peninsula to peninsula, cut up by tidal creeks and coves, the dowitchers and red-winged black birds—even the egrets—were on the move. Laurie no longer remembered which of them left first. It would be soon. She had stood at this very window, her *wishing-well window*, when she was still bleeding from the loss of her own motherhood. She too had been scared one night. By the time she had come there was something else to speak of. A man named Ken and a proposal called marriage. Mary was the only mother she had, so she had to come to her. Soon the snow would fly. Thanksgiving would come. Then Christmas. You had been mother to mother since the earliest time. Protecting Helen after her illness, forcing Tommy to do his homework, and the time Pop said, "How big is Daddy's girl? Soooo big!" Maybe that's why you need motherhood, to claim at last your role as daughter.

Wishing won't make it so. Now who was it said that "a woman without maternal instinct is a sport in nature"? Why, Ken, of course. The last male Preston. In that scholarly paper that was turned down before you convinced him his normal, natural place was where he now is: a thousand miles from home as it happens, and headed even farther away in a week. I am possessed as surely as Mary is, I am possessed. As crazy as she is in her way, I am in mine. The doorbell rang. She heard Mary calling out the other window, "Come in, Doris, just for a minute." Laurie sensed secrecy in their greetings. Doris's eyes glittered and her voice was high pitched. Her lipstick was a shade too bright for her too-white skin. She seemed feverish. As Laurie went to the closet for her coat, she heard them whispering, and she saw the exchange between them in their eyes.

"Gloria is afraid of men. The doctor keeps saying all little girls her age go through it but it hurts my father terribly," Doris said as she drove. "The way she hides from him you'd think he was Jack the Ripper. Ma says I ran like that from Dad, but I don't believe it. It's Toby." Then Doris lapsed into silence, and Laurie asked, "What in hell is going on with Mary? Each time I see her she's worse."

"Not really. You know Mary."

No, I don't know Mary. That's just the point. "You two seem to be seeing a lot of each other."

"Well, I'm nearer than you and you've been real nice to us, sending that stock market letter."

"Nuts!"

"Besides, when Mary doesn't drink too much she's lots of fun. Like you." She went on quickly, "In a way, I mean." Doris told her how Mary informed everyone of the things she learned from Laurie about stocks. Though Mary never bought a single one herself, there were many people in Riverneck who were making money in the market thanks to her! That included the snips who worked for her. Once they got some information they usually quit. She asked about school.

"A drag," Laurie said. "Homework every night. At my age."

"Aren't you gaining a little weight?"

"Could be. Remember the way we used to eat preparing for exams? It's funny. When you do a thing you used to do, you also do the things that went with them." Somehow it led them to the subject of pregnancy. "Just don't rush into it," Doris warned. "The things you take for granted! Touching your toes, running up and downstairs without something always pressing on your bladder. I've had one on the arm and one in the belly for six years and I'm sick of it."

After a silence she said, "You're so much in love, you'll probably hate me for this."

"For what?"

"I have a boy friend. I see him once a week in Manhattan," Doris said, "and your mother covers for me. Toby thinks I'm with you. He's like a schoolboy. Bill, I mean." Her eyes were glittering again and she tumbled out the story in a desperate hurry as though if she didn't it would be too late. Then she was back on Toby, justifying, attacking. "Just plain rape, every time there's a fire. And afterwards he terrifies the kids, especially Gloria. Oh, I told you."

She went through a light, talking faster.

"And when he's not scaring everybody he's got his big fat feet on the table drinking beer, watching ball games, burning holes in the chair while all his jerk friends come tramping in and out and I'm supposed to play servant girl and raise his kids and walk his dogs."

"Stop the car. I'll drive."

"You don't really know Toby." Doris stopped the car. "If he ever found out about Bill or knew how I felt, he'd kill me. *God*, I hate him!"

Laurie controlled a smile. By Mary's definition, that meant she loved him. Maybe she did. The halt and the blind, all right.

"I have a date tonight. You sure you don't hold all this against me?"

"Why? Did Mary say I would?"

"Of course not! Honest, Laurie."

Mary *did* say so. Have I been that much of a pompous ass? "This Bill you love, I suppose he's married?"

"How did you know?"

Brother!

Doris went on. "But they're not Catholic, and if Bill gives his wife enough and lets her have the kids, he's sure she'll agree. It will take time, of course, and he has no money. Now, you see why I need advice?"

"Seems to me what you really need is money." More than you know.

"Please don't say that! You have so much, you don't realize the trouble it caused between you and your mother, just offering it."

There's lots I don't know but I doubt it includes mother Mary.

"Bill makes me feel important and happy in bed. Still, Mary says—" Doris hesitated.

"I know all about Mary. What does she say?"

"Before this—I mean, before Toby—there was never anyone. And it's been Toby all these years. Mary says many men make her feel that way, but it wears off, so I should think twice."

"At least twice," Laurie said. "Meanwhile slow down because nobody's killing anybody." Yes, money. With this Bill or without him. To leave Toby means she needs money. The market letter. Seems that everyone has a problem that gets cured by money. Everyone except us.

Maybe the trouble was that money trouble loomed so large you didn't realize your real trouble until you got it out of the way.

They had reached Peter's beauty parlor.

Doris sat under the dryer. She couldn't hear the conversation between Peter and the handsome woman in her mid-thirties who was there with a nine-year-old boy, his seven-year-old sister, and the older one, already a beauty at eleven, calm, clear-skinned, and poised. The girls were getting permanents. The boy sucked a lollipop as he looked aimlessly about.

"We haven't seen you for almost a year now," Peter said. "Since your husband died."

"Eleven months." The woman spoke with tight, clipped precision. "We've been south."

"It came as a shock about your husband."

Too bad she had acne. Otherwise she would be beautiful, like her older daughter.

"Yes. He died right in the middle of the afternoon." It sounded like a criticism. "A neighbor interrupted my shopping to tell me."

"Really too bad," Peter said. "He was a young man."

"Ten years older than me."

Laurie listened to the cold, hard voice and turned the pages of a magazine, pretending to read.

"He was never sick," Peter said.

"No. Never was. Just dropped dead without warning."

The woman's son sucked his lollipop and walked up to the magazine rack.

"Be sure your fingers are clean," the mother told him. He picked a magazine and she went on, telling the beautician, "The priest was waiting for me at the door. Don't make her hair any shorter. We went to Florida after the funeral. I'm back to sell the house."

Peter nodded sympathetically. "No use staying here."

"Indeed not," she said indignantly. "If a widower goes out and finds a wife, no one cares. But a woman!" Her face was as hard as her voice. "With three children. Unless a man has some of his own and wants more. More work. Not for me."

Both permanents were finished. The girls studied the result in the mirror. They didn't seem to be listening at all.

"Must cost plenty to rent places in Florida."

"My husband was heavily insured." There was a glint of cold satisfaction in the eyes.

When they left, the beautician attending Doris looked across at Laurie. "Did you ever?" she asked.

Laurie shook her head.

"Peter knows how to talk to them," the girl shouted over the dryer. "All the wives in Riverneck."

"The women in Riverneck," Peter corrected.

The girl raised the dryer and Doris came out from under it. "What have you been talking about?"

"Peter was telling Mrs. Preston—"

"About McHenry," Peter said. "He died in an automobile accident a month ago."

"I remember. Wasn't that awful?"

"That very same day, Peter told me—"

"Sally, why don't you go get some of that new spray for Mrs. Foote?"

"Have it right here. That same day he died Peter said to me, you be prepared for a real busy day tomorrow."

Peter gave up trying to stop her. "That's right," he said. "Poor Mr. McHenry's wife, mother, and sister and his two daughters. They all came in for permanents the next day."

He knows all about Doris, Laurie thought. Next stop Riverneck. If Toby ever finds out, big ape that he is—she saw Doris looking at her in the mirror.

One more traffic light and she was home. Love is the most perishable commodity there is and nothing exists that can take its place. All day long I have been engulfed in motherhood and mothers who hated their men and were faithless to them. Fathers too; men who weren't sterile and likewise, weren't capable of love. Was it last year, before they left St. Terese, when she was curled up in Ken's lap as they watched the big sun set behind the mountain? The symphony of birds and her love for him had filled her, and to stop the tears she had whispered, "Ken, how long does the honeymoon last?" He'd kissed her and said, "How long are we going to live?" She had felt his arms tight around her and the tears had spilled over in spite of everything. "I have married a miracle," he whispered into her ear, "a fabulous miracle I will never understand." If you are less of a miracle now, that is your fault, not his. As Wallie said. Of all things, Wallie! I don't want to think about it. Yes, but it *was* Wallie who spoke of his wife and told you, "It's easy enough for a woman to talk about mating like it was changing a shirt. But when a woman keeps drumming at a man about technicalities, such as having a kid or wanting one or not wanting one—it's like pouring ice water on a fire. You just put it out." That's how you became his weekend girl. "Technicalities" never came up between you and Wallie. Now that you think of it, has anything else come up between you and Ken for over a year now? You have all but talked passion to death. Maybe that's why you couldn't keep him at home, and that young fellow, Hawley, who looks like Nixon and Dana Andrews was *not* the reason you and Ken spent so little time together before he left. Getting away from ice water. You better learn to stop talking about it. Especially since nothing can be done. Not by Ken. She parked in the dead end.

Aunt Betty had called again. I can't face Ken, not now. All right, the prospect of walking into Pop in Chicago is also too much for me now. It's too far away and I have my exams. She returned the call explaining to Aunt Betty that Ken was still out of town and couldn't attend the hunt and, yes, she would be delighted to go. She had baked herself in: going to Caleb Island was safer. It kept her away from Chicago, away from Mary and Doris. Then she phoned the Atwater Agency. Kathy Hinkson was cheerful and friendly as always.

"I was beginning to worry. You know how they are about that non-stop flight to Chicago."

Laurie explained that she wasn't going. Exams. Her husband's family, the scheduled visit, and no, she definitely would not be going to Los Angeles the following week either. Too far away, what with school and everything. Kathy said she'd be glad to teletype Mr. Preston and Laurie told her that would be fine.

Then Kathy called transportation and told them to confirm the reservation to Chicago in the name of Kathy Hinkson. Yes, round trip. Just the weekend.

At least, so far.

The air smelled of hickory and apples, pumpkins and axle grease. The countryside had passed harvest, and was readying for winter in the white sun. Laurie was traveling with Aunt Betty, Alicia, and George.

The road was hardening with the first of the frost, but the air was almost balmy and the sky a clear blue. Their spirits stayed high as they passed one another, honking horns, waving, shouting, and laughing. There was little traffic and when one of the five cars stopped for gas or rest room accomodations the others caught up and waited till they came abreast of them at a traffic light. Then they leaned out of the windows, exchanging excited greetings like friends long separated and delightfully surprised at an unexpected reunion. Laurie did not feel the mounting anticipation shared by the rest of them. When they reached the roadside inn prearranged as their luncheon stopover, they threw themselves into animated argument as to whether or not birds would still be at Caleb: if so, George and Randy intended hunting woodcock before sunset. Morse would tell them. Good old Morse. He would know.

It grew colder as they entered Maine and colder still as they approached its northern border. The last leg of the drive was over frost-cracked roads that rose and fell abruptly, like an accelerated roller coaster. George took them at seventy-five miles an hour. Aunt Betty held on to the inside handle in the rear of the car and Alicia huddled against the door up front.

"How you feeling, Laurie?"

"Fine. How should I feel?" Actually she was getting quite sick at her stomach.

George laughed. "Some people get icky coming over these roads. Awfully."

Count me in, Laurie thought. I'm awfully icky of all of you and this weekend even before it's begun. The notion of just driving somewhere on the morning of a working weekday except in summer and what's more doing so to kill animals is too preposterous. She realized she had no impression of Caleb Island or even what it would look like, what was on it, or how the time itself would be occupied. They couldn't just go on shooting for seventy-two hours. Or could they?

"We're here first," George exulted.

Surprise. "And all in one piece, too," Laurie said.

George laughed. He, Aunt Betty, and Alicia agreed that the only sign of change since midsummer was the replacement of Swamp Gash Restaurant by an indoor hotdog stand and beauty parlor. Ugh. The aquarium removed last spring had not been replaced yet. Tsk, tsk. Last July the natives had advanced various explanations. Hurricane had broken through and released the sharks. The aquarium was removed to make way for a more important marine biology building. Its inferiority to the institute at Woods Hole was causing a natural death. Aunt Betty walked to the edge of the dock and called down to someone she addressed as "Sharkey," and Sharkey called back. The top of the ladder, flush with the dock, stood fully a steep hundred feet above the bobbing boat and the water. Now Laurie knew why she was the only woman wearing a skirt. The other cars were approaching almost in a straight line. They were honking their horns. George waved.

"This is Trubeck," Alicia said. From where the car was parked, Laurie saw mostly old, reddish-brown warehouses fronting on the Bay, badly in need of painting and repair. The smell of salt came powerfully from the old buildings; that and the smell of herring. What store windows she could see on Main Street announced their names in French and English. It seemed a strange town for the state of Maine.

"I'll take you across to the drugstore," Betty told her, "where you can change into slacks."

"Must you?" George asked, and the rest of the boys dutifully laughed. A handsome-looking woman walked by across the street. George nudged Randy, indicating her. "Remember?"

"Could I forget?"

"What?" Corinne asked. Randy and George were laughing. "Now tell us," she persisted.

George told them. It was the summer he had waited half one nervous weekend in Trubeck until Aunt Betty's approval was announced and he could appear at the house on Caleb Island as the accepted fiancé of Alicia. Randy had spent the time with him. Corinne remembered that. "Well, it was hard finding lodgings, and only one house had a To Let sign on the door. Next to it was a wreath. It was that lady's house." When they entered, they found her dead husband laid out in the living room and a maid briskly changing the linen on the one double bed in the one available room. They recalled their solemn faces until the maid left. Then it had all sent them into hysterics. "That's all. It was funny. Awfully," George said.

Remembering doubled them up with laughter again and the contagion of it made the others laugh too.

That's all. I'll bet. I'd like to hear the maid's version.

Aunt Betty walked into the drugstore ahead of Laurie and went to the rear. Laurie waited at the counter. Sitting beside her were two men in scarlet-colored mackinaws.

"Be the last time we make that trip in November," one said to the other in a lowered voice. "That old baster is leaving the Rock to die now and you can bet the others are too spleeny to go out there for gunning mid-November." When he saw Aunt Betty approach Laurie, he frowned, bit his lip, lifted his cap, and sullenly mumbled a greeting.

"You can go back now," Aunt Betty told Laurie, and then addressing the man who had spoken, she said, "Perkins, we're going directly to Goat's Head Landing."

The water had a frozen look though it boiled with currents. As the boat approached Caleb, a bank of clouds lowered, surrounding its outline in thick mist and fog.

"That's fine," George said. "Damper the better. Rain is what we need. Makes for quiet stalking."

"Sharkey, remove all the bags here. They're marked. Are yours marked?" Aunt Betty asked Laurie.

"There's just one with the initials L. P. on it."

Corinne giggled. "I'm sorry, Cousin Laurie," she said, "but L. P. reminds me of records. You know?"

At Goat's Head Landing three handymen waited, each with a horse and carriage. The handymen stayed behind to walk back. George, Randy, and Clarence drove the carriages. They followed one another up a winding path. The earth underneath had a hard, unyielding feel, like rocks struck by a pickax. The road ran straight up a high slope on either side of which was a lawn dotted with dried-up sheep droppings. The wind had swept the exposed field bare. Looming at the top of the slope, its width dark against the cold sky, was Mansion House of Caleb Island. The carriages stopped a good distance away. They all lowered their voices. As they approached across the lawn, a nurse dressed in immaculate, starched white walked toward them and then moved off a distance with Aunt Betty to converse in a whisper.

Betty returned to the silent group on the porch. "Cousin Theodore cannot see us. He isn't awake." They took the information solemnly. "He left word for us to come in and see the new painting."

The nurse waited at the partly open door and they all filed in quietly. Like a hospital corridor, Laurie thought, except that the foyer walls were dark and hung with discreetly lit paintings of the sea, boats, the harbor seasons, and the open sky. Specially lit and in a favored position hung the new painting of Mansion House as seen from the harbor they had just entered.

"The Secretary hoped you might want to see the book." The nurse turned a kindly and superior air on Laurie to explain, "It's the book signed by all the yachtsmen—the ones who gave the Secretary the painting."

They gathered round the book which rested on a narrow table in a small room off the dark foyer. Beside it a Chinese porcelain bowl stood on a delicate teakwood stand. The attribution beneath the bowl said that it was made by Syngchong in Canton, July 1812, expressly to celebrate the birth of Timothy Jeremiah Preston. Aunt Betty must have said something to the nurse for she now led Laurie with a proprietary air into a room past the small one in which the others still clustered round the signed pages of the book. A piano stood between the windows and on it an open album of sheet music. Gilbert and Sullivan. Laurie recognized the portrait on the wall above the piano as the face in Ken's silver box. Timothy Preston. But many years older. Beside it hung a painting of Timothy's wife at an earlier period. Either that or she had married a man old enough to be her father. It brought back Florida and fog, the first meeting with Ken, the plane, the fog clearing, and right now an alarming sense of time standing still once more. She turned away and faced the opposite wall. Against it the vast, bleached antlers of a buck were spread. She approached and read the information underneath. They stood twelve points. Above it hung the two long, crossed swords of swordfish. She leaned over the piano and looked at the sheet music. *Pinafore.* Opened May 25, 1878. There were hand-written notes in the margin. "Quaint." "Charming." "True." "Must write and thank dear W.S. Send him idea for satire on Bostonian false intellectuals? Professor of Metaphysics? Confessions of St. Brahmin? For instance:

> I am literally illiterate
> And understandably sick of it
> When students inquire
> I start to perspire—

Perhaps he would be offended. Presumptuous. No, don't send."

Laurie looked up again at the young girl's face. Not her. Ken's grandmother. This one was eager, delicate, lovely. His great-grandmother? She heard a faint movement and looked around. The nurse was no longer there. She'd forgotten about the nurse. Now, aware of being alone and of the musty silence engulfing her, she felt panic. A door led from the music room. She walked to it, opened it, looked into a bedroom. From its window one stared straight out to sea. The room was high above the steep cliff of rock. Her old uneasiness at looking down from heights returned. She faced the room. It was large and comfortable. In the center was a circular table. Drawn up to it was a chair; both were of hard maple. On the table were an inkstand, pen, ink, and stationery of "The Mansion House, Caleb Island." The green rug was threadbare. The plaster was cracked. She walked to the bed and pressed her palm against it and sat down. The mattress was thin and hard. She looked across to the opposite corner and saw two small glass enclosures on a triangular-shaped table made of oak.

In one enclosure stood a high hat, in the other, a formless linen one. Underneath each was a plaque. She walked across the room. Under the formless hat was the statement, "Worn by General U. S. Grant when he stayed in the guest room of Mansion House, Caleb Island, the 28th day of August, 1874." Under the other, written in black ink, she read, "Worn by Abraham Lincoln and sent as his gracious token of the time he stayed at Mansion House, Caleb Island, 1863. Not to be touched or used, by order of Timothy Preston."

At the wall nearest it was a door she had not seen before. She opened it. Beyond it in a tiny space some inches from her feet she saw a trap door. She bent and pulled it open. It led into a darkness and a narrow, circular staircase. She took a few steps down and then hesitated, afraid that the trap door might close over her. She had a sudden wild feeling of being in danger, of being lost. She stepped back and let the trap door fall. Its loud noise startled her. She hurried from the bedroom back through the music room to find that no one had heard the noise or missed her. In the room beyond, they were still examining the book signed by the yachtsmen.

"Nurse says we may visit the first two floors if you'd like to now."

"No," Laurie said, "I'd rather not."

"We'll be back when Cousin Theodore can see us." Aunt Betty led the way and they trailed out in pairs. "Why don't the rest of you go on ahead, change and meet us at Aunt Sarah's? Laurie and I will just stop off for a moment to see Cousin Arthur if George will drive us. Nurse, would you please call Cousin Arthur and tell him we're on our way?"

The other carriages descended the narrow road that cut the lawn and turned off to the left, winding away from the side of the island that faced the Atlantic, toward the harbor.

At the harbor's edge a telescope mounted on heavy brass pointed toward the mainland. Close by stood a small white cottage. After Mansion House, it gave the impression of a child's plaything. Cousin Arthur was waiting on the porch to welcome them. He was a man in his late eighties, with merry blue eyes, a weather-beaten face, and thick, gray hair, tousled and hanging forward in a cowlick over his high forehead. He was lean and slight and yet somehow strong and shaggy. He wore faded blue denims with a jacket to match which he kept buttoning and unbuttoning as they approached. He showed them in as he fingered his bright red bow tie.

"And where is Cousin Ken?"

Aunt Betty started to answer and stopped, turning her attention to Laurie.

"He's out of town on business," Laurie said, her face flushed.

This information amused Cousin Arthur considerably. "On business? Well." His eyes twinkled and he repeated it several times. Then, still buttoning and unbuttoning his jacket with one hand and fingering his red bow tie with the other, he ushered them into the cottage where he stood in the center of the small sitting room and watched them all carefully, as though conducting an experiment. Laurie followed a frieze of paintings high on the wall close to the ceiling. They seemed to tell a continuous story of catching sheep, the difficulty of handling high-spirited horses, the delicate young fawns, their maturation, and the inevitable killing of the hunt. There was humor about them. It made her smile till her eye came to rest on a large sheep in the foreground, heavy with wool, and a small, solitary human figure with a large, pale moon behind him.

"They're not good, are they?" he asked, his blue eyes twinkling.

"They're nice," Laurie said. "I like them."

"Really? I painted them. I did all but that one over the door, by itself. Cousin Ken did that. He was—let me see now—nine years old at the time."

She looked up at the pathetic little crayon drawing of a boy on horseback with a sheep watching. She smiled tenderly and all at once Cousin Arthur, his experiment apparently successful, took her by the arm and led her to the couch. "You'll have tea or coffee or a drink, perhaps?"

Aunt Betty said, "No, really, Cousin Arthur, we're just on our way to pay our respects to Aunt Sarah. But we did want you to meet Cousin Laurie."

"The tea kettle's boiling."

"Very well. Tea then."

He brought out a tea tray and a Dr. Johnson's Educator Crackers tin with an assortment of cookies in it. Laurie was looking down at a glass-enclosed tray with a collection of stones and Arthur, seeing her interest, opened it at once. "They're not pasted down. You may lift any one of them, but do place them back at the appropriate cards. You see?"

She lifted a green stone. The card read: "$CuCo_3 \cdot Cu(OH)_2$" and the year 1919. The next card read "$(2CuCo_3 \cdot Cu(OH)_2)_1$." "What does that mean?" she asked him.

"Oh, that?" He said it innocently, like a small boy enjoying a prank. "Good heavens, I thought everyone knew what *that* means. Now here's —George, isn't it? Our engineer? You can tell Cousin Laurie what it means."

George looked at the card, forced a laugh, and said, "You know I'm not a mineralogist, Cousin Arthur."

"Oh," Arthur said. "Well, that's malachite. The blue one is azurite. Both from Bisbee, Arizona. It says so right on the card. Well, bless me! You've been looking at the wrong sides."

He reversed the cards to reveal the simple words *malachite* and *azurite*, plainly inscribed.

"This one's gold," George said.

"Yes. Neither the rarest nor the most valuable of metals." Arthur turned now to Laurie who found herself smiling with him in a conspiracy, the nature of which she could not describe.

It delighted him. He squeezed her arm and pointed out the various stages of polishing to which he had brought the stones. "There are four steps, you see, and in no case have I gotten beyond the third." His merry eyes twinkled again. "I haven't the time. Would you like to see where I work?" He bustled in a world of his own making, hurried to the door, opened it, returned to the couch, and in passing picked up a piece of circular wood, carefully shaped with shells embedded in it. "Napkin ring," he said, handing it to Laurie. "Nobody uses them any more. Come, let me show you where I work."

"We really can't now, Cousin Arthur," Aunt Betty said. "I've asked the girls to meet us at Aunt Sarah's."

"You can run along then. I'll bring Cousin Laurie over."

"Why don't we stay for just the length of a cigarette, Mother?" George said. He seemed uneasy about Laurie and Arthur's being left alone together.

"For the length of a cigarette," Cousin Arthur repeated, cocking his head to one side as though translating a measure of time into slow burning tobacco and paper, and finding it sufficient.

"You'd better light one," he told George, "because I don't smoke. Come, it's this way."

He took Laurie's arm. Aunt Betty and George followed out the back door to a rear porch and he led them down a few steps to an alcove shielded by the house where his workbench stood. There was a table, also a surface grinder, clipping shears, sea shells, and a barrel for refuse. He lifted a shell from the bench, snipped it adroitly with his shears, and ground it into a quick symmetry, working the pedal for the polisher with his left foot. Beside the bench was a collection, also unfinished, of inch-long sailboats made of the shells. "Now." He preceded them up the stairs to the back porch. "Have you started your cigarette? Yes. Good." He motioned them to porch chairs, turned to Laurie and, when she had sat down, did so too. "What parts of the world have you been to?" he asked.

"None. I haven't even seen most of my own country."

"What country is that?"

"America."

His face danced with amusement. "I'm disappointed. I surely expected an exotic young lady like you to have come from some strange place."

"Strange enough." She smiled. "Calterston, Long Island."

"Good heavens! You *must* have been out of place there."

Before she could answer, he launched into a story of his visit to Shanghai in 1907. "There were two ladies wearing hats with birds on them. One with the wings stretched this way and the other with the wings stretched that. The Chinese were, as always, most polite. They waited until the ladies passed before they permitted themselves to smile." He laughed at the recollection, now almost fifty years old. "They'd surely have been out of place anywhere. But they were especially so in Shanghai. Well, I see Cousin George's cigarette is almost finished."

He rose.

"Don't bother," Aunt Betty said. "We'll find our way."

"No, no," Cousin Arthur insisted. "I mean to come with you." He took Laurie's arm and squeezed it again.

He pointed out the birch trees all shorn to an unnatural size by storm, growing in an unusually widespread, horizontal fashion, to make up in width what they had lost in height.

"Have you trees as strange as that in Calterston?" he asked. "These are the result of the big hurricanes of nine hundred and twenty-four and nine hundred and thirty-seven. We should require an army of five thousand men to chop down all our dead birches, rowans, and privets. And no one, not even Sarah, has devised a means for doing that at no cost."

"You could declare war on the United States," Laurie suggested.

He laughed. "Yes. Then the army would occupy Caleb and do it for us. And after postliminium we should have a perfectly reclaimed forest. But I really don't think Theodore would approve. The worst hurricanes hit Caleb. They always have. There was the one in eight hundred and sixty-six, that Emerson or someone else, I forget who, now, celebrated in a poem. The text concerned losing his breeches in the wind, I believe. I forget that now too."

Arthur began to unhitch his horse, but George assured him there was room enough in their carriage.

"You are quite fortunate," he told George. "Nothing but rain each morning for the past four days and a real line storm three weeks ago with slow, steady wetting ever since."

"Makes for great driving," George said.

"I always thought still hunting was best on Caleb," Aunt Betty said.

"Either way," Arthur said, "it's perfect weather for murder." He turned to Laurie. "As in Mother Goose, the misty, moisty days."

On their way he fell silent. Sad, Laurie wondered? No, simply quiet, she decided. He's only coming because of me. That's nice and he's nice. She tried to remember what Ken might have told her about Cousin Arthur and could recall nothing. It puzzled and disturbed her. Hurricane of nine hundred and thirty-seven or eight hundred and sixty-six, give or take a thousand years. They crossed one bridge and then another. Presently the carriage was surrounded by children. A pony behaving more like a dog lay on the lawn watching and then rose to his feet to join the group, nuzzling and prancing about in their midst, threatening to drive their horse and carriage off the narrow road.

"Back, Dream Boy, get back!"

The pony ignored the command from the woman on the porch, pretending not to hear, and trotted alongside them. So did the children. The sound of the sea was stronger here than it was at Arthur's. This cottage faced the ocean. The woman on the porch wore a formless, faded dress, a hair net, and a pair of grass-stained white shoes on stockingless feet. She brought her hand to her remarkably lined suntanned face to shield her bright, piercing blue eyes from the sunlight. Then her lips parted to show strong white teeth.

"Why, you look all re-entrenched," Aunt Betty greeted her.

"We haven't left yet."

"In all this cold?"

"Only cool. Make way, children. Dream Boy, get back on that lawn!" She tucked a gray strand under her hair net. "It's been quite fine. What with Theodore staying on for the hunt I thought it best not to leave him. Or for him to make the journey twice." She turned her sexless but completely defined face toward Laurie. "And this is Cousin Laurie?"

"Yes, I'm Laurie." She accepted the firm, masculine hand defiantly.

There were no chairs on this porch, in fact, no furniture of any kind. Here, too, a telescope pointed away from the Island, in this case out toward the ocean. The living room itself was small with a narrow black couch, a few hard chairs, and some straw ones. The only ornament was a charcoal portrait hung over the fireplace. Laurie recognized the face from her grade-school library books. His poems had been required reading along with Emerson and Longfellow.

"And how have you been, Arthur?" Aunt Sarah asked.

If I have it straight, they're first cousins and the man in the portrait is her husband's great-grandfather, Laurie thought. She and Cousin Arthur both live on the island. Yet the greeting had a distant sound of acquaintances meeting again after a long interval.

"Very well," Arthur told her. "Quite busy. I see you have claimed the rocking melodeon after all."

"It was mine," she said.

He smiled. "Theodore had already given it to Waldo."

"Waldo is the caretaker at Mansion House," Aunt Sarah explained to Laurie. "The melodeon is one of my eccentricities and enjoying my eccentricities is one of Arthur's."

"Are you claiming the *haut bois*?" Arthur asked, lifting the melodeon from the mantelpiece.

"It doesn't work and can't be fixed."

"That never stopped Tom Eayres." He placed the melodeon on his knees and struck a chord.

"Be careful," Aunt Sarah warned.

"Come now. I play both piano and organ. It's you who should be careful." His eyes twinkled. He replaced the instrument on the mantelpiece as the room filled with children. Behind them came their parents and their parents' parents. Aunt Sarah introduced them in the order of seniority. Her married son, Tiffany. He was a thin, tight-lipped man in his early fifties, with a rope around his waist, not so much to hold up his faded blue denims but more as an insignia, she felt. Her unmarried daughter, Eleanor. Her grandson Morse, and his wife Gert and all the many children. "This is your Cousin Laurie," she continued to say to each of them.

To hell with trying to remember all these names!

Tiffany announced to Sarah that he was fairly sure now as to the exact size of the cistern. "Twenty-one cubic feet."

"I should say it was more like twenty-four cubic feet," his sister Eleanor said.

"No, I doubt it. Twenty-two at the most."

Children, grandchildren, and great-grandchildren remained attentively silent while this discussion continued. When they had narrowed their range of disagreement down to twenty-three or twenty-two and a half cubic feet, Aunt Sarah cleared her throat and stopped the discussion. She suggested the grandchildren be readied for dinner, which emptied the room almost instantly, leaving only the visitors, Tiffany, and Eleanor.

Before the others left, each one of them carefully acknowledged having met Laurie, repeating without variation, "Glad to meet you, Cousin Laurie," and shaking her hand.

"Now, how is Cousin Ken?" Aunt Sarah asked. "I expected we would see him."

Laurie was aware of Tiffany's careful, resentful scrutiny. Why was her answer to this question so important to him? Laurie explained again that Ken was out of town on business.

Tiffany received this information skeptically. Laurie thought, he resents me because his name is not Preston and mine is. For his not to be is to deny his existence and to say that mine is, is to lie like hell. You won't believe this, Tiffany, but I agree with you!

"Really? Business?" Where it had amused Arthur, it surprised Sarah.

"Well, then, of course," Sarah said. "Someone will have to explain that to Theodore."

This last was for Betty, who nodded.

"Centuries seem to reverse patterns," Aunt Sarah continued. "In the nineteenth, men did all the things they didn't want to at first; then afterwards they were free to do the ones that interested them."

"I don't think Ken did what he wanted to at first." Laurie's heart beat in her throat as she said it. She was frightened, she couldn't say why. Perhaps it was the way they all watched her and listened.

"Then he's doing what he wants to do now?" Aunt Sarah asked.

"I hope so," Laurie said. "I'm not sure."

"Still," Tiffany said, "he's quite different now, from what I hear."

"He's in love," Arthur rose and moved across to Laurie. "Tiffany, have I told you of my purple finch experiments?"

"No. I heard about them but not the results. Do you have results?"

"Oh, yes. Excellent results for an amateur." Arthur's eyes twinkled and he acknowledged Laurie's silent gratitude for changing the subject.

"The purple finch isn't purple at all," he told her. "The male is extremely dull." He smiled. "A very, very dull, rosy red. The female, as might be expected, is drab—a tiresome brownish gray. My experiment is quite remarkable," Arthur went on, telling Tiffany. "It concerns the ability of the male bird to avoid mistakes and learn from past errors when not confused by the presence of other birds of his breed. You will have to see the charts. In essence, the male bird, when left alone can sample and avoid noxious food and generally exercise experientially induced judgment. However, once placed with the female, it loses judgment. The loss increases anywhere from one hundred to two hundred per cent."

"And the female?" Aunt Sarah asked.

"The female does not lose her judgment at all, whether alone or as part of a male-female community."

"I don't quite follow it," Tiffany said.

"Oh, I follow it," Aunt Sarah said crisply.

"You do?" Arthur asked innocently. "I did not know of your interest in such things."

"The deleterious effect of congeners on a lone individual in any species has always interested me." She turned to Laurie, changing the subject. "Have you met Cousin Theodore yet?"

"No," Aunt Betty said. "He couldn't see visitors."

"But you saw the painting?"

"Yes."

"I'm sure Theodore will meet you before you leave."

"Aunt Sarah is our family genealogist," Arthur said. "And a connoisseur of its individual members. Her aunt wrote the story of Cousin Ken's great-grandfather, Timothy."

"She was Timothy's daughter," Aunt Sarah said. "Most scholars claimed she was too close to see him. I don't agree. She detailed his birth at the time his father and grandfather were digging pits in Boston in eight hundred and twelve, to his death in nine hundred and five. His self-education, varied experience, friends and enemies, tastes in architecture, decoration, music, art, his philosophy and attainments. What else is left? And who was in a better position to describe these?"

"No one," Arthur agreed. "The criticisms had to do with accounting for his motivation."

"Any effort at analyzing men like Grandfather Timothy would be false."

But you are Ken's father's sister, thought Laurie. I'll get it straight yet.

"They lived without introspection," Aunt Sarah went on. "They were too busy. They focused outward. They were doers. They had no time to consider themselves. If they had complexes, they coped with them privately."

Arthur's eyes twinkled. "You mustn't sound so irritated, or Cousin Laurie will think *she* is responsible. Now don't you agree, Sarah, it was easier to live without emphasis on inner, private frustrations when there was that much breathing space, mostly in the West—and all that innocence?"

"No doubt," Sarah said. "But the facts remain. They knew the difference between right and wrong. The rules by which one lived were fixed and it gave them freedom to apply themselves. They *thought* alike but were different. Round Green School played a big part in shaping them and unifying their ethic. More so than Groton or Harvard, I think."

"I know that Ken didn't go to Round Green School," Laurie said.

"Didn't he? I hadn't realized. I'm sorry."

"I'm not."

"I'm talking too much," Sarah said. "At least that hasn't changed. Women talk, men *do*." She smiled. It lit up her face and the family resemblance to Arthur came clear. "So Cousin Ken is away on *business*?" She gave the word a strange emphasis, half uncertainty, half self-reassurance. "You might mention that to Theodore tonight."

Aunt Betty was surprised. "You mean we're having dinner at Mansion House tonight?"

"Of course, that's part of what Theodore remained on for. The night before the hunt." She rose. The others rose. "I'm very pleased that Cousin Ken is out of town on *business*." Again the strange emphasis. "It's important to move out among others. Very unhealthy to stay apart." Her face lit up suddenly with humor. "Of course, Caleb is the worst example of isolation. We live here as a people apart." Her swift glance at Arthur was full of criticism. "Perhaps it's quite unhealthy. Still a thing is many things and a person many people." She took Laurie's arm as they walked toward the door. "One must accept all of them. You find us comical?"

Laurie, unprepared for the question, blushed. "Why, no."

"You may," Sarah said. "We are. Also we are not, because a thing is so many things. For instance, I gain an impression of loveliness, youth, uncertainty. Then another of eagerness, readiness, susceptibility. Then strength, stubbornness, a capacity for self-possession. But above all, youth. They don't refute each other." They stood on the porch.

"I'm twenty-three," Laurie said simply.

"You're fortunate. Still, people stay much younger now. I recall my father. I always thought I should never live to be that old. I'm already twenty years older than he was when he died. They looked older in Father's day. The women too, with their bodies thoroughly covered, always carrying parasols out in the sun. On the other hand, I saw a newspaper photograph of a young woman walking down Charles Street in what's called a bikini bathing suit. That's equally unhealthy. Perhaps more so. But mostly in those days it was the fact that everything was fixed. Settled. Fixed goals, fixed duties. That aged people. Do you like sailing?" she asked unexpectedly.

"Ken tried to teach me," Laurie said. "But I'll never be good at it."

"Then you golf?"

Laurie nodded, lying by agreement.

Aunt Sarah smiled. "Yes, quite. Golf, tennis, and shooting." This pleased her. Fixed. Everything fixed.

Her great-grandchildren were at the upstairs windows with their parents, waving them off.

At Aunt Betty's the young people were having cocktails. George was explaining to Laurie that one addressed Cousin Theodore as "Mr. Secretary." He had been a member of the Cabinet for seven years and an ambassador after that. A book exposing the administration under which he served assigned him the relatively benign epithet of paternalist, where other Cabinet members earned such labels as fanatic, crook, autocrat, and reactionary. It reminded Sarah's grandson, Morse, of a story currently going the rounds in Washington where he worked. The minister of Monaco had sought American loans and the terms were finally agreed upon at lower levels. When he met the Undersecretary of State who expressed sympathy for Monaco's difficulty with Communists, the minister said, "We have no Communists," and the loan was promptly turned down. So the minister flew to Paris and reminded the French president of how helpful Monaco had been on many occasions and said, "France must lend us fifteen hundred Communists." The French president replied, "I'm sorry, but at present we need every Communist we've got."

Morse's wife told Laurie how they loved Washington and only spent a few weeks of the year at Caleb.

Reggy said, "I'm sick of the subject of Communists," and went out on the patio while Randy brought out a book on indoor bird watching, full of labored cartoons, such as a cowardly man huddled in a corner frightened by a tomcat, captioned "the yellow-bellied titmouse."

There seems to be one hell of an effort to convince me of something, intended, in turn, for me to convince Ken. But, of what? That they too are visitors here?

Reggy ran in from the patio. "Deer!" she shouted and everyone rushed outside. They took turns at the telescope, and binoculars were passed from hand to hand quickly midst excited disagreements as to the size of the buck and whether the doe still retained her white spot.

"Tremendous buck!"

"God, yes!"

"And wasn't the doe the most graceful, lovely, shy, charming thing?"

"I can't wait!"

"Let's leave early tonight. Last year I was sleepy."

"Well, Randy, which will it be, stalking or still?"

"Still."

"I'm for stalking in the burned-over area."

"No, the wild raspberry bushes."

"I'd suggest the beech scrub," Morse said. His voice carried authority. "And if it's still hunting, I'd take the apple orchard."

"I'm for driving," George said.

"George, remember last year."

"Last year was dry, Al. The wet down now is perfect."

"You really think the orchard is better than the ridge top? There's real black growth up there."

"Well, yes," Morse agreed, "the nubbles are fine but I still prefer the apple orchard."

"Damn pity we can't hunt in October. It's not as though we were on the mainland."

"Just part of the union, darling."

Everyone was talking at once.

"The doe still had her white spot."

"A child bride."

"The buck certainly looked satisfied."

"Isn't a child bride the biggest thrill?"

"Corinne, you're a little devil!"

"Here, give me your glass. There's more scotch in the pantry."

"No, look, seriously."

"All right, seriously. Birds do *not* have extrasensory perception."

"Extrasensory equipment."

"Where?"

Laughter.

"Morse, put down that rifle and settle this argument. You know all about birds."

"Well, no, but Father does."

"We're talking about woodcock. Don't they have a tactile sense in the beak?"

"Not exactly. Father says they have an eye on the top of their head. As a lookout for danger. There's a soft extension on the beak connected to the fifth nerve."

"There!"

"Well, honestly, George, I don't see where what Morse said and what you said—"

"It's no use, Al, I've made up my mind. I'm hunting woodcock."

"The olfactory ducts of birds are the same as any other."

"Birds use them for taste, not smell."

"Really, Morse?"

"The woodcock! Awfully!"

"Morse, if you say the apple orchard's best, then that's it. After all, Morse, you know."

"Well, no, not really, but Father does."

Laurie was moving toward the door. No one seemed aware of it.

"I mean if the average male is male, he's masculine. How can he help but?"

"I'll explain it later, dear."

"No scotch. Here's bourbon."

Laurie pulled the door shut behind her and stood on the porch. A fine, icy rain fell over the bleak, black trees, revitalizing the color of the firs. She bent and peered through the telescope, pointing it to the spot where they had seen the big buck and the small slender doe. Child bride. The biggest thrill. There was nothing there now, only dead leaves falling. That and the naked austerity of the leafless trees into which the deer had fled, outlined cold and lifeless against the black, stark sky.

She lay in bed, shivering. Some night, girlie. I'll say. Some reception. Some dinner party. Some evening. It hadn't been marred for them until Aunt Sarah's grave announcement that Theodore could not join them. Then they'd sat at the long, mahogany table with a servant in attendance for each three guests, all quiet and somber till Margaret remembered eating dinner alone with Theodore once when she was sixteen. Scared to death and in an evening dress, a servant all to herself, standing behind her chair at the far end where Arthur now sat with Theodore in his dinner jacket in the place Aunt Sarah now occupied, and it seemed just *hundreds* of candles flickering in between. She told it in a whisper. After dinner the men dispensed with cigars and brandy in order to be rested for an early start. They had been totally entertained and entranced with one another. Constantly. They *couldn't* have been more delighted with one another. Infatuated, transported, and carried away with their small talk, fun, and games. They genuinely enjoy what and who they are. If such people were bored to death, it would be natural. But they're not bored. Everything I've ever heard about "such people" paying for their privileges with boredom and loneliness is sour grapes. God knows they're boring enough, but not to each other. Because they've been handed the gift of self-acceptance—breathed it in with the nursery room air. All of them except George. Before dinner she had gone to the study, with a fireplace big enough to hold a small, burning tree, which was exactly what it was doing, when suddenly, the disconnected conversations had become too much for her. *Anna Ella Carrol. She did win the Civil War. She didn't. She did create the Tennessee River campaign. She didn't. The river flowed north. It flowed south. Congress was supposed to and wasn't supposed to hear Lincoln introduce her but he'd been assassinated in between.* Unanimous agreement. Tiffany versus Eleanor.

Those who disapproved of working with Communists in the thirties and forties unconsciously favored Fascism. They didn't. Those who now opposed working with Neo-fascists favored Communism. Ridiculous. Eleanor versus Tiffany.

Morse, please talk to Randy. Randy, please talk to Morse. Tiffany, please talk to Randy and Morse. Talk up a chemical storm on spraying the broom that overruns Caleb Island. I do wish you wouldn't call it the Rock, Randy dear. Rock means Alcatraz or Plymouth and Caleb is neither. Morse, raise it with the Department of Agriculture. Make a note. About the broom, *dear. Randy, you must tell Aunt Betty that Charlotte Baldwin left our fund a legacy of thirty thousand dollars for improvements. It could be used to install a float and repair the old wharf if someone would contribute another twenty thousand for fighting the broom. You will remember, Randy? That's Charlotte Baldwin who passed away three months ago. Not even a Preston or married to one. Tiffany, you will follow up on Morse and Randy. Remember, you're the chairman of the board now. Sarah. I say still. Stalk. Drive. Kill. Randy. Clarence. Tuffie. George. We must be prepared to be branded Fascists. But how can Dr. Schweitzer be the greatest moralist if he retreated to Africa? Oh, yes, it was Emerson. The view of Transcendentalism taken by State Street that it seeks to eliminate contracts, that was Emerson. Arthur smiles, Arthur twinkles, Arthur wanders and he listens. That's funny. It's very funny. Let's stalk. I'll drive. Hunt still. Let's kill. Can't wait to thrill. Young bride. We'll stride, we'll kill, we'll thrill, we'll hide. . . .*

I hid. But George came right in after me, George, who's so happy he's part of all this he just can't stand it. Just can't keep away from it. And can't keep away from me, if I'm any judge. He'd better. Here by design and engineering while God help me, I'm only here by accident. Accident from the very, very beginning. That chatter of his. You will be chattering soon: your teeth will. Well, you'll get accustomed to it. Like hell. Oh, in the summer when all twenty-five cottages are used and it's warm, you will get accustomed to it. Not to it and not to you, George. Just offering my friendship, dear girl. A fellow countryman in a hostile land is useful. Awfully! Like hell. I know what you're offering, dear *boy.* On the make, on the prowl, before the hunt and the kill. Now they're all sleeping and I'm freezing. Sleep for the hunt. Tomorrow. Tomorrow they'll kill what they found endearing today. The handsome buck. The shy, soft doe. Lunatic and criminal, incomprehensible. When you love, you protect. Even when you only *like.* Perhaps my need for motherhood distorts my outlook. The charms of destroying life are lost on me. I don't care if millions of people, women as well as men, kill for sport, for pleasure, and then go on to explain how you killed each time you ate anyway or someone did for you and even vegetables have life so what's the difference?

Now you sound like Ken about his cat at St. Terese with the chip-munks, over twenty-five years ago. That's the way I love Ken. I don't need to kill for pleasure. Life, not death is my need. I want my child. Oh, how I want my baby. Life owes me a child. I'll sleep and pray that whatever is missing in Ken that's needed for giving life to what's inside me can be reached. I'll sleep and I'll pray. I'll pray, but will I sleep? Not if this room is going to be this cold all night. Do you see yourself here at all, I wonder, in this little room on this narrow, hard, prisonlike bed with the ceiling that slants so close to your head, if you sat up abruptly in the middle of the night, you'd crack your skull? Every wild wind of the Atlantic is blowing through this house, with nothing between you and it but some clapboard tired from doing this for two hundred years. You are a speck on a speck. No matter. You will freeze to death long before morning. She put the light on. Another speck. Thomas Alva Edison has only been granted tentative citizen-ship here. Poor devil. Pushy. Self-made man and all that and just years and *years* after the Revolution, my dear. Well. By the light of this lamp one might find the switch to put on a light by which one could actually read. Watch your head! You should have brought your home-work. You know there's a good chance you *will* freeze to death tonight. Think of it. What an excuse for missing the exam on Tuesday! But what would Ken do? There *must* be a book here somewhere. God, this floor is cold. I didn't think anything in this room could be colder than I am. Eureka! A book. Now, if we only had a light. Don't worry. The pages are uncut. And the same for the next and the next. Books are for filling bookshelf spaces and the Atlantic Ocean is what the United States and I are between the Pacific and. . . . Well! A book. At last. An actual cut and opened book, meant for reading.

She crawled back into bed, held the book close, and read the title: *Beauty Aids for Ladies.* The cover was cracked, the leather stretched beyond much more endurance on the rack of cardboard. You and me both, she told it. On the inside page, she read, "Fub-head on *Fituations Moft Diftreffing* to *Unaffuming* Ladies." Yeow! Now don't tell me, I'll guess. *F* stands for S except at the end of words. Published in 1791. All right. I will *affuredly* freeze to death unlefs I am *refcued*. I sure as hell am a maiden in *diftrefs*. I am a maiden facing *difafter*. Beauty hints for facing harfh climate and its *difeafes*. Winter is more *fevere* than *fummer*. Agreed. I am all for *fummer*. God, how I wish for *fummer*! Read on, girl. All that stands between you and the glacier age is your eyeballs so read on and keep the frost from covering the windows of your foul. *Soul.* Your foul-soul. Keep reading, girl, it's that or *fleep* and with *fleep* comes certain death. A fight for *furvival*. Fortitude in your *folitude*. Ah, here's a chapter.

Marriage. Ladies are ſuddenly placed by marriage in a new circle and the utmoſt reſpect is neceſſary as you turn to this new ſituation. Now, isn't that a fact? Well, I *am* turning. Blue with cold and hunger and rage. I'm mad. I'm mad as hell. All right, stay mad and you stay warm. Give it its head. You are mad at Ken. You are mad at him for placing you in this spot. You are mad at him for being away. For not preparing you. For being sterile and not knowing it. You are mad at yourself for coming. Oh, glory be to God, you could kill, you're that mad. And you are only that mad because you won't kill. Ah-h, to hell with them all. You came on a hunt. A hunt for what? Hunt means search. Seek and ye shall find. Hunt doesn't only mean kill. Search for what? What's here to find? Nothing. That word again. You are not going to let these bastards intimidate you. You are not going to hunt. All those clothes laid out for you there, the cap, the parka, the shirt, the boots, the hell with 'em all.

She went to the table, found paper and a pencil and wrote out a note. "Please don't wait for me and don't wake me. I'm not going hunting." She put on her robe and slippers, walked to Alicia's door, stuck the note under it, and returned to her room. All right now, ſleep or freeze. At least you will be maſter of your own foul soul. "Virgins' Milk for the skin," she read. "If the face is waſhed with this milk, it will be calling the purple ſtream of the blood to the external fibres of the epidermis and produce on the cheeks a beautiful, roſy color." I'll take death. She put out the light. It was a beautiful, broad-shouldered, thick, longhorned buck. A handsome boy and a lovely, lovely doe. My life with Ken demands its tangible expression, our fusion. My confusion. How can it happen if Ken can't make it happen? You want to grow up *and* reclaim your childhood by becoming a mother. *That's* confusion. You're here so as not to be somewhere else. More confusion.

She slept.

Chapter 5

SHE woke to hear their voices. The dawn mist vanished quickly and the wind blew the clouds from the sky, leaving it a brilliant blue. The air was clear and crisp. It carried the smell of salt from the harbor along with that of the leaves from the wood. The horses pawed at the earth outside the barn, and balked as they were hitched to the wagons. While the handymen fed the horses, the cook poured steaming coffee from the huge, flagonlike thermos. The hunters' scarlet and yellow caps, bright shirts, and gloves were matched by their cheeks, rosy from the wind and the flushed expectation of blood. They fastened short axes and long knives at their belts, examined their shotguns and rifles, laughed, joked, and sang.

For a moment, hugging the blanket, Laurie felt that it was cowardly of her to have come this far and not joined them. They could well be laughing at her right now, having just heard of her note and finding it hilarious that she had slunk out during the night to leave it. She could no longer recall exactly what she'd written—no doubt something childishly defiant, pathetic, and inappropriate. If she hadn't wanted to do this thing, she shouldn't have come at all. She stood at the window, watching from behind the curtain, and smoked a cigarette. Then one of them looked up and she pulled away. God, how you shouldn't have come!

When the carriages drove off, the wheels struck sparks against the hard stones and she could hear their voices as they moved out of view. She dressed in heavy slacks, a flannel shirt, and her leather jacket.

Downstairs the maid greeted her with surprise and Aunt Betty, appearing from outdoors, said, "Good heavens, don't tell me they left without waking you?"

"I left Alicia a note asking them not to."

"I understand completely," Aunt Betty said at once. "It was a relief when I could use my age as an excuse for no longer going." She joined Laurie at the table. "I admire your courage. I wish I had just said no at the beginning, myself. Now they won't ever bother you again."

After breakfast she took Laurie down to the dock in time to see the boat landing. Fifteen horses and carriages waited as handymen picked up food and supplies for the shepherds who would remain the winter. Then they placed trunks and suitcases aboard for shipment.

"There will be another landing at noon," Aunt Betty said. "Closing up Caleb for the winter takes a bit of doing."

They drove around the island across the old bridge down to the abandoned wharf where Aunt Betty hitched the horse. They walked on the beach facing the ocean across a stretch of sere grass flattened by wind and passed a handyman painting a kayak a bright red. He doffed his hat. Then they came upon two bubbles from Flying Fortresses.

"Strange," Aunt Betty said. "I never saw those before. I can't imagine how they got here." It reminded her of the time when Corinne was only eleven, and had done shore patrol during the last war. On this very spot she had come across the corpse of a sailor from the Murmansk run, who had jumped ship and had his neck broken by the life preserver.

"How do you like Caleb?" Betty asked.

"I don't really know."

"It takes a while but then you love it." Aunt Betty sounded as though it were important to her that Laurie should. Then, embarrassed, she led them back to the road where Dream Boy was trotting by himself, his nostrils turned away from the stinging wind and still following some scent, perhaps the smell of their mare. He trotted alongside them as they drove back.

Arthur was waiting on the porch. He tapped the telescope. "I've been trying to spy on our young killers. Would you like to come for a walk?"

"We've just been," Aunt Betty told him.

"Yes, but I'm not tired," Laurie said.

So Aunt Betty went in and Arthur led Laurie to the harbor side. There was quite a difference between it and the ocean front, but islands have neither sides nor fronts, only an outer circle surrounded by water.

"This is no time to be at Caleb," Arthur said. "Death is on the minds of the old and sought out by the young. Spring is the good time."

A rustling, crackling sound made Laurie turn with a start.

"Leaves on the wind," Arthur said. "I recall a forum on the play called *Death Takes a Holiday,* in which one discussant kept wondering where death goes when it takes a holiday. I wanted to tell him that if it was after Labor Day, I knew. Death comes to Caleb. But spring here can leave an imprint with a word, a lilac bush, or the sound of a thrush. There's nothing quite like the smell of young, green grass on Caleb. Or the sight of our newborn fawns. The sun is all the more

palpable for the cool air it must penetrate. Those are the things I try to
remember at this time of year. Wriggling tadpoles, frogs sitting on cold
stones no longer frozen, teeming life in the sea. When you see Caleb
now you see it at its worst, without the syringa, forsythia, or young
sheep and clover. This may be the truer picture, but it's not the only
one."

They walked in silence.

"How did you know I wouldn't be on the hunt?" Laurie asked.

"I hoped you wouldn't. Why aren't you?"

"I hate killing."

He nodded. "I always shot in the air. Cousin Ken never liked it either.
But of course we had to go."

"Last night they all loved the grace and charm of the deer they saw
through that telescope. Then why kill them?"

"Oscar Wilde. 'Each man kills the thing he loves.'"

"I don't go in for paradoxes."

"No? Are you sure?" His blue eyes were twinkling again. "You have
gone far in for one of the oldest paradoxes I know. Ken has been a
paradox for thousands of years." He looked at her, enjoying her bewilderment, then went on, "Yes, *Ken*. The Ancient Egyptian word
meaning 'weak-strong.' *Ken* for weak. *Ken* for strong. They used
hieroglyphic pictures with the word. *Ken* for strong was the picture
of an upright, armed warrior. *Ken* for weak was man bowed over. It
was their way of admitting that each thing is by virtue of having been
something else. Ah, dogfish!"

He ran to the bridge and Laurie followed, in time to see a three foot
long fish cross under them. "It's convenient to be cold-blooded," Arthur
said. "I sometimes wish I were." And then, "So Cousin Ken won't take
over Mansion House?"

"No."

"Good. Though it will confuse things when Cousin Theodore dies."
He smiled a faint, far-inside smile that made him look more like a
child than ever. "Of course they'll go at me again to take it over but I
was born here. My museum days are done. Caleb is my home." He
looked at her with his startling blue eyes bright and clear. "And that
leaves Ken. And Ken won't." It amused him, satisfied him too. "And of
course someone has to tell that to Theodore, so that's your mission here."

Only then did Laurie realize why Aunt Betty had insisted she come.
"All right," she said belligerently. "I don't mind."

"Timothy came as close to putting Caleb in entail as one could under
American law. Unfortunately for him, in getting rid of the British, one
also lost their method of all but forcing the eldest son of each generation to take over on penalty of losing everything else if he didn't. No

such force can be imposed here, except that it will affect everyone's attitude toward Cousin Ken's taking over the assorted investments when Theodore's firm is closed down."

"I didn't know that—Theodore—" she hesitated over the name, "was handling investments or that anyone planned for Ken to take them over. I'm sure he couldn't care less."

"I see that *you* don't," Arthur said. "I hope he doesn't either. The fact is I'm quite pleased with you. But like the Mother Queen, you may still have a son to go. Should the eldest male Preston turn down the privilege of assuming Mansion House, in the event he had a son, that son may correct the mistakes of his father by taking over when he reaches majority, regardless of who inhabits Mansion House or how well they may have run it. Like most efforts at immortality, it proves unsuccessful. Do you follow it?"

"Almost."

"Well, this much is simple. I imagine Cousin Ken doesn't relish Alicia's man taking over."

She shrugged.

"When Betty tried to prevent the marriage, she had a report drawn on George," Arthur went on. "It disclosed that his father had been a clerk of some sort in Allentown, Pennsylvania, and during the steel strike of '36, he organized strikebreakers. A blow on the side of his head from a lead pipe cost him his hearing. The mill owners expressed their gratitude with five hundred dollars, a job as night watchman, and a scholarship for George which included a trip to Europe. That's how George became an engineer. He chose to go to Germany and when he returned he sang the praises of Hitler. While there, he studied neither science nor languages but fencing, riding, and polo. He hunted in the Black Forest with guides to give him lessons in shooting and diligently learned the names of things, aristocratic practices, and the care of all manner of guns. I engaged him in conversation once and he told me the people his father had served so well did not even know his name."

They walked in silence again.

"Ken made a fine suggestion to Aunt Betty about Mansion House," Laurie said at last.

"Yes?"

"Tear it down."

Arthur's blue eyes widened and he laughed a sneezy, throaty laugh. "I do believe we would all prefer that to Alicia's man. But unfortunately that's illegal under the trust. It's been a source of regret to Prestons before that even Caleb is under the law. They cannot breach trusts, nor hunt deer in October, nor on Sundays, nor without a license —except for me of course. I was the only one born on Caleb." He examined her face. "Don't you understand? I'm making jokes about the family fortress surrounded by the rising waves of democracy."

Laurie nodded. "I get the idea in a general way."

"I do believe Cousin Ken was lucky to have misled you into marriage."

"Thank you. But why must it be George for Mansion House?"

"Because my only son died in the war of nine hundred and fourteen."

"There's Aunt Sarah's son, Tiffany. He's the oldest. And he is a male, isn't he?"

"Yes, but Sarah isn't. Though she wishes she were. It was unfair really, her not being a male. I've often thought that Sarah's daughter, Eleanor, remained an old maid as penance for her mother's transgression into marriage. Sarah and Alicia were born Prestons and rate as such, once we run out of males, but Tiffany is not a Preston, and nothing can make him one. No, I'm afraid it's Alicia's, which means George. Besides would you really prefer Tiffany to George?"

She grinned, but did not answer.

"In all fairness to Sarah," Arthur said, "that name for their only son was her husband's idea. The only one he had, to my knowledge, and like all things done without practice, unsatisfactory like Tiffany himself. At all events you see, Timothy's plan has run awry. As I say, he never foresaw a time when there would be only one male Preston save for Theodore and myself, who no longer count. It was inconceivable to him that if there were only one remaining male Preston, he would not wish to take over Mansion House."

"The whole thing is ridiculous. Why should an old house have mattered that much to a man like Timothy?"

"What do you know of Uncle Timothy, lost Laurie?"

She smiled. "My father called me lost Laurie as a child."

"Don't be disturbed by it. The most any of us can expect to find is acceptance of the strangeness of our unknowable surroundings, with enough curiosity to play the game of cataloguing and sampling. I once thought Cousin Ken understood that. Men like Uncle Timothy never did. They believed themselves miracle makers. I imagine that's the essential difference between Cousin Ken and myself, apart from age, appearance, and capacity, of course. Cousin Ken tortures himself with the conviction that Timothy and some of the others were infallible. I have my grave doubts. Perhaps his more generous endowment makes it easier for him to believe it. We are always the victims of our own strength. Fortunately, nature pulled my leg a bit and that helped me enormously. Oh, I do think they were on the track of something—our great-great and grand fathers and equally grand and great uncles—and

I try to surmise now and then what it might have been they found or thought they found and surely lost and which we never had at all. With Ken's superior equipment I might have come closer to a clue. That's why it would have been better if Cousin Ken had stuck to his mutton. He should have adhered to scholarship, to exploration, to inquiry, regardless of how little those things are valued by others nowadays."

"That's my fault, if it is a fault." Laurie said. "My intentions were good. But then, to coin a phrase, the road to hell was paved with good intentions."

"To coin another, there's a fiery short cut paved with bad ones. Knowing Cousin Ken, I'm sure it couldn't be your fault. He abandoned scholarship almost twenty-five years ago." He paused and from under dead leaves picked up one that was inexplicably green. He twirled its stem and handed it to her. "I suppose there is no more use posing one way of life against another than there is posing the past against the future," he went on, "but there *is* use in posing a right way of living and working against a wrong one. The life best suited to you is the one that draws out your greatest potential and achieves your recreation in work. The argument that society needs more plumbers at one time and more mathematicians at another should mean nothing to the individual any more than the problem of overpopulation should lead sane men to commit suicide or cease to have children. If a man is naturally suited to something productive and can't afford it financially or morally, that is society's crime, not his. Whatever he does to correct it is proper. Should his emergency measures of correction prove to be evil or lawless, the crime still remains society's against him, not his against it. Only when a majority persist in believing that and behaving as though society is there for them, and not they for society, will society improve. The only way I know for meeting our duty to the future is by meeting it to ourselves. All else is snare and delusion. I never saw a tyrant yet who urged eating grass today so that there might be fruit tomorrow, who went without his own jellied preserves at tea time. But perhaps you find such talk old-fashioned? Full of generalities about life and work, society and love?"

She gave her head a small, hard shake.

"One must apologize these days," he said, "for believing in things that have survived for more than fifty years. Newness is a religion: its god a combination Tin Woodsman and brass monkey." He paused and listened. They heard the distant sound of shooting. "I still find love the most beautiful, shocking, and masculine force there is, whether for one's woman, one's friend, family, country, or oneself. But a wholehearted willingness to live or die for love demands the opportunity to develop such capacity for desire, the ability to recognize it, and the right to act upon it."

"My trouble is I don't see how anyone can be sure of what they want or don't want till long after they've had it," Laurie said. "Something like what Ken often says about investments in securities: even the best is a calculated risk."

"But it's an *un*calculated risk. And one in which we must lose in the end, obviously. Look at it. As children we refuse to grow up while insisting we be treated as though we already have. As young people we try not to grow old though laying claim to knowledge that comes only with the experience of age, while old people of course try not to die and nonetheless yearn for the peaceful state which only death can bring. In the face of all that, what can we do but anticipate our absurdities and defeats, learn to endure them, and avoid the mummery of laying claims to comprehension we simply don't have? Now, how can this be done save by listening for and respecting the small voice which sometimes, mind you, *sometimes* says I want, *really* want *that*. The dictates of that voice are the only reality you can possess! That's why Ken should not have let his restless tail touch the floor of his cage. Don't you recognize it?" He smiled. "The leopard, the tiger, the puma in captivity. So long as the tail swishes at the air and won't settle on the ground, he has refused to admit that the bars of his cage exist. That is as close as we can ever get to freedom." He peered at her. "Or perhaps Ken's protest is not yet over?"

"I don't know. He struggled hard all during our first summer."

"Against the tyranny of love?"

Laurie blushed. "No. Against returning to Wall Street. I told you that was my doing."

Arthur plainly remained skeptical. He quoted:

> My love must be as free
> As the eagle's wing
> Hovering over land and sea
> And everything.

"Though I must agree with Emerson's final verdict. Thoreau's poetry, while admirable, was also abominable; parlando where it meant to be profound. Poetry should reconcile opposing forces, discordant qualities, syncretizing a more than usual state of emotion with a more than usual state of order. Another paradox, I'm afraid. Coleridge's, I believe. Yes." He laughed his sneezy laugh. "And to complete the paradox, he went on to say the language of Shakespeare's gentlefolk was too indecent and full of coarse allusions such as one expects to hear in the meanest taverns, to be translated. No. If Cousin Ken struggled, it was with the tyranny of love. The Wall Street folly was his own."

"That's not so," Laurie said, flatly. "I made him go back, I tell you."

"Most unlikely."

"It's true."

"You've returned to college, I hear. Isn't that so?" He made it sound as proof she could not have influenced Ken in any such fashion.

"Not back," she corrected. "I never got past high school."

"Even more conclusive. I went back. I was fifty. It was most valuable. However, if you insist, we all do, did, and will do something we shouldn't. The question is, once having done it what next?" He paused, apparently over a random thought. "Perhaps Ken never could abide hunting because of his father's insatiable appetite for the blood of all lower mammals. Once Cousin Ken's father steered his yacht all through the night, going round and round the lighthouse and returning to the same spot, his guests getting more and more alarmed. Only toward morning did Cousin Ken's mother discover a walking stick with metal in it placed above the compass where its magnetism distorted direction. I put that walking stick there—deliberately. Of course, the guests were convinced he was insane—which actually, he was—and never came back." As Laurie laughed, he added, "I don't believe I've ever quite forgiven him for the petulance of suicide. Naturally it caused Cousin Ken to assume burdens for which he had neither taste nor talent. Perhaps that's why Jonathan did it, though. For men of action, nothing is more persuasive than force. So, now. What makes you think you sent him back to Wall Street?"

"He couldn't make up his mind between scholarship, which was still nebulous, and Wall Street, which was definite. By insisting he decide at once, wasn't I insisting that he go back?"

"You did not make scholarship indefinite. His father and grandfather had already done so. However, there is no need to speak in the past tense. If he is still capable of love, Cousin Ken is only a boy. Forty or fifty. We Prestons live to alarming old ages when we don't invite disaster too loudly and accept the principle that most of the process is simply a series of false starts. In Cousin Ken's case, false starts are compounded by an obsession to be like Timothy, which is now a heritage. A study of genius and heredity was done on Prestons. It stopped with Timothy. And that's been a sore point with all of us who came later, festering more with each succeeding generation. It caused Cousin Ken's father to join second- and third-rate societies, final clubs as they are called, since Harvard abolished fraternities, though obviously, with his status, he could have joined the best. Better top man among third-raters than third man among the best, you see.

In later life, it drove Jonathan to surround himself with men who were beneath him, and it was his undoing. All part of the tradition."

Laurie's mind jumped to Coogan and McBride. Compared to the type of men Ken had told her about on the Street, either swindlers of majestic proportions or men whose unwitnessed handshake was sufficient for them to make good on transactions that cost half their fortunes, and others like them who had forgone profits to meet avoidable but morally mandatory buy or sell orders from customers, both Coogan and McBride *were* third-rate. But Ken did *not* want to be first. If he was trying to now, that was only because he thought she wanted him to. And then, of course, there's me and his choice of me. How do I rate?

Arthur seemed to sense her thoughts, for he said immediately, "In marrying you, I suspect Cousin Ken struck his first real blow for freedom. Now, others may follow."

Laurie smiled. "Each time I try to find you laughable, I find you lovable."

He made a small bow and fingered his red tie. "Almost the same, lost Laurie. We can genuinely laugh at what we love, but only pretend to laugh at what we fear. What we fear, we hate." He put his arm through hers.

"What's a *haut bois?*" she asked.

"What? Oh." He laughed. "Like a flute."

"And who is Tom Eayers?"

"Son-in-law of Paul Revere. He went mad. Among other things, trying to play the flute soundlessly was part of his obsession."

"And what in God's name is postliminium?"

He frowned, remembered, and laughed. "The restoration of civil and other rights to a country that has lost them to a conquering enemy. Quite often impossible."

"You sound like Ken used to."

"Not unnatural, save for the past tense." He squeezed her arm. "Shh!"

She stopped. He pointed. The bird that stood on the rock looked like a creature in some fantasy. It was a foot long, with a beak that was half its face, laterally flattened, broad, and bright vermilion. Its legs were red and the rest of its short, stubby, toylike body was white, with blunt black wings.

"He looks like a black collar and cap on peppermint sticks," Laurie said.

Then, suddenly the bird let out a wheezy groan followed by a grunt, and took off with speed despite its comic dumpiness. Soon it rose over the cliff and out of sight.

They walked on.

"The puffin bird on his way to Long Island for the winter," Arthur said.

"Why yes," Laurie said, suddenly excited. "I never knew its name."

Arthur smiled. "At least we have a clown in common, lost Laurie. Ours for the summer, yours for the winter. Old bottlenose."

"I just want Ken to be happy."

"You just want the impossible but that, too, is not unnatural. Who can tell? Cousin Ken has already survived so many of the weakest things in our line. Why not value a man at his highest potential?"

"I value Ken by my love."

"The highest potential of all, the truest miracle. And only those who believe in miracles are capable of them, you know." He took her hand. They had reached the front porch to find Aunt Betty waiting in the carriage.

"You certainly took a long walk," she said. "Cousin Theodore can see you now."

"Would you like me to come along?" Arthur asked Laurie.

She nodded.

"Perhaps you'd better change into a skirt first," Aunt Betty suggested.

Arthur winked. Laurie ran upstairs to change.

Once again they drove up the road that cut the lawn leading to the top of the high hill. This time Laurie saw the ten-foot model of *Silver Box* on the side of the porch. It was complete in every detail from bowsprit, hawse lips, and chain plates to fife rails and summer mast. Off to the left, at first glance looking like shirts and towels flapping in the wind, were many small models of double-masted sailboats. The nurse in starched white was waiting at the partly opened door. "Don't keep the Secretary too long," she said. "He's under extremely heavy sedation."

Laurie was aware of him before she actually saw him. He sat in the small room to the left, dressed in a black suit, custom-tailored to the style of fifty years ago, with some strange white apparel underneath it reminding her of bandages or a tightly ruffled dinner shirt. He sat perfectly straight, staring ahead, a heavy figure of majesty and force.

Aunt Betty approached him first. She bent and kissed his cheek. "This is Cousin Ken's wife, Laurie."

Laurie felt Arthur nudge her forward gently. Despite his ninety-three years, his illness, and the overpowering sedation, Theodore roused himself. The effort brought a suffusion of deep purplish-red color to his face. It was a large, heavy face with a thick nose, bushy eyebrows, and hanging jowls. Laurie stood before him, not knowing what to say or do, transfixed by his wandering eyes that reflected his fight with death and his mind's reluctance to surrender as it sought the subject before it.

"Yes," he said, not hearing. "Yes. Cousin Ken. You will want to see the painting." He looked beyond her, speaking slowly, struggling to remain coherent. His sentences seemed unbearably long. She felt dry-mouthed and lightheaded. It was like having an audience with an ogre, a king, an ancient tribal head, and she was a child or a captive. Both. In his struggle he barely knew what he was saying, and in her fear she barely heard.

"They made this painting of Ram's Head Harbor. Four hundred yachtsmen. They all signed the book. What bore are you using?"

Laurie turned frantically to Arthur.

"Which would you suggest?" Cousin Arthur asked.

"The .30-.30. Or the .300 Savage. Anything from .25 up will do."

Laurie continued to look at Arthur. He nodded reassuringly.

"You may take your pick from my gun room," Theodore said.

"Thank you."

Plainly, he didn't realize this was Saturday, the hunt was on, and she was not part of it!

"Pay no attention to any tracks my deer make that are many feet apart. You will never find a Virginia buck when he is running that way. Look for a zig-zag trail."

She had an almost uncontrollable need to laugh.

"Your colors should be brighter. Young people are careless nowadays. And no white kerchiefs. If you pull one out, it will look to another hunter like a deer's tail flashing. Move only when the wind blows. Keep your hands high when you can, so your movement is down, the way leaves fall."

"There's been lots of rain," Arthur said.

"Yes, good hunting, still or stalking." Theodore smiled. "But if a girl brings down one of my two hundred pounders, it won't be the first. My wife did several times." He was trying to see Laurie.

"Where is Cousin Ken?" he asked.

"On business."

Some tremendous inner effort cleared his brown, red-tinted eyes. "You must see the Tower." He could see her now at last, she realized. "See the Tower," he said and it was an order. "The Tower and the catwalk."

"I will," she promised.

His effort was spent and so was he. "If you come face to face with a buck, keep your eyes partly closed. Animals don't like to be stared at."

The nurse nodded now, and Arthur led Laurie and Aunt Betty through the foyer into the room with the book signed by the yachtsmen. Neither Laurie nor Aunt Betty told Arthur they had already seen it.

Aunt Betty whispered, "He gave you a lot of time." She was clearly relieved that the audience was over. "He can no longer see things up close. He sees better at far distance."

Laurie followed Arthur from the small room to the music room she had visited yesterday, leaving Aunt Betty behind. This time she saw a photograph that looked as though it might have been Ken in his teens. It was Cousin Theodore with a pipe and a dog in a shack in Colorado. Beside it was the larger photograph of him she had seen yesterday. In it, his face already looked sensual, stubborn, and accustomed to command.

"The picture above the piano is Timothy," Arthur told her.

"Yes, I know. I recognized him."

He looked surprised.

"Yesterday." She explained. "From the daguerreotype in Ken's silver box."

"Oh, the Revere box. Yes. How is that dag holding out?"

"Ken says it's fading."

Arthur walked on into the guest bedroom and she followed.

"I was here yesterday too," she said.

Arthur opened the trap door that led to the circular staircase. "The Raleigh Walk," he said. "Originally used to take refuge when Indians came. Later, it hid slaves. Don't worry. There are no ghosts. Only dust." He preceded her into the blackness and found the low light. "You see? Nothing but a printing press. It was one of the first in America." The press had turned a strange, mosslike green. Beside it under glass were leaflets rousing the good citizens of Massachusetts to monetary support of the first all-Negro division of the Union Army. She followed Arthur up the circular stairs and re-entered the bedroom.

"Still," Arthur said, "there's something to Longfellow's statement. 'Old houses wherein men have lived and died are haunted houses,'" he quoted, as Laurie lingered at the table under the glass enclosed hats, listening. "'Through the open doors the harmless phantoms on their errands glide with feet that make no sound upon the floor.'"

There were magazines on the table. She had not noticed them yesterday. *National Geographic, Political Science, Oceanographic Review.*

The dates on all of them were 1932. A shiver ran up her back. Phantoms. She had once yearned for time to stand still. Here at this moment it did and it terrified her. The trap door fell. She turned. Arthur's smile did not reassure her. She walked back into the music room and stopped at the sound of Cousin Theodore's voice. She could see his massive profile. At the opposite wall, thirty feet away, the nurse sat so that he might see her.

"Did you show her the picture?" he asked.

"Yes, Mr. Secretary. She was most impressed."

"Good. Did you tell her to visit the Tower?" It seemed less difficult for him to keep his mind focused now. It was almost as though he were alone. "Yes, Mr. Secretary, I reminded her."

Laurie felt like an eavesdropper. Or worse. The feeling that he was speaking to himself could not be shaken. The nurse saw her and pretended not to. She hopes I'll have the delicacy not to appear within Cousin Theodore's line of vision, but she's not sure, Laurie thought. She was afraid to move lest he hear or see her.

"You must make sure she visits the Tower," he said again. "The Tower and the catwalk."

"Yes, Mr. Secretary."

He means me. He knows I'm Ken's wife and he thinks I'm moving into Mansion House. He wants me to see the Tower. Laurie suddenly felt very proud and Ken's suggestion of tearing down Mansion House seemed absurd. I don't believe he meant it. He couldn't have. Arthur was beside her. She followed him back into the foyer, relieved that Cousin Theodore had not seen them leave. Aunt Betty joined them and they went up to the first floor landing where authentic thirteenth- and fourteenth-century furniture and statuary from France, England, and the Orient were all properly marked. Everywhere in odd corners were models of schooners, brigantines, and square-rigged sailing vessels.

"Theodore made all those models when he was a young man," Aunt Betty said and Laurie suddenly remembered that Aunt Betty had once lived in this house. That seemed even more ridiculous and, if possible, more blasphemous than Ken's suggestion that it be torn down. "You don't have to go to the Tower," Aunt Betty said. "It's a long, steep walk from where the elevator stops, and very drafty."

"I promised."

Aunt Betty shrugged. They walked to the third floor. On the landing stood the marble bust of Timothy and beside it the three-volume work on *The Life and Pursuits of Timothy Preston*, compiled by his daughter.

Aunt Betty said, "I'll wait here," and Arthur led Laurie to the foot of the stairs to the Tower.

"It was built in a hurry without care for comfort in eight hundred and twelve, when Maine was the most heavily attacked part of the Union."

She ran up ahead.

"Save your breath," Arthur called after her. "The stairs are steep."

In the Tower, winter was already an accepted fact, and the wind stormed about its stony head. She saw her breath escape in quick jets and heard Arthur stop on the stairs below. The Tower was circular, like Caleb Island itself. A scroll hung on the wall, protected by glass. She recognized the handwriting and the black ink as she approached it. It was dated 1859.

> Our family's close association with the French makes the choice of Caleb Island for our summer abode an appropriate one. To the north, it touches that portion of France known as Canada, and to the south, at an equal distance, our own New England. To us Canada will always be French regardless of its occupation by the British. To us also New England will ever remain the beginning point of our nation despite a treasonable South or the continuing dreams of empire with which our own free land is still coveted on Downing Street. This tower has served many functions and served them well since 1812. May it in future time serve only the peaceful purpose of ennobling, farsighted vision which is democracy's highest denominator and prevent that mean expediency which deteriorates all things to their lowest level and in which we find only the tyranny of the moment and the mob. Further north than this one cannot go and stay on Union soil. For the black man, fleeing from the South to the freedom of Canada, it is therefore the last moment before paying the price of exile for liberty. However long this condition exists, so long shall this Tower, this house, and this Island provide beacon, warning, and haven. The French have done much for Prestons. My grandfather's closest friend was a Frenchman, the son of Apollos Rivoire, by name Paul Revere. The best soldier in Revere's army was another French Huguenot, a Sergeant named John Thoreau, whose grandson, Henry David, I am honored to call my good friend. My wife, Claudette V'agnion Preston, is of French blood. So is my grandmother, the wife of Kenneth Fenimore Preston, who with God's grace joins us in taking this occupancy, her husband having passed on fifteen years ago at the ripe age of ninety-one.
>
> So much for the Island, the propriety of our choice of it, and the thing it stands for. Kenneth Fenimore Preston introduced our family line to this new world. He is our host and we honor him for

it. Therefore, choosing Caleb in a spirit of remembrance, I set forth a simple presentation of an occasion recalled in a like spirit by Kenneth Fenimore Preston, exactly as he tells it to us in his journal. It took place in the year 1791, the fifteenth anniversary of the Declaration of Independence, on which occasion he invited to his home his closest, dearest comrades of those earliest days.

This is what he says:

"After we had supped well and drunk much, each guest rose in his turn and reviewed in rhetorical fashion where they and Boston, the capital of New England, now stood. The mariner extolled his industry and the navigable rivers no longer red with blood, and the wet crop beneath their surfaces, as well as the treasure afloat in their boats to and from the far shores of the earth in ships flying a nation's flag of free men. Then a builder of bridges recounted his particular pride—new landmarks and structures that connected all the vital growing parts to the mighty whole; cleared at last of all trace of carnage and no longer shaking to the echoing stamp of the redcoat boots."

You will mark that this was before the contrary evidence of 1812.

"So he spoke of the bridges spanning the Housatonic, Chicopee, and Merrimac, Pentucket Falls, connecting Haverhill and Bradford, West Boston to Cambridge, and many others that joined the state to all of New England. Whosoever spoke, boasted of the prosperity, peace, and growth from the point of view of their particulars. Thus, the scholar recited literature and its authors while pedagogy spoke of schools, the lower relating to the higher: Dummer, Phillips, Bristol; whilst the clergy with an open heart rejoiced in all their houses of worship, nineteen for the public in Boston alone: Congregational, Episcopalian, Baptist, Friends, Sandimanian, Universalist, Methodist, and Roman Catholic. After their distinguished manufacturer had gloated over rum, beer, sugar loaf, spermaceti, and all the rest, and their masterful military man recounted the strength of their militia in detailed numbers of regiments, brigades, and troops that formed a well-trained body of fifty thousand infantry, seven thousand cavalry, and fifteen hundred artillery, then at last did Paul Revere rise to his feet in his natural turn as the last to speak, and he said:

" 'I am a goldsmith, as you all know, working in silver and have little much else to boast of and a scarcity even of that as my works belong to others except for my foundry, now three years thriving at Lynn and Foster Streets where I cast my own hardware so as not to acquire it from the British. I cannot much boast of that, either, I must confess, for as yet I do it but poorly. So I must return to that which I do well. And in this craft I have fashioned for each of you a small and valueless object as memento of this occasion.'

"Then he gave to each of us a small silver box with our initials on the fluted face, made by his own hand, which hand he raised, lest we think he was finished, and said:

" 'I know of nothing we truly possess nor anything we can share with each other more valuable than the precious memory of our birth. Without birth no living thing can have a past. Without a past, no living thing may have a future. Without both, there is no living thing at all: there is no life. Children tend to forget their birth. For them it is a time of indignity and helplessness, and it suits their impatient and unseasoned pride to forget. They try to. They pretend to. But when the fully grown man has fully forgotten his birth, he dies. That memory we possess. That is our treasure. It and it alone, dear comrades-in-arms: the labor pains, the flesh and birth of life are ours. Surely posterity possesses more than we do the medals and evidences of it all, in bridges, ships, industries, and harbors. But we alone possess its earth and roots. That birth is ours. All external evidences give witness to the fact that noon is but the harbinger of night. Only the dawn stands beyond blemish. Let us not forget our origin, nor sin against its design. It is our only immortality.'

"These were the words of Paul Revere, a workingman and comrade, son of a Frenchman, as I recall them."

So reports Kenneth Fenimore Preston. It is true that his good wife even now does state that so much did her husband drink that night she doubts he would recall things as they were or even as he should have liked them to be. Still that is his statement in his hand and Kenneth Fenimore Preston earned the right to believe it and to command our family's faith. According to him, Mr. Revere then invited his friends to examine the small silver box he had given to each in token of the occasion, as remembrancers against the slugs of time, lest any of them suffer themselves to forget in all the subsequent glory.

This silver box is my proudest possession and it shall follow its course from Preston to Preston, from son to son, as shall this Island. For even as is this Island, such is each of us at birth a small, poor, wild thing, surrounded by vast turbulence and all the tides and hidden but prevailing terrors of the deep unknown, through which however far a distance we must travel, shall we always risk the danger of return to that starting shore from which all our journeys are made, else we are lost. We shall remember the salt and blood, the cry that came when first we suckled, crawled, then walked, strode, then ran, knowing that if we do not, however strong we may appear, we shall surely perish. Should any of us fall behindhand, may this Island joining our origins crowned by this Tower, erected against the dangers of afterbirth in their aggregate remain our continuing remembrancer. So may it please Almighty God. Amen.

Arthur was standing at her elbow, examining both her and the scroll with a quizzical smile. "Interesting how even in his fervor, Timothy lists statistics with care. So did his grandfather. Every Preston who ever drew breath also drew charts. It's an inherited disease. There was a British captain named Preston," he went on, "accused of ordering his troops to start the Boston massacre. John Adams was the only Yankee lawyer with enough courage and faith in due process to defend the very symbol of his enemies. Preston was finally acquitted and returned to England, as I assume any college history major knows. What no one knows and Aunt Sarah has seen fit not to find out in her passionate genealogy is whether this Preston and whoever the British prison ship *Preston* was named after are blood relatives of ours."

"How do I get out on the walk?" Laurie asked.

"You don't have to. Theodore will never know."

"I want to."

"The doors are concealed. Always. It is a characteristic." He walked to a place in the circular wall. "Revere's father married into a family something like ours," he went on. "The Hitchbourns. And poor Rivoire lost his identity. All his children were named after Hitchbourns, and when he died, they buried him in the Old Granary, surrounded by Hitchbourns. Except for Paul. Paul was named after him."

"Why do you ridicule all this?"

He made no reply.

He has to or it would break his heart, she realized. He's a Preston. She recalled the time when she first met Ken, the protective coloration with which he concealed from himself what this burden meant. A Preston. *The* Preston, as it turned out. Namesake to the primary, initiating Kenneth Fenimore Preston. They all had to ridicule: it was too much for any of them to carry in its naked form.

"Timothy knew how to wait," Arthur was saying. "He waited for Caleb for almost twenty years, having charmed the widow who owned it so that at her death she left it to him for the nominal sum of five thousand dollars. He was a man of strong staying power and persuasive charm. Still he was more generous than Revere's great-great-grandfather, Tom Dexter, who bought Nahant from an Indian for a suit of clothes, possibly in retaliation for the fact that one generation earlier, Captain Woody, also on Paul's mother's side, was murdered by Indians off Pemaquid."

"Please open that door," she said. Though she understood his need to scoff, she was getting angry.

"What do you expect to find?"

"I don't know. What does Ken expect to find?"

"God knows. All Prestons expect something. Perhaps because all men have been taught to have faith in progress—a God-given process toward perfection in an ordered universe; civilization. But we are not 'all men,' we are Prestons. And that as you can see has some special feature. How does a Preston advance when this is how high they stood to start with? For Timothy and his grandfather, freedom and riches, your own free soul's salvation, and society's security were all of a solid piece. Poetry and politics, worship and warfare were all one. Birth was in the air to keep one young. At the age of seventy in eight hundred and twelve, this Kenneth Preston could still stand shoulder to shoulder with boys digging pits in Boston because the British were coming again. Power and money were by-products. Timothy's love of the French endeared him to his good friend Abe Lincoln, whose father's cousins, Amos and Jedediah Lincoln, loved the French so much they married Revere's daughters, Deborah and Mary. For us these aren't monuments, you see. They are our family and their close friends. Perhaps if we could find behind the silver box, the scroll, and all the rhetoric some cheap and devious fraud, it might help. Otherwise"— he opened the door and the wind blew in a ferocious gust carried over the ocean—"otherwise it might be the notion of progress itself which is the fraud. What other alternative? That we latter-day Prestons are inferior or that our land has ceased to grow? Perhaps progress and everything connected with it, religious, scientific, social, and ethical are an agonizing, idiotic delusion and noon is indeed the harbinger of night; a fact of nature that stands by itself. A series of unfortunate choices, you must admit, and all quite personal. For you as well as me, lost Laurie. You are Mrs. Preston. This may be metaphysics, abstract history, or philosophy to others, but not to us. Neither to Cousin Ken out in the hinterlands beating the drums for money as an end in itself, nor for me. It's our daily companion. It gnaws like a worm, gives no rest, and there is no escape from it. Not even in the pesthole of eccentricity or skepticism. Even at my age. At least I have the personal anodyne that every man, whatever his origin, has a dream in which he believes, believing equally that no one else's will be attainable save his. It is my particular unattainable dream that before death reaches me, I will reach the stage at which I will have no dream at all, and no need for one, because I find sufficient delight in the simple privilege of being alive."

He stepped aside. His eyes suddenly twinkled again, filled with a laughter based on knowing that in the face of tragedy, the best of men must be a fool and that only time had taught him this and he would never be able to explain it. His cry of "Be careful!" was shut off by the door slamming behind her.

Laurie pushed against the gale and held her face to one side, still swallowing gusts as the wind swept up her skirts. Afraid to look down and white with the fear of it, she stopped and placed her hands on the low rail and forced herself to look out. Below, to the southwest was Maine, to the north lay Canada, and out eastward was the ocean's wild, white water blown by the winter wind. The tossing yachts in the harbor were small toys. On the Island itself the cottages were like dolls' houses, their blue-gray shingled roofs and white sides against the water, or nestled in the trees, bare and gaunt sticks of gray, black, and silver with intermittent evergreens, some turning yellow. The wooded place where the killing was going on was an ugly smudge marring the clean definition of land, sea, and air. A smell of burning logs came distantly on the wind from Aunt Sarah's, Cousin Arthur's, and Aunt Betty's houses, the only ones open now save for the one on top of which she stood, surveying all the rest. Cut logs were still being piled in front of the farmhouse that would give shelter to the shepherds for the winter. It looked no bigger than her fist. For a moment fear returned. She brought her face closer to her chest, but her eyes remained open and she stared down at the stones of the catwalk, well-worn and smooth under her feet. Then she turned her head again and looked out. You could see everything below in moonlight or by day, through fog or snow, rain or hail, and the heat and fertile green of summer when the smells were soft on the breeze and one took lunch from a knapsack and marched the walk. Her mind ran to sentries, fortresses, alerts, and alarums. Was this what Cousin Theodore wanted her to see? Had anyone ever jumped from this walk? Had any Preston chosen that solution? Ken's father chose his gun room. It took so little to raise your knees. Had one of them stood here and thought, I was born for failure, and then shut his eyes? The rocks below were sharp and high. What love had found itself within this narrow circle, shielded with a blanket, a pillow, a lover's coat, close to heaven, caressed by the sweet smells and pure air, the wild cry of birds come from over the sea? Life itself could begin here, or death, and dreams of hate or longing, the far visions of the near solitude, companionship, or reflection, food, drink, lust, all in this narrow circle! It might be equally true of any place but not this way. Origins. One could not see and feel and know them as one did here. To be frightened but secure, high yet low, surrounded and free. To be of this place was to know what was most permanently yours to defend and cherish. Mine? Yes. His name is mine and my love his. Mine!

Suddenly the fear of being out there was too much. She leaned toward the Tower, walking carefully, her head away from the rail. She could not find the door. She pounded against the Tower. Her fist made no impression. She shouted and the gale swallowed the sound. Her body hugged the Tower circle closer and she pounded, frantic now, as she went round, mouth-breathing. Just as she stopped, the door opened and her body fell inward.

Arthur caught her shoulder and they stood that way facing each other.

"I used to watch the birds from the catwalk," he said. "Their songs come to you strangely up here."

The door was still open. She turned her head away from Arthur but rested against him and looked out at the sky.

"No one seems to know how to reclaim it," he said.

Why should that bring back the moonlight flooding our bedroom when I cried and wished that time stood still? What happened that day? What was lost? Everything and nothing. *Nothing.* That word again. I spent my day unpacking clothes, and he packed up his dreams. First day. He came home two hours late and I began my menstrual period. Both of us chatted. Then we went to Aunt Betty's for dinner. Small talk and Ken's foolish argument with a drunken ex-Communist. *Nothing* happened. Same word. What needed reclaiming? What of alarm or tragedy has transpired? Same word. But big things, you said, *can* happen without incident and have been happening for almost two years. Things transpire in the night of the soul and you know they happen because of what you are afterward. Noon, the harbinger of night. We have been anxious, uneasy, and guilty of something that has not yet happened. It is connected with my wanting a child to the point of obsession, while knowing that having one won't change it, and whatever makes him go away, run away, though he knows he shouldn't, and that doesn't change it either.

The answer was here.

Arthur was looking at the scroll. She pulled the door shut with unexpected strength. Then there was only the deep, time-nourished silence of the Tower.

"I don't want to scoff," Laurie said.

She raced down ahead and he followed slowly. She didn't stop until she reached the foyer. Her heart was beating quickly. Where man has lived and died there is a haunted house. Perhaps the answer would never be found.

She saw the massive, brooding figure again. He had not moved from the chair in the small room; a profile with both hands on the cane. He believed that he and he alone understood.

Aunt Betty appeared from the small room. Arthur was walking unhurriedly down the stairs. "Shall we say good-by?" he asked.

They entered the room. Once again Theodore exercised the major effort to focus. "Did you like the downstairs guest bedroom?"

"It's a fine room," Laurie said.

"So? You liked that room?" The tortuous, slow process of making a coherent statement began. "The carpet is old. The paint is cracked. I am putting in a new carpet. It will be green. The walls will be painted to match. It will be suitable." He seemed to fade away, then rally. "Did you see the painting?"

"Yes."

"It is a beautiful painting, Cousin Ted," Aunt Betty said.

"The painting is for permitting them to use the harbor. I hung it in the foyer of Mansion House because that seemed most suitable."

"I'm sure they deeply appreciate your permitting them to use the harbor," Aunt Betty said.

"I couldn't prevent it. It's a harbor," Theodore said.

"I'm sure you would have permitted it even if you could have prevented it."

"You're sure?" He turned his gaze on Aunt Betty. An insect. "Yes," he said. It was not in reply to her but to some question of his own. He looked at Laurie. She felt his vast dissatisfaction, his conviction that no one understood his anger at his impotence and inability to take command. How strangely this figure, thickened by time, hardened by authority, and weakened by age, compared with the young man's picture of him at the age of eighteen, in a hunting lodge out West, sitting with his dog and looking so much like Ken—a young, thin, sensitive and brooding, vulnerable, unsure Preston.

"Did you go to the Tower?" he demanded.

"Yes. And out on the catwalk."

Something altered in the determined, desolate, despairing figure.

"You can see everything from there."

She nodded. The nurse stirred. It was time to go.

"As to painting the guest room," Theodore said, "Cousin Ken may wish to do otherwise when he assumes occupancy."

Arthur placed his hand on Laurie's arm and Aunt Betty's shoes scraped the hard floor.

"If he ever does," Laurie said.

"It is time to rest now, Mr. Secretary." The nurse glared at Laurie with hatred.

"What was that?" Theodore asked.

"Ken isn't sure," Laurie said unsteadily. "Because of my ignorance and because he's not sure of himself."

The massive figure of Theodore altered again. The eyes with the brownish, reddish tints in them seemed elsewhere. "Not sure? If he wishes to paint the room another color, he can change the orders at any time." He smiled.

Aunt Betty bent and kissed his cheek hastily. Arthur found his hand and pressed it. Laurie touched his cheek with hers and held her face against his for a moment. Then she hurried out ahead of them. Leaving Mansion House, they passed the children's playhouse. The tiny dishes, chairs, and tables inside it all stood intact, in a state of readiness for an event that had not taken place and perhaps now never could. Laurie sat down on the bench in front of it and Arthur, holding Aunt Betty's elbow, moved with her past Laurie, further up the hill where he stopped, and they stood and waited.

Laurie looked back at Mansion House. The nurse was helping Theodore into a wicker chair on the porch. His old felt hat was straight on his head and a thick blanket was thrown across his lap. His gnarled hands rested on the head of his carved stick. A statue. Morse's wife was approaching, coming up the lawn, walking rapidly. Had he been seated earlier, Theodore would have seen her at a distance and recognized her. She was too near now.

"Who's that?" he demanded.

It sounded like a sentry's alert, tense and on the ready, until the proper password had been spoken.

"Gert. Morse's wife. May I cross the lawn to the dock? Boat's coming in and I'm late."

"Go wherever you wish."

She approached the porch and bent forward to kiss his face. It took on a tolerant expression which vanished by the time she straightened and hurried on. He stared straight ahead, unaware that Laurie sat close by at the children's playhouse, watching him.

That night Laurie could not sleep again. The past was alive about her and death was more in the present. The past held a promise and strength that the present had not delivered. But all this had to do with knowing clearly, as she never had before, what Ken expected. In expecting, she thought, he seeks, *needs* something from me; that completeness in love Arthur spoke of. If I fail to provide it he will seek it elsewhere. He'll have to. Now that I sense, not really understand but *sense* what torments him, I know that the only crucial thing I can bring on this journey is love. Without it there is no answer. He still has the capacity to grow, to seek and believe that which was lost so long ago in Theodore one way, in Sarah another, in Arthur a third, and that which the others who came along later never had at all. *Hold your hands high when you can and keep your eyes partly closed. Animals do not like to be stared at.* But at St. Terese, when Ken spoke in a flat monotone because it disturbed the birds less than a hissing whisper did, he said, "Take a step during each song. Most birds are so lost in their song they will not notice." Another time, as we listened to the soft, very faint sounds of cooing, he said, "Keep your mouth slightly open the way music lovers do, or sweethearts when they kiss, and you will hear them better." The same secrets but seen differently because of love and the need for it. Something has been fading and that is the part I must nourish with emergency measures. It is the part that must not fade till death do us part, or it will keep getting replaced with the *nothing* we spoke of. It is the hidden thing that can join us as one and by so doing make each of us more clearly and separately defined as individuals. Arthur's paradox. Our barrenness itself might well be the result of the fact that it is fading, and whose very personal history is this? Against all reason, I know we will have our child! It's all still too vague and confused. But I know that here is a tangible meaning. We missed some vital turn in the road. Before I might have thought it could not be undone. I do not think so now. Both of us knew it though neither would mention it as we kept speeding on without direction. It can still be corrected. What arrogance and ignorance lay in my assumptions when I drove him back to a work and way of life not meant for him!

But there's this about ignorance: it can be cured by knowing.

It seemed to her she had just fallen asleep but the sun was shining. She had gone to sleep Laurie Dugan, to wake up Mrs. Kenneth Fenimore Preston. They would have a child! The floppy sweaters, the bobby sox and flats, and all other forms of unfinished business lay behind her on that other side of a bridge she had crossed in the night. She would not look back.

She bathed, singing a song, dressed quickly, and ran downstairs. She felt a need for haste, to make sure she would not miss something. The table was empty and fully cleared.

"Where is everybody?" she asked the maid.

"Church."

Yesterday that would have made her feel out of place, out of step, an object lesson in what not to do or be. But something had happened during the night.

"Will you be having just coffee?"

"No, I'm hungry. I'll be having breakfast."

She was not surprised as she finished her second cup to find Cousin Arthur at the door.

"Everyone's at church," she greeted him. "Coffee?"

"Yes, I'd like coffee. Morning, Elsa," he greeted the maid, and sat down at the table. "In Japan I learned to worship under a widespread cherry tree. When I came home, our storm-shorn beech trees reminded me of it, so I naturally took to worshiping there until I realized I was not worshiping God, but my youth and its delights in beauty." He sipped. "There's a chapel at Mansion House. It hasn't been used since Cousin Stuart took it over."

The maid had left the room. He continued: "Or, rather, from the time it took over Aunt Betty. She was so anxious to do things right, inevitably she did them wrong. Whatever was it? Oh, yes. The chapel is circular, built in six hundred and thirty on the basis of some unorthodox theories concerning witches. A witch could not survive in a house of God and for that reason would not knowingly enter one. Built in a circle with the door concealed would make it harder for a witch to stumble upon the chapel, and, once inside, more difficult to escape. It seems Betty once confused the door to the chapel with the downstairs bathroom in an emergency and couldn't get out." He was laughing. "Would you like to see it?"

"After coffee," Laurie said.

The entrance to the chapel was down the flight of rear stairs fronting on the harbor. There were bits of glass and pebble in the plaster covering the woodwork that made it glisten. It had its own gambrel roof and a spiracle connected to the great chimney of Mansion House. Quiet as it was everywhere, the silence here was absolute. The door shut out the sound of surf, wind, trees, branches, even the rustling of dead leaves. The old benches, polished by care and use, had a reddish hue. A lectern faced them from a slightly elevated platform, to one side of which was an organ and, to the other, the pulpit. Small wonder such people had believed in witches: as Arthur said, they could believe in miracles both good and bad for they themselves had performed them. At either end, flanking the benches, were boxes such as one sat in at the opera. Surely they were not meant for worship.

As though reading her thoughts, Arthur asked, "You wonder about the boxes? The original landlord of Caleb acquired them in France. His first purpose was a theater. It was his love. But the witch hunters frightened his wife. Though they were wealthy, the fever left no clan, age, or sex out of its path, so the room was promptly altered to become a chapel."

The room was an almost perfect circle. Now that the door was shut, its form and color being the same as the rest of the walls and wood paneling, it all seemed to have neither beginning nor end, entrance nor exit. The back porch of Mansion House jutted out above the second story, throwing a heavy shadow over the stained-glass windows where the chapel faced the harbor.

Arthur had placed his hand gently on her head and then walked noiselessly in his sneakers to the platform. He stood at the lectern for a moment, then disappeared to the left.

Laurie sat on the bench looking at the floor. Entrance and exit, endings and beginnings: she could find neither. Then the sun appeared, throwing rectangular designs on the rich red-brown woods, and Arthur, who had opened one window near the organ, sat down and struck a chord. The sun's brightness there gave the circle its lie. That was the exit. And this, she thought, is the west and there's the harbor and here the ocean, and though I cannot see it, between them stands the door.

The organ's soft reverberation blended with the silence, lending it its own tone. Blessed silence. With soundless lips, Laurie repeated the Lord's Prayer. Suddenly a throbbing sense of sound rather than sound itself shook her body, and with it came panic. Only then did she realize that Arthur was reappearing at the open window, to greet someone. The throbbing sound that shook her was the motor of a boat.

"How's the catch?" Arthur asked.

"Best ever," someone answered, with a strange accent. "Don't think there's any more chance of another like it than there is of catching a white weasel sleeping."

Arthur shut the little window and in an instant the circle had neither opening nor closing again.

"It's the seafood for the cookout," Arthur explained.

Guided, so it seemed to her, by a mysterious knowledge, he found the door's opening. She followed him out, up the stone stairs and then down a path which placed them on the beach under the second-story porch at the rear of Mansion House. The fisherman, who had stopped the motor and anchored out at the edge of the moss-covered dock, was untying a big rowboat full of lobsters and clams. He had the face of a young man, almost beardless, but his hair was snow white. He swung the rope attached to the ring in its stem into a round, loose knot that fell over a big rock, then pulled it tight, jumped to the narrow, moss-covered plank leading up to the dock, slipped, waved his arms to recapture his balance, and continued walking quickly up the slippery boards.

"He fishes the bay waters," Arthur said. "It's so cold none of them have learned to swim. Fear of drowning makes them nimble-footed as goats."

They approached halfway up the dock to where it was still dry and waited.

"How was your summer?" Arthur asked.

"Started poorly but by August the hogsheads piled up." The man removed his hat when Arthur introduced them.

Handymen were appearing now in pairs, carrying big, heavy logs which they threw into a crater of rocks on the beach directly below the back porch that jutted twenty feet above. Laurie and Arthur watched as the fire was started and shepherds joined the handymen, bringing more wood which they piled on the rising fire. The fisherman had emptied the rowboat of all its catch, and now the Mansion House servants appeared to remove the seaweed from the bottom of the boat as they laughed and exchanged gossip. Each was quite clear as to his place in an unspoken division of labor.

Toward noon the fire had begun to build a thick, glowing carpet of red-hot coals and heavy, smooth stones were placed upon them. *Silver Box* appeared, coming from the mainland with the family on board. Laurie could see Theodore, seated with a blanket over his legs, staring straight ahead. The nurse stood beside him, the wind blowing her blue cape and tossing the streamers of her cap.

"They'll all be coming here presently," Arthur said, anticipating Laurie's thought.

The Mansion House servants appeared, disappeared, and reappeared, carrying trays with cocktails, and shortly Theodore emerged on the porch above with Aunt Sarah and Aunt Betty on either side of him. The nurse wrapped the blanket around his legs and placed another over it, and the rest of the family joined Arthur and Laurie on the beach.

Clams by the hundreds were laid on the hot stones and covered with a thick wet blanket of seaweed. Everyone drank cocktails, talked, and laughed as the wind swept the waters. Toward midafternoon the first of the lobsters was laid on seaweed and covered by it. The red glow deepened as the sun entered the western sky.

By the time the moss-covered part of the dock was submerged in the tide, dozens of boats appeared, and standing in them, red-cheeked, wearing heavy mackinaws, parkas, and gloves, were the grocer, shoemaker, butcher, vet, doctor, postmaster, and their families: every person in Trubeck, actually, who had in any way served Caleb Island this summer.

Then the pure, young, bell-like voice of a girl began to sing a strange, uncomplicated melody to words that sounded part English, part French. As the boats moved on toward Goat's Head Landing, bushels of eggs were spread and began to bake. The people both on land and on water joined in the singing that continued as they docked their boats, secured them, and walked the length of the beach to the crater and the fire. They nodded to Theodore, who sat up above, greeted one another, and accepted their drinks around the flames. Their songs seemed to Laurie to tell a story of times and places no longer existing, of manors and manners, wenches and knights, tall forests, firs, winter, and highwaymen's roads. Though no one conducted nor chose their order, nor the keys in which they were sung, everybody knew his assigned place in melody or complex obligatos, as they sang in a chorus against the wind, waves, and winter.

The cold stung Laurie's cheeks and the heat ran through her from the drinks and the fire. The sun pulled down in the west.

"Ken should be here," she said.

"He should have been here the summer you married," Arthur said.

"He asked me to. I was afraid."

"I'm still afraid," Arthur said.

"I remember your paintings."

They were singing again. Laurie looked up. Theodore was singing too, his gaze fixed high over their heads, out at the blackening waters. He starts the songs, she realized. They are all aware of him without looking up and he of them without looking down. Yesterday I would have felt alone here, isolated, a stranger. Yesterday.

Now, Aunt Sarah lowered a small net secured by a rope. The first of the baked eggs was placed in the net by the fisherman and Aunt Sarah pulled it up. Then, Cousin Theodore removed one glove and cracked the hard egg against the porch rail. When he commenced to peel it, the feast began. Eggs washed down with drink, drink washed down with song, song washed down with waves. After the eggs came the clams, both with wine, and then came the lobsters and more wine. Then, harder drink. The smell of seaweed and burning spruce mingled with salt, food, heat, and the cold night air as the songs continued, and Laurie imagined embraces in the shadows and whispers as the first evening star rose and the sun set. Fresh logs were thrown into the crater over the steaming stones and on the glowing coals. The flames rose and danced, revealing, concealing—creating and destroying.

From up above came George's voice.

"Awfully."

She laughed aloud. Yes—George, of all of them, at the porch, his back to the rail, would be the only one to presume upon Theodore.

You first-rate fake, she sang inside against the sight of him groveling before the majestic figure. You think Ken will let you—that I'll let Ken? She felt a sharp, primitive desire to spit at him, trample him, scratch his face with the lobster claws. Fake. Plunderer. Son of a strikebreaker.

"Easy, lost Laurie." Arthur's face was close to hers, red and glistening from heat, drink, and wind. He can hear my silence, Laurie marveled, and the things it is shouting.

"Easy?" She laughed aloud. "Easy enough." They laughed together.

"I didn't kill my deer and it's disappointed me. Awfully."

Their laughter grew louder. They held onto each other, laughing.

"Do you really," she asked Arthur, shouting above the wind, "do you really think that Ken is a lost cause?"

"Not in his natural place," he shouted back. "Not with you."

"No. Not with me. Good. I'll drink to that."

A servant walked by, they picked up filled glasses, and Laurie said into Arthur's ear, "I drink to you, Cousin Arthur. I am on to you. I know who you are. You play the organ in perfect circles and laugh at scrolls and give strange names with numbers to simple rocks and stones, but I know you. Your mask is off. I see you. You were born here, you said, and worshiped like a pagan under cherry trees in Japan. Ageless and timeless, the flames are your brother. Cousin Arthur—*you* are the Devil!"

"Lost Laurie, you're drunk." He was laughing again now and so was she.

She hiccupped.

"Yes. I am drunk and you're the Devil, Cousin Arthur. I see you. The bed of love was in Salem Town and you were born on this Island. You *are* the Devil."

Arthur smiled, looking hard at her.

"Lost Laurie, is that how you got him? By being even crazier? Is it madness that makes you sing?"

She shook her head. "I don't know your songs. Only my own. And I'm singing you, Cousin Arthur—drinking you. Here's to you! Eternal laughter and damnation, Cousin Arthur, I drink you down." They drank again and then again, seizing full glasses from the passing servants.

"Yes, I am the Devil," Arthur said, "but what are you? Why weren't you here the first summer of love?"

"I told you, Devil, didn't I? And I'm in the lair now, so isn't that enough? It's not too late. I told you I was afraid. To see too much, to know too much of the weight of what I was in for. I feared meeting you and made a fool of myself instead. I went to New York for safety

where a white worm with a red face made a pass at me and I returned
to St. Terese and Ken." She hiccupped again. "Ken weak. Ken strong."

"You're here now, lost Laurie."

She looked at him. "I'm not lost any longer and what's more, I am
now going to kiss you, Cousin Arthur."

"No, no, still wrong. *I* am going to kiss *you*." He did so and then
with his face next to hers, he said, looking up, "Behold Alicia's stud
horse staring like a hoot owl into a thunderstorm. He's been dismissed."

"Yes, he's a case. Case dismissed!" she shouted.

She laughed and spilled some wine. Dismissed, dismissed. She
staggered against Arthur. "Devil, Ken should be here now." My Prince
Charming, who came in a coffin instead of a carriage, my young man
preserved in ice against time with the fire of his heart intact. Not with
his back to a Coney phoney Island wall in Manhattan. Not where he
is now.

"Then bring him back," Arthur said.

"I will." I'll wake him and bring him back. To be what he will be,
what he was beginning to become and release him from the sorcery
of the little silver box in which he is trapped with a fading image.
"I'll bring him back, Devil."

Fire, air, and water. A figure flew against the red sky. "Look," she
said. "Our puffin bird. Old bottlenose—the winged clown we share."

Arthur raised his glass to it. They were singing again. Now the songs
were elegiac and the language incomprehensible, a French beyond
any French she knew. Yet she understood. Not sounds and syllables but
the unfinished business of her heart. Were there whispered lusts in
the shadows suggesting things happening, hands doing, flesh touching,
or did she only imagine it? No one would care. This was the end of
the hunt and in its midst each was private, together, and separate, in
communion and union. They had timed it to the sky from the sun high
in the east to the stars with no moon and night's blanket of secrecy.

She leaned against Arthur and whispered, "What is this called?"

"It has no name," he said. "But it's never been missed since the first
Kenneth Preston began it. It may even have been before him. No one
knows. Perhaps it was the Merry Mount."

"What's that?"

"*Mere Mount*. Where worshipers of the senses danced round a pole
adorned with buck's horns, drinking, loving, and debauching until
dawn." He laughed softly. "Its founder, Captain Wollaston, built his
home next to the Adamses. As the Pilgrims faced the unknown to
glory in the spirit, so did they to glory in the flesh. The Pilgrims drove
them out but perhaps one of them who managed to stay behind was a
Preston."

"I knew you were the Devil."

He shrugged. "Then again it may have been Thanksgiving by the old calendar, ten days behind the present Gregorian one. With fifty of them and ninety Indians led by their king, Massasoit, they entertained and feasted three days. It was the Indians who killed and provided five deer for the occasion."

"I like that explanation better."

"The ladies, God bless them, always do."

She laughed and he rejoined the singing and held her hand.

Still singing, Theodore rose, helped to his feet by the women, leaning on his two canes. They finished the song and fell into silence. The waves murmured softly. The flames licked at Theodore's image, not quite reaching it. His eyes sought out the blackness beyond them.

"Another season has come and gone at Caleb," he said, "and for what each has done in its behalf, I thank you. And in behalf of all I thank Almighty God."

The women helped him back into his wheel chair. The blankets were restored to his legs, the hat replaced on his head, the gloves put back on his hands. Laurie thought he looked down at her and smiled. Then he receded from the light into the shadows. Blackness enveloped him and he was gone. It wrenched her heart. She wished the waves would stop, the fire stay high, the feast go on forever, but the fire cracked and boiled now, spitting the wet salt of the sea. The waves rose higher and the flames sank lower. The townsmen with children were taking their leave, still eating, drinking, talking. Voices called out. There was laughter at Goat's Head Landing.

A woman's voice said, "You're too fat to get in," and another woman said, "You're so thin I can pitch you clean through a flute," to which a man replied, "Or pitch a flute clean through—" Then there was the small sound of a motor against the waves and wind and the first of the boats pulled out with its small, feeble lights pointing toward the mainland.

"Well, of course, it won't start not without it's fueled," someone said.

"It's the boat, I tell you!" Then a bargain was reached. There was the sound of fuel pouring. "All you children jounce down in the corner!"

The many small boats moved like a fleet, their small lights braving the blackness. From shore to sea, from sea to shore, they still sang in unison while the shepherds began to haul and remove things. Sarah, Tiffany, Eleanor, and Betty were down on the beach with the others. Tiffany yawned. Sarah told him to go home. She would stay to the end as Ted used to. Arthur told Sarah's children he would take her home by carriage. They thanked him and left.

The servants had retired, leaving the windows open. Their laughter was heard on the beach as the others packed what remained to be removed after the sun rose. At last there was no one left on the beach but the family and of that only the young people. A voice called out, "Your hands are too cold now." The young people were still drinking. One of the girls began to sing a folk song learned at school. "Saturday night and Sunday too, true love on my mind."

"I'll drive Aunt Betty and Alicia home," Arthur told Laurie. "George is too drunk."

"I'll go with you."

"Stay with the young people. We'll only be a few minutes."

"I won't stay," Laurie said.

"All right, then."

The carriage lantern flickered and Alicia drew a flashlight from her purse to throw a beam ahead on the road. At Aunt Betty's they said good night, then sat silent on the way back. Their carriage wheels struck the stones and the galloping hooves sent up sparks. The carriage was now ascending the road to the lawn with the dry sheep droppings.

"Cousin Theodore looked sad," Laurie said.

"His last hunt."

"I understand."

They reached the top of the hill. There was still a red glow in the sky and they could hear a disorganized chorus of popular songs. It was a thin sound with everyone singing the melody. When they reached the beach, Sarah was on the porch sitting where Theodore had been, but the flames had licked the air to their capacity and now spread low over the glowing coals. Sarah was only a shadow.

All at once a hissing sound came from the fire. Rain was pouring thick and cold. The hot coals hissed louder and steamed and glowed as white smoke rose. The shepherds were out again, moving things, pulling them under the protection of the wide, long porch overhead. Laurie waited in the carriage while Arthur went to fetch Sarah. Then the three of them drove off.

Behind them the young people were clustered under the porch. One sang with nostalgic self-pity:

"I loved her in the morning and I loved her at night,
I loved her in the evening when the moon was shining bright,
I loved her in the winter and I loved her in the fall,
But last night on the back porch I loved her best of all."

"That's George," Aunt Sarah said.

"Everything is George," Laurie told her.

"I hope not."

"So do I."

"That's half the battle," Sarah answered.

They reached Aunt Betty's in silence. Looking back, they saw only the faintest glow. They could not hear voices, but there was a light burning somewhere at the top of Mansion House. It could not be the Tower: it had to be the bedroom. No, it was too high for the bedroom. But how could it be the Tower?

They heard Aunt Betty's voice through the partly opened window saying, ". . . doing this gratuitously cruel, unpardonable thing! Telling Cousin Theodore that Cousin Ken would definitely not take over Mansion House."

"And what did Cousin Theodore say?"

"He pretended not to hear. The girl is hopelessly N.O.C.D."

"We'll come in with you to say good night," Arthur said.

"What's N.O.C.D.?" Laurie asked him.

"A vulgar abbreviation," Sarah said, "used by Betty, her daughters, and parasitic husbands. It means 'not our class.'"

"Not our class, *darling*," Arthur corrected.

Laurie laughed. Then Arthur laughed and Sarah joined in. All three of them laughed helplessly and hysterically, standing out there in the night, and the horse shifted in his harness and neighed.

"She's right, I'm not," Laurie said. "And thank God I'm not."

"Amen to that," Sarah said.

"But we'll come in and say good night just the same," Arthur said.

They mounted the stairs noisily. When they entered, the lights were still on in the living room. But it was empty.

"We are sorry Cousin Ken didn't come."

"I'll tell him, Aunt Sarah."

"Also tell him he missed nothing by not waiting for our new museum. Just endless bickering since it's opened."

"I will."

"But say that when I took over Thorpe I knew nothing," Arthur said. "They appointed me director only because they were convinced I would make a stupendous financial contribution."

"Which I made for you," Sarah reminded.

"As did Theodore. But in the end I made my own. Because finally I knew the things they never thought I would know. Little as it was, I left the musuem wiser than before I came to it. You will tell Ken?"

"*Cousin* Ken to you," Laurie said smiling.

Arthur smiled back. "Cousin Ken."

"Now go away," Sarah told Arthur. "I want a few minutes alone with Cousin Laurie."

"In a moment."

"It's a miracle to me," Sarah said, "how a man who gets as drunk as you do at the cookouts remains so sober all year long."

"Everything is a miracle," he told her. "As a genealogist, you know that. Lost Laurie, you tell Ken, that is *Cousin* Ken, I'm very glad I contributed what little I did to Thorpe. When next Cousin Ken comes, make sure he brings the silver box. I've heard of a process for restoring the dag which has to do with working from a print. He'll understand. When you touch the surface of a dag directly, it is permanently blemished. Will you remember?"

"Why should she?" Sarah asked. "When the image fades, what will be left is pure silver."

He took Laurie's hand, kissed it and fingered his red bow tie. "Don't you claim *all* the errors. You must leave a few for God or He'll be offended." He left.

"While anatomically inaccurate, I am pleased to find the future of Prestons in your hands," Sarah said.

She kissed Laurie's forehead and Laurie knew that neither she nor Arthur would be present in the morning to prolong farewells. She did not want Sarah or Arthur to leave. She feared that the night would vanish like a dream. Sarah and Arthur. Two wonderful people and I love them. But they are backwards somehow. Important things in them are mixed up. Sarah, like a man and Arthur so like a woman with his unexpectedly revealed and as quickly concealed facets of charm; the mocking way he smiles and the light that flashes on the muscles of his eye and then vanishes. He had been married and a father. It seemed to have left no trace. But they are wonderful and Ken can set them straight and I'll see to it that he does. She laughed recklessly and ran upstairs to her room.

She threw her clothes on the chair and stood before the open window where rain beat against it and her. She welcomed its cold needles, thinking, that is my house. Here is my work and my lesson. Arthur, Sarah, Theodore. Three fully formed individuals, each denying the existence of the others by his own choice, yet all together! A fully formed human being was a complete education, a signpost, a call to arms. The very existence of such a person was a miracle; nature's revelation of the special role of humankind and the place of choice in being, becoming, and remaining human. Ken was not yet fully formed. Because he refused to face that part of him which still remained beyond his reach, untapped, unused, surrounded in a kind of sleep.

I can't sleep. I don't want to sleep. This night must spin on and on like my head spins. As the earth spins. Does the universe spin? *The last male Preston.* When Ken had said it during their courtship, it sounded completely, utterly ridiculous.

She threw herself on the bed. Its hardness felt good to her. She turned on the light again, slipped on her robe, and opened the door.

The bathroom was directly opposite. Alicia appeared, then stepped back.

"Go on," Laurie said to her. "I can wait."

"No," Alicia answered.

Laurie entered the bathroom, was there a few minutes, and came out.

"Let's have a smoke when I'm through," Alicia said. Laurie left her door open, sat on the bed, and waited. When Alicia came out they lighted cigarettes.

"All that wine and whisky," Alicia said.

Laurie nodded.

"We'll leave early," Alicia said.

"I'll be awake."

"Well then, good night."

"Good night."

"About my mother—"

"Yes, what about her?"

"She's in conflict, you see, so don't pay any attention."

"What would she know about conflict?" Laurie asked.

"We are both in conflict," Alicia said. All at once her face showed it. "George needs Mansion House now that he knows it's there, but he doesn't belong in Mansion House. Cousin Ken does. As Theodore did. Since Cousin Ken loves you, you belong there too." She stopped, then spoke again. "One has many loyalties. George isn't a fool. At least not altogether the fool he appears to be. When I mention it, he says it's the role best suited to him, in these circumstances. Still, he's my husband and I love him."

The rain had grown wilder. Alicia said good night and left. Laurie returned to the window. She could see nothing outside, only blackness. Suddenly, for all of the wind, she felt hot. She threw off the robe again and stood by the window with her back to the door and breathed deeply. Then she heard a creak. Only the bottom of the old keyhole was obstructed from inside by the key. She stepped out of its line of vision, put on her robe, and approached the door from the side. Then she pulled the door open abruptly and stepped out into the hall. She could see the door to Alicia and George's room closing. The wet imprint on the floor below the keyhole where a little puddle with sand in it had formed was a large one, made by a man's shoe. She locked her door, stuffed paper into the open part of the keyhole, removed her robe, put out the light, and walked back to the window.

On the outside, not looking in, is where you belong and are going to stay, *friend* George. It's my fault if Ken isn't here tonight. Not all accident is bad. I came to run away from Ken and from myself. Instead I found both of us. Miracle of miracles, I'm needed. The Prestons need me. You need me, Ken. The least and the most. After honeymoon comes marriage *in order to form a more perfect union,* the miracle that syncretizes and demands full postliminium for the joining of forces so far apart which means I must accept, respect, and cherish all of you. *Ken-weak. Ken-strong.* See what I have learned here? The Dugans of Dublin once owed their lives to Great-grandfather Timothy. Mr. Sands told me. Now so do I and in a way no one could have expected except possibly Timothy himself. I share his faith: How our child will come I do not know but it will come. A living token, a remembrancer. Yours and mine, ours. This island is not a prison, nor Mansion House a tomb. Your heritage is not a burden. All over again and for the first time, I, Laurie Dugan, do thee wed.

Chapter 6

"PRESTON speaking."

"Mrs. Preston speaking," she imitated.

"Is that you, Laurie?"

"Any other Mrs. Prestons you know, hey?"

"Laurie, what's the matter with you? And where are you?"

"Nothing's the matter. I'm happy, that's all and I'm in our bedroom. Our bird has gone south and there's absolutely no one here to hypnotize me. Caleb was marvelous. I just got back this minute."

"Laurie, are you sure you're all right?"

She laughed. "Very. And I'm also sure I love you and Cousin Arthur and your Aunt Sarah and even Cousin Theodore. But mostly I love you. Where are you?"

"At the hotel."

"I know that, goose. I called *you*. I mean *where*. I want to see you." She could feel him smiling.

"In my sitting room."

"Go pick up your phone in the bedroom."

"Now, Laurie—"

"Are you alone?"

"Yes, but—"

"Then you just go and pick up the phone in your bedroom." She smiled as she heard him put the phone down then lift the other and hang up the first one.

"All right, crazy. I'm in the bedroom now."

"You know what? I miss you. And do you know who misses you most of all?"

"Laurie, are you drunk?"

"Very likely, oh, very, very likely. But don't go changing the subject. I was starting to tell you who misses you most of all."

"I'd better guess or the operator will disconnect us."

"No one will ever disconnect us, hey, ever again! Not even me. And each and every one of us passionately says *amen*."

"You all have company," he said. "Now what is this?"

"*This?* This is I know what I should have known in the beginning. But I know now. That's what matters, isn't it?"

"You know *what?*"

"Something terribly important."

"Laurie! You're pregnant."

"No. But it's just as important. Even more so, I think. When will you be back?"

"Now, Laurie, you tell me."

"No. When will you be back?"

"Nine, ten days. Thanksgiving."

"That's too far away."

"I have the broadcast tonight, the press tomorrow, and the staff meeting Wednesday. Then I'm off to Los Angeles Thursday morning."

"Isn't seeing me more important?"

"Much."

"You should see me now. I'm taking off my robe. Wait. There. Hold on. Hold close. Everything's off. My head's on your pillow. The curtains are blowing. The sky is clear. It's still light out. And that guitar is playing across the river."

"Laurie, that's not fair."

She laughed softly. "I don't want to be fair. I want to see you. Do you really plan to wait till Thanksgiving?"

"I could try to cancel the press. That's tomorrow."

"Tomorrow and Thursday I have exams. Wednesday, I'm free."

"I'll skip the staff meeting Wednesday. I'll be in tomorrow night and leave for Los Angeles Thursday early."

"Do, oh, please, please do."

"I will. They'll raise hell but I'll do it. Why can't you tell me what's important?"

"I love you. Isn't that important?"

"Yes. All right. Say good night to everyone."

"Now *that's* not fair."

"I'll say it myself tomorrow."

"Tenderly?"

"Very."

"You sure you won't mind missing that miserable staff meeting Wednesday?"

He laughed. "I'll tell them tonight after the broadcast or first thing tomorrow."

"The guitar just stopped. I have to go to school for just a few hours. I love you wildly and I hate to wait. This is the longest we've been apart."

"I love you, Laurie."

"I love you!"

She hung up and turned with surprise to the window. She heard the guitar again. It hadn't stopped. It was only that the wind had shifted.

Laurie paused at the door to fumble in her big purse. She put her books down, balancing them between her feet. The idea of Mrs. Preston home from school, books and all, struck her as funny. Cecil opened the door before she found her key and told her that Mr. Hawley was waiting. She greeted him at the foot of the stairs.

"Your houseman told me to go directly to Mr. Preston's study, but I thought I'd better wait." Hawley said. He explained that four files were needed downtown. He had left them in Mr. Preston's study in their last conference before the tour.

"You certainly should have gone right in."

She ran upstairs to get rid of her books and get out of what she privately called her uniform. Then she came down and suggested he stay for coffee. "Find what you were looking for?"

"All but one. I imagine Mr. Preston has that with him."

She was about to say that Ken would be in tomorrow night and stopped herself. Unless Ken informed them, they wouldn't know. No business. She wanted him to herself. She went out of her way to be nice to Hawley. She had been ungracious before Ken left and none of this had been Hawley's fault. She asked how things were going and whether the date for his wedding had been set. It had. He asked her how long it had taken for her to grow familiar with the Street.

She smiled. "I never did. And Mr. Preston's been very patient."

"That's encouraging. I thought it was me."

"How is that—" She groped for the word and laughed. "I'm proving my point—specialty?"

"Specialist?"

"Yes, that you talked to my husband about."

"The noncompetitive specialist's book?"

They both smiled.

"I wouldn't try that on your fiancèe for a while," she advised him.

"There won't be any need to. I've decided to stay with Preston and Company."

"I gathered from my husband it was quite an opportunity."

"There's no opportunity like working for and around a man like Mr. Preston. Not because he's your husband but because it's a fact. And no discourtesy meant to Mr. Coogan."

"You mean you're staying with Preston and Company because of my husband?"

"That's so. I don't suppose another specialist's book like the one I've been offered will come along for ten years, but then you can't have everything."

She liked his sincerity. What a state she must have been in to have found him so obnoxious only four weeks ago. "What would you do if Mr. Preston left?" she asked.

Hawley laughed. "Just so long as he doesn't for the next five years."

"But what if he did?"

"I'll take my chances that he won't."

She poured more coffee. "I should think you'd talk it over with Mr. Preston before doing anything drastic."

"I'm afraid I've got to give my answer this week. I pretty much have made up my mind. In fact, you might tell Mr. Preston when you speak to him."

She put down her cup. "It's possible Mr. Preston may retire," she said.

Hawley smiled, puzzled. "You mean from the Street, going into public funds? I hope so. It's not the Floor I'm interested in, it's finance."

"I mean finance." Then she said impulsively, "He'll be in tomorrow night, just for a day. Please don't tell anyone. It's not business. I'll mention this to him. If there's something you should know, I'm sure he'll call you."

At the door, he thanked her for the coffee and told her how much he had enjoyed the visit. She ran up the stairs whistling. Tomorrow night! Mrs. Preston, decorum please. Just two steps at a time. She wondered about what she had told Hawley. Well, you do feel sure, don't you? The thought of Coogan crossed her mind and vanished. The sky was fat with snow clouds. By tomorrow night the city might lie under a blanket of white while they—how nice it would be!

Leatrice Coogan looked across at her husband's bed, separated from her own by the night table. A few moments ago he had struck the glass on the table with his arm and the shock of the cold water hitting her chest had made her gasp and sit up with a start. The wet sheet was now in the bathroom and she had on a dry nightgown. He still slept, the blankets up over his head. He moaned. She pulled at her eyebrow, a habit she had when extremely irritated. Frightening her out of sleep that way! And he *would* smoke too many cigars whenever his cronies came, no matter what anyone told him. She turned off the light, convinced she would stay awake the rest of the night. Then she promptly fell asleep.

Pat Coogan was fighting his way out of a dream. It was all mixed up. A moment ago, freedom and balmy breezes. Then, tropical rains and mud. Now no longer barefooted, he was wearing boots and sank deeper into the mud, up to his hips. All at once it was cement hardening as it rose to surround his throat, choking him. Soundlessly he cried out "Help!" against being buried alive and then, with a forward lunge, broke out of the tomb into wakefulness. There was a cold, rocklike lump at the pit of his stomach. Freezing cold. He felt on either side of him. The mattress. My bed. My bedroom. The wind must have seeped through the window.

He belched, not yet really awake, and rubbed his stomach. His daughter, Melanie, gently reproving, came back. "Too many cigars, Daddy. Altogether too many cigars."

But something pretty important had happened tonight: either that or a bad dream. No, wait. Yes, a dream. How did that sequence go? Flowers, mud, cement, concrete. It was a warm place, then cold. South Sea Islands. Balmy. Natives in grass skirts. Balmy also means nuts. But something had happened. It was coming back now. Of course. Something? You have been building toward this for months, years, in some ways a lifetime, and it had taken less than three hours in the study tonight while the women sat in the living room exchanging dirty jokes, comparing hysterectomies, and listening to his youngest, Geraldine, play the piano badly. Melanie sat in the study with the men, holding side bets on the TV wrestling matches. Amazing girl. Perfect timing. He felt the rock at the pit of his stomach again. After Leatrice had knocked on the door and said, "Break it up. We're sick of our hen party," while Melanie opened the window to clear the room of cigar smoke, practically as they were leaving, he'd reintroduced the subject of Eisenhower and the incredible effect his heart attack had had on the market. "Actually, we profited from it. You see, we sold out all our positions by Friday before the President took ill." An explosion of questions, admiration, and incredulity followed. "Just luck," he told them. "Instinct, call it whatever you want. A technical sell-off was in the making. It happened in one day instead of a month." Hawley confirmed that it had actually happened and Pat smiled good-naturedly. But what had that to do with his dream? The natives. Smiling, shaking their heads while they danced and welcomed him with wreaths of flowers. Lovely women. Honey-colored. No—*money*-colored. The same feeling of anger he'd had in the dream before danger began came back. No—*henna*-colored. He had shouted it. Not honey-colored, damn niggers. Money-colored!

But they weren't Negroes at all. Just honey-colored. *Henna*-colored. It contradicted him, refuted, confused, and infuriated him all over again. Damn near drove you crazy trying to make yourself understood in a language you couldn't speak. Now that's plain silly. You're making a lot out of nothing, aren't you? If you didn't know their language, how could you possibly know what they were saying? You knew. For that matter, they couldn't understand what you said either. The room wasn't cold, it was hot. Needed air, in fact. Your pajamas are damp. Cold sweat? Maybe you're sick, but you don't feel feverish. Too many cigars. And why, for God's sake, *henna*-colored?

Pat fumbled his way to the bathroom in the dark. Still half asleep he changed his pajamas. Then he stood holding the sink with both hands, his head drooping forward till it rocked back and his eyes opened abruptly. He saw his face in the mirror, the bags folded under his eyes, and the creases in his neck due to the lack of resilience in his flesh. It angered him. An affront by nature to record decay in a man so full of future plans. Then all at once he was wide awake and both dream and reality were one with the rock at the pit of his stomach.

Hawley. Of course. Damn fool, treating the information so lightly! Telling it to me as we left the room where the others might even have overheard. If he had told me sooner, it might have had considerable bearing on how I broached the subject of enlarging the firm's capital. Naturally I emphasized Preston. Preston was the major attraction. In describing the luck of selling on Friday before Ike's Saturday heart attack, and that black Monday of seven weeks ago with its near fifty-point sell-off from 488 to 439 on the Dow Jones averages in one trading day, I placed that piece of instinct at Ken's door, gave it the Preston label. On the other hand, how *could* Hawley attach significance to Laurie's telling him not to build his plans on the proposition that Ken would remain on the Street because *she* wanted him to quit? You had to know Ken and you had to know her to realize that four generations of Prestons on the Street or not, and Ken's authority and intelligence to one side, she did have this influence on him. She *could* do it: you ought to know. Two years ago she succeeded where you failed. Hawley had said it so lightly, so amused in fact that you smiled: you even joked about it.

He took an Alka-Seltzer, splashed his face with cold water, smoothed out the wrinkles on his throat, and watched them fall back into their permanent folds. Pat nodded at the sight, accepting it as a fact. He left the bathroom by the opposite door and entered his study.

This girl was the flaw in Preston's independence and character. Her existence threatened everything. Ken could not quit. Not yet. Lucky he'd invited Hawley over. He wanted the potential investors to see the sort of clean-cut young man who was replacing McBride. A nice, decent, God-fearing Catholic lad, that Hawley, as honest as the day was long. He could afford to be. Explaining that McBride was no loss proved superfluous. It was common knowledge how after pulling all his cash out of the firm, in the week that followed, Mac had reinvested in the weakest part of the market, and been murdered in the sell-off of September 26, then panicked and sold out at the bottom.

You are wide awake now.

He turned on the television set, selected a cigar from the humidor, clipped the tip, and lit it. Then he reviewed the brief exchange. After the others left he had questioned Hawley carefully. "You sure now Mrs. P. didn't say she'd like him home and wanted him to quit the tour?" Hawley, still amused but clear about it, answered, "No, sir, she was talking about Mr. Preston's retiring from finance."

Pat slumped in the chair. The room still smelled vaguely of stale cigar smoke. Sometimes the best of things come out of near disaster: who could deny for instance that Eisenhower's sudden illness that rocked the financial world with the worst single market day since 1933 had proved the blessing that brought his cronies to the invisible line where the issue of investing in the firm could at last be raised? The thought of 1933 brought back the spasm in his stomach. Honey-colored, money-colored, henna-colored. He belched again. They were ready to match the firm's capital, in return for a trivial six per cent on their money, without interference. One year of that and you won't need customers or customers' men. *Customers'* men was almost accurate. These newcomers belonged to the customers, all right, not to the Street, and their real address was Madison Avenue. Customers' *boys*, custom-tailored dummies with a crease in each trouser leg and a hole in each head. It would be a day to celebrate when you needed neither them nor their customers—when you no longer needed Preston. One year. With twice the capital you've got now, you won't need anybody. Three million the day before Eisenhower's heart attack when positions were all sold out and you sat with cash. Then buying back at the bargain prices for that second ride up as the market returned to its highs: in less than a week, three and a half million! with McBride and his share of the profit out of the way. Laurie could have her retired husband, a year from now, but not now. Now you need him, and now, by God, he's going to stay. You don't actually *know* she wants him to quit. How could Hawley, who understands none of this, be able to gauge the information? He just found her too cute for anything. Still you can't assume he was wrong to find out later he was right. Too late then. So assume it. Ken's been away for weeks so his wife has had it and wants him to quit. No, that doesn't add up. I gave her a crack at that before Ken left. She could have made him cancel the tour and she didn't. The tour's almost over now. Then why? All right, something else. It doesn't matter. What matters is you still need Preston. These men are putting up their money on a combination. The main ingredient is Preston, and not just the label, either. Somehow he's reversed roles with you. I don't know how exactly. Ken has never been more active and I've never felt his pressure less or his presence more. Queer. Busy, not active. Getting things done but not accomplishing anything and yet getting more results than ever. Preston has a charmed life. Your cronies are voting for that as much as anything else. Getting out of positions to get rid of Mac sooner because of the soy bean spread, and agreeing to the likelihood of a technical sell-off all coming together a few days before an unpredictable heart attack suffered by the President of the United States! It has nothing to do with knowledge, reason, or planning. Luck. As self-made men your cronies believe in luck because they know how large a role it plays, how being lucky is part of a good man's inexplicable equipment. So do you. Hardheaded men, not dreamers, they measure each inch of ground before they walk on it. Just like you do. They judge things without panic. A loss or a gain neither makes them nor breaks them, and you can rest easy in their company without fear of being hit for a loan. Part of this know-how was a faith in luck, which in turn was a faith in Preston and that was all the more peculiar in view of the fact that the Floor had taken over. The feet are replacing the head in a vast stampede on the part of the unseen, unthinking customers outside the market who are making it. This should be the season for men like Mac except it is Ken who has advanced in it.

In a world full of mysteries all that Coogan could hold on to was that he still needed Ken. Ken had assumed an authority beyond the label, beyond tradition, and far from the rubber stamp. Black Monday shook you, Pat thought, not him. Yes, we were out of it. But the mere fact that it could happen was terrifying: it told you the kind of hands securities were in now. The rabble. He'd had to get away from the office, just to get away from the tape, and when he came back after the bell, there was Ken, calm, cool, and indifferent, working on some data, somehow seeing through him and a little amused. Ken's name had unexpectedly ceased to be his greatest asset. He was a man on the move—thanks to what people call "falling in love." Her asset, no one else's. Hers to do with as she saw fit and you can't let her. Not yet. You can't stop playing second fiddle either. Not now. When stakes run high, problems are complicated. But solutions are always simple. That's the thing people get backwards, out of fear.

All right. She wants him to quit. I don't. That's the problem. What could complicate it is the reason she does that I don't know about.

What could complicate it further was the fact, known now, thanks to Hawley, that Ken was coming in for love's own sake tomorrow night. No doubt she would make her wishes known to him then. If she had already, that would be a further complication.

Yet solutions are simple. They usually require taking a chance and that's not new to you. You sized her up once: overambitious, oversexed, overconfident—that hasn't changed. It's harder to believe she married him for love than for money. Not only for you—for Ken too.

Solutions are simple and call for taking a chance. But you have faced that before. A couple of years ago when you were worth less than a half million dollars, you took chances with the SEC, the N.Y.S.E., the Texans, and Tamiamians. When these two married and you worked on her, you took a chance too. You've taken chances and you've solved problems. Ten years ago, when you had less than a hundred thousand dollars, or twelve years ago—he smiled. Yes, indeed. You've had a little luck of your own. Being out of the market Black Monday was your luck too. A day in which twelve billion dollars were lost in values; a day of disaster excelled only by Black Tuesday and Thursday of '29 or that terrible nine million share day in 1933.

Suddenly a jet of fiery acid flamed through his insides like a blow torch and *honey-colored, money-colored, henna-colored,* came back with a rush. 1933. He took a deliberate breath, saw his crushed cigar, clipped and lit a fresh one. Henna-colored was the biggest chance you ever took. You don't have to take such chances now. She wants him to quit. If you let him, you'll have to give up what you've planned from the beginning that is now getting very close.

He frowned. I despise people who rummage around in the junkyard rust of recollection! It's a sure sign of no faith in the future or of losing your nerve. Same thing. Is this another case where Preston and I have reversed roles? I hope not. Junkyards were Ken's specialty: the bankruptcies of the thirties, reconstructed and reorganized in the forties and fifties. Tarnished treasure, retreads, the last of which was WHIP. He searched the room for the morning newspaper. Leatrice's books lay about. Another thing he despised. Novels were an addiction like sleeping pills or drink. Now where the hell is that newspaper? It's too late for news on TV now. Sh, here we are. I knew damn well Melanie would pick it up and leave it here. He puffed his cigar and scanned the headlines. "West Renews Pledge to Soviets To Curb Germans." When the West makes pledges to the *Germans* to curb

Soviets, it might be news. "Stevenson Stresses Prosperity Flaws." "New Synthetics Used in Skirts." "The market recovery from the worst one-day sell-off since 1933—" He tossed the paper aside.

This isn't the first time henna-colored money-colored Nelly Granger crossed your mind since 1933. In the excited atmosphere of the office that sell-off day last month it had come back. The customers' men had advised all their customers to sell simply because the firm had! The absence of a market letter with sell recommendations or the fact that the firm's primary purpose was to get rid of Mac and then take advantage of the soy bean spread meant nothing to them. An object lesson in the role of rumors and what he meant about the new breed of customers' men. That day the atmosphere around the shop was the kind one finds in an airport waiting room among passengers who narrowly missed the plane that just crashed or were ticketed on the next one, all safely gathered at the gate watching the flaming debris. It had started a talkative flood of recollection. Then one of them asked, "Where were you the autumn of '33?" Some were in college, others in high school: one was even in kindergarten! The moment you asked Ken, you realized your error: that was the time of his father's suicide. So he got off the subject by asking you and you, gulping your drink, said, "San Francisco." There's no use carrying on. You've taken chances since. Hell, the time you hired the Ajax Credit Investigating Company, you took a chance. You told their man you expected Ajax to look for weak spots, just to see what sort of an edge they could get on you as a customer. When he started to protest, you raised your hand and told him not to deny it. "I'll tell you now there are no weak spots, not in Mr. Preston or Mr. McBride or myself. But my saying so won't convince you. No protests, please! If it did, I wouldn't hire you. So that's your first job and we'll pay for it. Do it thoroughly." All it had turned up were some indiscretions of McBride's.

He was breathing calmly again.

Nelly Granger had been the living proof: problems were complicated; their solutions were simple. *"I get paid in dimes, quarters, and dollars, lovey, but they all add up."* When he'd first gone to work in her garage and repair shop on West Farms Road, they had added up all right, but not for him. She was fifty, and he was twenty-six: just a few months older than her oldest son. All four of her sons worked in the garage. Nelly sure was henna-colored. Never mind the way she dyed her hair: she really was, as he'd found out. Nelly's four sons were wire-tight muscled and consumed in angry silence, their tongues thickened by rage as they worked and watched the terrain. A crisis in warfare had been reached to continue longer than anyone had expected—to the breaking point and past it.

He recalled: It was still intensifying in the beginning of '33 when you rushed on your way out of the Depression, into Nelly's garage to serve as half bookkeeper, half mechanic, and smelled a crime in the making. Nelly with her gray, greedy eyes, spindly arms, gaunt face, and lantern jaw, offered you coffee to help swallow the dry, wilted lunch time sandwiches. In winter, hot coffee. In spring, lemonade. Finally she invited you to supper. It brought a gleam to her eye, made of both fear and satisfaction, as she watched her four sons and how it fed their fury. You knew that your presence was hastening something. Had the crime already hatched? Where was her husband, for instance? Had the sons killed their father? Had she? Or had they all done it together? More likely Granger, aware of what surrounded him, had run. Nope. In the depths of a depression, to abandon a business that took in several thousand a week was impossible. So you had properly estimated that the crime had yet to happen. Its goal was the business located at the junction for all trucks, buses, streetcars, and subway transfers to Pelham Bay and City Island. Her sons were not waiting for Nelly to die, not unless they determined the time and circumstances. The chance you took was really no different from the one you took with WHIP, though how far apart they seemed! In both, daily combat and passions confused judgment and the coolest mind won. In both, you took chances. In one case, regulations, financing, law, and plenty of territory—Texas, Florida, South America, London, Paris. In the other, a dirty, greasy garage and repair shop, lawlessness mounting with each turn of the crank and blow of the hammer, and less and less room as the four sons encircled while Nelly desperately offered the unspoken proposition that had to do with more than animal needs still churning under her grease-covered overalls. One morning he had shown up for work to find a carpenter knocking out the wall between kitchen and office. Another bedroom was being built alongside of Nelly's. The sons slept upstairs over the shop. Then he knew she had made her firm offer. That night the brothers snatched at their food around the table in their semicircle, never speaking a word, like snakes possessed of some other means of communication. There was more than the usual sullen greed in their eyes as the half dollars, quarters, dimes, and nickels received for tightening fan belts, simonizing, lubricating, repairing cylinders, crank cases, and axles were piled high in the huge iron washtubs in the kitchen. After supper, the coins were hosed with grease remover and then left overnight to soak in hot water. The dirtiest of the singles, five-dollar and ten-dollar bills were washed, then hung up to dry, to be exchanged the next day for gold pieces. He stayed that night but refused to satisfy her.

One did not enter a deal without knowing particulars.

"Each has a different father," she told him, "and each of their fathers is dead, God rest them. Now they want me to divide the business, but once I do they'll throw me out. Instead of hating each other, they hate me. Help me run it and out they go, Pat. You'll get your share." From then on there was wild humor in their eyes. They laughed at him, deciding he was a fool, after all, as they ate like wolves, heads bent forward over their plates, stoking their fires as they stabbed their forks into the meat and their bread into gravy, never adding a pound of flesh to their bones. He encouraged them to believe what they would, take him for a fool. Perhaps she had killed these husbands. Was that the reason for the hatred of her sons—murder done and yet to be done? He had tried to find out where she kept the gold pieces. Not in a bank. She feared all banks, since so many had failed. But she wouldn't tell him, fearing men even more. Each night, lying in his own bed in the room next to hers, he stared at the bills that hung on the thick cord running the length of the kitchen fastened by paper clips, and the mounds of coins that gleamed dully in the tubs by the light from the lamppost outside. He had considered the pros and cons, slowly, carefully. Alliance with the sons? Impossible. Satisfying Nelly equally so. No hope of being taken into her confidence, and he would not make love to her. No meeting ground with anyone. Then he would work alone. Abruptly, on April 5, came President Roosevelt's announcement prohibiting the hoarding of gold and pronouncing May 1 the last day for the report of all gold pieces and their deposit at Federal Reserve banks.

First he thought that hesitation had cost him his opportunity. Then he discovered the difference between decisiveness and desperation. His chance would be the sensible one and theirs the one of folly. He learned the further lesson: when you have an enemy, make him lose his head. Then, just before this leads to his explosion—act! He waited for the long Decoration Day weekend, when truck income was at its heaviest on Friday, passenger income on both Saturday and Sunday, and all of it at its peak on Monday, with the banks still closed and the coins and bills accumulating for four days. Monday, he hired a car from an old pal on Tenth Avenue and kept it parked two blocks away from Nelly's garage. Throughout the long weekend he moved his burlap bags. At the end of each work day, he hid them under rags. On the last night they lay in the corner of the garage office nearest the kitchen, under his ledgers. That night he gave Nelly the relief she had sought: payment in advance. She drank heavily and fell asleep. While she slept he dressed, all but his shoes. He controlled the temptation to take coins still in the tubs. He took only those in bags, ready for deposit, as well as wrapped bills and those still hanging damp on the line. The brothers were awake. He could hear them pacing overhead. With his shoes in his pockets, he carried all the weight he could bear in one trip—a burlap bag on each shoulder— and slipped out the door. It was the hardest five thousand dollars he had ever earned. Then came June, July, August, opening various savings accounts, depositing small amounts in each of them—and then, finally, at the end of August he'd left for the West Coast.

He had known all along that none of her sons would call the police, and that in her uncertainty Nelly would lose the advantage and hesitate until it was too late. In San Francisco, reading the business opportunities, he found and entered a partnership in a small auto repair shop. He made no friends and kept to himself. Each day he received the *Bronx Home News* by mail and read the obituaries. It came at last in the week of the big sell-off in the fall of 1933. Nelly Granger, age fifty-one, dead of heart failure in her sleep, mourned by her four loving sons, John, Abner, and so on. It was clever of them not to list their last names, each one different from the rest. That might have drawn the idle curiosity of a homicide dick with an empty hour or two to spend on speculation. So many fathers for so many loving sons, with only one dead widow leaving behind so much nice money! Nelly had not known how to trade and it had cost her her life. Her sons had not known how to reason—and that had cost them their peace of mind forever. He had taken his chances within fixed boundaries, so his safety was a certainty. He'd met Leatrice in San Mateo, married her, and returned to New York in time for his son to be born, his five thousand now ten, his credit good for twenty, secure in the knowledge that he could meet any of Nelly's sons on the street and laugh in their faces. If you must commit a crime, compel your enemy to commit a greater one. He remembered Nelly, trying seduction, telling him what the doctor had said: Sound as a rock. Young as a woman of thirty.

Gray streaks danced up and down on the television screen to a hissing, deserted, atmospheric sound. Interesting.

If the sons had worked willingly, she might well have given them the whole damn thing. But it was not in their nature to toil in their youth when they wished to enjoy the rewards that might come later. So. A person whose passions remained under control was the winner. It was true then. It has been true ever since. It's true now.

Mac hates Ken and this hatred demands release. Ken needs Laurie. This need demands satisfaction. Don't forget the Hinkson girl. Now Laurie, for reasons unknown, for *passions* unknown, wants Ken to quit.

The spasm in his stomach was gone. He felt better. He turned off the television set. The hissing and dancing stopped. The sound died. The wheel of light grew smaller, became a dot, and vanished.

Remember this: you have the edge. The red-hot branding iron left its mark deep in your guts. You are one of the breed who faced, fought, and won the fight for survival. That girl is only a girl, and Ken came from the backwaters; far from the storm centers.

Stamina, yes, intelligence, yes. Instinct, too. But the ability to live between grinding wheels and not cry out when safety itself was at stake? Not Preston! That took more than intelligence, stamina, or instinct. Lucky he had invited Hawley. Well, you had a bad night but who doesn't? A bad night is a small event in a long life.

So Ken was coming in tomorrow night. He hadn't told Devlin yet, because Devlin had called earlier from Chicago, right after Ken's broadcast, to report on listening response and hadn't mentioned it though he did say the broadcast was sensational. He hadn't been able to tell Ken yet how delighted they all were. But they'd be together tomorrow morning when the boss met the press and he'd certainly tell Preston then! You had used Devlin's call as an excuse for getting on to your subject with your guests.

Step number one: keep Ken in Chicago. Step number two: stay close to Laurie. Step number three: stir up the animals, including McBride and that Hinkson girl. Take your chances. You know what you want and for it you'll gladly give up any hopes of stopping the tour. You want Ken to stay in this business until you don't need him any more.

These men were buying a team at the head of which stood Preston and that's what they'd get. If the alternatives shook down to Ken quitting the firm or quitting Laurie, he would quit Laurie.

The picture of Melanie sitting on the arm of his chair earlier in the evening came back to Coogan, now. She had squeezed his shoulder and given him that private, crooked, winning smile. She knew he was up to something, felt its direction like a dog on the scent. The power of Ken's temporary spurt belonged to him. He had fanned it, nursed, nourished, and brought it to this point. Nothing would stop him or the market either. Not tight money, the Senate hearings, nor stiffer margin, raised from fifty to sixty and then in April to seventy per cent, or Ike falling ill and the sell-off in bonds last week that wiped out all the tortuously slow advance since August. Nothing! The romance got caught in a little thunder shower on September 26—that was all.

Unprepared, he thought. Like you were tonight. No matter. Every ingredient for victory existed. The bull market lay ahead, their banner record behind like money in the bank and all necessary additional capital within easy reach. Mac was no longer grabbing one third of the pie, and we have all the required personnel. You don't have to like them: the customers do.

So we have everything—providing Ken stayed with it. He'd stay. You were looking the wrong way when through the winding back streets of troubled sleep, Nelly Granger appeared, surrounded by her murdering sons. It had served the purpose of reminding you. All these soft shnooks, including Hawley, created an atmosphere. The way Hawley smiled, in the feeling of triumph the evening had created, you almost missed the significance of it. When that happened and a man got soft, it was time to quit.

I'm not ready to, I'm not soft. The unpleasantness is over. Set the alarm for seven. Six, Chicago time. Get to Devlin first. Simple.

There would be no more troubled sleep tonight.

Chapter 7

AT SIX-THIRTY A.M. Chicago time, Coogan had Devlin on the phone, explaining why he couldn't talk last night. Company. Big doings. Now. In view of the tremendous result and the vital role of Chicago in the whole setup, what had Devlin and his colleagues arranged by way of demonstrating their appreciation to Ken and making the financial community cognizant of it? Nothing? Didn't Devlin think something was indicated? Oh, yes, absolutely. Well, he was glad to hear that because in every other city so far there *had* been something. Devlin said he was sorry he hadn't thought of it; part of the stiff-necked thinking Mr. Preston had talked about. But they had Mr. Preston scheduled for the staff meeting Wednesday. They could still get hold of the agency and network people today, and even call the Detroit office.

Coogan's tone altered. "Good idea. So we don't take the bloom off it, let's forget we ever talked this morning."

"Right!"

"You know what Preston is like. Don't tell him about it till you've got the wheels rolling or he'll just stop you from going to all that trouble."

"Right!"

"You really go to town now."

"Right!"

By noon, New York time, Pat Coogan had visited Mac on the Floor to learn he was scheduled to appear before the Board of Governors for fist fighting. Pat offered to help in whatever way he could. By the bell, Devlin had called back to report that everything was fine. At first it had looked bad. Mr. Preston said he'd planned to cancel the Wednesday staff meeting, to which Coogan replied he didn't doubt it: being offended, that would be exactly Ken's way of showing it. No, Devlin went on to say, it was all right now. It was all set. It was going to be one hell of a party. Right!

By six o'clock, Ken reached Laurie. She reminded him that she'd been at the school all day, taking exams, and asked what time to meet him at the airport. Then he told her.

"It seems they've been planning this for some time. A surprise. The office, the network, the agency are all involved. Colleagues and associates from the Board of Trade. Detroit's in on it too."

"And Thursday you go to Los Angeles."

"Darling, it's only one week to Thanksgiving."

Silence.

"They've gone to a great deal of trouble," Ken said, "and I am head of the firm. It's only a week."

"Only!"

"Sweetheart, come on. Can't what you were going to tell me wait?"

"Sure," she said. "It can wait!"

She hung up. She told Mamie to forget about dinner and she went to a movie.

She returned before midnight to find six messages from Ken, and Mamie asleep. She turned off her phone.

Next day, she tried to study. She tried to feel outraged. She tried to feel justified. By noontime she only felt chastened. By midafternoon, she felt foolish. After all, he still was Preston of Preston & Company. He was in Chicago on business. He couldn't just leave. They *would* be together in a week. By late afternoon, she was trying to reach him. The hotel did not know where he was. She left a message. When she phoned before dinner, he still wasn't in and they still didn't know. She ate, bathed, had coffee, and phoned again. He still wasn't in.

She phoned Coogan at home and asked, did he know they were throwing a party for Ken in Chicago? Yes, of course. Did he know where? No, he didn't. Had she called the agency or their branch office? No. Then he would do so and call her back. He called her back. The branch office was closed and so was the agency. If she had phoned a few hours earlier. . . . However, so long as she left a message at the hotel, Ken would doubtless get it. Was something the matter? No. She just wanted to reach him. Was everything all right? Yes, everything was fine.

She lay in bed reviewing material for tomorrow's exams and waited for Ken to return her call. Granted he'd called six times last night. Granted she didn't call back and that he may even have called again after the phone was turned off. Even so, he might have called again today or checked the hotel for messages.

She sighed. You have exams tomorrow and it's eleven-thirty. She put out the light and reviewed her scant knowledge of French again.

At one-thirty she phoned the hotel in Chicago. Mr. Preston wasn't in. Now that I go to school, I have my schoolgirl habits. She cursed her schoolgirl habits and went down the three flights to the kitchen, where her fumbling about woke Mamie. Mamie poached eggs, sliced tomatoes, boiled tea, and toasted bread for her. Then they had a cigarette together.

"All those messages yesterday," Mamie said.

Laurie sighed.

At three o'clock she took a pill, dozed for half an hour, and was suddenly wide awake. She phoned Chicago. Mr. Preston still wasn't in.

"Is he not in or did he leave a do-not-disturb?"

"We are ringing the room. There is no answer. Would you care to leave a message?"

She left word he was to call Mrs. Preston whenever he got in, regardless of the hour. By four o'clock, she was thinking of calling the Chicago police. That was hysterical. She knew it. She *was* hysterical. At five o'clock she called once more. No, Mr. Preston had not come in, nor had he picked up any of the messages and yes, they certainly *were* in his box. She insisted that they go to his room and see if he was there and whether something was wrong. Nothing was wrong. He wasn't there. It was close to six when she fell asleep. The alarm was set for eight.

It rang at eight and she called Chicago ten minutes later. The messages were still in Mr. Preston's box. Then she phoned Coogan.

"I still haven't been able to find Ken."

"You stay right there and I'll call you back."

He did. "I spoke to Devlin," he said. "They had this party out in the country and a small group of them went to the home of the agency fellow. Seems Ken didn't get a minute to himself and he was so tired, he slept over. Said he hadn't closed his eyes Tuesday night."

Touché.

He gave her the number. "You can reach him there."

She thanked Coogan, hung up, and hesitated.

Sulking again? You sulked all Tuesday night and most of Wednesday and he didn't sleep because of it. You want to grow up? You want to be a woman, not the kid in the bobby sox?

She called the number. Then a young, firm, sleepy, female voice said to both operators, "Ladies. Yoo hoo! I'm *trying* to tell you Mr. Preston is not available. If you leave a number, he'll return the call in an hour."

Familiar voice. A slow, blind anger was rising. "Operator, I'll speak to the party on the line in Chicago."

"Do you wish to cancel your person-to-person call?"

"It doesn't matter. I'll talk to the person who's on."

More negotiations. "I'm sorry but you'll have to cancel this call and put in a new person-to-person call or cancel this call and put in—"

"Look, you idiot, this is an emergency. Just get off the line!"

The sleepy female voice was amused and awake now. Also alert.

"Is this Miss Hinkson?" Laurie asked.

"Yes. Who's this?"

"Is Mr. Preston there?"

"Yes. Mrs. Preston? I'll wake him."

"Don't. And when he wakes, tell him not to bother returning the call."

She hung up. Her heart was pounding. If tears were running down her face, she didn't know it. Her ears burned as though they had been hit. She stared at the phone, a loathsome, dangerous object. Let's start all over again? Just back from Caleb, Mrs. Preston. Remember her? *Hello, Ken, Ken dearest, you* are *my dearest. But I know you're at the hotel, goose. I called* you. *Now go to the bedroom. Oh, you* are *in the bedroom. Well what are you doing in the bedroom?* What does any man do in a bedroom? What are bedrooms for, modern marriages included? Modern males in modern marriages with a modicum of monogamy. Having a wonderful time. Wish you were dead. As she looked at it, the phone rang and she picked it up slowly. Expecting what?—God, to tell you it hadn't happened, wasn't true. Ken—to say there is more to it than that. There always is. But at Caleb, I understood. *Ken you don't have to measure up or down to what others were or are or want to be. You were right. Ken, I'm only reminding you. On the Island, I understood.* Now it was lost in the fog, its spell over. A memory. Just another island: like Long Island or Manhattan. Not my island: it never was and now it never will be. That's how the other half did it. All they had in common was a dumpy bird, a winged clown. Theirs for summer. Mine for winter. It's winter.

It was Coogan. "Did you reach Ken?"

"He was still sleeping."

"Laurie, before you go jumping to any conclusions—"

So Coogan knew. Who else knew? Anyone who was at the party and said good night to both of them, like Devlin, faithful reporter to the home office. Now Wall Street might know and the Pit she was at the bottom of.

"—Laurie, you are a headstrong young girl and I'm old enough to be your father. You and I in New York can jump to conclusions but we both know Ken better than that."

"I don't know what you're talking about."

"Yes, you do. And I want you to have lunch with me."

"No. I have exams today." Tests. I have had my tests.

"I won't take no for an answer. I'm coming up in the car and get you."

What difference could it make? What difference could anything make?

The door to the conference room of the Board of Governors shut Mac out. His shoulders and the back of his skull leaned against it. He had been fined five hundred dollars. Before that, they had debated, and in the waiting room he caught snatches of the arguments that deliberated his punishment. Everyone knew he was one of the few Floor men really hurt in the Eisenhower sell-off of September 26. In at top prices and out at the bottom: the day of despair had driven him to panic selling. He had lost a million, give or take a few thousand; a third of all he possessed. Twice the percentage ratio of the sell-off. All low-priced stocks, the ones worst hit. He had appeared on the Floor each morning ever since like some dumb brute, watching the trades day after day as the stocks he had sold rose and the averages miraculously recovered. He didn't buy and he had nothing left to sell. Even those who despised Mac sympathized. Floor men who liked him avoided him like a pestilence that could prove contagious. When he moved into a crowd, they parted. He had every opportunity to make a trade if he was up to it. But he would only get as far as holding his coin ready to match. Then in that split second of decision, he stood aside and his vast paw of a hand clenched the unused coin until his white knuckles ached. Last week, without provocation, he had struck Chip Turner so hard there at the post that Chip lay on the Floor unconscious for fully five minutes. When they asked Mac to explain his conduct, he couldn't.

Chip specialized in a book at the post adjacent to the one at which Mac had been in the days when he was still a specialist. It had been good, being a specialist. You had the advantage of knowing something, holding the book, seeing the good-sized bids and offers, and to hell with the long view and hocus-pocus of charts, all beside the one-point, two-point, half-a-point profit you were after on the shortest terms the market had to bid or offer. Each morning for fifteen years Chip had been in the most competitive book in Murderer's Den. He began each day by pretending to smoke a fake cigarette, half burned down with a false ash at the end, and every single morning of the six years that Mac had stood beside him, fifteen hundred mornings, when the tape appeared with its very first announcement—the statement that it was ten A.M. of such and such a month, day and year—Chip would treat the particular month as the name of a stock, the date as its price, and exclaim, "What do you know! November is up one from yesterday, selling at nine!"

Out of habit Mac had returned to his old post and stood beside Chip, waiting for the tape and the bell. Then Chip said, "What do you know! November is up one from yesterday, selling at—"

And the next thing Mac knew he had wheeled and struck Chip, who now lay stretched out at his feet on the floor.

No one made anything of the fact that ten days earlier, Mac had punched an order clerk in the jaw for looking at him in the men's room mirror. That was understood and by-passed. The superstition was shared by many. With Mac's losses, he was entitled to that minimum of understanding: any Floor clerk who didn't know *that* deserved a physical education! But Chip? And without being able to give any reason. It was then that Kehoe recommended suspension, and the raised voices came through so Mac could hear them outside. Kehoe was paying him off. Five years ago as a prank, Mac had snatched his matching coin as it flipped into the cuff of Mac's trouser, never to return it. Paying me off, he thought, Kehoe started paying me off years ago when I was still a specialist and he first became a governor. In a rough buyers' market, I tried to duck a few trades and Kehoe, a husky boy in his own right, tapped my shoulder with some force and said, "Don't turn your back on this market, McBride. You're in it."

In the waiting room Mac had heard Kehoe warning: "McBride's been around long enough to behave like a pro and he's strong enough to kill somebody when he behaves like a fool."

It was true.

When they called him in to announce their verdict, the five-hundred-dollar fine, the stern reprimand and warning meant nothing. Even the scorn in the eyes of others meant nothing. In the downstairs lobby he walked to the entrance of the Floor. There, at the din, the shouting, the bells, and the scurry, he flinched and stopped. *That* was the issue. *There* was the gross injustice, the intolerable.

I died, over a month ago. September the twenty-sixth was my burial day. Why didn't anyone tell me? Now all at once I know it. I'm dead. Sucked out, drained of the will to act. My corpse stood before the governors who sat in judgment and my soul pleaded guilty but not to the crime they're concerned with. My crime is cowardice, the result of folly. Good God, why didn't they throw me out?

Why did they let what was left of me stand like a harmless dog, a castrated eunuch, sulking, condemned by myself? To prove me alive, they should have meted out a man's punishment, the punishment a man should be able to take.

What could he say in his defense? What had they expected him to do but stand there, his head hung low in silence while behind his eyes he felt the hot vacancy that might once have been tears, as the running out coldness in his veins might once have been blood. There *had* to be some way. His furnace lay heavy and shut, chilled with the dead weight that made breath impossible. Inside he whimpered and shivered. It was worse than death, and if there were no way to act, no means for achieving revenge or failing that, to forget it, he would act against himself. You bought. You sold. If you hadn't bought, you would have been a hero; but once you did buy, if you hadn't sold, the losses would have vanished in less than a week. Panic. The one thing some dark inside corner always warned you against had happened. In defense of your manhood, impatient to prove you could act on your own, you did. You bought. Then in fear and panic, you sold. Before that were the four brief days, Tuesday, Wednesday, Thursday, and Friday, the last of it on September 23. Exhilaration, freedom, a kid out of school playing hooky, on vacation, heels in the air, head in the clouds, a song in your belly, and lights in your eyes. You went up and down that Floor like a trackman readying for the main event. Free! Free to destroy yourself. From the moment you heard The News, you began to die. Slowly, like rolling lava it got through to you. What could this do to the market? To the closed, unalterable, unreachable market, viewed by a frantic world of finance, in for a long weekend of woe. Trapped, you faced Monday. You faced going down to the whole, horrible day that cost what was left of your ability to function. In the camaraderie of welcome-back-Mac, as you went from post to post like a kid in a candy store—getting in deeper each day in those days just before you died, who could have predicted this? You died of noncomprehension. Two shores, Friday the twenty-third and Monday the twenty-sixth—as far apart as day and night, north and south, life and death. How did you start from the one and get to the other? Only one thing connected them—Kenneth Fenimore Preston! You sold: that is *they* sold and gave you your cash. Then you bought and *then* you sold. But you've been over all that. After the first shock, the remorse of loss, by sheer will you brought yourself around to accepting it. You lost a third of all you were worth, after fifteen years of trying with the aid of drunkenness and a girl's soft belly here, a dimpled buttock there, and a pair of breasts between in which to bury your face; you drank your way through to sweating it out. All right, you're a man and a man can take it. Never mind how many lifetimes were involved in this tax structure and the market as it now stands to acquire nine hundred thousand dollars net. It's all part of the game, the fortunes of war. You thought you had conquered yourself: instead you had simply resigned to catastrophe. It settled inside you, demanding that room be made for it, and after the amputation, submission grew slowly like a thick, ugly skin at a raw place where some vital part of you no longer existed. In that gap the vermin of self-accusation nibbled, gnawed, multiplied, and festered. You, not Preston, had urged the shortening of positions—their sale, in fact. You, not Preston, had foreseen this sell-off. If it were Preston who had left and you who remained with Pat, together as in the old days, then Preston, not you, would have been out of the market, driven as it rose to new highs to enter underpriced stocks as you had done. Lightning would have struck *his* portfolio. How had it wound up this way? Questions shouted, answers whispered. Taunts and confusion. Worse than death. He had said he wanted out from under: the image frightened him. It gave him the now-familiar feeling that he wasn't a man any more, that worse-than-death feeling. You wanted out of bondage. Out of positions. Out of the market. What sleight of hand, what black magic was involved here? That was the thing he could not bridge from shore to shore. The direct result of this should have been Preston's loss and his gain. An evil miracle. Black Monday had made him its victim. It was beyond him like the things heretics taught, the results of Black Mass, of going to sleep a boy and waking up a man. Good things and bad things alike happened all at once, abruptly: they lacked rhyme or reason. History was arriving at the place opposite to the one you intended to reach. Experience was being victimized by unpredictable, senseless change. A man was a grain of sand carried from one place to another on the wave crest of a wild moon tide.

There was no use attempting to reconstruct events, he thought. I was once determined and stubborn, tenacious. Now I merely hold on. I lack strength in the head. I am too stupid to understand what has happened to me: I cannot trace these sequences. So I am doomed. All I know is I fought like a bastard to get out of this market and I did. I fought to get out of that firm and I did. I had the guts to get back into positions because you watch the tape, and watching the tape is the only answer. They *were* underpriced stocks. The way they rallied since Black Monday proves it. You don't buy stocks, you trade numbers.

There was no use now going back over it seeking answers from charts and technical levels or tops and bottoms that did not connect to an act of God. A man gets sick. He happens to be the President. That's all. But it isn't. There's more; all in a circle. The more I try, the more unclear it gets. It's a hash made up of Uncle Jim on the Floor every day of his life, capable of resisting though he played numbers too and your wife stretched out beneath you for years un-yielding, and now worse—wide with pity. Drink—burning your belly and leaving ice in your spine. Freedom—giving you cash and liquidity that liquefied your brain, leaving you now deprived of judgment. Way back, far back, a moment of decision; the moment you sealed your fate. A blond girl in a black sweater in a dark hole. Public. A telephone booth, and a sky full of stars. A clock striking four-thirty when Uncle Jim used to take his first drink. Now you stand here swaying from side to side like the polar bear does at the zoo. You violated the holy law: you lost your nerve. Is that what the bear felt like? Did it sway all day and all night as it stared out from behind bars because runts wearing glasses with notebooks in hand by some minor maneuver had trapped it, and then inspected it every day of that long journey from the fiery snow of the Arctic to the sweat-stinking, indoor smell of a zoo? Bears and bulls. Trapped and gored. I must have sinned. This punishment is for violating some deeper law. I lied in Confession. I sinned. Good Merciful God, on bended knee I beg forgiveness, and will forever if you will be my Merciful God, and Son of God, dear Holy Ghost and Virgin Mother, Blessed of Women and only Pure Woman to live in eternal grace, whose Son died for men: I am a man! Let me die or live and act like one. I must bust out or burst—put all this together or come apart. I hold to one thing: mine are the sins of the flesh but this injustice goes beyond punishment. I read the signs. I fought for them and being right, lost—as Preston, being wrong, won. God could not mean this. Such a Gethsemane I have not earned. Here, while I am still flesh, I must get my vengeance and then, not ever again, do a violent deed, or commit a carnal sin, I swear it on the fact that I have never witnessed such injustice in all my life.

Crybaby. Calling on God for that which is your own business! Idiot, whipped dog, yellow belly, you witnessed nothing. *They* witnessed on that Floor—all of them—twelve hundred men, your colleagues. You were the bear who walked on the stage on his hind legs balancing a ball on his nose, and fell. Your wife witnessed. Barkeepers, B girls, runners, clerks—above and beyond all, Preston witnessed. You stood up to him, toe to toe. Now here you are on your knees, while he's off on a trip, getting kudos, rewards, projects, and profit. . . .

Mac heard his number called.

He still had a number, even if it no longer meant Preston & Company

as when it became Preston & Company, it had no longer meant Coogan
and McBride; no longer a specialist or a trader. Just Francis Xavier
McBride, the slob who owned a Seat but not a head, spine, or legs
to stand on. Had the Board of Governors decided to suspend or expel
him after all?

For a moment, hearing Pat's voice on the phone added a tinge
of active nightmare to the daydream: nothing at all had happened.
Things were as they had been. These two years and the three before
them hadn't happened. Five years younger, full of plans in the time
when his lucky jacket still fit. No. Coogan was asking how it had gone
with the Board of Governors. Good old Pat. If only Preston hadn't
stepped between them. Now Coogan was saying—why did he have
to mention that name? I still can't live around the name: it robs me
of my ability to think. Preston's *wife?* Yes, he still knew the guy. Wallie.
Saw him often, sure. Why? No, Wallie didn't talk about her. He still
had his pride. Most men did who had something to take pride in.
Still married. Not doing bad. Two kids. His mind was not suited to
complicated ideas now. Ruffie's Restaurant today at one o'clock? What
about it? No. Impossible. Somewhere he knew that what Pat was saying
would once have been simple, would have made him smile with anticipation. Not now, he thought, I'm too far gone. Then abruptly it opened
like a crack in the mountainside cleft by the hand of God. Revenge!
Good old Pat. His pal, his buddy. He was offering him a hand from
behind the unpartable.

He laughed. "Yes, I get it! Sure, Wallie will come. He'll come if I
have to carry him. Ruffie's Restaurant. Today. One o'clock. One-thirty."
He laughed again and nodded at the phone. "I got the score, I got it,
Pat."

He hung up. Three hours. Was that all it was, ten-thirty? A new day.
He reached Wallie. He was eloquent, salacious, even smart. He was
successful. He went back to the Floor, plunged into a crowd, took a
few chances, elbowed and shouldered his way. At eleven o'clock, still
lightheaded, he showed a profit of one hundred and fifty bucks. You
are worth two million, stupid. You are still a millionaire. If you don't
have two balls, at least you have one. Well, get on it, and stay on it!
If your scalp itches, go to the barbershop. He went. Shave and a
haircut, shampoo. I got a hard on for you. He smiled. Hot towels,
cold towels. I just picked up the towel I'd thrown in. Pile 'em on, boys,
make it hot. Oh, there is a God after all. Who ever said there wasn't!
Hadn't they always told you that He worked in strange ways His
wonders to perform? Say what you would, Pat was a pal even though
Pat was not of the faith. He was nothing like Preston—not at all like
that piss-pure Protestant bastard, shit heel, stone-chiseled son of a

Plymouth Rock bitch. Yes, there was a God! Pour on the towels, hot, cold. Pour! Lunch for me and him for breakfast. I have an appetite for life again. Protestant Preston. I owe you something. Policy, piety, poles, and purposes apart. I.O.U. and you owe *me*. As my word is my bond, you will pay up and so will I!

He was looking at his feet. He could stand on them again. Crazy maybe, but if he did this act, he could. The Floor would be his once more. He was still wearing his broker's shoes.

"Boy," he said, "go down to my locker and get me my street shoes." He handed him the key.

"Excuse me, Mr. McBride, but aren't them your street shoes you got on?"

"The Floor and the Street are not the same. These are my *Floor* shoes," Mac said. "You been down here long enough to know that difference. Any sucker can walk the Street."

He felt combative again. Argumentative. Headed for home.

Pat lifted the silver cover from the steaming bouillabaisse. He smiled across its vapors and said, "Now, Laurie, please. It's not fattening. Nothing but fish. And it's the very best in town."

He returned Phil Powers' smiling bow of thanks for the bottle of wine he'd sent over. Serving Laurie, he continued to tell her in a firm, earnest tone that all or most men went through this sort of thing in their forties. Good Lord, if every wife in America broke up a good marriage for *that,* homes and families would become as extinct as the buffalo! When Phil half raised the wine bottle out of the ice bucket, Pat indicated the card that went with it. The card read, "Happy Birthday. I'll come over to pay my respects later." Seventy-five. Old crook. Now that old Phil was twenty million ahead, with one foot in the grave, he looked innocent as a baby. Some baby!

On the way to his table, someone had told him it was Phil's birthday. Ruffie's was patronized by bankers, heavy traders, Street men without Seats, Board followers, and those risen beyond the point where they had to accept the restrictions that went with Exchange membership. He answered questions on volume and prices and introduced Laurie. Many of them had heard of her but none had seen her before. Their appreciation was evident. Now Pat sat facing the door. He wanted to see Mac first.

"The smart woman ignores it, Laurie, believe me. You make an issue of an indiscretion and you can only lose. A man far from home is under pressure and a pretty girl on the make knows it. She's ambitious and takes advantage. Now Ken is headed further from home, three thousand miles away, and that girl is still with him. This is no time to be headstrong."

He saw Mac and the man with him. You could understand a girl like Laurie reacting to *him*. Too late now to wonder what Mac had told him.

Pat looked up with a proper show of surprise as Mac approached and introduced Wallie, "an old friend of mine." Then Wallie was saying, "Long time no see," and Laurie went deathly white.

Pat had risen to shake his hand and Phil, responding as Pat expected him to, called, "Now, you come on over here, Coogan, and sing happy birthday."

Pat said, "Excuse me," took Mac by the elbow and walked the distance, three tables away against the opposite wall. Smiling blandly at Phil, out of the corner of one eye he saw Wallie sit down. Then the waiter brought two more wineglasses. Phil told them of the many wires he had received, rewriting the history of his life and believing every word of it. If he lived much longer he'd be selling fairy stories as autobiography. Pat shifted slightly in his chair. *An old friend of mine.* Friend of Mac, of Laurie, Ken, Devlin—I am everyone's friend.

There was heightened color in Laurie's cheeks now and the pained, clouded, troubled expression in her eyes lent mystery to the glisten that illuminated them. It gave her face an indescribable sadness and vivacity. No denying she was beautiful.

"That so?" Pat said to Phil. His eyes seemed fixed on the waxy, old, sun-lamped face and he seemed duly impressed by Phil's tale of acumen in avoiding an offering of stock rights that looked good, first rate, y'understand but as it turned out—

Pat saw the pulse beating in Laurie's throat. That was a big man. Even she, sitting beside him, had to tilt her face up for their eyes to meet. Her lips were slightly parted. In Wallie's place, I'd read that as an invitation and the pain as explanation: he was, too. He won't take no for an answer and not out of tenderness, either. He gave a fair imitation of it though. To someone in her state it ought to look good. Go to it, girlie. Tell yourself it's fate, destiny, life's strangeness and what's sauce for the gander. Tell yourself you didn't start this, didn't step in the middle here, didn't bring your two-bit plan to bear on *my* whole life's effort. Do that, girlie. Whip it up. Didn't you once say you never ran from a fight? That was all well and good in your schoolroom safety. I never got very far at school myself. You wanted in the middle. So. You *are* in the middle. Let me tell you, honey, you are *really* in the middle.

Phil had finished his story and Pat raised his glass. Yes, indeed. The tougher things get, the more complicated the problems, the simpler the solutions. Just tap what exists. Nature takes care of the rest.

Phil had finished his story and Pat had raised his glass.

"Happy birthday." Old crook!

The three of them drank.

Chapter 8

OREE, *Oree, Oree-ay. So early in the morning.*

It was a week since she had phoned the outskirts of Chicago, and that mocking voice had answered the phone so early in the morning while Ken still slept. *Mr. Preston is not available.*

And so very much had happened. She sat with her brother Tommy in the living room. *The* living room, not hers, while Tommy, his college roommate Mel, and Mel's girl friend Dot kicked around the universe. Brother! Tom explains to Dot what Dot insists she knows, down to the heart of the principle: *matter in uniform motion and matter at rest are indistinguishable.* Much matter, no motion. She knew.

Laurie had gone round and round to stand absolutely still. She would leave Ken, leave home, leave school. She would go back with Wallie. Leave life. Go to hell. Why not? Didn't everybody?

All things are relative, Tom says. He's my blood relative. Another relative by marriage; my husband. Ma too: she's a relative.

Wallie wanted me to, but I didn't, which is more than Ken can say. It was far from dead. But all the same, it was "How do you do, and don't call me. Thanks for the compliment, but don't call. No, *don't.* No 'whys.' Just don't." But Wallie has been calling ever since, and ever since I've still been saying no, which is also more than Ken can say he said. Wallie was all concern: a new role for him. All our roles are new. Interested in my studies and how come no kids and *are* you really happy is all I want to know. Two days ago when she wouldn't speak to Wallie for ten phone calls running, with Cecil on instructions monotonously and unconvincingly repeating, "No, sir, Mrs. Preston is *not* in," a phone call came after dinner from Mary. "What gives?" Mary asked her. "Wallie tried to reach you *here.*" If I don't, I don't for *me.*

Wallie continued to call but Ken had stopped days ago. It had been agreed that he would be home on Thanksgiving Day but that was in another world before all this happened. She had turned down Aunt Betty's invitation, Mary had turned down hers, though Tom, who was coming in to see Mom, had accepted, providing his roommate Mel, who was driving him in, could come along with his girl friend, Dot. Then this morning, she had received Ken's wire. He would be in.

Dot was giving them what for, now, on Copernicus. Nice young people with equations where their youth should have been. But Dot had plenty of dash and kept things going. Dot dot dot dash; the space age answer to the Floradora Sextet. Three students in search of a future. Very wise. Why look at the past? Thanksgiving looked at the past, and Thanksgiving was no national holiday; just a national excuse for overeating. Commemoration only to a high and mighty handful and the scroll in the Tower was not a national charter. Not mine—not Laurie Dugan's. Not until she got so soft in the head, old in the heart, and sprung in the rump, that any special sanction for gorgeous gorging was sufficient reason to be thankful.

It could be a thankful day for children. Sweet kitchen smells, hilarious laughter; a day you could go down on your knees, when only pageantry and ritual could express a fullness of heart. But my pilgrims never landed, old calendar or new.

A bell rang and if that was Wallie, lost Laurie's answer would still be "Get lost."

Tom is growing, she thought. Past nineteen. The way he looked at you, through those bifocal lenses. The thick glass magnified his eyes into weird, oblong shapes, lifelessly detached, yet intense. Ken would be home, and what was there to say? Laurie, I was going to come home but Miss Hinkson arrived. So, O.K., you didn't. Happy Thanksgiving. Have a turkey sandwich. Mary once sent Pa off with two dry pieces of bread in his lunch box. Between them was a piece of paper and on it the words "You stinking bastard," and Mary had filled the thermos with hot water.

After this week of pain, jealousy, and hating, exhaustion followed. Now the wish to strike out and destroy was gone. It was a week like the one after Helen had killed herself and they waited with her poor young body lying above the earth for the rest of the week until her schoolmates could come and see her. By the time she was buried your heart was numb. It was numb now too. A dangerous impartiality had set in. A sense of justice; totally self-destructive.

He betrayed you. The word didn't fit him, only the deed. *But only because you betrayed him first.* So if Ken is a time bomb ticking down to zero, you supplied the fuse and the match. Too late now to realize the results of trying to make him prove for *your* sake not his that he was top man on someone else's terms. Not *someone*—Wallie—who turned you down, except on a dog's terms, as you in turn almost turned down Ken, and treated him no better. Ken repaid you. You're even. Suppose that's so. Where and how does one pick up? Does one say that life being what it is, given a man and a girl alone together for some days and nights in a strange place far from home, with the girl no doubt bent on getting the man, something is bound to happen, and does. Why should it matter this much? It just *does*. At first you wanted to cause him such pain that his cries would be heard around the world. What you felt now only proved that no one can live for long with that much destructiveness.

The young people were still talking. No longer the universe, down to earth now—in fact, *under* the earth. The atomic submarine that could circumnavigate our globe in fifty days on a two-pound lump of uranium, the size of a golf ball. You'll miss this room with its soft greens, yellows, and browns. What a lovely room for the smell of pumpkins, autumn leaves, the excited sounds of . . .

The front door opened and her heart jumped. Tom examined her mildly.

She said, "That's Ken," and as she heard him call out "Laurie?" from the door, she went to the landing.

"We have guests," she told him formally. "Tom and some friends of his."

She walked back into the room. It was the first time in two years that their greeting had not been an embrace and a kiss.

Ken entered the room, shook hands with each one, and turned to face her.

She said, quickly, "I suppose you'll want to wash up."

Cecil was carrying his bags to the bedroom and Ken followed.

He looks haggard and disturbed, she thought. Naturally. He doesn't like hurting people! She went to the kitchen.

When she returned, Ken was mixing a drink, always the gracious host, listening, as Tom ran on, "That's why the average man can't do it. He relies on his sense of touch, taste, smell, and sound, along with sight. But only sight is usable in outer space."

Three Univacs, one universe. God, how furious Ken is!

"How are you?" he asked, conversationally, looking up.

"I'm fine. You?"

He nodded.

"I wasn't sure you'd be home," she said.

His eyes flashed anger and hurt.

"—just as Laurie's generation after you feared hunger and another war."

"How did I get into it?" she said.

"And we fear a third war, of course. It would mean total extinction. But we equally fear finding ourselves ridiculous."

Then your wildest fears are realized, Laurie longed to tell him.

"—perhaps being ridiculous is the price of dedication. That's why we're not dedicated. Your decades were full of dreams. Ours are full of doubts. We heard your various crashes."

Tom's eyes were alive with death. "All we see in history is warnings, not precedents. And we realize that for the older generations the world is overwhelming. But we believe that so long as we act on our own fresh perceptions, it is all quite manageable, providing we check our premises." Cecil appeared to say that dinner was ready, but Tom insisted on finishing. "Our integrity must be arrived at through our own minds. It is impossible to hand us anything."

At seven o'clock, Mel and Dot said good-by. It included fifteen minutes of involved arrangements concerning Saturday morning, how Tom would be picked up, and when they would leave town.

As Laurie was seeing them to the door, Cecil appeared to inform her, "That gentleman is on the phone."

"Tell him to call later." Mel and Dot left. "You might bring more coffee to the living room." She turned to Ken. "Tom and I are going out to see Mother, so I'll have to get dressed now."

Ken smoked a cigarette. He felt Tom's eyes on him. He permitted a discussion of epistemology to begin, then abruptly he excused himself and went upstairs.

Laurie was out of her housecoat. She was in her skirt and as Ken appeared, she turned her back to put on her blouse.

"I didn't expect people," he said.

"I'm accustomed to guests on Thanksgiving. If you'd come home last week, I could have told you. We might even have invited Miss Hinkson."

"I tried to call. Several times."

How another man would have bitten on that one, she thought. Not Ken. Even when he's in the wrong.

"Your father seems a very decent fellow."

She faced him, the blouse fully buttoned, and walked angrily to her dresser.

"Aren't you interested?" he asked.

"Fascinated. How did he and Miss Hinkson get along?"

Again he ignored the sarcasm.

"Your father is attempting to get transferred back to New York. He asked my help. Apparently our association with Selective Insurance Company is fairly well known in Chicago."

"All your associations in Chicago are fairly well known."

He stared at her. Then he shook his head.

"Well?" she demanded.

She opened the drawer to get her brown leather jewel box and saw a silver cigarette case.

"It's a gift," Ken said. "I received it at the party."

She read the inscription. "*To a new and exciting personality, Kenneth Fenimore Preston, Chicago, 1955.*"

"Well, I'm glad it's silver," she said. "You and silver get along so well. I don't suppose you remember the young man who brought his Nuremburg clock to the museum the first time we met and you came in with silver?"

Ken spoke quietly. "Laurie, I *had* to stay there. The party was planned over a month ago. A surprise. Not to stay could have wrecked all the work I did."

"I read in the papers that he finally *did* sell that clock to the museum," she went on, musingly. "He's going to use the money to invest in the market. Aren't you pleased?"

Ken tried again. "Laurie, we are not a boy and a girl having a lover's spat. We are a husband and wife who haven't seen each other for over two weeks."

"Nineteen days," she said. "Your family loves silver too. Though I don't know how they'll react to this gift. They're terribly interested in the silver box." She took it out and placed it on the dresser. "Your cousin Arthur says he's found a new process to prevent the picture from fading but Aunt Sarah says, why bother? She's right."

"Laurie—please!"

"Please, my ass." She stormed across the room. "Oh, I forgot. You don't like such words."

"You said there was something important to talk about," he said. "Isn't it important any more?"

"No! Nothing is important any more except that tight, snug little New England ass that kept you warm in Chicago. And if you don't like the way I talk, get out. Don't let my kid brother fool you. We Dugans weren't raised to conceal what we mean behind three-syllable words."

The phone rang. She had put on the suit jacket. Now she strode back to the jewel case and hunted for a pin.

The phone continued to ring. She flung the door open, walked to the landing and shouted down. "Answer that, God damn it!"

Ken picked up the phone. Cecil was on and Ken heard the other voice saying, "—Mrs. Preston."

That voice.

St. Terese. The honeymoon. Her mother. The night she braved the boat and lied about the checkbook. If you went away to find out, you just found out. Mac was right.

Ken extended the phone to Laurie silently. She looked from it to him and understood. She held it defiantly and then hung up.

Ken stared at her. She stared back.

"I don't have to explain," she said.

"No, you don't."

He started for the door and she shouted after him:

"A man's a man but a woman's a woman. Is that it, you pompous, arrogant, blue-blooded son of a bitch? For you an aristocrat's diversion but I'm only Laurie Dugan, an interloper on Sheep Shit Island, is that right? My legs would spread at the slightest suggestion: all right, what if they did? Just tell me, what if they did? I asked you, is Miss Hinkson going. You said no, five weeks and three days ago. I'm sorry I imposed myself on the weekends. The waiting must have been a strain on both of you. But at least you made up for it the minute I left. Why say you were coming back? Why lie? I called your hotel room every hour on the hour until five in the morning, my time, to tell you I was hasty, it was wrong of me, sure it could wait, and why you were right the first time. I was sorry if I blew my stack—and a man had to do what he wanted to. Well believe me, that's exactly what you did."

He turned at the door, very quiet. "Now I can understand why you *must* believe that."

"You can!"

"I can."

"You were going somewhere?" she said. "I'm about to leave."

"If you're leaving, I'll stay." He crossed over to the window.

She walked to the door.

"I went on tour," he said, facing her, "as president of my firm. That was your idea."

"And you mean to make me pay for it!"

"Believe whatever filth you wish, but please remember. It was *your* idea."

"Hinkson?"

"I won't stoop to answer that. I repeat, this house, this way, this tempo, this folly, this waste and fraud were all *your* idea."

He turned his back.

"Not Hinkson!"

He turned again.

"You once said you played house, Laurie. You still play house. Not knowing who you are, what's entailed, what you want, or how much it costs."

"Oh, I know what I want from now on. I want *my* life to matter."

"So do we all, Laurie."

"Not we. *Me*. My life!"

He nodded. "Yes. I know. *Your* life. Singular. Was that the important thought you wished to communicate? Now that you were lonely, I had been right and you wrong and I should quit the Street? Too late for that. There's a time for doing something and when the time passes, so does *it*. You can't push a man's life around as though it were an old chair. Just seeing everything in terms of your own self-centeredness. But you do and it distorts your view of everything. Me, you, us—your inability to have a child."

"*My* inability! Did it ever occur to you, the great Kenneth Fenimore Preston, that you are the last male Preston and the big parade ends with you because of *you?* For your information—it does!"

She ran from the room.

As he heard her steps down the stairs, he turned and shouted, "It was your idea. Yours. Not mine!"

The first time they'd met was *not* at the museum. It was in a Florida fog, when the old Amish gentleman wanted to go on that journey, Lord, and leave without saying good-by, and even a bitter reality would have been reassuring to end your battle with ghosts. Then came love, and the impossible was possible, burning away not only winter's moss but the shadow of it. Here was reality.

Two phone calls. Two strangers.

You'd returned expecting the kind of argument married people are bound to have one day. Hubby is out of town on business, wifey wants him home. Promise? I promise. I can't.

Wifey is disappointed and angry. Hot words, tears, then, warmest of all, the embrace of reunion.

But McBride had known better.

The argument itself was nothing. You *did* tell her Kathy wasn't going, and you *didn't* tell her when Kathy arrived. How could you? You weren't at the hotel room.

Another conventional argument. Jealous wife, blameless husband—"But darling, I swear now, look at me, can you honestly believe—"

And then reunion.

So if you're as wrong about her as she is about you, nothing has happened.

Nothing very important *has* happened.

She can believe that of you and you can believe it of her. Such words can pass between you. And aiming it like a dagger at your heart, she can taunt you with sterility. Nothing of the greatest importance has happened. You once told her: we can adopt a child. Yes, but that's not what *she* told you. *For your information.*

He picked up the cigarette case. Despite his resentment of the party in Chicago at the time because it kept him from Laurie and led to the argument, before it was over it had touched him deeply. It summarized the warmth, the friendship and acceptance he had found wherever he had gone.

A great one for silver is right. The price of silver thirty-six years ago to the day was a record high of $1.38 per ounce. And the year before that, these United States had decided to make silver available to Great Britain, and so. . . .

Stop it. Stop your statistics. Stop trying to forget the reasons for your pain by hiding behind facts—*to Great Britain so they in turn could supply the need for rupees in India.*

Stop it, damn you. Stop!

Do you believe Mac was right? His taunt was in fact a prediction. Can you *not* believe it? You picked up the phone!

Melting one-quarter of a billion dollars worth of silver out of currency into pure silver.

Nothing is pure. Nothing stays pure. Images are created only in order to fade.

And pure silver results from the resistance to atmospheric oxidation. It is harder than gold, softer than copper, the best conductor of heat.

I say you do not believe Mac! I say all you believe is what you heard because she told you.

At the turn of World War I silver, important, became unimportant, and then became important again, and in World War II, Natalie teased you, and you thought when she said that sometimes one and one make three, she might be carrying your seed, not knowing that you had none. Sterile. Add that to the attrition of daily existence which began when you proposed by saying that she was too young and you were too old, sitting in another man's car with his girl who had destroyed his child and hers, and then to hold her dreams down to size and her desires in check she said yes *we have no bananas, and isn't the symmetry adorable, Major. And haven't you been on a treadmill, Major? And haven't you completed a circle, the symbol for zero, Major? And aren't you squarely in the middle of it?*

Laurie's original sin was ignorance, and yours not indecision, as you so fondly tell yourself, but *inadequacy.* Sterility. You and your public and its funds! Nine million American gamblers in behalf of 38,700,000 others shooting craps on the say-so of soothsayers like you, with you near the head of the parade and the big parade stops with you. The last male Preston. Nothing has happened.

Your efforts. Nothing. No half-hearted effort or earnest minimum. The only all-out effort you have ever made or will ever make again— all for love of Laurie, and it had taken all the inner reserves that only faith and devotion could create. You were prepared to expend life itself to prove yourself worthy and adequate.

Nothing.

Your acceptance by others in five cities. Nothing. The beginning of the bridging of the gap between you and others. Nothing. Your feeling that there was a way to make prosperity aid and deepen the national moral sense instead of corroding it—nothing!—and Kathy's unannounced arrival in Chicago to begin preparation for the New York broadcast that would follow Los Angeles and wind up the tour—less than nothing!

It was all seen now in its true light, epitomized by the two old people who stopped you on the street after the Chicago broadcast. They circled, recognized, whispered, approached, congratulated, and shook your hand. "Take care of yourself," the old woman said. The love of a hungry dog for a bone: if you read random numbers from a telephone book from coast to coast now, they would flock, wag, bark, and listen.

He heard her start the car with her usual mistake of racing the motor.

Yes. Absolutely nothing had happened.

He sat in the darkening bedroom and looked out the window at the trees and the river.

So long as we can act on our own fresh perceptions we believe the world to be manageable.

What a sweet, innocent, and heartbreaking conviction!

"Well, what's the latest shattering news from outer space, may I ask?"

Tom smiled, stirred his coffee, and offered:

"There's reason to believe the earth isn't round."

"See?" Mary turned to Laurie. "That's what I get for asking a foolish question. So it's flat after all. That explains plenty."

Tom doesn't realize how drunk she is, Laurie thought. Watch this. If you can.

"No, not flat. Pear shaped," he corrected seriously. "Of course, we won't know for certain until we place instruments for corroboration in outer space."

We. Watch Mary.

"I can't wait. How about you?" she asked Laurie.

Laurie forced a smile. "I'm all agog. First flat, then round, now pear shaped." Like a tear falling from the eye of God and rolling slowly through space. "Later square. And finally a speck," she finished.

"Less than that," Tom agreed confidently. "Our entire galaxy is much less than that in an expanding universe."

"Good," Mary said. "I hate being crucial."

Because you can't, Laurie thought. I can't; no one can. And Tom tries so hard. Too hard.

What satisfaction did it give him to believe he had a mission? The new priests and altar boys of science, robbing us of the last vestige of mystery. Was certainty worth it? Has certainty done *you* any good? Are you *really* that certain? Ken seemed so outraged. Only the innocent —what a terrible thing you said to him. And if what you believed wasn't true, by behaving as though it were, you will make it true. You should be back with him.

"I can't stay too late, Ma. Ken's alone."

"He's not a bad guy, you know," Tom said. "Just a little weird. I mean, his not coming down to say good night." He said it quizzically.

"You're an expert on weirdness," Laurie told him.

"Pop likes him too."

As I stop being Preston the Dugans get around to meeting my husband. Tom was saying Pop told Ken something and Ken helped.

Had she walked out on Ken? Was it over?

Too late she realized what she should have known sooner, Tom knew and was telling Mary. She couldn't stop him. ". . . so it looks like Pop's getting transferred back to New York."

"That so?" Mary stirred her coffee and peered into it. From the look on her face, she seemed to see the pink-cheeked, gray-haired, slightly overweight image in it. "So the bishop masquerading in civilian clothes is returning to his parish, is he?" She turned to Laurie. "Thank your husband for butting into my business."

"He thought he was helping."

"Every time a man tries to help, another woman gets crucified," Mary said. "So he's tired of sleeping around Chicago."

"Take it easy," Laurie said.

"I wasn't talking about *your* husband, I was talking about *mine*. And he's *my* business."

"Maybe if you behaved as if he really were, everyone else could butt out."

"Everyone else had better butt out. I want no part of your father."

"Why? You find being bored that much better?"

Mary's eyes glittered. Plainly she remembered the reference.

"Much!" Suddenly Mary hurled her coffee cup at the wall.

"All right," Laurie said. "Don't rain all over me or Ken. You got to start flipping, go to your room and flip with your bottle."

"I pay for *my* bottle," Mary snapped.

"What does that mean?"

"Just means what it says. *I* pay for my own. I've never asked you for anything and I'm not asking you now!"

"Do we have to have all this melodrama?" Tom asked. "I only come a few times a year."

"Every time you come you bring the stink of your father."

"That's better than the smell of a whorehouse," Laurie said.

"If you think yours smells better, go back to it. I don't have servants to handle the traffic, or people on the outside to take my calls."

Mary rose and stormed out of the room.

"She needs the crutch of religion," Tom said. "That's what holds Pop together."

Laurie looked at him coldly. "You've said enough for one day. Why don't you shut up?"

"This is too ridiculous," Tom said. "I think I'll leave."

"I think you won't. You and your father, always ready to leave. This time you'll stay."

He smiled. "Threatening me again, Laurie?"

"Don't try to find out. Everyone treats Mary like a charity case. Me with advice. You with your precious company and your father playing policeman, long distance. Why did you have to tell her about Pa? Couldn't you see she was drunk?"

They heard the front door open and shut. When Laurie parted the kitchen curtain, they saw Mary standing at the curb.

"Now what?" Tom asked. "Does she walk around the block and fall down? Or do we go out and get her?"

"She goes to the store and gets drunk and someone brings her home. Paul, if we're lucky."

"Why don't we just go out and bring her in ourselves?"

"Because she's not the evening paper," Laurie said. "Insulting herself is the only act of self-respect she has left. If you want to leave, go on. I'll stay tonight."

"What is she waiting for?"

"Paul, probably. Here he comes."

She dropped the kitchen curtain. If Paul saw her, he would want to talk to her. "Just for a little moment, Miss Laura, about the stock market and your husband's weekly letter now—"

I don't want to know, ask, or answer *"How is the market?"* ever again!

I don't care any more.

May God eternally damn the God damn market!

"She'll know eventually, won't she?" Tom asked. "Why isn't New York big enough for both of them?"

He went to the window and they watched in silence as the cab drove off.

"How long does this take?" he asked.

Laurie said, "There's no schedule. It's like the Long Island Railroad. As long as it has to. Till she doesn't care."

"What did you mean before, 'if she's lucky' she'll come home with Paul? Does she get drunk and go around picking up men? Is she that far gone?"

"She seeks affection, like any stray dog," Laurie said quietly. "If you don't want to stay, you can leave, Tom. It's all right."

She wished Doris were here and Tom out of the way. But it was *Tom* who mattered. After poor Helen it was Tom. We love those who are helpless. Tom is, though he doesn't know it. I robbed Mary of something. I could read and write at four and handled this kitchen better than she did when I was ten. Practically a woman at twelve, and earned more than Pa did when I was sixteen. A daughter who can't ask her mother's help kills her mother's ability to give it. Powerful Katinka. Like hell.

"Don't just stand there, Tommy. Take a walk or read a book . . . this takes time."

He studied the pattern of the linoleum on the floor. "You go through this often?"

"Not as often as I should. Doris does. I rile Ma."

"I had no idea she was this bad."

"Well, she is."

"She's sick."

"No kidding!"

"Shouldn't she be put away?"

Laurie turned on him. "Not by you or anyone else. She runs her own business without help. Who does she hurt but herself?"

"How does your husband feel about this?" Tom asked.

"He doesn't know."

Silence hung between them.

"It's ridiculous," the boy said.

"That's right, Tommy. Lots of things are ridiculous. Why don't you go to your room?"

Headlights flashed against the window as a car sped by and Laurie walked out of the kitchen.

She stood at the window of her old room thinking, my wishing-well window. You expected something. Now, you don't even know what it was. Helen and I, faces pressed against the pane looking out at the ice and snow, the bright moon, and a wide expanse of space. Waiting for Santa Claus. But there ain't no—very late—until almost nine P.M. you waited. Then very early, almost at five, tiptoeing down together. Poor little Tommy, too small to walk. There was Ma, on her way up. "Be very quiet. Your daddy and I are going to bed. We were up all night talking about you to Santa Claus."

Her doll. Glory be! Playing house.

Years later, the Madame Queen stage. Dressed and scrubbed from the skin out. Tommy, then seven, poured a pail of water on you from over the porch door. Out you went, grandly, then zoom went the pail! Down came the water. He laughed and ran and you ran, with his boy scout ax in your hand. He shinnied up a drainpipe, and you followed. He jumped to the ground. So did you. Patch ran after you, tail wagging, barking his head off. Then Ma and Pa, hilarious. They caught up and all of you lay down on the grass, gasping for breath. Laughing.

Christmas. Springtime. Thanksgiving. Football. Pop brought home the team he coached. You fed them. Two hundred cream puffs. Count them! And weren't you ever proud.

Yes. You were.

Tom's view of the past: history is a warning, not a heritage. Whatever it warned you of was here now. Drowned in the wishing well—far too deep for anyone to see the bottom. Ken sterile and unfaithful. You wanting him to quit. How had you reversed roles?

Tom was in his old room listening to the radio. When Helen was small she used to sing herself to sleep. Even then Ma couldn't. Doris and Toby and all the rag doll tatters of childhood on your far-off island, too far out to sea to ever find the shore.

Tom was listening to the news broadcast, suffering the sports roundup. The phone rang. Mary ran out into the night like you did. Pa is coming East for nothing. Like Ken did.

"Laurie, that phone is ringing."

She was about to say something, thought better of it, and picked up the phone.

It was someone from the fire house, asking for Mrs. Dugan. When Laurie told him who she was, he told her what had happened.

The phone's ringing rose shrilly over the muffled tugboat sounds outside. Ken answered and it was Laurie, incoherent and hysterical. Only one thing remained clear after he hung up. She needed him.

It wasn't until he was in the cab on the way out to Riverneck that he fully realized it: Laurie needed him. She had turned to him and in that, all his bitterness vanished like paper in a flame. The cruelty of her statement to him before she left was only her pain in believing he had turned to another woman. Mac's taunt and its confirmation in that voice at the other end of the phone, realities both, were both lies. The truth lay only in what she revealed by whom she turned to in her moment of agony. He was certain: in body and spirit she had been faithful.

Toby Foote cursed and took the phone from Doris. Right in the middle of the roundup of all the holiday football results. He listened, grew grim, and hung up quietly.

"A three-alarm fire," he said. "The row of stores to the west side of Main from the bank building at the corner of Pickerel. Cleary's place."

"My God. Mary Dugan's store!"

"That's right."

Toby's eyes had the brightness fear always gave them. The light-headedness was there too and the painful cramp in his calf muscles. Soon as he swung into it, he'd be all right. You can bet this would be another one of those "After you, Captain" deals. You're a lieutenant. You're in.

He circled Doris with his arm and lifted her off the floor.

"Toby. Don't! They'll be here in two minutes."

"I can boff you in one."

"Let me down."

He let go, and she dropped a foot to the floor. He went to his room and slipped swiftly into his spare uniform; the asbestos shirt, pants, jacket, and boots. They would bring his hat. In the boots he stood almost seven feet tall. He looked down at her from the door. They could hear the siren approaching.

"Are you laying for somebody?"

"No," she whispered.

"I can snap your neck like a twig between two fingers. So don't lie to me. When did you lose your appetite or did you just change your diet? Hot pants is how come you got me. How come I'm a fireman instead of a basketball pro."

The animal wail of the siren screamed round the corner.

"You look scared," he said. "Scared I'll die, or scared I won't?"

The small red car was slowing down. They wouldn't stop. It was time to be outside, to hop in as they slowed.

"Tell me later." He nodded his head in short bobbing motions. "You used to say, 'Come back safe.' "

"Toby, they're outside."

He pointed a warning finger. "Don't play it otherwise." He left the door open, and the siren picked up again, tearing the night.

"Die," she said silently to the screaming siren. "Die. Die. Die. I hope you die!"

The Captain's way of walking was a forward stumble. A half-running, disjointed thing that made his arms swing too freely at his sides, like a fast-moving ape. It made Swannie look breathless, but Toby knew Captain Swanson better. He wasn't moving thoughtlessly, either: that was just his way. Physical aim. A ramrod at the target. He used his own body to break down obstacles. The Captain really believed in himself. He made you think there was more of him than there was of his equipment—more force than there was in locked and bolted doors, smoke, heat, or flames.

It was an "After you, Captain" deal, sure enough. He moved up the stairs following the Captain. He could feel, almost hear, the flames gathering on either side. Still safe, but he knew how things stood with this back stairway up to the two floors over Cleary's bar. A few feet to the right down below was the restaurant kitchen with all its grease and gas. A few feet to the left was the storeroom over Mary's music shop with its woods, plastics, and papers galore and below that, all those live, hot, plugged-in wires. What went on to the left and right of that for the rest of the block didn't matter. Not yet. But these lousy wooden stairs did, rising over the bar where plenty of alcohol that could burn like holy hell was mixing freely with the flames now. Even two steps higher, Swannie stood shorter than he did. In the war, Swannie would have been that firing-line general everyone made movies about and no one ever met.

Lead the way, Captain. There's almost seven feet of me and five and a half of you, but lead on. If I was nuts like you, I could believe in myself like you do and I'll bet *she* would, too. I'll bet the bastard who certified this nonfireproof building is safe and cool.

The wall was buckling. A gradual change in the atmosphere had set in. There was a far-off, sizzly sound to the right and below from the kitchen. Then the flames burst through, up on the first floor landing and Swannie was almost surrounded by them at once. They both turned to the sharp crash of sound below.

"Get it!" the Captain shouted.

Toby ran down to the bottom and pulled at the door. "Locked," he called back and saw the flames stick their long tongues deeper into the stairwell from both sides. Now grease fire to the right, short circuits to the left. He watched the Captain being engulfed. Suddenly Swannie was on fire.

The stairs between the first floor and the ground floor landing weren't burning yet. Weird. An air shaft maybe. Toby took the stairs four at a time, reached into the flames, and dragged the Captain, bumping down.

Singe, scorch, sting, and guts turned inward on themselves—like scorpions. The stairs were suddenly burning. Big laugh back at the firehouse. "Smoke gets in your eyes."

He knelt over the Captain, stretched on the ground floor.

Try the door again. You'll choke on dryness, not smoke. You need extra holes in your nose, a razor blade to slit your throat. Oxygen.

There goes the skin of your hand.

Lay over the Captain, boy. Put him on his side, knees up, face down—cover the crotch, your last earthly treasure like the day you both were born.

Don't breathe. Shut your mouth. Shut your eyes.

A hum. A hush. Too much of you. Don't stretch. Too much.

The fire had begun like all newborn things—red, wild, and hungry. Then it grew swiftly, nourished on melting metal, and changed color as it spread. They found the man responsible for keeping the back stairway exit clear and picked up Toby and the Captain five minutes afterward. To judge by their condition at the time, they were either dead, or dying. Hands, arms, legs, ears, and necks were burnt beyond recognition.

Ken stood beside Laurie and tried to prevent her from making it worse. She screamed, "Why aren't your men in there?" and the Assistant Commissioner answered, "My men *are*. They *have* been. One died and another's dying because Mrs. Dugan left those lights on, with all those live wires, and lit cigarettes, and poured alcohol all over the place. *That's* why my men are in there."

The Assistant Commissioner turned on his heel and moved away. Ken could not help believing they would jeopardize very little in an effort to find Laurie's mother. In their eyes, she probably was what the cop killer is to policemen.

The heat had rolled across to the gutter where the passers-by stood. Their faces were bathed in bloody hues and their eyes gleamed as they watched.

The fire had found its voice now. A crackling, ugly sound made by the munching, tearing, and swallowing of wood, plastic, and metal. It had spread beyond Mary's store to blaze through the real estate office, the gas and electric company display room, and into the basement below the Riverneck Bank to rise through it to the eight-story office building that stood above at the southwest corner of Pickerel and Main. It was moving less rapidly northward up Main: The flames had not yet reached the stationery store, jewelery shop, photography shop, ice cream parlor, or movie theater at the far north end of the block. The cold wind that had brought the temperature down to thirty-eight degrees since eleven-thirty was determining its course. The fire fattened and chattered like hordes of hungry insects eating smaller ones still wet with the juice of life and the nourishment was turning the orange, red, and yellow to phosphorescent greens and swollen-bellied purple. Tongues appeared out of its many heads over an ever-widening area. What else was slaking its hunger?

Ken kept his hand on Laurie's shoulder. Any moment now the police deputy would tell them they were standing too close. Whatever it was, she had not left him out of it this time. But he should have known sooner. Much sooner.

"Ken." Her voice was level and flat. "Make them find her, Ken."

"I will."

He signaled to Tom and Tom approached. He had stood farther back, nearer the roped-off crowd.

"I want you to phone your father," Ken said.

Tom nodded, the flames reflected in his glasses. His eyes were separate forms of life, each struggling in a hell of its own, unbelieving, lost.

"I'll get you through that mob and back again. There should be a public phone in the drugstore on that corner. You see it? Here's change. If it's not enough, make the call collect. Tell your father what's happened. If he doesn't hear from me in half an hour, he's to fly in without waiting any longer."

Ken had taken a small notebook and envelope from his pocket. He wrote two numbers on the envelope. "The top number is my branch manager's home in Chicago. Your father should call him and say that I want Dan on the next nonstop to New York. If there are no more planes tonight, let them charter one. I'll pay for it. This second number is mine. Your father should phone it when he arrives at La Guardia regardless of the hour. Someone will be there to tell him where to go. Is all that clear?"

"Yes."

"Good. Tell your father we have hopes nothing has happened to your mother. But in that case she still faces the charge of starting a fire, and there's been one death already."

Tom nodded again.

Ken walked to the policeman and tapped his shoulder. "This young man's mother may be trapped in the music shop. His father must be notified in Chicago. I am Kenneth Preston. That's Mrs. Preston, the boy's sister."

The officer hesitated, then he reached into a leather bag hanging at his side and pulled out an armband.

"Wear that," he told Tom. "When you come back, look for me."

The officer raised his voice.

"All right—open it up—make room. Let this man through. Make room!"

The crowd parted reluctantly and then closed ranks again.

Ken removed his coat and put it around Laurie's shoulders.

"You'll get sick," she said, starting to wriggle out of it.

"Wear it," he ordered.

He buttoned it around her.

"We'll do what must be done," he said.

"I couldn't tell you about Ma."

"That doesn't matter now."

"I didn't know about Ma when we married. Later I was ashamed."

He held her and kept looking up and down the burning buildings for some sign of men coming out of the flames. The fire had reached the third floor on the corner now.

"I'm ashamed of me now. Not her," she said.

"In two years I never asked or found out anything about your family or friends."

"There's Doris."

He looked.

"All right. Wait here."

He ran up the line in front of the roped-off, watching people.

"Stand back," a fireman shouted. "That roof's coming down!"

The spectators pushed one another, crowding wildly to pull away. Some tripped against the curb of the opposite sidewalk.

"God damn!" the Assistant Commissioner shouted. "Move all those bastards back."

Ken continued running, reached Doris, took her by the hand, ran back to Laurie, and drew them both away as the hardwood of the supporting beams of the restaurant building's roofing collapsed. Brick and plaster slid and then crashed to earth in an almost straight line with a terrible shudder. None of it catapulted past the sidewalk.

"Where is Toby?" Laurie asked.

Doris was wild-eyed. "He's burned all over. Black, skinless, and hairless, in a mobile at the corner. All smeared with something. All over. All over. All over," she whimpered.

Laurie took her arm. "Doris—"

Ken hurried to the corner.

"We need a doctor."

"Who's we?"

"I'm Ken Preston. Mrs. Foote is back there with my wife, hysterical."

"Wait—damn it . . ."

A young doctor in white uniform appeared.

"Where are these hysterical women?"

"Just one," Ken told him.

He walked swiftly. The doctor ran to keep pace. When they reached Laurie and Doris, Doris was repeating, "I wanted him dead. I prayed for it."

"Take it easy," Ken said.

Then the doctor told him, "You're wasting your breath. Just hold this coat and keep the sleeve out of my way." He swabbed Doris's arm and inserted the needle. "Now take her back to the corner to one of the mobiles. She'll be out in a matter of minutes."

"Can you manage it?" Ken asked Laurie.

She nodded.

"I'll wait here for Tom and keep an eye on those buildings."

As Laurie led Doris to the corner, she remembered the beauty parlor: the placid, indifferent children and Doris deaf under the dryer. In all these years you never said to Mary what you said tonight. You never felt the way you felt tonight. No excuse. Why must everyone fix blame?

Firemen were coming out where the door to the restaurant or the music shop had been, coughing and choking. Laurie saw Ken approach the Acting Captain, and she left Doris in the mobile to run back. She reached Ken as the Acting Captain walked off.

"What did they say?" she asked.

"Very encouraging. No one's in the restaurant. There was a man in the bar, and no one in the music shop."

Actually the Captain had told him, "We picked up a dead man in the john near the bar."

Ken had seen two of them carrying him out wrapped in asbestos. When he asked, "What about the music shop?" the Captain said, "Minor explosions. Can't really say until the fire's over. But no one's alive in there any more. That's certain."

"They're doing everything," he assured Laurie.

"Doris isn't asleep. She's in a fog," Laurie chattered. "She's talking crazy. I hope no one pays any attention to her. Ken! What if my mother's in there?"

She seemed about to lunge forward. Ken seized her arm.

"I'm all right," she said, mechanically.

He said, "Here comes your brother. You're sure you're all right?"

"Yes. Go get him through."

Ken left her and she stared at the flames. Fire, air, water, and against the red sky a bird. The puffin, old bottlenose, our winged clown: the thing we share. Summer there, winter here, both islands. *A small, poor, wild thing surrounded by the vast turbulence.*

Mary is a child.

Children in their impatience and unformed pride seek to forget their birth.

If Mary couldn't grow up, she was not the only one.

The wind rose higher from the north, pushing the flames. A strange hose had appeared, standing at right angles to the earth, with an added elbow pointing at the fourth story of the corner bank building. The only way the fire could go now was up. Cold air blew. Water spouted. The fire roared, still rising. The puffin bird circled against the bloody sky, matching soot, smoke, and flames.

And we must always risk the danger of return to that starting shore from which all our journeys began, else we are lost.

Mary was. Totally lost. Locked in there. Dying or dead. Mary had started it. Smoking, drinking, whoring; wanting to die, to forget— Mary had started it. No, Tom, by telling Mary of Pop's return. Pop started it. Asking Ken to help get his transfer so he could try again. Ken started it. A Preston, a presser of buttons, a mover of men, a man who mattered, by trying to help. No, no, I started it. Pushing Ken back to where he didn't belong or wish to be. Demanding he make good at it. *I* started it. So did Wallie, by planting the seed and making me kill the fruit of my unborn child. Helen by killing herself, Ken's father—even the dead started it. Ken's great-grandfather, and *his* grandfather, cousins of Abraham Lincoln, daughters of Paul Revere:

everyone started it. The Prestons' love of the French and the Irish: a mixture made of the stuff of hell instead of heaven and surely never meant for earth.

On this Thanksgiving night, new calendar, who had started it? Where did the crime of suicide and murder begin? In the fairy books Mary read to me, or those her mother failed to read to her? Who set fire to Cleary's bar? For every crime that ever happens everyone is guilty whether trying to help or be helped, running to or from the scene, recognizing guilt or failing to. Each feeds the flames, drops a twig, stirs the wild wind, rubs the flint. No one and nothing is innocent. United we fall. And the guiltiest are the greatest victims.

"Your father knows," Ken was saying. "Now, Tom will stay with you and I'm going to see where your mother might be. I'm sure she's alive and not in there."

He sounded so convincing.

"You wouldn't even recognize her," Laurie said.

"I remember her face very well," Ken said.

Why don't I rush through? In only a moment I could see for myself, for everyone.

"You behave yourself," he said, and kissed her forehead. It was cold and damp.

Doris lay in one of the mobiles, Toby in another, his transfusion completed. They had covered him with antibiotics and sedated him with morphine; now he was in an oxygen tent. The doctors were hopeful.

Before leaving, Ken went back to tell Laurie that Toby was expected to live.

"You see?" he said. "Everything's going to be all right."

Firemen reappeared from inside the building at the corner, their faces black, their eyes bloodshot and red. One retched and another hopped on his right foot like a swimmer after swallowing water or a boxer rocked by an unexpected punch. Now, all the hoses were turned against the burning buildings.

"They've given up," Laurie cried. She rushed forward and Ken raced after her. Two policemen closed in simultaneously, but Ken reached her first and dragged her back.

She was screaming, "They didn't even look. Town drunk. Town whore. She's my mother!" She kicked at Ken. "What do you know about it?"

Ken held her, breathing unevenly. "Go get the doctor," he told Tom, and Tom ran to the corner.

"You all think she did it," Laurie screamed. "If *she* did, *we* did. Let me *go!*"

A cop was approaching.

"I don't need help, thank you," Ken told him.

"It's not my Thanksgiving," Laurie shouted.

The same doctor in the white uniform reached her, gave the same instructions, and performed the same procedure.

"Is her mother the one they couldn't find?" he asked.

"Yes. And she's not unconscious, doctor," Ken said. He turned to Tom and said, "Stay with Laurie. I'll find you later. Just don't leave her side."

"I'm taking her to the mobile," the doctor said.

Ken nodded.

As they moved off, Ken said, "If they find your mother in the next ten minutes, phone your father. Tell him the truth, whatever it is. Understand?"

Tom said yes but no sound came from his lips. His lost eyes seemed suddenly to have found something and what they found would not release them: they were dying in its grip.

Ken asked, "Which way is the Riverneck Hotel, and what are the other bars in town?"

Tom blinked away mist. "The Riverneck's that way—nine—ten blocks. I don't know about bars. Ma wasn't this way when I—"

"All right," Ken said. "The hotel will know about bars. And one last thing: If your mother's in there, she's dead. I'm telling you so you'll know what you're up against. You're Laurie's only blood relative here tonight."

Tom nodded. Ken moved off.

Chapter 9

A BLOCK from the Riverneck he had found a bar, went in, and asked the bartender, "Has Mary Dugan been here?"

One customer snickered, "Her boy friends treat her better than that."

The bartender said, "No. And you better stay away from her tonight, Jack. She burned down a block corner Pickerel and Main. There have been deaths."

At the Riverneck he named the bar he had been to, asked the doorman whether there were any others in town Mary Dugan might have gone to, and had he seen her tonight?

"You a newspaper man?"

Ken reached into his pocket, took out a bill, handed it to him.

"Did you?"

"No. I just came on two hours ago. They tell me she's dead."

Ken went through the bar and searched the lobby. He looked carefully in all the alcoves of the now darkened restaurant. He asked the hat-check girl to search in the ladies' room. Then he approached the desk clerk.

"Was Mary Dugan here tonight?"

The clerk removed whatever expression had been on his face.

"Is she a regular guest, sir?"

"She's my mother-in-law. She may be dead in that fire on Main Street, and she may have started it. Is she here? Has she been here?"

A flicker came and went in the clerk's eyes.

"Maybe. With one of our guests, a few hours ago. In the cocktail lounge."

"What's the guest's name?"

"Have a heart, man. I'm in no—"

Ken dropped bills on the counter.

"Room 715. Harry Bickward."

Ken headed for the elevators.

He looked up at the transom of room 715. Dark. He looked down at
the sill where there was a slight crevice above the floor. Dark too. He
heard himself sigh. Silence. He knocked on the door. It was open. He
went in and put on lights. Napkins with lipstick smear. Glasses with
melted ice. A sweating bucket. Crumpled silk stockings on the couch. A
bottle, almost empty—not quite. Scotch. The bed was open, pillows
and bed sheet used. He touched them. Cold. The bathtub was wet.
There was powder on the sink bowl and long black hairs inside it.
The sink was dry and the towels damp. He went back to the living
room. Under the tray he found a photograph. Pornography. Two men,
one woman. He searched the entire suite again. Nothing. He picked up
the phone.

"Room service?"

"Room service. Good evening. Can I help you?"

"I want the waiter who brought dinner to room 715."

"715. What was it you had, sir?"

He looked at the tray. Melted ice and plates. Two forks. Two
spoons. Two knives.

"Service for two. Sandwiches, coffee, and drinks."

"What time was that, sir?"

He felt the dishes, toast, and coffeepot. It was midnight now. Two
hours since the fire began. He should have asked Tom what time
his mother left home. Laurie walked out a little after seven—an hour
or more from Manhattan to Calterston made it eight-twenty; say half
an hour for bitterness and pain inflicted on each other. About nine.
Then drinks in the lounge.

"About nine-thirty," he said, and waited.

"Yes, sir, Mr. Bickward." Another voice now. "About ready for me
to pick it up?"

"Not yet. Did you serve the drinks?"

"No, sir. That's a bar order. Bellboy."

Ken flashed the operator.

"Bar service, please."

"Sorry, Mr. Bickward. We're not permitted to serve drinks after
midnight."

"Get me the bell captain."

Nine-thirty. The fire started at ten. It could have taken her fifteen minutes from the store to the hotel. It took me five. Three blocks. Not ten.

Say she was very drunk. She goes to the store. She opens a bottle.
Lights a cigarette. *Let's have another.* You embrace, stagger, knock
an ash tray over, and leave a burning cigarette behind. Or you go to
the store, and you don't drink, you don't smoke. You just leave all the

lights on: the drugstore clerk said so. So did the candy store owner
and the corner cop. She did it all the time. *Everyone* said that.

He looked at the pornographic picture again. Two men, one woman.
"Bell captain speaking."

Ken repeated the request and the time, and waited. The fire would
be out by now, the wet ruins hissing. Perhaps a more careful search
was already on to find the arsonist who caused the loss of a fireman's
life. If they brought up a charred lump, this was the wrong end of
all this. I should be back *there*.

When Laurie woke, if bones and ashes were found, and Tom lost
in the finding, with her father in the dark early winter sky, trapped
at a speed too slow for tragedy begun so long ago; I belong *there!*
If the right bellboy wasn't found at once—

"Yes, sir, Mr. Bickward. You said not to bother with 715 or 927."

"That's right. I called to say so again."

He hung up.

927. He ran from the room to the fire emergency stairway, and took
the steps four at a time.

You're too high. This is ten.

He ran down. Nine. He opened the heavy green door, turned left,
and ran. 922—24—26—28—

Wait. Even only. You want odd. To the right then.

He ran to the right. 919—21—23—25—

He stopped. Transom lit. Space between the floor and sill lit. He
listened. A male voice sang:

> "Mid pleasures and palaces, though we may roam—
> Be it ever so humble, there's no place like home."

No other sound. Odd. Very.

He lunged against the door. One man in a chair. Whisky bottle.
Hairy legs. Folds of fat hanging from his naked hips.

"Home, home—sweet, sweet home . . ."

On the bed another man and a woman. The man's back was sickly
white. Very odd.

"Say—"

Ken hit the man who sat in the chair, and his head met the wall
with a resounding crack. The other man half turned.

Laughter.

Ken held him with one hand and hit him with the other.

Careful. You'll kill him. That won't help. She may have killed before
she came here. Two naked men on a hotel room floor, both unconscious. Blood.

He covered the woman with a sheet. She was pale. Chalk white, dead white. Red-gashed lips, smeared. Eyes vacant as plaster. Was she human? She was young. Younger than you. God help me, that's Laurie's mouth! Laurie's face. A charred body would be better. Steady.

"You're one too many. Who invited you?"

"I'm Laurie's husband."

"Oh, sonny. Hello, sonny. You next?"

He slapped her face hard. It snapped his murderous half-dream state.

"Get dressed," he said.

He heard his voice. No dream. That's me. Calmly me. Always calmly.

Her mouth was bleeding where he hit her.

"Were you at the store tonight?"

The bed sheet had fallen to her middle. Breasts like Laurie's, smaller, but similar; shape, contour, color. He pulled the sheet up and held it tight against her shoulder with a cold hand.

"Listen, you demented creature. You may be arrested for arson and charged with manslaughter. Doris's husband may die. His captain is dead already. Another man too. People say they saw your store lights on tonight. Everyone says you leave cigarettes burning and liquor bottles opened. *Did you go to the store?*"

"Glass can't burn," she said. "Fireproof files."

Her face was a tight, small viciousness. The line of her mouth hardened. Her eyes became suddenly wily and old: an animal out-smarting an enemy.

"Fireproof. Nothing burns. Glass won't melt."

He shook her.

"Stop babbling and listen! Your lit cigarettes could have started a fire."

"I wasn't there. Went to the bar. The bar. The bar!"

"Which bar? The one that burned next door to your store?"

"Hotel bar." Her voice suddenly rose. "Chicken-shit millionaire. You're not so surprised," she shrieked. "Two men, one woman—that's no news to *you!* At least I go to a hotel!"

His hands were before him, trembling. Seeing his fingers, he was able to keep them away from her throat.

She's drunk and insane. That night at the lake when the young birds were born has nothing to do with this. Nor the checkbook on the dresser. Nor Wallie on the phone. Nor McBride and two men, one woman. She is drunk and insane.

One man stirred. Illegal entry. Assault and battery. This similar, smaller, older face, body, and voice were a poisonous lie: she was better off dead. Who wasn't?

These men were her evidence of innocence.

Innocence! Your world is mad at last. Still, one must do what is at hand. He searched for her clothes and found everything but her stockings and underwear.

That other room. The couch. Crumpled stockings. Room seven something. It's a statistic: bring it back. 715. Perhaps the underwear too.

"Get dressed."

She sat motionless. You will have to touch her. Laurie's insane, obscene, and lying mother, a mirror—and you will have to touch this mirror! You are wasting time. Just dress her.

He did. Then he retched. A fireman had retched smoke and near death; nightmare things. You retch reality—if any of this is happening.

He supported her down the emergency fire stairway to the seventh floor, re-entered 715, and found the stockings. The underwear was covered by pillows on the couch. He would have to touch her again.

He found the garter belt and tightened the stockings. The underwear he stuck in his pocket. Then he slapped her face with a cold wet towel and wiped the smeared lipstick from her mouth. Her lips were blue.

"Your son and daughter think you're dead. So does your husband. He's on his way in from Chicago. Everyone believes you started the fire. Two men are dead already. Toby may die. Do you understand anything I'm saying?"

The animal look died in her face, leaving behind lines and the web of crow's-feet at her eyes, all mercilessly exposed.

"Yes. I understand. I'm dead. I started a fire and died in it."

"Did you or didn't you go to the store?"

"I came here. I kept a date. First I canceled it to see my children, and they gave me the usual, called me the usual—"

She looked at him.

"I kept a double date," she said.

Life returned to her eyes, dirty, angry, and without strength.

"You're very sick."

"All dead people are sick."

She began to shiver. He rubbed her face and neck with a dry towel. He helped her to the bathroom and held her head over the sink.

"Yes, I'm very sick, but I didn't start a fire. I came here drunk, and got very drunk. I kept a date on a dare. For a month he's been daring me . . ."

She looked up at him with eyes so much like Laurie's he had to turn his face away.

"You need a doctor," Ken said. "But right now, you must see your children."

"I can't!"

She held onto the sink and bent her head forward and trembled. "You know I can't."

"All your children need know is that you're alive, weren't at the store, and didn't start the fire."

He took the underwear from his pocket and put it on the table in the living room.

"Can you manage that?" he asked, without turning his head.

"I'm dizzy," she answered.

He moved toward her, his head still averted.

"Lean on me."

They walked down another flight. Then they took the elevator and went to the bar.

"Give Mrs. Dugan a straight scotch."

"Sure thing."

The bartender watched Ken suspiciously.

"Would you remember what time Mrs. Dugan came in with Mr. Bickward earlier this evening?"

The bartender looked at Mary.

"Tell him," she whispered.

"Nine-fifteen or nine-twenty. Paul dropped her off."

Paul. The cab driver Laurie mentioned. The one she had put on the firm's list for their market letter. Thank God for Paul!

"What time did Mrs. Dugan and Mr. Bickward leave?"

"Heck, I wouldn't know. It was four or five drinks apiece."

He looked at the wall clock as though it might help him. It did.

"I'll say eleven o'clock."

The fire was in full blaze by then. He was already there by eleven.

"All right," Ken said. "Paul will confirm that, and you may have to. There was a big fire on Main Street."

"I'll say."

"It began at ten. Some people claim Mrs. Dugan was there and started it."

"At ten o'clock?"

Ken nodded.

"Mister, she was right here from nine-fifteen to eleven. I know that damn well, because I listened, and heard them say—"

He stopped.

"He's my son-in-law," Mary said. "Ken Preston."

"Alf Mendorf."

Alf extended his hand. Ken accepted it with his left one. He was supporting Mary with his right.

"Mrs. Dugan was here, all right."

"You started to say—"

"Tell him, Alf. I don't remember anything. But whatever it was, tell him."

"Well, Mrs. Dugan said to Harry Bickward she'd take him up on the—double date idea, and to go upstairs now. Before they left, Mr. Bickward told me if Mr. Martin came looking for him, round eleven, to go straight up to his room—that the big party was on."

"Thank you. I know you won't go into any of this unless it's absolutely necessary."

"No, sir. Mrs. Dugan's a nice lady, but you know how it is with some folks. They got to have it, then they can't hold it and they will keep trying."

The bartender saw Ken reach for his pocket and shook his head quickly.

"Don't do that," he said. "Someone's liable to say I got a special interest."

Mary drank the scotch and winced. He felt her shudder. She stood at the bar while he phoned the taxi service and was told that Paul was home and asleep, but they gave him Paul's number.

He woke Paul, explaining who he was, what he wanted, and why.

"Sure, Mr. Preston." Paul cleared his throat of sleep. "I'll dress and be right over."

Mary said, "Thanks, Alf," and Alf told her earnestly, "Take it real easy."

Ken stood outside with Mary. Once he told her to breathe deeply and she tried. Then Paul showed up and on the way to Main Street in his cab, he confirmed picking Mary up at the house at nine o'clock and taking her straight to the Riverneck Hotel. Ken said that he appreciated Paul's coming out at this hour and being so helpful and Paul told him, "You folks have been real decent to me. I'm just about fixed to go in for myself again, Mary, a new project of private houses out past the bay. No monopoly and they need servicing—"

He stopped himself short. This wasn't the time or the place.

The crowd had all but disappeared. Tom saw them first. He ran and put his arms around Mary and began to cry in that noisy, convulsive way boys who are almost men and unused to tears will.

"Holy Christ, Mom. Mom! For Christ's sake, Mom."

Laurie was laughing or crying, Ken couldn't tell which.

Ken stood in a semicircle made up of the police captain, the acting fire chief, assistant commissioner, and two plainclothesmen from the arson squad. Paul stood behind Ken, belligerently ready. A man stood off some distance away, hovering.

Ken told them the pertinent facts. Mrs. Dugan arrived home at eight-thirty. The proof. She left again at nine. The proof. She went straight to the Riverneck bar and was there from nine-fifteen to eleven. The proof. No proof was needed beyond that. But if it were and only if it were, and they would have to prove that to him and the law firm of Riley and Caldwell, *then* proof would be given as to where Mrs. Dugan was from eleven o'clock until this very moment.

Apparently, Ken had stated his name enough times for them to have done some checking and when Captain Fisbee said, "I don't see how the issue of where Mrs. Dugan was from eleven o'clock on is pertinent, do you?" his tone made it clear that nothing impertinent was contemplated.

"Who is that?" Ken asked.

The police captain looked. "Reporter for the *Long Island Herald*."

Ken turned. "Would you come over here, please?"

"Come on, Dave," the plainclothesman said. "This here's Mr. Preston."

The reporter approached. "Evening, Mr. Preston. They get you in from Detroit or Chicago?"

"My wife and I were spending Thanksgiving with my mother-in-law."

"Uh-huh. Any comments?"

"I think I'll let Captain Fisbee make the comments. I may have something to say off the record."

Captain Fisbee said all the evidence pointed to a fire that started in the men's room at Cleary's bar. Really a fluke. What must have happened was the drunk was sitting on the can in the john. He leaned forward and fell asleep. Damnedest thing. His cigarette set fire to the toilet paper. The exhaust fan blew some of the burning tissue, which set fire to the mop, and the mop set fire to the beaverboard. Then the fire crept up the wall closest to the music shop: it had to be that way. Once the live wires started burning, there you were. The drunk was dead and as yet unidentified. The tragedy of Captain Swanson was in the line of duty. So was the heroism of Lieutenant Foote. It looked as if Foote was going to make it, though you could be sure, before these antibiotics and what not, he'd have been dead. Lucky. If he'd been up in front of the Captain instead of the other way around, their places would be permanently reversed. Hard to estimate the dollar loss in property. There'd be a follow-up story tomorrow.

Dave's eyes had remained on Ken and he had made no notes. "Now, off the record, Mr. Preston?"

"Off the record, some reckless, slanderous statements were made here tonight, under pressure of crisis and tragedy," Ken said. "We are prepared to forgive and forget them because of the circumstances. But the faintest innuendo in print, by word or inference, from this moment on, will be neither forgiven nor forgotten."

Dave nodded slightly.

"Were I in your place, *I* would take me most earnestly," Ken said.

"I'm not in the market for trouble, Mr. Preston. Just a good by-line story. I almost had it." Dave smiled coldly and shrugged. "And speaking of the market, any hot tips?"

Ken returned the smile, equally cold and hostile. He didn't answer.

The police captain told the one about the fellow with the hot tip, which under the circumstances led to several other jokes.

"I sure could use a hot tip, Mr. Preston," the Assistant Commissioner said courteously.

"Who couldn't?" Captain Fisbee was wistful.

"So could I."

"We're recommending Herrington Mills," Ken said.

"Can I have that again, Mr. Preston?" It was one of the plainclothesmen, who had whipped out a book and pencil.

"Herrington Mills."

Dave had out an envelope and was scribbling the name.

"I'll remember that," Captain Fisbee said.

"So will I," the Assistant Commissioner said. They all laughed.

"I think I had better collect my family now." Ken asked Paul if he would go to the airport to pick up Dan Dugan. Paul said that he would and then asked, "Was that Herrington Mills, Mr. Preston?" Ken said it was.

Doris was awake, standing white-faced outside the mobile. Toby had not been moved.

"I'm glad your husband's doing well," Ken said.

"I hear Mary's alive. How is Laurie?"

"She's fine. Yes, Mary is alive and she wasn't anywhere near Main Street or the bar or her store at any time tonight. She had absolutely nothing to do with the fire."

"Thank God for that." Doris looked up at him quickly. "You're a nice man."

If I were, he thought, I'd have met Laurie's close friends and family long before this. "I don't suppose any of us have made mistakes we can't correct," he said.

"I hope not," Doris said in a small voice. "Look, tell Laurie and Mary they're taking Toby to the hospital now and I'm going with him. I'll call tomorrow."

"Laurie's mother is coming to our house," Ken said.

"I'll tell Toby we finally met."

Ken waited at a distance until Tom beckoned to him. Mary and Laurie were still crying.

"Your father should be getting in at five-thirty," Ken said. "If we leave now, we'll be home by three."

Lights were on all over the Preston house and Mary was in bed in the second-floor guest room.

Before falling asleep, Mary said, "Laurie, get me to a doctor who doesn't know me, who'll just help without feeling sorry for me. No matter what I say tomorrow, please do it."

"I've got a really good doctor, hey." She fumbled for a handkerchief. Ken gave her his and in his eyes she saw love enough for all her pain.

"I said crazy things tonight," Mary said. "Ugly and untrue."

Ken left them and joined Tom in the living room. The phone rang. It was Laurie's father calling from the airport. Ken told him Paul was there and gave Dan the good news and the address.

"This is a very big room," Tom said.

Ken looked up at the ceiling. It was. He said, "Let's go down to the kitchen."

They drank coffee. Gray streaks were forming in the sky. Over-the-road trucks rumbled on Second Avenue: tug whistles sounded hoarse, low, and distant.

"You seem to understand modern physics," Tom said.

"In a hazy way."

"It should be remarkable when an intelligent man doesn't. Instead, it is when he does."

Somewhere a cat upset a garbage can cover. From the blocks of stone came the cry of a wakened child.

"For instance," Tom said, "why should false ideas like immutable time and infinite space, separate and fixed, be easier to grasp than the constancy of light?"

A personal world in pieces.

"Truth violates common sense," Tom was saying. "The old boy really nailed it then. Really. What could be plainer?"

Twice reassembled. Twice destroyed. And the night still not over.

"The light from a star that died in Plato's day travels and that takes time. How else is it to reach our field of naked or instrumental vision?"

"Tom," Ken said.

"Or you take the indistinguishability of matter in uniform motion or at rest on the one hand and accelerated velocity or gravity on the other—"

"Tom!"

"Yes?"

"I've done that sort of thing all my life. It doesn't work."

"What's that?" Tom's eyes shifted.

"It doesn't work, Tom. Whether capital goods or the universe, it doesn't work."

Outside, the sounds of preparation for a waking city were gathering.

"Well, what's the point?" Tom asked. "I mean, looking and looking again and again. Is there a point?"

"Yes," Ken said. "You look till you know why and where you fit."

"That's sound scientific practice," Tom said. Then he flushed and faced Ken and smiled.

"First encouraging thing I've heard about science in years," Ken said.

Laurie entered the kitchen. "Hungry?"

"Starving!" Tom said.

A cool silver moon was dying in the sky when Dan Dugan rang the doorbell. Paul waved and drove off. Dan shook Ken's hand, started to say something, couldn't, and asked, "How's Mary?"

"Asleep. I'll show you to her room."

Dan Dugan hesitated. "I'm afraid I'm not needed here now."

"Hi, Pop." Laurie stood at the kitchen door, her father at the out-side door, and Ken between them. Ken stepped aside.

"You look well, Laurie," Dan said.

She grinned at him. "Considering the hour. Let's see if Mom's awake."

He followed her up the stairs. Tom came out of the kitchen.

"You think any of this really happened?" he asked.

"I'm not sure," Ken said.

"I hope so," Tom said.

I hope not, Ken thought. I know things I don't want to know. I have felt things I don't want to feel. We are all of us what we were and will be and they are mutually exclusive: that is why any man, every man, is unreliable and terrifying as no other animal can be. We are neither beasts nor gods, but hybrid monsters in unpredictable and dangerous transition. Half flesh and half dream. A hypothesis that disappears as you propound it and the part that is flesh in its yearning seeks the dream by looking up. But the dream is not there, nor even straight ahead: it's *down*. To see a dream one looks into its depths through a misty surface that is nearest the heart's eye, and past that to its core. Far down. To do so you must stand at the brink, bending over, and take the full chance of falling through all the space between you and it.

Half an hour later Ken and Laurie were alone. Mary was asleep again. Pa had spoken to her, then he and Tom had gone to their rooms. Strange how they all behaved. As though Mary had killed or been killed and was the center of a staggering tragedy when neither was true. And yet both were. But how could they know that? What did they know? Ken called the hospital to learn that Toby was resting. Doris was staying on. Her parents were in from New Jersey to take care of the children and the patient was doing well, the special nurse assigned by the Fire Department said. Ken hung up and told all this to Laurie.

Then she leaned her head against his shoulder.

Ken has taken over at last, she thought. Once I would have had to do all this and die a little more, blaming and hating Mary a little more for making me be mother instead of daughter, while doing so in some mysterious way diminished my femininity. Now I have Ken and he has taken over at last.

"How did you know Ma was alive?"

"I just did."

"When you found her, what was she doing?"

"Nothing."

"Ken, let's never use that word again! I saw her too."

"All you saw was a woman very drunk and unhappy."

"What did she say that was ugly and untrue?"

"N— she was out of contact."

Laurie said, gently, "Ken, I wish your parents were alive tonight so I could love them and help you know them and them, you. I love you more tonight than the first time in St. Terese. Tonight you could be a streetcar conductor, a shoeshine boy, or the corner grocer and you'd still be my whole life. Do you know that?"

St. Terese was a bad thing for her to bring up. As you said, one looks *down* to see a dream: into dark waters and even darker nights past voices and the bodies they came from. Two men, one woman.

"I believe you about Kathy," Laurie said.

"When you set up the doctor's appointment for your mother, set one up for me, too."

"Don't, Ken, please."

"I love you," he said with anger. "So let me finish. If I am sterile, we'll adopt a child and start to build our own family."

At Caleb, doing so with another's issue was unthinkable. Now, not doing so was. No truth stood still, withstood every test, or appeared the same in every light.

Still leaning against him, Laurie wept quietly. He understands. Having seen what he saw tonight, he understands our need. A family.

Ours. Not an either-or family of Dugans who never got started or Prestons coming to an end. A his-mine family.

He led her to the bed. "Help me undress," she murmured.

Thank God, oh, thank God, she sang in sacred silence. This Thanksgiving is mine, and my thanks to Ken for taking over and making over as he did once before and for understanding, and to Tommy who just this once behaved like a brother and called Mary mother so that she knew at last she wasn't alone, and Mary for not having done it and not dying, and Doris for being where and what she had to be tonight. "Does it always take tragedy to bring people together?"

Ken kissed her forehead.

"Hold me," she said.

He held her. The blood ran from his limbs to leave his hands icy distant things. Face. Form. Voice. *Mary.* Larger but the same. Younger but the same. You cannot erase it. You cannot erase a mirror, nor fuse love with loathing. But you don't believe in heredity! That's Aunt Sarah's arrogance. All we inherit is life: the rest we do to it as it does to us. So says the mind. And the mirror? Mirrors are liars, revealing only one side. Sight is not the whole truth. But dismissing it one way only gave rise to it another. Lying there, stretched out. Sitting up. Bed sheet falling. Slowly and forever. Falling. Falling. The red-gashed mouth. My son. Sonny. Two men, one woman, shifting images that summarized something not in her. Sonny. *A mirror shows one oneself.*

"I know I don't have to say this, but from the first moment I became your wife and for every single moment thereafter, I have never—"

"I know," he said, "and you know that is exactly how it has been with me."

"Yes." Her tension fell away. She was getting drowsy but intensely alive. We are face to face, almost. Together. Each of us. Two yet one, and that alien body occupying no space that still could stand between us had been made of something she could almost name now. Not only childlessness, planlessness, empty hours, days cluttered like scrapbooks with scrawls and meaningless accumulations, and for him the added weight of all that past and the things it made him seek and expect of himself. It was all that and something more. Being strangers. Until people know the worst about each other, they are strangers, and strangers cannot be one. The frightening barrier was almost gone. This too: he said you grew up too soon and you agreed, whereas pretending to and being told you had and behaving as though you had, you couldn't grow up at all. Playing house, like Mary. A good deal more like Mary than you ever cared to recognize. Going to school in a sweater and bobby sox, hanging on to childhood, yearning in the way you did for a child of your own, a doll. Union began by facing the worst. Then it included the ordinary, the flat, the dull, the tiresome, each with its important place in a thing called living.

No more weekday schoolgirl and weekend bride.

"The man who died," she said sleepily. "Have they found out who he is?"

"Not yet. I'll ask. If we can help, we will."

He held her.

Thanks. Yes, thanks. I have as much to be thankful for as any wishing-well child ever did and it's safe to fall asleep now saying thanks. Because we are no longer strangers.

If I cannot forget it, I cannot touch her again. Pity in the place of passion and where desire was, disbelief. Faith in her fidelity vanished in that mirror and the truth of Mac's taunt and that voice on the phone gave sound to the two-faced image.

"I know I don't have to say this but from the first moment I became your wife and for every single moment thereafter, I have never—"

I can't believe it now. Everything blurred, faded, and died but the sight I saw in that mirror. She could not answer why she married you. Her confessional before the vows included this. Then later there was the further confession that in your arms she had to imagine, pretend, and daydream. Imagine what? Pretend to be where? Daydream of *whom?* Though she had said, "I can tell you now only because it's over," *she married you not loving you.* That was the confession, before, during, and after. Of such honesty are deadly weapons made. She loved the men who took and tore, terrorized and left welt lines on her cheek, missing buttons on a blouse and the single handkerchief in the hamper smeared with her own lipstick. If this continues you will go mad.

"Anyone can cheat on anyone. Biology makes us that way." Who said that? She did; in the far-back courtship time.

You are exhausted but you can't sleep, and will not hide behind your barricade of statistics. Light is that constant in the universe which moral law is to society and love to the individual. Therefore? Without each there is bedlam and all ceases to exist.

He seemed to lose track of time sitting there. Then suddenly something on or above the dresser glistened in the dark with a life of its own. It made the hair rise on his neck. The mirror? More mystery? He walked to it and his back blocked the window. The glistening stopped. He stepped aside and it glistened again in the first feeble dawn. It was his silver box.

THREE

Chapter 1

A DRY, thick snow fell steadily but the wet wind blew it like fine powder out to sea. The hill on which Mansion House stood broke the bitter north wind somewhat and the small group clustered on the beach behind Arthur's cottage. To the west, the evergreens were a dark tracery against the sky. The gathered company stood with heads bowed, the men hatless. It included the shepherds, a few townspeople, and what was left of Prestons after the past year's misfortunes. It was the day after Thanksgiving. The cremation had taken place at First Grace Lawn Memorial in Auburn three days ago but there had been too much weather to cross from the mainland till this morning. It tore the brown and red leaves that still clung to the low branches and dropped them in the thin layer of snow where they were held upright like full-bellied sails upon a frozen ocean. Only the sheltered, lacy network of berry bushes was weighed down with snow. They bowed toward Arthur's cottage, pointing earthward like oriental fans falling from unseen, sleeping hands. The wind was punctured only by the distant complaining of the sheep and the old voice of the minister burdened with cold and age as he quietly read: "And now, Lord, what is my hope? Surely my hope is even in Thee. Deliver me from all mine offenses and make me not a rebuke unto the foolish."

Cousin Arthur would controvert all finalities even to the end, Ken thought. He *was* a rebuke unto the foolish, including the foolish in himself. ". . . *that I shall be cremated and my remains scattered on the waters off Caleb where I was born, and mind you, Cousin Ken, to be careful that you hold a wet finger to the wind before you discard my ashes. There is nothing more painful than a cinder in the eye.*"

"Hear my prayer, O Lord, and with Thine ears consider my calling. Hold not Thy peace and my tears."

No tears except for Laurie's. Laurie, who *was* my wife. Laurie, the stranger. This is no time for self-pity. Is there ever for one who despises and abominates it?

"Soon as Thou scatterest them they are even as asleep or fade away suddenly like the grass."

I do not pity myself; I place myself. I must. I have. Mother is dead. So is Father. Likewise Theodore, Sarah, and even poor Mr. Sands. Now Arthur. How strange Eleanor looks with her lashless eyes, like shining buttons in her unlived face and that perpetual look of a forming smile. Without tears she too is crying.

"The years of our age are threescore and ten and though men be so strong that they come to fourscore—"

The ice lay thin on the harbor water close by. It was bunched up in rough surfaced ridges. Beyond it rolled the black waves, gushing, churning, and driving. He would have to use the boat to comply with Arthur's last request. Even at the landing there was ice and the wind blew shoreward.

". . . and what shall we say of this man? In Deuteronomy it is written: I have set before you life and death, blessing and cursing, therefore choose life, that both thou and thy seed may live. Arthur Jonathan Preston left no seed. But he left strong works. Life was his choice in so many ways."

I never found out from Cousin Arthur how to prevent the image in the silver box from fading. Now it is too late. Strangers. And she among them. She will not look at me.

". . . special student of New College, Oxford, in 1888. Harvard University, LL.D., in 1924. Director of the Thorpe Museum, 1906 to 1936—"

Cousin Arthur *did* choose life. Even there in the oldest book we have, freedom and life are defined in terms of choice, and how rarely is this choice what we think it to be. Out of opposite needs, striving not to compromise, we always end with an unexpected third. Now what will happen to Caleb? Arthur was the only one who really belonged here. This cluster, this quorum, Aunt Betty and her brood, George the intruder, measuring, watching; Sarah's survivors, Arthur's associates, townspeople, farmhands; all of them focus on me with the unspoken question: what next? I do not know. *I* am the stranger. I stand alone. So much alone that out of her sleep Laurie once had asked: Why do you have no friend?

I rejected my society and was rejected by the rest of it; all epitomized in George, who was my best man.

The minister handed Ken the small jar. The others stood on shore as Ken eased the boat out by himself. With heads bowed, they watched as he rowed. The wind had shifted. How many times the statement "dust to dust" has failed to make clear how little is left of a man

when the immeasurable part of him is over. Arthur would laugh as
Mother did: *Bargaining, I am forever bargaining, and shall be to the
end.* The minister, facing toward the water, was earnestly speaking, but
the wind's voice was louder and Ken could not hear.

He wet his finger and held it above his head. There, Arthur,
I have sampled the winter wind. Now, to accept your wise counsel,
I must turn my back on them. He opened the jar. And so to your
Renaissance, your history and inquiry, your laughter and love, there
is the cold winter sea. Good-by.

The wind blew up, carrying the ashes so that they trailed parallel
to the waves, falling ever more distantly till at last they all sank
out of view.

Probate was a mere formality. The custodians were prepared to
receive bequests in behalf of the museums, magazines, scholarships,
and historical societies they represented. Ken and Laurie were present. Arthur had provided that those involved might take a vote on
whether they desired the first two pages of his will read aloud. The
lawyer, unaccustomed to such proposals, voiced it with embarrassment:
with embarrassment the vote was taken. Then, upon its decision, the
pages were read.

"When you hear this, that which lies ahead of me will lie behind.
I hope I bore the event in proper spirit, and am fortified by the knowledge that I have been preparing for it for quite some time. Death
never comes at once. All the same there is that special moment—the
one calling for self-respect, stamina, and curiosity. Should I lack them,
remember: I tried. Now what shall I say? I am an authority on
nothing. No one is. We live neither long enough nor strong enough.
As an amateur then, a word for each. For those who expected my
money, it is neither mine to give nor yours to take. Therefore in the
main it belongs in impersonal hands for possible use. That is the
least offensive disposition thereof. For you who expected nothing,
something. To lost Laurie, the impatient one, an amount small but
sufficient and defined elsewhere, and should you wonder why, it is because I believe that having your own is the best way to cure your pre-
occupation with it. Also a package, worthless by itself, on which, too,
more later. For my colleagues, a warning out of the conceit that death
permits: little as I knew, it is more than you might think. Follow me
with caution. Now, lastly, for Cousin Ken a simple word of counsel:
all-sided does not mean spread thin and everywhere at once. In the
end there must be choice and I believe that if one could ever succeed
in exploring fully all there is to know about a blade of grass, he

might well find that he has discovered and described the universe. All that lies ahead. Behind there is still the question of Caleb. That is also one of choice. Yours, not mine."

The lawyer felt its unfinished nature. He cleared his throat and proceeded to the more practical and specific details, drawn in his own language, and soon both his voice and manner took on a less self-conscious air.

Hail beat against the windows and continued an incessant rhythm on the roof. Mr. Perkins had already told them that leaving the Island today was quite impossible. They would share the farmhouse with the shepherds until morning. Family and guests had assembled in the one sitting room where the fire blazed. The townspeople were in the shepherds' quarters. Ken had already advised the lawyer that he was taking Mansion House. Eleanor sat alone with her Bible. Tiffany stood by the door with Morse and Gert. Aunt Betty's brood huddled together closest to the fireplace, all but George, who looked out a window. Laurie, with Arthur's small package unopened at her feet, was reading the cryptic letter that went with it.

Tears she had not shed made her body ache. If there had been the wax of Arthur, something to kneel beside with a scarf over her head, say the Lord's Prayer for, and then cross herself, she could somehow know that Arthur was at an end: her grief would have been liberated. Now it seemed just another one of Arthur's pranks, at the bottom of which lay an undefined wisdom. He only claimed to be dead. He made you consider it, sample it. But it had gone as far as she could bear. It was time for Arthur to appear with his eyes twinkling, gray hair tousled on his forehead, fingering his red bow tie, only he wouldn't. He was dead, and the picture of Ken in the boat with the jar in his hand, turning his back at the last moment, would have to serve memory to the end of her days. That was Arthur's point. Only his life was real. She felt Ken watching her from across the room and folded the letter. It was the first time she had seen him since their separation six months ago. Before that, ever since Thanksgiving night in '55, exactly a year ago, he had never touched her. At first not understanding, she fumbled toward him, offering herself. Then she waited. Later she threw herself upon him. After that, incapable of understanding, she brooded. At last she decided that what he had been and done on that Thanksgiving night was simply Ken honorably meeting his duty. His body was pledged to someone else: it could not be shared with her. Kathy after all, she had decided. In spite of what he said and she had told herself that night last November, it *was* Kathy. Then followed shame, offense, and anger, until that morning in April when she announced, "I'm leaving." Ken, his face pale, had nodded wordlessly, and she had left: another death in which the body could not be found, in which why it happened could only be guessed at, the question unaskable and the answer never spoken. He cannot even look at me. His face is turned as it was when the last of Arthur disappeared forever, hooded in that way I now know so well. He had demanded something he couldn't name and expected love to both find and provide it. The unfairness and maddening frustration made me do and say things he couldn't forgive. I blame him for my failure and hate myself for having hurt him in a way beyond repair. That was the reason beyond Kathy, the mutilation no effort could undo. Yet each of us gained from the other in unexpected ways. I will be a teacher and have at last learned the excitement I never understood in history. He has succeeded beyond the expectations of anyone including himself.

She saw Ken approaching and forced herself to look up into his face. They shook hands formally. He was delighted to hear that she would be graduating from Teachers College at Columbia next June. History, really. And it was nice to know that her family was fine. She was looking very well. Then the silence and the ache of this other unburied dead, and then nothing.

Darkness followed dusk. Eleanor came from behind, tapped her shoulder gently, and said, "It is time to sleep, my dear. Let me show you to your room." At the bedroom door she gave Laurie her Bible.

"*For the lips of a strange woman drop as a honeycomb and her mouth is smoother than oil, but her end is bitter as wormwood, sharp as a two-edged sword.*"

In Ken she felt no lust, no love, no pleasure or joy of life. That bitter end had already come. Whatever there had been with Kathy Hinkson was over. He was left as was she with the fullest measure of the meaning of that now familiar word, defining the only thing they had ever truly shared.

Nothing.

Why had he done it? Not the infidelity—that no longer mattered: but the other. Why had he driven her back into the arms of Wallie, where she found only shame, vengeance, and at last the ridiculous. It had lasted a month. Since the end of last term she had lived like a nun. She remembered, of all things, parochial school days and Sister Louise, devotion, piety, and perfection until one morning on her blemishless skin a blackhead appeared and suddenly Sister Louise became human. Later, hairs appeared above her upper lip and the other kids called her Groucho Marx. Work and sleep. Sleep and work. The knowledge that she had continued to, had been able to, in spite of it all sustained her. But may God help the poor children who will look to me to teach them!

Lying in the frozen dark, she remembered Betty's cottage and her room. Same island. Etiquette for Young Ladies. Hints on Marriage. "To *fleep* perchance to dream." There's history. Ancient. A world away.

She did not understand Arthur's letter. *"Decide for yourself if you wish to pursue this."* This? Whatever was in that package. She had no desire to open the package and she did not want his money. She was not a Preston. Not any more. Or ever.

Story of her life. Begin vividly, clearly, and end without ending. Were anyone to ask and were she to try to answer, as indeed Doris had asked and so had Mother, she couldn't answer. "Well, what happened between you? I mean, what went wrong?" Yes, what? And when? Before the tour? After it? And before Ken—Wallie? Before him others. And before them? Mary and Pa, together and separate. Helen, and now this, here, tonight. A funeral that was not a funeral, an end without form or substance. Somewhere a voice was muttering in the old, drafty house and elsewhere another was crying. The sounds closed over and were lost in one another.

Ken sat. He had been sitting. He still sat. The sun had fallen, a cold moon had soared, night advanced, and still he sat. His collar was damp with mist or tears: a trance of despair and the wish for death. You want to mourn Arthur. Instead you mourn yourself. You cannot do otherwise. After promising the limitless, his energies had stopped and betrayed him. He had the familiar feeling that all this had happened before. For a cause that no longer existed he had thrown himself into something alien to himself and now both cause and battle lay in the past. His very existence lay in the past. There was no room for him in the present. The present had room for liars and scientists, historians and falsifiers, the prematurely old who lived obscenely on and the arrogant young demanding what they had not earned. Failures, phonies, fanatics, and incident makers in the daily war of life. There was a welcome somewhere for each and every creed, color, cruelty, crippled cretin, or carnivore. Only his crime was special. He corresponded to no concrete catalogue, had fealty to no fraternity. The present made room only for those who knew what they *would* tolerate, accept, or demand. For those who only knew what they did *not* want, there was no room. How different seemingly similar materials are in their response to identical pressures. One sinks where another rises. Still others move slowly when their opposite numbers race, and where one is overcome, another emerges stronger. Always and either way, these major changes come imperceptibly, unimportantly, and all the more so in the case of disaster. Triumph takes hard work and constant effort. There is less chance of it arriving unheralded. You waited for something too long. It probably appeared and you did not recognize it. If so, it vanished and you still don't know it and all that remains is your utter disgust with yourself and your inability to change who and what you are.

She looked at you as something faintly remembered. Yes, I know. It was I who would not touch *her*. I could not: could not shake the double image or drape black across the mirror. It was I who could not rid myself of what finally became an obsession. That she married me to forget him. That in marrying me, she was for a time transported by the sheer biochemistry of relief at achieving a legitimate union. That what was more longlastingly true in her needs reasserted itself and only because this was wrong by the moral code she had learned, did she attempt to deny it. That finally she could do so no longer and her mother knew. It left him with no charge of guilt against her. *He* was the guilty party. In the end it no longer mattered whether she had or had not slept with Wallie. That was a mere physical detail, as the nightmare evening with her mother was a mere incident.

What survived the confusion, passion, and pain of the moment was the fact of his inadequacy and sterility. What made it survive and rendered it irreconcilable to the things one did in the face of such a condition was the value she had placed upon it and the use to which she had put it. A knife straight to his heart. An act of disgust, contempt, anger, hate, and outrage prompted by her deepest evaluation of him; her deepest disappointment in him for not making her forget her more basic needs, the things that made her whole, the warm, if you like, greasy and sweaty things that had once made her whole, which I did not. You scorned her partial needs, with which she tried to reconcile herself to what you were. You lay by her side unyielding, only an inch from release, cold under a passionate control, firm in that strange suicidal satisfaction of knowing you could reject that less than totality of self she offered. Each day it continued, you knew you were guaranteeing the permanent loss of her and waited for it with perverse anticipation. When she finally told you, you nodded in acknowledgment, your purpose achieved, knowing that the last remnant of hope and reason for living had died.

It was many months after Laurie left that Kathy, as junior account executive on Preston Public Funds, came with him to Boston for the first full-dress meeting of the merged staffs of Cousin Theodore's firm and his own, an event staged for the public with dignity and a certain amount of pomp. Afterward came the reception, then a word with the press, drinks, and good talk. Later they walked along the Charles River, each of them remembering college days. Finally, at the hotel, she brought her television and radio summaries to him and they sat in the living room of his suite. There after several drinks, she said, "Well, now I know what Disraeli felt like when he cabled in code, 'The celery is ripe to be cut,' only this is much more than the Suez Canal, isn't it? Two ends of a dynasty knotted together. What does it mean to you?"

"To me, truly, very little," he had admitted.

Then there was silence, her incredulity, and for a moment she seemed to understand. It created a closeness in which she fumbled for words. "A girl should not give herself to mean and petty things," she said.

Then more silence.

She was pale when she turned to face him. "For God's sake, what does a woman have to do?"

"The most you could be to me is reassurance and ritual," he told her. "Something like tearing up old love letters, and that's less than fair."

First she trembled, then she cried. Finally she laughed. The following week, he was advised by Mr. Atwater that at her own request Miss Hinkson was being transferred from the Preston Funds account.

In a blade of grass, discover the universe? What could Arthur have meant by that? He was not one given to rhetoric or mysticism. Even his round statements could be grasped and verified. It was Arthur who had taught him to recognize specific birds and concrete species of flowers, as well as how one could discern in the first spring budding the ultimate result in autumn, down to the last definable color and exact shape. It was Arthur too who had taught him to look upon his life with the eyes of a pilgrim: nor was there ever in this the slightest suggestion of living apart from, or not participating in, but seeing even as you lived it.

After the reading of the will, the lawyer left them and these strangers, custodial beneficiaries, had spoken of Arthur with such personal affection and closeness to his actual living presence. So many things about Arthur he had never known!

Far out at sea, miles from their shore, he could see the lighthouse in the blackness, an illuminated sentry warning whatever reckless mariner might be afloat on such a night to keep well away from Caleb. Wise counsel. Yet you have taken Mansion House.

That is because you mean to die. When Theodore died, Arthur

took Mansion House. But he was born here and lived here. He started and ended here, and in between he had used the whole of himself.

You have learned so much from Arthur. Yet you have learned nothing because you failed to learn the main thing and what that is, you still don't know. He had imparted more to strangers. They were more capable of receiving it. The man who had been trained by Arthur and was now director of the museum in Florida had recalled how in his callow youth he had invited Arthur to his shack, a horrible, uncomfortable place for a man in his seventies, as Arthur then was. Still, Arthur had left the comforts of Caleb to accept his invitation along with the improper plumbing, poor weatherproofing, insufficient light, and abundant mosquitoes, as though it were a privilege to be bitten, roasted, and dehydrated. Then the older man, now Director of Thorpe, and the elderly lady, once Arthur's secretary on some mission to the Near East, both recalled Arthur's strange, wonderful, sometimes vexing and unpredictable characteristics. Once because he had been "a real ladies' man and all the girls loved him and she was jealous," she had dubbed him Arthur Don Juan Preston. The following Christmas Arthur had sent out printed cards signed exactly that way! They reminisced about dining in foreign restaurants and how Arthur believed he knew the exact difference between one native dish and another, and how offended he was if you did not eat the strange and usually horrible concoctions. The silk-woolen underwear he wore, down to his elbows and under his knees. The time he had refused to walk the length of the railroad station and calmly stepped onto one of the hand-driven baggage carts to drive himself up to his train compartment.

The foreman of the shepherds had joined them, nodding as he listened, finding nothing unexpected in all this. "He was a great one for coupling things," he said. "Things and creatures and folks." He told them the story of the bachelor Kingsley, who lived with his father, and how women played no part in their lives except to stalk the kitchen. "Young Kingsley was in his late fifties. He and his pa had a barn dance every Saturday night till the old woman died. Then they cut it down to once a month. Went on raising oxen and when the sun set lived in the basement next to a cider jug. Well, the word got to Mr. Arthur and when I visited town—not Trubeck," he was careful to add—"my town. He snuffed and sniffed around till he found this here theater group, what they called road shows, and this lady actress, Mrs. Gorham, in her forties though she didn't look a day over thirty-five. She was to the post office and Mr. Arthur walked Dave Kingsley in, knowing she was there. It was the day the sexton got his tie caught in the town clock while winding it.

Set the clock back two and a half hours all day. Well, Mr. Arthur introduced them and what with the clock and the tie, there was enough to talk about so that before the month was out, they were married."

They all laughed and nodded. There was so much love in their eyes. The present director of the Thorpe Museum had said that perhaps Arthur's most important contribution lay in his attitude toward the Renaissance.

"Very few think differently now," he said, "but back in 1893—"

He referred of course to Cousin Arthur's refusal to accept the convention that Petrarch was the father of the Renaissance, Da Vinci its son, and as the current director of Thorpe put it, "Erasmus its Holy Ghost. It was his north star and compass that guided him to appropriate selection of paintings and facts, individuals and trends, papal letters and correspondence that mattered."

Ken was familiar, they were all familiar, and if some, like the foreman of the shepherds, were not, they understood with their hearts. They nodded comprehension: Arthur had considered it more in keeping with the hidden flow of changing events that even as the child is father to the man, so was Da Vinci the father of the Renaissance. That made Petrarch exactly what Petrarch himself had said he was, "a man trapped between eras."

"A most unfortunate place to find oneself," the Reverend Winthrop said, and he looked straight at Ken.

Arthur must have spoken about him to the minister. Trapped between eras. Very likely. And if so, quite beyond redemption. Arthur had said it not to you but of you and hit the nail squarely. Trapped between eras, you were incapable of joining Arthur at the incredibly amazing banquet table strewn with the dazzling jewels, feasting all of the senses with the foods and wines and helter-skelter of life in its earlier formation. You were equally unable to admire the costume jewelry, prefabricated feasts, cut-and-dried menus manufactured for multitudes and marveled at en masse. I tried. I made the effort. A clumsy effort, no doubt, but I made it. And it came to nothing.

The closed-end trust that Cousin Theodore founded. The open-end trust on which I foundered. I have faith in neither. I mourn you most sincerely, Cousin Arthur.

He heard the knob turn and the door creak. He could see nothing. He thought he smelled the faint passing of her perfume, heard the slightest rustle near the bed and then soft breathing. A dream. He rose and walked to the bed. She was there. In the sightless face of death, where there were no mirrors, in a spasm of necessity, he took her. Neither spoke: not a word was spoken. Then they both wept.

When he reached for her again, she was gone as she had come, unless it was a dream after all. He dared not put on the light to seek evidence and confirmation. Her perfume lingered faintly on the pillow or in memory.

In the morning, from his window he saw the spring-fed stream pushing under the ice and tossing white spray. The storm had ended and tall bare trees chattered where the wind rubbed their dry branches. The sky was a frosty blue and the ground was hard though the white sun shone. He saw Laurie, her cheeks red from the wind, as she looked up, saw him, and turned her head away.

That first time it was you who were out and about and she who woke later and came to the window. You called and she waved. You had left coffee at her side. Neither of you turned your heads away then. This must have been a dream. There was no trace of her perfume in the room or in memory, no mark of her head upon the pillow. There was only the feeling that it lay in the past like Arthur and other dreams of childhood on this island. The day you and he pretended to go on a vast journey, a daring escapade, as with lunch baskets you both walked through the wet, fearsome woods and ended triumphantly at this very shepherds' house: conquerors of a strange and alien place. The sun-bronzed, body-strong shepherds had smiled their affectionate welcome.

The last male Preston, in fact. Host by default.

At breakfast everyone was cheerful except Laurie. Somehow during the night even George had made peace with the fact that Mansion House would not be his. He was asking Ken what he thought of the current Near Eastern crisis and the staggering fact that the Federal government admitted to a pay roll of a billion dollars a month, mind you.

The dream sense continued until the point had come for them to leave. Then he told Mr. Perkins he would stay. At the dock the others took their first cognizance of the state of affairs between him and Laurie by going on ahead to the edge of the dock. They had that moment alone.

Laurie understood the question in his eyes. "Call it whatever you will," she said. "For me it was good-by." She extended her hand. "There's more to what separates us than there is to what drives us together."

Then she ran the length of the dock and Perkins helped her down into the boat. Ken stood watching as they moved off into the black waters between him and the mainland.

The wind shook the windows, swept the land bare, and whipped
dead debris out to sea. Ken sat before the fire. For days, weeks,
almost three months now, he had risen, eaten, sat, walked, eaten
again, and slept here on Caleb Island. The envelope with its various
enclosures from Mr. Sloates lay on the table. His formal declaration to
the board had been accepted by both Cousin Theodore's personnel and
Ken's from New York in silence. Only the bylaws were drawn to his
attention. His tender of stock and his resignation would be considered
at the next semiannual board meeting in July. His letter had come too
late for the February session. Mechanically he shoved the mail into the
wastepaper basket. Letters of condolence, inquiries, thoughtful and
thoughtless correspondence from many places. Mr. Sloates had discreetly marked the personal ones calling for Ken's personal acknowledgment with red ink: Coogan, Dan Dugan, Chanteuf, Doris and
Toby. The letter from Dr. Kirkland had a memo from Sloates stapled
to it. At first it was quite meaningless. Kirkland and fifteen thousand
dollars still due? The District Attorney and the American Electronics
Research Institute. Sloates's memo brought back the sallow-faced,
rickety embezzler who in his gratitude had rushed to the door of the
conference room, to kiss his hand, Ken was convinced at the time, so
that he washed it afterward in hot water. Kirkland's letter proposed
something in lieu of the money he owed, something that he was certain
would challenge Mr. Preston's sensitive imagination. A thing of
growth, strong in the present, gigantic in the future: Kempton Electronics. Sloates had thought to type the words "you do (do not) want
me to answer this." Ken crossed out "(do not)." Mr. Sloates's letter
had pointed out that the duties he performed were not worth the
twenty thousand dollars a year "now that you are retired. It seems
appropriate therefore that I seek employment elsewhere."

You are retired. The delay until July is sheer ritual. You retired
right after Thanksgiving, 1955. He put on his gloves and sheepskin
coat and went outside. This was the beach on Caleb Island he knew
least and remembered only with his own small hand held in that
strong and large one extending from above. Arthur's. The small stones
were brilliant in the brittle late February sunlight but in childhood
he had learned how their subtle beauty died when brought indoors.
Then the intense black of the smooth ebony ovals became gray. The
pure whites turned pale yellow. The bleeding red oblongs faded into
dull rust. Even as the stubble and stalks still peering above white snow

seemed golden, once the wind had its way their true color, a vomitous yellow, would be plain to see.

A voice called out, "Good morning," and a hammer striking metal rang in the crisp air. It was the foreman holding a spike with a beveled edge to a long slab of rock.

"Tunk it again."

The young man struck the spike at an angle. Impatiently the foreman took the hammer himself and swiftly completed the job. Then he short cutted and joined Ken on the beach.

"Those young ones get the heft of it," he said. "But it's not half enough." He told Ken the work in progress. Building an extension for the storing of fodder. Scouting for hay: the meadow grass had been a bit snug. Laying in extra wood to spring out on, what with the earliness and severity of winter. He reached under his mackinaw into his overall pocket and came up with keys. "Mansion House is dried out now and the heat's going. You can move in any time you want. The boys will cook for you till we can bring help from the mainland." He handed the keys to Ken.

The foreman was a man who valued silence. He was able to measure just how much and when there was need for the sound of the human voice. When Ken made no reply, he completed the tale half told over two months ago of the marriage Arthur had brought about.

The actress lady had introduced furniture, rugs and records, radio, phonographs, and television. Visiting folks came to the house, not the barn. Friends of her own appeared from New York.

"The Kingsleys went on raising oxen," he said, "but they smelled different. I ran into young Dave Kingsley at Jeff Mullet's funeral. Jeff's widow was more cheerful and social than ever. So Dave got to talking about the last job poor Jeff had done repairing oil burners at the Christian Science Church. The black smoke was pouring hot and heavy out of the chimney and that didn't bother Jeff till all at once he heard the fire alarm. Being a good volunteer fireman, he left the oil burner, raced around the corner into the firehouse, on to the wagon, and came clear around the block to where the black smoke was still pouring out of the chimney of the Christian Science Church. It was real thoughtful of Dave to talk up that way about the dead, so I said, 'Dave, you sure are a changed man now,' and Dave said, 'I sure am.' I said, 'Your missus has sure changed things on you,' and Dave admitted that was so and said he'd tell me the big change if I'd pass the good word along to Mr. Arthur. 'It's this,' Dave said. 'Things is all backwards now from what they was. Now Pa and I eat on the outside and go to the toilet on the inside.' "

It was the foreman's way of proving that Dave *was* a better man because he knew how to tell a joke on himself and even on his pa who, the foreman went on to say, "was a mirror-minded man, saying black when he saw white so, at the wedding reception out in front of one hundred and fifty guests, he said to Dave's mother-in-law, meaning it for a compliment, 'Well now! I see you're not as dumb as you look!' "

The foreman said, "You ought to wear a cap, Mr. Preston," and left him to cross over back to the farmhouse.

At the oceanside Ken walked up the hill at the top of which stood Mansion House.

Arthur had found something in every region and something worth while in every regional man. He had neither envied nor imitated, but admired, was amused by and enjoyed.

Ken paused at the porch. Ought to wear a cap. That weekend of sleet and snow—was it in 1929?—without overcoat or hat, rushing about New York, wanting to die and coming very close. That was in the days before antibiotics, to which Toby, as the fire chief had said, owed his life. When you recovered you had lost so much weight and strength and had so little will that in early spring you were still convalescing on the porch of the main house in St. Terese. While Father, who was responsible and didn't know it, watched from a distance, Mother, who welcomed your invalidism, stayed close. Arthur came for a visit. Then you saw it all through his eyes. Mother creating witty conversation, helping you collect silver and woodcarvings, and because the weather was still cold, covering you with that dark, black cape that was heavy and hung over your shoulders.

"Very romantic," Arthur had said. "All you need is the hunting cap gentlefolk wear on the Scottish moors."

Then caught up in his whimsy at the bottom of which there was always a purpose, he amused you as he painted the scene. "I can see you," he said, "all in good time with a colored servant who says 'good mornin', Massa Ken' as you look up from your book." He didn't have to say "and there was your mother, as sweet as she could be because she'd won." Instead he said, "Some charming feminine voice will ask, 'Did you have a good night, dear?' and you will kiss the lady's hand and say, 'Indeed I did' and go back to your book. A book like the one you're reading, which is what?" He looked at the book. "In fact *exactly* that book," he said. "Lao-tse and the theory of renunciation." Mother was standing there and so was Mr. Sands; Arthur was aware of both of them. It was Mr. Sands who asked, "What's that renounciation, Mr. Arthur?" and Arthur, as though addressing another class at Harvard said, "A form of Buddhism. It teaches that man is only a name. The body is but a compound of perishable organs. Therefore ignore your body and your self as illusions and heed only your karma, your deeds which do not at all presuppose action, for spirit and thought are also karma, the highest action. If you are sufficiently pure, renounce. That is to say run from life. Avoid it. Avoid pain by renouncing goals, passions, or desires."

Mr. Sands had removed his hard straw hat and with confusion more feigned than real, exclaimed, "Why, Mr. Arthur, that just sounds like plain dying."

"That's exactly what it is," Arthur had said. "The Indian rope trick of being buried before you're dead."

Mother had hated Arthur ever since. The next day you began to walk. The day after that you exercised. Within a week you began to plan. You enrolled in make-up classes and used the spring so well that you succeeded in completing the semester.

He opened the door and entered the foyer. At the far end was the game room. He entered it and paused at the mahogany card table. New green felt covered the scooped-out wooden receptacles made by hand and meant for shillings, a favorite of the first Kenneth Fenimore Preston, acquired by him in 1775 and brought here by his widow. At this same table, Arthur had confounded you as a child with his feats of magic. It was part of his way of laughing at the place and making it more accessible through funny stories and ghostly jokes. He remembered the story of the gray-colored flannels with the black thin stripes Cousin Theodore wore as a boy and how Arthur had made him laugh until Theodore wailed, "Oh God, I've soiled Grandfather's pants."

They were all gone from first to last and the things they made had outlived them. It summarized the senselessness of human existence. A gambling table, the source for Arthur's little jokes, had outlived everything and everybody.

Last week you went to Concord and visited the cemetery where Cousin Theodore lay, and Aunt Sarah. Also Father and Mother. As a boy, you walked the old Boston Post Road that passed it, in the heat of summer, surrounded by trees and flowers, brooks and blossoms, gurgling streams and the smell of rich earth, and listened to the songs of birds at Sleepy Hollow. As a young man, you started at the other end of the same Post Road, walking away from New York with Muriel. You have seen it coming and going. There was nothing new for you there or here even though Father never lived in Mansion House: Mother had seen to that while Father was away to the wars and he had called it betrayal. Could that fact in some way explain Father's senility before his time, or his desperate gambles that failed? He had never mattered in the family. It was something so solidly formed, so inexorably shaped against him that nothing he could do, not even gamble and die, had changed it.

Now you to whom it never mattered, or so you always thought, are Preston of Mansion House, Caleb Island. You tore down the main house at St. Terese but the past is not that easily escaped!

A sense of his irresponsibility, deeply hidden from himself, rose up. How much of what you are have you blamed on this house, this island, and all they stand for? You give the illusion of facing duty but you are irresponsible and always have been: your self-effacement comes from that. Father said that irresponsibility hides behind anonymity and though he did so in a very different context, it remains true. He spoke of those who attacked the Street and the Floor, calling it a jungle.

"It is a jungle, boy, but not the way they mean, and I will tell you in exactly what way. It had been part of his reminiscences before he died. *You learn to squat in the jungle, relax your muscles with just two slight shifts, and keep clear of wet surfaces and red bugs. A gunshot can frighten wild creatures for a few seconds, but once you cough or sneeze, you're finished. It lasts fifteen to twenty times longer and by then it's too late."*

Then he spoke of the jungle flies and one in particular with eyes that contained the exact scale of colors of a certain rainbowed butterfly. When the fly died, the colors faded and nothing was left in the open eyes but flat grayness. Then he said, *"A thousand wonders to be seen and conquered, son, so long as one walks alone. The collective won't do. There is no room in the jungle for committees of cowards, which is what your irresponsible seeks every time. If there must be a guide or companions, you go single file. Everyone waits while someone walks. The wild have poor memories. But if men move along together, jostling shoulder to shoulder, they hear and smell it and it's over. You are lost."*

Then Father smiled, recalling a time of self-respect and triumph, real or fancied. *"That's something to remember always on the Floor. Stand responsible. Avoid committees, collectives, joint accounts, too many partners. No shoulder to shoulder. Get counted for who and what you are or do. Hunt alone."*

You walked alone. You hunted alone. In that desperate journey, made urgent by time that cannot be frozen, for most of the distance you walked alone. Then for a while you walked with others and lastly with her. Now here you are: more alone than ever you hoped to be.

He had mounted the steep stairs to the tower. He glanced briefly at the scroll and turned his back to it. Empty words. A boat was fighting the wind, forcing its way into Ram's Head Harbor with supplies for the shepherds. The sun would soon set.

Standing above and apart. Away from. The Chinese girls, Sorbonne students in pullovers, smoked their cigarettes and laughed. Regardez ce ballot. Ballot. *Slang is the language of people who live, are of the present, shoulder to shoulder, together.* Ballot.

He threw his weight against the door, fighting the wind. The door swung to with a loud clang. His hands held the rail of the catwalk. The boat was still making slow headway against the current and wind.

Ballot is the democratic verdict of your peers. Above and alone, you stand at the edge of approaching old age, a man who never found himself, one whose skirmishes have always ended before they led to the major event. You never found the simple path to the center of your existence. At least Father believed in the jungle, describing its heights and pillars, lights and incense, aisles, altars, and silences as a temple where the delusion of change did not exist to mislead a man. You have always been at odds with nature, your own and everyone else's. When alone you seek companionship. When you have it, you seek solitude. Where you love, you demand perfection: the bargain is not for you. You cannot conform or will not. A man between eras in that vacuum nature abhors. Your sterility and inadequacy cover every highway and byway of what you are and are not.

Recall Father recalling his father, in turn recalling his father? *Never cut the balls off a stallion,* Timothy said. But that presumes their existence. You rejected the cloistered inaction Mother offered, the jungle paths Father urged, the cheap chest-thumping so dear to Laurie, and the stuffy role of oracle Theodore left behind. Even Arthur's world-wide amateur standing in which he took such pride you reject. You reject everything: everything rejects you. There is no meeting ground. You are a shadow of shadows, a ghost spawned by ghosts. There never was, there is not now, and there never will be direct, concrete, immediate, touching, living, breathing contact which can suffer all delusions including change or changelessness and willingly endure. Save once upon a honeymoon. But not a lifetime. And against the years that yawn, it is not enough. You are strong in a terrible way, young in a horrible way, like a dinosaur intact for the ice that a glacial age has wrapped it in. Incapable of any other action, can't you recognize the only action open to the likes of you? You are strong enough against this wind: do it!

He looked at his hands, strange objects refusing to let go of the catwalk rail.

You succeeded where Father failed. You shall fail where he succeeded. You will not drop your hand in mid-game. You will play it out, joker and all. The last and least pride at the end of the line. But to live you must forget what makes you want to die. And to do so you must destroy what makes you remember. Close Caleb. Sell St. Terese. Resigning from Preston Public Funds is only the beginning. Sell your Seat. Get your divorce. Leave New York.

He pulled the door open and ran. He was still running when he reached the dock where Mr. Perkins, having left the supplies, was about to depart.

"Wait," Ken said, "I'm going with you."

Ken lay on a big towel spread over the lawn grass, a cabana behind him on the shore of the Gulf of Mexico. He watched the little sandpipers play daring games with the incoming waves. After a week of sand, sea, sun, silence, and space, he had finally called Tess Peters, secretary of the local Chamber of Commerce and informant as well as intended liaison between himself and Moe Kempton of Kempton Electronics. Matthew Kirkland had vouched for the fact that Tess was hard as nails and thoroughly reliable.

To judge from Kirkland's appropriate appraisal of how Ken would respond to this project, it seemed plausible to rely on him for the rest. It was not only the fact that he owed Ken the money, he explained, and was unable to pay it. He knew Ken's involvement with power and light and his father's before him: electronics was the next logical step. Ken was a lone wolf. He thought he understood that. This was a lone wolf's dream. All that stood between Kempton Electronics and a fortune that staggered the mind was the four million dollars worth of needed financing, now that it had the government contract. More vital than the financing was solution of the contest between Kempton Electronics and the inventor Herb Stanley, whose basic patents their government contract was based upon. He had explained to Ken's satisfaction why the government would award the contract with this challenge unsettled and litigation pending. He had exhibited photostats of all the documents, including the special indemnification granted the government by Kempton. The company was located here on the west coast of Florida and the suing inventor in London. Tess Peters was the only point of contact in Florida. Kirkland himself was the path to Herb Stanley. Kirkland had explained the special process of direct ore reduction and its vital bearing on the increased aluminum and steel requirements of an atomic age. He proved the *bona fides* of the patents and made clear the underlying premise of the process: the physical principle that force is a fiction. Neither the company's claims nor the inventor's challenge was clear-cut. Surely the company's proposals for settlement were not unfair.

"Of course I knew you would have nothing to do with it if that were not so," Kirkland had said.

Small white puffs of clouds were blowing across the sky: it brought back the same healing he had felt once before from this nameless fragrance, blue-green water, warm, clean, generous expanse of beach, sea, and sky.

He turned at the sound of the beach boy's voice and saw the milky-white-skinned woman in her mid-forties coming toward him. She carried a huge straw pocketbook, and wore sunglasses and a wide-rimmed straw hat. Her hair had the same brittleness and color as the pocketbook and hat.

Ken rose to his feet. The beach boy set up two chairs and an awninged table.

Tess Peters said no to a drink and immediately got down to business. "Herb Stanley is cracked, but so is Moe Kempton. Moe has more than enough in the way of money. If he sweetened the figure too much, he might just as well quit. Still Herb has him over a barrel. But lean on a barrel hard enough and it breaks. Kempton built the company before Herb Stanley was born, but the government contract is based on Herb Stanley's inventions. No doubt about it. So Stanley holds one half and Moe holds the other and both have nothing if they don't get together. Moe can't seek financing with the litigation hanging over his head and that's the package. Nuts, isn't it? Get Moe to yield more, sell it to Stanley, and deliver the financing and you can damn near take the company away." She smiled. "Naturally I get paid by both sides. Moe and you." She shifted in the sun chair, showing a figure that might once have been very near perfect before age had thickened it at the hips. She raised her chin. It revealed sharp creases wrinkling her throat. "I'd better dig up all the material for you from the Chamber's files, City Hall, and the newspaper morgue."

Ken asked questions regarding Kempton's other contracts and general financing. He was surprised at how much of the company's information she possessed and understood. Then he queried her on the exact nature of Herb Stanley's contentions. He was equally impressed by her knowledge of the legal issues. He asked what strategic or tactical reasons might have prompted Herb Stanley to remove himself as far as London.

"To avoid the temptation of easy settlement. Or the need to work. He's divorced his wife. She's up in Connecticut. Maybe because he's a screwball. Ask Moe. I wouldn't know."

They talked for several hours.

"Now I'm thirsty," she said, "—if you're still offering to buy me a drink—"

She had four scotches while he had one. They had no visible effect on her. "I doubt you'll get anywhere," she said, "so while you're here, if you want to know about Gulf or inland property, citrus, fishing, or offshore oil, I'm your girl."

Ken asked if she would like a swim.

"Love it. We natives don't get into the water often. When I go back to town for that info, I'll pick up my suit."

She returned carrying a small suitcase. "There's a lot of this junk. For the local yokels it was big stuff."

Ken read reports, interviews, summaries, and legal briefs while Tess put away more scotch over rocks. She touched his shoulder at one point and said, "I'm using your cabana."

When she ran past him toward the waves, he caught sight of her unnaturally white body in the sunlight. Then he joined her in the water. She swam like a man with strong overhand strokes. When they reached shore, she was in no way breathless. She rubbed herself dry, lighted a cigarette. "How about buying me another drink?"

Now that he'd read the material, they could talk about the issues separating inventor and company, their inflamed and subjective expression through Herb Stanley and Moe Kempton, and the impersonal arguments based on fact, equity, and statute presented by lawyers.

"I should have thought," she said, "that you or Kirkland would have found out first whether Herb Stanley is willing to settle before trying to bargain with Kempton."

"Florida is closer than London."

"But Stanley is crazier than Moe."

"All the more reason. If I can't do business with the sane one, why bother with the crazy one?"

"You're not half so absent-minded, really, are you?" She smiled.

Ken asked how she came to know the company that well. "Since they seem to be in Florida for delivery reasons and their customers are national, what can the Chamber of Commerce offer?"

"Not the Chamber of Commerce," she said, blandly. "Me. And not the company. Moe. He's the only man down here who can drink as much as I do and still stay sober."

She left to keep her date with Moe for cocktails and dinner, promising to report back later.

Ken ate on his balcony. Then he walked the beach. He watched the clouds stretched across the southern sky from west to east like a fiery fan. A heron flew straight as an arrow into the blood of the sun. To accept life as it is is not so bad. Once you take it as it comes, there are interesting things to occupy one's mind.

When his phone rang, it was almost ten o'clock. Tess Peters was in the lobby with encouraging information. He joined her and they went to the cocktail lounge, where a man played piano and sang witty songs to the empty room.

"Moe knows all about you. He was surprised that I didn't. What have I missed?"

Ken shrugged.

"Moe says you retired from finance with a whirlwind record." Her eyes narrowed. "Now why would a man like you come down here to fool with this jigsaw puzzle when you have all of Wall Street to choose from?"

"I like the extra breathing space."

"Another screwball?"

"Aren't we all?"

She laughed.

The waiters were closing the room. "I forgot my bathing suit," she said.

They walked across the sand and shuffleboard courts, around the pool to the cabana. Her suit wasn't there.

"I must have taken it upstairs," Ken said.

He left his room door open as they walked in. The chambermaid had spread both suits in the bathroom.

"Why not buy me one more drink? Then I'll set up this date for you and Moe tomorrow."

When Ken was on the phone, she said, "You might just as well order my four scotches at once."

When the waiter knocked she retired to the bathroom. After he left and she heard the door shut behind him, Tess reappeared, naked and remarkably young in limb and flesh. She walked calmly to the bed, got under the covers, and reached her hand out for the first drink.

"Did I read the signals wrong?" she asked.

Ken handed her the drink in silence.

"O.K. I read the signals wrong." She tossed down the scotch. "I'll take the second one, please." She lay under the covers, unembarrassed, and talked about "me and my equally gorgeous identical twin." She may well have been gorgeous at one time. "Sis really knew what she wanted. Now she's stuck with it. A jerk of a husband and grown children who think *she's* a jerk. Life stopped at twenty.

I'm past forty and still on my way." She made lying in his bed seem perfectly natural. "How come a man like you never married?"

"I am married."

"So Matt Kirkland told me. But that's just a certificate. Marriages over forty don't count. They're done in cold blood or middle-aged lunacy. No offense."

Ken nodded slightly.

"I've had one child and twenty husbands with no certificates for any of them. At least the certificate for the child went with her to the people who took her while I was still asleep in the hospital. All you have to do to become a mother is lie on your back." She finished the second drink. "I like business. Now my sister envies me. She has to take money from a man she despises. I suppose if my daughter knows about me, she despises me too." She handed him the empty glass and waited for the third one. "The things women do to men out of love. They want their men to be heroes and they hate them when they are. Not book heroes, life heroes. Self-centered jerks. What else can you be if you have to succeed?" She looked at him. "You don't drink at all," she said.

"Not much."

"Do you smoke?" She smiled.

"I've stopped."

There was silence. She finished the third drink and extended her hand for the fourth. "I'm quite sober," she assured him.

"Out of one hundred and two million adults, sixty million drink in this country. I usually am with a minority."

"Snob."

"That, too."

"Go on. Tell me more."

"About alcohol? Twenty-five per cent of it sold in this country is moonshine and bootleg."

"You're kidding."

"No. It's all bathtub stuff. Refills in bona fide labeled bottles. Same as the prohibition days."

She sniffed the glass, was satisfied, and drained it. "That's weird. Why? Tax-free money?"

"Not worth the double jeopardy," Ken answered. "Why is the big real estate boom in Florida picking up where it left off in those same roaring twenties under the same water?"

"It is, too." She laughed and put down the glass. "Well, why?"

"Why are they doing the Charleston again? Reading F. Scott Fitzgerald again? Singing the same songs?"

She nestled in the pillows. "I don't know and I don't care." She saw his expression. "Don't worry. I won't fall asleep. I must remember that suit."

She got out of the bed and went to the bathroom. When she came back holding the suit, she was still naked. She passed the mirror.

"Mirror, mirror on the wall," she said.

She dropped the suit on the dresser and stood against him, the fingers of one hand opening the buttons of his shirt. "How did I get the signals that wrong?" she asked.

When he took her, she beat her fists against his chest and cried out. Her eyes were open but vacant, unseeing like those of one in a seizure of epilepsy. When he made a slight move away, she seized him and dug her nails into his back. Then she fell asleep and the reek of alcohol that came with her deep breathing was too much for him. He moved off the bed quietly, put on a robe, and went out on the balcony. At the last moment the milk-white color of her body had been altered by red splotches. They began like long welts on her throat.

He sat in the darkness, depressed. Peelings instead of fruit. The secret is not to stop or sit still. Don't stare or consider. Keep moving. Others do. Take it as it comes and when it's gone forget it.

He lost track of time. Several hours later he heard her moving in the dark room. She put on lights and opened the door to the balcony. She was dressed, fresh looking, her make-up in order, and she held her small suitcase.

"I'll see you home," he said.

"I know my way." Her tone was sharp. "Didn't give you much breathing space, did I?"

"I'm not a child."

"I imagine you'd like to get our business done and over with quickly and vamoose."

"Yes, I would."

"We can arrange a meeting for tomorrow. Actually today now. You'll hear from me before noon. Figure to see Moe at cocktail time."

"I would prefer to take you home."

"Suit yourself."

On the way, the smell of honeysuckle, palms, and oranges was thick in the night air. She let her head rest on his shoulder. "If you straighten out Moe, we could take a holiday," she said. "There's a real nutty guy, a Cuban. He and his son own a cab. They're a riot. Sonny drives and Papa gives orders. 'Stop for the red light. Turn left. Turn right.' His idiot son reads all the signs along the way out loud. Or we could take a plane to Cuba. Quite a spot since Castro."

She took her head from his shoulder, and saw the expression on his face. "Just worry about yourself," she said. "I grew up near the Everglades like an Indian or a hunter's boy, killing snakes and raising alligators. I didn't wear shoes till I was twelve."

"You misunderstood me," Ken said. "I just don't want to go to Cuba."

"No kidding?"

He shook his head.

"You remind me of an ex-heavyweight champ or an erstwhile movie star. Now that's wrong. You're not that old." She took his hand. "I know a great spot on the Keys. We'll have a wonderful time."

She ran up the stairs of the small house. Ken re-entered the rented car and drove away.

After two weeks of meetings with Kempton the issue of terms was "satisfactorily settled." Tess laughed when she used the words. They were at last lying on the hot deck of the chartered boat far out in the Gulf. Nothing was settled till Herb Stanley agreed and they were headed in a direction that would not get Ken any nearer to London.

For three weeks it was forgotten. Except when the captain docked for supplies and the one time they anchored for repairs, land itself was forgotten. Heat and the cool water, sun and the sky of stars, swimming, fishing, lying stupefied in the heat or dozing below with ice, gin, limes, and soda turning the revolving wheel of eventless timeless drifting.

One morning Tess looked at him soberly and said, "You've had it," and Ken turned away. Then they leaned on the rail and watched the porpoises. Closer to shore they watched the mating sting rays. It was mid-April and people straggled along the beach. They were natives taking advantage of Sunday.

Chapter 2

ON A DRIZZLING cold Tuesday, Ken arrived at the London airport. It took him two days to find out that Herb Stanley was in Paris. On the second day a housekeeper finally answered his phone. The cable had arrived from Dr. Kirkland in New York. She had read it to Mr. Stanley. He instructed her to give his Paris number to Mr. Preston when he called. She did.

Ken phoned Paris. A young Englishman's voice said, "Hang on." Then another young man apologized and explained, "Matt Kirkland didn't say when you'd be coming through. I'll fly right back to London if you like. Though you might enjoy Paris. It's only an hour by air. I've a good friend here and the weather's much better."

Ken said he'd fly to Paris and two hours later they picked him up at Le Bourget airport.

Ken assumed that the tall, wiry, blue-eyed young man with the precise blond mustache would be the Englishman. It turned out that the middle-sized, black-eyed, curly haired one who looked so Latin was. The other was Herb Stanley.

He introduced Jack Vincent, who said, "We'll all stay at my place. There's plenty of room."

"It's a piece of good luck for me your coming through," Herb said. "Matt says you're the only man alive can get my patents back from Kempton. If you can, just name your own figure."

They had crowded into Jack's small, bright blue buglike car.

"You mean Kirkland suggested I would aid you to divest Kempton of the rights to your patents?"

"What else?"

Ken frowned. "You must have misunderstood him. I saw Kempton in Florida and persuaded him to improve your royalty by thirty-three per cent. We agreed in writing that if I succeeded in getting you to accept it, I would receive a one-third share of the common stock as well as eight per cent income bond debentures for providing financing. I'm not passing through. I flew from the States for this purpose."

Herb's pale blue eyes darkened. He fumbled for a cigarette and tapped it rapidly on the big knuckles of his nervous left hand. His jaw muscles expanded and contracted. "Well, what do you say to that?" he demanded.

"Kirkland is a proper bastard," Jack said.

You start with an embezzler, Ken thought. Naturally he is also a liar and leads to a screwball. Action, yes; away from familiar places, public funds and brokerage, or the Floor. But where do you draw the line?

"You won't get anywhere with me," Herb said.

"Suddenly I'm not at all sure I want to," Ken answered.

A cab crossed their path. Jack leaned out the window and cursed in French. The driver cursed back. A few other drivers cursed both of them, one another, and various pedestrians. Jack felt better. "We were talking about molecules as your plane came in, at least Herb was. Quite fascinating. A molecule left to itself in no time at all becomes no molecule at all. I didn't know that. It started as an argument on the difference between alliance and union—West Germany and all that."

"Was Matt also lying when he said you were a major with O.S.S. and Jed?"

"Hardly."

"Herb was with your 508th," Jack explained. "They dropped lots of your chaps in South France."

"And a few of our own outfit," Herb said.

"I was with C.O.P.P.," Jack went on, "though I don't suppose you'd know about that."

"Combined Operations Pilotage Parties, wasn't it?" Ken asked. "Vanguard for Overlord."

"Good man!"

"Preparing for Anvil we kept close track of Overlord," Ken explained.

"And one hell of a fight between the two." Herb was cheerful again. "Which you lost and the brass have been writing bitter memoirs about it ever since."

The air was suddenly cleared.

"How about lunch?" Jack suggested.

"I wouldn't mind," Ken said.

The restaurant had whitewashed walls and dark wood. There were paintings and only five tables. Two were empty. A man sat at one, three girls at another. Ken and Jack ate. Herb drank wine. Jack was

curious about Ken's work in public funds and why he had left it.
Ken offered little enlightenment.

"Now that you Americans are bankers for the western world," Jack
persisted, "I should expect that being in charge of new depositors
would be an enviable position."

"For some, I'm sure it is."

"It would be for me," Jack said.

"Major," Herb said. "You're a windmill tilter."

Ken smiled.

"I know because I am too. That's why I hate Kempton. He's a
bloodsucker. Oh, I know I'm a spoiled brat and a young snot who
should think himself very lucky while Kempton is drenched in know-
how and has been for more years than I am old. Bilge. He makes
fifty bets at a thousand to one in his favor. So what if forty-nine go
down the drain? He pays dribs and drabs and keeps the lion's share.
He's the kind of a bastard I'd like to see dead."

"He takes chances too," Ken said.

"Bilge. I take chances. I can come within a hair's breadth and
end with nothing. I should think you'd see the difference."

"Easy, man," Jack said. "He does. Better than you do."

"At least I do see a difference," Ken said.

"I can't get over Kirkland. Matt was really all right when I first
met him. I suppose you don't tear down a civilized man all at once.
The apes have to kick him about for a while." Herb looked at Ken
shrewdly. "Now why couldn't your candor just be deviousness?"

"It could," Ken said, "but you needn't worry. My interest in Kempton Electronics has ceased to exist."

"I have an idea your Major needs your ruddy patents about as
much as you need two left boots."

"Seriously?" Herb asked Ken.

"Altogether."

"Fine. Then let's forget it."

"Gladly."

"You chaps belong in England for the reason I left. It's been full of
windmills for centuries. There was one in Haberdon for all tilters to
take on as far back as 1191. Set up by Dean Herbert in his glebe lands,
till an Abbot Sampson who had a water mill made him take it down."

"Is that the same Abbot Sampson whom Ralph Waldo Emerson
compared to Thoreau?" Ken asked.

"Damned if I know."

"Major, it's a stinking shame we had to meet under such stinking
auspices."

"We agreed to forget it."

"Right you are."

The bottle was empty. Jack called for another.

They sat at a boulevard café on the Champs Elysées. A group of young girls who should have been at school came out of the movies to add their color to the late April crowd. They laughed and giggled, held hands and chased one another to the crossing.

Then two whores walked by.

"Out early," Jack said in English.

One told the other in patois, "Before long if we wish to sleep with Frenchmen we shall have to go to a foreign country."

Herb and Jack laughed. Ken smiled. The two whores smiled back.

"Most of them already have," Jack said. "There'll soon be more Frenchies peddling it down Piccadilly than the home grown. They get rich in London and return to Paris to open millinery shops. I hate to admit it but our English girls can't compete, either *demi* or otherwise."

"That's why Jack lives in Paris."

"I live in Paris because the French are practical." He turned to Ken. "When did you get to London?"

"Two days ago. I went to Stratford. It was Shakespeare's three hundred and ninety-third birthday. I didn't want to miss that. They performed *As You Like It*."

"Not as *I* like it," Jack said. "Brevity is the soul of wit, to be sure. For the simple reason that a few extra minutes of it make you want to puke. Even great William's. There were ninety nations present, weren't there? They were expecting Malaya but she didn't turn up."

Herb was drinking cognac and wine alternately. "I have a theory," he said. "It explains England, Shakespeare, Churchill, everything."

"Now you should patent *that*," Jack said.

"What's blood, sweat, and tears?" Herb went on. "Salt water," he answered himself. "Red, white, or hot, at heart it's the plain blue sea, and England is our oldest island."

"He's getting potted," Jack explained amiably. "When he starts that tripe, he's well on his way."

"All right, I'll be serious. Major, why don't you take over Kempton, then I'll settle. What do you say? There's justice in that."

"The Major isn't interested," Jack reminded.

"Right. Well then, maybe we can interest you in taking your share of the refreshments." He refilled Ken's glass.

"I'm doing very well," Ken assured him. "Until quite recently, I was a one martini before dinner man."

Herb's blue eyes were taking on a milky haze. "What else did you do in London?"

"I went to bed early and I was awakened this morning at seven o'clock by a trumpet, saxophone, and drum under my hotel window playing Dixieland jazz. 'Five Foot Two.' It was the Salvation Army."

Herb and Jack began to laugh.

"What in hell is 'Five Foot Two'?" Herb wiped the tears off his cheeks.

"A popular song of the twenties," Jack said. "Only it's called 'Has Anybody Seen My Gal?' You like good jazz bands, Major?"

Ken shrugged.

"Great idea," Herb said.

Jack fished franc notes out of his pocket and rose. "Let's go."

They sat against a wall of stone. It was damp and cold despite the flaming fireplace, candles that dripped over the wine bottles on all the tables, and the close body heat. Someone was frying onions and bread. The four-piece band was playing in a disjointed, improvisational way.

"That's 'Diane,'" Jack said.

"Yes. From the movie *Seventh Heaven*. Came out in 1927."

"Ever been in a place like this before, Major?" Herb asked.

"Yes. Greenwich Village. Also in the twenties. 1928. It was next door to the headquarters of the King of the Hobos."

"Major," Jack said, "you ought to chuck it all and stay here. You could get a mansion in Cotswold for twenty thousand American, or in the south of France for a good deal less."

"I may," Ken said.

"Or both," Herb said. "Either that or get my patents back from Kempton and we'll both return to the States."

"We decided to forget that."

"I forgot." He laughed. "I forgot to forget."

"And you forgot to remember," Jack sang. "Aren't those the lyrics of the thing they're playing now?"

"No," Ken said, "but both songs came out at the same time. This one's called 'Always.' 1925."

"What I don't understand was how Matt got you interested in the first place."

"It was a means of getting out of something," Ken said. "It has served its purpose."

"I don't suppose that son of a bitch Kempton ever told you how he used my patents as a blackjack over the heads of big firms to get subcontracts and deliberately kept my stuff from being used for three years? Now the government wants it, he's eager to settle. He has to. I don't. Why should I?"

"Are you asking me to plead his case?"

"Yes, God damn it."

Jack grinned. "He's potted as blue hell now, so you might just as well."

So Ken traced the issues and the law which was not that clear cut, nor was the evidence. Kempton had in fact attempted to buck the big boys who used competing blast furnaces. There was a fair case for proving that while he attempted to avoid a crippling fight, he carried out their original purpose. The offer to increase Herb's royalties with an actual order on hand surely made up for any profit the firm might have enjoyed at the expense of delaying the use of Herb's patents.

Herb sighed. "I still hate Kempton," he said.

"But there's something to what the Major says."

"I'm not persuading you," Ken said. "I'm no longer interested. I answered your question merely for your own future use."

"Do you know that one?" Jack challenged.

"'Charmaine,'" Ken said. "*What Price Glory*. 1926."

"And the lyrics?"

Ken recited them.

"Are you a collector of popular songs?"

"I'm a collector," Ken said.

"The first time around on these tunes, I was still the Sunday punch in my old man's scrotum."

"He means he was born in 1926," Herb said. "So was I but I'm still a windmill tilter from way back. I didn't leave America because England is practical, but because I'm not. Now you've been divorced." He didn't wait for Ken's answer. "Women are taking over America. Like my wife took me over. They read the books, buy your clothes, live longer, marry twice, inherit estates and insurance, hold more stock, organize the vote, and raise the children. Damn bitch wanted me to settle with Kempton."

"Herb, now you're getting monotonous," Jack said.

"I'm struggling with the Major's proposition."

"Don't. I withdrew it," Ken said.

"To tell you the truth, I left America because my wife has lovely legs."

"Very potted," Jack said.

"I liked looking at them. She stopped wearing shorts one summer because the town elders didn't approve. Connecticut, after I left Kempton. I said God damn it, *I* approved. She didn't answer. So here I am."

"That's 'Barney Google,'" Jack said. "Isn't it something about being cross-eyed with a wife three times his size?"

"Yes," Ken said. "Now she's suing for divorce and he's living with his horse."

"The alcoholic art is getting through to you, Major," Herb said. "Brandy, cognac, wine, scotch."

"Jack, did you ever hear one called 'Doin' the Raccoon'?" Ken asked.

"No. Who does it and how and where and to whom?"

"To the raccoon. You wear a coat made only of his skins. With flappers and a hip flask in your flivver at the football game. Collegiates did it. Also in the twenties."

"What's with you two and the twenties?"

"And everyone's dispensed with the thirty years in between," Ken went on. "A remarkable feat."

"An impossible feat," Jack said.

"No. Remarkable. Not impossible. They're *doing* it. Everyone chooses to forget to remember and the result is we repeat what caused the thing we want to forget."

"Listen, God damn it." Herb struck the table. "Break it up. Major, I've thought it over. With you in the picture, I'll do it. But not if I have to go back."

Ken said, "Excuse me," to Jack. "I am no longer in it," he reminded Herb. "But if you settle with Kempton you *will* have to go back. That's a condition."

"With my best years ahead of me? Not on your life! I'm only thirty-one."

"Thirty lost years plus one," Jack said. "Where did it go, Major?"

"Not it," Herb said. "Me."

"It, we, me, same thing. Where are the lost years, Major?"

Ken raised a vague hand. "Just lost."

"I'm not lost," Herb protested.

"Yes, you are, boyo," Jack said. "And so am I."

"Forget and repeat," Ken said. "The lost generation second time around. Word for word. Chapter, place, and verse."

"Bilge and balls to the lost generation. A rose is a rose is a rosary."

"A rose is a rose is a crown of thorns," Ken said.

"More bilge."

"I'll tell you why I left England," Jack said. "Now that you know.

It's the fat sheep with their legs folded under them. Centuries of semesters. The Mitre. The pub and Kings Arms. The glory that was isn't but the melody lingers on."

"Going round and round the long trail awinding getting nowhere," Ken said.

"Exactly."

"Where do you suppose the Frenchmen go?" Ken asked.

Jack laughed. "Musical chairs. America?"

"I hadn't noticed. That's a game leaves one man always standing up, isn't it?" Ken asked.

"He may be the lucky one."

"But we're no damned lost generation," Herb insisted. "Lousy ambulance drivers and male nurses. I'm here to get away from all that television installment buying make yourself a bloody millionaire. No artists' models or rich fathers sending me the check on the first of each month."

"In the twenties, it was radio," Ken said. "Chapter and verse."

"Major, for an O.S.S. man you talk more God damn bilge. It was the *Student Prince*. They scratched a finger and howled for ten years. We get the score. We're turning it down."

"I call turning down the only turn we have loud complaining. Besides, our war ended twelve years ago."

Jack put his hand between them and filled their glasses, assuming the role of referee. "Gentlemen, proceed," he said, "with the blessings of Bacchus. And may the best man win."

"Bacchus was primarily god of fertility," Ken informed him. "And all on the side of women."

"God's always on the side of women," Herb said. "We agree there."

"The Orphic priests of Bacchus explained all lost generations thousands of years ago in an actual tablet they left behind," Ken said. "It contained instructions to the dead on what to do and what not to do when they reached the next world. On the left bank of the house of Hades, they said, is a wellspring called Lethe for forgetfulness. On the right is the lake of Memory and guardians who wait. The oracles instruct the dead to go up to them, identify themselves as children of earth, stars, and heaven, and beg for the right to drink from the cold, flowing waters of Memory. When you do that, the tablet says, the guardians will give you drink and you shall go forth among other heroes and have lordship forever. As for those who drink from the banks of Lethe left of Hades to forget, they forget nothing and remain lost in torment forever."

"In short," Jack said, "it's hell to forget, heaven to remember, and you must endure pain to reach paradise."

"Two, three thousand years ago," Ken said. "And we have been doing it backwards ever since."

The two young men said nothing. Ken looked at them and realized his years.

When Jack spoke again, his voice was thoughtful. "Major, how does a man like you come to be on Wall Street?"

"I was born there."

"Let's get going," Herb said. "It's time to celebrate the deal between the Major and myself. We have one, don't we?"

Ken shrugged. "If you insist."

"Good. Now let's get out of here."

"Where to?" Jack asked.

"Pigalle."

The whores of Pigalle were careful to obey the law against soliciting. Some stood in pairs, telling jokes and making comments on the sailors, soldiers, and tourists who walked by. Others stood alone at the mouths of side streets. They were of every age, shape, and size, from seventeen to forty. The sidewalk was littered and the air was damp. The man walking behind them gave up urging their attendance at the pornographic movie about to go on. The blinking lights of the clubs threw red, blue, and green shadows across the wide gutter. The smell of cheap whisky, perfume, and sweat came from the hallways and the open doors of saloons and cafés.

"I've agreed," Herb said, "and Jack's our witness so you can tell me the truth. Was that your purpose? Did you turn me down to make me want it?"

"Oh, knock off," Jack said. "Just leave it alone."

"The one question, Major, that's all."

"You really want the truth?" Ken paused and a whore misunderstood.

Jack laughed and took him by the arm.

"I don't know," Ken said. "I hope I didn't. I'm not so sure. There's someone I want to call," he said to Jack. "Will you remind me?"

"Why wait? Let's call her now. Or perhaps you prefer my brand?"

"He's a lawyer," Ken said.

A three-piece band played loudly. Ken searched his pockets. "I have his phone number. It's somewhere." He removed his jacket and they helped him search. "His name is Chanteuf. It's for you," he told Herb. "Finance."

Herb straightened Ken's lapel. "Now I swear I'm through with it," he said.

"Thank God," Jack said. He touched Ken's arm. "In there."

A well-groomed American matron dragged a mink coat and leaned against the far end of the bar. She watched the Negro bass player.

"I tell myself certain fictions that are not open to argument," Herb said. "Number one, I'm terrific. Number two, I'm fun. Number three, everybody is fun. Number four—"

Jack and Ken had walked into the bar. Herb followed.

"Noisy," Jack said.

The bar sloshed with water, whisky, and red wine. They ordered drinks and didn't touch them. The woman with the mink coat turned her head. She saw them and smiled. Jack smiled back but she was looking at Ken. Another girl joined her. She too was well dressed.

"This one looks Turkish," Herb said.

The dark, swarthy girl examined them.

"Now if there were a third to their party—"

"There is."

The third was blond and pale. Over the noise she cocked her head to hear what the dark one said. Then the three of them turned and looked across.

"If they follow us, let's make it a dawn patrol, with breakfast at my place," Jack said.

They walked to the corner. The girls were following.

"Dawn was the worst," Jack was saying. "If you missed your rendezvous or the tide carried you and you tipped your canoe with a mile or two to swim and the benzedrine wearing off, what with sentries practicing rifle shooting and your back to them and that damn gray light coming up—"

"For us it was the fog when we landed," Ken said.

They paused at the entrance to one of the night spots.

"They'll follow," Jack said.

The Master of Ceremonies wore lipstick. Just before the lights dimmed for the floor show, the three girls appeared. Jack signaled the waiter. They walked to a table and the six of them sat down. The naked girls stamped and wiggled, shook and marched. The champagne was bad and the show reached an unrehearsed climax when one of the performers, a girl under seventeen, staggering on very high heels and dressed as a bride, giggled, clutched at something invisible, and fell. From her dilated pupils, it was clear she was drugged. She hit the floor a dead weight. Ken rose to his feet but the M.C. left the prop wedding bed in his idiotic striped pajamas, and the bridesmaids, naked under their wardrobe, showed their bare buttocks and breasts ungracefully as they lifted her, blood trickling from her nose, and carried her off.

"She should be in a hospital," Ken said.

"Very dismal," said the girl with the mink coat.

"His saving grace was that he went from male to female," Jack was telling the blond girl. "Otherwise—"

"The brothels of Kentucky are the worst."

"How would you know?" the girl with the mink said to the swarthy one. "You're an Armenian."

"It's all part of big business. You're in big business. Am I right?" she asked Ken.

"You were never in America," the girl with the mink persisted. "How would you know? You're an Armenian."

"You dislike vulgarity," the Armenian girl continued in French to Ken. "You dislike it much."

"Much," Ken said.

"But you like beauty?"

"Also much."

"Everywhere, all the time?"

"Speak English," the girl with the mink coat said. "He's an American."

"Not when it's stuffed down my throat," Ken said.

"We can also agree on that," the Armenian said.

"A pig should be succulent," Jack told the blond girl. "Not truculent."

She turned to Herb and asked, "What does he mean?"

"It's the difference between being eaten or beaten," Herb explained.

"The brothels of Kentucky, particularly Newport," the Armenian girl was saying, speaking English again. "And they loved you men from Boston. Called them broad A's. They spent more and were perfect gentlemen."

"How can an Armenian be an authority on whorehouses in Newport, Kentucky, if she was never in America?"

"I was never in America." Her voice was soft and quiet. Her eyes were angry. "Do I have to be an American in America to recognize an American whore?" She smiled to Ken. "Do I?"

"So was my friend for a month," the girl with the mink said to Ken. "But this is too much."

"She came here because she couldn't face it," the Armenian said.

"I came to get a divorce."

"She has a plastic," the Armenian said.

"From an auto accident," the girl with the mink told Ken. "My face was marred and they all gave me up but I'm a long life buff."

"Boff," the Armenian corrected.

"Then this lunk in our squadron showed his fraternity ring to the men's room attendant and said, 'The bell captain told me you could find me lodgings.' The attendant asked, 'Are you gay?' and the chump said, 'Well, I'm happy.' Telling this to *us*, mind you! And on that, he says, the son of a bitch kissed me, and I punched him in the jaw, stuffed his head in a toilet, left New York, and came back to the base."

Herb, Jack, and the blond-haired girl brought their heads together in laughter.

"Five hundred million a year on the whores alone in Newport and most of it big corporation business to improve sales," the Armenian girl said.

Herb was shaking Ken's hand. "Don't forget now. It's a deal, Major. To you fellas on Wall Street, a hand shake's enough. You don't need a contract. Isn't that right? Now we shake!" He pumped Ken's hand again. "Synchronize our watches. Make it for breakfast."

They were out on the street, then in a cab. Herb and Jack and the blond girl were gone. Now the two girls were drinking brandy and he was drinking *café noir*. St. Germain. A waiter was mopping and another turned chairs upside down. There were still many people, much argument, smoke, and talk. One group was singing.

"You're making sweeping statements," the Armenian girl said. "You're lightheaded. Go home. Go to sleep."

"I'm not lightheaded. I won't sleep in your room any more, you Armenian bitch."

The Armenian smiled. "You're married," she said to Ken. "You're used to females. I can tell. Do you know Marlon Brando?"

"Does Marlon Brando know Marlon Brando?" the girl with the mink coat swung around. "Does anybody here know Marlon Brando for this Armenian bitch?"

"You are embarrassing our host." The Armenian girl's voice hadn't risen.

"We're Americans, right?" The girl with the mink put her hand on Ken's. "In a strange country. I mean *strange*. And her horning in. All right, fun is fun, but a month of her is more than enough."

Suddenly the two girls were fighting, rolling on the floor. Ken looked at them, puzzled. He rose and walked out. No one paid attention. The laughter and arguing, singing, and ringing in his head followed him.

Herb said make it for breakfast. But where? Jack's place. Where's that? No one had told him. Somewhere in Paris. That's where you are now, somewhere in Paris. A half a billion dollars in whoring in Newport, Kentucky, alone. Big business.

Always dominated, poor man.

That was a woman in her eighties, in Antibes. The niece of Gustave

Flaubert, Mme. Franklin Grout. That's right, the celebrated lady of "Lettres à sa Nièce Caroline." She was speaking of Turgenev to Mother. That's another time, another place. Help the starving Armenians for America is dominated by women who live longer and marry twice and going from male to female is what saved him. Man who has no fear is never lost. Have no fear.

He was standing with his fists clenched, held to his sides. If time joins place, you are overrun. Your cup runneth over. Overrun. Very drunk. Silly. Focus. Neither forget nor remember. Just focus on the present. On here. Where's here? He started to walk. Then he ran. A rat maze. They were all alike. Dawn soon. Breakers capsizing canoes. Sentries on a beach. X marks the spot and we are ready for a landing, Major. Rue St. Martin. That's what the sign says. This is Rue St. Martin. What? The street on which Daguerre lived when the Academie honored him in 1839. Remember Daguerre? He was the man who lost his voice on the day he was to accept his honor. He could not speak and someone else had to do it for him. The people had waited from midnight till noon to gain entrance for the ceremony, a great event. Oh, indeed it was. The freezing of time is a serious event. Rendering the perishable permanent is a monumental event. It seizes the instant and impales it for posterity to touch forever and ever, providing enough care, enough regard, enough caution is shown.

His wrists were pressed against his outside pockets. He opened his fists. The fingers ached. He brought them up slowly, pressing, feeling his pockets. They were flat. Flat! All of them were flat. A rose is a rose is a crown of thorns, but a vacuum is less than nothing.

What have you lost? What are you looking for? I forget. Remember!

He was down on all fours. Your money is gone. Which does not matter. For some strange reason, he searched the cuffs of his trousers. The silver box. *You have lost the silver box.* This is Rue St. Martin where Daguerre once lived. You came here because the silver box is gone. Slow. You are looking for something you lost and you have forgotten again. What are you seeking here on all fours on a dirty sidewalk? Think! You seek yourself.

No, only a box.

Misplaced, forgotten, lost. This never happened when you wore a vest. But someone said don't wear a vest. *Ballot.* Jerk, square. Get hep. Wake up. Get wise. In sickness and in health. Laurie, I thank you for this moment. Not ours or yours. Mine, all mine.

He ran blindly. The café at St. Germain des Prés. An occasional light appeared and disappeared. A cab cruised. He hailed it, and named the café. When they were there he hunted among the upended chairs. Nothing. A box, a small flat box of tin with rubber inside. Try the Champs Elysées. He would recognize the café. The cab came around through the Tuileries, past Fouquet's. Then it followed him slowly as he walked. Dawn. Light. Nothing. He got back into the cab.

"Pigalle."

"Monsieur has lost something?"

"Pigalle!"

Forget time, forget place. Focus on object. The silver box. You walked here. This was the night spot. Closed. Across the wide gutter is the saloon. Also closed. He retraced his steps. Once again the cab followed. We walked up this way and down that and the man was behind us—"a remarkable motion picture of women and dogs. Amusing for the gentlemen"—Now, wait. Herb had his arm around your shoulder and for some reason your jacket was off. Can't remember why. That never happened when you wore a vest. There was the girl at the side street who misunderstood and from the shadows presumed to display. He was down on his hands and knees again.

Then, crouched as he was, he was crying, with one closed fist against the dirty sidewalk. His body trembled. He opened his hand and looked. Yes, the silver box. A miracle. He had found it. That won't happen twice.

The cab driver helped him to his feet. "Perhaps Monsieur would like to go back to his hotel?"

"I have no hotel and my money is gone. You see, during the night—" He was taking off his watch. "You may have this—"

The cab driver shook his head. "I can see Monsieur is a gentleman. There is no need."

Ken looked at his watch. "I flew in this morning from London. The bank opens at nine. If you will wait with me until then and pay for my breakfast. I am greatly in need of coffee."

"Monsieur is not well."

"That's so."

"I think perhaps if you slept. You can breakfast at my home."

In the small apartment, a broad, strong looking woman prepared breakfast. Ken splashed his face, neck, and chest with cold water. The cab driver spoke of the Resistance. Yes, he had been in the south. Lyons. Finally Grenoble, too. Ken saw his face in the mirror and turned from it quickly. Later when the cab driver awakened him it was close to noon. They went to the bank on the Champs Elysées and crossed the street to the travel bureau with enough francs to pay for his ticket and the cab fare—the driver would not accept any more. At last they were shaking hands at the airport.

"Too much of a holiday," the driver said.

Ken entered the airport terminal. His baggage would be forwarded on from London.

You removed your jacket for a reason. You were seeking something. Someone you wanted to call. He stood in the phone booth. Can you remember now? Perhaps this wasn't it. He was calling Grenoble. The numbers no longer existed, neither the home nor Angi's novelty store. At the Hotel Splendide, the manager was gone. The present manager had been an assistant manager then, and he *did* recall the girl. Her mother was dead. Her father was gone, so was she. No, he did not know where. The Mayor? Oh, yes. He was dead, too. Ken hung up. That wasn't the call. But the other call didn't matter. He heard his flight announced, saw the passenger agent leading a group of Americans down the ramp. He felt the silver box in his jacket pocket and hurried to catch up with them.

Ken had started by car from New York City early in the morning so as to drive in daylight all the way. He had not expected the snow storm that overtook him at Lake George this late in the year, and he lost time putting chains on his tires. By early evening he had reached Keene and further progress was impossible, despite frequent pauses on level ground for clearing ice off his windshield and rear window. His area of vision was finally reduced to a few feet, the needles of snow blinding him through the glass. Then the car spun on a hairpin curve, careened off the road, and struck a tree.

He walked north against the storm until he reached a farmhouse. The two brothers who owned it permitted Ken to phone the state police and Mr. Sands's surviving son, Ben. One of the brothers drove Ken the rest of the way in their snowmobile. They passed Lake Placid and Saranac, Paul Smith's and St. Regis. Before they reached St. Terese, the snowmobile stopped at a farmhouse where Ken saw Ben Sands holding the curtain back, as he peered from behind the half-frosted window.

Dinner was waiting. Ben's daughter, Clementine, served it. Her husband, Hank, who helped his father-in-law with their small farm and the caretaker duties for camps along St. Terese, made the fourth at the table.

"Those damn Beery brothers are crazy," Ben Sands said. "Never should have done it. You could have been killed. Fact is there was no reason for you to come at all." He spoke with a barely concealed resentment. "You want the place sold, I could have talked to agents, handled repairs, and readied it all by myself."

"There are personal things at St. Terese I wish to do."

"How much them Beery brothers charge you?"

"Twenty dollars."

"I'd'a done it for ten."

"I didn't know you had a snowmobile."

"You can't handle the camps on the lake without one."

Clementine's eyes smiled at Ken and she gave the slightest shrug.

"Will we be able to get to St. Terese tomorrow?"

Ben Sands looked at him a moment with amazement. "You'll be lucky to get there next week. It's a long, late winter. The lake ice is half froze, half wet. You can't use boat nor snowmobile and there's no way to reach your camp by land."

"With a few of Brooks's men, we could try to hack a way through at the neck near the mainland," Hank said.

"Yeah," Mr. Sands said grudgingly. "We could try."

"I'll pay whatever it's worth to you," Ken said. He rose from the table. "I should like to leave as soon as possible. Could you put me up for the night? Otherwise I suppose I could get in at the country club."

"Country club's closed and Pa's room's empty." Ben Sands seemed mollified. "Clementine here will fix it up."

"You can warm up by the fireplace," Clementine said, "till I've done the dishes. If you're too tired, I'll do Grandpa's room first."

"I'll wait," Ken said.

He sat before the fireplace, reflecting on the degree of detachment he felt when the car began spinning, and indeed his total absence of interest before that as the whining, ice-laden windshield wipers kept giving ground. He set himself against what lay behind the indifference, and felt the bosom pocket of his jacket. The letter was still there. It was a habit of late, expecting to lose things, even unpleasant ones like this letter from Howard Leach, Attorney: "Re Mrs. Laura Dugan Preston versus Kenneth Fenimore Preston," it began, and then went on to say, "Mrs. Preston has forwarded yours of the fifth inst. with instructions to advise you of her continuing intention to sue for divorce. She will establish residence here in Reno immediately after Commencement Exercises, which I am told is now only a matter of some few weeks away."

Clementine appeared and before Ken could help her, she pulled aside the fire screen, lifted a heavy log, and with accurate aim, threw it into place on the fire. "Those Beery brothers sure are crazy," she said. She straightened her lean, well-formed body. Neither the apron nor the housedress could conceal its young, strong line.

"Last year they heard folks were fishing their pond on the north end where they couldn't see from the house. So they tore down a wall and replaced it with a big picture window. Then they took turns sitting at it with a gun. The first trespasser who ever showed up was scared half to death when he heard that gun go off!" She removed the apron. "You can follow me and wash up if you like. Only take me a few minutes." Ken nodded, rose, and followed her up the stairs. She was a few steps above him. Ken kept his eyes turned down.

"Fella who sells them fuel oil says the bill comes to $25.01 a month. Each brother makes out half, taking turns at the odd cent. Every once in a while the delivery men keep it even. Then they let the odd cent turn up again just to see if the right brother remembers whose turn it is. Would you believe it? They never forget."

She opened the bedroom door. No wonder Mr. Sands had preferred to spend Sundays and days off at St. Terese. This was much too small a room for anyone. Strange that neither Mother nor Father nor even he when he took over had visited the place where Mr. Sands lived, in all those years.

As Ken unpacked, Clementine took two pillows from the top shelf of the narrow closet, stretching for them. Her skirt rose. Then she turned and dropped the pillows on the bed and smoothed her skirt down, her hands lingering a moment over her thighs.

"How's Mrs. Preston?" she asked.

"Fine," he answered.

"Good thing she's not with you." The bed was no bigger than a cot. "Mattress is pretty hard," she said. She sat down and bounced for a moment. She had sat so that from where he stood he loomed over her. She pulled up her neckline at the shoulders. When she rose, Ken stepped back.

"We're separated," Ken said.

"I heard. Anything else I can do for you?"

"No, thanks."

"I'll be up for a while if you need anything. My room's that one across the hall, down by the stairs if you want something later."

"Thank you."

"Pity you're selling the camp. It's the nicest one on the lake."

"Oh? I wasn't aware you'd seen it."

She smiled. It gave her face a heart-shaped look. There was a level, sharp brightness in her eyes. "I've been going to St. Terese every year since I was six. That's seventeen years ago." She added, "And every summer after you left, I used your boat on the lake till Gramps once slapped me for it." She was challenging him to dislike it.

"He shouldn't have."

"I was twelve. Anyway, the next summer I started working at the country club."

"Yes. I recall his mentioning you were there four years ago."

"Two years ago. From my freshman year in high school till I married Hank." She hesitated over something. "Gramps once slapped my face after I grew up. *That* was four years ago."

Ken tried to visualize Mr. Sands, removing his hard straw hat to scratch his bald head, and the way his eyes would fill up with tears for no reason toward the end, slapping the rebellious young woman standing before him. It was difficult.

"Because I wanted to tell you something," she explained. "And he thought I was ungrateful to your bride."

"Oh?"

"It was my first year on the elevators. When you came on your honeymoon. I didn't know what Mrs. Preston looked like except later when I saw her again in town the next day. Then I knew it was the same one."

Ken stood frowning at her in the narrow space between cot and wall, like someone accosted on the street by a lunatic stranger, waiting for the unhappy moment to pass.

Clementine's eyes were very bright now and she held her face tilted up. It was a pretty face with well-formed features and a clear, unblemished skin. "Someone rang, on the second floor, and I opened the door. Right then I turned and saw this lady, bare, as Gramps would say. I mean up here." She touched her breasts. "With her lip rouge smeared all over her face. She was smiling. Then this big lug comes to the door wearing a kind of silk bathrobe wide open with nothing on underneath. After he shuts the door, she stops smiling and gets around to covering up out in the hall and wipes her face. There was nothing under that blouse, believe me. Of course, Gramps didn't. Believe me, I mean. Next day I saw her with you. Then Gramps brought me this bundle of used bras, step-ins, slips, and dresses and I told him it took more than secondhand goods to bribe me. So he slapped me." She moved forward. Ken leaned against the cot and she walked toward the door. "I thought if you were even half what Gramps said, how rough a deal can a nice guy get? I'm telling you because I know you're leaving her anyway and it doesn't matter to you anymore. Besides, it's good to get it off my chest." She stopped and took a breath. "If you want anything at all, just let me know."

"I doubt that I will but if I do, I'll let you know, thanks."

"You do that," she said. Hostility and invitation were still in her eyes.

He shut the door, looked at the small bed in the small room and wished again that he had known about it sooner. Poor Mr. Sands. His son said you didn't have to come at all to put St. Terese up for sale. You came to remove the personal things; to prevent their exposure to strangers' eyes and hands. He walked to the window. The icy needles of driving snow aimed straight for the light behind him, and brought back the hypnotic compulsion to continue driving into it. He pulled the shade down. You and Mr. Sands once tried to hack your way through at the neck of the peninsula: that was the time Laurie went to New York. It was hardly likely that Ben Sands, his son-in-law, and some hired hands would be able to do for money what you and Mr. Sands had not been able to do out of love. The door was sprung and he couldn't lock it. He lay there for the wakeful hours, looking up at the small light that hung from the middle of the ceiling and swayed in the wind that crept through the cracks round the window casement.

In the morning it was still hard to believe that May was well on its way, even though the snow storm had stopped and the chunky greenness of the pines peered cheerfully through the white blanket.

Outside the front porch, Ken saw tiny footprints and claw marks that left an even impression as they ran past the door round the house. He followed them, wondering what newborn creature they belonged to. Not a raccoon: they remain blind for the first six weeks. It was too far south for a wildcat. Perhaps a skunk or a fox. The trail stopped at the kitchen door. It was a fully grown squirrel, doing battle with another squirrel over two slices of white bread that lay on the outside mat. Their chests were puffed out to twice their normal size: they emitted ferocious, deafening cries as they circled one another to collide, and leap apart, never biting, clawing, or striking. It was a ritual dance done to piercing screams. The one that looked and sounded most formidable was the winner. Through the kitchen window, Ken saw Clementine sitting on a chair, watching, her knees crossed, her dress high above them. He nodded and turned his head away. Doing so, he caught a passing glimpse of the barn. Half inside it sat a rat. Its little eyes darted, missing nothing as the battle continued. Finally one squirrel charged the other, made it roll over and scramble to its feet and then race away up the snow-covered tree. The winner chased him, chattering threats from the ground as it looked up. By the time it had returned for the spoils, both slices of bread were gone and with them the patient rat.

Clementine opened the door. "They give me a charge," she said. "Never learn anything, so the rat always wins. It beats me."

Her silk dress seemed a bit premature in view of the weather outside.

"Your breakfast is ready," she said.

Ken walked up the stairs. She held the door open in a manner that conveyed mock servility.

"In the kitchen?" he asked.

"Heavens, no. That was Pop's idea. He's just a farmer, I'm afraid. So's my husband." She led him to the alcove. "At least it's a kitchenette," she said. "Pa and Hank are over to the mainland with Mr. Brooks."

"How is Mother Brooks?" Ken asked.

"Died a week after Christmas." She put down the warmed plate, hot biscuits, jam, and butter. "We don't have much choice but whatever it is, is fresh." She smiled. "Eggs? Flapjacks? Ham? Pressed chicken?"

"Just this and the coffee will be fine, thank you."

"Not long on appetites, are you?" She looked out the window. "The sun's warm. I walked down to the river this morning. Swollen with melting ice."

He ate part of one biscuit, drank his coffee, dabbed at his mouth quickly with the napkin, and rose. "When do you expect your father?"

"He and Hank won't be back for quite a while. Anyway, they'll phone first."

"I see. In that case, I'll go for a walk."

"I'll show you the way to the river."

"That won't be necessary, thanks. I'm sure I'll find it."

"I have nothing else to do."

"Thanks, no," Ken said. He faced her. "I said no, Clementine. Thank you, but no. I'll be back here in time for lunch." He looked at his watch. It was eight. "At noontime. Say between twelve and twelve-thirty. If that's inconvenient, I can find a place in town."

"It's not inconvenient." Her tone had altered to a chastened sadness. "I'm just trying to help, that's all."

"I appreciate it," Ken said.

As he went down the front stairs, she appeared at the door and called out, "It's a hundred yards to your left when you hit the state road and then right on the old foot bridge. The road's slippery."

Ken nodded without turning his head. He heard the door slam sharply behind him.

"Pa called," she told him at lunch. "He says you won't be able to get through today, that's sure."

"Was he at the Brooks' dock?"

"No, they close out after skiing and don't open till the ice melts off the lake. That's another week or two."

"I don't suppose there's a spare car here?"

"No," she said. "Pa and Hank will be home around dinner time. I don't guess you could help them any."

He frowned. "Can I get a cab? I'd like to go into town and speak to the real estate people."

She gave him the phone number of the cab service. "See the river?" she asked.

"Yes. Most of the ice is still frozen hard." He recalled the smell of frost and ice, dead leaves, and hay blown from lofts. The sky had been crystal clear and a car had appeared suddenly on the narrow country road, its driver ignoring the Go Slow sign. His front wheels were caught helplessly on solid ice and the car had skidded toward Ken, who cleared the fence. In that instant he saw the driver's face, the smile still frozen on it: no doubt he had been paying more attention to the funny story told him by the person next to him than to his driving. Along with the smile was the terror. It had all taken less than a second, including the narrow escape and the sight of the storyteller trying with trembling hands to light a cigarette.

"Take more than one day to thaw *that* out." A tone of defiance was still in her voice. "Dinner will be ready at six o'clock."

The cab took Ken to town where he saw the three real estate brokers, solicited their opinions as to possible price range, and offered nonexclusive authorization which only two of them accepted. Then he walked to the Brooks's boat dock fronting on Lake St. Terese. It was boarded up. The boats were hoisted on chains. The road leading from it to the peninsula was far too deep in snow and thick with ice. Attempting it in his city shoes and suit was impossible. He walked back into town wondering why there had seemed so much of it in the spring, summer, fall, or at the height of skiing time. A time between times. Yours. A state of suspension but no mystery now. Clementine was ugly in an attractive way, inviting if a slut could be, but too obvious for such subtle lying. Clearly that *is* what happened four years ago. Perhaps when you have finished your unfinished business it will not matter: meanwhile you may work at putting its shadow to rest.

If it was ridiculous to say that love destroyed a man, it was just as ridiculous to say that not the newness of love for a young and almost honest young woman, but the only world you knew destroyed you.

Everything was ridiculous. Both trying to forget and remembering.

At the river this morning the sun struck a melted stretch and glinted on the rocks beneath, and it brought back the dazzle of sunlight through a locker-room window at a beach somewhere north of the Bronx. Muriel—the towel held between you. It came back as vividly as though it were not thirty years ago and was connected somehow with mistakes made by others for which you paid. Why does everyone have to blame his mistakes on someone? Or for that matter, discover exactly why one made them and blame oneself? One way, you were absolved of error, the other the pain of remorse finally became sufficiently unbearable so that by escaping it you also escaped the fact of the mistake. But either way the consequences remained and it would seem you have learned nothing.

When he returned to the farm, Clementine wore a housecoat and her hair was piled high up on her head. There was a towel around her shoulders.

"You're early," she said. "The fire's out in the parlor but I can get one going right quick."

"I'll do it myself."

He was putting a match to the kindling when she entered the room, still in her housecoat, and stopped with one leg forward of the other. From where he knelt, he could see the receding whiteness and firm, well-formed shape.

"Pa and Hank are eating at Brooks's place," she said. "He can't help them tomorrow so they got flare torches from the ski jump house. They figure to be finished by eleven o'clock tonight."

"I see."

"Means you can leave tomorrow, maybe. That sun's going to go right on shining. All that snow and ice should be melted down. I can mix you a drink if you like."

"No, thanks. But if there's hot water, I would like a bath."

"You better let me collect my undies and get my hairs out of the tub. There's only one." The smile was not on her lips: it was behind her eyes. She turned and left.

There is nothing wrong with this girl and a good deal that's right. She's neither old nor ugly. She isn't hustling or seeking to confirm her attractiveness. Without sentimentality, she just *is*. Without investing that with unreal things, she offers her youth and energy. No sweet, wild music: nor the melancholy that lives behind them either, like a sickness. Accept the invitation. Be like the donkey, the horse— see the hay that hangs before you. Wear blinders and cling to the literal connection between A and B, snout and hay, the thing pursuing and the thing pursued. Unfortunately man has an imagination and he must learn to ignore it. Tell yourself whatever you must: when you lose this capacity for self-hypnosis, you have lost your capacity for life itself and I have already told you—

Clementine was back at the door. "Clean as an operating room now," she said, and disappeared.

Ken sat in the bathtub, letting the water run as hot as he could bear it. When he looked up at the rod parallel to the tub, he saw that there was no towel. Suddenly he felt quite ridiculous. At the door he realized he didn't even know her last name. Hank something. Mrs. hank-of-hair something or other. Formerly Sands' granddaughter. "Clementine?"

She appeared and he closed the bathroom door somewhat but not until he had seen the mocking humor in her eyes.

"Can I do something for you?"

"You might get me a towel."

"Oh, yes, a towel. I'm sorry. Bring it right in. I mean right to you."

She handed the towel through to him and kept her hand there, the palm up an amused and charming gesture of inquiry and invitation. He stood looking at the hand, the slender wrist, forearm, and greedy fingers. There was no evidence of a sleeve. *And then with the dazzling sun shining in his eyes, he saw Muriel drop the towel.* In the light of everything, what difference could it possibly make? He opened the door and they stood facing each other. Quite incredibly she turned away, embarrassed.

"I guess you think I'm some kind of a whore."

"Is that what you want me to think?"

"I don't care what you think." Her head was still turned away. "I love my husband. Marriage is more than sex or bearing children. Except if a man thinks they're his, he gives them the same love as if they were. No one would know but me and I don't care."

She saw the tension go out of Ken as he started to laugh.

"What's so darn funny?"

He picked up the bath towel and wrapped it round his waist, tucking one end under. "You little freak," he said. "Is that the point behind all this campaigning?"

"I don't have any point and yours is gone."

He took her by the shoulder. "Was all this a deliberate plan? Do I understand that your husband is sterile? Is that it?"

He felt her tremble under his hand.

She looked up at him. "There is no plan, Mr. Preston, no idea. I've been cooped up here all winter, a long winter. He's undersexed and thinks he's a great lover. I don't want to hurt him by saying he isn't. I love him and you send me a charge. Is that a crime?"

He shook her. "Sterility and impotence are two different things. Even you can understand that difference. Now which is it?"

"Who said it was either? I just want you to do it something awful. Anyway I did."

She wrenched herself loose. He watched the back of her naked body as she strode off and into her room. Her housecoat lay on the floor outside the bathroom door.

He sat in his room until she knocked on his door and said quite distantly, "Dinner is ready."

She was wearing a woolen dress.

"I should like to say that—"

"Some men don't talk enough. Others too much. Try not saying anything."

He placed his hand on her shoulder.

"You planning to manhandle me again?"

He removed his hand. "Clementine, you must understand, surely. I am in your father's house. He and your husband are working for me, as your grandfather did. You're a charming, attractive, beautiful young lady."

"Don't tell me, Mr. Preston, that you're going to seduce me after all?"

Afterward, her head on his shoulder under the covers, she said, "When I got married, I got pretty. That couldn't have happened if it wasn't a good marriage, could it?"

"Certainly not."

"I tease most men and then let them go soak it in water. But you don't make me have a chip on my shoulder. Those pigs who come up here skiing in winter and golfing in the summer. They're all so damned obvious. You're not really over her, are you?"

"I suppose I still love my wife."

There they were, lying in each other's arms, met yesterday, protesting their love for the people they were married to and weren't with. Most likely there's no answer to any riddle because all of us are insane.

"When is your birthday?" she asked.

"It was. April Fool. Why? Does it show?"

"Oh, God." She sat up, suddenly gloomy. "I might have known. April first. That's Aries, the ram, and I'm Cancer. We're incompatible this week."

He felt himself on the verge of laughter. "I suppose your husband was born at the right time?"

"Yes. You and your ram." She bit his arm gently. "Ever hear Mary had a little sheep?"

"No. Is that part of zodiac litany?"

"Everyone laughs at astrology till they know more about it. It's just a little twist on the old nursery rhyme."

"All nursery rhymes could stand a twist."

"You know how it goes, Mary had a little lamb. Well the way *this* goes, Mary had a little sheep. She took it with her one night to sleep. The sheep turned out to be a ram. Now Mary has a little lamb." She placed her small hands on his shoulders and sat up, leaning over him. "Don't be mad, Mr. Preston, but I do hope you made me pregnant. That's not why I did it but I still hope you did. I believe in blood lines—when you live on a farm, you know it's true. A kid of yours would be smart and strong and well put together. He'd have no fear."

Ken sat up and started to laugh. "I'm not mad at you," he said. "But you couldn't be more wrong on any and every score. Not possibly."

It had been raining all night. When he woke, there was still no sign of let-up. The earth had a reddish hue from the glistening, soaking dead leaves. Wind shook the young evergreens. Snow had melted in the small valley where the farmhouse stood. Water was running across the road outside the house and dripping from the trees and eaves. Ken dressed quickly, hurried down the stairs and out the front door. He had no desire to face them or her. The knowledge that he might be able to get to St. Terese today made him impatient to do so, find what he sought, and leave. They were to phone him when they were ready and a cab would pick him up. Two hours at the most. He was not hungry.

He wore his country shoes now and an old raincoat and walked swiftly through the puddles and rain until he reached the old road parallel to the river. Streams had appeared in new places. The one that had trickled through the ice yesterday to disappear under the road and re-emerge at the river's edge no wider than a finger now boiled and rushed, a caldron of white water filling a twenty-foot wide basin below the road and just this side of the river's edge. It churned up earth and rocks, carrying them to the river in a muddy gush. When the river was still frozen there had been shallows despite the previous snow storm: a full ten-foot drop from the banks above to the river. Now the wild water was lapping at the top soil. The yellow stalks that had been held in the embrace of the domes of ice shaped like gigantic petals now lay flat, wet, and matted. Much of it had been ripped away and carried by the current.

Ken walked down river. The moss bank that had stood three feet above was now submerged. There was no shore. The land was overrun. The frenzied force and violence of the river had destroyed all boundaries. It rushed close to the road where he walked. Its eddies and currents swirled and slapped the trunks of tall trees, ripped the bark and dislodged stones. The bridge crossing was submerged and a tree felled by the stream straddled it below waterline, its roots, partly visible, clutching at the air like the fingers of the drowned. There was the steady rumble and thunder of huge rocks pulled by the current and punctuating like shots each time they struck one another below the surface. Everywhere trees stood naked against the deluge, disfigured with splotches of sickly green winter moss and lichens from which fat beads of water dripped. Trees that were rubbed raw of all bark but still alive gleamed a livid, wet orange which turned abruptly black where frost and storm had amputated branches. The roots of some trees were partly exposed like raw nerves that still clung tenaciously to the soil. Dead ones without room to fall lay across those that had withstood the winter. The river ran brown: even its whitecaps were muddy. When the foam was lifted from its surface and lashed about by the wind, it turned white like the flecks that flew from the jowls of mad dogs. Rivulets ran swiftly alongside the road carrying dislodged topsoil and thousands of dead leaves catapulted from the hill above. The wind had turned warm but remained wild, driving sprays of water parallel to the earth, a low, fast-racing mist. Chunks of ice ripped from their hiding places had been tossed, pummeled, and melted to join the torrents that flooded the arable earth. Only at the underside of the road, shielded above by woods and facing the north was there still ice, thick and grimed with dirt, more like stone than frozen water.

Monuments. Walking into the wind, Ken recalled France and the tribute to the dead by the living. Later in the less inflamed hours, it would appear to be a costly gesture. But not then: not in the dead of night, the stealth of danger, the food of rebellion, as they built their monuments to their martyrs and then risked death again by placing flowers on these monuments. It had seemed necessary. It *was* necessary. Without it, caution and tranquillity were only surrender. He paused, standing in the midst of violence, surveying the carnage of battle, its nameless wounded and dead unmasked by frost and thaw, stark, twisted, snakelike with leaves chewed, ground, and spat by ice, frost, and wind, millions upon millions pulverized into the earth as the thundering patches of ice were drawn ever further west in the fast-moving, red, and muddy water. In the howl of the wind, he heard nature's cry for peace. The need to get to St. Terese was almost more than he could bear.

Ken was awakened by the *bida-beet, bida-beet, bida-beet-beet-beet* of a distant bird on the island west of his patio. He dressed quickly and went outside. It was still early morning but the slim dogwood tree and its slender branches were already shining copper-colored in the rising sun, the long, lean buds swelling. A hummingbird's nest still sat intact in the topmost branch from the past summer. It was wet and dripping. Even on St. Terese where the ice and snow clung longer, they had all but vanished.

He had declined the proffered services of Clementine, her husband, or father and tended the house himself. He chopped logs and cooked meals. What had begun as a stay of one day had drawn into weeks, during which he had supervised and planned repairs.

He alone had the keys to Father's workhouse and the desk inside it. Yesterday the carpenters had finally gone. Ken headed for the wooded section that had once prevented the sun from reaching the no longer existing original house and kept the workhouse cool. Here beards of ice still clung to branches and rocks.

He opened the door and stood at the entrance. You sat at that desk one summer day after picking up your lunch on the main house porch and gloated that you were happy. Later that day, a butterfly opened its dark, velvet-green wings and poised its slim, golden, yellow-green body on a leaf of the lilac bush, a mirage of sun and shadow like its resting place. Then a cool breeze filtered the hot sun and blew through the young maple so that it swayed and bent while each separate leaf shivered in a silvery green dance of ecstasy. So at last you stopped working and went back to the house for Laurie because it was a day more suited to reading the leaves than writing on dull yellow pages. You investigated the apple and peach trees, the berry bushes approaching ripening. It had all been part of a general deceit.

He went to the desk and removed drafts of the papers he had written that summer. There were letters from Coogan, from Preston & Company in the summers that followed. He threw them all into the fireplace. In the bottom drawer he found a letter in his hand-writing. Strange he had not seen it before. It had been caught between the drawer and a shaft. To Laurie? "Confidence abounds every-where," it read. "The first broadcast was thrilling and I was proud when General Eisenhower said that the underground resistance was organized and ready. Please don't worry." To Mother. Sounds more like husband to wife. She was not very much of either. He threw it into the fireplace, too. Father's file: the beginning of WHIP. After its end, Mother had brought up the subject of so and so who had just returned from Paris, having sold all his stock by sheer accident before the crash of '29 to chase, catch, and stay with some girl on the Left Bank. Now he was back, buying at bottoms and about to marry a *good* girl, one he *really* loved. When she left the room, Ken's face must have betrayed him because Father had said, "Son, when you envy your betters, you just widen the gap and when you envy inferiors, you close it."

Father had closed all gaps. He set his mind against itself and kneeling, hunted the open, empty drawers. That was all of it. There in Father's hand in ink lay the cold facts, potentials, and personalities who might promote a project based on power and light. It was Father's note, written to whom? Himself. "To bring light and power into places where they were not is God's work. For God made the light and it was good."

Ken put it gently in the fireplace. Then he could not find a match. He went to the main house and returned with matches. They were damp. He went back again. This time he found dry ones. A past within a past, an Eden in which the original sin had indeed proved to be ignorance so that when you returned to New York your past and hers, her family and yours, your separate failures and mutual omissions had led to disaster. The greater one's capacity for surprise, the higher the ecstasy. Also the lower the descent.

He set fire to the papers. The smoke descended to the stones and pushed out into the room. He bent, opened the flue, and watched the flames rise. Then he left.

This was the first of the necessary deeds. That and the divorce. Now the sale of St. Terese. Then closing down Caleb and offering it to the State of Maine as a public museum for the summers. The board meeting of Preston Public Funds would take place early in July, and with it, your resignation. Then learn to take what each day offers.

Facing north, the thin coatings of lichens and green moss had begun to fade. The lake itself was still agitated and beat against the shores. Tight red buds of the soft maple were forming in the smallest of clusters. In the days and weeks ahead, the long, thin, silky fingers would stretch, thicken, grow, as would all the others, each briefly revealing the color it would have at death before taking on an anonymous greenness as buds opened and leaves, blossoms, and fruit ultimately matured. Yesterday the forsythia branches were still gray and barren. Now they were turning a greenish gold, their swelling buds pushing inexorably to burst into bloom.

He heard the sound of a motor. Mr. Brooks was headed for the dock, delivering *Silver Box II.* He smiled his whimsical, apologetic smile and pronounced the lake safe for navigation.

"I heard about your mother," Ken said.

"That's right." A warm recollection woke behind Mr. Brooks's eyes. "It happened in her sleep."

"I was out of touch."

"Yes. Mother liked Mr. Arthur the few times he came. We wrote you."

They stood a moment.

"Seems a pity to sell St. Terese," Mr. Brooks said, "just when it's become part of the mainland, so to speak."

He got into the outboard, untied it, and drove off.

They had not mentioned Laurie.

Ken went out on the lake, examining the shore line for damage. No other camp was open yet. The absence of inhabitants gave him a strange and satisfied feeling. From the island that faced his patio, came the donkeylike *"ee aw ee aw"* sound of a bird. Ken smiled, stopped the motor, and listened. The symphony of sounds surrounded him, floating over the water. When the boat drifted too close to shore, he started the motor and kept it at a low purr. He docked and walked through the neck to the mainland where his car, fully repaired, was parked.

He had turned in on a side road nearest the river. All that remained now to remind one of the late winter was a thin ribbon of snow at the top of the highest hill, like a crown above the yellowing fields. The waters had drained from the bottom land. The straw was now stiff and glued into matted clusters. It reminded him of Tess, the drunken gorgeous identical twin, when she lay drugged in her alcoholic sleep. Currents broke every which way round rocks where the river was deep. Where it was shallow, the sun played on sand, pebbles, and small stones, making them gleam like gold dust. No spring birds were in sight yet on the mainland and that was curious for some had already landed at St. Terese where they always came last.

As a jet plane broke the sound barrier, Ken looked up to see its thin swath of white cut gracefully through the startling blue. The ferment of but two weeks ago had been reduced to small bubbles of foam and a minor spilling over of blue water where the river narrowed and bulged with the stones fallen into it from the hill. A last piece of ice floated round the bend from up-river. As he watched it approach, it thinned and disappeared.

Traces of convalescence were everywhere. The tarred road with its long, fine cracks kept oozing water. The buds of forsythia and lilac were as yet puny where only the eastern sun poured through. There was freeze underneath the mud and muck of oozing earth. Further down in the valley from the sudden warmth there was fog. He walked through it and came out at the other end, to be greeted by a blackbird singing its high-pitched, croaking song and the low warbling of wild canaries perched in young evergreens flecked with the gold of the sun. On his way back, with its rays in his eyes, the river's cascades formed rainbows.

Looking down, he saw a doll's bridge, three feet long, stretched across evenly cut strips of maple, the proper length for kindling. How had it survived? Then he drove into town to keep his appointment with the real estate broker who believed he had found a prospective buyer. Ken answered his questions in an absent-minded way. The broker told him his customer was expected to come up in person within two weeks. Ken controlled surprise at his regret. "I'll be gone by then," he said tonelessly.

Tomorrow the prospective buyer would appear. Tonight, Ken would be leaving. He had refused to consider additional repairs suggested by the agent. They would improve the drain system that ran along the sides of the main house roof but they would also alter its appearance. As a result, water still fell from it in fat drops on the back stairs.

Ken had not stopped to reckon what these weeks had done for him or to him. Now that the time had come to leave, he was aware that once again he was responsive to the small things outside, the fragrance of pines, the cleaner look of the earth, the difference between millions of chopped-up evergreen sprigs that lay dead and the short, new grass, alive and growing. Yesterday a flock of ducks flying low had passed him on their way further north. This morning yellow warblers had arrived to make their home in the big birdhouse between his front porch and the dock back of the lawn. St. Terese was alive with song, the bright *whar, whar, reep peep beep,* the deep throated *chu chip! chu chip!* an infinite variety of young, new, delicate sounds, untried and joyous, announcing that all the birds had at last arrived from the south. A dove cooed softly in the tree at his window.

His last day. He had traveled the entire lake in his boat. Now he docked at the mainland.

"Last night I heard peepers," Mr. Brooks said and smiled with a gladness he knew needed no explaining.

That was how it happened. The world hangs suspended. Then all at once each thing emerges with a tempo of its own, and you know it was never dead, only sleeping. Tiny trickles become currents. Currents submerge in rivers. Rivers reach the sea. Gray branches turn green, buds stretch thin fingers to assume small knobs that unfold into lush greenness. The tatters and remnants of winter are gone. In his car he passed picket fences defenselessly exposed, their battered slats in need of mending, hammering, and painting. There were patches where topsoil was gone and debris that needed removing. But the juices were aflow again and dead leaves fertilized live shoots.

He realized he had driven back to the river. It was no longer stained. Everything had an eager air. He needed to use his own legs even if he had no destination. He stopped motionless, his hand on the half-open door of his car, as a young doe appeared on the road, looked up and down, then cleared a fence with its hind legs high over its back.

He had not realized how hungry his eyes were for space and brightness, green, blue, brown, and gold, or his ears for the sound of the easy running water and the thoughtless cry of birds, his nostrils for the smell of sap, grass, and growth. His brain had been clogged for years with the veal gray death of the city's concrete. You are participating in spring instead of only observing it. Have you forgotten? No matter how well he remembered stern warnings, hunger rose in his mind, blood, heart, limbs, and spirit, as it did that morning worlds away in '44 in the Alps when despite the night's dead, he had awakened to a sense of promise. You have lived since then. You have heard the *pouree pouree* of birds through many seasons and seen promises turn to dust. Are you a puppy who needs only to smell the wind? Does it take this little to lead you afield? You know better. Or worse. But truer. If there is a purpose to viewing nature at all, it is neither for escape nor entrancement but simply because man-made society is one of thousands on earth and who knew how many hundreds of thousands in that universe of which we are most certainly *not* the center. We only dominate one small ball among many and thus far our custodianship, ability, and devotion leave so much, in fact too much to be desired at all. The source material confirms what man's makeshifts show: beguile and betrayal, senseless, defenseless repetition. *God made the light and it was good.* So the myth says! *Exerted His cosmic power: flexed His muscles of lightning and banished evil.* So says the myth, and Father ran singing his madness in its name to his death. Truth. Repetition. A treadmill. A repetitive charade from the first body song of Muriel in the bathhouse at the city beach and that next night in St. Mary's Park near where she lived, to Laurie. First days, first nights. Also last ones. The first day Muriel dropped her towel and cried against you till you were almost willing to forgo. Then, as you pulled away, she clutched and you knew that she cried

because she had learned a deeper, more fervent lesson than the words
written, printed, or imposed by those who had passed spring's young
sweet, unreclaimable time. Hunger and tears, laughter and youth and
then your betrayal of her or hers of you. But only after that first day
of love like the first one of creation when the spirit is truly made
flesh and the myth made real. With her tiny dots of breasts needing
your touch, her face shining with desire—what matter how or why
anyone betrayed? She learned who you were *and why hadn't you
told her and what was there to tell and do you expect me to believe
you intend to marry me?* By the time Mother and Father had finished with you, indeed *did* you? But first the towel fell, her eyes
dropped, tears rolled, her hair hung to her shoulders, and below she
enveloped you as your arms enveloped her above. That which could
not help but last forever, did not. Laurie's love which also could not
help but last forever, did not. As your love for Muriel hadn't, and
your love for Laurie wouldn't. But it never starts there: it starts like
this, with the lure into agonizing repetition.

How many songs and how many springs must mislead you with
senseless sound of infinite variety, as empty of meaning as the wind,
before you learn in a permanent way? *"My song has put off her
adornments, she has no pride of dress or decoration,"* simply means
that the man with the white, flowing beard, gentle brown eyes, and
long, sensitive face, who sat in your living room a thousand repetitions
ago, looking into your eyes, where he saw your heart's first wound,
was himself a child or a sainted idiot. At your request, he repeated
his naive song:

> "I take pride in this great wall and I plaster
> It with dust and sand lest a least hole
> Should be left in this name
> And for all the care I take I lose sight of
> My true being."

But you blasted the walls. You did throw away the name. You took
your chances. You sought your true being. Like the children he sang
of, you had your play on the seashore of worlds and cared not
whether you knew how to swim or cast nets, dive for pearls or sail
ships. Here in this very place, with your heart in your hands a second
time, a hundredth time, the only true gift you had to offer, you fool-
ishly offered and it was not enough. No matter how pleasantly sleepy,
or pink her ears, and taut the nipples of her breasts, how searching-
ingly hungry her hands: despite the emblem over the fireplace and
how soberly she asked and accepted its sacred meaning, as you trans-

lated from the French, "Here reigns love," it was not enough. Love reigned here with impatience and restlessness. It was not enough, as it never is. You dragged your nets. It was Natalie who said, "Love is not like war. To win you must surrender." Failing to surrender with Muriel, you lost. Not deigning to surrender with Natalie, you lost again. So this time you did surrender and for it Laurie destroyed your manhood by making you prove it, which is the surest way to do so, especially when it is done in the sweet name of love. Perhaps men who are unquestioningly adored by their women give largesse, not love, in return, because they are pampered and spoiled. But their manhood remains intact and they remain faithful. The ridiculous pollution of philandering is an act of self-doubt and in every spasm of confirmation, doubt is born anew. Women signaled invitations only to men who were no longer faithful. So in a world of poor choices, the better one is Clementine. In that inverted, backward, twisted, distorted thing you cannot express, Clementine or enough women like her may restore what Laurie took, and in time you will forget.

But we agreed that forgetting is not the way.

Yes, we agreed and this is not a chess game! We agreed, but to stay the observer, to hold yourself intact at all requires forgetting at one time and remembering at another. That is how one bears the prospect of living. Clementine gave no more thought to your lifting her skirts than she would to picking wild flowers. If her eyes clouded it was only with excitement. If her hands followed the line of you, it was not with reverence but simply as a small child fondles presents. When it was over, she spoke briskly of food. Except for some playful, light-hearted reminders, it might all have been just a good game of tennis. That vital drop of mercury, of magic, and the poison of participation that changed all this was what we were pleased to call love. If love was not like war, surely the consequences of surrender remained the same. You found them on a dirty sidewalk in Paris where you sought to find yourself. Repetitions aplenty. Pick one. Any one. The roaring twenties and the stammering fifties. A rose is a rose by any other name or game is just, *mot juste,* defeat. Repeat: *defeat.* Don't forget the seventies after the Civil War and another lost generation found by Henry Adams and William James. If there was none after the Spanish American War, that was only because not enough Americans were killed or made rich. As for '76 and 1812, one and the same: in a war of founding and finding a nation, the loss of one generation more or less could hardly be missed. Once for union, twice to make the world safe for democracy. A third time ought to do us in.

The ultimate in what is specifically private, love, and the ultimate in what is public for private and general alike: war. Anything else? Your father repeating his father repeating his father repeating back to the first Ken Preston, a cabin boy and the lash, and forward to the last Ken Preston, wasting the best of himself on WHIP.

Once you had come to terms with the comfortless hypothesis of an accidental universe in which man improvised certain makeshifts. Now you know that there is order after all and so much the worse that there is. For at its core is repetition. Even this moment is repetition. Every word of it has been said before and better. "Life is a tale told by an idiot." *"Thus spake Zarathustra* of the eternal return of all things." Men in all centuries and places have exposed and refused to accept this shell game. Those who do otherwise are as dumbly and obediently inhuman as rocks, twigs, and the wind.

Last night you woke to the magic of a first spring moonlight and walked out on the dock to feel the cold air touch your skin. You saw the shimmer of stars in the still water. Far to the west at the island, a low mist hung and wisps of it tread mysteriously away upon the water. The moon's round, silvery face lay motionless in the dark mirror at your feet. All at once you remembered that to see a dream you must look down, standing at the edge of doom. But you still forgot that the moon itself is a dead, cold place from which the rays of the sun are only reflected. In that pellucid pool you only saw the reflection of a reflection, the death of a death, the ghost of a ghost, the true face of a dream. Toss a stone into its bosom and you shatter all of it into the convulsed particles of bedlam. We never touch more than shadows. We mirror-read our sleepwalking way through existence, repeating and repeating and once again repeating. Another night of moonlight. Laurie at your side. Mist on the lake, the northern lights fracturing the sky and you are transported. You cleave to what comics call your "better half" without which one cannot be rendered *whole* as spelled by McBride. After Laurie, Tess and the nameless creatures, Florida and Paris. Now Clementine and there will be others. In the twenties, after Muriel, back at Harvard, it was Irma, a name and a face forgotten until this instant. Coarse and hard, the child prodigy of Radcliffe, at eighteen in her junior year, a chess-playing, chest-heaving, heavy drinking fool. New Year's Eve. Recall? More moonlight and water. Irma and before early breakfast both of you stripped at the banks of the Charles River under a cold, clean sky, crisp with briskly twinkling stars. You washed yourself with snow. Afterward she spoke of olfactory stimuli and repellents, reflexological response, and told you quite calmly, "I only did it to find out whether I was *hot*."

Hot. Cool. Bee's knees and the bitter. Only the words, clothes, and

other wrappings grow old-fashioned whisky sour grapes of wrath we tread in an endless circle till each permanent tourist falls and dies from exhaustion. Take no one's word or outer wrappings for it. Speak only of what you know in this thirty-year war in which twenty from fifty leaves nothing, from Dada to Dali to Doomsday, from Gilded Age to Gilded Age to Right Bank to Left right left right in an idiot's forward march to nothing at all but the bitter pride of *knowing*.

If Mother's negotiations with life were unrealistic, those she had with death were not. She may have slept less, smoked more, drunk too much, and overeaten but she knew all of it was preparation. The approaching rendezvous was clear to her. The day before it happened she had said, "I find this a bore. But my mother was worse. You see, *her* mother died of pneumonia so her fear of upper respiratory infection drove her to the use of Argyrol morning, noon, and night. Ten years before rigor mortis set in, her nose was as cold blue as marble." At the end, Mother returned to the First Congregational Church, not for salvation but for burial.

Almighty and ever-present God and so forth and so on. May the love that we have known bear us up through the days that are ahead. May our loneliness give way to fellowship and may our regrets give way to hope. Overshadow, we pray Thee, our despair with Thy divine peace. May we not look longingly back at our yesterdays but may we move forward eagerly to our tomorrows in the faith, hope and confidence of the love and grace, etc., etc.

Fine. Do not look longingly back. Look eagerly forward. If your eyes see far enough ahead, as I have told you again and again, you will see only the grave. We are all of us like figures in a wax museum with a hurdy-gurdy hidden in the background, all covered with spider webs, dank, and in rot, when a lean, hungry rat quite by accident trips off the starter with its slimy tail. Then the ghostly noise begins and the waxen dummies in grotesque postures move round and round.

Laurie once said that before the good fortune of meeting you, she had come to believe life began at the top and wound down and it was this that led the young, the greedy and the avid into false beginnings and endless promiscuous introductions to experience. Too bad your courtship disrupted her dawn of wisdom: she was right. The first Prestons were the top Prestons, the last Preston is the least. Your childhood was your best time, your manhood made of maddening mistakes. We win battles and lose wars. By being first to make that particular mistake, the flaming youth of the twenties had the charm of innocence. If Nietzsche was wrong, he erred on the side of hope. It is not quite repetition, for each repetition takes us one step lower. Hunger, hunger, hunger, death. Abundance, prosperity, material

needs beyond necessity and the monotony of despair. You once had the idea that given the animal needs of security and the benefit of love, man quite normally sought work that would serve a higher purpose. But all higher purposes end in the gutter. In short, some creature other than man is needed to protect and use the small fruits of his efforts. The labor of discovering nature's minor secrets has exhausted all his capacity for what is now needed most: the force and faculty for teaching heart and mind, instinct and consciousness how *not* to be seduced by nature. That seduction is her major secret. Planes, pneumatic drills, and atomic reactors came nowhere near the heart of the secret. We are born in a state of emergency and perpetuate that state by perpetuating ourselves. Each time an emergency is met, the reward is not triumph but triviality. We are at our best when circumstances are at their worst. When we succeed ever so slightly in getting the upper hand, we are the worse for having done so. Moses and the Promised Land. Just one more senseless repetition. No calipers or devices have yet been created for measuring or educating the human spirit.

I hear you. And in the silence I also hear the river and the birds.

He picked up a branch of maple, snapped it to a five-foot length and prodded the earth as he walked. It was soft. He slashed at the air and heard the sharp whine.

At least I have freedom: more than most. But what good is freedom when you don't know how to use it? The sheer fact of having it, I suppose. So long as I have it I can try. Freedom not only permits trial and error, it insists upon them. Freedom involves choice. Choosing requires not only giving up things but enough experience and therefore error to be able to confront oneself with the things from which to choose. Freedom means remembering truthfully, without the slightest discoloration. So freedom means the loss of one's right to escape pain. Without pain no life, without life no experience, without experience no error, without error no choice.

Without choice, no freedom.

Error and pain are part of the purpose, the sinews of freedom. You speak only for yourself. You speak privately. Yet a part of things remembered by any Preston remains public. Freedom is an institution and those who shaped it were in a state of grace to have so designed it to endure mendacity and permit amendments including those of the human heart that cannot be legislated. A divine institution, it is not yet liberty and never claimed to be. It is only the temple in which liberty might be found. It is liberty's precondition, protecting each person's privilege in its pursuit.

He looked up at the sky. It was as it had been before his eyes had

turned inward. If that is so, this is not senseless repetition. Rebirth and repetition are not the same. Perhaps nature provides that eternal second chance, the ninetieth, hundredth, and millionth time so that we may continue to try, and if you return to source material here, it is what any sensible workman does when derivatives wither, go wrong, or run down.

Suddenly the weight of it dropped from him. The cheerful vista and sweet air were as they had been. So were the songs of the birds. The things that oppressed him had fallen away, and he thought: standing here alone on a country road and hearing small birds sing, you are so very, very lucky, simply because you have the gift of life to lose, spoil, or cherish. You can choose. Some people live and die without ever having known this gift. Never having it, they cannot lose it: but nor can they find their way back to it. Enslaved by need, trapped by circumstance, chained to work, multitudes of mankind do not yet have the luxury to consider the meaning of life or their own existence. They don't even have the time to consider whether it is better to live or die! For them, that agony is as yet an unattained privilege. Now notice something. Listen. Only the river sound. Not even the birds. Observe. With this branch in your hand, touching earth and bare-headed, you are looking up. You said a dream is not seen from above or even equal to the eye but below. Yet you look up. Seeking guidance? Forgiveness? Wishing once more to be above? None of these. It is simply a natural gesture as old as man himself. It means something whether you can explain it or not. Not what is meant by men who use words like God or eternity as artillery, nor those either who by cataloguing, destroy or dissect to deny. Still there is meaning here, beyond the tyranny of man-made institutions past, passing, or yet to be formed. There is even meaning here beyond the permanent paradox of life ever springing from death, or trees for their branches to reach upward, needing roots that dig down, and nations being formed by small duchies opposing one another, as perhaps one world will yet be won out of the polarizing bitterness and menace that men now impose on each other: yet once more out of clashing hostile forces, an unknown, unexpected third new thing is born.

There is meaning here beyond all that. What appeared as repetition that defied meaning was itself evidence of meaning. Order. It has pattern as certainly as do the birds reading stars to find south in the frost or north in the spring and they no less than I prove this meaning. Everything is both lower and higher than we know. That is part of the meaning. So too is the illusion of ground up twigs of dead evergreen looking so much like newborn grass.

That all this was known to you as a boy does not make it senseless.

It is over thirty years since you last stood this way in the presence of the blessed, untarnished springtime of life and heard, tasted, felt, sensed, and knew its order. But neither springtime nor your boyhood betrayed this knowing: *you* did, as man must if he is to discover all the richness and treasure within himself. Then if he is lucky as you are, he passes yet one more winter and in sufficient time perceives the approach of still another spring. If all the pain and self-betrayal has cost you your youth and you can no longer accept your second chance, then this meaning continues without you. You have felt this before and forgotten. No doubt you will forget again. When you do so, at least remember you knew you would forget. Holding to that will bring it back.

Standing in the excruciating dead center between eras is not without value: it helps you to see what lies behind and ahead in a way that perhaps the slightest deflection in either direction might have made impossible. The vacuum it can so easily become is valuable just because it is intolerable. You must place yourself with accuracy or perish, and that is, was, and always will be both the problem and the privilege, for man's purpose is to know *accurately*. That is his business. To differentiate between things that look alike. To see small differences without exaggerating: *but not without rejoicing*. To see the difference between repetition and rebirth. This bush, this tree, that stream, your hand are all of different heights, depths, weights, lengths, and places. You may see a thousand springs and you will never have seen this one. To only observe, like to forget, is to forgo. This is your profane and blessed land and life and now you understand what you vowed on the catwalk. You shall not ever run from it again. Neither from the future, nor from the past that shines underneath the present, lighting the way for as yet unborn and unhatched dreams.

You failed her. She failed you. You failed each other. Love is a synthesis of many things known and lost, imagined and real. Loving Laurie means more than seeking the shadows of Muriel or Natalie and the wasted years. You know you love her because you seek her forgiveness and you forgive.

He was no longer looking up. He was running. A car passed him. The driver looked back and shook his head. Ken waved and hurled the branch in the air. As it fell into the bushes off to the side of the road, he laughed. Who knows how many thousands or millions of people are standing alone or running at morning, noon, or night, on some equally cracked side road, dead end, or catwalk, at this very moment discovering as you have, feeling, thinking, knowing as you do in their own tongue, language, passion, fable, and heart exactly

what is clearly revealed and illuminated for you in the sacred here and now.

My dreams are not for sale. St. Terese and *Silver Box* are mine. So is Mansion House. I will find Laurie. How, I do not know, but I will make her understand. He suddenly realized that the day after tomorrow he and Laurie had arrived here for the first time. Four years ago.

A raccoon leaped off the hood of his car. It was a baby with its eyes wide open, no longer blind.

Chapter 3

KEN stood at the entrance to the narrow street on Beacon Hill that wound to an end at the center of another exactly like it. He held his head up to catch the faint breeze. It smelled of young apples. Grass grew among the cobbles, and the sidewalks were made of old brick. Leaves on the branches of the tall oak threw their dappled shadows against the small houses, their white doors and shuttered windows. When he walked, his leather heels made a pleasant, echoing sound in the quiet summer heat of late afternoon.

He was filled with a sense of excitement and at the same time, peace. In half an hour, he would be speaking to Mary. It was bound to be good news.

At the end of the board meeting he had been given Mr. Sloates's message. Mary Dugan had left the number of a Mrs. McAfferty for Ken to call in Los Angeles after four o'clock his time. Since six weeks ago, when he first looked for Laurie in New York, and she had not appeared at her own Commencement Day exercises, the question of where she was had mystified, angered, and finally alarmed him. At her instructions the diploma had been sent to Doris for safekeeping but when he visited Doris and Toby, now on semiretirement pay, they did not know where she was. A few weeks later, her lawyer in Reno had heard from her by mail. She would advise him before she arrived in Reno to set up residence preliminary to bringing suit for divorce. Dan hadn't heard from her at all: he was still in New York, awaiting transfer back to Chicago. Mary had left for California once the mess with the fire insurance company was cleared up. Ken's weekly talks with Mary in Los Angeles, difficult for both of them at first, grew easier but no more fruitful. Then last week Mary called him to say she had received a letter from Laurie at last. She was well and was traveling. When she settled down she would let Mary know. The postmark was Albuquerque, New Mexico, which made no sense at all.

In thirty minutes now, he would be speaking to Mary.

The board meeting itself had left him with something to think about. He had come to resign and left without doing so; he had in fact undertaken assignments. It would be strange to find that he belonged in the very place he had tried so long to escape from, and for the very reasons he actually had not belonged all these years. What he'd said to the board was true. The new developments in the market, the dangers, and the opportunity did not call for high-pressure sales-manship and other things alien to his nature, no matter how hard he had once tried to do them. The need now was for facts, for careful, non-rhetorical inquiry and a willingness to endure the discomfort of probing the unpredictable.

He had witnessed a stormy session between Old Boston and New York; Cousin Theodore's colleagues on the one hand and Coogan with the men who had put up capital for Preston & Company on the other: they had stayed with the project when the firm left the Exchange to merge with Theodore Preston Associates and became Preston Public Funds. The announcement of his intended resignation, along with the fact that the big bull market was facing its first major test, had both served to bring the fight out into the open. A severe sell-off was in the immediate future. It could be followed by recovery. It could also be followed by panic and possible collapse.

The two factions had agreed as to appraisal but stood opposed on fundamental policy. Ken had tried to do nothing but listen. New York, led by Coogan, urged drastic expansion of both promotion and sales personnel to find new customers to replace those who would run: a program of selling bargains in a falling market. Boston favored re-trenchment and reduced positions to weather the storm. Toward the end, Coogan had turned to him. "I think we'd like to know just where you stand on this," he said.

"I'm not sure," Ken had answered. "A sell-off obviously. Twenty per cent. Conceivably more. But intrinsically that should be the limit. Neither Federal Reserve action and deficit spending nor unemploy-ment and the slowed down rising rate of production and earnings would justify anything more severe. From there on it should rise to new highs. But that's not the issue. Nor is it one of retrenchment which encourages panic or of trying to increase sales if the close to twelve million people now in this market run from it; that's one out of every nine adults in America. They have to be educated to the fact that they are no longer *in* the market, they *are* the market. If they run and it collapses, so will the economy and much else besides. And for the first time in financial history, whether that happens doesn't depend on cycles, cartels, or combines. It depends on *them*. How much of their unprecedented participation is confidence and how much fear of inflation is unimportant now. Regardless of why, they have accepted a franchise and like it or not, they can't turn their backs on it. Nor we on them." They had waited, expecting more. "That's all," Ken said. "Except for the need to disassociate ourselves from this circus atmosphere of girls in tights posting trades in cocktail lounges that breeds tips, rumors, and ignorant, speculative buying of dubious securities, simply because the price is low and the noise is loud. Solid clarification is called for so that they really understand why the market and economy are both absolutely sound and will continue to grow. I still hold my personal Seat on the Exchange and I'll be glad to request a discussion of it with the Board of Governors. I don't think it will be easy to explain to the public, but if they know the facts, I do not believe they will run."

The rest of the meeting had been devoted to ways and means; practical measures that would unavoidably require joint efforts with competitive funds, the various exchanges and even the hostile opposition in savings account divisions of banks and the insurance companies. Quite likely his associates would forget the implications of today's meeting. They would need reminding: who didn't? It was not easy to resign, feeling that way.

That issue still remained open. It hadn't been broached by them, nor had he raised it. Curious how even an indirect vote of confidence made you feel the obligation to earn it. For the first time, he could honestly say that he was looked *to*, not *at*. A heavy sell-off, no doubt; the first since the big bull market began, when his honeymoon ended, not counting the freak collapse on Eisenhower's illness. It brought McBride to mind. Poor Mac. He would probably hold out against panic selling this time, thinking he'd learned his lesson, but if decline lasted long enough, he would finally sell, to end where he began before WHIP. As *you* may, in matters far more vital than money. No. You mustn't believe that.

The woman who answered the number Ken called said Mary wouldn't be back for at least three hours.

"Is this Mrs. McAfferty?"

"Yes."

He could think of no plausible questions to ask a stranger.

"She's still at the hospital," the voice offered.

"Is she all right?"

"Sure. She's fine."

Now questions rushed in to confuse him. "May I have the hospital phone number?" he asked.

She gave it to him.

The switchboard operator said, "Wiltshire Hospital." He realized he did not even know whom to ask for. "Mrs. Preston, please," he was forced to say.

"There's no phone in her room."

"I see. How is she?"

There was a pause.

"We have instructions not to give out any information on this case."

"This is Mr. Preston," he said.

"Sorry." The voice was disinterested. Click. He flashed the hotel operator and asked to be connected with air transportation.

"I had a fare the other day, important fella," the cab driver said. "He told me soon there's gonna be rain or fog all the time."

They were driving through both from La Guardia to Idlewild. His Los Angeles flight had only one stopover in Chicago. "Onacouna the hydrogen bomb," the driver explained.

Once again Ken went round the unbearable circle. Laurie in Los Angeles. Laurie in a hospital. Mary unreachable and no longer at the number where she'd been last week. An accident? That was one way for Mary to have found her. But then why the message? "Nothing urgent." The thought that had crossed his mind before came back and once again he dismissed it. Laurie was in the hospital. But not for that reason—no more than he would be. Her sister, Helen, your father, and in her own way, Mary: but not Laurie.

"—who doesn't hate the city! But how long can a guy look at nature? You go to the lounge car for a drink and come back to your seat. You can't play cards with strangers. My wife hates flying and long train rides drive me nuts, so there you are."

At the terminal, he had just enough time to phone the hospital again. He asked for the superintendent and while he waited spread all the change he had before him. The first announcement of his flight departure came over the speaker. He told the superintendent who he was, that he was calling from New York on his way to Los Angeles, and insisted on knowing how his wife was doing.

"Hold on, please."

His flight was being called again. Then a woman's voice came on. Mary.

"What's the matter with Laurie?" Ken asked.

"She didn't want anyone to know."

"To know what?" he shouted.

"She's in labor."

They announced the final call for his flight.

"I'll be in Los Angeles at eight A.M. your time," he said.

"I don't know," Mary started to say, but Ken had hung up.

He stared at the phone. Outside the booth someone rapped impatiently. Ken opened the door and ran.

Slumped in his seat, he stared out at the puff of flame leaping incessantly beside the wing, a splash of vivid color against the blackness. The one thing you hadn't counted on: your one area of inadequacy for which there is no correction. No, she hadn't asked Mary to call you; not when she wrote to her lawyer in Reno regarding "the contemplated divorce" less than three weeks ago. Divorce me and marry the father; or delay the divorce so the child had a name. Yours.

Poor Mary. Trying to behave like a mother and not knowing where to begin, because she never wanted to be one, while Laurie who did, had gone to these lengths. No further than she'd gone the time you first met her. Only now it had reached fruition. As Tess said, all it takes is lying on your back. You don't have to love the man. You can even hate him. Raped women get pregnant. Did she like, love, or hate this man?

The Prado, Havana. An all-girl orchestra. A street corner bazaar and heated argument from their guide, who smoked cigarettes and bargained for the guitar Mother wanted. She kept smiling and shaking her head, willing to pay the outrageous price. "Over my dead body, señora," José said indignantly. "My reputation is at stake." José who was seven years old. *At two in the morning, world-wise and weary with a reputation at stake to be loyal to his innocent charges.* When you paid him where the Salvation Army band played at the foot of the dock and a laughing tourist shook the tambourine for contributions, there was that split second when little José's eyes met yours and held them in a wistful question.

That's how fatherhood begins: in the thing that lay behind that look and what it did to you. Direct animal descent was the least of it. In our similarities lay our humanity. But our differences depend upon our inner selves, and they are born in the heart, and shaped in the mind by the heat of emulation. When the child is full-grown, he who tended that garden is its father; that is the only lasting resemblance or true heritage. Had you taken José aboard that boat, he would have been your son. Remember where Tess said, "All it takes is lying on your back." In *your* bed, on *her* back, to say nothing of the others. If several women were not in labor that was only because as Laurie had said, your seed is dead. Wanting to kill the father, whoever he might be, solves nothing.

The plane hit earth. It rocked, squealed, and rumbled forward. For a moment, he thought they had reached Los Angeles. It was Chicago. The twenty-minute stopover.

He ran to one end of the terminal, then to the other. Finally he found an open restaurant where he got the necessary change.

The operator said, "Wiltshire Hospital, one moment please."

Outside, the indifferent voice droned over the loud-speaker, "For Galveston, at Gate Two." The gravelly sound bounced off the walls, reverberating in the emptiness of the terminal.

"Wiltshire Hospital. Are you waiting?"

"This is Mr. Preston. My wife is in labor. I'm calling from Chicago. I want to know how she is doing."

The droning voice continued. "First call for nonstop to New York Flight Four now boarding at Gate One."

"Mrs. Preston is fine." So Mary had changed the orders at the switchboard. There was a hiss of static over the long distance wire and then "—a boy."

He hung up. A violent constriction at the pit of his stomach made sweat break out all over his body and something like a steel cap tightened over his scalp. He went outside. A boy. Someone else's. Congratulations, Mother. When had the fog lifted? The sky was clear, the stars shining. There were things to hold on to. Then hold on. In St. Terese you knew you would forget that it was a privilege, that trial and error, pain and limitation were all part of order. But you had not expected it so soon. *You had not expected your wife to give birth to someone else's child.* Still the things you knew remain true. Hold onto that. And in spite of it all, hold onto Laurie.

The mist was light, the air sweet, and the sky blue. Tom was waiting at the gate. They shook hands.

"No luggage?"

Ken carried a small overnight bag. "Just this."

"You need a shave and a clean shirt."

It was too early for barbershops. They went to the men's room in the airport. Ken shaved and changed his shirt while Tom held his jacket. Other men impatiently waited their turn at the sinks.

"Laurie's the last person on earth I'd expect to want to be next to Mother for the big event." They were driving now. "And I thought you had more sense than to let her."

Apparently Tom didn't know. No one had told him of the separation, the impending divorce, or anything else.

"—at Stanford University. Not a bad postgraduate course at all."

"How is your mother?"

"Much better. Being near her sister Bertha helps. They were friends as kids. Then something happened. Though what comfort she gets out of Aunty McAfferty is way beyond me."

The closer they got, the stronger Ken's doubts. He had flown from

Boston to New York and then cross country. If she would have no part of him, then what? Do you love her enough to swallow this and never ask who, when, and why? All the things that had seemed worth saying were gone.

"—technical possibility of destroying mankind now exists, though of course, Einstein said it before it actually did. But by the end of this year, it will be a fact. The only question really is which one of us gets into orbit first. Not that it matters to anyone except politicians. And once it does happen, *they* won't matter. War will be outlawed and along with it nationalism and all the rest. In a decade, life as they know it will be over and all the noisy issues that rattle like pebbles in a tin can along with them. It's really amazing how unprepared they are."

They. I too long for certainties, Ken thought, even those of a fool.

"—and I'm the most relativistic guy there is. But when an issue is closed, it's closed. Like the dinosaur. Except all this souped-up passion without purpose, dog eat dog, and flag waving is going to end faster because it's a much more basic change." It struck Tom funny. "How can you occupy outer space and go on arguing about your own backyard? Of course, no one knows what's in outer space or how it will change us when we get there. But we *do* know we're going to and once we do, all this will vanish without leaving track or trace."

Perhaps that's why "they" go to see westerns, Ken thought. "They" are seeking track or trace.

Tom stopped the car. "The florist's shop is in the main lobby," he said. "Laurie's in Pavilion C, where you'll find all the mothers primped up and everyone carrying on as though the lower species haven't been doing it ever since species began. It was nice talking with you." He drove off.

Ken stopped at the door to the reception room. Mary stood against the wall under the far window. She seemed smaller and older. When Ken approached, she met him halfway and gave him her hand.

"How's Laurie?" he asked.

Mary nodded.

"And the boy?"

"Twenty-two inches, eight pounds, seven ounces. Laurie was mad as hell that I told you." She shrugged and raised her hands in a helpless gesture. "You know how many times I went over meeting you again?"

He nodded.

"Well," she said at last. "I'll go tell Laurie you're here."

"No," Ken said. "I'll tell her myself."

"Tell her whatever you have to," Mary said. "It's the last door on the left."

Ken walked down the corridor. Life as we know it will soon be over? Never. There are no ends or beginnings, only more or less awareness at given points. The past serves the present and is part of it as trees half a billion years old will provide the heat in tonight's coal. So even if Laurie will have no part of you, you are still part of her and will therefore always exist.

Outside the door, he hesitated, and knocked. "It's Ken," he said. Then he entered.

She looked the way she had the first time, the same drawn, pale beauty, and that strain of trusting no one. He started to close the door. "May I?" he asked.

She nodded.

"Tom will come by later," he said.

"This is all pretty square to Tom."

"I hear it's a boy."

"Yes."

There was a knock on the door. Laurie looked surprised.

"Shall I open it?"

She nodded. A nurse stood before him, holding a baby wrapped in blue. Its face was bright red and its eyes shut tight. It had an uncommon amount of hair.

"Grandma said Daddy was here," the nurse said. "Isn't he *something?*"

Ken nodded.

The nurse mistook his pain for confusion. "Yes, he's *something,*" she repeated and lay the baby beside Laurie. She said "congratulations" to Ken, winked to Laurie, and left.

"I tried to find you," Ken said. "I went to see Doris and Toby, I called your father, your lawyer in Reno, the school, your mother. I'll say now what I wanted to say then, when I didn't know about— that." He pointed to the child. "You said what separates us is more important than what draws us together. It's not true, not for me. Not even your child separates us more than what draws us together. You're still my wife and I love you. You have a child: I will love the child. I don't care who the father is."

"You ought to."

"No. Once it might have been important. Now it isn't."

"You are," she said.

"I'm what?"

"His father."

The night in Caleb, the dream, and good-by?

"I don't understand," Ken said. He did understand.

"You're not the last male Preston."

"Why didn't you tell me?"

"Would you have believed me? Do you believe me now?"

"Why didn't you tell me?" he repeated.

"I just said—"

"I heard what you said and you've got one hell of a God damn nerve."

She smiled.

"What's funny?"

"Us. You sound like me. I sound like you."

"I don't find it funny."

"That night in Caleb when I came to you, I came with hate. I wanted you to know there was only one Laurie Dugan. No matter what you thought I did or why you turned your back on me, when we were front to front, there was nothing else you *could* do. I was leaving you with something to remember. Something you'd hunger for, something you'd come back for, and when you did, I'd spit in your eye. Could I tell you? I went to Havana before Commencement when I finished exams but the doctor said no, it was too late. A month ago, I was still lifting things, knocking myself out, trying to lose it. That's why it came early. That's why I didn't tell you! Do you understand what I'm trying to say?"

"Yes," Ken said. "That you love me."

She began to cry.

He came to sit down on the bed. The fact of the infant sleeping there made him kneel instead. He held her hand in silence.

His head rested on the cover. Her hand touched his face. He saw the package wrapped in parchment on the lower shelf of the night table. "Isn't that Arthur's?"

"Yes. His letter said it's a valuable fragment, ancient, and pieces of it were all over the world. Fitting them together might prove something very useful, he said. He thought I might want to work on it. I thought to hell with Arthur and his gambits. I was all set to turn it over to some museum. But somehow I couldn't. Then Kenneth Fenimore Preston III started kicking, and I forgot all about it. Until last night when I went into labor. Then all of a sudden it seemed important. I still don't know why."

"Shall we open it now?" He reached for his key chain with the small knife on it, then patted both pockets. He looked up in surprise. His voice was bland. "I've lost the silver box," he said. Boston, New

York, Chicago, or Los Angeles. This time he had lost it for good. He was puzzled: it didn't seem to matter.

Ken sawed with the knife till the thick cord cut and the baby was suddenly crying. He howled with his fists clenched and his eyes shut. He shrieked.

"Is he hungry?" Ken asked.

"I just fed him."

"We woke him."

"He could sleep through Judgment Day."

Ken put the box on the floor. "Shall I ring for the nurse?"

Laurie smiled. "What for?"

"He may be sick."

"He's fine," she said.

"How do you know?"

"I just know."

"Well, it has to be something."

"Yes." Something. Not nothing.

Curiosity, perhaps.

"He just doesn't want to miss anything," Laurie said.

ABOUT THE AUTHOR

JAY RICHARD KENNEDY received his Honorary Doctorate of Letters from Ithaca College in 1957, where he presented his paper on "The Need for Know-Why in a Know-How Culture." He has had no formal education. During the mid-twenties, he worked variously as itinerant farmer in the West and Southwest; as longshoreman in both San Francisco and New York; and up and down the Eastern seaboard as housepainter, bricklayer, and printer. He was also a theater and night club manager at the end of that decade.

Since then Mr. Kennedy has raised cattle in Kansas and New Mexico, managed real estate in Delaware, New Jersey, and New York, and manufactured precision tools for the Army, Navy, and Air Corps. He has also produced and written for theater, radio, television, and motion pictures, and functioned as business and artistic advisor to prominent artists in these fields. For the past ten years he has been an Allied Member of the New York Stock Exchange, and he is president of the brokerage and security specialists firm that bears his name.

Mr. Kennedy's screen writings include "I'll Cry Tomorrow" and "To the Ends of the Earth." His "Man Called 'X'" was among the top fifteen radio shows for ten years and "The Heart of Trinidad," produced for television under his supervision, began the calypso trend in 1955. As song writer, he has seen his calypso ballad, "Eden Was Just Like This," join the list of all-time highs in sales of single recordings both here and abroad.

As Mr. Kennedy's first novel, *Prince Bart*, published in 1953, drew upon his direct knowledge of the foibles and folkways of the nation's motion picture capital, so *Short Term*, which was six years in the writing, draws upon his experience on Wall Street. With his wife, Dr. Janet Kennedy, and their teen-aged daughter, Susan, he lives in Manhattan and Connecticut. Mr. Kennedy's hobbies are history and, more recently, astronomy. He is currently at work on his third novel.

This book was set in

Caledonia and Baskerville types,

printed, and bound by

The Haddon Craftsmen.

Typography and design are by Larry Kamp.